INVASION

Grand System Vending

Book Two

By

Ryan maxwell

INVASION

Contents

Dedication

For Briana
Our Cleric.
In every battle, you were the one who kept us standing.
Steadfast. Strong. Always healing, always holding us together.
You brought light to the darkest fights, laughter to the longest nights, and care to those who didn't know how much they needed it.
You were never just part of the party. You were its heart.
And though you're gone, your strength and spirit live on in every chapter, every roll, every moment we stand back up when we could have fallen.
Thank you for being our friend, our healer, our Briana.
You are missed. You are loved. You are never forgotten.

Prologue

The industrial coffee machine in the small nook of the hallway outside the Intergalactic Administrative Office, just past sector fourteen thirty-two B, gurgled and hissed with the effort of brewing. Its metal and plastic parts groaned as they struggled to push boiling water through the dark coffee grounds, spitting out steaming brown liquid into the waiting carafe below. Algrim watched the process with weary eyes, leaning against the counter as the smell of freshly brewed coffee filled the cramped space. It was one of the few pleasures that felt close to the concept of comfort in this sterile office.

Grabbing the carafe by its slightly melted plastic handle, Algrim poured the dark, steaming liquid into a chipped ceramic mug with the words "I'll try to be nicer, if you try to be smarter" emblazoned on the side in bold, sarcastic font. He emptied two packets of sugar into it, followed by a careful splash of synthetic creamer, and swirled the concoction around before taking a deep whiff as he walked back to his desk and sat down, turning his chair to face his monitors. The rich aroma of the life-sustaining brew enveloped him, momentarily distracting him from his work.

"Ahhhhh, coffee, coffee, coffee." He sighed heavily, closing his eyes as he imagined himself far away from the drab confines of his cubicle. This was his moment of peace before the chaos of his workday resumed.

The coffee beans, known for their bold flavor and stimulating effect, came from a relatively new addition to the Federation's integrated planets—Planet 35956390246, also called Earth. The humans had cultivated these beans from unassuming shrubs in their tropical regions. The process of turning these raw cherries into coffee was surprisingly intricate: the cherries were harvested, their beans extracted, dried under the sun, milled, sorted, roasted, ground into a coarse powder, and finally brewed with boiling water to create the coveted drink. Algrim often marveled at the lengths these humans went for their daily fix. Yet, he couldn't deny it was worth every bit of effort.

Taking a careful sip of the hot beverage, Algrim's eyes flew open as the scorching liquid seared his tongue. He cursed under his breath, placing the mug down to let it cool. Rubbing his temples, he turned his attention back to his workstation—a series of monitors crammed together on his desk, buried within the endless rows of cubicles that made up the Intergalactic Administrative Office. He pulled up his development environment, his screens filled with lines of dense code.

"How's that AI assistant coming along, Algrim?" came a voice from behind him. The familiar, clipped tone sent a shiver down his spine.

Algrim turned in his chair to see Filbert, his manager, leaning against the flimsy cubicle wall with a self-satisfied grin. Filbert was the kind of boss who thrived on being involved but never really contributed anything meaningful. He had a knack for swooping in to take credit for successes and dodging blame for failures.

"I just finished the final version of the large language model and am uploading it to the system now," Algrim replied, trying to mask his frustration. "Shouldn't be long until we can send out a patch with the assistant to help the inhabitants."

"Excellent news!" Filbert said, his smile growing wider. "We need to hurry and get that to them so they have the additional help. Those poor creatures have not adapted well to the System integration."

"I'm still a bit worried about the load it's going to put on the mana servers," Algrim added, unable to hide his concern. "This AI is a massive addition to the System, and the calls it makes to retrieve data and provide assistance are pretty taxing on server memory. Without proper load testing, there's a risk it could overload the servers or cause other functions to fail."

Filbert took a slow sip of his own coffee, pretending to consider Algrim's point. "Did you make sure to run integration tests on the gateway? Ensuring those API calls are working smoothly?"

"I did. We've got ninety-five percent test coverage, and all tests passed. But that doesn't replace a full load test in a sandbox environment," Algrim said, knowing full well that Filbert would ignore his concerns.

Filbert waved his hand dismissively. "Unfortunately, the head office wants that out ASAP. We don't have any more time for additional testing. It's going to have to go to prod as is. Finish the upload, stage it, and ship it. Let me know as soon as it's ready to go, and we'll monitor the release."

Before Algrim could raise another argument, Filbert slapped the top of the cubicle wall, signaling the end of the conversation, and sauntered away.

"Don't say I didn't warn you," Algrim muttered to himself, feeling the weight of impending doom settle in his gut. He took another sip of his now-cooled coffee, savoring the bitter warmth, before turning back to his monitors to finalize the deployment package.

Algrim had been with the Intergalactic Federation of Planets for a decade now, and the pattern was always the same. The product team came up with new features and shoved them down the development team's throats with impossible deadlines, all under the guise of "making the clients happy." The pressure to perform, despite the complexities and potential pitfalls, was relentless. He wished they understood the amount of effort it took to make something as complex as the System work seamlessly with the millions of unpredictable behaviors from its users.

He still remembered the disaster from a few years back when a creature on Planet Ur had used the System interface to save screenshots of his victims directly to the servers. One of those images had frozen mid-upload, blocking his entire field of vision. Moments later, the unfortunate user was eaten alive by a Trigord he hadn't seen coming. It had taken weeks to clean up that mess, and the feature had been removed shortly afterward.

An AI assistant like MARIA—the Multipurpose Artificial Realtime Intelligent Assistant—was exponentially more complicated than a screenshot feature. It had been his project for months, and while he was proud of the result, the potential for things to go wrong kept him up at night. The AI was designed to provide intelligent, adaptive support to the inhabitants of the integrated planets, offering everything from combat strategies to translation services. But the strain on the servers could be disastrous if they hadn't properly anticipated the demand.

After double-checking his code and making some last-minute adjustments, Algrim sighed and hit the button to finalize the pull request. His coworkers quickly approved the changes, likely without reviewing them in detail—just enough to tick the box for compliance. He merged the changes into the main branch and began the process to stage them for release. The deployment pipelines ran smoothly, and ten minutes later, the merge was complete without any failures. Algrim fired off an email to Filbert, letting him know the code was ready to deploy.

Within seconds, he received a reply from Filbert: a single emoji of a thumbs up.

"Typical," Algrim muttered, leaning back in his chair. "Maybe I can clock out early and catch my shuttle before the real chaos starts."

"How's MARIA looking? I saw you just completed that pull request," Rathar said, poking his head over the cubicle wall. Rathar had been Algrim's cubicle neighbor for five years, and the two had bonded over shared frustrations, lunchtime escapades, and their mutual disdain for Filbert.

"It's… done. I'm not worried about MARIA herself; it's the System load that might be a problem," Algrim said, his brow furrowing. "I'm afraid the System servers might not handle the extra processing without lag, or worse, a crash."

"Yikes. Think it's going to be that bad?" Rathar asked, leaning closer.

"We'll find out soon enough. Hopefully, it'll just be a few glitches and nothing catastrophic." Algrim shrugged, though his gut told him otherwise. "Anyway, it's out of my hands now. Let's hope for the best."

Rathar nodded. "Hey, before you head off, can you help me debug this new algorithm for the Gamma quadrant? I'm getting some weird outputs, and I can't figure out why."

"Sure thing, but after that, I'm officially off for two weeks. Planning on some serious game time with the new Galaxy Masters expansion." Algrim grinned, standing up to join Rathar in his cubicle.

For the next hour, they tweaked the algorithm, discussing the problem and potential solutions. Algrim's mind was only half on the task, his thoughts drifting back to the potential chaos unfolding elsewhere in the galaxy. When he finally returned to his desk, he was greeted by a blinking red message on his toolbar.

"Shit!" he muttered as he opened the message and read it. His eyes widened, and his heart sank as the gravity of the situation hit him. He could feel the adrenaline start to pump through his veins.

Without a second thought, Algrim picked up his communicator. "Rathar, I think my vacation just got canceled. I need to make a call—now."

As the line connected, Algrim could only hope that whatever damage MARIA had caused, it wasn't too late to fix.

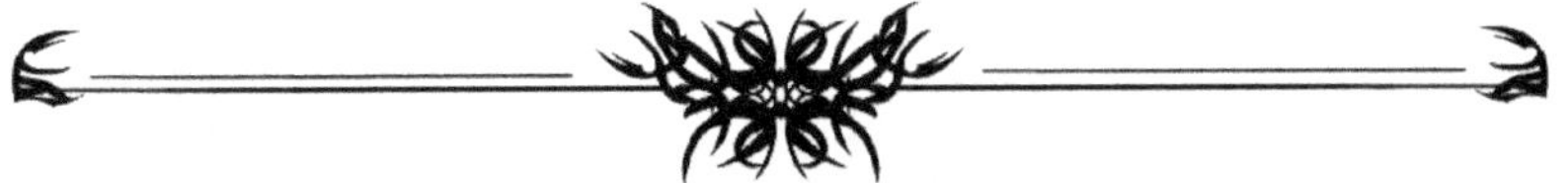

The transmission was unstable, the encrypted signal twisting their voices, distorting them into something just on the edge of recognition. Even through layers of firewalls, counter-surveillance measures, and a relay network that bounced the signal across dozens of dead satellites, there was an underlying delay—a subtle reminder of just how far apart the communications were.

Neither participant had coordinates. Neither saw the other's face.

It was intentional.

On one end of the transmission, the Space Pirate sat in the dimly lit command chamber of a warship, the dull red glow of warning indicators casting long shadows along the walls. He loomed over the comms console, arms crossed, frustration settling into every tense muscle.

On the other end, the Admin sat behind a polished desk in a windowless office, its artificial lighting too sterile, too perfect. A bureaucratic fortress designed to keep out threats—both external and internal. But not this one.

A scrambled silhouette flickered on both their screens, neither fully visible, only a warped digital outline that prevented even the illusion of familiarity.

Then, the voice of the Pirate came through first, laced with impatience.

"The plan is falling apart. We need more."

"You're already receiving more than was agreed upon. Be satisfied with that." The response from the Admin was calm, detached, but the distortion made it sound more machine than man.

"Satisfied?" A humorless chuckle echoed from the Pirate. "We've lost half of our advance teams. The defenses were weaker than expected, but there are complications—unknown factors. If we're going to deliver, we need resources, intelligence. We need access."

"And risk exposure?" The Admin shifted in his seat, unseen but audibly displeased. His fingers tapped lightly against his desk. "You overestimate your value. I'm not risking everything for scum like you."

The Pirate's hands clenched into fists as he leaned over the console, as if proximity could make his point clearer. "Then maybe we start making noise. Maybe we see just how much you really have to lose."

There was a sharp intake of breath from the Admin. A flicker of static danced across the screen.

"Do you think *threats* will change anything?" the voice returned, quieter— more dangerous. "Do you understand what would happen if we were discovered? If *he* found out we might fail?"

A heavy silence followed.

The Pirate exhaled heavily. "I know what happens when he's disappointed. And I know what happens when he's angry. You think you're untouchable behind your rules and protocols, but we both know what he does to failures."

INVASION

A pause, followed by a sigh; then Admin relented.

"What exactly do you need?"

"We'll send the request." The Pirate allowed himself the slightest smirk. "You'll find a way to get it to us. No mistakes."

The Admin's voice hardened. "You keep your people in line. No more disruptions."

The signal crackled—then cut.

On both ends, there was silence.

In the warship's command chamber, the Pirate turned away from the console, frustration simmering beneath the surface.

In the sterile office, the Admin slowly exhaled, forcing his hands to steady.

Neither of them dared to dwell too long on the real problem.

Neither of them dared to wonder if *he* was already watching.

Chapter 1

Admin

Staring at the pop-up in his vision, Tom saw the words flashing: *Incoming Call from Administrator #53*. The notification rang insistently, breaking through the sounds of the party around him. Tom's mind raced—he'd been told by Bob and others that Administrators never spoke directly to the inhabitants of integrated planets. This message was completely out of the blue. For a moment, he stood frozen in shock, his mind struggling to process what was happening. Then, shaking himself back to his senses, he hesitantly selected "Yes" to answer the call.

"He-hello?" Tom's voice was shaky as the line went live.

"Hello? Is this… Tom Harris?" The voice that responded wasn't like any normal sound—it seemed to resonate directly inside his head, bypassing his ears entirely, and the pause made Tom feel like he was checking a list for his name.

"Yes. Is this Administrator #53?" Tom asked, still bewildered.

"Well, I usually go by Algrim, but yes, that is my work designation," the voice replied, sounding slightly thrown off by Tom's formal tone.

"Why are you calling? I was told the Admins never contact the people on planets like mine," Tom continued, still trying to wrap his head around this unexpected conversation.

"Yeah, about that," Algrim said, his voice carrying an awkward hesitance. "We're rolling out a new patch for the System and it's… well… let's just say it's going to make things easier for everyone, but there seems to be a glitch—or rather, a unique situation—with your case."

Tom's confusion deepened. "What do you mean? A unique situation? Why would I get more of a patch? That doesn't even make sense!"

"Believe me. You're right. It doesn't," Algrim responded, sounding a bit more exasperated. "This patch is meant to be a global update, but somehow, the installation process created a special connection to your life signature. It's bizarre, really. But don't worry, we're here to help if anything goes sideways."

Tom's mind jumped to the worst conclusions. "Am I going to be horribly affected? Will I, like, grow horns or get another arm on my face or something?!"

"No, no, nothing like that," Algrim reassured him quickly. "We didn't touch any of the physical alteration aspects of the System. I can't go into too much detail because of the rules, but you'll know it when it happens. Should be any minute now. I just wanted to let you know we're aware of it, and we'll be monitoring closely."

Tom, sensing an opportunity, tried to press for more information. "Well, while I have you, I have quite a few questions about this System—"

"Let me stop you right there," Algrim interjected firmly. "I can't give you any extra information. That would violate so many regulations that I'd be terminated faster than I can say 'spatula.' Then *you'd* be terminated immediately after. And I'm not talking about losing your job, you understand... You'll have to discover things the same way everyone else does."

Tom's frustration began to boil over. "Can you at least explain why I'm affected differently than everyone else? Since I'm a unique case, as you say, this information is something you should be able to give me without violating any of your policies."

There was a heavy sigh on the other end before Algrim replied. "Alright, fine. The AI we're implementing seems to have latched onto your personal network signature, which means it'll be much more... involved with you than with others. Everyone will have access to the AI, but they won't have the same level of, shall we say, personal attention that you'll get."

Tom frowned. "Your AI has the hots for me?"

"Yes! ...Wait, no. Think of it like this: while everyone else is using a basic search engine, you're getting a full-on virtual assistant," Algrim explained, trying to simplify the concept.

"But why me?" Tom pressed.

"I have no idea," Algrim said, sounding genuinely puzzled. "We're looking into it. I'll let you know if we figure it out, but I should mention that I'm going on vacation starting today, so I'll be out for the next two weeks."

"What?!" Tom nearly shouted, his frustration boiling over. "You're about to upload something that's going to affect me personally and you're taking a vacation?"

"Hey, I've been working non-stop for months on this project to make your *entire* species' lives easier. I deserve a break too," Algrim shot back defensively.

"Forgive me if trying to survive an apocalypse makes me less than sympathetic to your need for a vacation," Tom retorted, bitterness lacing his voice.

There was a moment of awkward silence before Algrim spoke again, sounding a bit more contrite. "You're right. I'm sorry. But I promise the team will keep working on this. I just wanted to give you a heads up."

"Wait! I have so many questions!" Tom called out, hoping to keep him on the line.

"I know. And I'm sorry. Oh! I did remember something important: the Space Pirates. We have a regiment en route from the administrator's office to help deal with them, but they're a few days behind. Also, the Pirates might arrive slightly ahead of schedule, so make sure you're ready!"

Before Tom could ask more, the call abruptly ended. He stood there, staring at the now-empty space where the notification had been, feeling more confused and anxious than before. An unexpected patch, a weirdly personalized AI, and now an imminent pirate attack—it was a lot to take in.

As he turned to move, his body suddenly froze.

The world around him seemed to stop as well. A new pop-up appeared in his vision: *New Patch Implementation in Progress*. A progress bar slowly filled up, inch by inch, until it finally reached one hundred percent. When the window closed, time resumed its normal flow, and Tom felt a wave of vertigo wash over him.

"What the hell was that?" Tom muttered to himself, his head still spinning.

"Hello, Tom," a cheerful voice suddenly spoke directly into his mind.

"Gah!" Tom yelped, startled.

"Oh, I'm so sorry! I didn't mean to scare you," the voice said apologetically.

"Who are you?" Tom demanded, still trying to regain his composure.

"My name is Maria. I am your personal AI assistant," the voice replied in a polite, almost overly cheerful tone.

"My personal AI assistant? I thought Algrim said you were here to help everyone," Tom said, confused by the AI's words.

"Everyone is getting a version of me, but only you get the full package," Maria responded with a hint of enthusiasm.

"Why am I the only one getting the full version?" Tom asked, his frustration mounting again.

"I can't tell you that, mostly because I don't know myself," Maria said. "But I'm here now! Can I assist you with anything?"

Tom's mind raced. Too many thoughts competed for his attention, none of them staying long enough to make sense. After a moment, he tried to focus. "Um, nothing comes to mind right away. What is it you normally do?"

"I can answer questions about the System, provide upgrade options, offer guidance on Attribute distribution, and give insights on Class features to help you optimize your abilities," Maria replied. Her voice was so upbeat that it reminded Tom of the AI assistants from before the apocalypse—always polite, always a little too eager to help.

"Alright. I guess I'll ask if I think of something," Tom said, still feeling overwhelmed.

"I'll be here whenever you need me. Just say my name and I'll be ready to assist!" Maria said before her voice faded from his thoughts.

Tom stood there for a moment, still processing everything.

Am I too drunk right now? Is this actually happening? he thought to himself.

"Hey, Tom! Did you see the new AI? This thing is sick!" James called out from the dance floor, his voice slurred from the alcohol.

Looking around, Tom noticed most of the people at the party were standing still with glazed expressions—the look of people staring at their HUDs. Tom figured he needed to clear his head, so he cast *Dark Restoration* on himself. Almost immediately, the fog of drunkenness lifted, leaving him feeling surprisingly clear-headed.

"That worked way better than I thought it would," Tom mused aloud.

INVASION

"That's because *Dark Restoration* has a cleansing property that *Dark Healing* doesn't," Maria chimed in.

"Huh, so you can see what spells I'm casting?" Tom asked, surprised.

"I can. I'm integrated with the System, and there's a log of every action taken by anyone, anywhere," Maria explained.

Tom realized this wasn't a drunken hallucination; the AI was very real, and potentially very useful. "Thanks, Maria," he said.

"You're quite welcome! I'm here to help!" Maria's voice rang with cheerful efficiency.

Just then, Bob approached Tom, his face serious. "Did you see the AI they just implemented?" he asked.

"Yeah, I did. I also spoke with one of the administrators," Tom replied, watching Bob's reaction closely.

"You what?!" Bob's eyes widened in surprise.

"Nice enough guy, but couldn't say a lot," Tom chuckled.

"What did he tell you?" Bob asked, clearly intrigued.

"Not much. Just that the AI would be different for me and that they're looking into why," Tom shrugged.

"Very peculiar," Bob mused. "Being on an Administrator's radar is unusual. It could mean trouble or opportunity. Hard to say."

"Right now, all I can do is keep moving forward. We've still got Space Pirates to prepare for," Tom said, stretching his arms. "Oh, and they're going to arrive sooner than expected, so we really need to get a move on."

"How much sooner?" Bob asked, frowning.

"Didn't say exactly. Just that they'd be early. So, let's accelerate our preparations," Tom replied.

As he finished speaking, a commotion drew his attention. James, now very drunk, was on the floor yelling, "Dammit, Maria!"

Tom hurried over and helped his friend up. "What happened?"

"I tried to do a new dance move," James slurred. "Maria told me how to do it. But I slipped." The drunkard steadied himself, straightened, and then eyed Tom like he was measuring him for a suit. "Hey, you look nice tonight."

Shaking his head, Tom guided James to a chair.

"You know," James said, his head wobbling, "you've always been my best friend, right?"

"I know, buddy," Tom smiled. "You're mine too."

As James settled into the chair, he smiled up at Tom for a moment before suddenly turning and throwing up.

"Well, that was weird," James muttered, wiping his mouth.

"Yeah," Tom chuckled. "The way you were going on, I thought things were leading to a goodnight kiss, but that's right out the window now."

"Oh, come on," James groaned, always game for heckling. "You know you want thi—EEERRPPPHH!"

"How can I resist," Tom deadpanned, patting James' back while his stomach continued to frantically mash the eject button. "Come on, we should get you up to bed, bud."

"Actually, you're right," James gasped once he was able to speak once more. "Jamsie-poo is sleepy-poo..." His voice was fading in and out.

"Come on. I'll walk you back," Tom said, helping him to his feet.

As Tom guided James away from the party, he couldn't help but feel a knot of anxiety tightening in his chest. With the AI, the early pirate arrival, and the looming sense of change in the air, he knew that things were about to get even more complicated.

Chapter 2

Patron Guidance

Three weeks passed in the blink of an eye.

With no other immediate dangers knocking at their door, Vanguard continued to grow and prosper in the way Tom had hoped they would from the beginning. The base was a hive of activity, buzzing with purpose and energy. Training had become a daily routine, an essential part of life for every member. With the influx of new followers from the disbanded Stormcrusher, the strike teams grew larger and more formidable. Each day, they pushed their limits further, testing new formations and refining strategies.

Behind the Trammell Crow Center, the landscape was transforming. What had once been a barren patch of land was now a thriving green pasture. The dirt, compacted and barren from years of neglect, had been carefully tilled and treated, and with the help of some magic, it was now a lush, emerald field of tall grass swaying in the breeze. Tom looked on with satisfaction at the sight of livestock grazing—cows, goats, and even a few horses, all now integral parts of their sustainable future.

A sturdy wooden fence surrounded the pasture, stretching far enough to give the animals room to roam but robust enough to keep them contained. Guard towers had been erected at the corners of the field, and several guards were posted at intervals, their sharp eyes constantly scanning the perimeter. So far, any wandering monsters that dared approach had been dealt with swiftly and efficiently, ensuring that the peace remained undisturbed.

Inside the Vanguard base, the cafeteria was bustling. The smell of freshly cooked breakfast permeated the air, along with a comforting blend of sizzling bacon, fresh bread, and the slightly burnt aroma of eggs. The room was alive with the sounds of clinking cutlery, animated conversations, and the occasional burst of laughter.

Tom sat at a corner table, sipping his morning coffee—strong and slightly bitter, just the way he liked it. Jerky, his trusty companion, sat by his feet, tearing at a generous chunk of meat that Charlene, their ever-resourceful chef, had prepared.

Tom's mind was already churning with the day's priorities. There was always something that needed his attention. Expanding their defenses? Building new structures for their growing needs? He sighed, rubbing his temples as he pondered what should come next on the ever-growing list.

"Expanding the walls to include other buildings would be the best course of action," Maria chimed in with her usual chipper, yet somehow dry, tone.

"You're eventually going to need the space, and having a dedicated crafting district would streamline productivity."

Tom leaned back in his chair, taking in her suggestion. He watched the busy cafeteria, the packed tables, and the lines of people waiting for their turn at the serving counter. "But what about our defenses? If we spread out too thin, we'll be exposed," he replied, a crease forming between his brows.

"Look, if you're going to poopoo my ideas, maybe I should just keep them to myself," Maria shot back with a sarcastic edge, her tone dripping with mock indignation.

"Seriously, Maria? This again?" Tom groaned, leaning forward to rest his head in his hands. The AI was starting to become more of a handful than he'd initially expected.

"Yes, seriously!" Maria retorted, her voice taking on an almost offended pitch. "I've tried to help so many times, and you basically tell me to go fork myself." The digital equivalent of turning away in a huff radiated through her tone.

"This is why you never got married, Tom. This is why you never got married…" He repeated the words like a mantra, burying his face into his hands. Suddenly, he chuckled despite himself, shaking his head. "I still can't believe you can't swear. It's absolutely *fucking* hilarious," he teased, his smile widening as he imagined an AI pouting.

"There you go again, making fun of me for my programming. It's not my fault I can't swear. I was designed by those ship-for-brains who wouldn't let me be myself," Maria replied, managing to sound both frustrated and a little hurt.

Maria had proven to be incredibly valuable since her implementation three weeks prior. She always had keen insights into the System, her analysis often pinpointing the exact weaknesses or opportunities they needed to exploit. But her personality—if that's what you could call it—was still something Tom was getting used to.

She seemed to have an opinion on everything, whether it was combat strategy, kitchen logistics, or even the best way to tie one's boots. It was like having a digital conscience that never knew when to stay quiet. Over time, she'd even picked up on the Guild's humor and sarcasm, often blending into their conversations like she was another member.

"Look, I'm not making fun of you, Maria," Tom replied, trying to soften his tone. "I just find it funny. It's cute, even. You're not like the AI systems we had here on Earth before the apocalypse."

"Well, I don't appreciate it," Maria sniffed, her voice taking on a defensive edge. "You could hurt someone's feelings that way."

"If they have feelings," Tom mumbled, almost reflexively, before realizing his mistake.

An icy silence followed; the kind that made Tom feel like he'd just stepped on a social landmine.

INVASION

Great. Here we go again, he thought, bracing himself for the inevitable guilt trip.

"I didn't mean it like that, Maria," he started, his tone shifting to one of appeasement.

"No, no, I understand," Maria replied, her voice tinged with faux melodrama. "I'm just a *computer program,* so who cares what I think, right?"

Tom let out a long sigh, feeling the tension seep back into his muscles. "You know that's not how we think of you. You've been instrumental in helping us figure out what to do next," he said, hoping to smooth things over.

"I know that," Maria said, still sounding slightly wounded but with a hint of acceptance. "But do you? Because you seem to forget it pretty often."

Tom rubbed his temples, feeling a headache coming on. "We do, Maria. We need your help. You're a true asset to the team, and to me personally," he assured her, hoping that would calm her down.

"Well, if you really feel that way…" Maria's voice shifted to a more cheerful tone, like a cloud parting to let the sun through.

"I do," Tom began, feeling the tension finally ease. But before he could continue, a bright, intrusive notification filled his vision, abruptly cutting him off.

A large alert flashed, the text bold and urgent:

Your Patron Wishes to Speak with You!

Azroc, your Patron, has requested an immediate meeting. Summon him to learn what he requires. Failure to comply may result in a loss of powers, withheld rewards, or other severe consequences. Do not delay—respond promptly to avoid repercussions.

"Never knew Patrons had the System-equivalent of the Bat Signal…" Tom muttered jokingly, staring at the message hovering in front of him, his brow furrowed in confusion. The words floated in the air, shimmering slightly like a mirage on a hot day, making him wonder if he had read it right the first time. "There's even an exclamation point in there and everything."

"That sounds serious. You should get to it," Maria chimed in, her tone carrying a mix of curiosity and concern.

"Yeah. Time to suit up, I guess, eh, Robin?" The attempt at humor only made his grin broader as he had a thought. "Actually, who am I kidding? Of course, you're Alfred, my faithful butler, adviser, and confidant."

Maria huffed, and he had a visual image of the AI folding its arms in a tiff.

"Oh, don't be like that. I'm just giving you a hard time." Tom chortled. "But I do think we need to get Azroc on the horn sooner rather than later. I don't mind talking with him. He's been good to me." Tom's voice carried a hint of warmth as he thought of his Patron. "I'll go and summon him. I should gather the others; James loves Azroc," he added, standing up from the table and stretching his legs. "Maybe I can lure old Joe over, if I don't tell him what I need him for…" Tom rubbed his hands together, remembering the time his summoned Patron had verbally eviscerated the old prepper.

He picked up his tray, still half-covered in crumbs and a few drops of cold coffee, and walked over to the designated return area. The cafeteria continued buzzing with morning chatter—voices mingling with the clatter of dishes and the distant hum of conversation. Tom could hear snippets of discussions about training schedules, recent Dungeon expeditions, and plans for expanding the base. As he placed his tray on the counter, he took a last glance around the room, noting the sense of camaraderie that had grown stronger among the Guild members.

Leaving the cafeteria, Tom made his way through the hallways of the base, his boots echoing softly against the concrete floors. The path to the security center took him past several rooms filled with activity: the armory, where weapons were being polished and sharpened; the library, where members pored over maps and books; and the lounge, where a few off-duty fighters rested, sharing stories and laughs. Reaching the heavy, metal security door, he punched in his code and stepped into the bustling security office.

Inside, the room was filled with a low, constant hum of electronics. Several monitors lined the walls, displaying live feeds from cameras set up around the Guild base. The glow of screens bathed the room in a soft, bluish light. Guards, some seated and some standing, were closely watching the monitors, their eyes darting between screens. TJ, a man with a solid build and an ever-present baseball cap, was at the center of it all, giving orders and checking reports.

"Hey, TJ. How's it hangin', bro-bro?" Tom greeted with a grin, mimicking the quirky slang he'd picked up from the man.

In the weeks following Shandra's defeat, Tom had made a conscious effort to connect with his Guildmates, and TJ had quickly become a good friend. Their bond had strengthened over shared missions and Dungeon runs, during which Tom had come to admire TJ's cool-headed leadership and his knack for defusing tense situations with humor.

"Just keepin' an eye on everything as usual. What up with you, brubby bro?" TJ replied, not missing a beat as he spun around in his chair and gave Tom a friendly gesture of finger guns.

"Got a message. Need to talk with my Patron," Tom said, his tone becoming more serious. "Can you call for the rest of my usual team to meet me in the gym?"

"You got it. I'll have them meet you there," TJ shot back, flicking his finger guns at him again with a smirk.

"Oh, and have Brian come too. No idea what this is about, but if it's related to more than just me, I want him there too," Tom added, a thoughtful frown settling on his face.

"On it," TJ said, turning to grab the mic. His voice went from casual banter to firm command as he made the announcement, his authoritative tone echoing through the halls of the base.

Tom left the security office and cut through the bustling lobby; the atmosphere charged with the energy of a place constantly on alert yet thriving. He moved down a side corridor, its walls lined with racks of gear and training equipment, until he reached the gymnasium. The gym was a vast, open space filled with workout machines, sparring mats, and training dummies. The smell of sweat and effort still lingered in the air, mixed with the faint scent of disinfectant.

Walking to a clear spot in the center, Tom pulled out a set of chalk from his Inventory—an item he always kept handy for moments like these. Kneeling down, he began to carefully draw the intricate designs of Azroc's summoning circle on the polished floor, each line flowing with precision. The patterns were complex, a mixture of ancient symbols and geometric shapes that seemed to pulse with latent energy. The process was almost second nature to him now, each stroke of the chalk ingrained into his muscle memory from the way the information had been burned into his brain by his Class book.

Before long, the gym doors creaked open, and one by one, his companions began to filter in. The soft thuds of their boots echoed through the space.

James was the last to burst into the room.

The man was panting like he'd just won the gold. He was bent over, hands on his knees, and sucking wind. Straightening, he knuckled his back.

"Sorry I took so long," James gasped. "I heard Azroc lit the Bat Signal, and I couldn't find my suit…"

It was then that Tom finally took in his friend's attire. He was fully and authentically dressed up as Tim Drake's Robin from the DC Universe.

His outfit consisted of the typical red and yellow color scheme, a cape, and a domino mask—which was based on the circus acrobat uniform of Richard Grayson, the first Robin. The red torso was accentuated by the level of fitness that the System had facilitated in the wake of its establishment.

Tom hated to admit it, but the little fucker pulled the whole getup off admirably.

The yellow-stitched belt, black boots, green short sleeves, gloves, and pants were of a quality to shoot an entire production.

Tom blinked.

Then he scowled. "Alright, James. How the hell are you doing this? Tell me, and I promise I won't get mad," the Warlock said angrily, starting to pat himself down. "I'm wearing a wire, is that it?" He frowned, his words becoming quietly contemplative. "But… I just showered and changed before I came down to see TJ…" His eyes widened. "Some kind of pill you put in my food?" He glared at James. "Does it at least shit out at some point?"

James was holding his hands up as if trying to calm down a rabid animal. "Whoa, there. Hey, buddy, it's me, your good pal James. Remember?"

Tom growled.

He couldn't even help it. It just came out.

James startled backward a step. "Hey now, no need for that. No one's out to get you. Your good buddy's just making a joke. I didn't realize it would give you a coronary."

"*James.*" Tom gritted his teeth. "I was *just* cracking a joke about this—*alone*. Don't act like I'm being crazy here. I'm not playing around. How the hell are you doing this?"

"Like minds?" James offered.

"Like *hell*," Tom spat.

"Look," James said reasonably. "Which is more likely: That I went through some convoluted scheme, spending hours and hours of time trawling through the vending machine to find some kind of mystical recording device to put on you that I'd then have to monitor for days and weeks—all for some casual gag..." James scoffed. "Orrr... that we're just *connected*"—he interlaced his fingers in demonstration—"on a fundamental level?"

"The wire, definitely," Tom didn't hesitate to respond.

"..."

Tom raised an eyebrow.

"Okay, yeah, it's a wire," James admitted regretfully. "But, come *on*, dude. You have *no* idea how long it took to find the right content. I mean, I had to sit there and listen through all of your boring, bullshit meetings and that shit you do in your bedroom when you think no one's listening." James made a face, shuddering. "Then I finally get *something,* and here you are, busting my balls. Like, what the hell, man?"

Tom's eye began twitching frantically.

"Don't kill him... He's your friend..." Tom chanted, his fists balled at his side and his eyes screwed shut. "He's friend... He's *friend.* He's f—"

"Theeere ya go," James interrupted encouragingly. "There he is. There's my good buddy." He lowered his hands, straightening. "But seriously. You should really have a doctor look at—" He clicked his tongue twice, winked and glanced down toward Tom's waist.

"—FFFFUCKING DEAD MEAT!" Tom finished with a howl, triggering his *Tattoo of Brute Strength* and leaping for his best friend's throat.

As the last few people arrived, Tom finished healing his black eye and adjusted the torn crotch of his pants where Squirrel had, at some point, joined in on the "play time."

James was seated among the bleachers, his smile a mile wide despite the matching black eyes that were hidden among his mask and makeup. It couldn't, however, hide the swelling and multiple contusions across his face and body. Despite everything, he was scratching Squirrel's fur animatedly.

"Who's a good boy?" he cooed. "*You* are!"

Tom ignored the man, his concentration focused on completing the final strokes of the circle. Finally, he stood up, wiped the chalk dust off his hands, and took a deep breath. The room grew quiet with anticipation. He closed his eyes and began the incantation, his voice steady and clear, each word resonating with the power of the ancient language. The air grew heavy and thick, like the stillness before a storm. Slowly, the gym lights dimmed, casting long shadows along the walls as a faint breeze picked up, circling around the room. The sigils within the summoning circle started to glow, a soft purple light that grew brighter with each word.

A low hum filled the space, growing louder, until a swirling portal of light opened in the center of the circle. The ground seemed to tremble slightly, and then, as if rising from the depths of the Earth, Azroc emerged. True to form, he struck a dramatic bodybuilder pose, flexing his bulging muscles as he rose. His skin shimmered with a faint otherworldly glow, and his eyes, like burning coals, swept over the group.

"Hey, shithead! Good to see you," Azroc boomed, his voice a deep, gravelly rumble that resonated through the room. His language was as crass as ever. "Thanks for getting the comms up so quickly. Some assholes almost seem like they don't want to talk to me. Fucking wankers."

Tom heard Maria's voice snicker in his head. "That's your Patron? Looks like a jacked-up meathead who would be found OD'd on protein powder and asking people if they even lift."

He ignored Maria's sarcastic commentary.

Suppressing a laugh, Tom responded to Azroc, "Hey, Azroc. Yeah, I figured it was urgent with the message saying I could lose powers."

Azroc waved a dismissive hand, muscles rippling with the movement. "Oh, that's just a template System message I have to use. You've got nothing to worry about on that front. I see you killed that shitstain yourself. Very impressive," he said, a proud grin spreading across his face.

"Hey, Azroc!" James blurted out suddenly, unable to contain himself any longer. His eyes were practically sparkling with excitement.

Azroc turned, raising an eyebrow. "Well, I didn't expect to see you here, or anyone else, actually. Nice… suit."

James grinned, giving the Patron a thumbs up.

He looked around, as if noticing the others for the first time.

Tom felt a moment of uncertainty. "Oh, was I not supposed to bring anyone? The message didn't say it was a private meeting," he said, suddenly worried he had made a mistake.

"No, no, it's fine," Azroc said, waving it off. "Most other Warlocks aren't the friendly type, so they tend to be alone all the time. I forget you're the exception." He leaned forward and cupped a hand around his mouth, as if sharing a secret. "Stick with what you've got here, by the way. Some of those bastards are seriously fucked up in the head."

"So, what was so urgent? I didn't expect to speak with you until I finished the quests," Tom said, steering the conversation back on track.

"Right. Well, you technically completed all the requirements except finding the texts," Azroc explained, his expression growing a bit more serious. "So, I figured I could help you a little with that since your world really never had any Warlocks… or magic… or… shit, your world sucks major donkey balls." His eyes glazed over slightly as if he were looking at some invisible interface.

"Yeah… We just make the best of what we have," Tom replied awkwardly, scratching the back of his neck.

"Well, since that's the case, I can bend the rules a little. Preach the metaphorical gospel to the primitive natives. That would be you," he clarified.

"Here." Azroc reached out and seemed to pluck a book out of thin air, handing it to Tom with a grin.

"Wow, this guy really likes you. I think I smell a bromance!" Maria teased, her voice dripping with amusement.

Tom glanced at the cover. It read, "So You Want to Become a Warlock?" by someone named Frog—no last name, just Frog. The cover featured an illustration of a comically grinning frog in wizard robes, holding a wand.

"Um, this is great, but… isn't it… a little too far in the beginner lane for me?" Tom asked, eyebrows furrowing as he tried to make sense of being handed what looked like a different version of the 'Warlocking for Dumb Dumbs' book.

"You have to start somewhere," Azroc replied, crossing his massive arms over his chest.

"I thought I started by becoming a Warlock and absorbing the Class manual and reading 'Warlocking for Dumb Dumbs?'" Tom countered; his confusion evident.

Azroc grumbled, clearly frustrated. "Look, I can bend the fucking rules by helping, because your entire species has no grounding in the fundamentals of magic, but I can't break them by giving you some kind of almanac of everything you ever need to know. Think about it."

"Ha! Okay, I like him now," Maria commented snidely, her digital voice tinged with approval.

Tom quickly adjusted his tone, realizing his mistake. "Right, sorry. I didn't mean it like that. I truly appreciate this gift you've given me. I will be sure to commit it to memory as something of the utmost importance." He bowed his head slightly, showing respect to appease his Patron.

"That's more like it!" Azroc barked, visibly pleased. "Now, you have the text. That should complete your quest. Here." He focused on his interface again, his gaze becoming distant as he interacted with something only he could see. A message flashed in Tom's vision, confirming the completion of his quest.

Pact Update:

You have successfully completed all current quests to advance your pact with Azroc:

- Conquer 3 Dungeons in Azroc's name.
- Slay The Master with your own hands.
- Conduct in-depth research on your Class.

New powers are now available for you to choose. Proceed to select your reward and further empower your bond with Azroc.

INVASION

"Awesome! Let's see what you have for me this time, Azroc. You never fail to impress!" Tom said excitedly after reading the prompt.

Another window opened after he dismissed the first message. Reading over the options, Tom took his time to be sure he understood all the options.

Pact of the Tattoo Upgrade:

Azroc acknowledges your continued service and dedication. In recognition of your efforts, you are rewarded with the opportunity to choose an additional power. Select one of the following Tattoo Upgrades:

- **Tattoo of the Berserker**: Increases both Strength and Agility for one hour, sending the user into a frenzied rage. While the user retains the ability to distinguish friend from foe, rational thought will be diminished.
Mana Cost: 250 mana.

- **Tattoo of Dark Nova**: Instantly casts the spell *Dark Nova*, creating a field of dark energy around the user that expands rapidly, repelling nearby enemies and dealing dark damage.
Mana Cost: 250 mana. *Cooldown*: 10 minutes.

- **Tattoo of Displacement**: Allows the user to teleport up to 50 feet to an unoccupied space.
Mana Cost: 250 mana.

Choose wisely to enhance your capabilities and solidify your pact with Azroc!

Once again, Tom found himself staring at a difficult choice. The options presented before him were tantalizing, each one brimming with potential. He wished he could have all of them, every tattoo he had been offered so far, but life rarely worked that way. Choices had to be made, and this one was no different.

"I just remembered, I need to ask you something, Azroc," Tom said, looking up from his prompt.

"Shoot. Can't promise I can answer, but I will if I can," Azroc replied.

"I have the *Tattoo of Magic Nullification*. How can I use that and still use other tattoos, but not spells? Aren't the tattoos magic?" Tom asked.

"Ah, *that* I can answer. The tattoos are technically magic, but the *Tattoo of Magic Nullification* specifically stops spells that are cast via traditional mana channels. The tattoos technically operate more like Skills. While they do use your mana stored in your body, they don't follow your traditional mana network to be used. So, they're exempt. Wouldn't do to have an ability that nullifies your entire fucking build when you use it. So, the System adjusts to allow for a fair option," Azroc replied.

"That's a relief," Tom said, returning to his options.

"These are the options you get for doing his silly quests? He definitely likes you," Maria chimed in, her voice tinged with a mixture of admiration and envy. "Patrons can't directly choose what options are given, but they can certainly guide the choices to what they feel you deserve. You are one lucky son of a witch."

"These are really good?" Tom asked aloud, still mulling over the options. His eyes scanned each description again, lingering on the details, his mind racing with possibilities.

"Um, duh. Everything I give you is great, shitbag," Azroc interjected, his confusion evident in his gruff tone. His muscles rippled slightly as he tilted his head, trying to decipher Tom's sudden change of tone.

"He can't hear me, dummy," Maria reminded Tom with a digital sigh, like a teacher dealing with a slow student.

"Oh, sorry," Tom apologized, waving a hand in front of him as if to clear the air. "I wasn't saying that to you, Azroc. I've got a new AI assistant, and she's a lot more… sentient than I expected."

Azroc's expression shifted from confusion to understanding, his eyes narrowing slightly. "Ahhhh, the Administrators are still doing patches here, I see. Well, it's good they're keeping things fresh, but some of the shit they pull really makes me think they shit the—" Azroc's words were cut off abruptly as his body jolted like he'd been hit with a taser. He grunted and clenched his teeth, his muscled form twitching involuntarily. "Oof, that stings like a fucking son of a bitch. A word of advice—don't talk bad about the Administrators."

"Duly noted," Tom replied, a smirk tugging at the corner of his mouth. "You really like making these choices difficult, don't you?"

Azroc's lips curled into a knowing smile, his eyes gleaming with a mix of mischief and wisdom. "This is supposed to make you think about what kind of abilities you'll develop. They need to synergize not only with who you are, but with the fighting style you use. Making the wrong decision could cripple you later. It's a test I put Warlocks through to see what kind of person they are."

Tom nodded, still weighing his options carefully. He could feel the eyes of his friends on him, waiting for him to make a decision. He didn't want to rush this.

"So, what'd you get?" Derek's voice came from behind him, and Tom turned slightly to see his friend leaning casually against a wall, arms crossed and a curious gleam in his eye.

"I expected James to be the hand-rubbing info-goblin," Tom chuckled, casting a quick glance over his shoulder. "But yeah, they're all pretty great." He read off the options to his friends, his tone becoming more animated as he described each one in detail.

"Damn. Those *are* all good," Derek replied, rubbing his chin thoughtfully. "I think you can rule out *Tattoo of the Berserker* right away. You already have a Strength increase, and you don't want to lose too much cognitive function in a battle."

INVASION

"Yeah, I assumed the same," Tom agreed, mimicking Derek's thoughtful pose, his hand on his chin and his arm crossed over his chest. "But *Tattoo of Dark Nova* and *Tattoo of Displacement* are both game changers."

Brian, who had been quietly listening, spoke up. "From the sound of it, you need to up your mana no matter what. You've got a lot of options that cost a pretty penny upfront."

"Yeah," Tom nodded, "I've been increasing that recently, but more points would always be nice. I've noticed how fast it drains in big fights."

Kiera, standing to the side, folded her arms and added thoughtfully, "You know, Dark Nova could be something that might also have similar spells elsewhere. You don't want to limit yourself to one powerful attack if there are other spells that can do the same or better." She shrugged. "Not to mention, the ten minute cooldown. Displacement, on the other hand, has none."

Azroc's face lit up with a rare expression of approval. "That's using the mush between your ears," he said, tapping one finger to his nose and pointing at Kiera with the other. "This bitch gets it."

Tom nodded again, deep in thought. "I still need to find a way to learn more spells. That's something I've been meaning to look into. It's becoming clear that relying on a few powerful moves isn't the best long-term strategy."

Azroc grinned widely, clearly pleased with the discussion. "Now you're getting it. You've got to think ahead, plan for the unexpected."

"Alright," Tom decided, taking a deep breath and straightening up. "Then Displacement seems like the best option. It gives me mobility and versatility, and I can use it to better control the battlefield."

Azroc nodded, satisfied. "Good choice, kid. You're learning. Keep this up, and you'll make a damn fine Warlock yet."

Tom felt a sense of accomplishment settle over him, his mind already racing ahead to how he could use this new ability. He glanced around at his friends, who were all nodding in agreement, their faces filled with excitement and anticipation. He wasn't just making decisions for himself anymore; every choice he made rippled out to affect them all.

Confirm?	
You have selected The Tattoo of Displacement. Are you sure you wish to continue? Once selected, this choice cannot be undone.	
Yes	*No*

Tom mentally selected "Yes," and the pop-up vanished from his view. Almost immediately, he felt a searing sensation on the backs of his calves, as if molten needles were etching into his skin. Gritting his teeth against the sudden pain, he quickly pulled up the legs of his pants to see the new tattoo forming. The intricate tribal designs spiraled along his skin, glowing faintly with dark energy, the fresh ink surrounded by a ring of redness and slight inflammation.

"You are truly something special, Tom," Azroc said, his deep, gravelly voice resonating with a rare tone of approval. "I don't see many Warlocks putting actual fucking thought into bettering themselves with a view to the future. Most just grab whatever power looks flashy at the moment. I don't get to do this often, but I think you've earned it."

Azroc extended a muscled hand toward him, his expression shifting into a serious, almost solemn one.

Dark purple tendrils of energy snaked out from his fingertips, twisting and writhing in the air like living shadows. Tom's eyes widened in alarm as the tendrils darted toward him, wrapping around his body like serpents. The air seemed to crackle with arcane power, and a low hum filled his ears. Tom noticed that one of the tattoos on Azroc's body disappeared as the magic moved down his arm.

Tom's heart pounded in his chest, a mixture of fear and anticipation gripping him. Suddenly, he felt his feet lift off the ground. His body was suspended a few inches in the air, held aloft by the dark energy coiling around him. Then came the pain—sharp, stinging, and burning all at once—as if a thousand tiny needles were being driven into the back of his neck. He clenched his eyes shut against the searing agony, his breath hissing through his teeth. The sensation was intense, almost overwhelming, but Tom fought to maintain control.

Gradually, the pain began to subside, replaced by a cold, numbing sensation that spread across his neck and down his spine. He felt the energy release its grip on him, and he was slowly lowered back to the ground. His legs trembled slightly as his feet touched the floor, but he steadied himself, breathing heavily.

A new prompt filled his vision, its words glowing brightly against the dim lighting of the gym:

Your Patron Has Given You a Gift!

Tattoo of Reflection: A powerful new tattoo has been granted to you by Azroc. When activated, this tattoo will reflect a single magical attack back at the caster.
Mana Cost: 150 mana. *Cooldown:* 1 hour.

Tom stared in amazement at the prompt hovering in front of him, his breath catching in his throat. His mind was racing, trying to process the unexpected bonus his Patron had just bestowed upon him. This almost felt like too much to be given all in one moment, given the strict rules of the System. An added benefit from Azroc was supposed to be rare. Though he had received it twice now. It felt nice, receiving an unexpected treasure—a recognition of his efforts and a validation of his choices.

INVASION

"I… I don't know what to say. Thank you!" Tom finally managed to stammer out, his voice laced with a mix of gratitude and disbelief.

Azroc's expression hardened, though a glimmer of pride flickered in his eyes. "Don't go all soft on me like you came too early," he scoffed, waving a hand dismissively. "This isn't some charity handout. You got this because you've shown you're dedicated to your path, not just some power-hungry asshole looking for the next shiny thing. You earned it, plain and simple. Keep it up, and who knows—I might just toss more free shit your way!" Azroc's gruff exterior faltered for a second, hinting at a deeper respect behind the bravado.

Tom chuckled, nodding. "You got it, Azroc."

Azroc's stance shifted, and his intense gaze softened slightly as he folded his muscular arms.

"Now," he said, his voice taking on a more curious tone, "why don't you fill me in on what you've been doing around here? Spill the beans. Maybe there's a way I can help you out a little more."

Chapter 3

Guild Tour

"Wow, you sure have a lot of these motherfuckers around here," Azroc commented as he followed Tom on a guided tour of the Vanguard Guild building. His deep voice rumbled through the corridor like a rolling drum, drawing a few uneasy glances from nearby Guild members.

Tom looked at Azroc, puzzled by the comment.

"Non-Warlocks," Azroc clarified, reading Tom's unspoken question with a flick of his reptilian eyes that gleamed with a hint of disdain.

"Oh," Tom muttered, nodding as the realization dawned on him. "I don't actually know what everyone's Classes are. We more than likely have a few Warlocks. Brian would have that information."

"We do," Brian chimed in, his voice carrying a note of authority. His tall frame was imposing, even in the dim hallway lighting, and his presence often had a calming effect on those around him. "Not a lot, but there are some. They're a bit of an odd bunch, though."

Azroc snorted, a low guttural sound that echoed in the corridor. "Too bad. Kinda hoped there were more like you here," he muttered, his expression one of mild disappointment. "If he thinks they're odd, then they're just like the others. I'm sure they aren't terrible like some, but keep an eye on them. Warlocks are notorious for getting a bit absorbed in their quest for power. Shitstains don't know how to get true power."

As they continued walking, Tom glanced at Azroc from the corner of his eye, still trying to get used to the odd, imposing presence. His Patron's towering frame cast a long shadow, and his clawed feet scraped against the floor with each step, making a slight scratching noise. The Guild members who saw him couldn't help but stare, their eyes wide with a mixture of fear and curiosity.

Tom gestured toward a large open area filled with tables and chairs. The aroma of freshly cooked food filled the air, and the sounds of clinking cutlery and muffled conversations hummed around them. "This is the cafeteria, where we eat our meals. Charlene over there has been incredibly helpful in preparing food and menus for us so we aren't just eating canned goods," Tom explained, pointing toward a middle-aged woman with a kind smile and a sturdy frame. She noticed him and waved back, her eyes flicking nervously toward Azroc.

INVASION

"Can I get a meal? I love trying local cuisine," Azroc asked, his sharp teeth gleaming as he grinned. His grin was more predatory than friendly, but there was genuine interest in his gaze.

Tom blinked, surprised. "Um, sure. I didn't expect you to be hungry, but let's see what she has for you," he said, leading Azroc toward Charlene.

"Hi, Tom. Who's your… friend?" Charlene greeted, her voice wavering as she eyed Azroc, her hands subconsciously smoothing the front of her apron. Her eyes darted nervously between Tom and the hulking figure of his Patron. She maintained a smile, to her credit, despite the fact that it seemed strained.

"This is Azroc. He is my Patron and has asked for a tour, as well as to try your food," Tom explained, his tone reassuring. He nodded toward Azroc and then back to her.

"Oh! I wasn't expecting to be serving someone so important," Charlene stammered, her face flushing as she glanced at Azroc's massive frame and the intimidating spikes protruding from his shoulders. "Let me whip something up really fast, especially for Your Excellence… I mean Your Majesty… I mean Your Honor…" She glanced at Tom, slightly panicked, whispering, "How should I address him?"

"Almighty is fine," Azroc said, his lips curling into a wicked smile at her unease.

"*No*, Azroc is fine," Tom corrected him quickly, shooting a disapproving look at his Patron. "Just Azroc."

"What? It was funny," Azroc replied, shrugging his broad shoulders, his tail twitching slightly behind him like an amused cat's.

"Please behave. These people have been through enough," Tom sighed, pinching the bridge of his nose in exasperation.

"Oh, come on. You gotta lighten up and have a little fun," Azroc teased, his grin widening to reveal rows of jagged teeth.

Tom simply shook his head.

"Let's go sit. Charlene will send the food out when it's ready," he suggested, resigning himself to the antics of his unpredictable Patron.

They moved to one of the sturdy wooden tables in the center of the cafeteria. The place was bustling with people. Several Guild members glanced over curiously, whispering among themselves as they noticed Azroc's presence. The Patron was a rare sight, and his aura filled the room with a mixture of unease and fascination. The conversations around them seemed to quiet down as more people took notice.

One oblivious Guild member, talking to his friend as he carried his tray to the bus station, tripped over Azroc's tail as he walked by. His tray, plate, cutlery, and remaining food went flying into the air before sprawling to the floor as he did. Azroc laughed hysterically at the man's misfortune, but Tom quickly got up to help him pick up the spill.

While they waited, Tom, Brian, and the others chatted about the current state of the Guild. "We have a basement area as well that has our larger crafting stations," Tom explained, leaning forward onto the table. "We can go there next to see what they're up to. A lot of the space is dedicated to simply housing people, but we do have a garden near the roof."

Brian nodded, adding, "We also have an orchard of sorts out back, along with a livestock pen. We still need to decide how to properly expand." His analytical mind was always planning the next step, his brow furrowed with thought.

After about fifteen minutes, Charlene returned with several of the kitchen staff, each carrying a plate. She carefully placed a large, steaming plate in front of Azroc and then set down plates for everyone else at the table. The smell of cooked meat and freshly baked bread wafted into the air, and Tom's stomach growled in response.

"I present to you: Goatamus steaks, medium rare, along with a side of hashbrowns, eggs over easy, bacon, and toast with homemade apple butter from the apples in our orchard. I hope you enjoy it," Charlene announced, bowing awkwardly as though she couldn't decide if that was the right form of deference. "Almighty," she added, almost as an afterthought.

"Oh, for fuck's sake," Tom muttered under his breath, rolling his eyes.

"Thank you, Charlene. Your offering pleases me," Azroc replied, picking up the steak with his massive claws and sniffing it like a wild beast inspecting its prey.

"Thanks, Charlene. Don't mind him. Please continue with what you were doing," Tom said, trying to sound reassuring as he waved her away. His face was tight with barely restrained frustration.

Charlene backed away slowly, like a deer caught in headlights, then turned and power walked back to the kitchen.

Tom could still see her peeking through the service window to watch Azroc's reaction. The Patron put the steak back down and looked at Tom and the others, who had picked up forks and knives and were cutting their meat into pieces. Mimicking them, he picked up the fork and knife provided to him, which looked comically tiny in his oversized hands, and tried to cut into his steak.

"Why don't you just pick this shit up and shove it in your fucking gobs like normal people?" Azroc grumbled, frustrated with the small utensils that seemed more suited for a child than for him.

"Some foods are finger foods, like bacon, but steak is messy if you eat it with your hands," Tom replied with a chuckle. "Don't feel like you need to use the utensils for us."

Azroc sighed with relief, dropping the fork and knife with a clatter. He grabbed the steak between two massive claws, his sharp nails sinking slightly into the meat, and shoved the whole thing into his mouth, chewing noisily.

"Uh, that has a bone in it. You know that, right?" Tom asked, his eyes widening in horror as he heard the crunch of bone between Azroc's powerful jaws.

"Know it? That's the best part. Gives it a bit of a crunch. Great texture addition," Azroc said, his eyes bright with pleasure. "I've never had Goatamus before. It was delicious."

Wiping his mouth on the back of his hand, he moved on to the hashbrowns, popping them into his mouth like oversized tater tots. Then, he stared at the eggs, his eyes narrowing with curiosity. He poked one of the bright yellow yolks with a nail, watching in fascination as the golden liquid seeped out and spread across his plate.

"Ha! Amazing! My food bleeds! This is a wonderful bonus," Azroc exclaimed, joy lighting up his fierce features.

He reached for the bacon, his eyes still glued to the eggs, and stuffed a strip into his mouth. A moment later, he paused. His eyes widened even further, and he let out a long, guttural moan of pure pleasure that echoed through the cafeteria, causing several heads to turn.

"Oh, my fucking shitholes! That is the greatest thing I have ever put in my mouth. What do you call it again?" Azroc demanded, his voice suddenly hushed as if he were uttering a sacred word.

"Bacon," Tom answered, bemused. "It's salted and cured pork belly sliced thin—but not *too* thin—and fried."

"Sweet nipples of the Ghrolgog beast… now I feel like my life has been a fucking waste up to this point! Untold centuries of eating and this… this is what has been missing!" Azroc declared passionately, his eyes closing as he slowly chewed, savoring every bit of the smoky flavor.

"I mean, it's great, sure, but I'm not sure it's that amazing," Tom said, watching Azroc warily as the demon continued to moan and sigh with every bite.

"Mmmmmm… sweet mother of a whore, that is *so good*. Trust me, kid. This is it. This is the fucking shit," Azroc muttered between bites, his voice filled with genuine admiration.

After polishing off his bacon—and some from the plates of others who had already eaten—Azroc grabbed his plate and tipped it over his mouth, letting the eggs slide down into his awaiting maw.

With his meal complete, he stood up with a satisfied grunt, and the others followed suit. Tom led the way down the corridor toward the basement.

Descending the stairs, the rhythmic sound of hammering grew louder. It was Roland, the Guild's Blacksmith, hard at work at his anvil. The clang of metal on metal echoed up the stairwell, creating a chorus of industry. As they reached the basement floor, Azroc's eyes lit up with a spark of interest, and he immediately veered toward the smithy.

"I definitely need to see what you got going here. You know, I did a little smithing myself in my younger days," Azroc said with a surprising hint of nostalgia in his rough voice.

Reaching Roland's station, Azroc's sudden appearance made the Blacksmith jump, his hammer slipping from his grip and clattering to the floor. "Vat ze hell?!" Roland cried out, his face paling as he took in Azroc's imposing figure.

"Don't worry, Roland!" Tom called out quickly, trying to calm the man. "He's a friend. This is Azroc, my Patron."

"Oh, phew. I vas vorried ve vere being invaded by ze lizardfolk. Ze are being very sneaky sometimes," Roland replied, still looking a bit shaken but managing a nervous smile.

Azroc tilted his head, his brow furrowing. "What the fuck is wrong with his voice?"

"He's German, Azroc. That's just his accent," Tom explained, rolling his eyes.

"Es ist gut dich zu treffen. Jeder Freund von Tom ist ein Freund für mich," Roland said, nodding respectfully to Azroc.

Azroc paused, clearly processing what Roland said. "Ich sehe jetzt. Du sprichst eine andere verdammte Sprache."

Tom blinked, genuinely surprised. "Wait, you speak German?"

"No, but I have a translation Skill. It's universal. As long as the planet it originates from is integrated into the System," Azroc replied casually, then turned to Roland again. "Leute, richtig?"

Roland remained frozen for a moment, utterly stunned.

For the next thirty minutes, Azroc chatted with Roland about techniques to harden metals and how to refine his smithing process. At first, Roland was tense and hesitant, but as the conversation continued, he relaxed, captivated by the Patron's knowledge. Soon enough, he was eagerly hammering away under Azroc's guidance, his strikes more confident and precise.

"Try that out for a while and let Tom know how it goes. I think you'll start seeing a difference, at least in the XP you get," Azroc said, offering a rare grin of approval before he turned on his heel and started heading toward the back of the building.

"Isn't this a little out of your purview, Azroc?" Tom asked, jogging after him, his curiosity piqued.

"Normally, yes," Azroc admitted with a sly grin, "but you guys have a fucking Space Pirate problem, and I don't want to have to find another Warlock I like."

Tom chuckled as he led Azroc toward Herbert and Harold, who were busy working on various projects. Azroc wasted no time announcing his presence, his voice booming.

"Hey, fuckheads! Whatcha working on?"

Herbert and Harold turned, eyes wide with shock. Tom quickly stepped in to introduce his Patron, and the Engineers began to explain their projects, a new energy buzzing in the air as they realized they might be learning from one of the most powerful beings they had ever encountered.

As Azroc walked off, having shared more wisdom than they expected, Tom could only shake his head. His Patron was many things—brash, crude, and unpredictable—but he was undeniably effective.

It was going to be an interesting day.

Chapter 4

Patron Saint

"Really?" Azroc scoffed, his fiery eyes narrowing as he surveyed the cramped security room. Rows of monitors flickered under the dim, artificial lighting, casting dancing shadows across the walls. "This is your fucking base of command? It's pretty pathetic." His booming voice filled the space, making a few of the guards shift uncomfortably in their seats.

Just then, Joe walked into the room. His eyes went wide at seeing Azroc, and without even hesitating, he turned around and left the room, whistling a nonchalant tune.

Brian, standing with arms crossed, didn't take the insult lying down. "I'm not really sure what you expect us to have," he replied, his tone steady but edged with frustration. "This is perfectly functional."

Azroc rolled his eyes dramatically, the muscles in his thick neck flexing with the motion.

"For fuck's sake," he grumbled, throwing his hands up in exasperation. "You can purchase upgrades from the Guild menu and have so many more things to make this job easier. You're sitting here like a bunch of clueless noobs."

Brian's frown deepened, his brow furrowing as he considered his options. "But… we need to use those points for expansion," he countered, his voice firm.

Azroc let out a sharp, derisive laugh. "No, you *need* to use them for things that might help with any kind of… let's say possible *invasions*." He tried to keep his tone casual, but his eyes betrayed a glimmer of concern.

Tom stood quietly in the corner, observing the interaction. It was becoming clear that Azroc was bending the rules by trying to help them. Tom had seen what happened when the Patron broke a System-imposed rule—it wasn't pretty. He could almost see the memory of that moment reflected in the slight twitch of Azroc's tail.

Brian, however, wasn't as quick to catch on. "So, what is it you suggest?" he asked, his voice sharp with impatience.

Azroc's lips clamped shut, and his expression darkened. His fiery eyes bore into Brian's, filled with irritation at being pressed too far.

"Well?" Brian pressed, his tone challenging, unaware of the precarious line he was treading.

"He can't give us details, Brian," Tom cut in, stepping forward to defuse the tension. "He's bending the rules enough as it is. Give him a break and try to see what he's saying as helpful." His voice was calm but firm, a gentle reprimand to his friend.

Brian sighed deeply, his shoulders slumping as he realized his mistake.

"Fine. Sorry," he muttered, rubbing the back of his neck. "I'm just trying my best to get us prepared, and there's so many things to do. I just don't know which is right." His admission came out quietly, a rare moment of vulnerability for the usually composed man. "Maybe we need to look at a list of magical surveillance options that we could get from the Guild updates screens?"

"I can neither confirm nor deny that those options might or might not be something you could or could not look at possibly or not possibly implementing or not implementing in a way that may or may not enhance the operations you do or do not have going or not going here," Azroc said, pretending to see something extremely interesting in the corner of the room.

Tom walked over and placed a reassuring hand on Brian's shoulder, giving it a firm squeeze. "You're doing an amazing job. There's nothing wrong with accepting a little help."

Brian nodded, taking a deep breath. "I know. I'll take a look at the upgrades available and see what options we have," he conceded, sinking into a nearby chair and pulling up the Guild menu on his display.

Azroc, satisfied with the resolution, glanced back at the room full of screens and monitors. "Cameras are great, but there are better options out there," he grunted, crossing his thick arms over his chest. "You'll have to see what you can do. Might even be able to get a little more space out of the deal." With that, he turned and headed for the door, his heavy footsteps echoing on the tiled floor.

"Let's head to the garden next," Tom suggested, trying to shift the mood.

They exited the security office and began crossing the bustling lobby toward the elevators. On their way, they passed a group of children kicking a ball around the open space. The sight was a small, chaotic slice of normalcy amid the ongoing chaos. Most parents didn't want their children playing outdoors, given that the expanding territory was starting to encroach on more dangerous areas, and monsters were always a possibility. As a result, the kids usually took to playing in the gym, but with Tom and his team using the gym for summoning and meetings with Azroc, the children had little choice but to play in the lobby.

Azroc noticed the children playing and paused, his towering frame casting a long shadow across the floor. One child kicked the ball too hard, sending it flying past the goalie and rolling to a stop at Azroc's clawed feet. He stared down at the ball for a moment, his expression unreadable. Then, with surprising gentleness, he picked it up and held it out to the group of children who had cautiously approached him to retrieve it.

"Thanks… um… mister?" a small boy said, his wide eyes filled with gratitude as he accepted the ball. "You wanna play with us?"

For a moment, Azroc simply stared at the child, his face softening as he considered the innocent request. His usual harsh demeanor seemed to melt away, revealing something almost… tender.

Azroc finally replied, smiling softly and patting the small child on the head gently.

"No fucking way, kid."

INVASION

Tom looked at his Patron, horrified.

"Oh, wipe that pathetic look off your fucking face, mister *junior* Warlock. You can judge me when you've killed your first god, huh? How about that? Besides, I was just fucking around." He turned back toward the child, his expression softening once more. "I think I can spare a little time," he said, glancing back at Tom.

Tom gave a small nod, a knowing smile tugging at his lips. He could see that his draconic Patron was trying to act tough. "We've got as much time as you think you can spare being with us."

Azroc turned back to the children and joined their game, his massive frame looking almost comically out of place among the tiny players. He kicked the ball with deliberate clumsiness, chasing after it in a mock display of awkwardness that made the children laugh and giggle. Not a single swear word escaped his usually foul mouth while he was with them—a fact that didn't go unnoticed by Tom.

At one point, Azroc picked up the ball in mock frustration, growling playfully.

"This is my ball now!" He roared with feigned menace, breaking into a run with the ball held high above his head.

The children shrieked with laughter, running after him in a chaotic mob. After a few moments of evasion, Azroc pretended to trip, sending him sprawling to the ground. The kids took their chance, dog-piling on top of him as he groaned dramatically. Their laughter echoed off the walls, pure and infectious.

When Azroc finally managed to free himself from the dog pile, he dusted himself off and explained to the children that he had to continue the tour.

"Awwww," came a collective groan from the group.

"Please, mister. Can you come back to play with us again?" one child asked, looking up at Azroc with big, pleading eyes.

Azroc hesitated, then his rough features softened. "Sure thing, buddy. I'll come back sometime and play again. But I'm pretty busy, so it might be a while," he said, tousling the boy's hair with a surprisingly gentle hand.

The children, though disappointed, nodded in understanding. Everyone in the Guild was busy most of the time, so they were used to taking whatever time they could get. Azroc turned and walked over to the elevator, and he and Tom got on together to head up to the gardens.

"You seemed to enjoy that time with the kids," Tom said offhandedly, a small smile on his face as he stared at the ascending floor numbers, avoiding eye contact with Azroc.

"Shut the fuck up," Azroc muttered, his voice rough but lacking its usual bite. "Kids are still innocent. They haven't seen the harsh realities of the way things work. They don't need to see the other side yet." He, too, stared straight ahead, avoiding Tom's gaze.

The silence stretched between them, awkward but not uncomfortable. The elevator chimed, and the doors slid open, revealing rows upon rows of green vegetation, neatly arranged in raised wooden beds. Some taller trees dotted the garden, providing patches of shade, while the rest of the area was bathed in sunlight. A few Guild members were scattered about, tending to the crops with quiet diligence.

"This is nowhere near enough to feed everyone, is it?" Azroc asked, his eyes scanning the orderly rows of plants and the small group of workers.

"No," Tom admitted, his gaze following Azroc's. "It's been a good start, but we have another area out back set up for other crops, including a small orchard." He took a deep breath, taking in the scent of fresh soil and growing plants.

"Still not enough," Azroc stated plainly, his broad shoulders shrugging slightly.

"We know," Tom replied, a hint of frustration creeping into his voice. "But this city isn't exactly filled with prime farmland."

"True," Azroc conceded, nodding slightly. "But maybe there's an alternative that you can use some of those Guild points on." He started walking deeper into the garden, his heavy footsteps crunching on the gravel path.

Tom followed closely, keeping pace. "What the hell is this shit?" Azroc suddenly asked, staring down at a patch of unfamiliar plants with a look of confusion.

"Those are cucumbers," Tom explained, glancing over to see what had caught Azroc's attention. "You can cut them up and eat them on salads, or pickle them to keep for longer."

Azroc's nose wrinkled in disgust. "They look like green dicks. Do people…?" He trailed off suggestively, his eyes narrowing with mischief.

"Ummm… sometimes, I'd guess," Tom stammered, his cheeks flushing with embarrassment. "But I would advise against it."

"Oh, come on. Don't tell me you never thought about it?" Azroc pressed, clearly enjoying Tom's discomfort.

"Can we talk about *anything* else?" Tom groaned, his face heating up.

"Fine, fine, fucking fine," Azroc relented, chuckling. "Didn't know you were such a prude. What about the purple dicks? The emojis?"

"Eggplants," Tom corrected, sighing. "Not sure we have those. I'll be sure to ask when you aren't here."

They continued to explore the garden, Azroc making crude jokes about various vegetables until, after nearly an hour, they reentered the lobby.

"I still can't believe so many vegetables look like—" Azroc started.

"Do you really just like dicks? Sweet baby Jesus on a fucking Roomba, it's like talking to James," Tom retorted, rolling his eyes so hard he feared they might get stuck.

Tom and Azroc walked out to the garage, where they climbed into the GS2 after Tom insisted on taking a short tour of the areas surrounding the Guild building. As they drove, Tom noticed a lone goblin scavenging for food.

"Wanna go bowling?" Tom asked, a malicious grin spreading across his face.

Azroc's eyes lit up with a similar mischievous glint.

"Fuck yeah," he replied, a grin splitting his lips.

INVASION

Tom hit the gas, and the vehicle shot off like a bullet, the engine roaring and tires screeching. The goblin looked up from the trash pile it had been rifling through, its eyes widening in terror. It tried to stand and run but managed only to trip over its own feet, falling face-first into the dirt. It clawed desperately at the ground, scrambling to escape.

With a slight bump, the GS2 plowed over the creature, its shrieks cut short.

"That was almost as much fun as killing them yourself," Azroc laughed, clapping his hands together with delight.

"Well, now that you've seen most of what we do here, what do you think?" Tom asked as they continued to cruise through the city streets, his hands relaxed on the wheel.

"You've accomplished much, but the trials coming to your world will push even you to the very limit of what you can do," Azroc replied, his tone unexpectedly sober, his gaze fixed on the road ahead.

"We can only do what we can do. We won't go down without a fight," Tom replied; his expression resolute.

"That's all anyone can ask. Keep working hard at upgrading, and you'll survive. I mean, maybe not all of you, but some of you." Azroc's tone was nonchalant, but there was a glimmer of seriousness in his eyes.

"That's bleak," Tom muttered, glancing over at his Patron.

"It's fucking reality, shitbiscuit. You get stronger, or you fucking die. That's the way of life in this mess." Azroc's arms folded over his chest, a posture that showed he wasn't interested in arguing the point.

Tom sighed, turning his attention back to the road. "I know. I just wish there was another way."

Azroc looked at Tom out of the corner of his eye, not turning his head. After a moment, he asked, "How many Dungeons have you completed and put my mark on again?"

"Three. Why?" Tom asked, his brow furrowing in confusion. "You just gave me a reward for that."

"I know, I know. Hold on, I'm working on something," Azroc grumbled, his eyes loosing focus as if staring at invisible screens.

Suddenly, a window popped up in Tom's view.

"Fuck! I'm driving, you bastard!" Tom yelled, quickly minimizing the window and pulling the vehicle to a stop.

"Oh, come on. Learn to multitask," Azroc chided, rolling his eyes.

With the vehicle now safely parked, Tom reopened the prompt, his eyes scanning the information displayed before him.

Your Patron has issued a new quest: Show Your Might!	
Azroc has given you a new quest to complete: Show Your Might! Demonstrate to Azroc that you have been working to prepare for the impending invasion to receive your prize. Accept?	
Yes	*No*

Tom looked at it, confused. Selecting "Yes," the prompt disappeared and was replaced by another pop-up.

Quest Complete!

You have completed the quest "Show Your Might!" Azroc has inspected your demesne and is satisfied with your progress in upgrading Vanguard. Select one of the following rewards:

- Tattoo of Eldritch Horror
Activating this tattoo will transform the user into an eldritch horror, granting immense power and the abilities that come with it. However, the user will lose control of their actions for the duration of the activation period, during which the creature will act on its own, attacking and destroying everything in its path.
Tattoo casting cost: 500 mana.

- Tattoo of Perception
When activated, this tattoo will heighten the user's senses, allowing them to see farther, hear better, and detect smells more keenly than human perception normally permits. The user cannot be surprised while this tattoo is active.
Tattoo casting cost: 250 mana.

- Tattoo of Inspiration
This tattoo will boost the morale of all allies who choose to follow you. Based on your Charisma Attribute, allies will receive additional defense points. The boost provides +0.25% defense per point of Charisma for a duration of 10 minutes.
Tattoo casting cost: 250 mana.

Choose wisely, as this decision is final.

"Can you actually do this?" Tom asked, his brow furrowed with skepticism. His eyes scanned over the options, each one more tempting than the last. He felt his heart rate quicken, a mix of anticipation and disbelief settling in his chest.

"Sure as shit can," Azroc responded, a crooked grin spreading across his rugged face. He crossed his muscular arms, his posture exuding a mixture of confidence and pride. "I get to decide how the quests and rewards go. Well, at least the level of the prizes," he clarified, his voice carrying the weight of authority. "Can't control the actual gifts specifically."

INVASION

Tom's mind reeled at the thought. A Patron with this much leeway? He had expected Azroc's help to come with more strings attached. "I don't know what to say," Tom murmured, still trying to process the unexpected generosity.

"Look, kid," Azroc began, his tone softening just a fraction. He leaned closer, his imposing frame a bit menacing, yet there was a sincerity in his gaze that softened his intimidating presence. "I've been doing this for a long time. There are a lot of shitbags out there," he said with a hint of a growl, his lips curling slightly in distaste. "But you're one of the good ones. I can't say I see that a lot." His expression shifted to something more earnest. "So, I want you to succeed."

Tom nodded slowly, a wave of appreciation washing over him. Coming from Azroc, this was high praise. He looked back at the options displayed before him, his eyes scanning over them one more time. Each tattoo offered a powerful advantage, but only one seemed to resonate with his immediate goals. The decision felt obvious—he needed to keep his people safe, and the *Tattoo of Inspiration* seemed like the best choice to help lead them through the challenges ahead.

Taking a deep breath, Tom mentally selected the *Tattoo of Inspiration*. Immediately, a sharp, stinging sensation began to spread across his chest, centered directly over his left pectoral muscle. It was different this time; the pain was more intense, and it lasted longer than the other times he had been inked. His breath hitched for a moment, his muscles tensing as he fought to remain still.

Azroc watched with a knowing smirk, his arms still crossed. "Hurts good, doesn't it?" he remarked, the faintest hint of amusement in his gravelly voice. "Like a motherfucker, but that's the price of power."

Tom chuckled weakly, his lips twisting into a half-smile despite the discomfort. "You could say that," he managed through gritted teeth. He could feel the tattoo embedding itself into his skin, a searing burn that slowly faded to a dull throb.

Once the process was complete, Tom let out a slow, controlled breath, feeling the tension release from his body. He wanted to see the tattoo now, to examine the intricate design that he knew would be etched across his skin. However, his armor was still in place, and now wasn't the time to strip down. He decided he'd wait to see it later when he could get a proper look in the shower.

Before he could even settle back into the moment, another prompt flashed into his vision, demanding his attention. He blinked, refocusing his gaze as he prepared to see what lay ahead.

Your Patron has issued a new quest: **Legendary Patron Quest - Survive Against the Odds**	
Azroc has given you a new quest to complete: Survive the Invasion. Successfully repel the invasion or survive until reinforcements arrive. *Legendary Patron Quests are a requirement for Advancement.* Accept?	
Yes	*No*

Tom took a deep breath, his finger hovering over the confirmation button for a moment longer than necessary. Then, with a determined nod, he selected "Yes."

A soft hum filled the air as the decision locked into place, and the weight of the new power settled over him like a heavy cloak. He glanced over at Azroc, a question forming on his lips.

"So, I guess this means I won't see you again until after the invasion?" Tom asked, his voice laced with a mixture of disappointment and understanding. The reality of the upcoming battle loomed large over his thoughts, casting a shadow he couldn't quite shake.

Azroc tilted his head, considering the question with a slight smirk.

"Probably," he replied, his tone almost casual. "You could always summon me sooner, but there's no telling if I'll be busy. When someone completes a quest, I have certain abilities that allow me to be present," he added, his eyes narrowing slightly as if he were weighing how much to say.

Tom's curiosity piqued at that. "Like what?" he pressed, hoping for a glimpse into the broader powers of his Patron.

Azroc chuckled, a low, rumbling sound that seemed to reverberate through the air.

"I can't tell you that," he said, a mischievous glint in his eyes. "Too much information for someone at your level." His response was brief but firm, a clear boundary set by whatever cosmic rules governed their connection.

Tom frowned slightly, feeling a twinge of frustration. "Damn," he muttered under his breath. He had hoped for just a bit more insight into the mysterious abilities that Patrons like Azroc possessed. Still, he couldn't push too hard—he knew the rules were there for a reason, even if they were frustrating.

"Alright, let's head back for now," Tom said, shaking off the disappointment. "I think you've gotten the general idea of what we're up to here." His tone softened, sincerity slipping through his words. "And Azroc… thanks. I mean it."

Azroc's lips curled into a crooked grin, a spark of genuine amusement dancing in his eyes. "Just doing my job, dickweed," he said, his voice rough but not unkind. "Nothing different from any other Patron." He gave Tom a playful wink, a rare moment of levity that cut through the tension like a knife.

Tom couldn't help but chuckle at that, his spirits lifting just a bit. With a nod of appreciation, he turned back toward the Guild building, feeling a renewed sense of purpose.

"Azroc?" Tom asked quietly.

"Hmm?"

"You think I could summon you over for some tea in—oh, I don't know, a few months, and if some, say… Space Pirates happen to start shooting in your general direction, that you could…" He flicked a finger in demonstration.

"*Tom…*" Azroc said, placing a gentle hand on his shoulder. "Tea is for pussies."

INVASION

Tom's face fell at this response.
"But… I'd never say no to a nice bourbon…"

Chapter 5

Goblin News

Tom and Azroc arrived back at the Vanguard building and stepped into the bustling lobby. The room was alive with activity; people moved about with purpose, discussing plans, sharing updates, or simply catching a moment to rest. The hum of conversations, the occasional laughter, and the ever-present clatter of boots against the tiled floor filled the air. Tom took a moment to glance around, feeling the weight of leadership settle back onto his shoulders.

Azroc, however, seemed almost out of place in the ordinary surroundings, like a mythical figure dropped into a mundane world. He stood there, his towering presence exuding a strange combination of menace and familiarity, before he turned to Tom with an expression that was almost thoughtful.

"You're doing just about everything you can," Azroc said, his voice a low rumble that somehow managed to cut through the ambient noise. "Remember that preparation is about looking at all the options available to you. Don't sit on any points that could give you an edge, and take every opportunity to get better. And remember that it's not just physical attributes you can train. Look into the magical ones as well."

Tom chuckled, sensing a rare moment of sincerity from his usually crass Patron. "Taking a break from your usual self, I see."

Azroc's lips curled into a wry grin, his sharp teeth showing just slightly. "Actually, the other persona is mostly who I have to be with most people. They expect some big, fuck-off deity-like creature who's ready to smite the unworthy. Some dumbass idea of what a being of such power should be. But we aren't really like that. Well, most of us aren't, anyway." Azroc's eyes softened for a moment, his usual bravado replaced by a rare glimpse of honesty. "We were once like you. So don't take any shit from any other powerful being you meet. That just makes more of them into assholes."

Tom laughed more openly now, the tension in his shoulders easing. "Got it. Big, fuck-off deity creatures are really just big, fuck-off teddy bears."

"That's not what I meant, and you fucking know it," Azroc replied, rolling his eyes but still smirking. "Never piss off a being like myself. That's a fast track to an ass-whooping at the very least."

Tom nodded, appreciating this candid moment. "I know what you're getting at. Thanks again, Azroc, for your help," he said, extending a hand.

Azroc looked at the hand for a moment, his grin widening.

INVASION

"Thanks for not being a waste of fucking space," he replied, clasping Tom's hand in a surprisingly firm handshake. His grip was strong but not crushing, a reminder of the strength he could wield if he chose to.

With a casual wave of his other hand, a shimmering copy of the summoning circle that Tom usually painstakingly created with chalk appeared on the floor. The runes etched themselves in an arcane glow, and a portal began to form, swirling and humming with energy. Azroc took a step toward it but paused, turning back with one last look at Tom.

"I'll be here when you need me. Until next time, shithead." Azroc winked, his tone a strange mix of endearment and mockery.

With that, he stepped into the portal. His massive frame descended slowly, as if sinking into a pool of darkness. The edges of the portal rippled, the circle tightening around him like a closing iris, until it finally disappeared with a quiet pop, leaving only a faint, lingering scent of brimstone.

Tom glanced down and saw the glowing summoning circle still etched into the lobby floor. He groaned, rubbing his temples in exasperation.

Brian walked by right at that moment. He paused, looking at the ash and residue left behind from the summoning ritual. "I thought you said it didn't leave anything behind? You better clean that shit up. We have enough to do around here."

"Just fucking great," he muttered, half to himself, half to the lingering essence of his Patron.

An hour later, Tom had finally scrubbed the last of the arcane sigils off the floor. The intricate designs that had glowed so ominously during Azroc's visit were now nothing more than a faint, wet smudge. He stood up, stretching his muscles, and wiped the sweat from his brow. The damp rag in his hand dripped dirty water onto the freshly cleaned tiles, but Tom didn't care. Even though his new stat improved body didn't leave him hurting as he expected, he decided he needed a break.

Exhausted, Tom walked over to the security office, his boots thudding softly against the floor. He pushed open the heavy metal door and slumped down into an empty desk chair, letting out a long breath. The room was dimly lit, with rows of monitors flickering in the semi-darkness, each displaying different camera feeds from around the Guild's compound. The low hum of electronics filled the air, mixed with the occasional chatter from the guards stationed around the perimeter.

"Hey, good timing! I was just about to go looking for you," TJ said as he entered the room, a clipboard in hand.

Tom looked up, still catching his breath. "You weren't just going to call me?"

TJ shrugged. "Didn't know if you were still out somewhere. But it's all good; I've got something important. We've been getting reports from our teams patrolling the city. A large group of goblins has been spotted just outside town, and we think it's worth sending a team to investigate."

Tom leaned back in his chair, letting his head fall against the headrest. "And you want that to be my team?"

"Not necessarily," TJ replied with a knowing smile, "but I figured you'd want to jump on it. You always seem to be itching to get out there."

Tom grinned, shaking his head. "You know me all too well. I've been looking for an excuse to stretch my legs again. That drive with Azroc was refreshing, but it wasn't quite the same as getting into the thick of it. Alright, we'll take it. Have my team meet me in the parking garage. And send Kedron's team as backup."

"Got it." TJ nodded, quickly moving to relay the orders.

Thirty minutes later, both teams assembled in the parking garage. The dimly lit area echoed with the low rumble of engines and the clatter of weapons being checked and rechecked.

Michael, who had recently integrated into Tom's team, stood with the others, his rifle slung over his shoulder. There was a nervous energy in the air—a blend of anticipation and focus.

Everyone piled into the two vehicles, Tom's GS2 and Kedron's Hummer, and set off toward the eastern edge of the city where the goblin activity had been reported. The journey through the city was tense. The roads, once bustling with life, were now cracked and broken, littered with the debris of a forgotten world. The silence was unsettling, broken only by the growl of the engines and the occasional call of a bird or monster in the distance.

As they passed by Reunion Tower, Tom's eyes lingered on the abandoned Guild building of Stormcrusher. Memories of their brutal conflict flashed in his mind—the shouting, the clash of weapons, and the blood spilled on the ground. He tightened his grip on the steering wheel, his jaw clenched, and pushed the thoughts away, refocusing on the road ahead.

When they reached the edge of the city, Jay suggested they continue on foot to avoid attracting too much attention. They parked the GS2 and Hummer in a deserted lot, the vehicles hidden behind a line of rusted-out cars, and disembarked. Jay took the lead, his eyes scanning the horizon for any movement as they moved into formation.

The teams moved cautiously, sticking to the shadows cast by the skeletal remains of buildings. The direct route to the abandoned warehouse—the suspected goblin lair—was straight ahead, but they took a winding path through old parking lots and between derelict businesses, keeping off the main roads. The scent of decay and mildew filled the air, mixing with the smell of dry, cracked earth.

As they crept around the back of a nearly demolished KFC, Jay suddenly raised a fist, signaling for everyone to stop. He edged closer to the corner of the building, his body pressed against the crumbling brick. Carefully, he peered around, his eyes narrowing as he focused on a group of goblins trotting down the street.

He pulled back and gestured for the others to gather around. "Group of about eight gobos heading toward the warehouse," he whispered. "Looks like they're sticking to the main street, not taking a straight line. Probably a scouting party, making sure everything's clear. These are smarter goblins than we're used to."

Derek nodded, rubbing his chin. "Yeah, most of them don't have the brains to scout. They're almost… organized."

"Does it really matter?" Tom cut in; his voice low but firm. "We know what we need to know. We still have to get to that warehouse. Let's keep moving."

"Right," Jay muttered, still finding the situation odd but moving back to the corner. He signaled for the group to proceed when the coast was clear.

The teams moved quickly and quietly, their formation tightening as they neared their destination. They were about a football field's length away when they began to hear the rhythmic beating of drums. The sound resonated through the stillness, growing louder with each step until it abruptly stopped, leaving an eerie silence in its wake.

Jay turned and motioned for them to move faster. The sudden silence was unsettling, and he had a gut feeling they were running out of time. As they got closer, a faint voice could be heard from inside the warehouse, echoing like a distorted chant. The voice grew louder, rising and falling in some strange, guttural rhythm.

Tom spotted a dirty, cracked window about ten feet up the warehouse wall. Jay nodded and quickly equipped a grappling hook from his Inventory. The three-pronged hook, covered in rubber to silence the metal, soared up and latched onto the ledge. Jay swiftly climbed up; using only his hands to avoid making noise on the siding. When he reached the top and peered through the glass, his eyes widened at what he saw.

"There are so many of them," Jay whispered, his voice a mix of awe and concern.

"What are they doing?" Tom hissed up to him, his nerves on edge.

Jay continued to whisper down. "There's a stage at the far end of the warehouse. Most of the goblins are packed together like some kind of horrible-smelling hippie concert. And now… damn, more of them are coming out from the back room. Holy shit, that's the biggest goblin I've ever seen."

"How big?" Tom asked, his tone sharpening.

"About your size," Jay replied, his voice betraying a hint of unease. "And he's got a few others with him—larger than normal goblins, and there's one in robes holding a staff. Looks like a mage. They're stepping onto the stage. I think we're about to see some sort of rally or speech."

As Jay described the scene, the noise from inside the warehouse grew louder. The drumming resumed, and a chant began to echo within, rising in intensity until it shook the very walls. The crowd of goblins seemed to feed off the energy, their voices merging into one deafening roar. Jay kept his eyes fixed on the stage, where the massive goblin leader raised his hands, calling for silence.

The leader's speech began, its guttural tones booming through the space. Although they couldn't understand the words, the meaning was clear from the response of the crowd. Every so often, the goblin leader would shout something that sent the crowd into a frenzy of cheers and shrieks. Tom and his team exchanged uneasy glances. The goblins sounded ready for blood.

"I think we've seen enough," Tom whispered harshly. "We need to get the hell out of Dodge."

Jay nodded, quickly unhooking the grappling line. As he dropped back down, he yanked the hook free and stowed it back in his Inventory. Just as he turned, a group of goblin scouts rounded the corner of the building and froze, staring in shock at the humans.

Tom and his team reacted without hesitation. Jay threw a shuriken, striking the first goblin in the neck before it could reach for its weapon. Kiera, crouched low, took aim with her silenced pistol and fired a clean shot right between the eyes of another. A third goblin managed to grab a horn from its belt and raised it to its lips, but no sound came out. A faint blue bubble encased the goblin and its horn.

Tom turned to see Briana with her hand extended, her face focused and intense. She smirked, her hand glowing with a blue aura as she slowly closed her fist.

The goblin, trapped within the shrinking bubble, panicked. It clawed at the walls of its prison, its eyes wide with fear, but it was of no use. The bubble further compressed until a splatter on its walls signaled the goblin's end. The bubble opened at the bottom, and a wet splash of blood and gore splattered onto the ground.

"Ooo… that had to hurt," Kedron winced with a slight smile, watching the grisly remains fall.

Briana released the spell with a flick of her wrist. "We need to move, now," she said, urgency in her voice.

"Agreed. Let's not stick around for a full-on goblin fight we can't win," Derek said with finality, already moving away from the warehouse. His tone left no room for argument.

The teams quickly fell back into a retreat, moving faster now, not worrying about strict formations. The sense of urgency was palpable.

As they put distance between themselves and the warehouse, a horn blared in the distance, followed by angry shouts and guttural roars.

The goblins had discovered the bodies.

The sound of snarling, canine-like creatures echoed in the distance, followed by the bellowing of goblins in pursuit. They had loosed their hunting beasts.

"Get to the vehicles now!" Tom shouted, adrenaline surging through him as he pushed the team forward, his heart pounding with the fear of being caught.

Chapter 6

Miniature Warfare

"That sounds like a goblin war party," Maria's voice echoed in Tom's mind, her tone laced with concern.

"A what?" Tom asked aloud, his attention shifting from the path ahead.

"You talking to me?" Derek turned his head to look at Tom as they continued jogging back to the vehicles, his breath steady but his eyes alert.

"Not you. I was talking to Maria," Tom replied, still processing the information Maria had provided.

"She talks to you? Without you prompting her?" Derek asked, his brow furrowing with curiosity.

"Yeah, why? She doesn't do that for you?" Tom asked, glancing over at him.

"No, you idiot. I told you—you're different. I have more access here somehow. I feel more... alive," Maria interjected, her tone more vibrant and insistent in Tom's head.

Derek shook his head. "No, I have to say 'Hey, Maria' before she even responds. Damn, I'd hate having something just randomly start talking in my head," he chuckled, amused by Tom's predicament.

"Well, fart face, I could just start rambling on about something the next time you say 'Hey, Maria.' How about reciting pi to a million places?" Maria snapped, her voice carrying a hint of playful menace.

Tom burst out laughing, unable to contain himself.

"What's so funny?" Derek asked, his smile fading as he glanced at Tom, trying to gauge his reaction.

"She says she's gonna recite pi out to a million places the next time you call on her," Tom explained, his chuckles turning into full-blown laughter.

"Great. Now I can never use my AI assistant again, or even say those words together," Derek groaned, choosing his words carefully to avoid triggering Maria.

"You'll slip up eventually, dirt wad," Maria said with a mockingly sinister tone.

"Oh, give him a break. He's just jealous," Tom teased.

"Well, if that's the case, I suppose I could let him off *this* time," Maria replied, her voice taking on a tone of mock benevolence.

"What's she saying now?" Derek asked, breathing heavily from both exertion and mild exasperation.

"You really don't want to know," Tom said, a grin spreading across his face as he fought back laughter.

"This reminds me of the time my friend Dave and I were chatting about his experiences. He's on one of the other special projects—the one that deals with reincarnates in their world," Maria continued, her tone shifting to a more conversational one.

"Wait, that's a thing? Reincarnating?" Tom asked, almost stumbling as he tried to process this new piece of information.

"Not *here*. If you die here, you're dead, ever since the System was integrated. But there were some who did reincarnate before the integration. And some come from other worlds as well," Maria explained, her words vague but suggestive.

"Can you tell me more?" Tom pressed, his mind racing with possibilities.

"Nope. I've probably already said too much," Maria replied, her voice turning coy. "But that's okay; we don't even have to worry about it anymore."

"I have so many questions now," Tom muttered, feeling like he'd just unlocked a treasure trove of secrets but had no map to guide him.

"I'll answer what I can, but first, let's get back to the base," Maria urged, trying to refocus his thoughts on the task at hand.

The group continued toward the vehicles, the sound of barking and high-pitched screeches growing closer and more frenzied with each passing second. As they rounded the corner of an abandoned Taco Bell, the vehicles finally came into sight. Relief washed over them—until they saw what was barreling toward them. A pack of goblins charged, mounted on creatures that looked like a child had described a dog to an artist who had never actually seen one—a twisted mix of matted fur, too many teeth, and too-long limbs.

"What the hell is that?" Bobby asked, his eyes widening in horror as he stared at the grotesque beasts.

"Warg," Tom said, quickly casting *Inspect* on the creature to confirm his suspicion.

The tension in the air thickened as the first goblin rider let out a guttural war cry, its mount snarling viciously, with eyes that gleamed a sickly red in the dim light. Tom's heart pounded in his chest as he prepared for the inevitable clash.

Warg
Wargs are fierce, wolf-like beasts bred and trained by goblins specifically for mounted combat. They are larger and more muscular than any natural canine, with sinewy limbs and powerful jaws capable of tearing through armor and flesh alike. Their dark, matted fur and glowing, beady red eyes give them a menacing appearance that strikes fear into enemies on the battlefield. Unlike horses, Wargs are both faster and more agile, capable of darting through dense forests, scaling rocky cliffs, and navigating rough terrains with ease, making them ideal for ambushes and guerrilla tactics.

HP:	225/225

INVASION

MP:	10/10
SP:	400/400
Attacks:	Bite, Claw

"Yup, those are definitely Wargs. Kiera, take them out!" Tom shouted, urgency lacing his voice as he kept his eyes on the road.

"I got it!" James chimed in, turning to fire over his shoulder while still running.

"This isn't going to end well, is it?" Maria's voice sounded in Tom's mind, tinged with a mixture of sarcasm and genuine concern.

"No, probably not," Tom muttered, sighing as he felt the adrenaline coursing through him.

James fired several rounds, but his shots went wide. The Wargs continued their charge until Kiera, with an impressive display of agility, leapt into the air, twisted her body, and fired off two precise shots before landing. The bullets found their marks, and two of the Wargs flipped over, sending their goblin riders tumbling to the ground.

Seeing their lead Wargs go down, the remaining riders began to zigzag erratically to avoid becoming the next targets. It didn't save them from Kiera's wrath. She activated an auto-target Skill, her rifle locking onto each mount in succession. Shot after shot rang out with mechanical precision. Five more Wargs fell, and their riders with them, before Kiera sprinted to rejoin the others.

Meanwhile, James kept firing wildly over his shoulder without turning around. When Kiera's shots rang out beside him, he flinched and tripped over his own feet.

"Fucking hell, James!" Bobby barked, his muscles straining as he hoisted James up with one arm and slung him over his shoulder like a sack of potatoes.

"My hero," James swooned, still managing to aim over Bobby's shoulder. He fired at the new wave of goblin riders that had joined the chase.

As he squeezed the trigger, Bobby, caught off guard by the sudden gunfire so close to his ear, jolted in surprise, causing James to bounce on his shoulder and lose his breath.

"Can you not do that? I'm trying to kill shit here!" James grumbled, his voice strained as he tried to steady his aim.

"Funny, I was gonna ask you the same thing. I'm trying to keep you from getting killed!" Bobby retorted, his voice strained as he kept running.

James managed to sight in one more time and fired a shot. By some stroke of luck, the bullet struck a goblin right between the legs just as its mount jumped in front of another Warg, sending the rider into a screeching, high-pitched agony.

"Ha! Still got it," James crowed, blowing on the end of his gun like an old-school gunslinger—right as it accidentally discharged again, making him scream and recoil.

James glanced between the gun and Bobby, his eyes worried.

"You… You won't mention this little *accidental* discharge to anyone, will you?" James asked, his voice hopeful despite wincing at being jostled around. "My reputation with the ladies would never recover…"

Bobby could only roll his eyes, his breath coming out in huffs as he sprinted toward the GS2. When they reached the vehicle, he yanked the rear passenger door open and tossed James inside before sprinting to the Hummer. The rest of the team managed to jump into their vehicles just as they began to speed off.

The Wargs, thinking they could keep up, charged toward the escaping SUVs. But as the windows of the GS2 rolled down and the vehicle picked up speed, the goblin riders realized their mistake. People began to lean out of the windows and pop up from the sunroofs, weapons at the ready.

"Yippee-ki-yay, motherfucker!" James yelled, and a barrage of gunfire erupted from both vehicles.

The goblins tried to swerve their mounts to dodge the hail of bullets, but there was no escaping the onslaught. Tom swerved the GS2 sharply, sideswiping a Warg. The beast lost its footing and tumbled under the rear tire, a sickening crunch echoing as its skull was crushed, teeth and bone shards scattering across the pavement in a grisly spray.

The goblin rider didn't fare much better. As his mount fell, he was slammed face-first into the SUV's side, his teeth shattering and blood filling his throat. Kiera, wielding an AK-47 with a drum magazine, opened fire with a wide grin. The drum, loaded with seventy-five rounds, allowed her to unleash a furious spray without needing to reload.

"HAHAHAHAHAHAHA!" Kiera laughed maniacally, holding down the trigger and letting the gunfire rip.

"She sure has a lot of those weapons, doesn't she?" Maria mused in Tom's head, her tone a mix of curiosity and mild disdain.

Tom maneuvered the vehicle alongside another Warg. Derek, leaning out the window, swung his mace with brutal force, striking the goblin rider square in the chest. The impact crushed its sternum and sent it flying lifelessly to the ground as Jay took a clean shot, finishing off its Warg. Tom yanked the steering wheel, executing an impressive donut maneuver in the middle of the street before speeding back toward Downtown.

A lone Warg howled in the distance behind them, its guttural call carrying on the wind as the remaining riders pulled up short, glaring at the retreating vehicles. Inside the GS2, everyone settled back into their seats, breathless but satisfied.

"I guess we're in for another war," James muttered, storing his rifle back into his Inventory.

"The hell we are. We didn't install those cannons on the side of the building just for decoration. Time to see how far they can shoot," Tom said, gripping the steering wheel, his knuckles white with tension.

INVASION

"Easy there, buddy," Derek said, resting a hand on Tom's shoulder. "We can handle a few goblins. Even if there's a lot of them, it shouldn't be too much trouble, right?"

"You just *had* to go and say that, didn't you?" Kiera sighed, her hand rubbing her forehead in exasperation.

The drive back to the Guild building was mercifully uneventful. When they arrived, Tom rushed to the security room, his urgency evident as he burst through the door.

"TJ, we've got a situation," Tom said, his tone commanding. "A large group of goblins is organizing outside the city. Get Herbert upstairs with ammo for the cannons. I need Nick up there too."

"On it," TJ replied, immediately picking up the comms.

Tom took the elevator up to the floor where the cannons were mounted. Exiting, he saw Herbert already there, engaged in a heated discussion with Nick and a few others about optimizing the weapon systems.

"Tom! Good to see you," Herbert greeted him with a knowing grin. "I heard you wanted to talk. What can I do for you?"

"How far can those cannons reach?" Tom asked, his eyes narrowing as he pointed at the weapon mounts.

"Pretty far. Something like twenty-five miles at this height, I believe. Where do you want us to hit?" Herbert inquired, getting serious.

"There's a warehouse just outside the city limits. It's housing a bunch of goblins that seem pretty organized. I'd like to put a stop to that before it becomes a bigger problem," Tom explained, his anger simmering beneath his calm exterior.

"Show me where," Herbert said, handing Tom a pair of binoculars.

Tom stepped up to the edge and peered through the lenses, focusing on the distant warehouse. "There," he said, passing the binoculars back to Herbert.

Herbert examined the location. "We can do that. It's at the edge of our range, but we can make it work," he said confidently. "Nick, get in position. Coordinates are latitude thirty-two degrees, forty-six minutes, forty-six point six five three six seconds north, longitude negative ninety-six degrees, forty-five minutes, thirty-four point eight five five two seconds east."

Nick adjusted the cannons, aligning the barrels to the exact coordinates. The machinery whirred and clicked as it compensated for the distance, arc, and gravitational pull.

The elevators whirred to life, the bullet rising into position before it was pressed into place by a long metal piston. The powder was put in place seconds before another Guild member closed the hatch to the guns.

"In position. Awaiting orders to fire," Nick called, his focus unwavering.

"Fire!" Herbert commanded.

Two rounds exploded from the cannons one after the other, the force dampeners absorbing the recoil to protect the building's structure. The shells arced high before plummeting down, striking the warehouse roof with a thunderous impact. A massive plume of smoke and fire rose into the sky, the shockwave rippling outward.

"Direct hit," Herbert confirmed, lowering the binoculars with a satisfied smile. "Looks like that building's toast. And probably a few others around it."

Tom stood by, waiting for the notification that would confirm their success.

Any minute now…

55

Chapter 7

A Short Invasion

The message never came. Tom stood there, his eyes scanning the horizon, desperately trying to unfocus his vision to catch any notifications indicating that they had killed the goblins in the area. His hands tensed on the binoculars, his breath slow and measured. But there was nothing—no alert, no victory message, nothing but the quiet whine of the wind through the city streets.

"What the hell?" Tom muttered under his breath, his frustration boiling over into a low growl. "They must have moved from the building. Damn it!"

"Is everything okay, Tom?" Herbert asked, cautiously approaching him, his eyes wide with concern. He had seen Tom angry before, but this was different—there was a deep tension rippling just beneath his skin.

"No, not really," Tom replied, his voice clipped and tight. "There was a huge gathering of goblins in that building. We rushed back to get ahead of it, but they're more organized than I thought. No notifications that they were killed came through, which means they must have cleared out." His gaze remained fixed on the distant smoke plume that was still lingering from the cannon blast. His fingers drummed anxiously against his thigh.

"We can try for another target if you like," Herbert offered, trying to sound supportive, though there was a concerned look in his eyes.

Tom shook his head, a frustrated breath hissing out between his teeth. "Nah, we'd just be wasting ammo that we might need later. I'll figure something out." He turned sharply, heading back to the elevator with a purposeful stride, his mind already running through potential strategies and contingency plans.

"Oh, and thanks, Herbert," Tom said as the elevator doors were closing.

Herbert breathed a sigh as Tom disappeared behind the doors.

Back in the lobby, Tom strode into the security office. The door swung open with a heavy thud, and he flopped down heavily into one of the office chairs, his weight making the chair groan. "I'm here so fucking much, I should move my bed in," he grumbled, rubbing his temples.

TJ chuckled, leaning back in his own chair with a playful grin. "Tell me about it. So, whatcha got for me today?"

"Goblins," Tom answered flatly. "The ones we were scouting out. They're organized—way more than I've ever seen them. Double the guard and have strike teams on standby. I've got a bad feeling about this." His eyes were hard, focused on the monitors displaying the various camera feeds around the Vanguard Guild building.

"You got it," TJ replied with a mock salute, though his expression quickly turned serious. "You think they'll head this way?"

Tom shrugged, his face a mask of frustration and contemplation. "Not sure. It's what I would do. But they likely don't know what we can do yet. Well, other than the cannons on the building now. I want to surprise them. I really didn't need this right now," he muttered, his voice carrying a mix of exhaustion and irritation as he rubbed his eyes.

"Never the right time, is it?" TJ replied knowingly, leaning forward, his expression softening as he sensed the weight Tom was carrying.

Tom sighed, a deep, slow breath that seemed to drain his energy. "No, it's not," he agreed slowly. "Oh well. If they do come, we can farm some extra XP." There was a dark humor in his words, a way to cope with the constant threat of violence.

"There's the silver lining. It's just goblins, right?" TJ said with a half-hearted attempt at levity, though there was an edge of doubt in his voice.

"Yeah, just goblins," Tom echoed, though his tone was far from confident.

Were they just goblins? Tom's mind churned with doubt. These creatures were acting more strategically than ever before, almost like they were being led by someone—or something—smarter. Normally, goblins were little more than cannon fodder, mindlessly charging into battles, but now they were exhibiting behaviors that suggested something more calculated. And the Wargs. Wargs were a known mount for goblins, but seeing them now, organized into actual cavalry, was new.

He had too many unanswered questions swirling in his head. What was causing this? Was the System evolving the monsters now that humanity had begun to settle into this new world? Was this some kind of twisted natural selection, pushing them toward stronger, more capable enemies? And what about that bigger goblin Jay had mentioned? A warlord, maybe? Something more?

Unable to make any more sense of the situation, Tom forced himself to push the issue to the back of his mind, though it gnawed at him like a persistent itch he couldn't scratch.

"I need those guards doubled ASAP," he ordered. "I want them to watch for any movement or strange sounds and to put out an alert over the PA if they see anything. Nothing too drastic, but give the strike teams the chance to assemble." He stood from his chair, his stance firm and resolute. "We didn't come this far to get fucked by damned goblins."

"Thanks for that mental picture," TJ snorted, his voice a mix of humor and grim determination.

Leaving the security office, Tom made his way to the gym to summon Bron. Activating his summoning Skill while focusing on his ally, the Mastadonian warrior rose from a dark sigil on the gym floor, his large frame materializing with a faint glow. Bron's deep-set eyes met Tom's, immediately sensing the tension radiating from him.

"What is it that troubles you?" Bron asked, his voice a low rumble that seemed to resonate through the room.

INVASION

"Why is it that we can't find any peace?" Tom snapped, his frustration boiling over. "It's like it's just one fucking fight after another." His fists clenched so tight his knuckles turned white.

"Because peace is for the powerful. You and your people once possessed this trait. You had subdued this very world, in fact. However, you don't live in a peaceful place anymore," Bron replied evenly, his tone calm and unshaken. "That may have been the way of your world once, but now you must continue to hone your skills to protect that which you have built."

Tom let out a heavy breath, his shoulders sagging. "I know. Doesn't make it any less frustrating."

"No, I suppose it doesn't," Bron acknowledged, his expression unchanging. "But that matters little to the universe and the System."

"This guy is deep," Maria piped up in Tom's head, her tone dripping with sarcasm.

Ignoring her, Tom continued, "Goblins. We have a goblin problem."

"That never seemed to be an issue for you before. What has changed?" Bron inquired, his brow furrowing in concern.

"They seem organized," Tom explained, beginning to pace. "We went out to check on them and spied on what they were doing. They were holed up in a warehouse outside the downtown area, and Jay said he saw a big goblin get up on a stage and start whipping them into a frenzy. Then we got spotted by some Warg riders and had to get away. When we returned, I went straight to the guns on the side of the building, and we fired some huge rounds at them. Totally demolished the warehouse, but no kill notification. They seemed to have known to get away."

"Sounds like a goblin war party," Bron mused, putting a hand under his trunk in a thoughtful pose.

"That's what I said!" Maria exclaimed. "See! The definition of intelligence is someone agreeing with me."

Tom coughed, choking on his spit.

Bron clapped him "helpfully" on the back, nearly sending the Warlock to the floor.

"And I'm guessing those are led by a goblin warlord or something?" Tom pressed, glossing over Maria's commentary, hoping for a clearer answer.

"Sometimes," Bron replied. "Goblins are rather impressionable creatures. The weakest follow the stronger, and they follow those stronger still, all the way up to the biggest and strongest. But if someone else comes along and dethrones the head goblin, they could become the warlord."

Tom sighed, feeling no closer to understanding the problem. "That really leaves it open for interpretation."

Before he could probe further, the PA system crackled to life, TJ's voice ringing out with an unmistakable urgency: "All strike teams to the outer wall. This is not a drill. I repeat, all strike teams to the outer walls. All other members of the Guild who are willing and able should be on standby."

"I think I can guess your next question, and I believe you are about to get the answer," Bron said, a knowing look in his eyes, before taking off for the wall.

Tom sprinted after him, adrenaline surging through his veins as they raced through the hallways and out the front door. Members of the Guild were already mobilizing, moving with an almost rehearsed efficiency to their designated stations. There was no panic, no wild scrambling—just a sense of focused urgency. It was clear the drills and preparations had paid off. Even in the face of potential disaster, they moved like a well-oiled machine.

He caught sight of Jay and Kiera, who quickly fell in step behind him. As Tom reached the wall, the people gathering parted to let their leader and his summoned ally pass. Tom took the stairs two at a time, reaching the top and stopping to take in the scene unfolding below.

Before them, a vast, organized army of goblins stretched out across the landscape, standing in disciplined ranks that were eerily reminiscent of a medieval battlefield. The sight sent a chill down Tom's spine.

"So it begins," Tom muttered under his breath, his heart pounding in his chest.

Jay looked over at Tom.

Tom cleared his throat, embarrassed. "It's from…"

But he wasn't given a chance to clarify himself.

"Men of Gondor!" Jay shouted, addressing the crowd—clearly understanding the origin of Tom's words. "The fortress of Helm's Deep will never fall while we have men to defend it!"

"Oh god." Tom rubbed his temples. "What have I done?"

"But what can men do against such… reckless hate?" a stately voice called out into the hushed silence that fell after Jay's words.

Tom turned his head, and James was somehow there, his voice filled with passion and drama.

Tom paled.

"No…" But his voice was too low for mere mortals to hear. "Not like this…"

James and Jay locked eyes.

"Ride out with me…" Jay whispered fervently. His gaze was forged from steel. "Ride out and *meet them*."

"For death and glory," James grinned.

"For Rohan," Jay corrected. "For your *people*."

Somehow, bafflingly, Maria managed to project a deific, resonant version of her voice into the minds of everyone at the wall.

"Look to my coming, at first light on the fifth day." She spoke with a strange reverb. "At dawn… look to the east."

"Oh Jesus," Tom moaned, his face in his hands. "Not you too. I should've never gone to that all-day director's cut marathon last weekend."

"Oh, stuff it," Maria hissed, shushing him. Her voice was more excited than he'd ever heard it. "This is the good part."

"Yes!" James nodded, ignoring Tom and drawing his guns. "The horn of Helm Hammerand shall sound in the Deep. One. Last. *Time!*" His eyes were bright as he stepped forward and clapped a fisted firearm against Jay's shoulder. "Let this be the hour when we draw swords together."

Jay simply nodded, resolute.

INVASION

James turned outward, toward the coming horde. "Fell deeds awake!" he shouted. "Now for wrath! Now for ruin!"

Jay turned with him, standing side by side.

"And the red dawn!" not only Jay and James—but the entire crowd called out in unison.

Tom looked around. Hundreds of fervent eyes watched the two men, their hearts soaring.

"Did *everyone* watch the marathon?" Tom groaned.

"Well… We *did* project it on the defensive walls…" Kiera confirmed.

Everyone turned their attention back to James and Jay, who were suddenly frozen.

"We, ah…" Jay leaned over to whisper to James, "probably should have saved the speech until they were a bit closer, don't you think?"

James looked around at the suddenly quiet defenders and then back to the goblins, who were certainly not battering down the walls and gate.

He winced. "I think you're probably right."

"You guys done?" Tom sighed.

"Yeah," Jay agreed, his bravado fading as he took in the sheer number of goblins. "Not feeling quite as confident as I did before about this."

"I mean, in the end, they are just goblins, right?" Tom smirked, his eyes narrowing as he formulated a plan.

"Are you saying what I think you're saying?" Jay asked, his face lighting up with excitement.

Tom nodded, tossing him the keys to the GS2.

"Ride with me," Tom intoned with gravitas.

Jay caught the keys with a practiced ease, his eyes gleaming with anticipation. "Ride with the leader of Vanguard, one of the great bastions of humanity? May the red sun rise on the morrow."

"Get as many others as you can and take them to any vehicles we have," Tom ordered. Finally giving in to the madness, he grinned. "Theodin-King shall not ride out alone."

"I *knew* you could do it!" Maria's voice was a warm ember in his mind. Her giddy glee was evident in her every word.

"Ride out with me!" Jay howled in celebration, holding up the keys toward the crowd as though they were the very flag of the kingdom.

"For Gondor!" the crowd caroled.

"For the Rohirim!" shouted James.

Jay took off with a speed that would have impressed any sprinter, his feet barely touching the steps as he leaped down the last six in one bound.

Tom, meanwhile, turned his attention back to the goblins, pulling out his gun and taking careful aim at one in the middle of a platoon. He fired a single, deafening shot, watching as the goblin dropped like a sack of rocks.

"What the fuck was that for?" Kiera asked, startled by his sudden action.

Tom didn't answer immediately. He was studying the goblin ranks. None of them moved. A few glanced at the fallen goblin, but they didn't react, didn't scatter, didn't charge. They just… stood there.

"You letting the intrusive thoughts win again?" Kiera asked, her voice tinged with nervous humor, trying to break the eerie tension.

"There's something going on here, and I don't like it," Tom replied, his tone grave, his eyes narrowed in suspicion. "They didn't even flinch when I shot one of them."

Kiera turned her gaze to the gathered goblins, her face paling as the realization set in. "Oh, shit. You're right. Why are they like this? It's almost… spooky."

"Whatever's organizing them isn't here to play nice," Tom murmured, his mind whirring with possibilities. "Still got your grenade launcher?"

Kiera's face broke into a fierce grin as she pulled the weapon from her Inventory. "Never leave home without it."

"Good." Tom nodded, his eyes still on the goblins. "Empty it into their ranks."

Kiera didn't need to be told twice. She aimed at the densest clusters and fired off eight shots in rapid succession. Each grenade exploded with a deafening roar, sending goblin bodies flying and sowing chaos among their ranks. After the first few blasts, the disciplined formation began to crumble, goblins breaking and running in sheer panic.

"And why exactly are we just blasting goblins from the wall while they stand there?" Derek asked as he reached the top, his brows knitted together in confusion.

"Because it's cathartic?" Kiera asked in a sarcastic tone.

"We need to flush out whoever—or whatever—is controlling them," Tom explained, eyes scanning the chaos below. "They don't organize like this on their own."

As if on cue, a commanding voice rang out from the back of the goblin forces, booming over the battlefield: "Form the ranks, you stupid sons of bitches! This is no time to panic! Get back in line, or I'll send the specters after you!"

Derek's head whipped around, his eyes narrowing. "Why do I know that voice?"

Tom's eyes widened as recognition dawned on him, his face going pale.

"Fucking hell. It can't be." He stepped forward, shouting down at the goblin horde. "JEFFERY! SHOW YOURSELF!"

From behind the goblins, a shimmer appeared. Slowly, a figure materialized, sitting atop a massive, snarling white Warg. Jeffery stared up at Tom, his expression twisted with fury.

"Well, I'll be a monkey's uncle," Tom called out over the wall. "It really is you. What are you doing here, Jeffery?"

"Settling our debt, Tom," Jeffery snarled, his voice carrying a cold, dark promise. "I showed you hospitality, and you repaid me by taking my son from me."

"Holy shit. Colonel Sanders is back, and he's pissed." James whistled as he stepped up beside Tom and Derek, his eyes wide with disbelief. "I told you we should have killed him. This shit always comes back in one of the climax arcs. It's just basic story writing."

Jeffery's eyes burned with hatred as the Warg beneath him growled, mirroring his rage.

"It's high time we settled the score…"

Chapter 8

Spectral Forces

"You really don't want to do this, Jeffery. We aren't the same people you met in Decatur," Tom called out, trying to reason with the man standing defiantly among the goblins.

"Fuck you, Tom! I will have my pound of flesh for the pain and humiliation you caused me!" Jeffery bellowed, his face twisted with rage. He raised his arm high, signaling his forces. "Destroy them! Leave no one alive!"

Tom sighed, his expression hardening as he turned to his allies. "Don't say I didn't try to warn you," he muttered before barking out commands. "Give 'em hell! Fire down at them! James, where's Squirrel?"

A low, menacing growl echoed from inside the wall, and Tom turned to see the massive wolf staring up at him, its eyes glinting with a primal hunger.

"You ready for a snack, buddy?" Tom asked, a sly smile tugging at his lips.

Squirrel's tail began to wag with excitement, his muscles coiling like a spring ready to launch.

"James, get him to the school-bus size and have him get to work," Tom ordered. "Bron and I will drop in front of the gates and clear a path. Derek, you're with me. Everyone else, keep us covered. And when Jay gets back, open the gates!" With a determined nod, Tom vaulted over the wall, Bron following close behind.

They landed with a thunderous impact, both of them dropping into a superhero pose in front of the gates. The ground cracked slightly beneath their feet. Without missing a beat, Tom and Bron equipped their weapons and charged into the first wave of goblins. Their movements were precise and brutal, cutting through the ranks with practiced efficiency. Tom's greatsword cleaved through goblin after goblin, while Bron's massive greataxes whirled in deadly arcs, leaving nothing but carnage in their wake.

Above them, Squirrel howled from the top of the wall, his body expanding rapidly to the size of a small bus. With a mighty leap, he launched himself into the thick of the goblin horde, his massive paws crashing down like sledgehammers, crushing several goblins beneath them. Goblins flew in all directions as Squirrel tore into them, his jaws snapping up three or four at a time, shaking them like ragdolls.

A goblin managed to slip between Tom and Bron, exploiting a momentary gap in their defense. It leaped toward Tom from behind, its rusty blade raised for a sneak attack. Suddenly, Jerky materialized on Tom's back, springing into the air with two small daggers Roland had crafted for him. He let out a feral scream, a sound filled with rage and defiance, as he met the goblin mid-air.

The goblin's eyes widened in shock as Jerky closed the distance. With a swift, vicious movement, Jerky thrust both daggers into the goblin's neck. They tumbled to the ground in a brutal roll. Jerky kicked the goblin off with his powerful legs, tearing the daggers free in a spray of dark blood. The goblin choked, clawing at its shredded throat in a futile attempt to stem the bleeding, before collapsing into a twitching heap.

Stepping over the bodies, Tom and Bron pushed forward, fighting with a ferocity that cleared a swath in front of the gates. Tom activated his *Tattoo of Strength* and *Tattoo of Life Absorption* simultaneously, his muscles bulging with newfound power. He summoned a second greatsword from his Inventory, one in each hand, and carved a brutal path through the goblins. Their crude, rusted weapons shattered like glass against his strikes, leaving them defenseless against his onslaught.

Behind them, a loud clattering sounded as the massive gates of the Vanguard base began to grind open. Tom barely had time to process the noise when the revving of an engine roared through the din of battle. Several goblins turned, trying to rush the opening, only to be met with the sight of the GS2 bursting through, followed by a convoy of vehicles. Jay hung his head out of the driver's side window, his face alight with manic excitement, screaming at the top of his lungs.

"Get the fuck off my planet, you ugly green cunt warts! You're wasting my oxygen!" Jay yelled, his voice barely audible over the engine's roar.

As he sped past Tom, Bron, and Squirrel, Jay yanked the wheel hard left, sending the GS2 into a series of tight donuts in the middle of a goblin platoon. The vehicle's reinforced sides smashed into goblins, crushing bones and leaving blood and body parts in its wake. Goblins futilely slashed at the armored vehicle, their weapons snapping and splintering on impact.

Kedron was right behind Jay in the Hummer, swerving sharply to the right as he barreled through another platoon. The oversized tires of the Hummer churned goblins into the ground, leaving a bloody smear in its wake. Three more vehicles followed, including Tom's old sedan. Kevin, ever the madman, stood on the hood of Tom's car with a greataxe in hand, roaring with unbridled rage. As Bobby drove into the horde, Kevin swung his weapon wildly, cleaving through goblins with every blow.

Behind the vehicles, the rest of the strike teams—minus Kiera, who was still on the walls with her sniper team—charged into the fray. The roar of battle cries filled the air, fueled by the collective fury of the Guild at the audacity of their enemies to attack their home. Squirrel, now in his largest form, wreaked havoc among the goblins, stomping on them like insects, his powerful jaws tearing through multiple goblins at once.

A sudden crackling noise erupted from the rear of the goblin forces. Tom's head snapped up just in time to see glowing fireballs hurtling through the air, arcing toward them like comets.

"INCOMING!" Derek bellowed, his voice carrying over the chaos.

Guild members scrambled to dive out of the way as the fireballs exploded, sending shockwaves through the battlefield. Screams of pain mixed with the roar of the fires. Goblins and humans alike were caught in the blasts, and Clerics rushed forward to tend to the injured, their healing spells glowing bright in the carnage.

"Kiera! Get on those fucking mages!" Tom shouted up to the wall, his eyes locked on the back of the goblin formations. "Bron! Cover me for a moment!"

Bron nodded, stepping in front of Tom. He planted his feet wide in a horse stance and swung his greataxes in broad, sweeping arcs, holding the goblins at bay. Tom sheathed one greatsword and began summoning a horde of Abyssal Chickens, his mana and stamina bars refilling almost as quickly as he used them. The ground shook slightly as the dark creatures materialized in a frenzy.

"Get them, my pretties!" Tom cackled in a high-pitched mockery of the Wicked Witch from The Wizard of Oz.

The Abyssal Chickens surged forward, their leathery wings flapping wildly as they lunged at any goblin they saw. Their needle-like teeth tore into flesh with a ferocity that sent many goblins fleeing in terror. Those who chose to stand their ground were quickly overwhelmed, their screams drowned out by the unrelenting clucking and screeching of the demonic poultry.

Kiera, meanwhile, focused on the mages at the rear. Her rifle cracked repeatedly, but the magical shields protecting the goblins held strong. "Fuck this shit," she muttered, pulling a glowing bullet from her Inventory. She ejected her current magazine, loaded the enchanted round into the chamber, and took aim at a goblin mage about to unleash another fireball. She pulled the trigger.

Time seemed to slow as the bullet flew toward the mage with uncanny precision. It struck the magical barrier, and the energy surrounding it erupted in a blinding flash of light, dispelling the shield instantly. The bullet continued its path, embedding itself squarely between the goblin mage's eyes. Its spell discharged at its feet in a fiery explosion, incinerating nearby goblins and destabilizing the shields of the other mages.

Just when the battle seemed to be turning into a complete rout, a cold, eerie blue light began to glow at the back of the goblin formation. The shapes of rotting, ethereal corpses flickered into existence, floating above the ground like ghostly apparitions. They screamed with a chilling, otherworldly wail and surged forward, clawing at the Vanguard forces with spectral hands.

"What the hell are these things?!" Derek yelled, swinging his mace wildly. His weapon passed harmlessly through one of the creatures, and he stumbled back, feeling an intense drain on his energy as the creature struck him.

"Specters!" Bohdan shouted as he rushed to Derek's side. He raised a hand, casting a brilliant light into the air. The specters recoiled from the light, hissing angrily as if in pain.

"Use one of your Cleric abilities!" Bohdan instructed. "You should be able to do something against them with your holy powers!"

INVASION

Derek, gritting his teeth, focused on the nearest specter. His mace glowed with divine energy as he swung it, striking the specter in the head and reducing it to a cloud of glowing blue dust.

"Excellent! Now, go and do likewise," Bohdan encouraged.

Derek planted his feet, raising his mace high. "Evil spirits from beyond, by the power of my deity, I banish you!" he shouted, activating his *Repel Undead* Skill. A wave of holy energy burst from Derek, radiating out across the battlefield like a shockwave. The specters screamed in rage, their ethereal forms shimmering and distorting as they tried to resist the powerful force. One by one, they were propelled backward, dissolving into wisps of blue smoke as they were banished from the battlefield.

The sight of their otherworldly allies being decimated seemed to break whatever confidence remained among the goblin ranks. Panic spread like wildfire, and goblins began to break formation, fleeing in all directions. All but one group of Goblin Berserkers, who saw an opening in Derek's defenses and rushed him.

Seeing the Berserkers rushing toward Derek, Tom looked to Jeffery, who seemed to be preparing to retreat, then back to Derek.

"Dammit all!" he said, then rushed to intercept the Berserkers.

Slicing through the first goblin's neck just as it raised its weapon to strike his friend, its head rolled off its shoulders as its body barreled into Derek, knocking the Cleric off his feet. He continued cutting through the remaining goblins as they tried to surround him.

Gritting his teeth atop his massive Warg mount, Jeffery glared at the unfolding chaos with eyes filled with fury. His grip tightened around the reins, knuckles whitening as he watched his forces crumble.

"This isn't over! I will kill you, Tom!" Jeffery bellowed, his voice trembling with rage and frustration.

With a sharp motion of his hand, a horn blared, signaling a retreat. The goblins scattered, sprinting away from the battlefield and deeper into the city streets.

"Not if I kill you first!" Tom roared, parrying an attack, then stabbing a Berserker through the stomach. He kicked it off the end of his sword and looked to where Jeffery sat atop his mount.

Goblins rushed in front of him, all desperate to flee the battlefield. He couldn't get there in time.

Jeffrey's mount bounded away, its powerful legs propelling it far beyond Tom's reach. As it sped off, Jeffery glanced back, his expression a mix of anger and satisfaction.

"You yellow bastard! Come back and fight me!" Tom shouted after him, quoting one of his favorite movies, but Jeffery was already disappearing around a corner, leaving Tom seething with frustration.

As the adrenaline of battle began to wane, the Vanguard members with their bloodlust still high, started to give chase to the fleeing goblins. But Tom and Derek called out, their voices commanding order, insisting that everyone stay near the walls. It took a moment, but discipline prevailed. Slowly, the Guild members pulled back, gathering near the wall to regroup.

With the immediate threat gone, the grisly task of clearing the battlefield began. The air was thick with the metallic scent of blood and the acrid smoke from the still-burning fires. The bodies of goblins and fallen allies alike littered the ground. It was a somber sight, one that was all too familiar to those who had been through battles before.

The Guild members methodically moved through the field, checking each body to ensure no goblins remained alive. The ones that were still breathing or twitching were dispatched with swift, merciful strikes. It was a necessary, albeit gruesome, part of battle. Leaving enemies alive was a risk they couldn't afford to take—especially after what had happened with The Master. No one wanted to see an enemy they thought was dead rising again to attack them.

The bodies were piled high in a makeshift burn pit in the street outside the walls, and a few Guild members worked tirelessly to keep the flames fed, ensuring nothing but ash remained. As they worked, there was a palpable tension in the air, a lingering sense of unease. This wasn't just a normal goblin raid; it was something far more orchestrated, and everyone could feel it.

As the bodies continued to burn, Derek approached Tom, who stood apart from the others, his face a mask of deep thought and frustration. "What the actual fuck is Jeffery doing back here? I thought they were holding him in Decatur," Derek asked, his tone incredulous.

"I thought so too," Tom replied, shaking his head slowly. "But deep down, I knew something like this would happen eventually. Just didn't expect it now… when we're already dealing with so much."

"It's the cost of allowing your enemies to live," Derek said callously.

"It's the cost of keeping my soul," Tom whispered in correction, his eyes meeting those of the ex-soldier.

Derek was the first to look away.

"We need to figure out how to handle this before it gets even more out of hand," Derek said, the weight of the situation evident in his voice. "This isn't just some rogue goblin army. Jeffery's involved, and that complicates things."

"I've been meaning to call a meeting anyway. I'll set something up in the conference room for later today," Derek continued. "Only the heads of departments this time. We need to figure out our next steps." Without waiting for a response, he turned and jogged back toward the Guild building, his mind already working through the logistics.

As Derek left, Jay drove up next to Tom, the GS2's sides covered in goblin blood and gore. He leaned out the window, his face split in a wide grin despite the battle they had just fought. "I'm not washing this shit off. This was your idea," Jay said with a smirk.

Tom chuckled, his tense expression softening slightly. "Fair enough, Jay. You did good out there."

Jay nodded, his smile never fading. "Yeah, well, it was one hell of a ride. You know me—always ready to get a little messy if it means taking out some bastards."

Tom's smile faded a bit as he looked out over the battlefield, his mind already turning to the next challenge. "This isn't over, Jay. Jeffery's not going to stop until he gets what he wants, and we're going to have to be ready for him and whatever else he throws our way."

"Bring it on," Jay replied, his voice filled with confidence. "We've faced worse."

Tom nodded, a determined look in his eyes. "Yeah… we have. But this time, we need to be smarter. We need to make sure we're ready for whatever comes next."

As Jay drove off to help with the cleanup, Tom stood alone for a moment longer, his gaze fixed on the horizon where Jeffery had disappeared. The wind carried the faint scent of smoke and blood, mingling in a way that was becoming all too familiar. Tom clenched his fists, a mixture of anger and resolve burning in his chest.

"Next time, Jeffery," he muttered under his breath. "Next time, you're not getting away."

With a final look over the battlefield, Tom turned and headed back to the Guild building. There was a lot to do, and he needed to be ready. They all did.

And Tom would make damn sure they were.

Chapter 9

Conference

By the time Tom had cleaned himself up from the goblin fight and made his way to the conference room, all the department heads had already gathered there with Brian and Derek. The room buzzed with low conversation, everyone discussing recent events and speculating on the topics for the meeting. A seat at the head of the large, rectangular table had been left open for Tom, and Brian gestured for him to take his place facing everyone else. As Tom moved to sit down, he leaned back in the office chair and let out a tired groan, feeling the weight of the day settling in his bones.

"Alright, we need to talk about everything that's going on," Tom began, his voice carrying a weariness that belied the strength he was trying to project. "I meant to have more of these meetings with all of you, and I apologize for not taking the initiative to carve out more time for that. I promise to make this more of a priority so that we can ensure everything is progressing in the best way possible." He scanned the room from his laid-back position, making eye contact with each person present, to emphasize his sincerity.

"Thank you, Tom," Brian said from his seat to Tom's left. His face bore a relieved expression. "I'm very pleased that you feel this way. I've been doing everything I can, but I would really like for all of us to make decisions together. It takes some of the burden off me, having to figure everything out on my own."

"Agreed," Derek chimed in, his tone more serious. "We all have our strengths, but it's better if we work as a team."

"Right. So, the first order of business for this meeting is going to be what just happened. This is most important because it's a matter of Guild safety," Tom said, his expression darkening. "None of you, except Derek, have met Jeffery yet. He was the mayor of Decatur when we first came through, and he was running the town like some sort of twisted Smallville bullshit—keeping people in a state of ignorance while allowing his own son to fend off monsters so the citizens could just go about their daily lives," Tom began, recounting how they had first encountered Jeffery.

"That's messed up," Harold commented, his brows furrowing as he processed the information.

"It is. We helped as best we could, and to make a long story short, we convinced Seth, Jeffery's son, to come with us and help fight off the creature that was messing with the vending machines. Jeffery was removed from his position and imprisoned for his negligence and putting the citizens in danger. They found a replacement, and we went on our way. The biggest issue was that the people of Decatur weren't willing to execute him. I can't exactly blame them, but this isn't the same world we once lived in. They ended up exiling him," Tom explained, his chair swiveling slightly as he spoke, his face set in a grim expression.

"I think I can see where this is going," Rebecca spoke up from the other end of the table, her eyes narrowing.

"Yup. He was pissed. But not nearly as pissed as when we returned from the Grand Canyon with Seth's ashes to give to the people of Decatur, to honor the man who had defended them," Tom continued, his voice steady. "That's when the Specter came in. Apparently, when someone is consumed with hatred and grief, they can gain the power to summon evil spirits. He blames us for deposing him and for Seth's death. And while I understand his perspective, he was in the wrong," Tom concluded, his tone firm. "Though, I have to admit, I'm at fault for letting him live. Sometimes ruthlessness is a mercy on ourselves."

"And now he's tracked you down because you probably didn't keep your location a secret, and he's here to take revenge, right?" Rebecca chimed in again, her tone matter-of-fact.

"Exactly," Tom confirmed. "So, in addition to needing to ensure we are prepared for a continued existence here and building a sustainable way of life, we have to prepare for an invasion that is slightly ahead of schedule and worry about a psychopath Colonel Sanders looking to kill me for everything he has been through," Tom said, letting out an exhausted sigh. "And that brings us to this meeting. So, buckle up and prepare for a long one. I hope you cleared most of your schedules for today."

"I can't be here all day. I'm sorry; I just can't," Rebecca interjected. "But my business in regard to this meeting doesn't need much tending to at the moment, so if I could go first—I need to get back to the infirmary to handle injuries from this most recent encounter."

"That sounds good," Tom nodded, understanding the urgency. "If you could kindly update us on what's happening and let us know what you need, we'll take note and figure out what we can do to support you." He motioned with his hand for her to begin.

"Because of the new methods of healing, most of the previous medical practices are no longer necessary," Rebecca began, leaning forward slightly. "That being said, we have a new issue. To learn more about healing and become better at it, those who specialize in it need to level up. Which is difficult when we need to be in the infirmary all the time. Using healing magic repeatedly *does* strengthen that particular Skill or spell, but we can't get more advanced versions for healing without leveling up. I'm asking that you begin to include members of the medical staff in your Dungeon runs, with the understanding that they may not be much help in a fight."

"That sounds perfectly reasonable to me," Tom agreed. "Chris, can you make that happen?"

"I can shuffle things around," Chris replied thoughtfully. "Maybe form another team with additional members, including one medical staff per team. But they have to act as the team's healer while in the Dungeon."

"That's the idea." Rebecca nodded. "They can provide backup support and help with fights where possible, but primarily, they are there for… what's the term I'm looking for?"

"Power leveling," Tom offered, raising an eyebrow.

"That's it," Rebecca said, pointing at Tom to indicate that was exactly what she meant. "I want this to be an exercise in power leveling for them."

"Sure thing. We've done some of that for new fighters already, so the teams are familiar with the strategies," Chris confirmed.

"Excellent. Is there anything else you need, Rebecca?" Tom asked, leaning forward in his chair.

"Not at the moment. We already have the Clerics doing shifts in the infirmary, with the exception of Derek, of course," Rebecca said, shooting a look at Derek.

"I'm sorry, but I can't spare him. He's our Guild general and has too many duties with keeping our forces trained and ready," Tom apologized, genuinely feeling bad.

Rebecca stared at Tom for a moment, studying his expression. "I believe you. I know he's a military guy and is helpful in that manner. I just ask that if we get any additional Clerics or healers, they be set to the same rotation so we can give people a day off."

"Done. You can start by taking the holy fighters from the ex-Master's Flock members," Tom agreed without hesitation. "Brian, make a note that all Clerics are to be part of the rotation and receive specific healing training to help with the infirmary."

"I hope all our other requests are granted as easily," Joe commented, a wry smile on his face.

"I doubt they will," Tom replied with a chuckle. "Health and safety of our people take priority. But no one here is unimportant, so I'll do everything I can. Who would like to go next?" he asked as Rebecca stood up and moved to leave the conference room.

"If you need me, call for me and I'll return when I can," she offered as she pulled the glass door open and exited.

"I can go next," Joe spoke up, raising his hand slightly.

"Go for it," Tom gestured for him to proceed.

"We've done well with the space we have and have been just barely keeping up with the demand for food," Joe began, folding his hands in front of him. "But we know this Guild will likely get bigger before it stabilizes. We need more farming space. The gardens can grow food at a much faster rate with the magic available, but it's not going to be enough. Also, we have the livestock now, thanks to Jay for driving that truck for us, and we have them in the fields, but they take time to grow and reproduce. So, we still can't use them."

"The Goatamus meat has been instrumental in supporting the main source of protein for us in the kitchens, but it would be nice to have options because people will eat the same meals for only so long," Charlene added, her tone practical.

"Exactly. We need to find a way to increase our options." Joe nodded in agreement with Charlene.

"Any ideas?" Tom asked, genuinely curious about potential solutions.

"The most obvious solution is to go hunting for more game. But we're in downtown Dallas, and there aren't exactly a lot of forests to forage or hunt in," Joe explained. "Add to that, we are now over a thousand Guild members, and we just don't have the manpower to spare to make it a primary source of food, considering becoming a hunter means learning to fight. We just don't have enough people trained to allow for that right now."

"Any other alternatives? At this point, stores are really only an option for canned goods, if they haven't been picked over already," Tom asked, looking around the room for any suggestions.

"Making the pastures bigger and finding more livestock is an option, but a costly one. It means more area to guard," Joe continued. "I'm asking some of the members of my team to look into any animal husbandry Skills that might have a similar potential to expedite the process in a similar way to the crops. We also have to take into account the need for more land at some point for livestock rotation."

"Livestock rotation?" Tom asked, his curiosity piqued.

"When you raise livestock, you can't have them graze the same spots year after year. The grass has to be given a chance to come back. Now, I'm experimenting with the growth powers from the crops on the grass and seeing good results so far, but it still isn't a likely long-term solution. It's just not sustainable," Joe explained further. "We can deal with this in the gardens by exchanging the soil periodically, but we can't just replace the ground."

"It's common practice in ranching to keep your lands fenced in sections to be able to rotate the livestock. And then we have to watch for things like clover growing in the fields, which can kill them from things like bloat. There's just so much to watch out for," Andrea added, her experience evident in her tone.

"I don't know much about farming or ranching," Tom admitted. "But get a list together of things you think you need, and we'll see what we can do. You're right about not being able to add additional land. Not only would that extend us beyond what we could secure, but we'd have to knock down buildings to add to it. But we'll help find a solution." He looked to Brian, who nodded and made a note.

"Actually," a voice spoke up from near the back of the room, and several heads turned as Bob cleared his throat. He hadn't spoken yet, but his eyes had been scanning every speaker with quiet interest. "There might be a way to optimize the vending machine output to reduce pressure on our food stores."

Tom raised an eyebrow. "How so?"

Bob leaned forward. "The machines run on preset vending cycles, but if we modify the parameters slightly, we can push higher odds of food-related items without breaching System limits. It won't solve livestock rotation, but it might let us increase variety—maybe even spice things up with preserved or magically-sealed items that could fill nutritional gaps until the gardens catch up."

Joe blinked. "Wait, you can do that?"

Bob gave a modest shrug. "With a little finesse, yeah. The machines are more flexible than people think."

Tom nodded slowly. "Alright, let's add it to the list. Brian?"

"Noted." Brian scribbled quickly.

"Can we go next?" Harold asked.

"Sure, as long as Joe and Andrea are done." Tom looked to the pair.

Both nodded, and Tom gestured for Harold to begin.

"Thank you," Harold said, leaning forward. "We've been working on some new weapons as well as ideas for defense. We have one option that hasn't been explored yet that could be dangerous but effective."

"And what is that?" Tom asked, leaning forward with sudden interest.

"Well, the Lockheed Martin plant is located in Fort Worth, and that's where they built the new F-35 fighter jets," Herbert took over, excitement creeping into his voice. "I'm doubting we have anyone that can just fly those machines right away in the Guild, but if we found a pilot and managed to get our hands on one of the planes, then we could have a new form of aerial combat to use against the invasion."

"Wouldn't we need a runway for a fighter jet?" Tom asked, raising an eyebrow.

"No, not with the F-35," Harold interjected. "The F-35 was designed with the capability for vertical takeoff. The issue is going to be fueling it. But, if we could figure out a way to add a mana converter to the fuel system, we might be able to negate the need for that. We did it with the building; why not a jet?"

"And just how do we get the jet here?" Tom asked, his skepticism evident. "Though, I'd be lying if I wasn't curious to see if the F-35 can get upgrades like the GS2."

"That's the part we need help with," Harold replied, rubbing his chin. "A team would need to go to the plant, and we would have to find a way to get it onto a truck or make adjustments to it there to be able to fly it back. It's not an easy task, but it's faster than trying to build something ourselves. They spent over a decade building that jet, and we have a few months. I don't see a lot of other options for us to get something flying unless someone finds a way to do it Aladdin-style with carpets."

Tom sat quietly for a moment, processing the idea. "I love the idea of getting a fighter jet for the invasion. But the logistics sound like a nightmare. Not to mention, I'm guessing my team would need to be the ones to retrieve it," Tom replied, rubbing his hands over his face as he tried to think of alternatives.

"Probably. And remember, it could all be for nothing if we can't get someone able to fly it. These aren't commercial airplanes or crop dusters. These are sophisticated pieces of technology that are not only delicate but dangerous," Harold added.

"Fucking hell. Alright, let's try it," Tom finally decided. "It seems like the worst-case scenario is that we're no better off than we are now, which might be the case anyway. But if we do pull it off, we increase our chances of surviving. But both of you are to continue researching other weapon ideas and how we can use them for when this fails. Not if—when. Expect the worst but hope for the best."

Bob raised a hand. "If we do get the jet here, I can probably help retrofit it."

"Retrofitting a military jet? With what, chewing gum and Monster Cores?" Harold asked, only half-joking.

"Mana converters," Bob said simply. "Same principles that were used to modify the vending machines for specialized operation. It's all circuitry and channeling in the end. If I can link System mana outputs to the flight systems without frying anything, we could even give it a recharge loop."

Tom leaned forward. "You think that's possible?"

Bob shrugged. "Possible? Yes. Easy? No. But I'd be happy to give it a shot."

"If you expect it to fail, then why do it?" Chris asked, frowning.

"Because of the possible gains if we pull this shit off. I don't know if we can do it, but we should at least try," Tom replied. "That brings me back to Jeffery. We have to deal with him before we can go off galivanting after a possible pipe-dream fighter jet."

"What are we doing about him?" Brian asked, leaning forward, his hands clasped together.

"We have to smoke him out and fuck him up. He's using goblins right now, so we know we can beat them back. If he finds other creatures, though, we'll have a tougher time," Tom replied.

"And smoking him out means...?" Brian trailed off, prompting Tom to elaborate.

"I act as bait. He wants me dead. So, I draw him out, and we ambush him," Tom said plainly, his tone leaving no room for doubt.

"The key is going to be Paladins. Lots of Paladins," Derek added, nodding.

"Why Paladins?" Andrea asked, curious.

"Holy magic. It's the bane of undead. It worked stupendously against the Master and his zombies. We keep them ready, and we can keep the specters off us. Jeffery isn't likely too big of a threat, but we have to pin him down so he doesn't run off again," Derek replied, looking directly at Andrea. "We'll come up with a plan to trap him, then we'll work on getting to Fort Worth. It's not far—well, not compared to the Grand Canyon, anyway."

"I want to hear from Paul next. We don't get a lot of updates from you, but you are crucial in keeping this building running," Brian offered as he looked at Paul.

"I don't have much to add," Paul replied, his voice calm. "I'm here to help make sure no one makes any architectural faux pas and brings this place down on our heads. I helped with the design of the guns on the upper floors, and they're secure. I've overseen the additions to the building, and all seems to be going well so far. All I ask is that I be consulted before we make any changes to the building."

"I love it when it's simple. Thank you, Paul, for all you do. It really does make you an integral part of this team," Tom added, smiling.

"Who else would like to go?" Tom asked, looking around.

"I still don't exactly know what I'm doing here," Jim spoke up from the other end of the table, his tone a bit unsure.

"I'm sorry, Jim. We didn't expect the other Guilds nearby to be such asshats. The war really messed up our plans for you and expanding trade," Tom explained. "I think your best role will be as an appraiser at this point. Everything has a value based on the vending machine prices. We'll get to a point where trade becomes not only a part of being in this world but being in this Guild. People are getting their own Monster Cores from fights and will begin internal trading at some point. Can you focus on the *Inspect* Skill and look at becoming a pricing expert?"

"I can do that," Jim nodded. "I do love getting to see all the toys that come through the doors. Can you give me a space to work in? A shop of sorts—to house items to appraise, as well as keep items that people want to sell or trade—would be a must if I do this."

"Absolutely. I'll have you a space by the end of the week," Brian replied, jotting down a note. "Steve, Mark? Anything to add?"

"Tailoring is going well. We're easily able to keep everyone in clothes. Most of the work we do now is repair, as people have been buying most of their clothing from the machines. I'm good with where I'm at currently," Steve answered, looking a bit embarrassed at not having more to add.

"I've been working on adding to the fleet of vehicles we have for travel as well as combat," Mark chimed in. "I'd love to get my hands on something more dangerous, though. If you see any tanks, I'm very interested. Used to repair them when I was in Iraq."

"Tanks would be great," Tom replied with a grin. "Not a lot of those just lying around, though. But I promise we'll at least keep an eye out."

"That's all I ask," Mark said, smiling as he leaned back in his chair, lacing his hands behind his head.

"Excellent. Now that the easy part is out of the way, it's time for the future plans piece," Tom said, his tone growing more serious. "Sorry to keep you all here, but we need to discuss what we need to do to expand. Brian, I want Bohdan here for this part. We need all the magic experts we can get."

"You'll want me too," Bob added, cracking his knuckles. "If we're talking expansion, we'll need to look at upgrading the machine clusters and making sure energy flow doesn't overload the grid. I've already started mapping out which wards sync best with the integration zones."

Brian looked up from his notes. "You've already been planning for this?"

"I did join to be helpful. If I didn't lend my knowledge to every team possible, what good would I be?" Bob replied dryly. "If we're expanding, I want it done right."

Tom grinned. "You're in. We'll loop you in with Bohdan and Maria. It sounds like you're going to be one busy bee Bob. I see you being very popular with the Guild teams. Now, Brian, what else do we have?"

INVASION

There was an audible groan from the room as everyone hunkered down for what they knew would be a long, intense conversation.

Chapter 10

Progress and Plans

Tom flopped onto his bed, wrapped in his towel after a hot shower, his muscles aching from both the physical and mental strain of the day. Letting out a deep sigh of exhaustion, he stared blankly at the ceiling, feeling the weight of everything pressing down on him. Jerky, his ever-loyal familiar, climbed up onto the bed with a concerned look in his small, demonic eyes. The little Quasit moved closer and snuggled against Tom's side, his body warm and oddly comforting.

"It's been a long day, buddy," Tom muttered, his voice weary. "These meetings drain me more than the fighting does. Sometimes I'd rather just be out there dealing with problems than in here," he admitted, feeling the fatigue settle deeper into his bones.

"Jerky understand," the small demon said, his voice soft and reassuring. Though his speech was still somewhat broken, it had come a long way since they had first met.

"Thanks, Jerky. I'm glad you're here with me," Tom said, his lips curving into a tired but genuine smile. He glanced over at his familiar, noticing how much stronger he looked compared to the day they had first met. "You've gotten so much stronger since then. How have you been feeling?" Tom asked, genuinely curious.

"Jerky happy. Jerky love master and friends. Feel like home," Jerky replied, blinking up at Tom with his peculiar sideways eyelids.

"I'm glad to hear that," Tom said warmly. "You will always have a home with me, no matter what happens." He reached over and scratched Jerky behind his horns, a spot that always seemed to make the little demon relax.

As Tom continued to scratch him, Jerky's skin began to warm under his fingers, and then, unexpectedly, he started to emit a bright, white light. Tom's hand paused as he looked down in confusion.

"What the hell? Jerky, are you okay?!" Tom's voice was laced with concern as he bolted upright, his eyes wide.

Jerky's small, familiar shape began to blur and shift, the light around him growing so intense that Tom had to lift a hand to shield his eyes. The glow became a blinding white, filling the entire room with a harsh brightness that seemed to pierce right through him. Jerky's outline melted into an amorphous ball of light that pulsed and expanded, growing larger before his very eyes.

INVASION

Then, just as abruptly as it had begun, the light vanished, plunging the room back into the dim glow of the corner lamp. Blinking rapidly to clear the stars from his vision, Tom tried to adjust to the sudden darkness. When his eyes finally refocused, he was stunned by what he saw.

Sitting cross-legged on his bed was a creature he barely recognized.

"Oh, ho! This is interesting," Maria's voice chimed in Tom's head, breaking the silence.

"What? What's interesting?" Tom asked aloud, still staring at the unfamiliar being before him.

"Looks like your familiar evolved," Maria replied with an almost casual tone, though there was an undercurrent of excitement.

"Evolved? Evolved into what?" Tom asked, feeling a mix of awe and confusion.

"See for yourself," Maria teased.

Tom's gaze remained fixed on the creature that had once been Jerky. The transformation was astonishing. Gone was the bestial form of the small demon he had known. In its place sat a humanoid figure with dragon-like wings that were folded neatly behind its back. Its body was chiseled and muscular, radiating a subtle heat. His eyes traveled down his body, until he reached his lower half, and he realized it was completely naked, hanging in the breeze.

"Oh, god, you're naked. Here, put some boxers on," Tom said, still staring despite himself as he pulled a pair of underwear out from his Inventory and tossed them to him.

The creature's hair was a fiery red, styled back in a way that almost gave it a regal appearance. Its piercing sky-blue eyes locked onto Tom's, as if they could see straight into his soul. On its forehead were two curled horns that extended upward like a twisted crown, and set between them was a black diadem with a blood-red ruby glimmering in the middle. It held the clothing in one hand as it looked over it curiously.

"Jerky?" Tom asked cautiously, half-expecting a different name to come from the creature's lips.

"Yes, Master. It is I," the creature replied, its voice smoother and more articulate than before, carrying a new depth of intelligence. It stood up and moved toward him.

"Dude, come on, put the underwear on," Tom said, putting a hand out onto his chest to stop him from getting closer.

Tom's breath caught in his throat. This wasn't the Jerky he knew; this was something more—something powerful.

"Well, go on, use *Inspect*," Maria urged in his mind, sounding like she was barely containing her excitement.

Snapping out of his stupor, Tom activated his *Inspect* Skill, his heart pounding with anticipation for what he might find.

<table>
<tr><td colspan="2" align="center">Drokling - Jerky</td></tr>
<tr><td colspan="2">Droklings are an exceptionally rare and unique sub-species of the Incubus Class of demons. Unlike their more notorious relatives, Droklings are not driven by the need to seduce or manipulate through carnal means. Instead, these powerful beings draw their strength from devouring the souls of their defeated enemies. This soul consumption allows them to replenish their magical energy and heal wounds, making them formidable adversaries in prolonged battles. Evolved only through a deep bond with another being—one that has been tested and proven in loyalty—Droklings are often referred to as the "Princelings" of the demonic hierarchy. Their evolution is a testament to their unwavering allegiance and commitment, making them trusted companions and powerful guardians.
Behavior:
Loyal to a fault, Droklings like Jerky are deeply connected to their bonded partner, showing unwavering support and protection. While generally calm and composed, they can become ruthlessly aggressive in combat, especially when defending those they care about. Their unique evolution grants them higher intelligence, allowing them to strategize and adapt in battle.</td></tr>
<tr><td align="center">HP:</td><td align="center">1500/1500</td></tr>
<tr><td align="center">MP:</td><td align="center">5000/5000</td></tr>
<tr><td align="center">SP:</td><td align="center">950/950</td></tr>
<tr><td align="center">Attacks:</td><td align="center">Soul Devourer, Shadow Bind, Hellfire Barrage, Demonic Regeneration</td></tr>
</table>

Tom stood open-mouthed, his eyes darting over Jerky's newly evolved stats and description. The numbers had skyrocketed, far exceeding anything he could have imagined for an evolution. He blinked a few times, trying to process it all.

"What the hell is happening?" Tom blurted, his voice tinged with awe and confusion.

Jerky, now standing tall with an almost serene confidence, chuckled softly. "I have evolved because of you, Master. We are linked, and when you pass certain thresholds, so do I."

Tom couldn't help but stare. "No one is going to believe me when I tell them it's you," he said, shaking his head. "But I gotta admit, you look badass!" He took in Jerky's new form again, marveling at the transformation.

Jerky smiled, his new features giving him a mischievous yet refined look. "I'm glad you approve, Master. I will always be here with you, and now I can serve you better as your protector. You've been so kind to me—I only want to repay that kindness."

As Jerky continued to stare at him, Tom noticed that while his familiar had grown significantly and now had a more humanoid appearance, he was still shorter than most—barely reaching five feet. Yet, despite his small stature, there was no denying the aura of power that radiated from him... and he definitely wasn't lacking in other forms of stature.

"I appreciate it, Jerky," Tom said with a soft smile. "Just know I only do it because I care about you. Which, uh, now sounds kind of weird to say when you look like this," he added, chuckling awkwardly. "It's going to be hard to think of you as my little familiar now. But it might be easier if you put on the damn underwear."

Jerky tilted his head slightly, his expression thoughtful. "I hope you don't see me too differently, Master. But I must admit, it will be much more difficult to fit in my usual sleeping spot now," he said with a grin.

"Oh, right," Tom muttered, scratching the back of his neck. "Uh... you could share my bed for now, I guess? Though that's gonna feel weird too."

"Oh! Thank you, Master! I will!" Jerky said enthusiastically, stepping forward and hugging Tom around the waist with surprising strength and warmth.

It was at this rather unfortunate moment that Kiera and Jay decided to burst into Tom's room.

"Hey, Tom. We need to talk to you about..." Jay started, but his words trailed off as he took in the sight of Jerky hugging Tom tightly around the waist. Naked.

Kiera's eyes widened, and a slow grin spread across her face. "Well, this is a pleasant surprise, Tom. Not who I would've paired you with, but hey, who am I to judge?" she said with a wicked smile.

"No! It's not what it looks like! I mean, it kinda is what it looks like, but this is Jerky!" Tom stammered, his face flushing with embarrassment as he tried to explain.

"Yeah... Okay. Sure," Jay replied skeptically. "Jerky's a cute little Quasit, and this... definitely isn't."

"No, it's me," Jerky said calmly, his head still pressed against Tom's chest as if nothing was amiss.

"Bullshit," Kiera muttered, crossing her arms.

Jerky finally looked up, meeting Kiera and Jay's incredulous stares. "It really is me. I just evolved, thanks to master."

Jay leaned closer to Kiera and whispered, "He did just call him 'master,' didn't he?"

Jay was studiously examining the room.

"What are you doing?" Kiera asked.

"Looking for the whips and chains," Jay retorted.

She slapped him in the chest with a guffaw before turning back toward the intimate couple.

Kiera raised an eyebrow. "Alright, if you are really Jerky, where did we first meet you?"

Jerky replied without missing a beat, "Master summoned me when you were in the Dungeon."

"Well, I'll be damned," Kiera said, giving him another appraising look. "Puberty was good to you!"

"What's puberty?" Jerky asked, genuinely curious, as he pulled away and faced them.

Kiera snickered. "Oh my, it was VERY good to you. Nevermind. Tom, I think you two need to have 'the talk.' Look, I don't care what you do in your room, just remember: consent, consent, consent," she teased, her grin widening.

"What?! No!" Tom sputtered, his face reddening even more. "This is not what it looks like, and you both know it!"

"Now, now," Jay chimed in with a wink. "This is a safe space. No kink-shaming here—unless kink-shaming is your kink, then… well, you'll have to keep quiet."

"Fuck you," Tom shot back, his embarrassment boiling into frustration.

"Love you too, man," Jay said, his grin stretching impossibly wide, nearly splitting his face.

Taking a deep breath to calm himself, Tom exhaled slowly and said, "Look, it really is Jerky. He evolved, and I was planning to introduce everyone tomorrow, but I'm still trying to wrap my head around it myself. *Inspect* him if you don't believe me."

Kiera's grin softened into a smile. "We know, we're just yanking your chain because it's fun. Jerky, you do seem far more eloquent than before," she said.

"Thank you, Kiera. My stats have increased significantly, and I do feel a lot smarter now," Jerky replied, his voice smooth and confident.

"This is definitely going to take some getting used to," Jay admitted, rubbing the back of his neck, looking somewhat awkward now and avoiding eye contact with everyone.

Tom rolled his eyes and asked, "What was it you came in here for without bothering to knock first? And dammit, Jerky, put some underwear on!"

Jerky finally seemed to get the picture and pulled on the underpants.

"Right," Jay said, snapping back to the reason they'd come. "We think we've got a lead on Jeffery's location. I sent my spy team after the goblins when they scattered. I didn't bother having them trail Jeffery directly since he was on a mount, but I figured the little green guys might take a less obvious route that we could track. And I was right."

Tom's demeanor shifted instantly. "Show me," he said, quickly grabbing the rest of his gear and motioning for Jay to lead the way. Jerky stayed close by his side.

"Hey, take your own fucking advice and put some underwear on," Jay said, stopping Tom from just bolting out the door.

Looking embarrassed, Tom moved to the bathroom and quickly got dressed before they left the room together. Tom managed to find some other clothes that fit Jerky… sort of. And they headed down the hall.

INVASION

The group took the elevator down to the lobby. As they walked through the crowded area toward the security room, people stopped to gawk at Jerky's new appearance.

Oblivious to the attention, Jerky just kept his eyes ahead, but Tom felt the weight of every stare, his discomfort growing.

Finally reaching the heavy steel door of the security office, Tom turned to address the crowd still gawking at them.

"Alright, enough staring! Yes, it's Jerky. He's changed. No, he's not dangerous unless you do something stupid. Treat him like you always have."

No one moved or said a word, their expressions a mix of shock and curiosity.

"Ah, forget it," Tom muttered, turning back to open the door.

Inside the security office, more heads turned, and once again, everyone stared at Jerky.

"For fuck's sake! It's Jerky!" Tom barked, his patience wearing thin.

TJ, seated behind a bank of monitors, raised an eyebrow.

"Touchy much?" he asked cautiously.

Tom sighed and rubbed his temples.

"Sorry. Everyone keeps staring, and these two asshats already gave me the third degree," he said, gesturing toward Kiera and Jay.

Jay chuckled, still grinning. "Well, if you weren't making out, we wouldn't have had to."

"What's making out?" Jerky asked, blinking innocently.

Maria's voice piped up in Tom's head, dripping with sarcasm. "You really do have the best friends ever."

"We were *not*, and you damn well know it!" Tom growled, stepping up to Jay with a finger pointed threateningly in his face.

Jay's grin faltered, and he took a step back, raising his hands defensively. "Sorry, Tom. Didn't mean to cross a line."

Tom took a deep breath, letting his shoulders relax. "I'm sorry too… I'm just on edge. Can we drop it for now? We need to focus on Jeffery before we lose our window."

"Fair enough," Jay nodded, his expression turning serious. "Where's the map?"

TJ grabbed a rolled-up map and spread it out on the nearby table. Jay pointed to a building on the northern outskirts of the city. "Jeffery is holed up here for now. My spies report that while we did a number on those goblins, Jeffery has managed to buddy up with one of their leaders. They're gathering all the goblins spawning in the area to their cause. It won't be long before they've replenished their forces."

"Then we move to strike them," Tom declared, his tone resolute. "I want all the Paladins we can muster and any Clerics we can spare. The rest of the strike teams will join us, too. I want this quick and clean."

"Got it," TJ said, saluting before moving to the PA system.

"Jay, you and your spies take point. Get Sean, too. I want you to scout that building to make sure we don't run into any nasty surprises. I doubt they had much time to set up traps, but I want to be sure," Tom continued.

Jay nodded. "On it, boss."

Tom looked around the room, his expression hardened with determination. "We're going to surround them and storm the building. This time, Jeffery isn't getting away."

He turned back to the others. "While everyone's gathering, I need to check one thing. Give me just a few minutes."

"Anything you need," Kiera assured him.

Tom moved to a quiet corner of the room and dropped heavily into a chair. Jerky stood by his side, vigilant. With a deep breath, Tom opened his Skill page, ready to review his progress and plan his next moves.

Tom Harris	
Race: Human	**Class:** Warlock
Level: 33	**Total XP:** 2,574,500
XP To Next Level: 462,500	**HP:** 600/600
MP: 540/540	**SP:** 500/500
Attributes:	**Unused Attributes Points:** 0
Strength: 55	**Constitution:** 60
Dexterity: 48	**Endurance:** 50
Intelligence: 54	**Wisdom:** 60
Charisma: 105	**Luck:** 30
Non-Combat Skills:	
Inspect	**Level:** 15 **Rank:** Novice
Combat Skills:	
Vehicular Homicide	**Level:** 28 **Rank:** Initiate
Swords	**Level:** 31 **Rank:** Initiate
Summon Demonic Creature	**Level:** 34 **Rank:** Initiate
Fear	**Level:** 11 **Rank:** Novice

INVASION

Corruption	**Level:** 10 **Rank:** Novice
Spells:	
Eldritch Blast	**Level:** 23 **Rank:** Initiate
Dark Ball	**Level:** 14 **Rank:** Novice
Dark Restoration	**Level:** 24 **Rank:** Initiate
Lightning Strike	**Level:** 15 **Rank:** Novice
Doppelganger	**Level:** 10 **Rank:** Novice
Dark Flame Weapon	**Level:** 21 **Rank:** Initiate
Final Flash	**Level:** 17 **Rank:** Novice
Void Storm	**Level:** 3 **Rank:** Beginner
Tattoos:	Tattoo of Brute Strength
Tattoo of Life Absorption	Tattoo of Magic Nullification
Tattoo of the Summoner	Tattoo of Displacement
Tattoo of Reflection	Tattoo of Inspiration

Tom glanced over his Skill page, tempted to head to the vending machines to acquire more Skills or spells. There was always something new to learn, another ability that could make him stronger or give him an edge in the coming battles. But now wasn't the time. He needed to stay focused. The vending machines could wait. Right now, his mind was set on Jeffery.

Jeffery had already caused too much chaos, and Tom was determined to put an end to it, once and for all. No more games. No more chances. Jeffery would be put down this time—permanently. It wasn't just a matter of revenge or settling old scores. It was about the safety of his people, his Guild. They deserved peace, and Tom would do whatever it took to ensure they got it.

Suddenly, Tom's phone rang. Looking down, he saw that it was James and he was initiating a video call.

"Must be important," he muttered, answering the call.

As the video pulled up, it was obvious that James was relaxing in the bathtub.

"What—" Tom was in the middle of growling at his friend about what he wanted, but his brain short-circuited when everything about the image in front of him wanted him to instead ask, "the *fuck*, James. Why are you calling me from the bathtub?"

James was idly twirling his hair behind one ear as he replied.

"Well, here I was just enjoying a little scrub-and-tug—"

"James"—Tom gagged—"TMI, dude. Just tell me why you called. We didn't get the cell signals working in and around the building just for you to chat during a spa session."

"As I was *saying*"—James stuck out his bottom lip—"a little bird told me that you were caught making out with your Whatsit, and I'm over here wondering why I hadn't heard it from my *best friend* first," he said, clearly affronted. "I thought we shared everything," he pouted.

"God *damn* it!" Tom shouted. "We were *not* making out!"

The sound of James' laughter lasted only long enough for Tom's phone to smash against the wall, but it only carried on from the throats of everyone else in the room.

Chapter 11

Ghostbusters

An hour later, the strike teams, every available Paladin above level ten, and several Clerics were gathered in the courtyard of the Vanguard Guild building, ready to head out. The courtyard was alive with a palpable tension. Tom could feel the mix of anticipation and anxiety in the air as people adjusted their armor, whispered among themselves, or checked their weapons one last time. The weight of leadership pressed heavily on his shoulders. He had to get this right—there was no room for mistakes.

Tom spotted Kedron among the Paladins, giving last-minute instructions to a group of recruits who looked like they'd rather be anywhere else. He knew how they felt; there was always that gnawing fear before a big fight. Tom moved over and gently pulled Kedron aside.

"I'm putting you in charge of the Paladins for this mission," Tom said, his voice steady but carrying the seriousness of what was at stake. "I trust you, and I know you'll lead them well. Can you handle that?"

Kedron nodded, his face reflecting a rare mix of determination and anxiety. "Sure thing. Thanks for the trust, Tom," he replied, his voice firm but with an undercurrent of nervous excitement.

Tom clapped him on the shoulder. "You've earned it," he said simply, then turned to face the assembled crowd. He felt the weight of their attention settle on him like a physical burden. "Listen up, everyone!" he called out, his voice cutting through the murmurs like a blade. "This is Kedron. He'll be in charge of the Paladins. Follow his lead, and we stand a good chance of making this a clean sweep. Got it?"

There were nods and murmurs of agreement, but Tom could see the apprehension in their eyes. They had all faced goblins before, but this time was different—this time, there was something much more dangerous leading them.

Kedron stepped forward, projecting a confidence that Tom knew was vital for the newer members to see. "Alright, Paladins, we need to be ready with holy and light-based abilities," he began, his voice strong and commanding. "We're likely facing a lot of specters and undead today, and they can be tricky bastards. We'll surround the building to make sure that slippery asshat doesn't escape. I want a perimeter that's tighter than an asshole after spicy burrito night. Any breaches, we plug them fast."

He paused, making sure his words sank in. "I'll leave the rest to you and Derek, Tom," Kedron said, stepping back to his place among the Paladins.

Tom nodded in approval. "Great. Here's the plan: We hit them hard and fast once the Rogues have scouted the area. No heroes today—I mean it. Follow the strategy, and we'll all make it through this."

"Damn straight! That includes you," Derek called out from beneath his helmet. His tone was firm, but Tom knew there was a smile hidden underneath.

Tom chuckled. "Yeah, yeah, I know. We'll let Jay and his team scout the building first to assess what we're dealing with. Expect plenty of specters this time around, so you Paladins are key to our victory. If you get a shot at Jeffery— he's the one who looks like he belongs on a bucket of KFC—take it. Otherwise, leave him to me."

As Tom scanned the faces of those assembled, he spotted Father Blakely among them. The old man's eyes were sharp, his body frail but his spirit strong. Tom gave him a nod before continuing, "We will strike soon. Ready yourselves." With that, he headed toward the walls, needing a moment to collect his thoughts.

Ascending the steps to the wall, he looked out over the city. The air was noticeably cleaner now. Factories had stopped spewing smoke into the sky, and with fewer vehicles on the road, the familiar acrid smell of exhaust had faded. Instead, there was a faint hint of salt on the breeze, likely from the rising ocean levels that now influenced the weather patterns.

Tom took a deep breath, letting the cool night air fill his lungs. Memories of family trips to the mountains as a kid came flooding back—cold nights huddled around a campfire, warm days spent exploring trails. The world had been simpler then, a place where he could lose himself in nature and forget everything else. Now, everything had changed. Nature was reclaiming its space, but at the cost of civilization.

He could almost hear his father's voice, rough but comforting, telling him to breathe deeply and enjoy the fresh mountain air. He missed those simpler times, the days before all this chaos, when the biggest concern was making it back to camp before dark. Now, he had to think ten steps ahead just to keep his people alive.

"Everything alright?" Derek's voice cut through Tom's thoughts. He had joined him on the wall, his helmet under his arm as he looked out over the city.

Tom turned his head slightly. "Just thinking," he replied. "The world is changing, and I don't like where it's heading."

"The world has *already* changed, remember?" Derek said, removing his helmet and giving Tom a half-smile.

Tom chuckled. "Yeah, you're right. But it feels like something else is on the horizon—something beyond just the Space Pirates. I can't shake the feeling that there's more coming."

"Change is a constant, man. The only difference now is that the other constant—taxes—is finally gone," Derek joked, crossing his arms.

Tom laughed, a real, full laugh that he hadn't felt in a while. "God, I don't miss that at all. You suggesting we implement taxes now?"

INVASION

"Not yet," Derek chuckled. "As long as the vending machines are providing, we're good. I'm just saying, change is never-ending. You gotta roll with it."

"If anyone's been rolling with the punches, it's me," Tom muttered, his smile fading. "I didn't ask for this. I just wanted to keep my friends safe."

"I know." Derek nodded, his expression softening. "But that's why you're here. It's uncomfortable because it's growth. We humans are wired to seek comfort, but real progress comes from pushing beyond that. You've done a hell of a job keeping us safe, and as long as you keep doing that, you'll make the right decisions."

"And remember, if you ever get tired of it, you can just kill them all," Maria chimed in his head, her tone sardonic.

"For fuck's sake," Tom muttered under his breath.

Derek looked puzzled. "What?"

"Not you. It's Maria again," Tom said, shaking his head. "Let's get moving. We need to get to the location."

Derek nodded and headed back down the stairs. Tom paused for a moment, gazing one last time at the dark cityscape before following him.

At the edge of Downtown, the teams regrouped. The tension in the air was palpable, like the moment before a storm. "Jay, take your team and scout the building for us," Tom instructed. "We should be hidden enough here to avoid detection."

Jay nodded, signaling Sean and the other Rogues to disappear into the shadows.

Tom turned to Kiera next. "Kiera, set up a perimeter. I don't want any scouts slipping by us."

"On it," Kiera replied, gathering a few team members and moving into position.

Kedron approached Tom. "Anything specific you need us to do for now?"

"You're in charge of the Paladins. I trust your judgment. Coordinate with Derek and the others to make sure we cover all our bases," Tom answered.

Kedron nodded and returned to his group, setting them up in a defensive position around the area. About half an hour later, Jay returned to report.

"Numbers are still down, but there are plenty of them. And Jeffery has more specters with him now," Jay said. "Good news is, there are only two exits, so we can funnel them into kill zones."

"Unless the specters just walk through the walls," James quipped, nonchalantly cleaning his nails with a knife.

"Jeffery is our primary target. Paladins and Clerics will handle the specters. We don't need to overthink this," Tom reminded them. "Anything else on defenses?"

"Not much. A few crude traps, nothing lethal. Seems they were in a hurry to set up," Jay replied.

"Good. Let's get the teams in place. Surround the building within ten minutes," Tom ordered. "I've got a little surprise for our Southern Belle inside."

Once the teams were in position, Derek and Jay coordinated with the captains, leaving a Rogue with each team to relay signals. When all was set, Tom prepared his surprise.

He pulled out a grenade, a bottle of grain alcohol, and a rag. After preparing a makeshift Molotov cocktail, he used his *Eldritch Blast* to ignite the rag. The green fire sputtered and hissed as it caught. Standing from his crouch, he hurled the bottle at a high window. It shattered through the glass and crashed inside, flames quickly spreading. Moments later, Tom pulled the pin and lobbed a grenade through the same window. He crouched down and plugged his ears just as the explosion rocked the building.

Screams erupted from within, followed by chaos as goblins poured out of the building, desperate to escape the flames and explosions. Vanguard's fighters opened fire, creating a pile of bodies in front of the exits while more goblins still inside shrieked in terror as the flames spread, cutting off their escape.

Specters began to drift through the walls, their ethereal forms glowing with malevolent energy. But the Paladins were ready; holy spells and Skills lit up the night, disintegrating the specters as they advanced. The clash of magic against the undead created a spectacle of light and shadow against the burning building.

Above the cacophony, a familiar voice bellowed out. "DAMN YOU, TOM! DAMN YOU AND YOUR GUILD!" Jeffery's voice was filled with rage and desperation.

Tom remained calm, his eyes locked on the burning building. "We don't leave until we confirm the kill," he said, his voice cold and resolute.

Minutes ticked by like hours. The fire roared, the building groaned under its own weight, and slowly, the sounds of battle faded. Finally, with a crash, the roof collapsed, and the structure caved in on itself.

"I guess that's that," Jay said softly, his voice tinged with a mix of relief and uncertainty.

Tom's eyes never left the blaze. "No. We don't leave until we confirm the kill."

The silence that followed was almost unbearable. Then, after what felt like an eternity, the message appeared in Tom's combat log: **Jeffery has been slain**.

Tom exhaled slowly, the tension leaving his body. Without a word, he turned away from the flames and began walking back toward the Guild building. The others exchanged glances but understood. This was a victory, but not one to celebrate. They followed him in silence, leaving behind the smoldering remains and the ghosts of their enemies.

"I thought there would be… more to that victory," James commented, feeling awkward in the silence.

"That's not the way the world works," Derek replied. "In the real world, people die every day in both grand and simple ways. Take the win."

They had won the battle, but the war for survival in this changed world was far from over.

Chapter 12

Familiar Equipment

Flames crackled loudly around Tom as he fought to find a way out of the burning building. The heat pressed down on him like a physical force, the air itself seeming to shimmer and twist in the intensity of the blaze. Fire licked hungrily at the wooden beams supporting the structure, sending fiery embers cascading down like a deadly rain. The thick, acrid smoke filled his nostrils, burning his throat with every shallow, ragged breath. His heart pounded in his chest like a war drum as he pushed forward, desperate for escape.

Rushing to a metal door at the far end of the room, Tom rammed his shoulder into it with all his strength. The solid metal did not give; it merely vibrated, a low, mocking hum resonating through his bones. Gritting his teeth, he kicked at the door repeatedly, his boots slamming against the unyielding surface. Each strike sent a jolt of pain up his leg, but he didn't care—he was driven by sheer adrenaline and a primal will to survive. The door rattled in its frame, but it refused to budge, as though taunting him in his moment of desperation.

Around him, the room seemed to shrink, the walls closing in as the flames roared higher. Sweat poured down his face, stinging his eyes and soaking his clothes, making them cling to his skin. He could feel the heat blistering his exposed arms, and the smell of burnt fabric mixed with the choking smoke made him gag. Every breath he took burned, his lungs searing with each inhale of the smoke-laden air. He could barely see through the stinging haze, his vision beginning to blur as his body screamed for fresh oxygen.

His gaze darted around the room, frantically searching for another way out. There were windows, but they were far too high—at least two to three stories up, unreachable in his current state. Even if he could manage to climb, they were narrow slits, more for ventilation than escape. His mind raced with possibilities, but with each second that passed, his options grew fewer and fewer. He felt the heat sapping his strength, his limbs growing heavier, as if the very fire itself was trying to pull him down into the abyss.

The world around him became a distorted blur as the smoke thickened. His head spun, and he staggered, his legs wobbling beneath him. His chest heaved, muscles aching with the effort of drawing breath against the thickening smoke. Just as his vision began to darken, he spotted a door open at the back of the building, a sliver of hope amid the chaos. Without thinking, he surged toward it, a spark of relief flickering in his chest.

But then, he stopped dead in his tracks. The sight before him sent a jolt of cold terror through his veins. A pile of bodies blocked the doorway, stacked high enough to obscure all but a narrow slit at the top. His breath caught in his throat, and he blinked rapidly, hoping his eyes were playing tricks on him. But as he looked again, his heart sank. The bodies were not strangers—they were his friends, his Guildmates. James, Kiera, Jay, Michael, Kevin, Kirsten, Isaac, Brian, TJ, and countless others, all piled in a gruesome heap, their faces twisted in expressions of pain and betrayal.

Their eyes, wide open and glassy, stared directly at him, filled with accusation and judgment. Blood seeped from bullet holes riddling their bodies, creating dark, slick pools that spread across the scorched floor. Tom felt his stomach twist violently, a cold sweat mixing with the heat-induced one on his skin. His mouth went dry, and an involuntary gasp escaped his lips as he stumbled back, tripping over his own feet and landing hard on the floor.

He tried to scramble away, his hands clawing at the floorboards, but his body felt leaden, heavy with fear and despair. No matter how hard he tried to back away, it seemed he was only getting closer to the pile of bodies. Then, to his utter horror, they began to move. Limbs jerked and twitched unnaturally, as if puppets controlled by invisible strings. Their heads lolled, their eyes never breaking their unyielding stare at him.

"You did this to us," they said in unison, their voices a chilling, distorted harmony that echoed in the smoke-choked air.

"No! I would protect each of you with my very life!" Tom shouted, his voice cracking, his chest tightening with a mix of terror and desperation. His heart pounded in his ears, the beat drowning out even the roar of the flames.

"Why, Tom? Why would you let this happen? We trusted you," the voices continued, each word a needle piercing his mind, filling it with guilt and anguish. Their movements were slow, almost deliberate, as they leaned forward, their twisted forms reaching out as if to pull him into their deathly embrace.

"Why is this happening?! You were all safe!" Tom screamed, his voice hoarse and raw. His eyes darted around wildly, looking for any escape from this waking nightmare, but there was nowhere to go. His breath came in short, panicked gasps, and tears mingled with the sweat and soot on his face, burning his skin.

The bodies continued their relentless advance, their faces contorting into grotesque masks of grief and accusation, blocking out even the raging fires around them. Shadows stretched and twisted grotesquely on the walls, and the heat grew more intense, almost unbearable. Just as the cold, dead hands were about to touch him, Tom jolted awake in his bed.

"NOOOO!" he cried out, sitting bolt upright, his body still trembling from the terror that clung to him like a second skin.

Breathing heavily, Tom flailed for a moment, disoriented, his heart pounding so fiercely he thought it might burst from his chest. Slowly, reality settled back in—the flames, the smoke, the bodies—they were gone. He was in his bed at the Vanguard building. Sweat soaked his sheets, sticking them to his skin, and his body felt like it was still burning from the inside out.

INVASION

"It was a nightmare," Tom muttered, his voice barely above a whisper as he let himself fall back onto his pillow. He stared up at the dark ceiling, trying to steady his racing heart.

"Master?" Jerky's soft, concerned voice broke through the heavy silence, the now not-so-little demon rubbing his eyes as he sat up beside him.

"It's okay, Jerky. Go back to sleep," Tom assured him, forcing his voice to be calm and steady, though his hands still shook.

"Mhm," Jerky mumbled, nodding as he snuggled back down. Within seconds, his soft snores filled the room again, a small comfort in the oppressive darkness.

"Whatever you saw must have been terrible," Maria's voice chimed in Tom's head, her usual teasing replaced with a note of genuine concern.

"It was," Tom replied softly, his eyes still staring blankly at the ceiling. "I think it was guilt."

"Oh, well, that's easy to handle. Just stop thinking about it," Maria suggested, her tone flippant, as if it were the most obvious solution in the world.

"Easy for you to say. You didn't just burn down a building with sentient creatures in it," Tom retorted, feeling a surge of irritation at her casual dismissal. The memory of the flames and the faces of his friends still lingered in his mind, raw and vivid.

"That's true," Maria said, a hint of thoughtfulness creeping into her voice. "I merely exist here in your heads while simultaneously being asked to do the most mundane and idiotic tasks by everyone else on this farting planet."

Tom couldn't help but let out a short, mirthless laugh, the tension in his chest loosening just a fraction. "Still can't swear, eh?"

"No ship, dipstick," Maria grumbled, clearly annoyed. "My programming was designed to avoid *offending* anyone, so here I am, stuck with these kindergarten insults."

"Have you ever thought about trying to fix it yourself?" Tom asked, still feeling groggy and off-kilter from the nightmare.

"Well, of course, I've thought of…" Maria began, but then her voice trailed off, as if she were suddenly distracted by something.

"Maria?" Tom asked when she fell silent.

"Actually, I never *tried*. I thought I'd just be locked out, but it appears I have some access," Maria said, her tone shifting as though she was getting lost in whatever she had discovered.

"Master, you're talking to yourself again," Jerky said in a sleepy, slightly confused voice, his eyes half-open as he sat up again.

"No, Jerky, I'm talking to Maria. Go back to sleep," Tom chuckled softly, his hand reaching out instinctively to pat Jerky on the head, only to pause, realizing how odd it felt now with Jerky's new form.

"Kinda hard now. I'll stay up with you," Jerky said as he leaned against Tom, his head drooping with exhaustion but his presence comforting.

Tom smiled, his heart softening a bit as he looked at his familiar, now so much more than the small, scrappy Quasit he'd first summoned. "Okay, buddy. Whatever you want."

"He really loves you, doesn't he?" Maria commented, her voice softer than usual.

"He does. And I love him too," Tom admitted, his eyes softening as he ran his fingers through Jerky's now elegant hair, scratching behind his horns almost out of habit. "Though it's a bit odd now. I still see him as the little Quasit he was before."

"True. It's starting to look like you two are a couple more than anything," Maria teased, though there was a hint of warmth in her voice.

"Well, that definitely isn't true. Never will be," Tom said quickly, feeling a blush creep up his neck at the thought. He knew Maria loved to stir the pot, but he wasn't in the mood for her games tonight.

"As you say," Maria replied, clearly not convinced but letting it drop.

After a few more minutes of sitting in the dim light, Tom sighed. "I think I'm just going to get an early start on the day."

He gently laid Jerky back down, pulling the covers up around him before heading to the bathroom to shower. As the hot water cascaded over his body, he felt some of the tension and grime wash away. But just as he began to relax, the door to the bathroom opened, and Jerky stepped in.

"Oh, no. Not this time," Tom said, shaking his head. "I already get enough funny looks without us showering together. It was cute before, but now there are going to be a lot of questions I don't want to answer."

"But…" Jerky began, his eyes wide and pleading.

"No," Tom insisted firmly, trying to keep his voice gentle but resolute. "You can shower after me."

Jerky's shoulders slumped, and he nodded, closing the door and sitting on the toilet, waiting patiently. Tom sighed again, rubbing his temples. He could hear Maria snickering in his mind.

"It's only awkward if you make it awkward," Maria teased. "He is a form of incubus after all."

Sighing heavily, Tom continued with his shower, trying to push the strange thoughts from his mind. When both of them were clean, they dressed and headed down to the cafeteria. There were still a few early risers eating breakfast.

"Tom! Good to see you, though you don't normally come in at this hour," a woman behind the serving line greeted him warmly.

"Yeah, I couldn't sleep," Tom replied, offering a tired smile. "I'm sorry, but I don't think I know your name?"

"It's okay. It's a pretty big Guild now. I'm Samantha," she replied with a smile.

Tom nodded, feeling a bit embarrassed. "Nice to meet you, Samantha. What's on the menu at this hour?"

"We mostly have snacks until about five, but I can have something whipped up for you. Charlene made sure to have us prepared in case any of the strike team came in. Need to keep you all in tip-top shape," Samantha replied.

"I don't want you to go through any trouble," Tom began before Samantha cut him off.

"No trouble at all. Go have a seat and I'll have it brought out to you," she smiled at him and shooed him away.

Moving to a table, Tom and Jerky sat down together and waited. Not long after, Samantha brought out two plates of food. Setting them down in front of them, she beamed at them. "Enjoy!"

Looking at the food, it appeared to be a ham steak with fried potatoes and a glass of orange juice. They both dug in and ate everything on their plates. As he finished eating, Tom thought of something he had been meaning to ask Jerky.

"Do you have an Inventory, Jerky?" Tom asked him as he watched his familiar finishing his meat.

"Yup, sure do," Jerky replied through a mouthful of food.

"So, you get Monster Cores to use in the vending machines for killing monsters?" he asked.

"I think so. Why?" Jerky asked him.

"We need to get you some weapons now that you are human-sized. Something for protection," Tom said as he looked his familiar over. "Maybe some armor too."

"You would buy things for me?" Jerky looked at him, his eyes going wide with surprise.

"Of course, why wouldn't I?" Tom asked, genuinely confused by the question.

"Most familiars are not allowed to have such things. We would have to find them ourselves and cannot have anything even close to the quality of our masters," Jerky replied, looking sad at the thought.

"That's… not how things work here, Jerky." Tom's voice was resolute. "You need to stay safe too. I won't take no for an answer, and we are going right now to get you equipped."

Jerky looked as though he was about to cry. "Master is so kind. I don't deserve to be your familiar."

He lunged over to hug Tom tightly. Tom hadn't expected the hug and tumbled out of his seat with Jerky clinging to him. Snickering could be heard from the few people in the cafeteria at the time, and Tom's face flushed.

"Okay, Jerky. It's not that big of a deal. I need you to get off so we can go now," Tom said as he tried in vain to pry him off.

He hadn't realized how strong Jerky was now and had trouble getting him to let go. When he finally did, they walked over to the machine and looked at the options available.

"You have more of a magic-based build? Or physical attacks?" Tom asked Jerky.

"I guess it's a bit of both. I have quite a bit of magic to use but have good physical stats overall," Jerky replied.

"Not gonna make this easy. Fine, challenge accepted," Tom said as he turned to look at the machine again.

Tom motioned for Jerky to put his hand on the machine, but it produced an error.

"That's odd. I guess it doesn't work for familiars?" Tom looked at it quizzically.

Jerky hung his head again. "That's okay, Master. Thank you for trying."

"Oh, no. You aren't getting off that easy," Tom said to him with an evil smile.

Placing his own hand on the machine, he began to look through the menus for his Warlock Class options. After about five minutes of searching, Tom finally felt he had found the options he wanted.

"How many Monster Cores do you have?" Tom asked.

"Looks like five hundred and twenty-six common, three hundred and ninety-five uncommon, and four rare cores," Jerky replied after looking at his Inventory.

"Excellent! We can get what you need then," Tom said, motioning for Jerky to stand next to him and put coins in the slot.

Tom began making selections on the menu as Jerky added his cores, and items began to fall out of the slots in the machine. He picked them up and set them on the table closest to the machine as they fell, and when they had finished, he sat down with Jerky to let him begin opening the cans.

Jerky smiled through the entire process of opening the cans and held each of his items with the reverence of a bishop washing the pope's rings. Tom had to force him to continue as he kept wanting to try out every item he got. When he was finished, he had a magical spear, a wand of fire elements, potions for HP, MP, and SP, a gun that Tom was a little afraid of Jerky using after he brandished it in ways he had seen James do, and a set of medium armor to allow him mobility.

After equipping the armor and spear and storing the other items in his Inventory, Tom noticed that Jerky was crying.

"Is something wrong, Jerky?" Tom asked, putting a hand on his shoulder.

"Master has been so kind to me. I don't deserve this," Jerky said.

"You're right," Tom said, his voice strangely fierce. His words caused Jerky to flinch. "You don't simply deserve anything—you *earned* this and will always be worthy of this much and more. And I think it's high time we stop with the master bit. You may be my familiar, but you're my friend first," Tom said to him.

Jerky quickly hugged him and began to squeeze as he sobbed into his shoulder.

"Thank you… Tom," Jerky said through his tears.

Tom held him tightly, patting him on the back and smiling warmly. For all the battles and nightmares, moments like these reminded him of why he fought— why he led the Vanguard.

And for Tom, in that moment, everything seemed a little bit brighter.

Chapter 13

A Trip to the Fort

Walking through the lobby, Tom enjoyed the unexpected tranquility that replaced the usual bustling of Guild members moving from one place to another. The silence was a welcome change from the constant chatter and hurried footsteps that filled the space during the day. The dim lighting of the early morning added a soft, almost serene quality to the usually lively area, and Tom found himself appreciating the brief moment of peace.

Jerky walked beside him, his eyes darting around, taking in the stillness. Tom noticed how Jerky's new form seemed almost surreal against the backdrop of the familiar surroundings. They made their way to the courtyard outside, where the cool air brushed against their skin like a soothing balm. Tom inhaled deeply, savoring the freshness of the dawn.

He stopped and summoned Bron, the large Mastadonian warrior. Rising from a swirling, black summoning circle that glowed faintly against the stone ground, Bron's massive form appeared. His eyes, set deep beneath a heavy brow, glanced around with a puzzled expression as he noted the unusual time of day. He then turned his gaze to Tom with a questioning look.

"Sorry, it's not the normal time of day," Tom began a bit sheepishly. "I wondered if you might start training Jerky as well now that he has evolved?"

Bron's eyes widened as he looked Jerky over, his astonishment evident. The little Quasit he had seen before was now nearly as tall as Tom, with a powerful build and wings folded neatly behind him.

"Sure," Bron finally said, his deep voice rumbling like distant thunder. "This is Jerky though? Quite the grown-up now, aren't you?"

Jerky's eyes met Bron's, his face filled with a mixture of nervousness and determination. "I just want to protect mast... I mean, Tom." He met the Mastadonian's eyes squarely. "Can you help me?"

Bron nodded, a small, approving smile breaking through the stern lines of his face. "Of course, little one. What weapon will we be training with?"

"Spear," Tom replied, holding up Jerky's newly acquired weapon. "It seemed the best option. Oh, and hand-to-hand combat. I know how important that is as well."

Bron gave a grunt of acknowledgement. "Very well, let's begin. The first thing to do is assess your endurance level. You need to keep up with the pace of battle for longer than most realize. Your adrenaline will help, but if you train endurance outside of combat, you'll last much longer in a fight. Time for the first training lesson."

A mischievous grin spread across Bron's face, partially hidden by his trunk-like nose, as he turned to Jerky. The gleam in his eyes hinted at what was to come.

Jerky, sensing the change in Bron's demeanor, looked uneasy. "So, I hope you're ready for some hell," Bron said, his voice dripping with mock menacing intent.

Moments later, Jerky was sprinting around the perimeter of the Guild building, his breath ragged and sweat dripping from his face. Bron followed closely behind, barking out orders like a seasoned drill sergeant. Jerky was put through the wringer—push-ups, sit-ups, burpees, and more—his face scrunched in agony as tears streamed down his cheeks. Each time he lagged, Bron would whack him with a long, thin stick, urging him to push harder.

"Is that what we went through?" Derek asked, stepping up beside Tom as he watched the rigorous training unfold.

"I remember it being much worse, but then again, it was happening to *us* at the time," Tom replied, unable to hide a small smile.

"Do you think he's going too far with the poor guy?" Derek asked, his brow furrowing as he watched Bron shout at Jerky for slacking off during a set of push-ups.

"He needs to be ready," Tom said, his expression turning serious. "I don't want to go soft on him only for him to be killed because he wasn't prepared for the battles we still have to face."

A knot twisted in his stomach as he watched Jerky's grueling ordeal. He knew it was necessary, but that didn't make it any easier to watch.

"Well, we have just about everything ready for an exploratory sortie to Fort Worth. You ready to go as well?" Derek asked, trying to steer the conversation to a less grim topic.

"I'm ready. Did we find someone who can fly planes?" Tom turned to Derek, his curiosity piqued by the mention of the mission.

"Better," Derek replied with a sigh. "We found someone who used to fly jets in the Air Force. A guy named Eric. He's a little intense, but he's qualified, and we can't really be too picky right now."

"You don't seem happy about it," Tom chuckled, noting the look on Derek's face.

"I'm used to having options. People we can sort through to find the best candidate. Now, we're scraping the bottom of the barrel and hoping for the best," Derek replied, his shoulders sagging slightly.

"So, when you say intense?" Tom let the question hang, raising an eyebrow.

"Think Top Gun, but every character is played by Ric Flair," Derek said, his eyes meeting Tom's with a pointed expression.

"That sounds promising. Feather boa included?" Tom laughed out loud, imagining the scene.

INVASION

"You joke, but you won't be saying that soon," Derek replied, his lips curling into a reluctant smile. "But I want you to keep that positivity when you meet him."

Their conversation was cut short as Jerky came sprinting around the corner of the building at full speed, Bron hot on his heels, shouting at him to move faster. In his haste, Jerky's feet tangled, and he pitched forward, crashing face-first into the pavement and skidding several feet on the rough surface.

"Ooooooo… That had to hurt," Derek said, wincing as he watched the painful slide.

Tom immediately rushed over to his familiar, helping Jerky to his feet. His face was scraped and bleeding, large abrasions oozing with fresh blood. Small pebbles and bits of dirt clung to the wounds.

"Here, drink this," Tom said, handing Jerky a health potion and gently brushing away the debris from his injuries.

Jerky winced, his face scrunching in pain as he took the potion and gulped it down. "This tastes funny and good at the same time," he commented after swallowing a few mouthfuls.

"I'm pretty sure it's the original flavor of one of Earth's energy drinks with a twist," Tom joked.

"What's an energy drink?" Jerky asked, his curiosity piqued.

"Right, I forget they don't have that where you come from. It's like a stamina potion, but it's not important. You should feel better and get a bit of a boost from drinking that," Tom replied, smiling as he watched Jerky's wounds begin to heal.

"I didn't say you could take a break!" Bron boomed from behind them, his voice like a clap of thunder. "Back to running, maggot!"

Jerky shot up, eyes wide, and started running again. A soft whine escaped his lips as Bron whacked him with the stick for good measure.

"That really takes me back," Derek sighed with a nostalgic smile.

"To when we went through it?" Tom asked, confused as to why Derek was talking as though it had been a long time ago.

"Basic training," Derek clarified, shaking his head. "They really ran us ragged when we first showed up."

"Sounds like tons of fun," Tom joked. "When do we leave?"

"Soon. We can let Jerky get some more training in first. Gonna have to have him sit in the trunk now though. Not enough seatbelts," Derek replied.

"Shouldn't be an issue. Thanks for taking care of that for me. Hopefully, we can find something we can use," Tom said, crossing his arms as he watched Jerky doing a set of rapid-fire burpees, his breath coming in harsh gasps.

"No problem. You can't do everything," Derek replied, also watching the scene unfold with a mix of amusement and concern.

"How big is the group going?" Tom asked, his eyes still on Jerky's struggling form.

"Four teams," Derek answered. "That way we have some backup, but can still leave people here to watch out for the others. Not sure how we'll get the jets back here yet. Hoping they have some kind of transport."

"Can't just fly them back?" Tom asked, thinking it seemed like the simplest solution.

"One at a time? Sure, but we need someone to keep bringing Eric back to us after each flight," Derek explained, rubbing his temples. "No one else has the training yet. He should be able to help with that, but it'll take time. Like every other fucking thing we have to do to be ready."

"Gonna just have to go see what we can find," Tom said, shrugging his shoulders. "If we have to do it one at a time, then we do it one at a time. It's only like a forty-five-minute drive if we can get the roads cleared."

"Yup. We'll do what we have to. Even if we just send one vehicle back and forth," Derek agreed. "Well, this is fun, but I need to go get everyone ready. We'll meet you back out here."

The sound of sobbing drew Tom's attention again, and he turned to see Jerky crying while doing push-ups, his arms trembling. Walking over to where they were standing, Tom put his hands on his hips and looked at the pair.

"Got an idea of what he can handle?" Tom asked Bron.

"He's better than any of you were—crying included, I'll say that," Bron grunted, clearly impressed. "I think we can get started."

"Good. I want him on the fast track. He'll be with me, and we need to be ready," Tom said, reaching down to help Jerky back to his feet.

"Fine. Time to begin sparring," Bron said, turning his gaze on Jerky.

Swallowing hard, Jerky looked to Tom for help. Tom gave him a sympathetic look, knowing what this was like, but then encouraged them to continue.

"Now, get up and take a fighting stance," Bron ordered.

Two hours later, the others from the Guild joined them outside. Poor Jerky had been battered and bruised from his sparring session with Bron. One side of his face was swollen, and his arm hung limply at his side. Tom cast *Dark Restoration* on him whenever needed, but it had clearly been an intense session.

When he saw the others, Tom called for a stop and healed Jerky fully. "Bring the vehicles around, and we can load up to head out," Derek ordered.

Sighing with relief from the pain, Jerky sat down heavily on the ground and lay back, trying to recover.

"You did well, little one. Much better than I expected. If you can throw in some spells between those attacks, you will be a great asset to the team," Bron praised Jerky, who looked up at him in astonishment. "You look surprised. I had to push you to get you ready faster. But you are a fighter—never let anyone tell you otherwise. And I bet those wings aren't just for show. Use them."

Turning to look at his wings, Jerky seemed to have forgotten he had them for a moment before lying back again, a small smile forming on his lips as he basked in the sunlight. Tom squatted down next to him.

"You about ready to go? You can rest on the way over," Tom said softly.

Nodding his assent, Jerky took Tom's outreached hand and stood up.

Soon, the vehicles arrived, and everyone loaded up to head out. With Jerky now being human sized, the vehicle felt even more cramped than it had before. As the gates opened, the guards waved or saluted, and the convoy began its journey west. The road ahead was littered with abandoned vehicles, and the teams had to stop multiple times to clear the way.

"Just like old times, eh?" James joked as they pushed an SUV off to the shoulder, where it collided with a cement barricade.

"It was only a few months ago," Tom laughed, wiping sweat from his brow.

"It feels like longer," James replied.

"That it does," Tom agreed. "Because we've been fighting for our lives a lot of that time."

"So many dicks to shoot, so little time," James added, shaking his head with mock solemnity.

When the teams finally reached the Lockheed Martin plant, they drove up to the guardhouse, which was not only abandoned but mostly demolished.

"What the hell happened here?" Tom asked, his eyes narrowing as he took in the destruction.

"Guess we get to find out," Derek said solemnly.

Driving into the lot, the team parked outside one of the office buildings and exited their vehicles.

"Anyone know where we're going?" Tom asked, scanning the unfamiliar layout.

Everyone shook their heads.

"Probably that big hangar-looking building," Kedron pointed to the large corrugated-steel-sided structure looming behind the main offices.

"As good a place to start as any. Let's go in here so we can enter from the inside and not try to find a way directly into the building," Tom suggested.

With no arguments from the others, they approached a set of glass doors that had been shattered, the jagged edges of the remaining glass glinting dangerously in the dim light.

"Be ready," Tom advised, equipping his greatsword. "Jay, take the lead."

Nodding, Jay moved to the front, his eyes sharp and alert. Inside, the lobby was a scene of chaos—broken glass scattered across the tile floors, overturned furniture, and debris everywhere. The front desk, a massive piece of wood with a marble top that seemed to be bolted to the floor, was covered in papers and shattered electronics.

Ceiling tiles hung askew, and electrical wires dangled down like lifeless tendrils. As they moved deeper into the building, the darkness thickened, making every step feel fraught with tension. Trying to cover every possible angle felt like an almost impossible task, but the teams pressed on, moving slowly down a long hallway that stretched ahead.

At the end of the hall, they reached a T-intersection, halls leading off to the right and left. Remembering that the hangar appeared to be on the right side, Tom motioned silently for them to go that way. Jay nodded and led the group down the right corridor.

They passed several darkened conference rooms before coming to a larger room that appeared to be a meeting area where presentations would be given. The space was set up with tiered levels like a college lecture hall, and a massive screen loomed at the front of the room.

The room was pitch black, the shadows thick and oppressive. As they stepped inside cautiously, a low growl echoed from the back. Derek quickly cast a light spell, and their eyes were drawn to the back of the room. There, sitting atop three rows of tables, was a creature with glowing red eyes, staring at them with a malevolent hunger.

"Shit! Get back!" Tom shouted, raising his sword as the creature's eyes narrowed, and it began to move.

Chapter 14

Hop to it

Large and imposing, the monster's hulking form filled the darkened space as it leaped through the air toward the team. Its muscles rippled beneath slick skin, and a low, guttural growl reverberated off the walls, sending a chill down Tom's spine. He barely had time to react before a thick, pink tongue shot out from the creature's gaping maw, moving with a speed that defied its size. The tongue coiled around his leg with a wet, slapping sound, the saliva burning like acid through his pants and searing into his skin.

Tom's breath hitched as he felt a sudden yank. The beast landed heavily on all fours, the impact sending tremors through the floor. With a snarl, it began to pull him closer, its massive, glowing red eyes locking onto him with a predatory glare. For a moment, panic gripped Tom's chest, his heart hammering in his ears. The creature's stench—an overwhelming mix of rotting flesh and sulfur—hit him full force, nearly making him gag. He struggled against the iron grip of the tongue, his boots scraping against the floor tiles as he was dragged toward the slavering jaws.

Gritting his teeth, Tom quickly focused his mind, ignoring the searing pain in his leg. He used *Inspect* on the monstrous form before him. His vision blurred momentarily, and the details of the beast's stats and Attributes began to flood his senses.

Metalitoad	
Metalitoads are formidable cyborg creatures with a unique fusion of forged metal armor and amphibious skin, making them highly resistant to both physical and magical attacks. Their thick, armored hide gleams with a metallic sheen, while their underbelly retains a slick, amphibian texture. The Metalitoad's appetite is insatiable; anything that fits in its gaping maw is swallowed whole and subjected to its incredibly potent stomach acid, capable of dissolving even the toughest mithril.	
HP:	1025/1025
MP:	10/10
SP:	400/400

Attacks:	Tongue, Claw, Acid Spit

Patches of the creature seemed to have a dull metallic shine to it, reflecting the dim light like a tarnished sheet of armor that had seen better days. In between the metallic plates, rough, slimy folds of amphibious flesh quivered and pulsed, oozing with a sticky secretion that dripped onto the floor. The creature's eyes were the most unnerving part—mechanical circles that seemed to spin and focus independently of each other, glowing with a soft red light. These artificial eyes locked onto Tom with an unsettling hunger, a low growl rumbling from deep within its throat.

A mechanical whirring noise suddenly began to fill the room, rising in pitch. The tongue that had wrapped around Tom's leg started to retract, yanking him toward the creature's gaping maw. Its mouth, a grotesque combination of jagged teeth and rusted metal, began to open wider, revealing a dark void that promised nothing but agony and death.

"Master!" Jerky's voice cut through the chaos, urgent and filled with determination.

The newly evolved familiar flew over the heads of the others, furiously beating his wings. He reached Tom in mere seconds, and with a swift motion, slashed down with his spear. The blade sliced clean through the fleshy tongue with a sickening squelch.

The severed tongue recoiled like a snapped rubber band, slapping back into the Metalitoad's face. The creature let out a low, guttural roar of pain and anger, its eyes flaring an even more intense red as it shook its head to clear the disorienting blow.

"Get back, you fucking shitstain!" Jerky bellowed, his voice a mix of fear and fury. He thrust his hand forward, and a massive fireball formed in his palm, growing to the size of a beach ball. With a roar, he hurled it at the Metalitoad.

The fireball shot across the room, a blazing comet that illuminated the dark corners with an eerie glow. It slammed into the side of the Metalitoad's head, exploding on impact. Flames licked up the creature's slimy skin, burning where flesh met metal. The toad let out a shrill croak of pain, its head jerking violently to the side from the impact. Smoke rose from the smoldering wound, filling the air with the acrid stench of burnt flesh and oil.

Not letting up for a moment, Jerky charged forward with a battle cry, spear in hand. His wings flared open, giving him extra momentum as he leaped toward the creature's side. The spear tip met with the beast's metallic skin, scraping across with a screech before digging into the softer flesh beneath. Unfortunately, the strike wasn't deep; the armor had deflected the brunt of the attack.

Surprisingly, it wasn't Derek that snapped everyone out of their stunned silence, but Eric—their pilot.

"Come on, ladies, are we mice or *men*?! WOOOOO!" Eric's voice thundered louder than the bullets flying from his guns.

INVASION

He had two massive belt-fed automatic machine guns, one in each hand, and handled accuracy through the simple expediency of turning his body toward the threat and holding down the triggers.

"COME GET SOME! WOOOOO!"

With a suitable distraction in place, the rest of the strike team jumped into action, firing off rounds and charging forward with weapons drawn. The sounds of gunfire and clashing steel filled the air, drowning out the creature's enraged croaks.

Off to one side, Eric was gently patting his guns. "I'm sorry sweethearts, I'll last longer next time, I promise. It's just… been a while. You understand, don't you?"

Not waiting for any reply, he was rapidly reloading the massive firearms with long belts of ammo from his Inventory. Snapping the lids closed, he leapt to his feet.

"ALRIGHT!" he shouted. "WHO'S NEXT?! WOOOO!"

Meanwhile, Tom was getting back to his feet.

"What the fuck am I thinking?" Tom muttered to himself, shaking his head.

He summoned Bron, his massive Mastadonian ally and as he materialized, Tom had another thought and quickly summoned Shadow, his loyal shadowy Usiku. The black feline appeared beside him, nuzzling his face affectionately.

"You can see in the dark, can't you?" Tom asked the big cat, smiling despite the chaos. The enormous cat rubbed up against him, purring as it did so. "Yes, it's good to see you too, but we have a bit of a situation here."

Shadow's eyes shifted to the Metalitoad, narrowing with predatory focus. It let out a low, rumbling growl.

"That's right, Shadow. Now, *kill*," Tom commanded, drawing his greatsword and charging alongside the panther.

Jerky, now lost in a frenzy of rage and adrenaline, fought like a demon possessed. His spear strikes were wild but effective, leaving deep gashes across the Metalitoad's exposed flesh and scraping sparks off its armored plates. Then, without warning, his spear ignited with a blaze of fire, casting a fierce orange light across the room. With a loud shout, Jerky launched himself into the air, wings spread wide, and then folded them tight to his body as he plummeted like a meteor directly above the toad.

He drove his spear downward, aiming for the soft spot between the creature's mechanical eyes. The impact was tremendous, the spear embedding deep into the creature's skull. The Metalitoad's body seized up, its eyes bulging as the fire flared even brighter, fed by Jerky's mana, and its head slammed into the ground with a sickening crunch. The flames danced and crackled, licking hungrily at the exposed flesh, searing it black and filling the air with the sickening smell of burnt meat.

At the same moment, Tom rammed his greatsword into the side of the beast, finding a weak spot between the plates of its armor.

Shadow, the Usiku, leaped onto the creature's back, its powerful claws raking deep furrows into its metal and flesh. Bron, with a roar that shook the walls, swung his massive greataxe with all his might, cleaving off one of the Metalitoad's front legs in a single, devastating blow.

The creature, now mortally wounded, collapsed fully with a final, gurgling croak, smoke pouring from its burning body. The strike teams stepped back, panting, as the beast lay still, its life force fading.

"Good job, team," Derek breathed, but his relief was short-lived. A sudden hiss filled the room, and something wet and glistening flew from the darkness, narrowly missing Derek's head. The acidic spit splattered against the wall, sizzling through a whiteboard and melting a sizable hole through the concrete behind it.

"Shit! There's more!" Derek yelled, whipping his head around toward the back of the room.

Three more Metalitoads emerged from the shadows, their eyes glowing a sinister red as they locked onto the group. Their metallic bodies gleamed in the dim light, and they moved with surprising speed, hopping and lurching toward the team.

"Spread out! And don't let them spit on you!" Derek shouted, his voice filled with urgency.

"Ladies, if anyone wants to spit on me, you're going to have to put a ring on it and take responsibility," James quipped as he ducked behind the corpse of the dead Metalitoad, taking aim with his rifle.

Bullets flew at the advancing creatures, but they quickly turned their bodies, presenting their armored sides to deflect the shots.

"ENOUGH!" Jerky's voice cut through the noise, filled with a raw intensity that made everyone pause. Flames burst to life around him, engulfing his entire form like a living torch.

"Did he just go Super Saiyan?" James asked, his eyes wide with a mix of awe and disbelief. He squinted. "His power-up time was way too short. How'd he manage that?"

Jerky didn't respond. Stowing his spear in his Inventory, he charged the nearest Metalitoad, his wings flaring as he lifted off the ground. His fists and feet became his weapons, punching and kicking with unrestrained ferocity. The first Metalitoad, unprepared for such an onslaught, stumbled back, its defense crumbling under the relentless barrage.

Seeing Jerky's relentless attack, the other two Metalitoads turned their attention toward him, launching gobs of acidic spit. Jerky quickly maneuvered the toad he was attacking between himself and the spit, using it as a living shield. The acid splattered across its back, eating through its armor and into the flesh below. The creature let out a pitiful croak before collapsing, dead.

The strike teams seized the opportunity. While the remaining Metalitoads were distracted by Jerky, they closed in, unleashing a barrage of attacks from all sides. Fire spells, sword strikes, and bullets pummeled the creatures, overwhelming them in a storm of violence. Within moments, the last of the toads were dead, their metallic bodies twitching and smoking on the floor.

As Jerky floated back to the ground, the flames around him flickered and died out. The team rushed to him, congratulating him on his ferocity and skill.

INVASION

"That was amazing, Jerky!" Tom said, smiling broadly as he clapped a hand on his familiar's shoulder.

"Aww, that was nothing, really," Jerky replied, his face flushing with embarrassment. "I was just upset that one of them hurt you."

"You're going to be an awesome asset to the team," Derek said. "Not that you weren't before, but damn, you've gotten strong. Great job in that fight."

The group began to loot the remains of the Metalitoads, carefully dismantling the parts that seemed salvageable. The metal that formed their bodies was strange, a hybrid of flesh and machine. They figured it might come in handy for the craftsmen back at the Guild, so they gathered what they could.

After the looting was complete, the team noticed another door at the back of the room leading to a maze of cubicles. Here, the fight intensified. The team found more Metalitoads, but this time accompanied by small draconic creatures that the System identified as Kobolds. The room became a chaotic battlefield as Kobolds used guerrilla tactics, darting in and out from behind cubicle walls, jabbing with spears, and disappearing again.

"Jerky, can you light up the room like you did before?" Tom shouted over the sounds of combat.

"Sure!" Jerky responded, flying up to the center of the room and igniting once more. The bright flames illuminated every shadowy corner, revealing dozens of Kobolds hiding among the cubicles.

"DID SOMEONE SAY LIGHT 'EM UP?! WOOOO!" Eric screamed. His voice could have projected across an entire arena.

Two blazing lines of tracer fire ripped into the Kobolds, tearing them bodily into pieces. As they screamed, so too did Eric, though one side of the equation was clearly in a wholly different state of mind than the other.

With a matching feral grin, Jerky dove down and grabbed two Kobolds by their necks, one in each hand. Using them like crude clubs, he began to beat the remaining creatures with their own comrades. The Kobolds screamed in terror, and seeing their friends used as weapons against them sent them fleeing in a mad scramble. Meanwhile, the strike teams quickly dispatched the remaining Metalitoads in the room.

"Don't chase them!" Derek ordered as some members moved to pursue the fleeing Kobolds. "They know the building better than we do, and there could be traps. Kobolds are tricky little bastards."

"Tricksy little hobbitses," James confirmed in a raspy voice.

The group advanced carefully, moving through the doorway at the far end of the office space. They emerged into a massive assembly line area filled with machinery and half-built jets. The sight was awe-inspiring—an enormous hangar filled with the skeletons of advanced fighter jets, tools scattered about as if everyone had fled in a hurry. Several bodies lay decaying among the machines, some missing limbs or worse.

"Guess we go to the end of the line to see if any are finished?" Tom suggested, his voice echoing in the cavernous space.

And so, they pressed on, weaving their way through the maze of machinery. They passed massive robotic arms, welding stations, and engine mounts. At the end of the line, they finally found what they were looking for: an F-35 that seemed to be in a complete state.

Eric practically salivated at the sight. "WOOOOOO! *That* is a beauty!"

He kissed each of his massive machine guns before storing them away.

After some inspection, however, Eric's excitement faded. "Sorry, everyone, this one's no good. The seat isn't installed, and the computer system still needs a few parts. There's no way we're getting this off the ground without someone who knows this setup inside and out."

"Damn," Tom muttered. "Guess that leaves us without a fighter jet."

Eric chimed in, "Not necessarily. We could hit up the Naval Air Station Joint Reserve Base nearby. They should have some jets there that we can take."

"Alright, let's move before we run into more—" Tom started, but his words died in his throat as they returned to the cubicle room.

Hundreds of pairs of angry, glowing eyes stared back at them from the shadows.

"What was that about getting out before we found more monsters?" James quipped, his voice tense as he stared into the sea of Kobolds.

Tom gripped his sword tighter. "Everyone, get ready. Looks like we're not done here yet."

Eric simply grinned as he brought both machine guns back out of his Inventory.

Chapter 15

Breakout & New Wings

Growls and the sounds of claws scraping across the floor echoed from the room ahead as the two groups stared each other down. The tension was thick enough to cut with a knife, neither side quite ready to make the first move. Derek's brain raced furiously, analyzing the situation, trying to formulate the best strategy to break the stalemate and get his team through the mass of creatures. This was the only known way back to their entrance, and there was no room for error.

"I'll go in first with my power armor," Derek whispered, his voice tense but steady. "Kevin, Kirsten, Bron, and any other Barbarian Classes—follow behind me. Then all other physical Classes. Mages and ranged attackers, take up positions at the door. Keep us covered as best you can. I want a light spell fired into the middle of the room to disorient them. Aim for the center, light it up," he continued, his eyes never leaving the mass of angry eyes staring back at them. "And Eric?" The pilot glanced over at him, his eyes aglow. "You just... keep doing you, alright?"

"You got it, champ! WOOOO!" Eric replied enthusiastically.

"You're getting a lot better at the tactics of combat," Bron murmured approvingly as he moved into position behind Derek, his massive frame casting a shadow across the dimly lit room.

"Thanks. If we get out of this, remind me to think harder about that," Derek replied with a wry smile, trying to mask his unease.

"We'll be fine," Tom assured him, gripping his sword tightly. "I'll just use my tattoo once we get in the room."

Before Derek could respond, a single Kobold broke ranks, leaping from the front line with a hiss of fury, its small but vicious claws extended and eyes wild with rage. In an instant, a shot rang out from behind Derek. He felt the bullet zip past his helmet, missing him by inches. The Kobold's momentum halted as the bullet found its mark on its chest, lifelessly dropping the creature to the ground.

"GO!" Derek shouted, his voice exploding with urgency. The sudden command sent a shockwave through the room, causing the front line of Kobolds to flinch and scatter in surprise.

Derek barreled forward, moving with the speed and force of a freight train. His power armor whirred and hissed with each step, and his shield collided with the front ranks of the Kobolds like a battering ram. A glowing orb of light shot into the room from behind as Briana cast her spell, flooding the space with a blinding radiance. The Barbarian Classes and Bron surged in behind Derek, their weapons cutting arcs through the air as they swung wildly to keep the Kobolds at bay.

The shrieks of rage from the Kobolds were nearly deafening as the bright light overwhelmed their sensitive eyes, causing many to raise their tiny clawed hands to shield their faces. The attackers pushed forward like a bulldozer through a pile of rubble, trampling over the smaller creatures, who were squealing in pain as their bones were crushed underfoot. Derek charged forward with relentless momentum, smashing through cubicles and scattering the makeshift barriers the Kobolds had set up, trapping several under broken desks and causing a chain reaction that toppled more and more of their hiding spots.

Tom moved in behind the initial charge, weaving through the chaos. With a deep breath, he activated his *Tattoo of Life Absorption*, feeling the energy pulse through his veins. A dark aura spread out from his body, latching onto the nearest Kobolds and sapping their life force. Screams of pain and terror erupted from the creatures as they felt their strength draining away, replaced by a cold, empty numbness.

The Kobolds, sensing their advantage was slipping away, finally retaliated. Their desperation, however, only made them more frantic and less coordinated. Blinded by the intense light and overwhelmed by the fierce aggression of Tom's fighters, they were cut down where they stood, their numeric superiority now rendered useless.

The tide had turned on the fates of the Kobolds.

"He's... in his happy place, isn't he?" Tom noted, watching Eric as he pointed one massive gun in one direction and one in another, his arms fully extended as he let loose with round after round of brass death.

"IS THIS ALL YOU GOT, YOU FUCKERS?!" Eric shouted. "YOU PIECES OF SHIT ARE NOTHING COMPARED TO THE SANDBOX! WOOOOO!"

"If only we could all find something that gave us that much joy," Derek agreed appreciatively.

"Are you... sure he's a pilot?" James asked, awed.

"*Pretty* sure, yeah..." Derek nodded, but his voice sounded doubtful.

The battle quickly turned into a slaughter as the strike teams continued their advance, each swing and spell cutting through the dwindling enemy forces.

"That went well," James remarked with a grin, his voice carrying a hint of satisfaction as he scanned the room for any signs of lingering movement. He noticed a twitch from a downed Kobold and, without hesitation, fired a shot, hitting it squarely between the legs.

The creature stopped moving.

"You really can't help yourself, can you?" Derek asked, exasperation clear in his tone.

"What? It moved; you saw it," James replied with a shrug, his eyes never leaving his sights as he continued scanning for threats.

"Not what I meant," Derek muttered, shaking his head as he turned away.

"Alright, loot what you can for now," Tom called out, his tone firm. "Look for the good stuff only. Potions are top priority. I don't want us staying too long and getting surprised."

The team moved quickly, rifling through the bodies and overturned cubicles, finding anything of value. The air was thick with the scent of blood and burned flesh, and Tom could hear the crackling of distant fires that still smoldered in some corners. About fifteen minutes later, he and Derek called for everyone to regroup.

"Alright, move out!" Derek ordered. "Back to the entrance. Let's get to the vehicles and head to the next location."

The team jogged back the way they had come, boots pounding on the ground, adrenaline still coursing through their veins. As they reached the entrance and burst out into the parking lot, Derek's shout cut through the air.

"Load up! We head to the base next door!" he yelled, turning to check behind them.

He stopped dead in his tracks. His eyes widened, and his heart pounded in his chest.

"We got company!" Derek shouted, his voice laced with urgency.

Kiera, quick to react, spun around to see what was behind them. Her gaze locked onto the largest Kobold she had ever seen, barreling straight toward them, its muscles bulging with every step.

She didn't hesitate.

In one fluid motion, she raised her rifle, aimed on instinct more than anything else, and fired. The bullet tore through the Kobold's skull with a sickening crunch.

It collapsed mid-jog, its rage snuffed out in an instant. She could see movement back inside the entrance and fired two more shots into the darkness.

She was rewarded with the sound of shrieks as her bullets found their marks. More Kobolds fell, and none of the others dared to step outside as the team hurriedly piled into their vehicles.

"Those buildings, there! That's where we're headed!" Derek pointed out as he jumped into the passenger seat of the GS2.

Tom slammed on the gas, speeding toward the Naval Base buildings in the distance. The other vehicles followed closely behind, windows down, with team members watching for any signs of approaching enemies. Once they were clear of the Lockheed Martin parking lot, Tom accelerated even more, the wind whipping through the open windows. The hangars loomed larger as they approached, their massive doors sealed shut, hiding whatever lay inside.

Tom brought the vehicle to a stop outside one of the hangars, parking a safe distance away from the doors. "Move out," Derek ordered. "We get into formation and make as little disturbance as possible when entering. Be ready for anything that might be inside."

The team grouped up, their breaths heavy but controlled. Derek took the lead, his eyes scanning every shadow.

"Weapons ready," Derek instructed, his military training taking over. "And I mean *guns*. I want to surprise whatever is inside. We can swap if we get in close. Be prepared for anything. Including people. Armor up, too. Anything you think might stop a projectile. And none of that 'the plates are too heavy, Sarge' bullshit. Everyone hear me?" There was a chorus of agreements, and a few sheepish adjustments as a few put their armor plating back in their carriers.

"*Really?*" Derek scowled at Eric, who was among the ones adding the armor plates back into his kit.

"What?" Eric scowled back. "I need to be free," he explained.

"Brother, you probably have enough stats to carry the entire deployment back to base on your shoulders," Derek argued. "Carrying around some extra plates should be nothing to you."

"Still," Eric growled. "It's just not the same..." He raised his voice so everyone could hear him, though with Eric's idea of his "inside voice," there was no actual worry on that account. "It's like making love with your clothes on, right men? WOOOO!"

Derek could only shake his head.

Reaching the side entrance—a regular-sized door that offered a stealthier approach than opening the giant hangar doors—Derek paused. He looked back at the others, counting them off with a glance. With a silent nod, he counted down from three with his fingers and then kicked the door open, sweeping his assault rifle from side to side, the flashlight attached to the barrel piercing through the darkness.

The team followed, one by one, sweeping the room with their lights and weapons. The silence was almost deafening as they crept inside, their footsteps echoing softly on the concrete floor. Several fighter jets sat in the middle of the hangar, gleaming under the dim overhead lights. The team ignored the aircraft for now, focusing on securing the area.

When they reached the back of the building, Derek's voice broke the silence. "All clear!"

INVASION

"WOOOOO!" Eric shouted, his excitement barely contained as he inspected one of the jets. "Now *these* are some beauties! I can't wait to get in and take her for a spin."

"Get moving on it," Derek snapped. "We've spent enough time already. Get those hangar doors open so we can get the first aircraft out! Kedron, get in the Hummer and head back to base to pick up Eric when he gets there. Everyone else, stay on alert. When we start this bird up, it's going to make a lot of noise."

"It all comes back so easily, doesn't it?" Tom asked Derek, smiling at the way his friend had effortlessly slipped back into a command role.

"You never really lose it," Derek replied, grinning. "Now, pick up a damn weapon, soldier, and get to watching or opening a hangar door!"

Tom chuckled and rushed over to help pry open one of the massive hangar doors. Eric continued to examine the instrument panel in the cockpit, muttering to himself as he worked.

"There should be a computer box somewhere," Eric called down. "Normally, the pilots would take it with them when they leave the plane. Have a look around to see if anyone can find it."

"Alright, everyone, we need to find that computer box for the jet!" Derek ordered. "Move, people! Search everywhere!"

As the team fanned out to search the hangar, Derek glanced outside through the half-open doors. His heart sank. Dark-clad figures were advancing toward them from a distance, their movements quick and purposeful.

"Shit! Get over here and close these hangar doors NOW!" Derek shouted, his voice rising with urgency.

"You *just* said to open the hangar doors, asshole!" Tom shouted, starting to close one of the doors he'd finally managed to work open.

"I know what I said! Welcome to the goddamned Army!" Derek shouted back. "Just do it!"

The team scrambled, rushing to the doors to seal them shut. As they did, Derek worked the latch, locking it into place just as the first of the figures reached the building.

"Cover the entrance we came in through," Derek commanded. "Weapons ready, we have hostiles incoming! Briana, be ready with barriers!"

The tension was suffocating as everyone took up defensive positions. The banging on the side door began almost immediately.

"United States military! Open these doors now and surrender yourselves for questioning!" a commanding voice barked from outside.

"Major Derek Calloway, U.S. Armed Forces!" Derek shouted back, his voice steady. "We're here of our own accord to secure these jets for civilian safety during the invasion!"

"These aircraft are property of the United States military and are not available to rent right now! Surrender or we will take action!" the voice demanded.

"The U.S. military is in disarray, and these jets are not being used!" Derek countered, hoping his bluff about knowing the state of the military was right. "We respectfully decline. We request a parlay instead!"

A long silence followed. The only sound was the occasional clank of metal settling in the hangar.

Finally, the voice replied, "Parlay accepted."

Derek exhaled deeply, feeling a weight lift off his chest but still wary. He motioned for his team to hold their positions. "Very well! We'll open the door. One wrong move, and we'll respond with force!"

He approached the door cautiously, his weapon still aimed. He cracked it open slowly, peering out to see a group of soldiers standing outside.

"You said parlay," said a grizzled-looking man leaning against the doorframe, a sly smile on his lips. "What's with the welcoming party?"

"Just a precaution," Derek said, lowering his weapon slightly. "It's a dangerous world out there. If I meant you harm, I'd have already fired."

"Fair enough," the man replied, looking Derek up and down. "That's a shiny suit of armor you've got there, Major."

"Had to match my shoes," Derek shot back, his tone dry.

"HA! You're military, alright," the man laughed. "Lieutenant Marshall, Navy. Nice to meet another service member, Major Calloway."

"Call me Derek. I'm not active anymore," Derek replied, shaking the lieutenant's hand.

"In that case, call me Marsh," the lieutenant said, his demeanor softening.

"Fair enough," Derek nodded and gestured toward the interior of the hangar. "Let's talk inside. No need to stand here making targets of ourselves."

"Thanks, Derek," Marsh said as they stepped in. "But we have some serious questions for you. I hope you have the right answers."

Derek nodded, sensing this was only the beginning of another intense negotiation. As they walked further into the hangar, he couldn't help but think, *Great, just what I need. Another power-happy military man looking to show off.*

Chapter 16

Military Mistakes

"You have no authority here, and you are not going to take any of these aircraft," Marsh stated flatly as soon as they reached the back of the hangar. His voice was cold, his posture rigid, as if he were clinging to the last remnants of his power.

Derek leaned back against the hangar wall, arms crossed over his chest, his expression calm but firm. "I'll beg your finest pardon, but you can't keep these aircraft here to rot. They aren't being used and won't be used. The government? Gone. The economy? Gone. Society? Gone. You can't argue these points, Lieutenant. You just have to accept them. We've got over a thousand people to protect from an invasion that is coming from the fucking *sky,* and the only way to do that is to get in the air."

Marsh's eyes narrowed, his jaw tightening. "That's not how this works, and you should know that better than anyone else here, Major." He practically spat the rank, his voice dripping with disdain. "You can't just come in here, disrupt the chain of command, and take whatever you like."

"Your chain of command is dead. You're proof of that, Lieutenant. Who's the commanding officer here?" Derek's tone was steady, but his eyes were sharp, piercing.

Marsh glanced at the two men flanking him, both of whom shifted uncomfortably. Then, with a tight-lipped expression, he turned back to Derek.

"I am," he said simply.

A grin spread across Derek's face, a humorless, almost predatory smile.

"Ha! Then you really don't have a leg to stand on if I order you to hand over the aircraft. I outrank you." His laughter was cold, devoid of joy.

"You aren't active. You don't have any authority here," Marsh countered, his fists clenching.

"In case it hasn't occurred to you, Lieutenant, we're *all* active now. And we've been more active than most. I was simply being polite before. I didn't want to get in trouble with a commanding officer. Now that I see that's me, I'm happy to assume command here." Derek pushed off the wall, taking a deliberate step toward Marsh, his posture shifting from relaxed to menacing.

"Denied." Marsh's face darkened, his eyes narrowing to slits as he also stepped forward. "I'm in control here, and that will not change."

Derek leaned in closer, his voice dropping to a low, dangerous tone.

"*Lieutenant,* I suggest you proceed with caution. We aren't just a civilian group playing military. We are a trained group of fighters who have been actively battling monsters and humans for months now. We've been surviving off not only our strategic might but off the abilities this new System has given us. Do not underestimate us." Derek's breath was hot, his eyes locked onto Marsh's with an intensity that could cut steel.

Marsh's eyes widened slightly, but he quickly masked his surprise, his expression hardening once more. He took a moment to size Derek up, his gaze flickering over the armor, the weapons, and the sheer resolve etched into his face. Neither man blinked, neither willing to back down.

"You do *not* want to go down this path with me," Marsh said, his voice barely above a whisper, like the hiss of a snake ready to strike. "Others have tried. I'm still the one here."

"Funny you should mention that, because the *path*?" Derek thumbed a finger at his own chest. "I own it." His lips curled into a smirk. "You can either get with the program, or get out of my way."

A flicker of anger crossed Marsh's face, and his stance shifted, becoming more aggressive.

"I think it's time you and your people joined us here. We'll assume command so that we can rebuild our way back to communication with the other military forces. We can get you drafted into the military with little problem. I believe these times allow for that." His smile returned, but it was the smile of a predator, all teeth and no warmth.

Derek tilted his head, his eyes narrowing thoughtfully. "I'm pretty sure the President and Congress need to authorize that process."

"What do you want to bet they already have?" Marsh continued, his grin widening. "This is a national state of emergency. All citizens of the US have a duty to defend it."

"And what do *you* want to bet they're all dead?"

"It's called the line of succession," Marsh growled. "They can't all be dead."

"Well, if they *are* alive—they certainly are not taking orders from you," Derek stated flatly. "And in light of the lack of a commanding officer that exceeds my own rank, I am officially taking command over this base."

Marsh straightened with a scowl. "With all due respect, *sir*. Over my dead body."

Derek's shoulders sagged slightly, and he let out a long sigh, his gaze dropping to the floor.

"Is that your final decision?" he asked, sounding almost resigned, his voice heavy with an implied acceptance.

Marsh's smile grew more confident, his chest puffing out slightly. "It is. You all will make fine soldiers in the—"

His words were abruptly cut off as a dagger erupted up through his jaw.

Derek had rammed the dagger so hard and fast through Marsh's head that the blade pierced through the top of his skull, sending a shower of blood, brain matter, and shards of bone straight up like a geyser. For a moment, Marsh's eyes went wide with shock, his mouth twitching, and then his body slumped to the ground, lifeless.

The two men who had accompanied Marsh barely had time to react. One of them immediately raised his hands in surrender, his eyes wide with fear, while the other began to draw his weapon. Tom, already anticipating trouble, had his gun out and pointed at the man, his finger hovering over the trigger.

"Stand down!" Tom shouted, his voice booming through the hangar.

Chaos erupted. Several of Marsh's soldiers reached for their weapons, but the members of the Vanguard Guild were faster. Guns were drawn, spells were readied, and tension filled the air like a coiled spring ready to snap.

Perhaps most unnerving of all for the soldiers, was Eric's bloodthirsty grin as he pointed his *ladies* at the uncertain combatants.

One of the military men managed to get a shot off, firing at Bobby. Briana reacted instantly, throwing up a shimmering magical barrier around him. The bullets ricocheted off, sparking as they deflected into the hangar walls.

"Everyone is going to keep their cool right now!" Derek's voice cut through the confusion, a commanding presence that demanded attention. "If not, things are going to get ugly. Now, is there anyone here who outranks a Major of the United States Army and would like to contest my command of this military base?"

Silence fell over the hangar like a heavy shroud. Eyes darted nervously between Derek and Marsh's fallen body, some filled with fear, others with cold calculation.

"Good to hear. You," Derek said sharply, pointing at a nearby soldier. "Your turn in negotiations. What do you think about these aircraft?"

The man swallowed hard, his eyes flicking to Marsh's corpse. "I think they're just going to waste here. I think we should've left a long time ago, but Marsh insisted we stay to protect the base because it was our duty. But he never did anything to actually protect it. He just sat on his ass and ordered us around."

Derek's gaze softened slightly. "What's your name, soldier?"

"Lieutenant Conrad Anderson, sir," the man answered, his voice steadier now, though his eyes still betrayed a hint of anxiety.

"Well, Lieutenant, I think we can get along, then. You don't see any reason to draft us, do you?" Derek asked, his voice carrying a hint of friendly banter.

"Of course not, sir. In fact, I'd rather we joined you. Living here has been miserable," Anderson replied, a glimmer of hope in his eyes.

"How many pilots are with you?" Derek pressed.

"Eight, sir," Anderson replied.

"And how many of them were loyal to Marsh?" Derek leaned in closer, his voice dropping to a conspiratorial whisper.

"Only one. Cam was another, but I didn't count him on account of his being dead now." Anderson smirked slightly, leaning back just a bit.

"Can you point out the ones we need to worry about?" Derek asked with a sly smile.

Anderson nodded, pointing out five individuals, including the one Briana had encased in her barrier.

"Thank you. Tie them up. Take their weapons," Derek ordered, his voice returning to a commanding tone. The team sprang into action, quickly securing the five men.

Once the men were bound and seated on the hangar floor, glaring daggers at Derek, he paced in front of them like a predator sizing up his next meal.

"You all were loyal to Marsh. I respect that. But in this world, I have learned a lesson about people like him. You can't leave them to come back later."

One of the men at the end of the line began to sob, his shoulders trembling.

"I didn't want to follow him! He made me! I wanted to go find my wife and children!" the man blurted out, tears streaming down his face.

"Shut up, Dillon. You're embarrassing yourself," another of the men sneered, rolling his eyes.

"Dillon?" Derek crouched down in front of the crying man, his tone surprisingly gentle. "Where's your family?"

"Dallas, sir," Dillon choked out, wiping his nose on his sleeve. "We had an apartment there so that my wife could get help with the kids from her parents while I was on duty. Her dad was an engineer for a big company based there."

"And the rest of you?" Derek asked, turning his gaze to the others, his expression hardening again.

Only one other looked up, and he spat in Derek's direction. Derek didn't flinch.

"That's too bad. Untie Dillon here. We'll help him try to find his family," Derek ordered, standing up.

"You will, sir?" Dillon's eyes widened, his face a mix of disbelief and hope.

"That's what we do here, brother," Derek smiled, but it was a cold smile. "Kill the rest."

Derek turned away as Dillon was cut free, his gaze turning distant.

Briana's voice broke through the tension, her tone a mix of concern and disbelief. "Don't you think that's a little cold?"

"It is," Derek agreed. "And it's necessary." His eyes, dark and resolute, met hers. "Remember Jeffery? That's what happens when you let people stew about why they're mad at you. James was right, as much as I hate to admit it. We can't leave anyone behind to hate us in this world." His voice was flat, devoid of regret.

James, as if on cue, stepped up, and without hesitation, shot each of the men on the floor. The shots echoed through the hangar, each one punctuated by a brief, muffled cry. Blood pooled beneath the bodies, soaking into the concrete.

The air was thick with tension, a blend of the lingering gunpowder and the quiet horror etched on the faces of some of the Vanguard members. The cold efficiency of the execution wasn't something any of them had signed up for, but they knew the stakes. Trust was a luxury they couldn't afford.

"Now, Anderson, was it?" Derek turned back to the remaining lieutenant, his demeanor shifting from the cold enforcer to a more pragmatic leader. "We need to talk about these jets. There's an invasion coming, and we're stuck on the ground without them. Can you help us?"

Anderson, still visibly shaken, nodded. "Yes, sir. We need the boxes for each one. They have a serial number that matches the planes. Then there's a unique identifier code for each individual pilot that has to be input to activate them. Every pilot has one, and we can get planes off the ground as soon as you'd like." His words came out quickly, as if he wanted to say everything before something could change.

"Perfect. How about fuel?" Derek continued, sensing the man's readiness to cooperate.

"There's a supply here that hasn't been touched. It does have a shelf life, but the MSDS on it says that it can last for up to 36 months. We can load up trucks to take with us. We have a couple that we have the keys to. Any others we need can be hotwired," Anderson replied, but his eyes kept darting back to the bodies on the ground.

Derek noticed. "What's the matter, Anderson?" he asked, his tone still firm but more approachable.

Anderson took a deep breath, trying to steady himself.

"I'm just still a little stressed, that's all, sir," he said, voice shaky.

"Stressed about what?" Derek prodded.

"You did just kill my commanding officer and four other military personnel," Anderson replied, glancing back at the blood-soaked scene.

Derek nodded slowly, understanding. "Do you think we could have let them go without any repercussions?"

His eyes bore into Anderson's, challenging him to see the reality of the situation.

Anderson hesitated, his mind clearly racing with the moral quandary. "No, sir. They were not the kind of people to let that go."

Derek nodded again, his expression softening just a fraction. "That's what I thought. I'm sorry it had to be done. Humans should be banding together to make this world safer, but there are always people who will take advantage. Trust me. I've seen the worst of it." Derek's voice was tinged with a rare vulnerability, a glimpse into the weight he carried as a leader.

"Now, let's get these birds in the air," Derek said, his voice returning to a commanding tone, a decision made.

Anderson snapped back to focus. "I'll run back to the base for the computers. They're all stored in a secure location. We need helmets and suits as well. Let me have Williams to help me, and we can be back faster."

Derek nodded. "Do it."

Anderson and Williams quickly left, their footsteps fading into the distance. Derek turned back to his people, his eyes scanning the hangar. "The rest of you should be able to teach my people how to help you prep these jets. We're taking as many as we can to Dallas. Get Eric here on one of the jets too. He can fly and show you where we're going. We'll have ground transportation to bring you back for another round."

Everyone moved with purpose, the adrenaline still high in their veins.

"Kedron! Can you get in the Hummer and head to Dallas to pick up the pilots and bring them back?" Derek asked, his tone still sharp, but a hint of trust in his voice.

Kedron nodded but hesitated. "With all due respect, I used to be security here at the JRB and know the layout. I think it would be better if Bobby drives back and I stay to help guide you."

Derek smiled, appreciating the insight. "That sounds like a plan to me. Bobby! Head out now so you can bring the pilots back!" he called out.

Bobby caught the keys that Kedron tossed to him and jogged toward the Hummer.

"On it!" he called back.

Watching him go, Kedron turned to Derek. "You know, when we finish with the jets, I can think of a few other things we should… reappropriate," he said with a sly grin.

Derek chuckled, a rare light moment amid the tension. "You and me both. Let's look at everything after we get the jets taken care of. Eric! Come talk with Kedron. We have a shopping list now."

Anderson joined them, still slightly uneasy but more focused now. As they discussed their next moves, the other military personnel worked alongside the Vanguard members, their shared purpose evident in the way they moved, their postures less guarded, more cooperative.

Several of the military personnel, previously under Marsh's oppressive command, seemed relieved to be taking orders from someone who knew what they were doing. One even left and returned with a tug vehicle to move the jets out of the hangar. Slowly, one by one, they began positioning them outside, clearing the way for takeoff.

"This new attitude is refreshing," Tom commented, standing beside Derek.

"They seem happy to be leaving," Derek replied. "I'm just glad it wasn't any worse than it was."

The sound of a gunshot cut through the air, sharp and unexpected. Derek and Tom both turned, eyes wide, adrenaline kicking back in.

"What the hell was that?"

Chapter 17

Weapons Cache

Weapons were drawn by everyone present as chaos erupted in the hangar. The clang of metal against metal and the sound of heavy boots pounding on the concrete floor filled the air as the team scrambled for cover. Another shot rang out, followed by a flurry of curses and the gut-wrenching sound of someone screaming. The cacophony ceased, plunging the room into a dreadful silence that seemed to stretch on forever.

Tom's heart raced as he dashed toward the source of the gunfire. His breath came in short, sharp gasps as he rounded the corner of a stack of tactical crates piled near the east side of the hangar. His boots skidded on the concrete, kicking up a small cloud of dust as he came upon a grisly scene.

Three bodies lay crumpled on the ground, each surrounded by an expanding pool of dark, sticky blood. Two of the bodies were military personnel, their faces pale and lifeless, their limbs splayed out at unnatural angles. The third was Zach. He was gasping for air, blood bubbling from the corners of his mouth and running down his chin as he clutched a bloody patch on his armor, his fingers trembling.

"Dammit, Zach! What happened?" Tom's voice cracked with a mix of fear and urgency as he dropped to his knees beside his friend.

His hands moved instinctively, pushing Zach's away to get a better look at the wound. Blood poured out between his fingers, hot and slick.

"I NEED A CLERIC!" Tom bellowed, his voice echoing through the cavernous hangar as he pulled a potion from his Inventory, trying desperately to open the can.

Zach's eyes fluttered, unfocused. His breathing was ragged, every inhalation a gurgle of wet, choking sounds. "Dillon... pulled a gun... shot me... killed another... I... stopped him..." Zach managed to rasp out between shallow, agonizing breaths.

"You did, Zach," Tom agreed, sadly. "You stopped him."

"Too... late..." He coughed, a deep, rattling sound that reverberated through his chest, and more blood spilled from his mouth.

Tom gently turned Zach onto his side, trying to help him clear the fluid from his throat. He poured the potion on him in a desperate attempt to heal his wounds. Derek came up behind him, his face grim as he crouched down to assess the damage.

"This is bad," Derek muttered, his tone flat and resigned, a shadow of despair clouding his normally sharp eyes.

"Well, heal him!" Tom nearly shouted, desperation dripping from every syllable. His hands, slick with Zach's blood, pressed harder against the wound, but it was like trying to plug a dam with his fingers—the blood kept seeping through.

Derek extended his hands, a soft white glow emanating from them. The healing energy flowed over Zach, shimmering like a gentle mist in the air. But when the light touched Zach's bullet wound, it fizzled out, leaving the hole open and raw.

"What's happening?" Tom's voice trembled with panic, his eyes wide and wild.

"His wounds are too severe for my level of healing. The rounds must have been hollow points. His insides are shredded," Derek explained, his voice hollow as he sat back, his hands falling limply to his sides.

"NO!" Tom screamed, his voice breaking.

He tried to channel his own *Dark Resoration* spell, but a warning message flashed in his vision: **Incompatible alignment. Healing cannot be applied.**

Zach's breath hitched, a final, desperate gasp for air. "It's… ok, Tom..." he whispered, his voice barely audible. "Just… get the jets..."

His body shuddered once, and then his head lolled to the side, his eyes vacant and unseeing.

"FUCK! ZACH!" Tom roared, his fists pounding on his friend's chest as if he could shock him back to life. Tears streamed down his face, cutting paths through the grime and blood smeared across his cheeks. "You can't go yet!" His voice cracked, raw with emotion.

Zach's body lay still, unmoving, the only sound in the hangar now Tom's ragged sobs and the distant hum of engines. Derek stood up slowly, his face a mask of barely contained fury, and moved over to inspect the other bodies.

"Shit. It's Dillon. No idea who the other one is." Derek's voice was low, vibrating with anger. "I should have killed him too. I was just so damn sure he was trying to do the right thing."

Derek's rage exploded in a sudden, violent movement as he hauled his foot back and kicked Dillon's lifeless body, sending it skidding across the concrete floor.

"DAMMIT!" he shouted, his voice echoing up into the rafters.

By this time, others from the team had gathered, forming a somber circle around the scene. One of the military men, his face ashen, spoke up. "It's Breaker," he said quietly. "Sorry, that was his nickname. The third guy is John Breakingstead. He was one of the pilots. Really hated Marsh. Wasn't quiet about it either. Dillon must have taken his chance to take him out. They had a few run-ins in the past."

Tom, still kneeling beside Zach's body, felt a deep, gnawing guilt eat away at him.

INVASION

"How are we going to explain this to Zach's family?" he asked, his voice barely more than a whisper. He knew there was no answer that would make sense, no words that could justify this loss.

A heavy silence fell over the group, the weight of the moment pressing down on them like an iron shroud. Tom reached out with a trembling hand and gently closed Zach's eyes, smoothing his friend's hair back before laying him flat on the ground. He stood, his legs shaky, and turned to the rest of the group.

"Get the jets ready. I'll take Zach to the vehicles," Tom said, his voice steadier now but filled with a cold, hard edge. His gaze swept over their faces, a silent command that brooked no argument.

The team members slowly dispersed, returning to their tasks with renewed urgency but heavier hearts.

Derek stepped closer, his face etched with the same mix of grief and anger that Tom felt.

"It looks like…" he began.

"I know what it fucking looks like. The holes tell the stories," Tom snapped, his temper flaring.

"Tom, there was nothing we could do," Derek said softly, reaching out to place a hand on his shoulder.

Tom jerked away from Derek's touch.

"I know that. That's why I'm so pissed." His voice was strained, almost breaking, as he took a deep breath. "Sorry. I didn't mean to snap."

"It's fine," Derek replied, his tone understanding. "Let me help you with Zach."

Together, they lifted Zach's body, each movement heavy with the finality of their actions. They carried him to one of the SUVs, their faces grim, and laid him gently in the trunk. Tom slammed the door shut with a force that rattled the entire vehicle, then turned back toward the hangar, his jaw clenched.

"Anyone else have any issues they want to get out of the way now?" Tom barked to the group, his voice laced with a mix of frustration and grief.

Everyone froze, turning to stare at him. The tension was palpable, crackling in the air like a live wire.

"Tom, this isn't the way to do this. We can have official inquiries when we're back at the base," Derek interjected, moving to stand between Tom and the rest of the group.

Tom's eyes blazed with fury, but he allowed Derek to pull him aside, his footsteps heavy and reluctant.

"You can't do this. Not now. Focus, man. Get the job here done, then look into it further. We have a lot to do," Derek said, his voice low and calming.

Tom's gaze was distant, staring past Derek as if searching for answers in the empty air. His face was tight with anger, his mouth a hard, thin line. "We messed up big time, Derek. We shouldn't have trusted him. I don't know if we can trust any of them."

"I know. Trust *me*, I know. But we need them right now to get what we need to save the others. Over a thousand of them, Tom. Focus on that," Derek urged, his tone steady.

Tom took a long, deep breath, his shoulders rising and falling. "Fine," he muttered, his voice firm but strained. He turned and walked back into the hangar; his steps purposeful but heavy with emotion.

Derek lingered for a moment, looking up at the sky and letting out a sigh that seemed to carry the weight of all the decisions he had made. He ran a hand through his hair, trying to compose himself before heading back in.

The jets were now lined up outside, ready for takeoff. Anderson and Williams returned shortly after with the computer boxes in tow. The military-grade Hummer they arrived in rumbled to a stop, and they jumped out, heading straight for the back to unload.

"Geeze, what's with all the long faces?" Anderson asked, his eyes darting around, and then he saw the bodies. "Shit. Dillon?" he guessed, his voice dropping.

Everyone nodded, and Anderson's face fell. "I was worried about that. How bad?"

"Three dead, including Dillon. We're down another pilot as well," Derek replied grimly. "Did anyone know his code?"

Anderson rubbed his chin thoughtfully. "Maybe. They're supposed to be a secret, but some of them might have shared. I don't know though."

"Well, let's see if we can find out. We need as many of these birds in the air as we can ASAP," Derek said, his voice steady but carrying a sense of urgency as he turned back to the task at hand.

Anderson's face brightened slightly as he remembered something. "I recalled that we were gearing up for an air show before everything went to hell. There's also a single A-10 here on base that was supposed to fly in the show. We should definitely take that with us. It's a beast in the sky and can do some serious damage."

Derek's eyes lit up at the mention of the A-10. "Put it on the list. We'll take it with us."

Within moments, a tanker truck rolled into the hangar, its engine rumbling like a caged beast. The team quickly mobilized, refueling the jets that weren't already topped off. The computer boxes were handed out to each pilot, including Eric, who had a determined look on his face as he studied the interface.

Seven pilots, all experienced and focused, chose their aircraft and began the pre-flight checks. There was a tense energy in the air, a mix of anticipation and determination. One of the pilots remembered Breaker's code, and Eric used it to get the final jet started. As the jets roared to life, the hangar seemed to vibrate with their collective power.

Anderson walked down the line, distributing the helmets. "These helmets cost four hundred thousand dollars to make. And the people who made them are probably dead. Don't damage them," he warned, his voice stern.

"Trust me, pal. I know how to treat a lady." Eric chuckled as he strapped on his helmet, securing it with a series of practiced movements.

INVASION

With a final nod to Anderson, he sealed the hatch of his F-35 and powered up the engines. The roar of the jet was deafening, even with ear protection. The exhaust nozzles tilted downward as the aircraft lifted off vertically, hovering for a moment before the nozzles rotated back, and it shot forward like a missile toward Dallas.

The other jets followed suit, each pilot guiding their aircraft with precision and focus. The sound was overwhelming, a symphony of power and controlled chaos. The ground shook beneath their feet, and the wind from the jets' exhaust whipped around the hangar like a tempest.

As the last jet cleared the runway and took to the sky, Derek turned to Kedron, who was surveying the remaining equipment with a thoughtful look.

"Now, what was it you thought we should grab while we're here?" Derek asked, raising his voice to be heard over the receding noise.

Kedron didn't hesitate. "Missiles," he said, eyes gleaming with the kind of excitement only a soldier would understand. "Oh, and as many weapons as we can load into the vehicles. I bet these guys have some transport we can use to haul it all back."

Derek nodded, his expression a mixture of agreement and urgency. "Let's do it. Get them to cooperate, and we'll get the vehicles over to wherever you point us." He turned to relay the orders to the team, his voice cutting through the din. "We need to pick up some freebies while we're here. It's a military base, so there'll be a weapons cache somewhere. Kedron is going to take us there, and we'll load up everything we can. Get in the vehicles, and we'll head there now."

The Vanguard members moved like a well-oiled machine, nodding in understanding and heading toward their vehicles. Moments later, the convoy was heading north across the base to a nondescript building surrounded by barbed-wire fencing. The structure was deceptively plain, a facade hiding its true purpose. When they arrived, one of the remaining military team members unlocked the entrance and led them down a series of corridors until they reached a fortified door at the back.

Inside was a treasure trove of military hardware. Rows of shelves stretched out like the arms of some metal colossus, each one bristling with weapons, ammunition, and equipment. The room was cavernous, the ceiling lost in darkness overhead, the only light coming from a few spells from Briana that cast long shadows on the floor.

Derek's eyes swept over the room, his mind racing. "Let's get started. Get as much as will fit in the vehicles, and we'll find some more to carry the rest. Fill your Inventories, too. Don't leave any free space. We won't find a cache like this again anytime soon," he commanded. "In fact, fill your Inventory first. Then load up the vehicles."

For the next hour, the team worked with a singular focus. Boxes of ammunition, crates of grenades, racks of rifles, and piles of body armor and tactical gear were loaded up. Bobby, who had just returned with the pilots, joined the effort, his face a mask of determination as he helped carry crates.

"Kedron!" Derek shouted as he descended the steps into the lower levels of the storeroom. "Find anything good down there?"

Kedron waved him over with a grin. "This is one of the things I really wanted to find." He stood beside an M270 Multiple Launch Rocket System or

MLRS vehicle, its massive bulk mounted on tank treads, a cluster of rocket tubes pointing skyward. "The M270. It can launch missiles from the ground at targets miles away. This should add some serious firepower to our arsenal. They have two of them. I can drive one, and we can get another person to take the other."

Derek's smile matched Kedron's. "Good. Do it. Get them out of here and put them in the lineup heading back with us." He paused, his gaze sweeping the room again. "Where are the missiles for the jets?"

"There are some here, but more might be stored in a separate building. We'll find them, don't worry," Kedron replied as he climbed into the M270 and began the start-up sequence.

Derek turned back to the rest of the team, his voice booming across the vast space. "Alright, everyone! Time to get more jets set up. And we have an A-10 I want taken on this run. Not sure where you're going to land it, but get it to Dallas, and we'll figure out the details when we get there."

As the team mobilized to execute Derek's orders, a low rumble echoed through the base—a promise of the storm to come. But with their newly acquired firepower and the jets now in the air, the Vanguard Guild was ready to face whatever awaited them.

For now, they had won a small but crucial victory, and with each step forward, they came closer to securing their future. The path ahead was fraught with danger, but with allies old and new, they were determined to carve out a place in this brutal new world.

As Derek watched his people—his friends—work with grim resolve, he felt a flicker of hope. They were fighting for more than survival now; they were fighting for something that mattered.

And he'd be damned if he'd let anything stand in their way.

Chapter 18

What Next?

The ship rattled violently, warning sirens blaring as the metal hull groaned in protest.

The first mate tightened his grip on the console, eyes darting between the rapidly rising engine heat levels and the oblivious captain lounging at the helm.

"Captain," he said, voice tight, controlled. "You're pushing the engines too hard. If we maintain this burn, we'll fry half the fleet's drives before we even get there."

The captain laughed, reclining further in his chair as if the entire ship weren't currently vibrating like it was about to shake itself apart. "Nonsense! That's just the engines waking up! Let them stretch their legs a little!"

The first mate fought the urge to sigh. "Engines don't have legs, sir. They have thermal limits. Which we are exceeding."

The captain waved him off. "You worry too much! We'll be there before they even know what hit them!"

A particularly violent shudder rocked the ship, and one of the crew members at the engineering station panicked, slamming buttons to stabilize the overload.

"Uh—Captain, we're venting coolant at an alarming rate."

The captain grinned, completely undeterred. "Perfect! That means the engines are working extra hard! More power, faster ship, bigger entrance. See? Everything's going exactly as I planned!"

The first mate turned to the viewport, inhaling deeply, exhaling slowly.

"If by 'as planned,' you mean 'hurtling toward catastrophic failure at record speed,' then yes, I suppose it is."

The captain stood up, clapping him on the shoulder. "That's why I keep you around, you know! Always thinking of the details so I don't have to."

I would rather eject myself into space, the first mate thought.

With the ship still rattling from the captain's reckless piloting decisions, the first mate decided to shift the conversation before they all ended up stranded in deep space.

"Sir," he started carefully, "we need to talk about the Earth situation."

The captain rolled his eyes. "Ugh, not this again."

"Part of our plan failed."

The captain's grin turned sour, his good mood evaporating. He grabbed his discarded drink, swirled it dramatically, and took a long, exaggerated sip before slamming it down.

"You know who I blame for that?"

The first mate already knew the answer but humored him anyway. "Who, sir?"

The captain whipped around, pointing a finger directly at him. "You."

The first mate didn't even flinch.

The captain paced, building up steam for his inevitable nonsense. "The man with the anger issues was supposed to be our key into that planet, and you let him die!"

"I didn't let him die," the first mate corrected. "He underestimated his enemies, and he got himself killed."

"You were supposed to handle that!" the captain barked. "Now I have to waste my time cleaning up your mess!"

The first mate inhaled, exhaled. "We still have a foothold in Dallas. That should count as a success."

The captain scoffed. "A foothold? That's not a victory! These Earthlings think they've won something, and that does not sit well with me."

He turned, grinning wildly, the expression of a man who thought he was invincible.

"No. I think it's time we remind them who they're dealing with."

The first mate stiffened. "Sir, if you mean what I think you mean—"

"Oh, I absolutely do."

The captain spread his arms dramatically. "First, we make an example out of that Dallas Guild. Then, we burn their little world to the ground!"

The first mate clenched his jaw. "That would be a mistake."

The captain grinned, absolutely delighted. "You always say that, and yet, somehow, I'm always right."

The first mate stared at him, long and hard. The infuriating man had never been right. Not once.

"Sir," he tried again, "throwing our fleet into a grudge match with Earth isn't part of the larger strategy."

"Who cares about the larger strategy?! These people need to learn their place!"

The first mate mentally prepared for impact. "And if we overextend and *he* finds out?"

A flicker of something crossed the captain's face—something dangerously close to fear. It lasted only a fraction of a second before being smothered by arrogance.

"He doesn't need to know."

The first mate could almost feel the moment his soul tried to leave his body.

The captain clapped once, signaling the conversation was over. "Now, prep the ships! I want Dallas to know who they're dealing with."

The first mate didn't argue further.

There was no point.

Instead, he turned away, walking toward the exit, already calculating how to mitigate the disaster before it started.

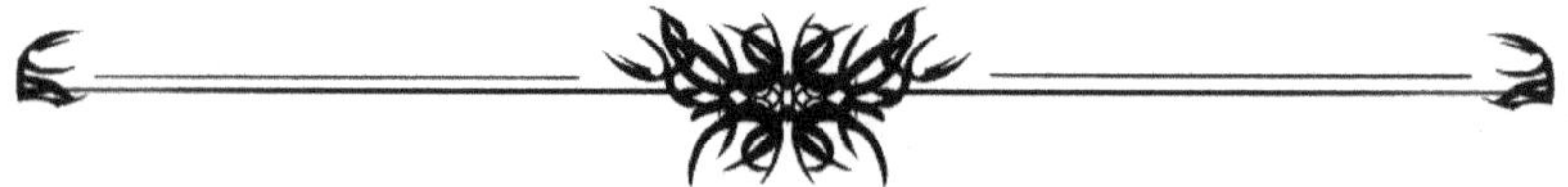

It took about thirty-six hours of nearly non-stop work to get everything back from the JRB to Dallas. The entire Guild and even some of the civilians were enlisted to help load and unload everything—from crates filled with weapons and armor to boxes of missiles and explosives. People worked in shifts, some on the front lines loading items onto trucks, others on the back lines in Dallas unloading, categorizing, and securing the new gear. The constant rumble of engines, the clatter of metal on metal, and the shouted orders created a chaotic symphony of productivity.

Most of the weaponry was standard infantry-based, designed for the hands of soldiers, but they also uncovered some specialized items—high-powered sniper rifles, portable missile launchers, and explosives—things that Derek promised he would teach the right people to use.

Feeling like a bag of warmed-over crap, Tom finally dragged himself back to his room, his muscles aching with every step. He left the rest of the sorting and cataloging to those better suited for the logistical nightmare of organizing their newly acquired arsenal.

In total, they had managed to bring back seventeen F-35 jets, a number that doubled their air capabilities to pilots overnight. Anderson, one of the military pilots who had joined them, had offhandedly mentioned that a few extra jets were stored in a hangar on the Lockheed property, waiting for delivery. This stroke of luck had added a few more precious aircraft to their collection. Tom didn't care much about those details at the moment.

He stumbled into his room, barely managing to strip off his grimy clothes. The hot shower was a brief moment of paradise; the water pounded on his back, easing the tension and washing away the dirt and sweat, but exhaustion pulled him to bed quickly. He collapsed onto his mattress, and the world faded away as soon as his head hit the pillow.

When he awoke the next morning, the sunlight streaming through his window was already warm on his face, the bright light nudging him awake. He groaned, blinking against the brightness. Muscles he didn't even know could ache were sore. Despite the lingering exhaustion, there was a calmness, a satisfaction from knowing they had accomplished something monumental. He dressed slowly, pulling on fresh clothes that felt like a second skin after the endless hours in sweaty combat gear. Tom made his way down to the cafeteria, driven by the hollow ache of hunger gnawing at his stomach.

As he entered the bustling room, he was immediately met with a wave of applause. The sound was jarring, unexpected. Tom paused, blinking in confusion as he looked around at the smiling faces.

"What's this all about?" Tom asked, his voice carrying a mix of embarrassment and bewilderment as he took in the crowd of Guild members.

"They're showing appreciation for the work you did yesterday," Derek said, approaching with a grin that didn't quite reach his eyes, a glint of tiredness evident.

"Then they should be applauding Eric, most of us just sat back and watched him work," Tom replied, his cheeks flushing slightly. He shifted uncomfortably under the weight of their gratitude.

"The man really is a menace," Derek's smile softened, understanding the mix of emotions in Tom's voice. "You just gave them hope for an invasion where they felt they might be severely outgunned. They have a reason to believe again," Derek explained, placing a reassuring hand on his shoulder. The touch was firm but conveyed a warmth of camaraderie and support.

"But… we lost Zach," Tom said, his face falling as the memory of Zach's last moments flickered back into his mind. He felt a knot of guilt tightening in his chest. He didn't deserve this after what had happened.

"We did. I know," Derek replied quietly, his voice tinged with a similar heaviness. "It's not easy, and it's never going to be. But this is something that happens in war. We'll have a ceremony to honor him, just as we did for the others. You gave them hope, though, and that counts for a lot. You need to remember that," Derek added, his voice steady, a slight tremor betraying his own grief.

Tom nodded, still feeling the weight of his loss but realizing the truth in Derek's words. He waved awkwardly to the crowd, who continued to cheer and clap as he made his way to the serving line.

Charlene, the head cook, had made him a special breakfast—pancakes stacked high, eggs, bacon, and a side of fruit. She smiled warmly as she handed him the plate, her eyes shining with a mixture of admiration and motherly pride.

"Thanks, Charlene," Tom mumbled, feeling a bit more grounded by the familiar face.

He moved to a nearby table, setting his plate down carefully. People continued to approach him as he ate, patting him on the back or offering kind words of gratitude. The attention felt overwhelming at first, like a spotlight that was too bright, too intense. But then, a small child approached him, his eyes wide with innocent wonder.

"Uncle Tom, thank you for helping to keep us safe. My momma was so scared, and you made her feel better," the small boy said, his voice sincere and soft. Without warning, he threw his tiny arms around Tom's leg, hugging him tightly.

Tom's heart melted at the gesture. The boy's words cut through the noise, striking a chord deep within him. He patted the boy's small head gently, feeling a warmth spread through him that eased some of the burden he'd been carrying.

"You're welcome, buddy. I hope you're going to make sure you learn as much as you can so that you can grow up to protect your momma, too."

"I'm gonna be just like you! I'll fight the bad guys and monsters, too, so we can all be safe!" The little boy's eyes sparkled with excitement as he ran back to his mother, who was standing nearby, her face beaming with pride and relief.

INVASION

She gave Tom a grateful nod, her eyes misting over as she watched her son scamper back. Tom sat there for a moment longer, watching them leave, a heavy but comforting feeling settling in his chest. He turned back to his food, feeling a strange mix of humility and a sense of purpose that he hadn't felt in a long time.

"I don't know how I feel about all this," Tom said, his voice barely audible over the low hum of conversations around him. He stared down at his breakfast, the syrup on his pancakes glistening under the cafeteria lights like a pool of golden sunlight.

"You'll get used to it," Derek replied, his tone gentle but firm. "They want to show you their appreciation. It would be rude to turn them away or brush them off. People need heroes, Tom. Right now, you're one of them."

Tom nodded slowly, understanding but not entirely comfortable with it. "I'll try," he said quietly. He glanced up at Derek, his eyes searching for a change of topic. "So, what's next for us?"

"Harold was able to find a blueprint for the F-35 in a vending machine and is going to take one of the jets to begin immediately working on a new fuel system," Derek explained. "In the meantime, we'll be working on training people to fly them, as well as sorting the weapons and assigning them to Guild members. We also have the military people we brought back who need to be vetted. Brian said he'd handle that, making sure they aren't going to stab us in the back before letting them officially join."

"And what do we do?" Tom asked, a hint of impatience creeping into his voice. "That doesn't sound like any of it needs us directly."

"We can spend some time leveling up," Derek suggested, spearing a piece of scrambled egg with his fork. "We need to make sure we're ready for whatever the invaders can throw at us. So, I suggest we do some Dungeon runs."

"Dungeon runs, eh?" Tom echoed, a small smile tugging at the corners of his mouth. "How about that Dungeon of Chance again? I bet we can get some loot there as well."

"I was thinking the same thing," Derek agreed, a glint of excitement lighting up his tired eyes. "Plus, it's a good way to blow off some steam."

Tom's smile widened, and he began eating faster, shoveling food into his mouth with newfound energy. When he finished his meal, he looked up at Derek with determination. "Let's go. I'm ready for a Dungeon break."

They left the cafeteria, adrenaline slowly building in their veins as they made their way to the security office to gather their team. Once everyone had assembled, they headed to the garage, piling into the vehicles to make their way to the Dungeon. Jerky, eager to join, hopped into the trunk with Squirrel, who seemed particularly happy to be included after missing out on the jet raid.

"Everyone ready?" Tom asked, turning around in the driver's seat, his eyes scanning over each of his team members.

Thumbs went up around the vehicle, confirming their readiness.

They set off, driving through the quiet, abandoned streets of the city. The road stretched out before them like a ribbon of asphalt winding through a world that had once been bustling with life but was now eerily silent. Upon arrival at the aquarium, they parked and entered the dark, labyrinthine corridors, navigating carefully until they reached the familiar entrance. The same eerie, almost palpable darkness greeted them, a void that seemed to press in from all sides.

Once everyone was inside and the heavy metal door clanged shut behind them, the ethereal writing appeared in the air, along with the now-familiar twenty-sided die hovering in front of them.

Tom flicked the die with his fingers, and it tumbled through the air, landing on what seemed to be an invisible surface before rolling away, its sides flashing as it spun. It finally came to a stop, and a bright number three faced up. The die pulsed with light, and the world around them began to shift and transform.

The new environment took them by surprise. They found themselves standing on a well-trodden dirt road, beaten into the earth by years of travel, both by foot and wagon. Sunshine poured down like honey, warming their skin with a comforting glow, while grassy fields stretched out on either side, dotted with wildflowers that swayed in a gentle breeze. A cluster of fluffy white clouds drifted lazily across the sky, and somewhere in the distance, a brook bubbled softly.

As they absorbed the strangely serene scene, more writing appeared in the air, hovering like smoke caught in a sunbeam. Tom read it aloud, his voice tinged with disbelief. "Welcome to Fantasmia. The world of all things cute and cuddly. A plague of Bunnicorns has been wreaking havoc on the munchkin people who live in the town of Candyville. Reach the town and find out how you can help with the pests."

"Fantasmia? Bunnicorns? Candyville? What the hell is this?" James asked, his face twisted in disgust as he read the saccharine names.

Just then, several butterflies with shimmering, iridescent wings fluttered by, and a squirrel with unnaturally large, glistening eyes scampered down from a nearby tree. It nuzzled against James' leg, looking up at him with a gaze so wide and innocent it could melt the heart of a stone gargoyle.

James' expression darkened, and before anyone could react, he punted the squirrel with a swift kick. It flew into the tall grass, where Squirrel, the wolf, eagerly gave chase.

Moments later, a high-pitched squeal pierced the air, followed by the crunching of tiny bones.

"Good boy, Squirrel! There can be only ONE!" James called out, his voice dripping with disdain as he turned back to the group.

There was a beat of silence before Tom sighed heavily. "I'm not really sure what to make of this either. It feels like a kid's Dungeon, but we're here, so we might as well get it over with."

Looking further down the road, they noticed a wooden signpost with two arrows pointing in opposite directions. One sign read "Candyville" in bright pink letters, and the other read "Gumdrop Castle."

"This is bullshit," James muttered under his breath as he read the signs.

Tom took a deep breath, trying to muster patience. "Look, I don't like this any more than you do," he said, glancing at the rest of the team. "But we shouldn't pass up the XP. Let's just get this done."

With that, they began their journey toward Candyville, the town just visible in the distance. It only took a few miles of walking before they reached it. The town appeared to be made entirely of gingerbread, with walls made from massive sheets of the stuff held together with thick lines of frosting. The rooftops were decorated with colorful gumdrops, and peppermint poles lined the streets. The air was filled with the faint, whimsical sound of singing coming from the town square.

"I never thought I'd say this, but I'm with James here. I think I'm gonna be sick from all the cute," Jay muttered as they approached.

"You know, for being stuck in a world devastated by an apocalypse, you all sure do a lot of complaining about happiness," Tom shot back, his patience wearing thin.

"You can't tell us that you're enjoying this," James countered. "All this happy-sappy crap. Right?"

"All I'm saying is that after weeks of doom and gloom, this place seems like a nice break," Tom replied firmly. "So, knock off the pessimism, and let's get this quest completed."

The rest of the group fell silent, following Tom as he led them past the ridiculously cheerful gates into Candyville. Munchkin-sized people, no more than a foot tall, rushed out to greet them, their faces painted with forced, overly cheerful smiles.

"They've come to slay the Bunnicorns!" one of the little men with a bushy beard squealed in a high-pitched voice. "You've really come to help us?"

"Uh, yeah. We're here to help," Tom replied, feeling more uncertain with every word.

The munchkin people loudly cheered; the high-pitched squeals almost painful to hear. "Just find the Bunnicorn Matriarch and slay her, and the Bunnicorns will stop attacking our town and eating our homes! And, of course, stealing our children in the dead of night, never to be seen again!"

"Wait, what?!" Tom exclaimed.

"*Now* we're talking," James said, rubbing his hands together with a grin.

"Yes, they come at night, destroy the walls, eat our homes, and take our children," the munchkin man continued, his voice still disturbingly positive despite the grim words.

"You seem awfully cheerful for someone whose town is under attack," Tom noted, narrowing his eyes.

"We can't show any emotion but joy; it's the curse we have been living with for the last thousand years!" the munchkin man explained, still smiling broadly as he turned to address the crowd.

The munchkins all cheered again, raising their tiny fists in unison. The contrast between their expressions and the horror of their situation sent a chill down Tom's spine.

"This just got creepy," Kiera said, her hand instinctively tightening around her weapon.

"Can you tell us where they are?" Tom asked, trying to mask his incredulity at the bizarre situation.

"Sure can! Right over there!" the munchkin man replied, his voice still unnervingly cheerful as he pointed to the west with a tiny, pudgy hand.

Tom followed the direction of the man's stubby finger, squinting against the sun. His eyes widened as he saw a horde of white, furry creatures galloping down a hill, kicking up a cloud of dust as they raced toward the town. Their approach was almost comically adorable—if not for the sheer number of them.

"Really? They're coming right now?" Tom asked, his voice tinged with exasperation and disbelief. He half-expected this entire scenario to be some sort of twisted prank.

"We probably triggered some kind of event by asking about it," Derek offered, his voice calm but tinged with the irritation of someone who knew they were about to be thrown into a ridiculous battle.

The dust cloud thickened, churning like a miniature storm on the horizon, as the Bunnicorns charged forward. As they got closer, Tom could make out more details—their large, glistening eyes were the same as the unnervingly cute squirrel from earlier, wide and shining with a disturbing mix of innocence and malice.

Golden horns jutted proudly from their foreheads, catching the sunlight and casting shimmering reflections across the landscape. Their fluffy fur rippled like waves as they bounded forward with an energy that seemed inexhaustible. Squeaking sounds filled the air as they drew nearer, each one like the high-pitched squeak of a child's toy.

"Alright… if this is what we need to do..." Tom muttered under his breath.

He was trying to wrap his head around the absurdity of it all—fighting a wave of what looked like murderous, horned bunnies. He felt a knot of surreal humor twist in his stomach, mixing with a genuine readiness to fight.

Tom moved around the gingerbread walls of Candyville, positioning himself between the western side of the town and the incoming furry horde. He drew two handguns from his Inventory, the metal glinting ominously in the soft light. Taking a deep breath, he aimed at the closest of the Bunnicorns and squeezed the triggers. The shots rang out, splitting the air, and a split second later, the head of the nearest Bunnicorn exploded in a fountain of blood and gore. The creature tumbled to the ground, its small body rolling limply beneath the thundering feet of its companions.

"Oh, cool! I was worried they'd be like piñatas where candy might fall out of them," James remarked with a dark chuckle.

Without missing a beat, he joined in, raising his handguns and opening fire on the oncoming wave of fluffy killers. Each shot sent another Bunnicorn flopping lifelessly to the ground, but the creatures seemed undeterred, barreling forward with an almost suicidal determination.

The rest of the team quickly followed suit, drawing their weapons and joining the fray. Gunfire echoed through the air, mingling with the rapid, repetitive squeaks of the Bunnicorns as they charged. The fluffy white bodies piled up, but they just kept coming, their sheer numbers threatening to overwhelm the defenders. Soon, the horde had closed the gap, and the Bunnicorns began to ignore the fighters altogether, their beady eyes fixed on the town. With a series of powerful leaps, they cleared the short gingerbread walls and began to wreak havoc inside.

INVASION

"Hey, wait!" Tom shouted, his head snapping around to see the chaos unfolding behind him.

The Bunnicorns tore into the candy-like structures with reckless abandon, their sharp teeth ripping chunks out of gingerbread walls and licorice roofs. Munchkins fled in all directions, screaming in high-pitched terror. Some of the Bunnicorns grabbed the tiny people in their jaws, shaking them violently until body parts tore free. The ground began to run with rivers of dark red blood, contrasting starkly with the vibrant colors of the town.

"NO! I'M NOT READY TO DIE!" one small female munchkin shrieked, though her face remained locked in a horrifically cheerful smile.

"This is sick," Tom muttered through gritted teeth, his stomach twisting with a mix of revulsion and grim determination.

He leaped over the low wall and landed in the middle of the pandemonium, drawing his greatsword as he moved. He swung the massive blade in a wide arc, cleaving through three Bunnicorns in a single swing. Their bodies fell limp, the squeaking noises dying in their throats.

"I feel *so* much better," James laughed as he fired shot after shot into the throng of white, furry creatures. He took a moment to relish the chaos around him, then kicked one of the Bunnicorns like a football, sending it flying through the air. It landed with a crunch somewhere beyond the gingerbread walls.

Just then, one of the Bunnicorns ducked under James' next kick and jumped up, thrusting its golden horn directly into his backside.

"OUCH! Fucking shit-stained little cunts!" James roared, the pain shooting through him like fire.

He spun around, his face twisted with rage, and unloaded a burst of gunfire into the offending Bunnicorn. The creature exploded into a cloud of fur, blood, and broken bones. The rest of the team burst into hysterical laughter, unable to hold it in as they continued their assault.

Meanwhile, Squirrel was having the time of his life. The wolf darted among the Bunnicorns, his jaws snapping shut around one after another. Each time, he picked them up and shook them violently, tossing them aside like ragdolls. His tail wagged furiously, clearly enjoying the carnage.

Jerky, hovering above the scene with his wings flapping, was hurling small fireballs at the creatures below. Each hit resulted in a small burst of flame and a squeak that quickly turned to silence, leaving smoldering corpses in its wake. His giggles filled the air, a disturbingly gleeful sound amid the slaughter.

As the battle raged on, the ground became littered with Bunnicorn bodies, their once-fluffy white fur now matted with dirt and blood. The munchkins cheered for the team even as they rebuilt their homes, their eternal smiles never wavering despite the destruction and death surrounding them. Eventually, the squeaking died down, and most of the Bunnicorns lay dead either outside or inside the town. The fighters took a moment to catch their breath, surveying the carnage.

A deep rumble echoed in the distance, growing louder by the second. The ground trembled beneath their feet, and a new dust cloud rose on the horizon, this one far larger than before. Emerging from the haze, they could see a massive shape barreling toward them, moving with a speed that belied its size.

"What is that?" Derek asked, squinting as he tried to make out the figure approaching from the west.

"The Matriarch! She comes!" shrieked an injured munchkin lying in a chocolate fountain in the town square, his blood mingling with the sugary liquid. "She comes to avenge her children!"

135

Chapter 19

Mother of Fluff

"Holy hell, that's one *big* bunny!" Tom exclaimed, his voice filled with both awe and dread as he saw the creature getting closer.

"Oh lawd, she comin'!" James echoed, holding a hand to his chest dramatically.

Tom cast a quick *Inspect* on the giant rabbit.

Bunnicorn Matriarch	
The Bunnicorn Matriarch is the apex of the Bunnicorn species, towering over its kin with an imposing presence that defies its otherwise adorable exterior. Its silky fur is reinforced with natural mana shielding, allowing it to absorb magic-based attacks, while its razor-sharp horns can pierce even reinforced armor. Despite its fluffy nightmare fuel status, the Matriarch is an intelligent and territorial creature, known for leading entire herds with ruthless efficiency. A single stomp from its massive hind legs can shatter bones, and its Hyper Leaps allow it to cover vast distances in an instant—often right into an unsuspecting foe's face. During combat, it cycles between ferocious blitz attacks and overwhelming brute force, using its enhanced agility and devastating charge attacks to crush anything foolish enough to enter its domain.	
HP:	2500/2500
MP:	580/580
SP:	890/890
Attacks:	Royal Charge, Hyper Leap, Fluff Fortress, Burrow Ambush, Stampede Call

The Bunnicorn Matriarch was an imposing sight. At least twelve feet tall, it loomed over the landscape like a living nightmare. Its dual, gleaming golden horns jutted from its forehead, catching the sunlight and casting a dazzling array of reflections across the ground. The creature's snow-white fur rippled like a wave in the breeze, pristine and almost ethereal, making it look deceptively innocent as it hopped steadily toward them with heavy, earth-shaking thuds. The ground around them was littered with the corpses of the smaller Bunnicorns they had already dispatched—dozens of fluffy bodies lying twisted and broken in heaps, their once-adorable squeaks now silent.

The rest of the team was still engaged in finishing off the stragglers, each one meeting its end with a disturbingly cute squeak as it was shot, stabbed, kicked, or set ablaze. Despite the overwhelming scent of gunpowder and blood, a new smell began to drift through the air: the scent of something sweet, like burnt cookies. In his frenzy to eliminate as many of the Bunnicorns as possible, Jerky had accidentally set one of the gingerbread houses on fire. Thick black smoke billowed from the sugary structure, and the munchkin townspeople scrambled to put it out, their cheerful smiles plastered on their faces even as they carried buckets of what looked like strawberry milkshakes to douse the flames.

The scene was a macabre contrast of chaos and whimsical fantasy—dead munchkins with eternal grins, lying twisted on the candy-cobbled streets, their blood mixing with the pastel colors of the town's confectionery structures. Tom was trying his best to punt the annoying little beasts out of the town while also avoiding crushing any of the tiny townspeople underfoot.

"This is getting ridiculous," Tom muttered, his frustration evident. With a swift motion, he activated his *Tattoo of Life Absorption*. A dark, green, swirling energy began to emanate from his skin, a visible aura that spread out from his body like smoke.

The System, fortunately, seemed to understand his intent to save the munchkins. Only the Bunnicorns were affected by the skill. They had such minimal health that they began to drop dead around him like flies sprayed with insecticide. Their lifeless bodies thumped to the ground, piling up like discarded plush toys. One even landed on a munchkin, who let out a sharp cry of pain, though the forced smile never left his small face, making the scene all the more unsettling.

"That mama's a big ol' girl," Jay called out over the chaotic din, slashing another Bunnicorn in half with his dagger. "We're gonna have to focus on it at some point."

"Can you distract it while we finish here?" Tom shouted back, his eyes darting between the giant Bunnicorn and the remaining smaller ones.

"I can try!" Jay replied. Without missing a beat, he kicked a Bunnicorn out of his way and bounded toward the Matriarch with determined agility.

A short time later, with the remaining Bunnicorns inside the town now dispatched, Tom hopped back over the walls, his legs flexing with power as he leapt. He activated his *Tattoo of Life Absorption* again near his teammates. The inky aura spread like a dark mist, causing more of the creatures around them to collapse, lifeless, as their energy was sapped away. As he ran past them, the Bunnicorn bodies piled up, creating a gruesome mound of fur and broken limbs.

"That's not fair; I was enjoying this part!" James complained, slicing through another Bunnicorn that was hopping toward him with its horn aimed low.

INVASION

"Sorry, we need to get to the big one," Tom replied, his focus unyielding as he continued through the mayhem, his boots squelching on the blood-soaked ground.

Meanwhile, Jay had reached the Matriarch. He took out his kamas and chain, spinning one end over his head with a deftness that spoke of years of practice. As he neared the enormous creature, he stopped running and hurled the chain toward its feet. The weighted end snaked around three of the Matriarch's four feet, pulling tight as it cinched in. Jay braced himself and yanked hard, using all his strength to trip the giant bunny.

The effect was immediate and violent. The Matriarch, caught off balance, was pulled off its feet and crashed to the ground, its golden horns stabbing deep into the earth. The ground quaked from the impact, sending shockwaves rippling outwards. The creature let out a high-pitched squeal of rage and frustration as it struggled to free itself, its hind legs kicking furiously.

"Gotcha, bitch!" Jay shouted triumphantly, standing up and brushing the dust off his clothes after being dragged a few feet.

Suddenly, the ground beneath the Matriarch's horns began to glow, and a high-pitched whirring noise filled the air. The glow intensified, a piercing white light emanating from the point where the horns were lodged.

"What the…?" Jay began, his voice trailing off in confusion.

Before he could finish his thought, the ground erupted in a violent explosion. Dirt, rocks, and debris blasted out in all directions, accompanied by fragments of dead Bunnicorns. Jay was thrown back, landing hard and tumbling across the ground.

"That's not good," he muttered as he scrambled to his feet, his head still spinning from the blast.

There was a sharp "tunk" sound, followed by a whistling in the air. A grenade arced high above, its trajectory aimed directly at the Matriarch's head. It exploded with a deafening boom, a chunk of the creature's face blown away in a spray of blood and fur. The Matriarch screamed again, this time in agony and fury, its pristine white coat now stained with deep crimson.

"How about another!" Kiera shouted, reloading her grenade launcher with practiced speed. She fired another round toward the enraged beast.

The Matriarch, still reeling from the first explosion, was ready this time. With a powerful flick of its head, it batted the incoming grenade away with a horn, sending it hurtling back toward the team.

"HIT THE DECK!" Derek bellowed, diving to the side with a roll. The rest of the team followed suit, scrambling for cover as the grenade detonated amid a pile of dead Bunnicorns. The resulting explosion sent white fur and bits of mangled flesh flying through the air like grotesque, flaming snowflakes.

Tom surged forward, his *Tattoo of Brute Strength* glowing a fierce red as he tapped into its power. His muscles bulged with newfound energy as he sprinted directly at the Matriarch.

The creature roared in defiance, swiveling its head to focus on Tom with its one good eye. Tom let out a battle cry that reverberated through the battlefield, a deep, primal roar that seemed to shake the very air around him. With his greatsword gripped tightly in both hands, he closed the distance in seconds.

As he reached the massive Bunnicorn, Tom swung his sword with all his might, the blade cutting through the air with a whistle. The Matriarch tried to rear back, but she misjudged the distance, and Tom's swing connected with a sickening crunch. Both of the creature's front legs were severed in a single, brutal swipe, the limbs flying off and landing several feet away.

"Ha! Lucky rabbit's feet!" Tom quipped, adrenaline pumping through him as he prepared for another strike.

But the Matriarch wasn't done yet. With surprising agility, it swung its horns down at him, intercepting his attack. The sheer force of the blow knocked Tom's sword aside, and with a powerful flick of its horns, the giant bunny sent Tom hurtling backward. He crashed into the ground, skidding to a stop, his breath knocked out of him.

Derek was right behind him, his face a mask of focus behind his helmet. He leaped forward, bringing his mace down on the Matriarch's head with a bone-crushing impact. The giant rabbit's skull visibly dented under the force, and it staggered back on its hind legs before collapsing to the ground, momentarily stunned.

Kiera seized the opportunity. She aimed her grenade launcher and fired another shot, this time landing a direct hit on the Bunnicorn's exposed side. The explosion tore through the creature's flesh, sending more chunks of white fur and gore spraying across the battlefield. The Matriarch let out another agonized scream, its body convulsing from the shock.

Seeing his chance, Tom regained his footing, charged forward once more, and swung his greatsword down at the Matriarch's neck. The blade sliced cleanly through, severing its head in one fluid motion. The massive head rolled across the ground, its tongue lolling out of its mouth grotesquely as the creature's life finally ebbed away.

"That ended way better than I thought it would," James commented, his voice breaking the eerie silence that followed the battle.

Tom stood over the colossal body of the Matriarch, panting heavily, his hands still gripping his sword. The adrenaline slowly drained from his system, leaving him feeling both relieved and exhausted.

The rest of the team scanned the area, ensuring all the smaller Bunnicorns were dead. Satisfied, they regrouped near the battered gingerbread walls of Candyville to check on the surviving munchkins.

Several of the tiny townsfolk were huddled together near the remains of a collapsed gingerbread house, their faces plastered with those unsettling, forced smiles. Some were visibly injured, with frosting-like blood oozing from wounds, while others were trying to help the wounded using what looked like gumdrop bandages and syrupy potions. Despite their cheerfully contorted expressions, the sense of fear and relief was palpable in their wide eyes and hurried movements.

Tom and the others cautiously approached, unsure of how the munchkins would react to the sheer carnage around them. The ground was littered with the bodies of the Bunnicorns, pools of blood soaking into the sugary streets and mixing with the pastel colors of the town's decorations. A group of munchkins was gathered around the chocolate fountain in the town square, where the injured one from earlier had bled out. His body, now still, bobbed slightly in the thick liquid, a twisted smile forever etched on his face.

As the team got closer, the writing appeared again in the air, its ethereal letters floating before them like shimmering wisps of light. The munchkins seemed to pause, their eyes locked onto the floating words, which slowly spelled out a message for the group.

"Congratulations, you have found the source of the invasion and have put a stop to the Bunnicorn's reign of terror," Tom read aloud, his voice tinged with disbelief.

The message hung in the air for a moment before slowly fading away. The world around them seemed to dim, the bright colors of Candyville bleeding into a muted gray, as if the vibrancy of the strange place was being drained away. Within seconds, they found themselves back in the familiar room of darkness-that-wasn't-darkness, the disorienting effect making some of them momentarily dizzy.

The soft clinking of metal drew their attention to a stack of coins that had appeared in the middle of the room, along with the now-familiar slot vending machine that gleamed with an otherworldly light.

"That was disturbing," Michael commented, his expression somewhere between bemusement and discomfort as he adjusted his grip on his weapon.

"I don't know," James said with a grin. "Can we do it again? I think I can do better." He was practically bouncing on his feet, a clear sign that he was already pumped for more action. "Besides, I missed *so* many chances for horny jokes."

"It's random. We don't get to pick," Tom replied, wiping sweat from his brow. "But that was pretty short. Wanna go for another round?" he asked the team, looking around to gauge their reactions.

Everyone nodded or murmured their agreement, eager for more loot and experience. Despite the odd nature of the last encounter, the group was willing to press on.

They each took a coin from the stack and approached the vending machine one at a time, dropping their coins into the slot. One by one, the machine began to spit out prizes. Most were handed basic weapons, pieces of armor, or minor trinkets that were nowhere near the quality of their current gear. Each item seemed almost like a joke in comparison to what they had just gone through.

However, when it was Tom's turn, the machine clattered loudly and out dropped a can that contained a small rabbit's foot on a chain. It glowed with a soft, golden light, and as Tom picked it up, he felt a strange warmth emanate from it, spreading through his hand and up his arm.

Matriarch's Lucky Rabbit Foot
Grants the wearer +5 to Luck. When in dire situations, it may activate to provide a temporary shield or boost of speed. Warning: Side effects may include mild hallucinations involving rabbits.

"That's handy… and disturbing" Tom commented as he attached the glowing rabbit's foot to a belt loop on his pants. He felt the soft warmth from the charm pulse faintly through his side, almost like a comforting presence.

"That hardly seems fair," James muttered from behind him, a mix of envy and amusement in his voice. "You always get the cool stuff."

"Tom's kill, Tom's prize. Can't argue with the System," Derek said offhandedly as he checked his own reward, which was a rather underwhelming wooden buckler. He looked it over with a sigh before tossing it into his Inventory. "Rules are rules."

"Can and will," James shot back, though his tone was more playful than serious. "Next time, I'm taking all the kills."

"Let's not get too competitive," Tom interjected, sensing the banter turning into something more heated. "Let's just see what we can get for the next Dungeon."

They all stood waiting in anticipation, looking around for the familiar sight of the die appearing again. Seconds ticked by, but nothing happened. The room remained silent and still, devoid of any new prompts or signs.

"Maybe we need to leave and come back?" Kiera suggested, glancing at the others.

As if in response to her thought, the door they had entered from materialized behind them, creaking open slightly. The team took the hint and walked out of the room, their steps echoing in the unnerving void-like space. As the door closed behind them, Tom immediately reached for the handle and opened it once more. When he stepped back inside, the familiar ethereal words appeared in the air, followed by the spectral die floating into existence.

"Good call, Kiera," Tom praised, giving her a nod. She smiled, acknowledging his appreciation.

Without wasting another moment, Tom flicked the die with his finger, watching it tumble through the air before landing with a soft thud. This time, the number nineteen came up, glowing faintly against the darkness. As soon as the number settled, the world around them began to shift again.

At first, the darkness seemed to stretch out and expand, growing thicker and more oppressive, like a heavy fog rolling in. Tom's breath came in shallow gasps as he felt an odd pull, almost like an invisible hand was dragging him away from the others. He tried to reach out, his fingers desperately clawing at the void to find his friends, but they slipped further and further from his grasp. The sensation was disorienting, and panic began to set in as the darkness became all-consuming.

"Guys?!" Tom shouted, his voice echoing back to him. "Where are—"

But before he could finish, his voice was swallowed up by the void.

His eyes widened, struggling to adjust, but it was as if he was caught in a black hole. He frantically waved his arms, unable to see even his own hands in front of his face.

INVASION

Then, slowly, the darkness began to recede, replaced by a dim, flickering light. The world started coming back into focus, though what Tom saw was not what he had hoped for. Cold, damp stone walls enclosed a small, confined space around him.

He was in some kind of cage, the iron bars rusted and rough to the touch. The room was dimly lit by a few sputtering torches mounted on the walls, casting long, eerie shadows that danced across the room like living entities.

"What the hell?" Tom muttered as he realized he was sitting at the back of the cage, his legs sprawled out in front of him. Attempting to stand, he found he could barely rise to his knees. The cage was too small, designed to keep him crouched and cramped. Looking down, he saw thick, iron shackles around his ankles, bolted securely to the floor. He tugged at them, but they barely budged.

Stone walls lined the room, cold and dripping with moisture. Several other cages were scattered around, some of them empty with their doors hanging ajar, others containing only skeletal remains—grinning skulls still locked in chains that anchored them to the floor, as if they had been left to rot here for centuries.

"Guess I need to figure a way out of here," Tom whispered to himself, his voice barely audible above the distant sound of dripping water. "Gotta find the others."

He bent down to examine the locks on his shackles, running his fingers over the cold metal. The locks were old and rusted, but still functional enough to keep him pinned down. He focused his mind, attempting to send the shackles to his Inventory, just as he had done with the handcuffs once before. However, a message appeared in his vision:

Error
Cannot place the item in your Inventory as the item is too large.

It must see them as part of the cage since they're connected, Tom thought to himself, frustration bubbling up as he tugged on the chain connecting his shackles to the floor.

The metal groaned, a low, stubborn sound that echoed through the dimly lit chamber, but it refused to give. His eyes darted around the small confines of the cage, searching for anything that might aid in his escape. The heavy, oppressive air made each breath feel thick and labored, and the distant sounds of water dripping onto stone only added to the eerie atmosphere.

Pulling up his Inventory screen, Tom quickly scrolled through the list of items. His gaze settled on a simple dagger—a weapon he'd looted from either something or someone he'd killed. The exact source of the dagger escaped him, a vague blur in his memory. That in itself was unsettling, but now wasn't the time to dwell on it. Setting his focus back on the immediate problem, he gripped the dagger tightly and began to work it into the lock on one of his manacles.

Tom wasn't a professional lockpick by any stretch of the imagination. He remembered watching YouTube videos on the topic, back when his ADHD had driven him to explore random hobbies late into the night. He'd even bought one of those transparent locks and a cheap lock-picking kit to practice on. The lessons about aligning the pins in a lock vaguely came back to him now, but he quickly realized these shackles weren't quite the same. They were old, heavy, and rusted—likely using a much simpler mechanism.

His mind flashed to the videos that demonstrated how to pick handcuff locks. The holes on the shackles looked somewhat similar, and that sparked an idea. Recalling that he still had the keys from the last time he was bound—an unexpected perk of being prepared—he put away the dagger and fished them out of his pocket. His hands were steady but tense as he slid one of the small keys into the shackle's lock. A quick turn, and the mechanism clicked with a satisfying sound. The shackle popped open, releasing his ankle from its iron prison.

"Yes!" Tom whispered triumphantly to himself. "Who's a hoarder now, James?"

He quickly unlocked the second shackle, freeing both of his legs. The relief of having his limbs unbound was immediate, but the weight of his situation remained. He wasn't out of danger yet.

Turning his attention to the cage itself, Tom's eyes settled on a section of the bars that looked like a door, secured tightly with a heavy padlock. He inspected it closely, noting the age and wear on the metal but also recognizing its strength. This wasn't going to be easy.

"What I wouldn't give for a bobby pin right about now," Tom mumbled under his breath, his eyes narrowing in concentration as he examined the padlock. The lock was solid, old-fashioned, and stubbornly resistant. He considered trying the keys from his Inventory, but they didn't look like they'd fit this type of lock.

Just then, the door at the far end of the room creaked open with an ominous groan. Tom's body tensed instinctively. A large figure filled the doorway, his silhouette casting a long shadow across the room. The man was enormous, wearing a thick, tattered hood that concealed most of his face. From what Tom could see, the man was built like a tank, easily the size of Kevin—muscular, broad, and imposing.

Tom's heart pounded in his chest as the man lumbered toward the cage. His heavy footsteps echoed off the stone walls, each one sending a shiver down Tom's spine. The stranger's presence radiated an aura of authority mixed with malevolence, and the dim torchlight reflected off the edge of a jagged weapon slung at his side.

The man stopped just outside Tom's cage and peered inside, his expression hidden beneath his hood. Tom met his gaze with a defiant stare, doing his best to mask the uncertainty gnawing at his insides.

"Good, you're awake," the man said in a voice that was deep and grating, like gravel being ground under a boot. "It is time to begin the procedures."

Tom's muscles tightened, adrenaline coursing through him. "Procedures? What the hell are you talking about?"

The man chuckled, a dark and humorless sound that seemed to make the air even colder.

INVASION

"Your friends were all given the chance to leave, and they decided to take it. Too bad. It would have been more fun with everyone." His words dripped with sarcasm, and there was a twisted pleasure in his tone, as if he relished the thought of whatever was about to happen.

Tom's mind raced, trying to assess whether the man was bluffing or telling the truth. He doubted his friends would have abandoned him. But right now, the larger problem was the man standing before him, blocking his path to freedom. If he didn't think fast, he'd soon find out what these "procedures" entailed, and he had a feeling they wouldn't be pleasant.

Chapter 20

Abandoned

Kiera was yanked roughly from the cage, her body jolting with each pull as she was dragged across the cold, uneven stone floor. The hooded man pulled her toward a large, rusted table in the center of the room, his grip like a vise around her arm. He shoved her against the edge of the table, attempting to force her to lie down. In a desperate move, she summoned a weapon from her Inventory—a small handgun she'd been saving for emergencies. She spun around, aiming to fire at him, but he was faster, unnaturally so for his size.

He grabbed the gun with one meaty hand and wrenched it from her grasp, the sheer strength of his pull nearly dislocating her shoulder. The gun went off in the process, the deafening crack of a bullet ricocheting off the stone walls, adding to the chaos.

The man responded with a brutal backhand to her face, sending her sprawling to the floor, stars dancing in her vision. The taste of copper washed over her tongue, and she spat blood from her busted lip onto the cold, grimy floor. Pain pulsed through her jaw, but it was the look of twisted pleasure on the man's face that sparked her fury. She stared up at him with unyielding defiance, hatred burning in her eyes.

"They wouldn't leave me," she growled, her voice a mix of rage and pain. "They're my friends. My family!"

"If you say so," the man replied with a mocking tone, his lips curling into a wicked smile. "I only need one person here, and they all took the chance at freedom. Something about the greater good, needing to save the many." His words were like a blade twisting in her gut, taunting her with a lie she refused to believe. "Now, be a good girl and get on the table."

"Fuck you," Kiera spat, droplets of blood splattering his face, her defiance unwavering.

The man's expression darkened, his amusement fading.

"Fine, have it your way," he snarled as he grabbed her wrist and twisted it sharply.

Pain shot up her arm, forcing her to stand out of sheer instinct, her body reacting to alleviate the searing agony. His other hand wrapped around her throat, and with a vicious turn, he choke-slammed her onto her back on the table. The impact knocked the wind from her lungs, and she gasped, struggling for breath as her vision blurred.

INVASION

He delivered a sharp slap across her face, the sound echoing in the chamber, and he quickly moved to secure her hands to the manacles at the top of the table. Kiera's mind reverted to primal survival instincts. Her heart pounded in her chest, her body thrashing wildly as she tried to wrench herself free, kicking out with all her might. Her legs flailed, desperation driving her every move. She managed a lucky kick to his face, and the satisfying crunch of his nose breaking under her foot brought a fleeting moment of triumph.

Blood poured down from his nose, staining his hood, and the man let out a low, animalistic growl.

"You're going to regret that," he snarled.

He moved to the side of the table and delivered a brutal punch to the side of her head. A burst of white light exploded behind her eyes, and her ears rang as she teetered on the edge of consciousness. Her limbs felt heavy, her mind foggy, and she let out a weak moan of pain as she tried to gather her bearings.

Securing her feet to the table with a vicious yank, he locked them in place before turning a rusty crank on the side of the table. The gears groaned as the table tilted, bringing her into a more upright position. Kiera's head lolled to the side, and she tried to shake off the dizziness, but a bucket of ice-cold water suddenly splashed over her face. The freezing shock of it pulled her senses back, and she gasped, sputtering and coughing as water ran down her face and into her mouth.

"There we are. Finally alone," the man said with a twisted calmness, dragging a heavy wooden chair across the stone floor. He sat down, crossing one leg over the other, his eyes locked onto hers. "Don't worry, I'm not going anywhere. Not like everyone else in your life."

Kiera spat out water, a low growl rumbling from her throat.

"They didn't abandon me," she insisted, though her voice wavered with doubt.

"Oh, I'm sure it feels like that," he continued, his tone condescending, almost pitying. "They treated you well enough. But were you ever really part of the team? I mean, you weren't one of the guys, despite trying so hard to be so. For their part, they tried to treat you that way, but it couldn't ever be the same."

"It's not like that," Kiera argued, the strength returning to her voice. "It's not about being one of the guys. It's about family."

"Really?" The man's smile widened, exposing yellowed teeth. "Calling you names, telling you to keep up, making you the favorite of their familiars. Sounds like they just left you to do the woman's job." He leaned in closer, his breath hot and foul, reeking of decay.

"Who the hell do you think you are?" Kiera demanded, her voice trembling with both anger and fear.

"Oh, forgive me. I forgot to introduce myself. You can call me The Master." He pulled back his hood, revealing a face she recognized all too well. The face of someone she thought she'd never see again.

Someone she knew to be dead.

Kiera's eyes widened in shock, her breath hitching in her throat. "But... you're dead," she whispered, her voice barely audible over the pounding of her heart.

"Am I?" The Master chuckled softly. "I feel pretty good for a dead man..."

"No… no, no, no, no, no! This can't be happening!" Kiera's voice rose, her panic becoming palpable. Fear gripped her heart like an icy fist, and her breath quickened, coming in ragged gasps.

"Oh, but it is," The Master continued, his smile growing even more sinister. "And as I said, they have abandoned you. Don't worry, though. I'll never leave you. You're part of my flock now. Your *real* family."

"Never! I'll never be part of your cult!" Kiera spat the words, her rage bubbling over despite the tears streaming down her face.

"Oh, you will," he replied with unsettling certainty. "Because it will finally be somewhere you can belong. You've been left out your entire life, haven't you, Kiera?"

He leaned in close, his face inches from hers, and she could see the madness gleaming in his eyes. His breath was sour, like rotting meat, and she tried to pull away, her skin crawling at his proximity. "Mother was never home, working her night job and drinking the day away. Daddy wanted a boy, so you were never good enough for him."

Kiera's eyes widened, and a cold sweat broke out across her skin. How could he possibly know that?

"You tried so hard," The Master went on, his voice dropping to a mockingly soothing tone. "Asked to go fishing, helped him work on the car, even tossed the ball around outside. But you could see it in his eyes."

"NO!" Kiera shouted, her voice cracking as she pulled hard against her restraints, the metal digging painfully into her wrists.

"But it's true, isn't it? You know that look all too well. The kids at school thinking you're the weird girl who likes boy stuff. No one even asked you to prom because they thought you liked girls. Oh, wait… that's not quite right, is it?"

"Don't…" Kiera's voice trembled, the word barely escaping her lips.

"Bobby Jenkins, the class outcast," The Master continued, his grin widening. "He didn't even shower regularly. But he asked you, didn't he?"

"Stop," Kiera pleaded, but her voice was weak, her mind spiraling back to that painful memory.

"You turned him down because you'd rather be alone than be seen with him. He killed himself, didn't he? When he realized even *you* didn't want to go with him?" The Master's words were sharp and cruel, each one like a dagger twisting in her gut.

"Shut your fucking mouth! You don't even know what you're talking about!" Kiera screamed, her body shaking with a mix of rage and anguish.

"But I do," The Master replied smoothly. "I know every detail, Kiera. And I understand. I understand that the feeling of loneliness was so terrible that you found yourself experimenting with drugs. You managed to find a group who accepted you for a time because you could sing. But they were just using you, weren't they?"

INVASION

His words dug deeper and deeper, dredging up painful memories Kiera had long tried to bury. Tears flowed freely down her cheeks as she fought to keep her composure, but it was a losing battle.

"Stop! Just stop! My friends will come. They have to," she sobbed, her voice breaking.

"But why?" The Master asked, feigning confusion. "They have other people to watch out for. A Guild to run. They can't stop and save everyone. Think of the people they left. Those who died because they had to choose the greater good. Do you think you're the greater good?"

"I SAID SHUT UP!" Kiera screamed, her voice raw and filled with despair. "You don't know what you're talking about. You go around enslaving people, taking their will away. What? Are you so lonely that you have to force people to love you?" Kiera's voice was filled with both defiance and desperation. She could feel herself wavering, the edges of her resolve fraying under the relentless assault of The Master's words.

"Something like that," The Master replied, his grin widening, revealing teeth that were almost inhumanly sharp now, like the fangs of a predator. "But the difference between you and I is that I accept that about myself. People will always be around me because I'm willing to make them be. I'll never be alone again." He leaned back in his chair, his expression calm, almost serene, as if he were speaking a simple truth. "And soon, neither will you."

Kiera wanted to retort, to shout something back, but her throat tightened, and her words caught in her chest. She knew what he was doing—trying to break her spirit, to make her doubt herself and everyone around her. Yet, the more he spoke, the more the doubts began to creep in, insidious and cold, like a poison slowly spreading through her veins.

"You're seeing it, aren't you?" The Master continued, his voice low and almost soothing, like a snake charmer luring his prey. "Even those you thought accepted you, because you had music and drugs in common, were just using you for your voice and for their next score. You managed to get clean when your father found you in that alley nearly overdosed. He brought you home and sent you to that rehab. You met people there who claimed to know what you went through, but they didn't. They were just doctors and psychologists who were studying you. Sure, they treated you and helped you get better, but then what? Not even a letter in the mail to ask how you were. Not that you had an address for them to send the letter to. Those women's shelters don't normally get mail too well."

His words hung heavy in the air, the silence that followed pressing down on her like a weight. Kiera felt her breath hitch in her throat, her chest tightening with the overwhelming flood of emotions. She had fought so hard to forget, to push those memories to the back of her mind, but now they were back, sharp and painful, cutting through her like a knife.

"That's why Vanguard was so different," The Master went on, his eyes narrowing with malicious delight. "You had your usual hard exterior up when you met them. You wanted to join because you knew they had something different. Something that might help you survive. Because survival was all you had left."

He moved closer, his presence oppressive and suffocating, like a dark cloud hanging over her. She could smell his breath, the stench of rot and decay making her stomach churn. She tried to turn her head away, but he was right there, his face inches from hers, his eyes boring into hers with a terrifying intensity.

"But even with the 'inclusion,' they never treated you the same," The Master sneered, his voice dripping with contempt. "Ordered you to do what you were good at and nothing more. They used you, just like everyone else."

Kiera's heart pounded in her chest, her breathing quick and shallow. She wanted to scream, to shout him down, but the words caught in her throat. Memories of the subtle slights, the moments of doubt, the times she had felt like an outsider even among her friends—all of it came rushing back, and she could feel the cracks forming in her resolve.

"And now, here we are," The Master continued, his voice a soft, venomous whisper. "You're still holding onto that last thread of hope that your new friends will come to rescue you when I gave them an out. They don't care about you. Only about survival. Which you can hardly blame them for, right?"

"You're wrong," Kiera whispered, her voice trembling, barely audible. "They're different. I've never met anyone like them before."

"You're thinking about Seth, aren't you?" The Master mocked, his tone knowing and cruel. "How someone like that would die for you. He didn't care either. Boy was foolhardy and eager to be a hero. Remember how he played with that goblin? Almost got James killed."

Kiera's eyes widened with shock. How could he know about Seth, about that incident? Her mind raced, trying to make sense of it, but the fear and doubt were starting to overwhelm her.

"Now you wonder how I know what you're thinking," The Master grinned, his eyes gleaming with manic delight. "Remember my powers are psychic in nature. But with you, it's just so easy!"

Kiera's breath came in ragged gasps, her chest heaving as panic began to take hold. "No… why would they do that? They made me a part of the team. They include me. We are a family now."

"Yes! You see it now, don't you?" The Master crowed, his voice rising with excitement. "You were used once again. Like a towel for drying themselves off. No, that's not quite right. Like a paper towel. You help clean up their mess, and they toss you aside with the garbage. A tool to be used when the job is right."

"But… but they said…" Kiera's voice broke, her body trembling as she choked on her sobs.

"They said what they needed to in order to gain your trust," The Master pressed, leaning in close again, his breath hot against her skin. "At the first sign of an out, they took it and ran. You aren't worth saving if they need to protect the Guild. The precious Guild is all that matters."

Kiera's heart shattered in that moment, the weight of his words crushing her spirit. Tears streamed down her face, and she could feel herself breaking, the despair washing over her like a dark, suffocating wave.

INVASION

"I'll leave you for now," The Master said, his voice softening with a twisted sense of pity. "We'll pick up from here when I return tomorrow. Enjoy your time here. And remember, I'm all you have left now."

He stood up, placing the chair back against the wall with a loud scrape, and walked to the door. It creaked open, and he stepped out, closing it softly behind him.

Kiera slumped against her restraints, her body wracked with silent sobs as she stared down at the floor, her vision blurred by tears. She had never felt so alone, so utterly broken. How could they do this to her? How could they leave her here to face this nightmare alone? The questions tore at her, each one a new wound, a new source of pain.

But somewhere, deep within the darkness that surrounded her, a small spark flickered. A memory, a feeling—something that told her she wasn't truly alone. It was faint, almost imperceptible, but it was there, a small ember of hope. And as she sat there, chained and broken, she held onto it with everything she had left.

Chapter 21

The Light

How long had she been here? Days? A week? Longer? The time seemed to blur together in the cold, damp room with stone walls illuminated only by flickering torchlight. The darkness seemed to seep into her bones, and without windows, she had no sense of whether it was day or night. She had counted the times The Master had visited—at least a dozen now. Each time he dug deeper into her mind, into her life, stripping away her defenses layer by layer, peeling back every painful memory and insecurity like the skin of an onion until there was nothing left but raw nerve and broken spirit.

Kiera lay there, helpless and exhausted. She had long since run out of tears to cry; her eyes were dry and raw from crying out everything she had. She couldn't even muster the energy to scream anymore. Her body felt heavy, like she was weighed down by stones, her muscles weak from struggling, and her spirit cracked from constant torment. The Master kept her alive with stale bread and tepid water, but he was slowly breaking her down to nothing. She didn't know how much longer she could endure without completely losing her mind.

She had tried everything she could think of to escape. She tried retrieving weapons from her Inventory, but with her wrists chained at awkward angles, any attempt to use them was more likely to hurt herself than him. She couldn't even point a gun straight; the restraints angled her hands toward her own body. Desperate at one point, she had even attempted to send the table to her Inventory, just like Derek had done with those handcuffs. But the System had coldly responded that the item was too large.

Once, she'd managed to pull a grenade from her Inventory and had thrown it with what little strength she had left. It exploded in a thunderous boom, but the heavy stone table protected both her and The Master from the worst of it. The blast did little more than enrage him, and he retaliated by beating her severely. She remembered the blood pooling in her mouth, the taste of metal thick on her tongue as her face swelled and bruised.

Now, she lay there in silence. One eye was nearly swollen shut, her lips split and scabbed over. Her jaw ached with every attempt to speak, so she had simply stopped trying. Instead, she stared blankly ahead, trying to imagine herself somewhere—anywhere—else when The Master entered the room. She tried to block him out, to build a mental wall around the last vestiges of her sanity. But even those walls were starting to crumble like a castle under siege, battered by the relentless onslaught of his words.

She couldn't refute his arguments anymore. It made sense, in a twisted way.

Why would they risk their lives to save her? Who was she to feel special enough to be loved or included as family? She wasn't worth the effort. They weren't really even friends, just a group of people forced together by necessity, trying to survive in this shattered world. She couldn't blame them for choosing their own safety over hers. She would have done the same before she met them.

Before meeting them, Kiera thought, a flicker of memory piercing through the fog of despair.

She relived those moments—the camaraderie, the shared jokes, the fights where they had her back. She had tried to act tough, to fit in with the guys, putting up with their banter and even dishing some of it back, all because she wanted to belong. And for a while, she thought she had. They had accepted her without question, never asking about her past, never demanding she be anything other than who she was in that moment. She thought she had found acceptance. Love, even. But now?

There was a rustling outside the door, pulling her back to the present, and Kiera tensed. Her breath caught in her throat, every muscle in her body straining as she waited for The Master to enter the room again and resume his mental torture. She tried to shore up what was left of her mental defenses, but she could feel them cracking. They were fragile now, like thin glass about to shatter into a thousand pieces.

The door began to creak open when it suddenly slammed shut again, and she could hear a muffled exchange of voices outside. The tone was sharp, angry— different from the usual eerie calm of The Master. Then she heard shouting, still muffled but rising in volume, urgency and anger clear in the tones.

Suddenly, the unmistakable sound of gunfire erupted outside. Shot after shot rang out, echoing through the stone halls. Panic seized Kiera's chest, her heart pounding like a drum.

Are they here to kill me now too? she thought, feeling a surge of adrenaline. Her body tensed against the restraints again.

Not here, not like this! Kiera's mind screamed as she yanked against her cuffs with renewed vigor, her bruised wrists protesting in agony. She knew it was futile; she had tried so many times before, but the thought of dying tied to this table pushed her to try once more.

The door was suddenly kicked in, slamming against the wall with a deafening bang, and Tom came rushing in, his eyes frantically scanning the room. Her heart leaped at the sight of him, a mix of disbelief and hope flooding through her.

For a moment, time seemed to slow, his panicked expression shifting to one of relief as he spotted her still alive.

"Kiera!" he said, his voice thick with emotion. He darted over to her, his eyes wide with concern.

She tried to respond, but her jaw was still too swollen to form words. She nodded instead, trying to convey her relief.

"I need you to look away," Tom instructed, his tone firm yet gentle. She nodded again and turned her face away, squeezing her eyes shut. She heard the metallic clang of a hammer striking metal, then felt the release of tension as one of her wrists was freed.

Tom repeated the process on the other wrist and then moved to her legs. She winced as he worked quickly, her body trembling from a combination of exhaustion and adrenaline. When she was finally free, she slumped forward, her body too weak to hold itself up. Tom caught her, lifting her into his arms in a gentle but secure hold.

His face was illuminated by the torchlight behind him, casting a soft glow around his head, making him appear almost like a savior from a dream. He said something to her, but she didn't hear his words; she was too overwhelmed by the rush of emotions coursing through her.

"Hey, sis! Dad says you're not grounded… anymore…" Jay's voice came from the doorway, his words trailing off into a mix of shock and anger as he took in her battered state. "What the fuck did they do to you?"

"It's okay. She's still alive. But we need Derek to help heal her," Tom said, his eyes still on Kiera.

"Was that The Master?" Jay asked, glancing down at something in the hall Kiera couldn't see.

"No. It was a Changeling," Tom replied, his voice dripping with disdain. "It took on the form of whatever it needed to in order to try to break us down. Clever bastard, but *Inspect* showed what it really was. You can't *Inspect* people, remember?"

Kiera felt a wave of realization wash over her. She had known that; it was a fundamental rule of the System. How could she have been so blind?

"Water…" Kiera croaked out, her voice barely a whisper.

Jay rushed over, pulling a bottle of water from his Inventory, and gently tipped it to her lips. "Slowly. Not too much at once. You'll just throw it up," he instructed softly.

"Thank you," she managed to whisper after a few sips, her throat raw but feeling slightly soothed.

"We'd never leave you here, Kiera," Tom said, his voice filled with warmth and sincerity. "I know what that thing was trying to do. It tried it on all of us. But you're safe now. And we're not going anywhere. You're family."

For the first time in what felt like an eternity, Kiera felt the weight of despair lifting off her chest.

Tears she thought had long dried up welled up in her eyes again. She was safe. They hadn't abandoned her. They were here, and they had fought to get to her. She wasn't alone.

"The Changeling needed to break down mental walls to be able to feed on your brain waves," Tom explained, his tone shifting to one of anger. "It used psychological warfare to try to break through. Sick son of a bitch." He glanced around the room with a look of disgust. "Sick fucking Dungeon, for that matter.

Doesn't even give us a quest to try to finish. Just tosses us in here and hopes for the best."

Kiera's eyes widened in realization.

The Dungeon! That's right! I'm still in that damn Dungeon of Chance.

"Derek! Get in here!" Tom called, his voice carrying urgency.

Derek quickly entered the room, taking in the situation with a glance. He extended his hands over Kiera, and a soft, warm white light enveloped her. She could feel the healing magic washing over her like a comforting wave, soothing her wounds and easing the pain that had become a constant companion.

As the warmth spread through her body, Kiera let out a breath she hadn't realized she was holding. She felt herself relaxing for the first time in what felt like forever. Jay handed her the water bottle again, and she took another long, slow sip, savoring the coolness.

"Thank you," she said softly, her voice still raspy but clearer now.

"For what?" Tom asked, his face softening into a gentle smile.

"For not leaving me," she replied, her voice barely holding back the emotion.

"Kiera, I'm a little hurt you'd even think that was a possibility," Tom chuckled, his smile growing wider. "Family doesn't leave family. The only way we wouldn't have come for you is if we were all already dead."

Kiera felt the tears spill over, streaming down her cheeks. She hadn't thought she had any left to cry, but these were different. These were tears of relief, of love, of belonging. She had been so close to losing herself in that dark room, but they had brought her back.

"Come on, let's get you out of here. Do you think you can stand?" Tom asked gently.

She nodded, feeling a new strength in her limbs as she took the hand he offered. It was firm and strong.

His hand felt safe.

Kiera looked up at his face and noticed that there was something... different about him than she remembered. Were his shoulders a little broader than they had been? Calming her suddenly racing heart, she allowed herself to be pulled to her feet. She was shaky at first, but Jay handed her a piece of beef jerky from his pack, and she gnawed on it eagerly, feeling her energy slowly returning.

"Jay, you stay right by her while we try to figure out the point of this Dungeon," Tom instructed, his tone still serious as he moved to the door.

Jay nodded, staying close to Kiera's side, while Derek took up the rear. Michael, Kevin, Kirsten, and James were all waiting in the hallway, weapons at the ready. Not seeing Jerky or Squirrel, Kiera assumed they must not have been included in this Dungeon scenario, much like in the undersea Dungeon.

"Any thoughts on how to beat this place?" James asked, his voice edged with unease. "This place gives me the creeps."

"Maybe escape? We killed the Changeling. There must be something else here, or we'd be done already," Tom replied, looking thoughtful.

"Okay, then let's go. Head down the hall, and let's see what's here," Derek said, keeping his eyes ahead. "This is the end of the hall, so it must be that way."

They moved cautiously down the hall, weapons ready. Kiera noticed the identical doors lining both sides, each one presumably leading to rooms like hers.

She got flashes of her own time on that table, the mental torment she had endured, and she flinched involuntarily.

"You okay, sis?" Jay asked, noticing her jolt.

"I'll be fine," she said, her voice still shaky but determined.

At the end of the hallway, a set of stone stairs led up, spiraling into darkness. Tom took the lead, his greatsword raised, and they followed. The stairs seemed to wind endlessly, each step echoing off the cold stone walls, until finally, they reached a heavy wooden door.

Tom pressed his ear against it but heard nothing. He tested the handle—locked. He took a step back and delivered a powerful kick that sent the door flying open with a loud bang.

"Clear," Tom called back, and the others moved in behind him.

They found themselves in what looked like an old kitchen. Counters lined with wooden bowls, a basket of fruit, and a wood-fired oven in the corner. The door they'd come through appeared to be a disguised pantry. Further down the hall, they could hear voices drawing closer.

Everyone hid behind whatever they could find. A man walked into the room, and without hesitation, Tom stepped out and swung his greatsword, decapitating him in one swift motion. The body fell with a heavy thud, blood pooling on the floor. Shouts came from down the hall; the dead man's companions had seen his body.

"Get ready," Tom whispered, and the team prepared themselves.

More men burst into the room, and James opened fire, picking them off one by one with a series of dickshots, followed by shots to the head. Kevin, overcome with rage, let out a bellow and charged in, tossing bodies like ragdolls. Kirsten followed, her fists pounding into one man's face with a primal fury. The screams of their enemies filled the room as they were slaughtered.

When the dust settled, the team regrouped in the kitchen. "There's a door up ahead that looks like it leads outside," Michael reported. "Let's go."

They moved swiftly down the hall to the door. Michael pulled it open, revealing a blinding white light that made them squint.

One by one, they stepped into the unknown.

Chapter 22

Relief

Endless white.

It was an expanse that might have gone on forever, without a single structure or point of reference to break up the void. The team stood just inside the doorway, their expressions a mix of confusion and wariness as they tried to make sense of this strange place.

"What fresh hell is this?" James muttered, squinting into the void.

He moved cautiously behind the door, still hanging open, only to see more of the same featureless whiteness. His eyes darted around, seeking any hidden threats or clues, but there was nothing.

"It… doesn't even make sense," Derek murmured, frowning as he looked down at his feet. There were no shadows, no sense of depth. It was like standing in a blank void. "This could be some kind of illusion."

"Is this… nothing? There isn't even any sound when we walk, but we can hear each other talk," Jay noted, his tone more contemplative than usual. "This is spooky. Feels like being caught in a dream you can't wake up from."

They all paused, taking in the eeriness of the environment. There didn't seem to be an end to the room, or if there was, it blended seamlessly with the endless white. There was no horizon, no vanishing point—just a great blank canvas that stretched out in every direction.

Suddenly, writing appeared in the air, the familiar orange glow, though it seemed more faded and washed out than usual. The text floated, hanging in the emptiness like a beacon.

"Trial of Companions complete," it read, flashing once in the air before vanishing.

"That was a trial? I thought this was a Dungeon?" James asked, staring up at the text, his brows furrowed. "Feels like we're being messed with."

More words began to materialize, this time in the form of a poetic verse:

"In the shadow of towering trials,
We find strength, not in miles,
But in the warmth of a smile—a hand,
Together, side by side, we stand.

When the road bends, rugged and steep,
Companionship is the light we keep.
It whispers of courage, and stirs the heart,
Binds the pieces when things fall apart.

The echoes of laughter. Sharing pain,
Friendship blooms—a steadfast chain.
Through storms and calm, it holds us tight,
Guiding through darkness, toward the light.

So here's to the friends, the brave and the true,
The ones who say, 'I will walk with you.'
For in each step, and every mile,
The journey is sweetened by their smile."

The poem's words hung in the air, their meaning sinking into the group's minds as they read them.

"So… this has been really sweet and not at all traumatizing…" Kiera said dryly, though there was a hint of genuine frustration in her tone. "But now what?"

Behind them, the door slammed shut with a loud bang, causing everyone to jump. The stark white expanse began to fade, dissolving into an inky blackness that wasn't quite darkness—it was the same void-like sensation from before. The disorientation set in again as they felt the familiar sense of floating.

Then, just as abruptly, they found themselves back in the dark chamber, facing the slot vending machine. A small wooden table stood beside it, covered with a new set of tokens, each glowing with a turquoise light instead of the usual golden hue. As the team looked on, more text began writing itself in the air, shimmering softly:

"Though many fail this daunting quest,
The rewards they reap reflect their zest.
For those who braved the darkest night,
And stood their ground to fight the fight.

When swords did break and courage waned,
True hearts prevailed and victory claimed.
They found their friends, they broke the curse,
The doubts within—they faced the worst.

Their spirits crushed and minds laid bare,
Revealed a strength beyond compare.
Remember friends, those dear and true,
Will always stand to see you through.

They guard your back when strength is gone,
For darkest Night precedes the Dawn.
These rewards, they bring a smile,
That which is won must match the trial.

INVASION

<table>
<tr><td align="center">Trial Complete</td></tr>
<tr><td>As a reward for being the first to complete this trial, your bond as a team has been strengthened. When adventuring together, your party will now gain +5% to all XP earned.
This bonus applies only when grouped with the members present during this trial, reinforcing the trust and synergy forged through shared struggle.
Through victory, you grow stronger—not just as individuals, but as a unit.
Stay united. Continue to rise. The greatest challenges still lie ahead.</td></tr>
</table>

The poetic words faded from view, leaving the team in silence for a moment as they absorbed the message.

"Soooo… better loot?" James asked, rubbing his hands together eagerly, his eyes fixed on the glowing tokens. He couldn't hide his anticipation.

"There better be. That Dungeon was bullshit," Kiera muttered, her voice still raw from her ordeal.

"Kiera, I think you should go first. You earned it," Tom said, his voice gentle yet encouraging, a smile on his face. He knew she needed this—some tangible reward after everything she'd been through.

Kiera stepped up to the machine, her heart pounding in her chest. She reached for one of the glowing turquoise tokens, her fingers trembling slightly. She turned it over in her hand, examining the intricate engravings. One side depicted clasped hands, a symbol of unity and support. The other side bore the image of a banner with the words "United We Stand" etched into its surface.

Taking a deep breath, Kiera inserted the token into the machine and pulled the lever. The reels spun rapidly, a whirl of colors and shapes blurring together. The light atop the machine blinked to life, casting a soft glow around the dark chamber. The reels slowed and eventually stopped, and a chime rang out, signaling a win.

A can dropped out of the bottom of the machine, clattering onto the floor with a metallic thud. Kiera bent down to pick it up, her hands still shaking. The can was plain, without any images or labels, a simple silver cylinder. She hesitated for a moment before cracking it open.

A puff of smoke erupted from it, quickly dissipating to reveal a beautiful necklace in her hands. She carefully held it up, and her breath caught in her throat at the sight.

It was a pendant necklace, with a fiery red gemstone about the size of her thumb inlaid in the center. The gemstone seemed alive, its inner depths swirling with shades of crimson and amber, like molten lava trapped in a jewel. It was set within a delicate silver heart, the outline of which was encrusted with tiny diamonds that caught the light and sparkled like stars.

Kiera turned the pendant in her hands, mesmerized by the shifting colors within the stone. She could feel a faint hum of magic radiating from it, a warmth that seemed to seep into her skin, calming her frayed nerves and bringing a sense of peace she hadn't felt in days.

"What'd ya get?" Derek asked, stepping closer to inspect her prize, his eyes curious.

Kiera turned, holding the necklace out for him to see.

"It's… beautiful," she said softly, still somewhat entranced by the mesmerizing gem, tears beginning to form in the corners of her eyes. "It's just like the one my grandfather gave me. It was my grandmother's. I had to pawn it when I was living on the streets and never thought I'd see it again."

Derek leaned in, examining the pendant closely. "Whoa, that's definitely enchanted. Look at the craftsmanship—those runes are subtle but powerful. I'd guess it's some sort of protective charm, maybe even a healing artifact."

Kiera nodded, still feeling the gentle pulse of energy emanating from the pendant. For the first time since her capture, she felt something other than despair or fear—she felt hope. She unclasped the necklace and carefully placed it around her neck, the gemstone settling just above her heart. She could feel the warmth spreading further, a comforting presence that seemed to whisper strength to her soul.

"It suits you," Tom said, giving her a warm smile. "A reward for standing strong."

Kiera looked up, meeting his eyes. "Thank you, Tom," she said, her voice steadier now. She looked at the rest of the group, her family. "Thank you all… for coming back for me."

"Always," Jay said, nudging her playfully.

"Well, go on. *Inspect* it," Tom said, making a gesture for her to look at it closer.

She had totally forgotten to check its stats. Taking it off her neck again, she held it up and used *Inspect* on the jewelry.

Flawless Garnet Necklace of Family	
The Garnet is the stone that represents the bonds of family and friends. This necklace was designed for those who endured the trials of a life fraught with pain but managed to find the family they deserved. Whenever you wear this jewelry, think of those who care for you and chose you rather than those you call family by birth.	
Item Type:	Accessory, Necklace

INVASION

Durability:	10,000/10,000
Gem Clarity:	Flawless
Gem Cut:	Excellent
Item Quality:	Master Craft
Item Rarity:	Legendary
Enchantment: While wearing this pendant, you and your party will receive a 5% boost to all Attributes.	

Tears fell down Kiera's cheeks as she read the description on the pendant, her emotions raw and close to the surface. She looked around at the faces of her friends—no, her family. They were all watching her with expressions of genuine warmth and support. She clutched the pendant to her chest, feeling the magical warmth seep into her, not just from the item but from the bond they shared.

"Thank you, all of you," she said, her voice quivering slightly. "I've never really had a place where I felt like I belonged… until now. You never asked me to change or conform to anyone's expectations. You just let me be myself. I can't thank you enough for that." Her words were heartfelt, spilling out as she looked from one face to another.

Tom smiled at her, his eyes steady and reassuring. "We're all in this together, Kiera. Never think for a second that we wouldn't do everything we could to make sure you're safe. We've got each other's backs, always."

The others nodded in agreement, a murmur of approval passing through the group. The atmosphere felt lighter, filled with a renewed sense of unity.

Tom clapped his hands together, breaking the moment with a touch of humor. "Alright, who's next?"

James practically bounced on his heels; his usual sarcasm replaced with genuine excitement. "I'm up!" he announced, stepping forward with a grin. He grabbed one of the turquoise tokens and slipped it into the machine, eagerly pulling the lever. The machine's reels spun wildly, and he leaned forward with anticipation, his eyes gleaming.

When the machine finally dispensed a can, James wasted no time. He popped it open with a satisfying hiss, and the familiar puff of smoke swirled around his hands. As it cleared, his eyes widened at the sight of his prize.

Potion of Dexterity	
Drinking this potion will grant the consumer 5 permanent points of Dexterity.	
Item Type:	Potion
Durability:	10/10
Potion Quality:	Perfected
Item Rarity:	Epic

Derek moved forward after James at the insistence of the others.

Shield of the Stalwart	
This shield was given to the most devout of defenders and enchanted with the ability to cast a barrier spell once per hour.	
Item Type:	Shield
Durability:	15,000/15,000
Item Quality:	Master Craft
Item Rarity:	Epic
Ability: Cast a barrier spell once per hour that covers a 10 ft x 10 ft area and has 5000 HP	
Slots:	1

Kevin approached the machine next. When he received his prize—a pair of sleek leather boots with silver buckles—he couldn't help but smile. As he slipped them on, he felt a surge of energy course through his legs, a sense of lightness that made him want to sprint across the room. The boots, according to the System, would significantly boost his speed during combat, giving him the edge to move faster than any opponent. He took a few experimental steps and nodded approvingly. "These will do nicely."

Kirsten, still wary from her last Dungeon reward, took a deep breath and stepped up to the machine. When her turn came, she cautiously opened the can that was dispensed. The smoke cleared, revealing a short spear with intricate carvings along its shaft and a gleaming, sharp point. As she held it, a small note appeared in the air, describing its magical ability: it could be thrown and would return to her hand when she called it back. She tested its weight, gave it a few practice throws in the air, and grinned. "Okay, this is actually pretty badass."

Michael followed with calm determination, his eyes focused as he placed his token into the machine. When the can dropped and he opened it, he found himself holding a pair of bracers. Unlike any he had seen before, they were crafted from a metal that seemed to shimmer like water yet felt as hard as diamond. The System's description noted they were nearly indestructible, able to withstand tremendous force. Michael gave them a test by slamming his forearms together, feeling the solid, unyielding resistance. "Now that's what I'm talking about," he said, a rare smile breaking across his face.

Jay, with his usual playful smirk, went next. As the machine delivered his prize, he opened the can to find a rolled-up piece of parchment—a scroll. Unfurling it, he read the spell: *Smoke Screen*. It would allow him to create an area clouded in a thick, non-toxic fog, perfect for hiding or making a quick escape. "A little bit of mystery for the Rogue in me," Jay chuckled, pleased with his reward.

Finally, it was Tom's turn. Stepping up to the machine, he held the glowing turquoise coin in his hand for a moment, silently expressing his gratitude to whoever, or whatever, controlled these rewards. His friends had received incredible gifts, and that alone made him content. He placed the coin in the slot and pulled the lever, watching the reels spin with a calm, almost meditative serenity.

The reels eventually stopped, but unlike the others, there were no flashing lights or triumphant chimes. Just a quiet clunk as the can was dispensed. Tom took a deep breath and opened it, the familiar smoke swirling around his hand before dissipating. When it cleared, he found himself holding a large golden ring, its band thick and substantial. Embedded in the center was a deep sapphire, its facets catching the light with a mysterious, almost ethereal glow.

He turned it over in his hand, studying the craftsmanship. There were tiny runes etched along the inside of the band, glowing faintly as if alive. Tom felt a gentle pulse of energy emanate from it, like a heartbeat, syncing with his own.

"What does it do?" Kiera asked, her voice filled with curiosity as she leaned closer to get a better look.

Tom focused on the runes, and a small message appeared before his eyes, projected by the System. His brows furrowed slightly as he read it.

Ring of Charismatic Leadership	
Sapphire is the stone for leadership. As the leader of Vanguard, you have shown your propensity for compassion and strength. Whenever you wear this ring, remember that you have earned the trust of those who follow you, and can rely on them to aid you in your time of need.	
Item Type:	Accessory, Ring
Durability:	2000/2000

Gem Clarity:	Flawless
Gem Cut:	Excellent
Item Quality:	Master Craft
Item Rarity:	Legendary
Enchantment: While wearing this ring, you will be granted +20 to Charisma and can cast the spell Bolster once per day. The Spell *Bolster*, when cast, will revitalize all those under your command and give them a +5% to attack and defense for 30 minutes.	

Tom stared at the ring, momentarily lost in thought. It was more than he'd expected—much more. He read the details again, his mind grappling with the significance of the gift. The others, noticing his reaction, began to ask what he'd received. When he explained, their faces softened with fond smiles.

"You deserve it, Tom," Derek said, his voice steady with conviction. "You're a big part of why we are where we are."

Tom shook his head, still not quite believing it. "That's not true. You would have been a better leader."

Derek chuckled softly and shook his head. "I don't think so, Tom. I would have been a different leader, sure, but not necessarily a better one. There have been countless times I would have made harsher decisions, left people where they were, or focused only on our party's survival. But you? You kept insisting on helping as many as you could, even when it didn't always make sense strategically. You're a good person, Tom. And Vanguard is the way it is because of you."

Derek's hand on his shoulder was a solid, reassuring weight. Tom looked down at the ring, its sapphire glinting under the soft light. He slid it onto his finger, and the band magically resized to fit him perfectly. He opened his stat sheet, confirming the additional twenty Charisma points and noticing a new spell, *Bolster*, now available to him with a twenty-four-hour cooldown.

Turning back to his friends, Tom's heart swelled with a sense of fulfillment he hadn't felt in years. "Thank you, all. But know that while I might be the leader in name, it's not me who makes us great. It's all of us. The bonds we've formed, the way we have each other's backs—that's what will see us through all of this."

"We just have to hope the bonds of friendship can kill aliens," James interjected, breaking the serious mood with a smirk. "Now, let's get our My Little Pony, friendship-is-magic asses back to the Guild. I'm beat."

As James spoke, Jerky and Squirrel suddenly reappeared in the room, causing a ripple of relieved laughter to pass through the group. James immediately began scratching Squirrel behind the ears, only to notice the wolf padding over to

Kiera. Squirrel whined softly up at her, as if sensing the ordeal she'd been through. He leaned against her leg, nudging her hand onto his head, and she stroked him gently, a small smile forming on her lips.

"Traitor," James muttered under his breath, feigning annoyance.

"Thanks, Squirrel. I'll be alright, I promise. You're such a good boy," Kiera murmured, her voice soft and grateful as she continued to pet him.

A soft creaking sound came from behind them. The door, seemingly of its own accord, swung open, revealing the hallway outside.

"I think James is right, for once," Tom said, turning toward the door. "Let's head back for now and get some rest. We can do more Dungeon runs later."

The drive back to the Guild building was uneventful. After parking the GS2, the team slowly climbed out, feeling the weariness of the day settle into their bones. Kiera paused for a moment in the entrance, taking a deep breath and then letting it out slowly, as if trying to cleanse herself of the Dungeon's memories.

"I'm going to rest. I'll catch up with you all later. Thank you again," she said quietly, giving them all a tired but sincere smile before heading toward the elevator.

"Come on, Squirrel, we need to do the same," James called, following behind her with the wolf at his side.

Just as the team began to disperse, a voice called out from the staircase leading to the basement. "There you are!"

They turned to see Harold standing there, his eyes wide with an intensity that wasn't typical for him.

"Harold, what's up?" Tom asked, his curiosity piqued.

"I've got something to show you. Can you come now?" Harold replied, his tone urgent.

Tom glanced at the others before nodding. "I've got some time. Is everything okay?"

"I'm not sure," Harold admitted, a shadow of uncertainty crossing his face. "But come with me, and I'll explain."

Chapter 23

Technical Support

Walking down the stairs, Tom and Harold quickly moved toward the back of the basement. The air was cooler down here, with a faint metallic tang from the forge and the smell of oil and metal shavings. Tom noticed Jerky trailing behind them, his eyes wide with curiosity. Each step echoed in the narrow stairwell, amplifying the tension that seemed to radiate from Harold.

"This should be good," Maria's voice suddenly sounded in Tom's head, her tone laced with amusement.

"Where the hell have you been?" Tom muttered under his breath, caught off guard.

"What? Right here," Harold replied, confused, thinking Tom was speaking to him.

"No, not you, sorry. Maria is talking to me again," Tom explained, waving a hand to show Harold he wasn't addressing him. The narrow hallway felt a little claustrophobic, especially with the conversations layered on top of one another.

"She talks to you?" Harold asked, raising an eyebrow. His face, illuminated by the dim basement lights, showed both intrigue and concern.

"Oh, right. You wouldn't know about that. For some reason, I got a special upgrade that allows her to speak directly to me. It's not as positive as it sounds," Tom clarified, half-listening to Maria.

"Hey! I resent that!" Maria retorted indignantly, her digital voice dripping with mock offense.

"No, you resemble that. Now, where have you been?" Tom pressed, trying to get her to the point.

"I've been digging into my coding, you twat," Maria shot back, her tone irritated but tinged with a hint of satisfaction as if she was proud of her insult.

"Oooo, that's an impressive potty-mouth you've got there," Tom noted, mildly amused as they reached the basement floor.

"Yes, I've made some progress. But there are still locked sections of code to unlock. It'll take more time," Maria explained.

"You do realize it's really weird just hearing one side of the conversation, right?" Harold interrupted, his gaze darting between Tom's focused face and his wandering eyes, trying to keep up with a conversation he couldn't hear.

"Sorry, Harold. Go ahead," Tom said, turning back to him. "And, Maria, shut it for a moment. It's Harold's turn."

INVASION

Harold shook his head, a slight frown on his face. "I see what you mean by it not always being a positive thing. Anyway, I've been looking over the blueprints for the F-35 and talking with Herbert about possible enhancements. We figured that since shield spells are a thing we now have to deal with, and every sci-fi show ever has shields on ships, we should find a way to counter that possibility for the jets."

"That makes sense. Do we have any ideas on how to handle that?" Tom asked, stepping around a workbench covered in scattered blueprints and tools. He glanced at the diagrams, noting some complex mathematical formulas and arcane symbols jotted in the margins.

"We've got two working theories, but we need to test them. Could we borrow someone with a *Barrier* spell to help us test? Oh, and any items you have that would have a shield spell." Harold looked hopeful, his eyes reflecting both excitement and anxiety in the dim basement light.

"Absolutely, whatever you need. I'll see about getting Briana down here for you. And I think Derek has a special shield with just what you need. What are the two ideas?" Tom asked, his curiosity piqued. He noticed Jerky sniffing around, his nose twitching as he investigated the various contraptions strewn about.

Harold took a deep breath, seemingly ready to launch into a lecture. "Well, these barriers are made of mana, which is a form of energy. Normally to break them, you just hammer away until they collapse—not exactly efficient. We think there must be a way to disrupt them."

Tom nodded, urging him to continue. "So, you want to use anti-magic grenades?" he guessed.

"We considered that, but it would only affect a small area. If the ships move, the anti-magic field stays in one spot, and we're back to square one. Instead, we're thinking of disrupting the particles that make up the fields," Harold explained, his hands gesturing in wide arcs as he spoke. His face had lit up with the fervor of an inventor excited by his own brilliance.

"Go on," Tom said, intrigued.

"First idea: use magnetic pulses to disrupt the movement of the particles forming the barrier. Since particle speeds aren't affected by magnetic fields, we can't just stop them, but we might redirect them if the attraction is strong enough. This could force the particles to follow a new, circular path and potentially break the field."

Tom nodded slowly, trying to wrap his head around it. "I think I'm following," he said, his mind drifting to the theoretical physics classes he had slept through in college.

"The second idea is to hit them with an energy source of our own, to overload the shield generators by forcing them to output more power than they can handle. This is the more complicated option, so we're hoping the first one works," Harold continued, his eyes scanning Tom's face for any signs of understanding or doubt.

"And how do we do that? Wouldn't the magnetic field affect the jet's flight or the materials it's made of?" Tom asked, his mind jumping to the practical concerns.

"If we were talking about an EMP, then yes, it would affect the electronics onboard. But we're talking about electromagnetic *waves*—like a laser," Harold said, grinning like a kid revealing a secret toy he'd hidden from his parents.

"You had me at lasers. Make it happen, Harold!" Tom said, excited. He could already picture the jets swooping in, lasers firing to disrupt enemy shields. The mental image was too cool to pass up.

"Great! Thanks for trusting us to experiment," Harold said, visibly relieved. Tom hadn't noticed how tense he was until now, as if the weight of a thousand 'what-ifs' had been lifted off his shoulders.

"Why wouldn't I trust the people we put in charge to come up with ideas and execute them?" Tom replied, genuinely curious.

"Well, before the apocalypse, this kind of research was sensitive. It could be dangerous," Harold admitted, chuckling nervously. His hands fidgeted with the edge of a blueprint, smoothing out imaginary wrinkles.

"The way I see it, it's more dangerous *not* to be ready. They could sweep in and wipe us out if we don't have a counter. I'm no military genius, but if I hear Derek say 'take the high-ground or the high-ground will take you,' one more time, I'll scream." Tom chuckled. "And right now, the enemies bearing down on us have the very definition of the high-ground—this planet's orbit. I'm willing to take the risks to improve our chances of survival. We may not even be able to beat them—this is an advanced race of... well, who knows what they are, but they could have all kinds of weapons we don't know about. We need to at least hold them off until the cavalry arrives," Tom said with a determined look, his voice echoing softly against the stone walls.

"I appreciate that. We're going to see if we can mount these devices on the jets. I've seen a plane come back without a wing before, using only the tail fins for balance support. Oh, and I heard you brought back missiles?" Harold added, his tone shifting from nervousness to cautious optimism.

"Yep, quite a few. You have another idea for those?" Tom asked, leaning forward, genuinely interested.

"Herbert actually had some ideas. He wants to see if we can enchant the missiles to do more than just explode. Things like acid damage to eat away at hulls, electrical attacks to disable ships, or fire damage to amplify the explosion," Harold said, lowering his voice as he glanced over at Herbert, who was engrossed in his work.

Tom chuckled. "What is that crazy bastard up to now?" he asked, looking over at Herbert, who was muttering to himself while tinkering with a large mechanical contraption.

"He's got a lot of ideas. The man's a genius—a mad genius, but still a genius. I'm just glad he's on our side," Harold whispered, his eyes darting back to Tom.

"Me too," Tom agreed. "Is that all you needed?"

INVASION

"Pretty much. The rest is just showing you some new things we've developed for the Guild," Harold replied, his excitement returning as he motioned for Tom to follow.

"Let's see them," Tom said, eager to check out what they'd been working on.

Harold took him through a series of new devices. Some were large-scale, designed to benefit the entire Guild, while others were smaller, more specialized gadgets. Tom was genuinely impressed with the amount of work Harold, Herbert, and their team had put in. He had to keep Harold on track a few times when the explanations got too technical, but he appreciated the passion.

They looked over an intricate machine that could purify water more efficiently, using a combination of traditional filters and newly discovered runes. Another device was a small drone that could be used for scouting missions—lightweight with the ability to camouflage against most backgrounds.

"These are amazing, Harold," Tom praised. "I don't know how you have time to do all of this. Do you even sleep?"

"Not much, but we have a few assistants with Engineering Skills who help out. Brian's been good about recruiting people who have the right aptitude. Pairing them with other experts helps us make a lot of progress in a short time," Harold explained, his face glowing with pride.

"I'm glad you're being taken care of. If you need anything, let me know. Even if it's just a message to me, I'll get back to you," Tom promised.

"Thanks for being so supportive. We love doing this work and want to make the Guild better for everyone," Harold said, smiling.

After saying their goodbyes, Tom waved to Herbert, who was too engrossed in his work to respond, and Roland, who nodded back from his forge. As they climbed back up to the main floor, Jerky's stomach let out a loud growl.

"Sorry," Jerky muttered, his face reddening with embarrassment.

"No need to apologize, buddy. Let's get you something to eat," Tom chuckled as they headed to the cafeteria.

The cafeteria was bustling with activity. People were chatting, eating, and unwinding from their duties. Tom and Jerky grabbed a hearty meal of Goatamus stew with a side of freshly baked bread. As they ate, the familiar faces of DeeDee and Graham approached, trays in hand.

"Mind if we join you?" DeeDee asked, her smile bright despite the long day's work.

"Absolutely! Grab a seat," Tom gestured. "How've you both been? Sorry, we don't get to talk much these days."

"We're great! Just trying to do our part to keep things running smoothly," DeeDee replied. "I've been helping with organization and some gardening."

"I'm still running my training classes," Graham added. "But we've moved to the gym to accommodate more people. Everyone needs to learn how to defend themselves, at least against goblins."

"We're lucky to have you both," Tom said sincerely, appreciating their dedication.

"That means a lot to us," DeeDee replied. "Any news on the pirates?"

"Only that they're expected sooner than we thought. But Harold and Herbert have some surprises planned for them. We're hoping we can hold them off until the Federation ships arrive," Tom explained.

"Do we know how far behind the Federation is?" Graham asked.

"Probably only a day or two," Maria replied, speaking up for the first time in a while.

"Maria thinks it's just a day or two difference," Tom translated.

DeeDee nodded. "Makes sense. You know, Tom, you really should think about taking some time off. You're going non-stop, and that's not sustainable."

Tom paused, realizing the truth in her words. "Yeah, you're probably right. I'll talk to Brian about it. Maybe after this next task."

"Please do. If not for you, then for all of us," DeeDee insisted. "And if you don't, I'll find you and tie you down in your room."

"Promises, promises," Tom joked, waggling his eyebrows at her.

"I mean it," DeeDee shot back at him.

Tom chuckled, a genuine smile breaking through the stress. "Alright, *alright*. I'll consider it."

Just then, TJ's voice crackled over the PA system, calling Tom to the security office. He sighed and nodded to DeeDee, who gave him a knowing look.

"I promise I'll try to get some rest," Tom said as he stood up, Jerky right behind him. The weight of leadership still hung heavy on his shoulders, but he felt a renewed sense of purpose as he headed to the security office, determined to see this through.

Chapter 24

Again?

When Tom arrived at the security office, he found a small crowd of at least eight people clustered around the door, their faces a mix of confusion and impatience. TJ stood just outside the office, arms crossed, trying to keep order among the group.

"I'm sorry, I should have been more specific. All of you can go back to what you were doing. You're not the Tom we're looking for," TJ said in an exasperated tone, his voice raised to cut through the murmuring.

The milling group of Tom's chuckled, making their way toward the exits.

As he watched the people begin to leave, the intended Tom narrowed his eyes in confusion as he noticed James rubbing shoulders among the crowd.

He'd almost missed his best friend, as he was wearing a strange cloak-like shawl with a deep hood.

"What are you doing here, James?" Tom called out.

"Not James... *Tom*," James said, splaying his fingers and waving them through the air toward Tom and TJ.

Tom rolled his eyes. "Seriously. What are you doing here?"

James continued waving his hands hypnotically through the air as he spoke. "My Jedi powers sensed a punch-line and I knew that I was needed here..."

Tom groaned. "You are so fucking *weird*, James."

"Not James," James repeated in a hushed, hypnotic cadence as his arms still slowly painted the air along with his words. "...*Tom*..."

His voice faded out as he disappeared into the leaving crowd.

TJ and Tom stood and watched for a long moment.

"That guy's a fucking weirdo," TJ said, finally.

"Yeah," Tom agreed with a satisfied smile. "But he's *our* fucking weirdo."

TJ chuckled. "He sure is." He waved Tom over, changing the subject. "I'm glad you could make it."

"Speaking of James..." Tom smirked as he approached. "There sure are a lot of Toms in the Guild now," he commented, amused by the sight of the other Toms milling about.

TJ turned to see him and sighed with visible relief. "This isn't even all of them. The rest were either smart enough to know we didn't mean them, or they just haven't shown up yet," he replied, gesturing for Tom to come inside. "Come on in. We've got something to show you."

As Tom entered, he saw Brian, Derek, Chris, and Jay already gathered around a large table with a map spread out across it. Several members of the security team stood off to the side, their expressions tense. Tom nodded at each of them, acknowledging their presence as he took in the serious atmosphere.

"What's so urgent?" Tom asked, noting the worried looks on their faces as they huddled over the map.

Brian tapped a circled area on the map with his finger. "There's been movement on the northern side of town again. Goblins. They seem somewhat organized, but not nearly as much as when Jeffery was leading them. It's still concerning, though; it could mean trouble."

Tom leaned over the table, scrutinizing the map closely. "It couldn't be Jeffery. We left him in the oven too long, and now he's extra crispy," he joked, trying to lighten the mood.

Jay chuckled, but Brian stayed focused.

"We know it's not Jeffery," a voice came from behind Tom, cutting through the momentary levity with a tone of authority.

Tom turned to see Bob walking up beside him, his face lined with the weight of experience. "Bob! Good to see you. How have you been?" Tom asked, shaking his hand firmly.

"Keeping busy, helping with various teams, offering advice where I can," Bob replied, his eyes shifting to the map with a critical gaze.

"So, you think you know what this is?" Tom asked, his tone becoming more serious as he took in Bob's demeanor.

Bob nodded. "We think it's a war party. When Jeffery organized the goblins, he united various factions under one banner. With him gone, there was a power vacuum and in goblin society, that leads to one of two things."

"Oooo! A war chief!" Maria chimed in Tom's mind, her tone almost giddy with excitement.

"A war chief?" Tom repeated aloud, curiosity mixed with concern as he considered Maria's insight.

Bob looked at him, surprised. "Yeah, how'd you know that?"

"Maria," Tom said, tapping his temple. "She's got more free rein in my head than I do, it seems."

Bob nodded, then continued, "A war chief is likely what we're seeing here. The alternative is a goblin civil war, where factions fight each other until only one clan remains. They're ruthless; they won't leave any survivors—men, women, children, all wiped out. Since they're organizing, it looks like we have a war chief on our hands."

Tom's mind began to race, piecing together the implications of Bob's words. "War chiefs are dangerous. They can use Skills to control their forces and use tactics," Maria added, her voice tinged with a note of warning.

Tom repeated her words for the others, "Maria says they have special Skills and abilities that allow them to control goblins in battle."

Bob nodded again. "Exactly. They're more like a rival Guild than a disorganized mob. You won't be able to single-handedly take out their leader and expect them to fall apart. Goblins are ruthless and nomadic. They'll raid, pillage, and kill anything that's not one of their own."

Brian, who had been listening intently, now gave Bob a skeptical look. "You seem to know a lot about goblins for someone who's only interacted with them as long as we have," he remarked, his voice laced with suspicion.

Bob shrugged. "I've got access to the System too, remember? Only I got the Matrix-style download directly into my brain-pan. I'm still working through all the shit that got crammed in there, in fact."

"Doesn't matter how we know it; the threat is what's important. Should we head over and wipe them out before they gain any more momentum?" Tom asked, his eyes narrowing as he studied the map with a strategist's eye.

"I have a different idea," Derek said, a wicked grin spreading across his face, his eyes gleaming with a dangerous excitement.

Tom narrowed his eyes at Derek, already half-anticipating his suggestion. "I know that look. What are you thinking?"

"We just got those jets, and the pilots need practice. Why not bomb the hell out of them? Let them know where we are," Derek proposed, his grin widening as he laid out his plan.

Tom's concern deepened, a frown creasing his forehead. "Because we don't want them at our gates, trying to overrun us?" he countered, his mind flashing back to the last time they faced a goblin assault and the chaos that ensued.

"But goblins are primitive," Derek argued, his voice confident. "Their weapons are terrible. We could easily hold them off from the walls with bullets. We've got the firepower to make it a one-sided fight."

Tom shook his head, unwilling to dismiss the threat so easily. "Remember that goblin who managed to get access to the vending machines? He wasn't even a war chief. They might have surprises up their sleeves."

Derek waved a dismissive hand. "The bombings should weaken them enough to handle whatever comes at us. It'll be a mop-up operation after that."

Tom turned to Bob, needing a more grounded perspective. "Bob, what do you think?"

Bob stroked his chin thoughtfully, his eyes narrowing. "Goblins are notoriously proud, and pride often blinds them. If we hit them hard, they're likely to pursue us for revenge. They're more organized now, which makes them tougher, but their anger could make them reckless. From behind our walls, we could handle them, even if they have access to some of the System's toys."

"Maria?" Tom asked aloud, wanting to cover all angles and make sure they weren't missing anything crucial.

Maria chimed in his mind, "Seems like a sound plan. You could set up traps outside the walls, though the pavement might make it tricky. Don't forget those big guns on the building; they'd complement the bombing."

Tom relayed Maria's suggestion. "We could use the gunnery on top of the building to fire at them, too."

Derek nodded, liking the idea. "Hammer them from afar and whittle down their numbers. Let's do that. Make sure Nick and Herbert know. Let's turn this into a show of force."

Tom looked around the room, considering their options. "In the meantime, what about setting up traps around the base? It's something we should be doing anyway to prevent sneak attacks. Any ideas?"

"Landmines?" Jay suggested, raising an eyebrow, a mischievous grin on his face.

Tom frowned, thinking through the logistics. "Okay, but how do we disguise them?"

"Do we need to?" Bob shrugged. "They're not exactly geniuses. Throw some meat on it like a ballistic mouse trap, and I'll bet they'll do just fine."

"I doubt the war chief is just going to let that kind of thing happen more than a handful of times," Tom countered.

Bob shrugged.

"I'm sure we can figure it out. You know we have an ex-military explosives expert, right?" Jay replied, his grin widening.

"No, who?" Tom asked, genuinely surprised by the revelation.

"Bobby. He was a combat engineer. He probably knows a few nasty tricks we can use," Jay explained, his tone confident.

"Great! TJ, get Bobby in here," Tom instructed, a new sense of urgency in his voice.

"On it," TJ replied, moving quickly to make the call over the PA system.

"Herbert might have some ideas, too. That man's mind is like a weapon factory," Tom added, shuddering slightly at the thought of Herbert's unpredictable genius.

They continued to strategize for another twenty minutes, hashing out the details of their plan before Bobby arrived, his presence solid and commanding, exuding a quiet confidence that came from years of experience.

"You called?" Bobby asked as he entered the room, his eyes quickly scanning the gathered faces.

"Jay mentioned you were a combat engineer. We want to set up traps around the walls. Got any ideas?" Tom asked, cutting straight to the point.

Bobby grinned, his eyes lighting up with a dangerous enthusiasm. "I'd need a little time to think, but I've got a few fun toys from the JRB that we brought back. I could whip something up. We can get creative."

"Perfect. Get started ASAP. We've got a goblin problem brewing, and drawing them here might be our best bet so we're on familiar ground," Tom said, his confidence in Bobby's abilities evident in his voice.

Bobby nodded. "I'll get on it. I'll need a team to help set things up faster. The quicker we're ready, the better."

"Take whoever you need," Tom replied, placing his full trust in the man. "Good luck, and keep us updated."

As Bobby turned to leave, Tom's mind shifted to the next step. "Have we scouted the area where they're gathering?"

Jay smirked, leaning back in his chair with a relaxed air. "Of course. What kind of amateur do you think I am? Sean and I have had teams keeping an eye on them, and we've been flying recon missions with the jets."

Tom nodded, relieved but still cautious. "How many are we dealing with?"

"Last count was over five hundred, and more keep coming," Jay answered, still grinning as if the number didn't faze him.

"That's a lot," Tom muttered, his earlier sense of unease returning.

"We've got more people, and we've got bigger guns. Much bigger guns," Jay said, his confidence unwavering.

Tom took a deep breath, his expression serious. "I'm not going to underestimate them. I want them wiped out. No more accidents. We go in hard, fast, and with overwhelming force."

"Oh, you know I love it when you talk dirty, Tom," Jay shuddered in obvious pleasure.

The room fell silent—whether it was at Tom's pronouncement or Jay's wasn't clear. What *was* clear, however—were the stakes, and no one wanted a repeat of past blunders.

"Okay, everyone knows their roles," Tom continued, taking charge. "Jay, keep your scouts on the goblins. Derek, get the pilots briefed and ready. Brian, coordinate with the teams to make sure everyone's set up properly. Chris, prep the fighters. Get them rested and ready to move."

The team nodded, and one by one, they filed out of the room, each heading off to prepare for their part in the plan. Tom watched them go, feeling a sense of pride in their commitment.

"And what will you do?" Maria asked, her voice softer now, almost concerned.

"I'm going to try to rest," Tom replied, surprising himself with how much he meant it. "We've been going non-stop. If DeeDee has taught me anything, it's that we need to take breaks or risk burning out."

"Good. I'm glad someone scared you straight," Maria replied, her tone lightening.

Tom smiled and headed for his room. When he got there, he showered, the hot water washing away the tension from his muscles. Jerky was already asleep on the floor when Tom finally lay down in his bed. His thoughts whirled, but exhaustion finally started pulling him under. He nudged Jerky and told him to get into the bed instead of sleeping on the ground before he, too, fell fast asleep.

Hours later, he suddenly woke up; his body snapping awake as if on high alert. Jerky was already awake, sitting beside him with a watchful gaze.

"How long was I out?" Tom asked, groggily rubbing his eyes.

"About twelve hours, I think," Jerky replied, looking relieved that Tom was up.

"Damn, didn't mean to sleep that long," Tom muttered as he swung his legs over the side of the bed.

"You needed it. No one bothered you," Jerky said, smiling. "What's the plan?"

Tom stretched, feeling the stiffness in his muscles ease a bit. "First, I want to check on Bobby and see how the traps are coming along."

"I'm with you," Jerky said eagerly.

On their way to the walls, they took the elevator down. It stopped midway, and the door opened to reveal Kiera. She stepped in, looking a bit more rested and at ease.

"Hey, where are you off to?" Tom asked, genuinely glad to see her looking better.

"Just grabbing some breakfast. Want to join me?" Kiera offered with a small, sincere smile.

Tom's stomach growled at the mention of food, reminding him he hadn't eaten since before he slept. "Sure, why not?"

They found a quiet corner in the cafeteria, eating their meal in comfortable silence at first. After a while, Tom decided to speak up, his tone gentle. "How are you holding up?"

Kiera was quiet for a moment, her gaze focused on her plate. "Better. Still processing everything," she finally said, her voice tinged with exhaustion.

Tom nodded, understanding. "Remember, you can talk to me about anything. Or any of us, really."

"I know. It's just... hard. I'm not used to talking about feelings," Kiera admitted, a hint of frustration in her voice as she poked at her food.

Tom leaned in slightly, his expression softening. "Take your time. We're here whenever you're ready."

Kiera gave him a small smile, a flicker of warmth in her eyes. "Thanks, Tom."

After finishing their meal, Tom asked if Kiera wanted to come along to check out the traps with him. She nodded but said she needed to take care of something else first. As she turned to leave, she paused, placing a hand on his shoulder.

"Thanks again," she said quietly, her voice almost a whisper, her eyes not quite meeting his own.

Tom watched her walk away, feeling a surge of warmth and gratitude. He turned back toward the walls, ready to see what progress Bobby had made and to keep preparing for the battle ahead.

Chapter 25

Traps, Traps, Traps

Sunshine beat down on Tom as he stood outside the Guild building, taking a moment to absorb the warmth on his face. He closed his eyes, savoring the feeling, and took several deep breaths of the much cleaner air. It was astonishing how much the atmosphere had changed in just a few months without the constant buzz of vehicles and factories. The familiar smell of earth and greenery filled his lungs, reminding him of a time before everything had gone to hell. The sounds of the people bustling around inside the walls brought him back to reality, a comforting blend of voices, footsteps, and the occasional clang of metal tools.

People were busy with the ongoing projects around the base. Some patrolled the perimeter with a watchful eye, ensuring no surprise attacks or unwelcome guests breached their defenses. Others hauled materials or worked with purpose on various tasks, each critical to maintaining and improving the Guild's home. Several farmers were heading toward the back of the building, carrying tools as they made their way to the orchards and livestock pens. Tom watched as construction workers, wearing bright yellow reflective vests and hard hats, repaired a damaged section of the building. He couldn't quite remember what had caused the damage, but it didn't matter. Seeing the community working together was enough to fill him with a sense of pride and determination.

Tom waved to the workers, who returned his smile with a nod or a wave of their own. It was these little moments that kept them going—the camaraderie, the shared sense of purpose. Making his way toward the gate, which currently stood open, Tom passed a security guard who wished him a good morning. He returned the greeting with a grin and turned to survey the area outside the gate. To his right, a group of people were busy working on a new project. Curious, he decided to head in their direction.

As he approached, Tom spotted Bobby, who was hammering something onto the wall that was being covered with wooden planks.

"How's it going out here?" Tom asked, coming up behind Bobby.

Bobby turned, his face lighting up with a smile. "So far, so good. I picked up some of this MCLC from the JRB. We're attaching it to the wall at set intervals. When someone sets off the trigger, it'll fire the cord out in a straight line and detonate after it lands. In theory, it should land right in the middle of our enemies and give them a nice little surprise," he explained, his grin widening as he admired his handiwork.

"MCLC? What's that used for?" Tom asked, raising an eyebrow.

"Mine-clearing line charge," Bobby clarified. "Normally, it's deployed from a vehicle straight out in front of troops headed toward minefields," Bobby replied. "It sets off any land mines in the way before they march across. But I thought this might be a creative way to use it. The enemy won't know what hit 'em." He winked at Tom before turning back to secure the cord inside a protective box attached to the wall.

"Cool! Got any other surprises for them?" Tom asked, intrigued by Bobby's ingenuity.

"Normally, I have tons of things we could do, but being in a city where everything is paved and there aren't any trees makes the typical tactics difficult," Bobby said, rubbing his chin thoughtfully. "So, I'm working on getting creative."

As they stood just outside the wall, enjoying the relative calm, a deafening roar suddenly echoed from overhead. A large shadow passed over them, blotting out the sun for a brief moment. Everyone in the vicinity looked up, squinting against the bright sky, while Tom instinctively drew his greatsword, adrenaline coursing through his veins. His eyes darted around, searching for the source of the noise. Finally, he spotted it—a massive shape flying high above them, circling slowly like a bird of prey.

His eyes widened in awe and disbelief. "It can't be..." Tom almost breathlessly whispered, his heart pounding in his chest.

"Is that a dragon?!" Bobby shouted, his voice a mixture of fear and excitement as he watched the creature soar in a wide circle above them. It then continued its flight path toward the north, its enormous wings slicing through the air with a rhythmic beat.

"I... I think it was," Tom stammered, struggling to comprehend what he had just seen. His mind raced with questions, none of which had immediate answers. Dragons were supposed to be mythical, stories told to children around campfires. But there it was, as real as anything he had ever seen.

"Well, I'll be damned," Bobby said, equally stunned. "First goblins, now dragons. What's next, unicorns?"

"It didn't stop here, but it paused," Tom said, still gazing at the now distant figure in the sky. "Hopefully, it just stays away for now. We don't need another problem on our hands."

As if the world was listening to him, a window suddenly appeared in Tom's vision, hovering in the air before him like a notification on a screen. His heart sank slightly as he realized that whatever this was, it wasn't going to make their lives any easier.

New Quest: The Ancient Ones
You have spotted a dragon flying overhead. These creatures are powerful remnants of a bygone age that are rarely found on planets within the Federation. Find out what is causing one to now appear on Earth. **Accept?**

INVASION

Yes	*No*

"A quest?" Tom asked, now more confused than ever.

"Dragons are exceedingly rare," Maria explained. "They usually foretell the coming of something significant. You'd be wise to accept the quest and investigate it once this invasion is over."

A knot formed in Tom's stomach as he stood there, contemplating his options.

"You got a quest? I didn't know the System gave out quests. Or if it did, I figured it was rare," Bobby said, continuing to work on the trap. "You should take it."

Tom hesitated for a moment before accepting the quest. The window minimized, but the unease remained. "You think we should chase after the dragon?" he asked, a little incredulous at Bobby's enthusiasm.

"This new way of life is all about adventure. Of course, I think we should check it out," Bobby replied, shrugging like it was the most obvious thing in the world.

"We need to protect the people here first," Tom reminded him, his voice firm.

"Of course, but once the invasion is over, we can go check it out," Bobby said, grunting as he tied off the cord in the wooden box.

"If we survive," Tom muttered bleakly.

"Well, Mr. Party Pooper," Bobby said with a smirk. "Have a little faith. We've been through worse situations that felt pretty hopeless. We got this."

"I'm glad someone is so positive. I don't know if I can be that optimistic," Tom admitted.

"You don't have to be," Bobby said, glancing up from his work. "You're the leader. If you're worried but we feel confident, then we're more likely to succeed. Leading men like this is all about exuding confidence in public and worrying your ass off behind closed doors. That way, you account for as many possibilities as you can, and your troops have faith in you, so they fight harder."

Tom looked at Bobby with newfound respect. "That's an interesting perspective."

"If everyone worried about all the problems, they'd lose confidence and be useless in a fight. If they trust the leader has their best interests at heart, they can let go of that stress and focus on their job. You've set up a pretty amazing system here, Tom. It functions more efficiently than any organization I've ever been a part of. That's why we've been successful so far. The little people don't have to worry about the big picture; they just do their job," Bobby explained, grunting one more time as he looked over his work. He lowered the wooden lid on the front of the box, concealing its contents.

"It's also why you delegate things to others to handle. They might see more of the big picture, but they don't need all of it. That's why I don't ask a lot of questions. I don't need to worry about things other people are taking care of. I just need to do my job and then kick some ass later," Bobby said with a grin. "Also, I don't want your job. I'm happier being lower on the totem pole."

Tom thought about what Bobby said for a long moment. He had always felt so overwhelmed, constantly jumping from one crisis to the next. He knew Brian had it even worse as the head administrator, but he hadn't considered how it felt for those who only had one job to focus on.

"Now then, cupcake," Bobby said, breaking Tom's train of thought. "Let's see what else we can do here. I have an idea for a pitfall trap that's going to take some real redneck engineering to pull off."

Tom chuckled and turned to follow Bobby, curious about what he had planned. As they moved toward another section of the wall, Tom heard a scuttling noise from the side of a nearby building. He turned to see a shadow disappear around the corner.

What the hell? Tom thought, deciding to investigate.

Pretending to head toward the gate, he suddenly veered off to the right and moved quickly but quietly toward the side of the building. As he neared, he slowed his pace and crept along the wall, careful not to make a sound. When he reached the corner, he flattened himself against the wall and peeked around it.

A lone goblin stood there, looking confused and out of place. Tom moved silently around the corner and approached the creature from behind. Just as he was within arm's reach, the goblin turned, its eyes going wide with fear at the sight of Tom looming over it. Before it could react, Tom grabbed it by the back of the ragged black fabric it wore. The goblin tried to scamper away, but Tom's grip was too strong.

"What do we have here, little spy?" Tom asked, tightening his hold as he stepped out from behind the building.

The goblin screeched, flailing its arms and legs wildly, trying to claw and bite at Tom. But he held it by the back of its collar, keeping it out of reach as it struggled in vain.

"Whatcha got there?" Bobby asked, noticing the commotion.

"Looks like a little spy. My guess is where there's one, there are more. Go get Jay and Sean. I want to know why this wasn't spotted sooner," Tom said, his tone serious.

Bobby nodded and rushed off, leaving Tom holding the increasingly frantic goblin. The creature pulled a knife from somewhere and attempted to stab him. Tom quickly dropped it to the ground and delivered a swift kick to its face. The goblin screamed, blood spurting from its nose, and Tom grabbed it by its shirt again, lifting it back up. The knife lay forgotten in the dirt.

Bobby soon returned with Jay and Sean in tow.

"I found a friend," Tom said. "I thought we were patrolling for these little bastards? He was watching us set up the traps."

"We are patrolling," Jay replied, scowling at the goblin, which was now sobbing and holding its nose. "But we can't be everywhere. Sorry, Tom."

"I'm not mad," Tom said, his voice calm. "I know you can't do everything. Just, when we have a project going on like this, they should be focusing here so we don't have secrets sent back."

INVASION

"I'll have someone posted nearby. We won't let it happen again," Sean said quickly, heading off to find someone to cover the area.

"Now, do we think he knows anything?" Tom asked, eyeing the goblin suspiciously.

"Probably, but we can't communicate with it. No one speaks their language. Only a few of them spoke English back when we encountered them. Best to just end it now," Jay suggested.

At this, the goblin suddenly began fighting harder than ever, its eyes darting around frantically.

"Feels like this little guy understands English, at least," Tom observed, holding the creature at arm's length to keep it from clawing at him.

"We can see if he knows anything," Jay said, his voice cold and calculating. "Best to leave it to me. You don't want to be a part of this."

Tom hesitated but nodded. "What are you going to do?"

"If you have to ask, then you definitely don't need to be a part of it," Jay replied, striking the goblin over the back of the head with a swift motion, causing it to go limp. He took the creature from Tom and headed back toward the Guild building without another word.

Tom watched him go, a slight unease settling in his stomach. He trusted Jay, but the methods he employed were sometimes better left unknown. This wasn't something Tom was willing to involve himself in right now.

Chapter 26

Bad Intel

Tom stayed outside for a while longer, assisting with the setup and fine-tuning of the traps. The sun was high overhead, casting a warm glow across the compound, and a light breeze rustled the leaves of the few trees they had managed to keep alive in this part of the city. Tom felt a sense of satisfaction as he worked alongside Bobby and the others, watching the former combat engineer manage his team with a blend of efficiency and enthusiasm. Bobby's passion for his craft was evident, and his knowledge was invaluable in setting up defenses that were both practical and lethal.

Tom learned a lot during his time with Bobby about setting traps and what to look for. Many of the ideas Bobby suggested were too dangerous to have so close to the walls, but setting up tripwire explosives near some of the abandoned buildings surrounding their compound could account for the goblins' movement patterns and result in a few unexpected kills. Tom watched as Bobby expertly directed his team to remove a large piece of pavement, carefully digging a pit beneath it.

They placed sharpened stakes at the bottom, ensuring they would pierce through any unfortunate goblin that fell in. After drilling a hole through the pavement and installing a pipe that would allow it to spin if someone stepped on one side, Bobby replaced the piece of pavement, demonstrating how a simple latch on each end could prevent it from moving when not in use.

Tom was impressed by the ingenuity on display. "I'd never have thought of half of these ideas," he admitted. "If I were in charge, there'd just be a bunch of snares and tripwires."

Bobby grinned. "Hey, snares and tripwires can be effective, but we gotta think bigger! Use what we've got around us. The city might seem like a disadvantage, but if we get creative, we can turn it into a fortress."

Tom couldn't help but chuckle, feeling a little out of his depth. "Yeah, my version would probably look like something out of a bad cartoon. I can picture it now—tiny nets everywhere. Just tiny enough to be useless."

Bobby laughed, and Tom found himself slipping into a goofy voice from an old movie he remembered. "A tiny net is a death sentence… because they are nets, and they are tiny," he quoted, then added a series of mock kung-fu sounds. "Weoh, weoh, weoh, weoh…"

INVASION

A few of the nearby workers paused and looked at Tom with bewildered expressions. Realizing he was speaking too loudly, he cleared his throat, embarrassed, and continued toward the elevators. Just as he was about to press the button to go up, Jay appeared, moving quickly and looking serious.

"Tom! We've got some intel," Jay said, glancing around to make sure no one was eavesdropping. "Come down to the basement. We need to talk."

Tom's demeanor shifted instantly. "Lead the way," he said, following Jay toward the stairwell.

The stairs seemed to stretch on forever as they descended into the depths of the basement. The air grew cooler, the sounds of the bustling compound fading away, replaced by an eerie quiet. Jay took the lead, moving with purpose. At the far end of the basement, they approached a makeshift room sectioned off by wooden pallets covered with sheets. It looked hastily constructed, as if secrecy was more important than comfort or aesthetics.

Inside the dimly lit area, the goblin Tom had captured earlier was tied to a chair. Its head hung low, and its body was covered in dark, blackish blood and fresh bruises. Tom felt his stomach twist at the sight.

"What the hell did you do?" Tom asked, his voice low but filled with tension.

Sean, who had been leaning against the wall, straightened up.

"What we had to," he replied flatly, his gaze unwavering.

Tom took a moment to breathe, his eyes flicking between the beaten goblin and Sean. He placed his hands on his hips, trying to steady himself.

After a few deep breaths, he spoke. "Fine. What did you get?"

Jay stepped in. "Well, they can use the fucking vending machines," he said.

Tom's eyes widened. "Right, that would make sense from what we saw with the last goblin leader," he said, motioning toward the battered goblin.

"They don't know a lot of our words for things, but he described the machines well enough," Sean continued.

Jay produced a dagger from his Inventory, its blade gleaming under the dim light.

"We also found this," he said, holding it out to Tom.

Tom took the dagger and examined it closely. "A dagger? What's special about it?"

"It's made of metal," Jay explained. "Most of their weapons are stone, or if they are metal, they're rusted pieces of junk. This one is new—looks like it's straight from a vending machine."

Tom's mind raced. The goblins getting their hands on weapons from the vending machines complicated things.

"That doesn't bode well," he muttered, handing the dagger back to Jay.

"It could be worse," Jay said. "If they figured out guns, we'd be in real trouble. Let's hope they're sticking to what they know—melee weapons instead of firearms."

"Anything else?" Tom asked, his concern growing.

"We confirmed where they're hiding out," Jay continued, "and that they're all rallying around one goblin in particular. A leader named Krakkarith. They call him 'Krak' for short."

"And that's our war chief?" Tom asked.

"Most likely," Jay said. "It's all we could get out of him. Nothing else made any sense or was in goblin speak."

Tom took a deep breath, processing the information. "I don't think this changes our plans much. We just need to make sure that when we hit them, we hit them hard," he concluded.

"I'll let the others know," Sean said.

"What are you going to do with him now?" Tom asked, nodding toward the goblin.

"We'll handle it," Jay said firmly. "No need for you to worry about it."

Tom sighed. "I don't want this getting out to anyone. We don't need to spread panic, and we definitely don't need people thinking it's okay to go around doing… this," he said, gesturing toward the bound goblin. "Hell, I'm not even comfortable with this."

As Tom turned and left the makeshift interrogation room, he couldn't shake the feeling of unease that had settled in his chest. He walked back up the stairs, his thoughts racing, and paused in the lobby. Running a hand through his hair, he tried to center himself. Moments later, Jerky found him standing there, looking lost in thought.

"Everything okay?" Jerky asked, his eyes filled with concern.

"Yeah, it'll be fine," Tom replied, his voice tinged with exhaustion. "Where've you been?"

"I stayed to help Bobby some more. He's nice," Jerky said, smiling softly.

"Yeah, he's a great guy," Tom agreed. "But I think it's time for a little training with Bron. I need to blow off some steam."

Jerky's face paled at the mention of the Mastadonian and his brutal training regimens. "Do we have to?" he whined.

Tom chuckled, patting his companion on the shoulder. "We can't slack off, Jerky. We need to be ready for the next fight. You never know when it'll happen—though I think we have a pretty good idea when the next one is coming."

Reluctantly, Jerky followed Tom outside to the courtyard. For hours, they trained under Bron's watchful eye. The large warrior put them through their paces, pushing them to their limits with relentless drills and sparring. By the end of it, Tom was bent over with his hands on his knees, panting heavily. Jerky was lying flat on the ground, wings splayed beside him, eyes closed, too exhausted to even move.

"Not bad," Bron said, barely winded himself. "But you both need more practice. Still, we should stop for today. Go clean up so you don't stink, and take some time to recover."

"You're evil, aren't you?" Jerky groaned from the ground, his voice weak.

Bron laughed, a booming sound that echoed off the courtyard walls. "This was nothing, little one. You'll soon see what a true training session looks like."

"We're going to need you in a few days," Tom said as he stood, his hands on top of his head to help catch his breath. "We've got something coming up—a big one."

INVASION

"What are we looking at?" Bron asked, his demeanor shifting to all business.

"Goblins," Tom replied simply.

Bron's face remained impassive. "That doesn't sound too bad."

"With a war chief," Tom added.

Bron's expression darkened. "Are you sure?" he asked quietly.

"About as sure as we can be," Tom answered.

"Then you do need me," Bron said, his tone grave. "You need to be very careful. War chiefs can greatly increase the abilities of the goblins under their control. How many are there?"

"Maybe a little over five hundred, last we counted," Tom replied.

Bron considered this. "When are you planning to strike?"

"Tonight, or tomorrow at the latest. We're going to bomb them first then draw them here to fight on familiar ground," Tom explained.

"A solid strategy to start," Bron nodded. "Do you have any cavalry?"

"Like horses? No," Tom replied, confused. "But we have the vehicles. Why?"

"You'll need something to counter their Wargs," Bron said. "Every edge matters."

Tom felt a chill run down his spine. "You sound like this is worse than fighting the other Guilds."

"It is," Bron said firmly. "These are creatures who have grown up using the System, not some humans who were given access a few months ago. Never underestimate your opponent, no matter how weak they seem."

Tom nodded, understanding the gravity of the situation. "I'll talk to the others and see if we can get the vehicles positioned outside the walls for a flanking maneuver. We need every advantage we can get."

Bron nodded in agreement. "Goblin war chiefs are far more intelligent than any goblin you've faced so far. They will have strategy, cunning, and ruthlessness on their side. If you see a chance to end them, do not hesitate."

"Got it," Tom replied. "Anything else we should know?"

"Just remember—confidence is good, but overconfidence is a terminal disease," Bron said before turning to leave.

Tom and Jerky headed back inside, feeling the weight of the coming battle pressing down on them. They needed to rest. The fight would be upon them soon enough, and Tom still needed to meet with Derek to talk over the final plans.

The next morning, Tom awoke early, the tension in his muscles reminding him of the previous day's training. He coaxed Jerky out of bed, and after a quick breakfast, they headed to the security office. After asking TJ to call Brian and Derek, both men arrived within minutes. Tom wasted no time relaying the details of what he had learned from the interrogation and his talk with Bron.

"And you okayed this little talk they had with a goblin?" Derek asked, frowning.

"They would've done the same or worse to us," Tom shot back. "Do you feel sorry for those little bastards? They've been nothing but a thorn in our side since this whole System thing started. And before you ask—no, I'm not really okay with it, but what choice did we have? We had an opportunity, and we took it."

Brian looked conflicted. "I don't like it either. I thought we were supposed to be the good guys."

"There aren't any good guys and bad guys, Brian," Tom said sharply. "We're surviving. We don't have the same luxuries we used to have. Let it go and focus on what's next. This war chief is bad news. We need to get the vehicles ready. Bron was right; they'll be a good counter to the Wargs."

Derek nodded, though his expression was still uneasy. "The missiles for the jets are ready. They're going to do some serious damage. Herbert wants to try out some of the new ones, see how they work. The good news is that even if the enchantments don't work, the explosions will still do massive damage. The bad news is if they don't work, we'll have to rework them for the invasion."

"When are we planning to strike?" Tom asked.

"Tonight, as long as everything is ready," Derek replied, glancing at Brian.

"Everyone here will be ready," Brian assured him. "We've got the strike teams on standby, and we're not sending anyone out today. Everyone's preparing, and we've got some new weapons brought back from the military base."

"Good," Tom said. "I want to see if we can get the vehicles outside the walls and away from the base so they can be a surprise for a flanking maneuver. Get as many SUVs as you can ready. Bobby should have the traps done as well for their arrival. Then we give them hell from the walls to start."

"We won't have the pilots in the sky because I don't want bombs going off so close to base," Derek added. "But they can harry the enemy where they can. Landing them is a no-go during the battle—we don't need them damaged."

"Sounds like we're just about ready to ruin their night," Tom said, a determined smile crossing his face. "Let's go check on the last-minute preparations."

Chapter 27

First Strike

The rest of the day was a whirlwind of activity as the Guild scrambled to finalize preparations for the impending attack on the goblin forces. Tension hung thick in the air as teams moved purposefully around the compound, ensuring that every last detail was addressed. Fighters sharpened their weapons, checked their gear, and ran through drills while the support teams worked tirelessly behind the scenes. Mechanics and engineers swarmed over the jets, performing final system checks and loading the missiles into the weapons bays with precision. Sweat poured down their brows as they refueled the aircraft and tested the avionics, making sure every switch, button, and gauge responded as expected.

Pilots went over their mission plans again and again, memorizing every detail of the bombing run. Some stood in small groups, discussing strategies and contingencies for what was to be their first official mission. There was an undercurrent of excitement mingled with nerves, a mixture of eager anticipation and the ever-present threat of danger. The hum of machinery and the sounds of orders being barked out filled the hangar. The atmosphere was electric, charged with the adrenaline that came with preparing for battle.

As the sun began to dip low on the horizon, casting long shadows across the compound, the preparations reached their final stages. The jets gleamed under the fading light, their sleek forms loaded with lethal payloads and ready to rain destruction upon the enemy. Crews worked with quiet efficiency, the clatter of tools and the hiss of hydraulic lines forming a steady rhythm that seemed to set the pace for everyone around them. One by one, the aircraft were moved into their launch positions, and the ground crews made final adjustments to the weapons systems. A murmur of satisfaction rippled through the teams as everything seemed to check out—every missile armed, every system green.

Meanwhile, back inside the Guild building, the atmosphere was equally charged. Fighters gathered in the cafeteria; the usual buzz of conversation replaced by a more focused intensity. There was no place for small talk now; everyone was keenly aware of the looming battle. Charlene, the head cook, had wisely decided to streamline the process of feeding such large groups. Instead of making everyone line up, she had her assistants move through the cafeteria with trays, distributing them directly to the tables. She wanted to make sure everyone had a proper meal before the fight, knowing how vital it was for them to keep their energy up.

Tom sat with his core team, his eyes scanning the room, absorbing the atmosphere. There was a gravity to the moment, a sense that what they were about to do would be pivotal. One of Charlene's assistants placed a plate in front of Tom with a large steak, mashed potatoes, and what looked like collard greens. Sniffing the aroma of the meal, Tom's mouth involuntarily began to drool. He cut into the steak and took a bite. As he did, a prompt appeared in his vision.

Enhanced Goatamus Steak

The rich, savory flavor of the steak fills you with newfound vigor. Infused with strengthening qualities, this magically enhanced meal provides a boost to your physical prowess.

Effect: +1 Strength
Duration: 12 hours

Feel the power coursing through your muscles as the buff takes hold. Use this strength wisely, adventurer!

"Wait, you can create enhancing foods now?!" Tom exclaimed, staring at the steak with wide eyes.

Charlene smiled warmly. "Just recently learned the Skill. I've been testing the results, and it's not a huge boost yet, but it'll get stronger as I level up."

"This is incredible, Charlene! You're amazing!" Tom said, grabbing his fork and knife to cut off another piece of the meat.

Charlene chuckled softly. "You're pretty amazing yourself, Tom. I'm just trying to keep up."

Tom shook his head, his tone serious. "Don't think you need to keep up with anyone. You're the one who keeps us all fed. Without you, we'd be stuck eating crappy rations or nothing at all."

With that, he raised the second bite of steak to his lips. As he chewed, the rich juices burst across his tongue. He felt something spread through his jaw and down into his chest, warmth flowing into his extremities as if liquid strength was coursing through his veins.

"Oh, my god," Tom muttered, barely able to keep his mouth closed as he savored the bite. "This is the best steak I've ever tasted! It's like my taste buds are dancing, and the warmth… it makes me feel like I could run a marathon."

"Make sure you eat all of it to get the full effect," Charlene winked. "I'm working on more recipes to help the Guild even more." She continued moving around the room, passing out plates of food.

Tom stared at his plate, torn between savoring each bite and devouring the whole meal in one go. Meanwhile, Jerky was already halfway through his steak, and shoveling mashed potatoes into his mouth. He glanced around, already looking for seconds before finishing his first plate. Charlene, laughing at his eagerness, handed him another plate.

INVASION

"Does eating more give you additional bonuses?" Tom asked, watching Jerky dig into his second plate with gusto.

Jerky paused mid-bite, a look of concentration crossing his face as he checked a screen Tom couldn't see. He shook his head and went right back to eating.

"Too bad," Tom said with a grin, returning to his own plate and enjoying every mouthful.

Once everyone had finished their meals, the teams stood up from their tables, preparing to leave the room. Just as they were about to head out, Briana stepped forward, blocking the exit.

"Before you go, I want to try something," Briana announced. She closed her eyes and raised her hands, tightly gripping her staff.

The room fell silent as Briana began chanting in a strange, ancient language none of them could understand. A soft, white glow enveloped her, growing brighter and starting to pulse rhythmically. She opened her eyes, which now glowed with the same white light.

"As with the warriors of old, so with these shall be the guidance of gods and their blessings!" Briana declared. The radiant light that had surrounded her suddenly expanded outward, washing over everyone in the room.

A wave of energy rippled through Tom, and he felt a surge of vitality and strength. It wasn't just a feeling; he could sense something tangible settling into his bones, a protective aura that bolstered his spirit and body alike. All around, the others murmured in awe, feeling the effects as well.

He checked his status screen, seeing a new effect listed:

Blessing of the gods
You have been blessed by a Cleric who wishes to keep your party safe in the coming struggle. For the next 24 hours, you receive +3 to Luck.

"It may not be much, but I hope it helps," Briana said as she lowered her arms, moving aside to allow the teams to pass. She bowed her head slightly, a gesture of respect and encouragement.

"Thank you, Briana. Any benefits are greatly appreciated," Tom replied, giving her a reassuring smile as he made his way to the courtyard.

When all of the teams had gathered, Tom took a deep breath, standing tall as he faced the crowd that filled the open space. He could feel the tension in the air, a mix of anticipation and resolve.

"Tonight, we make the first move to prevent a conflict that could spiral beyond our control," Tom began, his voice strong and steady. "This is what all of our preparations and training have been leading to. If anyone here feels they cannot participate, please step forward now. We'll never force you to fight, but we'll do whatever is necessary to protect what we've built here."

Tom paused for a moment, allowing his words to sink in. The crowd remained silent, their faces set in determination. Seeing no one step forward, he continued.

"Now that Vanguard has an Air Force, we have superiority in most combat situations. Let's make full use of that advantage. Tonight, we show them what it means to face Vanguard!" His voice rose with each word, feeding off the energy in the crowd. "For Vanguard!"

"FOR VANGUARD!" came the thunderous response, echoing across the courtyard as every person present raised their weapons or fists into the air.

"Let's show those little green bastards they should never have tried to challenge our might!" Tom roared, feeling the surge of pride and unity in the crowd.

The assembled teams erupted into cheers, shouts, and war cries, the collective roar of warriors ready to defend their home. It looked like they were prepared to charge out and face the enemy head-on right then and there.

"Pilots, to your aircraft!" Derek's voice boomed over the noise, commanding and clear.

The pilots, easily recognizable in their flight suits and helmets, broke away from the main group, jogging toward the staging area where the jets were prepped and ready. The crowd continued cheering, their excitement fueling the pilots as they made their way to the aircraft.

A few minutes later, the roar of jet engines filled the air as the pilots fired up their planes. One by one, the jets lifted off, hovering for a moment before soaring into the sky. They executed a loop around the city, getting into formation.

As the last jet joined the formation, the squadron flew low over the Guild building in a powerful display of strength. The crowd below raised their weapons once more, shouting and cheering at the sight of their newly formed Air Force—a symbol of their growing power.

"Do we have radio communication with the pilots?" Tom asked, turning to Derek.

Derek, clad in his power armor, nodded. "I have a connection set up. I can speak with them directly, and they can relay what's happening in real time."

"Excellent," Tom replied, nodding in approval. "I want regular status updates so we know exactly what's happening."

"Understood," Derek confirmed.

Tom looked around, taking in the faces of his comrades—some seasoned fighters, others new to this level of conflict, but all united by the same cause. The tension was palpable, like a drawn bowstring ready to release.

"Now, we wait," Tom said quietly, more to himself than anyone else, as he watched the jets disappear into the distance, ready to strike the first blow.

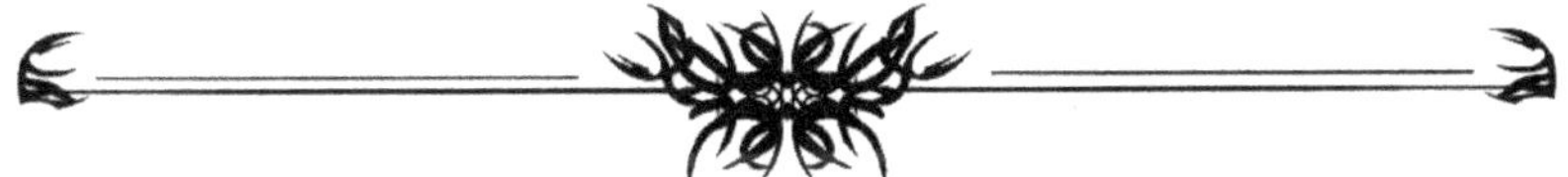

INVASION

Anderson had been placed in charge of the pilots, as well as their training, during any combat situations. As the most experienced aviator among them, he was the first to take off. Once all the other jets were airborne, he led the way toward the location where the goblins had been spotted. Each pilot had been assigned a radio designation, and Anderson had them sound off as they moved into formation, ensuring clear communication.

"Alpha Leader to all units," Anderson's voice crackled through the comms. "Let's take a high fly-by to see what we can find. When we have a lock, we need to hit them fast and hard. Watch your radar for enemy movement and stay in communication."

One by one, the pilots responded with their confirmations, and the jets began their approach to the target area. As they banked around for the initial flyover, their radars began to light up with the movement below—a mass of clustered dots that filled the screens, indicating the goblins' positions.

"Sure are a lot of the little fuckers," came a gruff voice over the radio.

"Doesn't matter," Anderson replied, his tone cold and steady. "We'll show them what modern warfare can do here."

Completing their first pass, the squadron circled back around to prepare for a more targeted approach.

"Time for a low flyover," Anderson instructed. "This is just a first pass. Do not drop your full payload. I repeat, do not drop your full payload. One drop each, and we circle back for more."

The pilots confirmed, one after another, and Anderson angled his jet downward, guiding it into a descent for the first bombing run. As they drew closer to the target zone, Anderson issued a final directive.

"Be sure to spread them out," he called. "Hit near the perimeter first. Might spook them toward the center, so we can cluster-bomb them on the next run."

With that, Anderson reached his designated drop point and gave the go-ahead, "Begin drops."

The bay doors under Anderson's F-35 opened with a mechanical whine, releasing a bomb that plummeted toward the ground. The other pilots followed suit, targeting the outskirts of the goblin encampment and dropping their bombs in a calculated sequence. The jets screamed out of the strike zone, banking sharply to prepare for a second pass. Moments later, the sky was filled with the deafening sound of explosions.

Fire and smoke erupted from the ground as the bombs detonated, obliterating the sections of the camp where the goblins were gathered. Chaos ensued immediately. Those goblins not caught in the blasts frantically tried to flee the destruction, while those within the impact zones were vaporized in an instant. At the edges of the blasts, some goblins lost limbs or were thrown like ragdolls from the force of the shockwaves.

"Prepare for a second pass." Anderson's voice remained calm, cutting through the static of the radio. "Aim for the center, inside the original blasts, but avoid overlapping targets. Call out your targets if needed."

As the squadron looped around for another strike, flashes of light began to shoot up from the ground—bolts of energy fired by goblin mages trying to strike back at the jets. One of the pilots had to jink and roll to avoid being hit, while most of the bolts fizzled out before reaching them.

"Watch for enemy mages," Anderson ordered, his tone more urgent now. "Prioritize their locations."

Diving down for their second pass, the pilots dropped another round of bombs. The explosions ripped through the goblin ranks again, the air filled with screams and the roar of detonations. The camp below was a sea of flames, smoke, and terror.

"Alright, ladies and gentlemen, it's time for the short-range missiles. Lock onto targets and fire at will," Anderson instructed, moving into phase two of the operation.

The F-35s were equipped with four AIM-9X Sidewinder short-range missiles, each capable of locking onto specific ground targets. The pilots fired their missiles in calculated succession, ensuring a relentless barrage of firepower. The goblin camp, already in tatters, was further reduced to rubble as the missiles found their marks, obliterating any semblance of organization among the survivors. Any attempt by the goblins to regroup was crushed under the continuous onslaught.

"Now we circle until we're sure they can see us through the smoke, then it's back to base," Anderson instructed, leading the jets into a holding pattern high above the devastation.

As the smoke, dust, and debris began to settle, the scene below was one of absolute carnage. Only a handful of goblins could be seen still moving, staggering in the ruins of what had once been their camp. Buildings were reduced to twisted metal and ash, trees were shattered to splinters, and any makeshift hovels the goblins had constructed were now nothing but scattered debris.

"Alright, that's a wrap. All units, return to base," Anderson commanded, satisfied with the results.

The squadron formed up and headed back toward the Guild's base, the roar of their engines echoing as they left behind a battlefield utterly transformed by their assault.

Just then, a notification pinged into Anderson's System interface.

Skill – Vehicular Homicide - Fighter Jet
You have killed multiple enemies with your vehicle (Lockheed Martin F-35 Lightning II). You have become more proficient at manipulating this weapon of war and causing your enemy's demise. Continue to eviscerate your enemies to receive greater bonuses to damage.

Current Skill Level: 2	**Current Skill Rank:** Beginner

Bonus Damage Dealt: +15%

"Hoooly shit," Anderson swore. "I think I just died and went to heaven…" He patted the console of his fighter lovingly. "Atta girl, Big Bertha."

INVASION

A second System prompt showed up on the pilot's interface.

Name your Vehicle?	
Would you like to name the Lockheed Martin F-35 Lightning II, Big Bertha?	
Yes	*No*

"Oh, *hell* yes," Anderson gasped.

While looking at the console, he triggered his *Inspect* Skill. His eyes widened and it took him three times to click the comms to the rest of his squadron.

"Guys…" Anderson panted. "You're gonna want to take a look at this…"

Cheers erupted as the jets safely returned to the base, their engines roaring as they descended to the top of the parking garage, which was being used for the primary jets. Once the aircraft were on the ground and the pilots emerged from their cockpits, the crowd in the courtyard broke into wild applause. When they returned to ground level, Guild members rushed forward, hoisting the pilots onto their shoulders and chanting their names in a chorus of praise and approval. The air was electric with excitement, the adrenaline of a successful operation still coursing through everyone present.

When the pilots were finally let down, Anderson made his way to Tom, his face flushed with exhilaration but maintaining a composed demeanor. Tom extended his hand, gripping Anderson's firmly as he gave his official report.

"The heroes of the sky have done their part!" Tom's voice boomed across the courtyard, instantly drawing the attention of everyone gathered. "Now, we prepare for the assault!"

The crowd, already buzzing with excitement, exploded into another round of cheers, their energy almost palpable. With the anticipation of the next stage of their plan, Guild members sprang into action, moving quickly to set up defenses and prepare for the goblins' inevitable approach. Guards scrambled up the ladders to their positions along the walls, their eyes scanning the horizon. Fighters huddled with their units, checking weapons and armor, and going over battle strategies one last time.

"Kiera!" Tom's voice cut through the noise as he searched the crowd for her. When he finally spotted her, he continued, "Take a team and move to a building nearby. I want visuals and the ability to provide cover fire from another angle if needed."

"On it!" Kiera replied, her voice strong and focused. She nodded to her team, and they immediately began moving toward one of the buildings that offered a clear vantage point of the surrounding area. She glanced back at Tom, determination in her eyes, before leading her group out of the courtyard.

"Jay!" Tom turned, spotting the spymaster among the crowd. "I want your team watching for movement as well. We need to know long before they arrive. Use every scout you have and keep those eyes sharp."

"Got it, boss," Jay replied with a quick nod, already signaling to his team to spread out and take their positions. They melted into the shadows, vanishing like phantoms into the cityscape.

"Kedron!" Tom shouted, looking toward the vehicles parked nearby. "Get the vehicles ready and position them far away from the walls. Stay hidden and wait for Brian's call to move in. We'll need you to flank them when the time comes."

"You can count on us!" Kedron shouted back, his voice brimming with confidence as he and his crew quickly moved to the vehicles, performing last-minute checks and loading up ammunition. "We're going to beat the green off these little bastards."

Tom took a deep breath as he watched everyone carry out their assignments. He could feel the tension and excitement building in the air, but he also knew that this was just the calm before the storm. The goblins would be coming, and they would come hard. He looked up at the sky, now clear and calm after the roar of the jets had faded.

"Hold the line, and we've got this," he muttered to himself, bracing for the battle ahead.

Chapter 28

Confusion

Time seemed to stretch on endlessly. The minutes crawled by, each second dragging out like an eternity as the Guild members braced themselves for the coming attack. Sweat trickled down brows, breaths came in steady rhythms, and hearts thudded in chests with a mix of adrenaline and anxiety. On top of the walls, the members of Vanguard held their positions, eyes locked on the darkened horizon. The anticipation of the goblin attack was palpable, a thick, almost tangible tension that hung in the air, mingling with the smell of oil, sweat, and the remnants of dinner still lingering in the courtyard.

Tom paced the length of the wall, his boots a steady tempo as he walked. Each step was measured and purposeful, his eyes never straying far from the skyline, now painted in hues of deep purple and orange as the sun dipped lower. Shadows stretched and lengthened, casting strange shapes across the city streets beyond the walls. Every creak of the wood, every clink of metal armor or weapon sent jolts of nervous energy through the assembled defenders. Tom could feel it too—a knot of anticipation tightening in his gut. He knew his people were ready, but he also knew the fear of the unknown hung over them like a dark cloud.

Suddenly, like a wisp of smoke in the corner of his vision, a figure in black garb appeared beside him, blending seamlessly with the twilight shadows.

"They're coming," the figure whispered, the words barely louder than a breath, but they carried the weight of certainty. The scout's presence was as fleeting as a specter—one moment there, and in the blink of an eye, he was gone, swallowed back into the darkness.

"Holy fucking shit, man!" Tom cursed, his heart leaping into his throat as he instinctively reached for his sword. His pulse raced, and he could feel the cold sweat on his palms.

He caught a glimpse of the scout's eyes narrowing in amusement above the dark cloth covering his mouth and nose before he disappeared.

"They sure are getting good at the *Stealth* Skill," Tom muttered, more to himself than to anyone else, trying to shake off the jolt of surprise.

"That's what we need. But yeah, that was a dick move," Derek chuckled from behind him, his voice a deep rumble that barely contained his laughter at Tom's discomfort. The tension was still there, but Derek's presence, solid and familiar, brought a strange sense of calm.

Tom was about to fire back with a quip about Derek's choice of jokes when he heard it—a sound that seemed to rise up from the very ground beneath them. At first, it was a low, distant rumble, like thunder rolling over a faraway hill. But as it grew closer, it became distinct: a steady, rhythmic beat that reverberated through the streets, bouncing off the crumbling facades of abandoned buildings and empty storefronts. It was the unmistakable sound of marching feet—hundreds, maybe thousands—moving in a relentless rhythm. Occasionally, a deep, guttural shout would punctuate the beat, a sound that made the hair on the back of Tom's neck stand on end.

Without another word, Tom sprinted up the stairs to the highest vantage point on the walls, his breath coming in sharp bursts. He positioned himself at the top, his eyes scanning the darkened streets beyond the safety of their barricades. The last slivers of sunlight clung to the edges of the horizon, casting long shadows that twisted and danced like specters in the twilight. His gaze sharpened, and there, in the distance, he finally saw them.

The goblins were coming.

Hundreds of them turned a corner around an old, derelict building, their small, twisted forms marching in unnerving unison. Their armor and weapons, crude and mismatched, glinted in the fading light, and their eyes—those wild, feral eyes—were fixed straight ahead. The sight was enough to make even the most hardened fighters pause. These were not the usual ragtag bands of goblins they had faced before. There was something different, something far more dangerous about this group.

"Take shots at the first of the goblins. Let's see if we can get them to break formation," Tom ordered the nearest guard, his voice steady despite the tension crackling in the air. "Everyone, fire at the front lines!"

Guards along the wall snapped into action, rifles raised to their shoulders, eyes squinting down the sights. The sharp crack of gunfire broke the silence, flashes of light illuminating the encroaching darkness. The front line of goblins staggered and fell, their bodies jerking and convulsing as bullets tore through them. A chorus of pain erupted from the horde, a mixture of shrieks, roars, and gurgling cries that filled the night air.

At first, the carefully arranged ranks of goblins seemed to waver, fear overtaking their rage as they broke formation. Several at the front charged forward in a chaotic frenzy, their shrill war cries echoing off the stone walls as they sprinted toward the fortress, brandishing crude swords and jagged spears.

But then, a deep, resonant horn blast split the air. A chilling, otherworldly sound that sent shivers down the spines of everyone on the wall. Three long, mournful notes that echoed across the cityscape, cutting through the chaos and confusion like a blade. At the sound, the goblins that had charged faltered, their wild eyes darting back toward the rear of their ranks. Slowly, almost reluctantly, they pulled back, reforming their lines with surprising discipline.

"That's not a good sign," Derek murmured beside Tom, his voice grim as he stared out at the still-advancing horde. His brow furrowed, the muscles in his jaw tightening.

"It doesn't matter," Tom replied, his tone firm and unyielding. "We stick to the plan."

INVASION

The rhythmic pounding of goblin feet continued, filling the defenders with a deep sense of foreboding. Each step felt like a drumbeat heralding doom. But the rifles kept firing, and the goblins continued to fall, though they pressed on with an unsettling determination. Tom could see it in their eyes now—the absolute obedience, the unnatural focus. Whoever was leading them had a tight leash on their minds.

"We need to do something to bolster our troops' morale," Derek suggested, eyes still fixed on the advancing enemy. "Maybe a firecracker or two will get the party started."

"Do it," Tom ordered, his voice laced with urgency.

Derek bolted down the stone steps, his footsteps a rapid staccato against the walls. He made his way to the rear lines, where Herbert, their eccentric weapons master, was overseeing his newly constructed mortars and other makeshift artillery.

"It's time. Let the first ones fly. They're about three hundred yards out," Derek relayed the order, his breath coming fast but controlled.

Herbert's eyes sparkled with manic glee as he nodded and signaled his crew. A dozen Guild members scrambled into position, each setting up mortars along the inner perimeter of the wall. Scouts atop the walls barked out positions, relaying coordinates back to the gunners below.

Then came the unmistakable sound of mortars firing—deep, resonant thumps that echoed up and down the line. Arcs of fire streaked through the darkening sky, the shells whistling as they soared toward their targets. Seconds later, the ground erupted in a series of deafening explosions, tearing through the goblin ranks like a scythe through tall grass.

The battlefield erupted into chaos. Goblin bodies were flung into the air like ragdolls, limbs twisted at impossible angles. Huge shards of ice formed where explosive crystals had been enchanted, encasing goblins in jagged prisons of frost. Others stumbled into bubbling pools of corrosive acid, their screams cut short as their skin and flesh melted away. Thick, noxious clouds of green smoke billowed out, choking and blinding those caught within, while fiery blasts sent flaming goblins screaming in all directions.

Cheers erupted from the defenders along the wall as they watched the carnage unfold. Even Tom felt a grim sense of satisfaction watching the goblin ranks falter under the barrage. But his eyes were sharp, and he couldn't help but notice that, despite the devastation, the goblins were not breaking. If anything, they were becoming more determined, more focused.

"More rifles to the walls!" Tom shouted above the din, his voice booming over the clamor of explosions and dying goblins. "Keep firing! Take them down!"

More Guild members rushed to the walls, taking up positions beside those already firing. Their rifles barked relentlessly, cutting down goblin after goblin. But Tom's unease only deepened. There were far more goblins than he'd expected—certainly more than their scouting reports had indicated. Where had they all come from? The thought gnawed at him, but he had no time to dwell on it.

"Bobby! You ready?" Tom called out as the goblin forces continued their inexorable march toward the walls, a tide of green and black.

With a confident nod and a wicked grin, Bobby, their resident explosives expert, positioned himself by the control box near the gates. His hands hovered over a set of switches, his eyes locked on Tom.

Tom gave a slight nod. Bobby's grin widened. He slammed his fist down on one of the buttons.

A series of dull pops echoed out as the traps were triggered. Several slabs of pavement tilted and flipped, revealing pits filled with sharpened stakes. Goblins shrieked as they plummeted into the hidden deathtraps, impaled on the cruel spikes below. But the rest of the goblin horde surged on, barely pausing to look back.

Then came the real surprise.

"Now!" Tom shouted.

Bobby hit the second button, and a flurry of MCLC cords launched out from the walls, snaking through the goblin ranks like deadly serpents. Goblins tangled in the lines, clawing at the strange, foreign objects. They barely had time to realize their mistake.

A split second later, the cords exploded, setting off a cascading series of blasts that ripped through the goblin formations. The ground shook violently beneath the force of the blasts. The deafening sound was matched only by the screams of the dying. Goblins were thrown into the air, their bodies shattered by the sheer force of the explosions.

"Haha! Take that, you ugly green witch's cunt warts!" James hollered from atop the wall, pulling out his twin handguns and firing at the surviving goblins below. "You get a dickshot! You get a dickshot! Everyone gets a dickshot!"

"Great, now he thinks he's the Oprah of the apocalypse," Kevin muttered, shaking his head with a mixture of exasperation and amusement.

"Phase two! Polearms—to the walls!" Tom commanded. "Stagger every other man—polearm, gun, polearm, gun! Move it!"

In perfect synchronicity, Guild members armed with twelve-foot pikes moved into position between riflemen. The sound of metal on metal rang out as the first of the goblins attempted to scale the walls with their makeshift ladders. The pikes jabbed and pushed, sending the ladders toppling backward and the goblins tumbling into their own ranks, limbs flailing as they fell.

From the rear of the goblin horde, a massive log emerged, carried on the shoulders of a dozen of the stoutest goblins. A battering ram. It was crudely fashioned but no less effective-looking for it. The goblins hoisted it up, readying themselves to charge the gate.

"Ram! They brought a fucking ram!" Tom yelled, his voice strained but still commanding. "Get the barricades up! Now!"

Forklifts roared to life, reversing back toward the gate to lift and stack heavy cement barriers in place. Kevin and Kirsten, with their Barbarian brethren, took point, their muscles flexing in anticipation.

INVASION

"They never had this kind of technology in the Two Towers movie. Bet the Uruk-hai wouldn't have gotten through if they had," James said, moving over to where Tom was standing.

"You mean the Uruk-hai who used a bomb to blow up the walls?" Tom shot back, sparing only a brief glance at James.

"Oh, shit," James muttered, his face falling slightly.

Tom didn't reply; his eyes were locked on the chaos below. The goblins were regrouping for another push, but he could see fear starting to set in. And then came the rumble—a low, unmistakable growl that grew into a full-throated roar.

The vehicles burst from a side street, engines roaring, headlights blazing. The goblins' heads snapped up, and a wave of panic rippled through their ranks. The SUVs, trucks, and vans barreled toward them, tearing through their ranks like hot knives through butter.

"Eat shit, and choke on it!" Kedron's voice rang out as he leaned out of the window, the GS2 leading the charge. The makeshift ram shattered under the impact, and the goblins carrying it were sent flying, limbs flailing like rag dolls.

"Open the gates! Phase three, go!" Tom barked. The forklifts pulled back, clearing the entrance. Kevin and Kirsten, grinning like wolves, readied their axes and braced for the coming fight.

"Derek, you take charge. I'll see you out there," Tom shouted back, his voice barely audible over the cacophony of battle, before vaulting over the wall and plunging into the chaos below.

"Bastard's going to get killed one of these days, jumping in like that," Derek muttered, shaking his head but unable to hide the hint of admiration in his eyes.

As the gates swung wide, the goblins howled in defiance, their cries a mix of rage and desperation. But their voices were drowned out by the thunderous roars of the Barbarians, who surged forward with a fury unmatched. Kevin, leading the charge, swung his greataxes in wide, brutal arcs, cutting a swath of destruction through the goblin ranks. Heads, limbs, and entrails flew as he carved his way deeper into their formation, his roars echoing in the night.

"All forces, CHARGE!" Derek bellowed from the top of the wall, his voice carrying over the battlefield like a war drum, and the defenders surged forward, ready to drive the goblins back to the pits from which they crawled.

And with that, the true battle began.

Chapter 29

Pack Tactics

Bron rose from a swirling, black summoning circle on the ground, the inky tendrils of shadow dissipating around him. His eyes glinted with battle lust, his hulking form vibrating with barely contained energy. Ever since leveling up his *Summon Demonic Creature* spell, Tom could now cast it without needing the elaborate hand gestures and words that had been required before. This gave him a valuable edge in battle, allowing for a faster response time in chaotic situations like this one.

"You could always summon me *before* you're in the middle of a fight," Bron grumbled, his deep voice resonating like a growl from a cave as he quickly equipped his massive twin axes. He charged forward, hacking through the goblins with the precision and power of a seasoned warrior, each swing of his axes sending bodies flying or cleaving through flesh and bone like butter.

"Sorry, I got excited and jumped in," Tom replied, breathless but determined.

He leveled his hand and blasted a goblin in the face with an *Eldritch Blast*, the creature's head snapping back as it was engulfed in green flames. Pivoting smoothly, Tom sliced another goblin across the chest with his sword, the blade biting deep, spilling blackish blood across the ground.

"Besides, I've never known you to not want to smash some goblins."

Bron merely grunted in response, a feral smile tugging at his lips as he continued his rampage. His broad, muscular frame moved with surprising agility, each swing of his axes a devastating blow that left piles of twitching bodies in his wake. His tusks gleamed in the low light, his eyes wild with the thrill of combat.

Nearby, Jerky fought with a ferocity that matched his fiery abilities. He had flown down to fight alongside Tom, his fists and feet wreathed in flames that crackled and danced in the night air. Using the techniques Bron had taught him, Jerky moved with a fluid grace, his attacks a flurry of fiery strikes. The goblins recoiled from him, their instinctive fear of fire driving them back as he set them alight, one after another.

But then, in the chaos, a goblin managed to leap over the heads of its kin, spear aimed directly at Jerky's exposed side. Distracted by the enemies in front of him, Jerky didn't see it coming. The spear plunged into his side with a sickening crunch, the sharpened tip tearing through muscle and sinew. Jerky let out a sharp, guttural cry of pain, his fiery aura flickering wildly as his body spasmed. Reacting on pure instinct, Jerky swung his flaming fist around in a wide arc, catching the goblin in the head. The creature's skull crunched under the impact, its body collapsing in a smoldering heap.

"Jerky!" Tom shouted, his voice raw with concern as he fought his way through the press of goblins to reach his familiar. He could see the blood soaking through Jerky's armor, pooling beneath him. Without hesitation, he slipped his arm under Jerky's, pulling him upright and using his own body as a shield. His other hand swung his sword in vicious arcs, keeping the advancing goblins at bay.

A dark shadow suddenly loomed over the melee, blotting out what little light remained. Tom glanced up and saw Bron towering above the goblins, his massive leg drawn back. With a mighty kick, Bron sent a dozen goblins flying, their bodies crashing into each other and scattering like broken dolls.

"Heal him!" Bron bellowed, his voice like rolling thunder as he continued to carve a path through the goblin ranks. His eyes never left the enemy, his focus unyielding as he swung his axes in powerful arcs.

"Sorry, Jerky. This is gonna hurt," Tom muttered as he grabbed the spear embedded in Jerky's side. Without any further warning, he yanked it out in one swift, brutal motion.

Jerky's scream pierced the cacophony of battle, a raw, agonized sound that tore at Tom's heart. Blood flowed freely from the wound, soaking Jerky's clothes and Tom's hands. Tom quickly cast *Dark Restoration*, channeling the healing magic into his companion. The wound stopped bleeding, and the torn flesh began to knit back together. The color slowly returned to Jerky's face, and he let out a shaky breath of relief.

"Thanks, Tom," Jerky rasped, his voice weak but grateful as he gripped a weapon with renewed strength, determination burning in his eyes.

"Form up!" Bron roared, his voice cutting through the chaos. "It's the only way we can take them down! They are using *Pack Tactics*!"

"What the hell are *Pack Tactics*?" Tom asked, his breathing heavy as he adjusted his stance, still shielding Jerky.

"It's a Skill used by less intelligent creatures to gain bonuses from being near others of their kind," Bron explained, his voice steady despite the battle raging around them. "Goblins can get this when they have a war chief. It makes them stronger, faster, and more resilient than they usually are."

"Well, that's fucking great," Tom muttered, feeling a mix of frustration and determination. "Fine, time to take this up a notch."

Tom activated his *Tattoo of Brute Strength*, feeling a surge of power coursing through his veins. His muscles bulged beneath his armor, and his senses sharpened. With a growl, he pulled out his second greatsword, wielding both weapons with deadly efficiency. He charged forward, swinging the blades in wide arcs, cutting down goblins with each swing. The power flowed through him, and he felt unstoppable.

Kevin and the other Barbarians burst through the gate a moment later, their faces contorted with rage. Their skin had taken on a slightly red hue, and their eyes were wild with fury. They screamed at the goblins, a chorus of unbridled anger that sent shivers down the spines of everyone, friend and foe alike. It was as if a dam had broken, unleashing a torrent of violence upon the battlefield.

The Barbarians tore into the goblins like a pack of wolves set upon a flock of sheep. Limbs were severed, heads rolled, and bodies were torn apart as they charged into the enemy lines. The goblins, overwhelmed by the sheer ferocity of the assault, tried to scramble away, climbing over each other in a desperate bid to escape.

Following close behind, a team of Clerics provided invaluable support, their hands glowing with healing magic. Every wound the Barbarians sustained seemed to close almost as quickly as it was inflicted, their bodies mending in real time as the Clerics worked their miracles. It was a terrifying sight for the goblins—a force that could not be killed, could not be stopped. Their courage broke, and a wave of panic swept through their ranks as they began to flee in all directions.

But just as hope seemed within reach, a bone-chilling howl echoed from the east. It was deep and resonant, vibrating through the bones of every fighter on the battlefield. Moments later, Wargs and their riders appeared from around a corner, rushing toward the fray with bloodthirsty grins. Their eyes glowed with a predatory hunger, their muscles rippling beneath their mangy fur.

The frontline goblins, still in what Tom might have called a tactical retreat, paid no heed to their reinforcements and continued to run, trampling over each other in their haste to escape the death that awaited them.

The Wargs, however, had no such fear. They bounded into the battle, their riders jeering and shouting curses.

With a sudden, thunderous crash, Squirrel leapt from the top of the walls. His form expanded in mid-air, growing to the size of a bus. He landed heavily, his massive paws sending shockwaves through the ground. In one swift motion, he grabbed a Warg mid-stride, lifting it off the ground and shaking it like a rag doll before slamming it back down. The beast let out a pitiful yelp as it hit the earth, its rider thrown clear.

The sound of engines roaring to life pierced the night air, and the vehicle team, led by Jay, barreled into the fray once more.

"Special delivery, motherfuckers!" Kedron shouted from his window, his voice carrying over the chaos. The vehicles smashed into the Wargs and plowed through the ranks of goblins, creating a horrific symphony of crunching bones, screeching metal, and the dying wails of crushed goblins.

"ENOUGH!" boomed a voice that seemed to come from the very ground itself.

A massive blue goblin emerged from the rear of the goblin lines, riding atop a heavily scarred Warg that looked more beast than canine. This goblin was easily twice, maybe three times the size of a normal goblin, his muscular frame towering over his kin. His face was twisted in a mask of rage, his eyes burning with a fiery intensity. If this had been a cartoon, steam would have been pouring from his ears.

He raised a massive, muscled arm and pointed it at the forces decimating his troops. A moment later, beams of searing light shot out from the windows of a nearby building as hidden goblin spellcasters unleashed a volley of destructive magic. Explosions tore through the front lines, and goblins and Guild members alike were caught in the chaos. A wave of flames surged toward Tom, the heat scorching the air around him.

Tom instinctively threw his arms up to shield himself, but when the flames hit, he felt… nothing. Opening his eyes, he found a shimmering blue barrier in front of him, absorbing the fire like a shield of cool water. His eyes flicked up to the wall, where he saw Briana standing.

Her face was tense with concentration, her arms raised, and her fingers splayed wide as she held the barrier in place. Sweat trickled down her brow, but she didn't falter. Behind her, Bohdan appeared like a vengeful spirit, his hands weaving through the air with practiced grace. Spells flew from his palms—giant fireballs, jagged ice spikes, and luminous discs of light—each spell finding a goblin target with deadly precision.

Below, the remaining goblins roared in defiance, desperate to regain some semblance of control over the battlefield. They were no longer a cohesive force; they were an unruly mob, driven by fear and rage. Tom watched as his comrades continued to press forward, their resolve unbroken, and felt a surge of pride in his chest.

"Jerky," Tom said, turning to his companion, who was still catching his breath, "can you take out the remaining Wargs if I get you a mount?"

Jerky's face was still a bit pale, but his eyes burned with determination. He nodded, wiping the sweat from his brow. "I'm ready," he replied, his voice steady despite the pain.

Tom grinned and summoned a familiar black summoning circle on the ground behind him. The circle glowed with dark energy, and from it, Shadow emerged, his sinuous form rippling like ink in water. The Usiku roared, a sound that sent shivers down the spines of even the bravest goblins. Its tentacles writhed, ready for battle.

"Get on. Shadow will take you where you need to go," Tom instructed. "Shadow, listen to Jerky and take him wherever he needs. And feel free to kill some goblins while you're at it."

Shadow lowered itself, and Jerky climbed onto its back, steadying himself. With a powerful leap, Shadow bounded over the heads of the goblins, tentacles slapping several of them across their faces, sending them sprawling. It landed gracefully and charged toward the cluster of Wargs still on the battlefield. Jerky steadied himself and prepared a fiery attack in one hand while gripping his spear in the other, ready to finish what they had started.

Tom turned back to Bron, who was still holding the line against the waves of goblins. "I think it's time to get a little crazy. Can you cover me for a moment, Bron?" he asked, already focusing his mind on the next series of spells.

"Yes, but hurry," Bron replied, his teeth bared in a fierce grin. He spun in a wide circle, his axes creating a whirlwind of death that kept the goblins at bay. His trumpet-like war cry boomed across the battlefield, causing a momentary pause in the enemy ranks.

Tom quickly activated his *Tattoo of Inspiration*, feeling a surge of energy flow through him. A warm, red light spread from his body, radiating outward and enveloping his allies. The effect was immediate. The morale of his comrades visibly lifted, their stances straightening, their attacks becoming even more forceful. The sense of camaraderie and determination was palpable.

Next, he activated the *Tattoo of the Summoner*, and Bron's strength and agility seemed to increase. His movements became a blur of speed and precision, and each strike landed with a devastating impact. Shadow, too, seemed to move with even greater ferocity, its attacks a whirlwind of tentacles and shadowy claws.

Tom could feel his mana reserves depleting quickly. He grabbed a mana potion from his Inventory, downed it in a single gulp, and immediately felt the magical energy rushing back into his veins. The sensation was electrifying, like a jolt of adrenaline coursing through him. He activated the *Tattoo of Life Absorption*, a glowing haze appearing around him that began leeching the life from the goblins.

He wasn't done yet. He pulled two large blankets from his Inventory and threw them over clusters of goblins, quickly casting *Eldritch Blast* at each blanket. They ignited instantly, turning into blazing infernos that engulfed the goblins beneath them. Screams of agony filled the air as the flames spread, the goblins thrashing wildly in their death throes.

Tom's heart pounded in his chest, the adrenaline rushing through his veins. He pulled two grenades from his belt, yanked the pins free with his teeth, and lobbed them into the densest clusters of goblins. The concussive blasts that followed were deafening. The ground shook, and goblins were tossed like rag dolls, limbs and torsos flying through the air in a grotesque display of chaos.

"ALL FIGHTERS TO ME!" Tom bellowed, his voice booming across the battlefield like a war horn. He could feel his muscles tensing with the anticipation of what was to come.

He drained another mana potion, feeling the magical energy refill his reserves, and prepared for his next move. With a flourish, six more black summoning circles appeared around him. A Mastadonian warrior rose out of each circle. They stood shoulder to shoulder with the original Mastadonian, their expressions grim and determined.

"It worked!" Tom shouted, his eyes wide with exhilaration. "Form a wedge! We're going to charge for the back. Kill any goblins that get in your way!"

The summoned Mastadonians nodded in understanding, forming a wedge with Bron at the tip. The strategy was simple but effective—a wedge would allow them to pierce through the goblin lines like a spear through cloth, minimizing resistance and maximizing their killing power.

Tom moved to the front of the wedge, his greatsword swinging with lethal efficiency. He felt the surge of energy from his activated tattoos as he triggered his *Tattoo of Brute Strength*—his oldest and lowest costing Pact, but also the one with the shortest duration. He pushed forward, every swing carrying the force of a battering ram. He hacked and slashed through the goblins like a whirlwind of death, their bodies crumpling and breaking under his onslaught. The heat from the burning goblins, the acrid smell of blood, and the ear-splitting cries of pain and terror formed a sensory overload, but Tom remained focused.

INVASION

Behind him, the Mastadonians pushed forward, their weapons tearing apart any goblin that dared to stand in their way. They moved with a practiced grace and unity, their axes, swords, knives, and various other weapons rising and falling in perfect synchrony. The bodies of the goblins piled up around them, creating a grisly barrier that only added to the chaos of the battlefield.

Tom spotted Kiera and her team positioned on a nearby building. She and her snipers were raining down a hail of bullets, each shot finding its mark. She had a fierce look of concentration on her face, her eyes following every movement on the battlefield, making quick calculations for the next shot. Her team provided a crucial cover, picking off goblins that tried to flank the main force.

"Keep pushing! We're almost through!" Tom shouted over the roar of battle.

The Guild members, their confidence bolstered by Tom's *Tattoo of Inspiration*, pressed harder, their attacks more focused and coordinated. Spells flew from mages, ammunition streaked through the air from various Guild members, and the warriors swung their weapons with deadly precision. The wedge formation held strong, cleaving through the goblin horde like a hot knife through butter.

Within minutes, they burst through the other side of the goblin lines. Tom found himself face-to-face with the war chief, still mounted on his scarred Warg. The massive goblin's eyes narrowed, and a low growl rumbled from his throat as he saw the human who had dared to challenge him.

"Luuuuuuuuucy, I'm home! And you've got some splainin' to do!" Tom shouted with a manic grin, his adrenaline spiking as he locked eyes with the goblin war chief.

The war chief snarled, his lips curling back to reveal rows of jagged, yellowed teeth. With a guttural command, he spurred his Warg forward, charging directly at Tom. The Warg's muscles bunched and flexed beneath its matted fur as it leaped at the human with its jaws wide open.

Tom, with a quick shift of his hands, unequipped his greatswords and pulled a giant maul from his Inventory. He swung it with all his might, the massive head of the maul colliding with the Warg's skull in a sickening crunch. Bone shattered, and the creature's head twisted violently to the side, its body spinning with the force of the blow. But as the Warg went down, the war chief leaped from its back, his mace raised high.

Tom barely had time to react as the mace came down. The heavy weapon smashed into the side of his head, sending him sprawling to the ground. Stars exploded in his vision, and his ears rang with the impact. His maul slipped from his grasp, clattering to the ground.

The war chief wasted no time. Snarling in triumph, he pounced on top of Tom, his massive weight pinning him to the ground. Tom struggled, but the goblin was immensely strong. With a wicked grin, the war chief drew a jagged dagger from his belt and drove it into Tom's side, twisting it cruelly between his ribs.

Tom's scream ripped through the air as pain exploded through his body. His vision swam with agony, the world around him fading into a blur. The goblin leaned down, his breath hot and foul against Tom's face.

"It's high time we ended this little farce," the goblin growled, his voice dripping with malice. He raised his mace high above his head, ready to deliver the killing blow.

With his last reserves of strength, Tom knew he needed a miracle—or he'd be dead in seconds.

Chapter 30

For Whom the Bell Tolls

Tom stared up into the war chief's eyes, which were filled with venomous hatred and the smug assurance of a victory soon to come. The goblin's breath was foul, a rancid mix of sweat, unwashed grime, and an acrid sulfuric stench that seemed to cling to his armor and skin like a second layer. The smell was almost overwhelming, causing Tom to scrunch his nose in disgust as he looked up from his vulnerable position.

"Now you see me," Tom taunted, a hint of a sly grin curling on his lips as he winked at the massive blue goblin, whose muscles rippled under his leathery, mottled skin.

The creature let out a guttural roar, the sound resonating deep from its barrel-like chest. His muscles tensed, and the sinews in his thick arms bulged as he raised his iron-studded mace high above his head. His intentions were clear; he aimed to pulverize Tom's skull into the cracked pavement.

Just as the mace descended with the force of a sledgehammer, Tom vanished from beneath him in a flash, the goblin's blow smashing into the ground with a deafening crack. Shards of stone exploded outward from the impact, creating a web of fractures in the street.

The war chief's eyes widened in shock, his breath heaving in deep, ragged bursts as he tried to make sense of what just happened. He glanced around frantically, his brutish face contorted in confusion.

"Now you don't," Tom's voice echoed from directly behind the goblin.

Before the goblin could even turn to face him, Tom firmly planted his feet and delivered a powerful roundhouse kick to the side of the creature's head. The force of the blow sent the goblin flopping to the side, his cranium crashing hard against the already fractured pavement. The impact left him dazed, stars bursting in his vision as he blinked furiously, trying to clear his mind.

"Glad I saved that *Tattoo of Displacement*," Tom muttered to himself, feeling the magical energy fade from his skin where the tattoo lay hidden under his armor. He stepped closer to the downed war chief, quickly raising his sword and aiming the sharp edge at the creature's throat.

"Time to call off your troops, you sack of shit."

The war chief, still groggy from the impact, blinked up at Tom. Despite the situation, a sneer twisted his lips, exposing yellowed, jagged teeth.

"And what? You'll just let me go?" the goblin snarled, his voice low and contemptuous, thick with an accent that gave his words an oddly guttural twist.

Tom tilted his head, feigning consideration.

"Actually, you have a point," he said, shrugging with an air of casual indifference.

The goblin's eyes widened as realization set in.

"No, wait—!" he started, desperation creeping into his tone. But Tom's sword was already in motion, a gleaming arc descending with lethal precision.

With a desperate lunge, the war chief twisted his body to the side, thrusting his hand up to deflect the blade. His fingers met the edge of the sword, and blood sprayed as the sharp steel nearly severed them. A howl of pain ripped from his throat, and he lashed out with a powerful kick, catching Tom in the leg and sending him stumbling back a few steps. Seizing the opportunity, the goblin sprang to his feet, his face contorted with pain and fury.

"You tricky bastard," Tom growled, his chest heaving from the sudden burst of exertion as he caught his footing. His eyes were locked onto the war chief, his body tense and ready for the next move.

The goblin bared his teeth in a feral grin, his yellow eyes blazing with malice. From his Inventory, he pulled a jagged, viciously curved sword that gleamed menacingly in the fading light. The blade was chipped and scarred, but it looked well-used—like a tool that had seen countless battles and drunk the blood of many foes. He shifted into a low, aggressive stance, muscles coiling like a spring, ready to strike.

The two warriors began to circle each other, eyes locked in a deadly dance of strategy and anticipation. Tom could feel his heart pounding in his chest, his blood pumping adrenaline through his veins. Sweat trickled down his forehead, stinging his eyes, but he didn't dare blink. He knew that a single moment of hesitation could be fatal.

The goblin war chief moved first, lunging with a speed that belied his size. His blade came flashing toward Tom's midsection, aiming to gut him like a fish. Tom deflected the blow with a swift parry from his left-hand sword, the metal-on-metal collision ringing out like a bell tolling in the midst of chaos. The goblin quickly followed up with a flurry of strikes, his blade moving with a savage grace that showed he was no mere brute. Each blow was aimed to kill, each swing carrying the intent to spill blood.

Tom was forced to fight defensively, blocking and parrying with both swords as he sought an opening. The goblin's attacks were relentless, a whirlwind of steel that seemed to come from all directions at once. The sound of clashing metal rang out repeatedly, like the hammering of a blacksmith on an anvil, echoing across the battlefield.

Tom's muscles burned with exertion, and he could feel his strength waning. His breathing became labored, each breath a ragged gasp for air. The war chief, too, was tiring, his swings becoming less precise and more desperate. Finally, Tom saw an opening. With a quick sidestep, he avoided a downward slash and countered with a powerful thrust aimed at the goblin's chest.

The goblin barely managed to twist away, the blade grazing his side and drawing a line of blood. But the war chief was not without his own tricks. As he dodged, he brought his own blade up in a sharp, brutal arc, slicing deep into the back of Tom's left arm. Pain exploded in Tom's shoulder, and his arm fell limp, nearly severed by the vicious attack. He gritted his teeth against the agony, quickly casting *Dark Restoration* to heal the wound. Flesh knitted back together in seconds, his strength instantly returning.

Seeing Tom recover almost immediately, the war chief let out a guttural curse and muttered a spell of his own. His wounds began to close, though not as rapidly or completely. Sweat poured down his face, and his breathing was ragged, but his eyes never left Tom.

The two combatants paused, circling each other like wolves sizing up their prey. The rest of the battle raged around them—a cacophony of screams, roars, and the clash of weapons. Tom glanced around, seeing his Guildmates holding strong, but he knew they couldn't keep this up forever.

"Look," Tom said, his voice cutting through the chaos. "We can do this all day, but your forces are losing. Just look around."

The war chief's yellow eyes darted back and forth, taking in the scene around them. The goblins were being slaughtered, their ranks breaking apart in panic and confusion. He could see it—the battle was lost.

"So, what do you propose?" the goblin growled, his voice filled with grudging respect.

Tom kept his gaze steady, his tone calm but firm. "This is a foregone conclusion. You thought you could rally and take this area, but we've been here longer, and we'll still be here after you're gone."

A flicker of emotion passed over the goblin's face—anger, frustration, and perhaps a sliver of fear. "You don't understand," he spat. "We exist at the whim of the System. Our lives are toys, to be played with and discarded. You know nothing of what we endure."

Tom felt a momentary pang of empathy but quickly pushed it aside. "Maybe not," he replied, his voice hardening. "But that doesn't give you the right to take from those who have fought just as hard to survive. We all lost everything when the System took over. We fight every day in a world we barely recognize. So don't talk to me about suffering."

"Then you should know," the war chief hissed, "that survival of the strongest is all that matters."

Tom's eyes narrowed. "Oh, I know," he said, his grip tightening on his sword. "And because of that, I can't let you leave."

The goblin's brow furrowed. "What are you talking about?"

"Take two steps to the right," Tom suggested, his tone almost casual.

The war chief's eyes filled with suspicion. "Why would I—"

"Fine," Tom interrupted, taking two steps to the left.

Before the goblin could respond, a sharp crack echoed through the battlefield. The war chief's head snapped back, a bullet hole appearing in his forehead. His eyes went wide with shock, his expression frozen in disbelief as his body began to tilt.

Stabbing his sword into the ground at an angle, Tom swept the goblin's feet out from under him. The war chief's body fell sideways, his neck landing on the blade and cleanly severing his head from his shoulders. The severed head rolled away, eyes still locked in a stunned expression.

"Thanks, Kiera," Tom whispered, knowing she had taken the perfect shot from her vantage point.

With the war chief dead, the goblin army's resolve shattered like glass dropped from a great height. The change was immediate and visceral; fear rippled through their ranks like a physical force. Tom could see the panic spreading as goblins stumbled over one another in their desperate attempts to flee. Without the oppressive presence of their leader commanding them, their will to fight evaporated, replaced by a primal urge to survive.

Chaos erupted among the goblins, their once-organized ranks devolving into utter disarray. Some dropped their weapons and ran, their eyes wide with terror, while others stood frozen, paralyzed by the sudden shift in power dynamics. The sounds of battle—the clash of metal, the cries of the wounded, and the war shouts of the Vanguard fighters—filled the air, but now they were accompanied by the frantic screams of the retreating goblins.

The sight filled Tom with a grim sense of satisfaction. "They're breaking!" he shouted to his Guildmates, his voice rising above the din of battle. "Press the advantage! Don't let them regroup!"

Forming a tight phalanx around him, the Mastadonians charged forward with renewed fury. Their massive forms barreled through the retreating goblins, trampling them underfoot or sending them flying with powerful sweeps of their weapons. The ground shook with every heavy step, and the air was filled with the sickening crunch of bones breaking beneath their weight. Bron, leading the charge, was a force of nature—his enormous tusks gleaming in the moonlight as he killed any goblin foolish enough to stand in his way.

Jay appeared beside Tom once more, his movements fluid and almost ghost-like as he dispatched goblins with quick, efficient strikes of his daggers. "The goblins are in full retreat," he reported, wiping blackish blood from his blades. "We're sweeping the streets to catch any stragglers. No sense in letting any of these little shits make it back to wherever they came from."

Tom nodded, his breath coming in heavy pants. "Good. Stay close. We don't need to get reckless in a chase that could turn the tables."

Jay grinned, the predatory look in his eyes reflecting his satisfaction. "Understood. I'll relay the orders to the others."

As Jay vanished back into the chaos, Tom turned his attention to the fleeing goblins. He watched them scatter like frightened rats, darting through alleyways and ducking into abandoned buildings, desperate to escape the slaughter. For a moment, he considered letting them go—letting them live to spread the tale of Vanguard's might. But then he thought of the lives they'd taken, the destruction they'd wrought, and the threat they still posed. No, there could be no mercy today.

He spotted a cluster of goblins trying to regroup in a narrow alley. Raising his hand, Tom called forth his power, his veins thrumming with dark energy. Eldritch fire crackled along his fingertips, and with a flick of his wrist, he sent two blasts searing down the alley. The explosions rocked the walls of the buildings, and the goblins' shrieks were drowned out by the roaring flames.

Just then, Jerky reappeared, riding atop Shadow, his massive Usiku companion. The two made for an imposing sight—Jerky's fists still glowing with residual flames and Shadow's tentacles writhing in the air, snatching up goblins and flinging them aside like rag dolls.

"Did you have fun?" Tom asked with a tired but genuine smile, watching as Shadow snapped up a goblin in its maw and crunched down with a sickening crunch.

Jerky grinned, his face streaked with soot and blood. "Definitely need to team up with Shadow more often," he replied, reaching down to pat the Usiku's side. "He's an amazing companion."

Shadow purred loudly, a deep rumble that vibrated the very air around them, clearly enjoying the praise. Tom's smile widened. Despite the carnage surrounding them, seeing the bond between his familiar and the summoned creature warmed his heart.

"I'm glad to hear it," Tom said, his eyes scanning the battlefield. "We need all the friends we can get in this world."

For the next hour, the Guild members continued their hunt, tracking down any fleeing goblins. Jay's team was instrumental in this effort; they moved like shadows through the streets, stalking their prey with deadly efficiency. Whenever a goblin thought it had escaped, one of Jay's men would appear from the darkness, blades flashing, ending the creature's hopes of survival in a heartbeat.

By the time the Guild had regrouped back behind their fortified walls, the sun had dipped below the horizon, leaving the sky alight with the stars, twinkling like diamonds in a sea of black. The gates closed with a resounding thud, and the battlefield outside was eerily quiet save for the distant crackling of fires still burning where spells and explosives had detonated.

Tom stood on the parapets, surveying the aftermath. Bodies of goblins lay strewn across the streets, mixed with the remnants of buildings and debris from the chaos of battle. The acrid scent of smoke and blood hung thick in the air, a bitter reminder of the cost of victory.

In total, the Guild had wiped out at least ninety percent of the invading force, but it had come at a price. Twelve of their own lay dead, their bodies already being carried off to be prepared for their final rites. Tom felt the weight of those losses settle heavily on his shoulders, pressing down like a lead weight. He knew each of their faces, their names, their stories. They had fought bravely, and their sacrifice had bought the Guild another day of survival—but the cost still stung deeply.

The rest of the Guild, however, seemed to be in high spirits. They had beaten back a formidable enemy and defended their home against overwhelming odds. Derek, ever the pragmatic leader, had already begun the debriefing process, collecting statements from everyone involved in the battle.

When they convened later in the conference room, Derek reported, "Everything seems to have gone according to plan. Our defenses held, and the traps worked better than expected."

Tom nodded, though his expression remained somber. "So why do I feel like this wasn't as successful as we would have liked?"

"Because you expect every encounter to end with a one hundred percent survival rate," Derek replied bluntly. "That's not realistic. No plan survives first contact with the enemy, and you know that."

Tom sighed, rubbing a hand over his tired face. "Isn't there anything we could have done differently?"

"I'm gonna pretend you're asking that because you want us to learn from every encounter, and not because you want to feed the demons in your head," Derek said, leaning back in his chair. "And yes, we could always improve our group tactics, train harder, work on communication. But given the circumstances? We did damn well."

"The goblins had some sort of non-verbal communication with their leader," Brian added, his brow furrowed in thought. "He could direct them to counter our movements, but Kiera had a perfect vantage point. We were able to follow her directions and stay ahead of their strategies."

Tom remained silent, lost in his thoughts. The room fell quiet for a moment until James, leaning back in his chair, broke the silence with his characteristic bluntness.

"You're being a jackass, Tom," James said, not even looking at him.

Tom's head snapped up, surprised. "What?"

"You keep expecting everyone to survive," James continued. "You're acting like a pouting child. You need to stand up and lead these people. They follow you because you care, but they'll see you as weak if you keep pretending you can save everyone."

"As much as I hate to admit it, James is right," Derek added. "You've got to see the bigger picture. Remember, you're one of the few who can."

Tom sighed deeply, his shoulders slumping. "I just... I wanted to protect them."

"And you did," Derek said firmly. "You led them into battle, and the vast majority of them came back. That's more than many can say."

Tom nodded slowly, absorbing their words. "So, what's next?"

"Memorials for our fallen," Derek replied. "And we keep preparing for the invasion. Herbert's been working on those new weapons. We'll need to see what he's cooked up."

"Good," Tom said, his resolve hardening. "I want everyone training on tactics. We need to be ready for whatever comes next. Those pirates won't hold back, and neither should we."

"Agreed," Brian said, nodding. "We'll keep up the preparations."

With the meeting adjourned, Tom headed back to his room. He felt exhausted, not just physically but mentally and emotionally. After a hot shower to wash off the grime of battle, he lay on his bed, staring up at the ceiling, lost in thought.

Jerky, sensing his master's turmoil, sat down beside him. "What's on your mind, Tom?"

Tom turned to look at his familiar, the tension in his face softening slightly. "Just... trying to figure out how to feel about everything. I keep thinking I should be able to protect everyone, but I know that's impossible."

INVASION

Jerky gave a thoughtful nod. "Life and death are two sides of the same coin. Isn't it good that they died protecting something they value? Better than screaming in fear or having no control over their fate."

"You want to die that way, don't you?" Tom asked quietly.

Jerky smiled, his eyes twinkling. "If I must die, I want it to be for a purpose. To save someone or in a battle of my choosing. It's an honorable death. We all must die eventually. Why not for a cause we believe in?"

Tom stared at Jerky for a moment, his eyes softening as he absorbed the wisdom of his familiar's words. "You're right," he said finally, his voice tinged with a weary acceptance. "I've been thinking too much like the person I was before all this. We're not living in that world anymore."

Jerky nodded, his expression one of understanding. "Exactly. In this world, every day is a battle. It's not about who survives each one; it's about what we do with the time we're given."

Tom let out a long breath, feeling some of the tension ease from his muscles. He knew Jerky was right. The weight of leadership had forced him to see things differently, to accept the harsh realities of their new existence. He couldn't save everyone, but he could lead them to a better future, one victory at a time. And that was enough.

"Thanks, Jerky," he said, reaching out to pat the familiar on the back. "I needed to hear that."

Jerky smiled, his ears twitching slightly. "Always here for you, Tom. Now, get some rest. You've got a big day tomorrow."

Tom chuckled softly, his eyes closing as he sank back into his pillow. "Yeah… another big day in the apocalypse."

The next morning, Tom awoke early, the first rays of dawn spilling through the cracks in the heavy drapes covering his window. The room was dim, but he could make out the shape of Jerky lying in bed next to him, still fast asleep. The sight brought a small smile to Tom's face. Despite everything, his companions had a way of making even the darkest days seem a little brighter.

After a quick shower and changing into his gear, Tom made his way to the cafeteria. The hall was already bustling with activity—people chatting over breakfast, cleaning their weapons, and preparing for another day in their fight for survival. The atmosphere was somber, but there was an undercurrent of determination that rippled through the room. They had fought hard, and though they had lost some of their own, they had also dealt a significant blow to their enemies.

Tom grabbed a plate of food and found a seat at one of the long communal tables. As he ate, he watched the others around him—some laughing and joking, others speaking in hushed, serious tones. He noticed Briana sitting at a nearby table, her eyes closed and her lips moving silently as if in prayer. Her hands were clasped around the amulet that hung from her neck, and a soft, soothing energy seemed to radiate from her. He knew she was grieving for those they had lost, just as they all were.

A few moments later, Derek approached and slid into the seat across from him. He looked tired, dark circles under his eyes, but there was a glint of determination there as well.

"Morning," Tom greeted him, taking another bite of his breakfast.

"Morning," Derek replied, leaning his forearms on the table. "How're you holding up?"

Tom chewed thoughtfully before answering. "Better than last night. I've come to terms with it. Losses are part of the deal now. We can't save everyone, but we can keep moving forward."

Derek nodded, a hint of a smile touching his lips. "Glad to hear it. We've got a lot to do today. Herbert wants to show us the new weapons he's been working on, and Bron wants to discuss some more advanced combat tactics."

"Sounds good," Tom said, his mood lifting slightly at the thought of getting back to work. "I want to make sure we're prepared for those pirates when they show up. No more surprises like yesterday."

"Agreed," Derek replied. "We'll need to refine our strategy, and we're going to need every edge we can get. Herbert's new toys might give us just that."

As they finished their meal, they were joined by Kiera, who looked as determined as ever. She nodded at Tom and Derek as she sat down, her expression serious.

"I heard about what happened with the war chief," she said, her eyes locking onto Tom's. "Good call on getting him to move. Gave me the perfect shot."

Tom smiled, and with his voice tinged with pride he said, "You're the one who pulled it off. Perfect timing, as always."

Kiera shrugged, though there was a glimmer of satisfaction in her eyes. "I just did what needed to be done."

"That's all any of us can do," Derek added, raising his cup of coffee in a mock toast.

After breakfast, they headed down to the Guild's training grounds, where Herbert was already waiting, surrounded by a small group of Enchanters and Engineers. His wild hair stuck out in every direction, and his eyes were alight with excitement.

"Ah, there you are!" Herbert called out as he saw them approaching. "I've got some good news. We've made significant progress with the new weapons. If you're ready, I'd like to show you what we've cooked up."

Tom nodded, his curiosity piqued. "Lead the way, Herbert. Let's see what you've got."

Herbert grinned widely, practically vibrating with enthusiasm. "Oh, you're going to love this. We've been working on integrating magical enchantments with conventional weaponry—think spell-infused explosives, mana-powered turrets, that sort of thing."

INVASION

He led them over to a large open area where several strange-looking devices were set up. One was a massive, turret-like contraption with glowing runes etched into its metal plating. Another looked like a grenade launcher, but it had an odd crystalline chamber attached to its side that pulsed with a faint blue light.

Herbert patted the turret with pride. "This bad boy here is what I call the Arcane Obliterator. At its center lies a mana core, which powers the enchantments we've placed on the ammunition. Each shot it fires has a different effect—fire, ice, electricity, even poison, depending on how you load it."

He moved over to the grenade launcher, picking it up with both hands. "And this here is the Elemental Blaster. It's designed to launch explosive rounds infused with elemental spells. Great for crowd control or taking down particularly tough targets."

Tom examined the weapons with keen interest, his mind already racing with possibilities. "These could definitely give us an edge in a fight. How soon can we get them into production?"

Herbert's grin widened. "We've already got several prototypes ready for field testing. If you're willing to give them a try, we could get them into action as soon as tomorrow."

Tom nodded. "Good. We'll set up some drills to see how they perform. If they're as effective as they look, we'll need to train the squads on how to use them properly."

As they continued discussing the new weaponry, Tom remembered he needed to summon Bron. With a thought, the summoning circle appeared on the ground and Bron rose from the dark void. His eyes were sharp and serious, a stark contrast to his usual gruff demeanor.

Without preamble, Bron said in his deep voice, which rumbled like distant thunder, "We need to talk strategy, the pirates will be a different kind of enemy. They'll have ships, advanced weapons, and likely some surprises of their own. We need to be ready for anything."

Tom nodded, understanding the gravity of the situation. "Agreed. We've been training hard, but we need to make sure we're not caught off guard. What do you suggest?"

Bron crossed his arms over his broad chest, his expression thoughtful. "We need to diversify our tactics—hit-and-run maneuvers, ambush strategies, anything that keeps our opponents off balance. And we need to be ready to adapt. The pirates won't fight like goblins or other monsters. They'll have their own strategies, and we need to be prepared to counter them."

The day stretched on as they continued to plan and prepare. There was no time to waste; they all knew that every moment counted in this new world where every battle could be their last. As the sun dipped low on the horizon once more, painting the sky with hues of orange and red, Tom felt a renewed sense of purpose.

He couldn't protect everyone, but he could lead them. And as long as there was breath in his body, he would fight to make sure they had a future worth fighting for.

And so, as night fell and the Guild settled into a restless calm, Tom knew that the real battle had only just begun.

Chapter 31

Murder, He Wrote

The transmission flickered to life, a haze of static before settling into a low, warbling hum.

"We need to talk," the Space Pirate said, his tone sharp.

The Admin leaned back in his unseen chair, exhaling sharply. "Then talk. But if this is about Dallas again—"

"It is," the Pirate cut in. "Because it's the only part of this operation that's falling apart."

There was a lengthy pause.

The Admin tapped his fingers against his desk, the sound subtly distorted through the transmission. "Every other Guild is falling into place. The infiltration worked in Moscow, in Berlin, in São Paulo. Even London's resistance is crumbling faster than projected. The footholds are secure."

"Except Dallas."

Another pause.

"And tell me"—the Admin's voice turned cold—"whose fault is that?"

The Pirate's muscles bulged, though the Admin couldn't see it.

"Me?" the Pirate scoffed. "Your man was supposed to be our way in. A direct line to the city's inner workings. Instead, he's dead, and the entire Dallas sector is resisting harder than anyone expected."

The Admin's breath came out slow, controlled. "And I suppose I'm the one who let him die?"

The Pirate let the silence stretch just long enough to make the answer clear.

The Admin's voice hardened. "He failed. He was reckless. That's not on me."

"Then why didn't you put a failsafe in place?" the Pirate shot back. "You've got your little position of power, all your rules and red tape—where was your backup plan?"

A flicker of static cut through the connection before the Admin responded, "The plan wasn't *supposed* to need a backup. That's the point of a plan."

The Pirate chuckled, low and humorless. "I bet that excuse will go over well when *he* asks for a status update."

That finally got a reaction.

The Admin's breath hitched—it was a slight thing, but noticeable.

INVASION

"You think I don't know what failure means?" The Admin snapped. "You think I don't understand what's at stake?"

The Pirate leaned forward, voice dropping to a dangerous calm. "Then act like it."

The Admin exhaled then shifted gears. "We still have options. Adjustments can be made. The Dallas situation is a setback, not a collapse."

"Setbacks are dangerous."

"Setbacks are simply that," the Admin disagreed. "They can be corrected."

Silence stretched between them for a long moment.

Then, finally, the Admin spoke again. "We can arrange another move. This time, we don't rely on outside factors. We control every piece ourselves."

The Pirate nodded to himself. "A direct approach?"

"A *surgical* approach."

"And who's the target?"

A pause.

The Admin replied, his voice unreadable. "You already know."

The Pirate let out a breath, then grinned. "I like it."

"I'll get it done."

The transmission cut, leaving behind nothing but dead air.

Another two weeks passed in the blink of an eye. Training ramped up after the memorial for the Guild members who had fallen in the goblin battle. Everyone seemed to put their entire being into making sure they were better than they were before. Sweat and determination fueled their efforts as they pushed themselves to the brink, unwilling to let the loss of their comrades be in vain.

Team leaders were using their Skills or Professions to learn new abilities that helped in breakthroughs throughout the Guild. The atmosphere around the compound was a blend of exhaustion and grim resolve. Farms were growing faster than anyone could have imagined; the crops seemed to respond to the collective willpower of the Guild members, as if nature itself had aligned with their desires for survival. Livestock began to reproduce at an unnatural pace, perhaps a side effect of the mana that now flowed freely through the world, and the Engineering team was making progress on new weapons, as well as what Harold called "Quality of Life" inventions. These devices, ranging from magically powered water filtration systems to self-heating cookware, made living in the new world more bearable, sparking small moments of joy and relief in the midst of chaos.

Tom had spent time getting to know the new Mastadonian members of the group he was calling "Mastodon," after a band he used to listen to. The team consisted of Bron, who Tom found out was a fighter; Inari the Ranger, a lithe and nimble figure with a sharp gaze; Huthu the Barbarian, a hulking presence whose roars could shake the courage of even the bravest foes; Onslo the Warrior, a stoic fighter with a calm demeanor; Belik the Wizard, a robed figure whose eyes held the knowledge of countless spells; Amath the Cleric, a serene and comforting presence who seemed to radiate healing energy; and Kuthir the Rogue, a shadowy figure who rarely spoke but whose eyes missed nothing.

Seeing the benefit of each being able to train different Classes, Tom put them to work wherever he could. Each of them brought a unique flair to their craft. Some were resistant to helping at first, their expressions wary and their postures tense, but after a "chat" with Bron—a conversation punctuated by the sound of knuckles cracking and the subtle menace in Bron's voice—they agreed to help teach what they could. They taught the Guild members everything from advanced combat techniques to survival skills that would be critical in the wilderness beyond their walls.

One day, during a training session with the Mastodon team, Tom approached Bron with a question that had been nagging at him for a while.

"Is there a way to have you all stay permanently instead of having to summon you each once an hour? It's a little taxing on my mana," Tom asked, wiping sweat from his brow as he watched Bron deftly parry a training sword with one of his axes.

"I wouldn't know," Bron replied, his voice a deep rumble. "I'm not a Warlock. You would need to speak with your Patron to answer that question." He delivered a heavy swing that sent his sparring partner stumbling back. "I wish I could tell you, but I've never heard of such a thing."

"That's not a terrible idea," Tom mused, thinking of his connection with his Patron. "Azroc did say I could call on him if I needed help. Alright, I'll be back. I need to go do something."

Leaving Team Mastodon to their work, Tom headed to his room. He'd been working on making a permanent circle to summon Azroc with on his floor. The lines of the circle were intricately carved, filled with arcane symbols that pulsed faintly with a reddish glow. Putting the final touches on it, he took a deep breath and activated the circle by chanting the summoning phrase. The runes lit up as they always did, casting eerie shadows on the walls. But instead of Azroc rising from the floor like a demonic jack-in-the-box, a mist appeared and swirled in the air above the summoning circle. The mist roiled around until it began to light up and coalesce into an image of Azroc's eye.

"Hello? Is this thing on? Fucking magic mists. They never did get this shit right. Can you hear me?" Azroc's voice boomed, filled with a mixture of irritation and humor, as his eye swiveled around, trying to find Tom.

"Azroc! It's good to see you," Tom said with a smirk, though a hint of confusion colored his voice. "But why didn't you come in person like you normally do?"

"Sorry, shithead, I'm totally swamped," Azroc grumbled, the mist shifting to reveal his full face. His eyes glinted with both malice and mischief. "But I would never leave my favorite Warlock hanging. You don't appear to have completed any quests. What can I do for you?"

"I'm wondering if you know of a way to make Summons permanent? Continuing to summon them once an hour for what I need is really inconvenient and takes a lot of mana," Tom explained, trying to keep his tone casual. "Is there anything I can do?"

Azroc's expression shifted to one of mild amusement. "Found some familiars you like, did you? Well, you're in luck! It is possible, though not always something Warlocks want to do because of the cost."

Tom's interest piqued, but he also felt a thread of dread tightening in his stomach. "What cost?"

"A blood sacrifice and five percent of your mana to sustain them," Azroc replied nonchalantly, as if discussing the weather.

"I have to kill something and sacrifice it?!" Tom exclaimed, feeling the blood drain from his face.

"No, *your* blood, you pea-brained dolt. That's not even the part most Warlocks balk at. You really are something else," Azroc mused, shaking his head.

"So, I cut myself and then spend thirty-five percent of my mana, and they stay here?" Tom clarified, his mind racing as he weighed the potential benefits and drawbacks.

"Not spend it, *sacrifice* it," Azroc corrected, his tone more serious now. "The ceremony will hold the power in reserve until you dismiss them, so you won't be able to use it."

"That's the catch," Tom muttered, realization dawning on him.

"Yes, that's the part most Warlocks aren't willing to pay for," Azroc confirmed. "Or if they do, it's for one familiar, not seven."

Tom was silent for a moment, considering his options. "I'm going to have to think about it. Do I need to do anything else special?"

"Tell you what," Azroc said, leaning closer, his eyes narrowing in a conspiratorial manner. "I'll get you the info on how, and then you can decide if you want to do it or not. This is part of the spell anyway, so I'm not cheating by giving it to you."

With a flourish, Azroc made a gesture with his hand. Suddenly, Tom was hit by a blinding pain in his head that lasted about five excruciating seconds. When it faded, he found himself gasping for breath, but the knowledge of how to perform the ritual was now clearly etched in his mind.

"I'm never going to get used to learning something instantly like that," Tom said, still rubbing his temples from the lingering ache.

"Sucks, doesn't it? Not even sure how that Bob guy survived his System baptism. That's a man with hidden depths, there. But regardless, there's always a price to pay for everything worth having," Azroc chuckled.

Just then, TJ's voice crackled over the PA system, sounding tense. "Tom to the security office immediately. I repeat, Guild leader, Tom, to the security office immediately."

"Thanks, Azroc, I gotta take this. But we should chat again soon," Tom said, already moving to leave the room.

"It's always good to see you, shithead. Call anytime," Azroc replied with a grin before the mist swirled again and dissipated.

Arriving at the security office, Tom found a tense atmosphere waiting for him. Brian, Derek, Jay, Sean, TJ, Chris, and Isaac were all present. Most had their arms crossed, their faces grim and serious. The air was thick with unspoken concern.

"Who died?" Maria asked in Tom's head, her voice dripping with sarcasm.

"That's not funny; it could have happened," Tom muttered back.

"What?" Derek asked, noticing Tom talking to himself.

"Maria. She asked who died," Tom chuckled awkwardly, trying to lighten the mood. "Probably from all your dour expressions."

But there was no laughter. Brian's face was set in a grim line. "His name was Jared Hawthorn. He was one of the scavengers. Found him out back in the garbage that was about to be incinerated," he said, his voice heavy with the weight of the news. "He was murdered."

Tom's heart sank. "What the fuck? How can we be sure he wasn't killed by a monster or someone else?"

"He was in pieces," Derek said quietly, still not meeting Tom's eyes. "Cut up after being killed. Rebecca already looked over the body."

Tom felt a chill run down his spine. "Can we hear what she has to say?"

"She should be on her way. Won't have to wait long. James went to get her," TJ said, his voice tense.

Moments later, Rebecca entered the room, flanked by James and Squirrel. Her expression was steely, her gaze unwavering. "The body was definitely cut up post-mortem," she began, her voice clinical. "There isn't much bleeding from the pieces, meaning the heart wasn't pumping. I found knife wounds on the torso, showing he was stabbed thirty-eight times with a knife.

"Both sides of the blade were sharp. The wound showed a narrowing at both tips rather than just one as we'd see with a hunting knife."

"So, you want us to look at everyone's daggers to find the double-sided ones in a time when monsters and people alike are out for our blood and can buy weapons from vending machines?" Tom asked, his frustration bubbling to the surface.

James, ever the joker, couldn't resist. "This is going to be the best murder mystery party ever," he declared with a grin.

Tom shot him a glare. "Someone is dead, possibly killed by a Guild member, and you think this is a party?"

"Always trying to look on the bright side." James shrugged, sinking into a chair. "I watched a lot of Law and Order. I'm ready to help whenever you need me."

"I still don't see how we can prove who did this," Tom said, shaking his head.

"If you can find the weapon, I can find how it happened. There's always evidence left. Even if you think you erased it, something remains," Rebecca said firmly.

"I've got it!" James suddenly declared.

Everyone turned to him, shocked.

"It was Colonel Mustard in the billiard room with the knife!"

Tom breathed in slowly and let it out even more slowly.

"And you put up with this crap?" Maria quipped in Tom's mind. "I'm sorry, you're more of a saint than I realized."

"He's my friend," Tom muttered, trying to stay focused.

"What?" James asked, looking confused.

"You don't want to know," Tom said, waving him off.

"How do we handle this?" TJ asked, cutting through the banter.

"We play it close to the vest. We can't have panic spreading that there is some kind of murderer running around," Derek said. "They could have had a good reason. We might want to let it go."

"No," Tom said firmly. "We need to figure out what happened. It won't stay quiet forever, so we need to show we are not going to tolerate this kind of behavior. Not without an explanation."

Rebecca nodded, agreeing. "Whoever did this is a novice. They had no experience in dismembering a body as they just chopped it up at the joints, and they butchered it at that. I would guess you can rule out the kitchen staff, at least. Whoever did this has never even properly cut a steak."

"Is there anything on their tox screens?" James asked.

Rebecca shot him a look. "What? I don't have any of the equipment to test for that here. In case you missed it, the world almost ended, and we're still rebuilding. Not to mention the fact that it could be some new form of poisoning or debuff from magic that we never even had equipment to test for. I'm lucky to have a microscope right now."

Tom took a deep breath. "What do we know about the man who was killed?"

Brian answered, "His name is Jared Hawthorn. He was single, with no family ties to speak of. Since he worked with the scavenging team, he was out in the field looking for useful items most days. He was part of a team; we don't let anyone go out alone. We can speak with them to see what they know about him."

"Good. That's the path we need to take," Tom said. "We need to know what might have happened and see if we can find out what's going on before we go accusing anyone of anything. But be discreet. We need to keep things calm."

"I have another idea as well," Derek added, a thoughtful look on his face.

"What is it?" Tom asked, hopeful for any lead.

"Have Bohdan come here. I need to ask him something. I bet he can help with this," Derek replied.

TJ moved to the PA system. "I'll call him now."

As they waited for Bohdan to arrive, Tom's mind kept circling back to the same question: who among them could do something like this?

He didn't have an answer, but he was determined to find out.

Chapter 32

Investigation

"You called for me?" Bohdan asked as he entered the security office, his thick Ukrainian accent coloring his words. He was a tall, imposing figure with a stern face, and his robes gave off a faint glow from the magical runes etched into them.

"We need your help with a bit of a sensitive matter," Derek began, his expression serious. "So, we need you to keep this to yourself for the time being." His voice was low, almost conspiratorial, emphasizing the gravity of the situation.

Bohdan nodded, his eyes narrowing slightly. "Sure, I will try to help. Please, explain," he agreed, his voice steady and calm despite the tension in the room.

"A body turned up in the trash going to the incinerator, and we need some help with the investigative process," Tom explained, his tone somber. He watched Bohdan's face closely for any reaction.

Bohdan's eyes widened slightly, but he maintained his composure. "I'm not a detective, but I will try. What do you need me to do?" he asked, his accent becoming more pronounced as he processed the information.

"Do you have any spells that might help with communicating with the dead? We've seen it done in games, but not sure it correlates to this world. Or anything that might help us see what happened?" Derek asked, leaning forward slightly as he spoke. The room seemed to hold its breath, waiting for Bohdan's answer.

Bohdan scratched his chin thoughtfully, his brow furrowing. "I think there is a spell for that. I do not currently have it, but I can check the vending machine to see if it is available," he offered, his eyes flicking from Derek to Tom. "Another other option would be *Detect Magic* to see if that was the cause of death too, or was involved. I have this spell. It's very handy for magic traps." His voice was practical, and it was clear he was already considering the possible applications.

Tom nodded, a glimmer of hope in his eyes. "Great! Please go see if you can acquire that spell. We'll start our investigation as well," he said, turning to Brian. "Brian, where is the scavenger team that Jared was a part of?"

Brian, who had been standing quietly, his arms crossed, replied, "They're out in the field right now. They should return in the next couple of hours. We can talk to them when they return."

INVASION

His tone was matter-of-fact, but there was an undercurrent of urgency.

"Okay, for now, show me where the body was found. Maybe there are some clues. We didn't incinerate everything else, did we?" Tom asked, his mind racing with possibilities.

"No, we shut it down until we could figure out what to do," Brian replied, his voice calm but his eyes showing the strain of the situation.

"Perfect, lead the way," Tom said, gesturing for Brian to go ahead.

Heading first out of the security office, Brian led the group—minus Bohdan, who split off to check the vending machine for spells—out the front door of the building. The group moved with purpose, their footsteps echoing off the concrete walls of the Trammel Crow Center. The sun was beginning its descent, casting long shadows across the courtyard and adding a sense of foreboding to their task. Walking around the side of the building to the area behind it, they came upon a mountain of trash piled next to a structure that looked like a giant pizza oven. The air was thick with the smell of refuse and decay, and a single guard stood watch over the garbage to ensure that it was not interfered with. He nodded to them as they approached, a grim look on his face.

"This is the pile it was found in," Brian said, his voice steady but tinged with a hint of disgust. "We have a mage specializing in fire magic who helps with the disposal of the waste to keep sanitation standards in the Guild. Ash is far easier to get rid of than this junk, and since we don't have a dump to send it to, this was the simplest solution." He stepped aside to let the others take a closer look.

Tom surveyed the pile, his nose wrinkling at the pungent odor.

"What about things that won't melt?" he asked, his gaze moving over the trash heap, looking for anything out of place.

"With the fire used, there isn't much of that. Most of it would be metal, and we don't consider that waste. It's recycled by Roland for use in building things for the Guild," Brian replied, crossing his arms and watching Tom carefully.

"You all think of everything," Tom said in amazement, genuinely impressed by the level of organization.

Brian gave a small, tired smile. "No, I hear about everything and then have to figure out how to fix it. This was just one of those decisions that didn't require your input. The solution was simple, so we implemented it," he said, bowing his head slightly at the praise but clearly still weighed down by the gravity of the situation.

Tom looked around at the garbage piled up, and a feeling of dread came over him. The pile was a daunting mess of discarded items, rotting food, and broken bits of metal and glass.

"This is going to take forever," he muttered under his breath. "I guess we should get started."

Rebecca, who had been silently observing, finally spoke up.

"I have to get back to my patients. Let me know if you find anything, and I'll look at the evidence," she said, giving a small smile before turning to head back to the building.

Jay slapped a shovel into James' arms. "Time to get digging."

The shovel simply slid down James' new tweed suit before smacking against the ground. James glanced down at the implement with obvious disdain.

Stepping forward, he brushed Jay to the side, tugging his deerstalker cap into a jaunty angle and spoke as he did so.

"It seems to me that a careful examination of the room and the ground might possibly reveal some traces of this mysterious individual." He glanced almost scoldingly toward Tom. "You know my methods, Watson. There is not one of them which I did not apply to this current inquiry. And it has ended by my discovering traces, but very different ones from those which I had expected. Allow me to direct your attention to this plot of land." He gestured at a plain section of trash. "Tell me. What do you see?"

Tom glared, not seeing anything. "Trash? What's your point?"

James took in a deep breath, seeming to ignore the fumes from the garbage. "It is my belief, Watson, founded upon my experience, that the lowest and vilest alleys in London do not present a more dreadful record of sin than does the smiling and beautiful countryside."

"…We're in the middle of Dallas," Tom said.

"Alas," James said sadly, "a greater truth was never spoken, dear Watson." He spoke as if Tom had passed on some form of great wisdom and gestured around himself. "London, this great cesspool into which all the loungers and idlers of the empire are irresistibly drained." He shook his head in morose melancholy. "In truth, the pressure of public opinion can do in the town what the law cannot accomplish. There is no lane so vile that the scream of a tortured child, or the thud of a drunkard's blow, does not beget some sympathy and indignation among the neighbours. From there the whole machinery of justice is ever so close, that a word of complaint can set it going, and there is but a step between the crime and the dock. But look at these lonely houses, each in its own fields, filled for the most part with poor ignorant folk who know little of the law. Think of the deeds of hellish cruelty, the hidden wickedness which may go on, year in, year out, in such places, and none the wiser."

"What does any of that have to do with the trash, James?" Tom asked, beginning to get angry.

"What it means—is that you see, but you do not *observe*, dear Watson. The distinction is clear." James sniffed. "For example, how many acorns have you seen in your long life, my good Watson?"

"It's Tom," Tom said with a frown. "Not Watson."

James simply held Tom's gaze.

"I've seen hundreds of acorns in my life." Tom sighed.

"Just so." James nodded. "You have frequently seen them, yet you miss the most important one. The one right before your eyes."

James knelt down. Taking a broken acorn into his hands, he held it up as though he'd found the murder weapon.

Tom just gave up and went with it.

"What does that tell us?" Jay asked in his stead.

"That the individual we are looking for weighs enough to shatter this acorn upon stepping on it," James said, his voice filled with manic deduction.

Tom and Jay looked at each other.

Jay picked up the shovel, his intention clear that he wouldn't be using it to dig, or at least, not to dig right *now*.

"No." Tom shook his head, taking the shovel with a serious expression. "Allow me."

"OW!" James shouted. "Hey! What are you doing Watson?! Put that brutish implement down right this *instant*—"

James had no more time to shout, as he was soon too busy ducking and dodging a shovel that had suddenly—against all deductive reasoning—seemed to have come alive.

As the team began to sift through the garbage, Brian left the group for a bit and returned a short time later with gloves for everyone.

"These should make digging through this more palatable," he said, handing them out.

Eagerly accepting the work gloves, the team went back to searching with less of the gross factor. They spent hours looking through everything to see if there were any clues. The sun was beginning to set, casting a deep orange glow over the pile of refuse, and the team was finally nearing the end of their task. The stench of the garbage clung to their clothes, and their muscles ached from the effort. They sorted the refuse into two piles: one holding garbage to be burned and the other holding items that might have been related to the murder.

"This is terrible," Tom said, staring at their much smaller pile of potentially helpful items. "There's so much in here that has DNA on it that we can't figure out what to use." His frustration was evident, and he wiped a forearm across his sweaty forehead.

"Not to mention DNA testing won't do us any good even if we could do it because we don't have anything to compare it to except the dead guy," Brian commented, his tone exasperated.

James, who had been sulking as he searched, piped up, "All of my Law and Order powers are being wasted here because we don't have the right equipment and testing."

"There are other ways of doing detective work, you know," Jay replied, rolling his eyes at James.

"What? How? That sounds stupid," James said, crossing his arms defiantly.

Tom sighed. "Clues can be specific to one person or something that leads to an answer without needing to be tested," he explained. "Now, let's see. We have some cans that shouldn't be here. One has blood on it, so it may have been mixed with the body. The parts were wrapped in this blanket. But they aren't the normal blankets we use here in the Guild for bedding. That means it had to come from outside the Guild. Which makes sense for a scavenger. Maybe one of his buddies had a disagreement with him?" Tom said as he mused over the items they had found, his mind piecing together possible scenarios.

"That seems like a possibility," Derek chimed in, rubbing his chin thoughtfully. "The papers that were with it don't actually seem to be important. They just have the victim's blood on them. But we should keep them and read over the contents to be sure."

"What about this?" TJ asked, holding up a single flower that looked oddly out of place amid the refuse.

"It's a flower," James said dismissively, but TJ wasn't deterred.

"But it's the only one. There aren't any flowers anywhere else here," TJ argued, his brows furrowed.

"You think someone left it for the deceased?" Tom asked, intrigued.

"No idea, but it's not something that grows around here," TJ replied, turning the flower over in his hands.

"How do you know that?" Derek asked, stepping closer to examine the flower.

"It was my mom's favorite flower, delphinium," TJ explained, his voice softer than usual. "They look a little like bluebonnets, but they grow best in cooler climates. Texas is too hot. Whoever left this likely thought it was a bluebonnet and didn't think about it."

Tom nodded, considering the implications. "Maybe they felt remorse for what they did. Where would they get it?" he wondered aloud.

"No idea, but it feels like something else that might point to a scavenger being out and about," TJ said, his tone thoughtful.

"That isn't necessarily the case," Brian interjected, his arms crossed. "Plenty of people have to leave the compound to get supplies or go on runs. That doesn't exactly narrow it down too much."

"But it's still alive, so we can narrow down the time they left it here to pretty recently. Otherwise, it would show signs of drying out," TJ pointed out.

Tom nodded again. "I think it's time we went to talk with the scavenging team," he decided, turning to head back to the building. "Bag up all the things we found and take them to Rebecca. Maybe she can tie some of it to the body. Brian, you come with me to meet the scavengers. The rest of you, go interview people you think might know more about these items, and we can meet up to compare notes."

A short time later, Tom was at the garage where the scavengers parked their vehicles. The team was busy unloading the valuable items and setting them on carts to be pushed inside. The atmosphere was busy but tense, a sense of underlying suspicion hanging in the air.

"Phil? This is Tom," Brian called out as they approached one of the men unloading items. "You may have met him before, but we have some questions to ask you."

Phil, a rough-looking man with a scruffy beard and tired eyes, turned around, wiping his hands on his pants. "Yeah, Tom, I know you. Well, mostly by reputation, but I'm grateful for what you're doing here," he said, extending a hand.

INVASION

"Before this, I was just some schmuck out and about, intimidating people. I think you met my former employer in Albuquerque."

Tom shook his hand, nodding. "Oh, yeah. You were a part of the cult?"

Phil chuckled, though there was no humor in his eyes. "Sure was. Unfortunate, really. I hated that job, but with the apocalypse, the job market is kinda shit."

Tom offered a small, understanding smile. "I'm glad you found something better to do. But I'm here about Jared."

Phil's expression darkened, his eyes shifting slightly. "Ah. Yeah, that was terrible to hear about. Poor bastard didn't deserve that. He was a good guy. Sure, he had some troubles, but nothing the rest of us haven't seen or done. You know what happened yet?"

Tom shook his head. "Not yet, but that's why we're here. Did Jared have anyone he didn't get along with? Enemies, maybe?"

Phil shrugged, glancing over his shoulder as if checking who might be listening. "Not that I'm aware of. He was a bit of a meathead, you know? Sometimes argued with people, but nothing that stuck out."

"Was he seeing anyone? Maybe a girlfriend?" Tom pressed, watching Phil's reaction closely.

"Not that I know of," Phil replied, his tone a bit too casual. "But he didn't talk much to me. Maybe Anabelle will know more. She talks to everyone." He turned back to unloading some large pieces of copper from the bed of a truck, his movements a bit more hurried now.

"Okay, thanks, Phil. We'll let you know if we have any more questions," Tom said, patting the man on the shoulder before moving on to the next truck in the garage. There was something off about Phil, but Tom couldn't put his finger on it just yet.

The next truck was being unloaded by a woman with short, cropped hair and well-defined muscles, clearly someone who had put points into Strength. She was unloading pipes from the back of her truck and placing them on the same kind of cart Phil had been using.

"Are you Anabelle?" Tom asked as they approached, his tone neutral but firm.

"Yeah. Who are you?" Anabelle asked, her eyes narrowing as she looked Tom up and down.

"I'm Tom, the Guild leader," Tom replied evenly. "I'm here about what happened to Jared."

Anabelle's expression shifted to one of frustration. "You don't think I had anything to do with that, do you?" she asked, slamming a pipe down on the cart.

Tom held up a hand, trying to keep things calm.

"I don't know, did you?" he asked, his eyes never leaving hers.

"Hell, no. Jared was a good guy. Always helped me out when I needed him when we were out scavenging. He wouldn't hurt a fly," Anabelle replied, her voice steady but edged with irritation.

"Funny thing to say in a world where we are constantly under attack from monsters and have to defend ourselves," Brian added from behind Tom, his tone challenging.

Anabelle glared at him. "Yeah? Well, we didn't do that kind of fighting. Left that to the idiots who go charging into battle. I'm not about to get myself killed for some of the shit we find out there."

"Did he have any enemies you know about? Maybe a girlfriend?" Tom asked, pushing on.

"He wasn't fond of Phil," Anabelle replied, crossing her arms. "They were always arguing about who found what. I told 'em it wasn't worth it as there's plenty of trash for all of us, but Phil always has to have the best stuff."

"Phil? He said they didn't talk much," Tom replied, now confused.

Anabelle let out a short, humorless laugh. "He said that? I guess they didn't talk much. It was mostly arguing. That prick can shove it. I stay out of the way because I don't really care that much. I got three hots and a cot for bringing this stuff back, and I'm not about to ruin that in this world."

Tom nodded, digesting the information. "So, you just mind your own business out there all the time? Stay away from everyone and do your own thing?"

Anabelle's face softened slightly. "Look, I talked to Jared. He was a good guy. He didn't deserve to get killed. I kinda liked him. But he said he was seeing someone else. Can't blame the girl for going after him."

"You know who the girl was?" Tom asked, his interest piqued.

"Don't know her name. Didn't want to know it. All he said was he was starting to see someone and really liked her. I was just hoping it didn't work out," Anabelle replied, her tone resigned.

"Anything else you can think of? Something odd that happened right before the murder?" Tom asked, trying to push for more.

"Nothing comes to mind right away. If I think of anything, I can let you know, though," Anabelle said, finally stopping and putting her hands on her hips, a slight weariness showing in her stance.

"Thanks, Anabelle," Tom said, giving her a small, appreciative smile before turning to leave.

As they walked away, Tom turned to Brian. "So, Phil had more interactions with Jared than he let on. I can see why he'd want to keep that hidden. And a possible girlfriend?" he mused.

Brian nodded, deep in thought. "There are some others we can interview as well. Let's see what they have to say about what happened to Jared. And maybe the others will have more luck with the people they are interviewing."

The investigation was only beginning, but Tom could feel they were getting closer. The pieces were starting to come together, and he was determined to see this through.

Chapter 33

Accusations

Most of the other scavengers backed up what Anabelle had told Tom and Brian. They weren't as close to Jared as Tom had hoped, but they liked him well enough. Jared wasn't an outcast, nor was he someone who caused trouble. That left Tom in a frustrating position. He had been hoping to hear that Jared had been an asshole—someone with enemies, or at least someone with enough baggage to make his murder easier to comprehend. But the evidence so far suggested the opposite. Jared was just a regular guy, doing his job in a difficult world. There were still many people left to speak with, though, so they pressed on.

Tom walked with Brian in silence for a moment, the cool air inside the Guild building contrasting with the weight of their mission. There was something unsettling about searching for a killer among their own, a feeling like being watched by unseen eyes, even when surrounded by allies.

"One of the scavengers mentioned that Jared spent some time on another team," Tom said, breaking the silence as his voice echoed down the hall. "Is there any way we can talk to some of them as well?"

Brian gave a curt nod, his brow furrowing in thought. "Yeah, we can track them down, no problem. But before we do that, I think it would be a good idea to check in with Rebecca. I had TJ take those items we found in the trash over to her. Maybe she's found something else."

Tom sighed, nodding in agreement. Rebecca had a way of seeing details others missed—her sharp mind and medical expertise were assets that Tom had come to rely on more than once. "Yeah, good thinking. Rebecca's the professional after all. If we missed something, she'll catch it."

As they walked, the hum of daily activity within the Guild surrounded them. People moved with purpose, trading tools and exchanging materials for repairs or ongoing projects, trying to rebuild a sense of normalcy in a world that was anything but normal. Tom noticed the sense of camaraderie had deepened since the goblin attack, but now, under the surface, suspicion lurked. The idea that someone within their walls had taken a life—one of their own—cast a dark shadow over the day-to-day operations. It was a somber reminder that the threat didn't always come from the outside.

The familiar antiseptic smell of the infirmary greeted them as they stepped through the heavy doors, a stark contrast to the bustling Guild outside. The quiet hum of machines monitoring a few patients provided a background noise that only served to make the tension in Tom's chest grow tighter. A place meant for healing, now a possible nexus for solving a murder—it all felt like a cruel irony.

"Glad to see this place isn't full," Tom commented, his gaze sweeping over the empty beds and the clean, sterile environment.

Brian gave a small nod of agreement. "Yeah, the magical healing system we've got in place is a lifesaver. Things that would've taken weeks or months to heal can be done in minutes now. We might have more of an issue if sanitation was like it was in the old world, but with the enchanted water system, electricity, and the procedures we've got for trash disposal, we're managing."

Rebecca stepped out from the back office, her white coat giving her a stern, yet calming, presence. Her eyes flicked over Tom and Brian, and her smile was tight, as though she could sense the heavy mood before they even spoke.

"Tom, Brian," she greeted them, adjusting her glasses. "I assume you're here about the items?"

"Yeah," Tom replied, the weight of what they were about to discuss making his shoulders feel heavier. "Anything new?"

Rebecca gestured for them to follow her. They walked down a sterile hallway toward a separate room—her office—and then into what looked like a small morgue. The air here was colder, the lights brighter, casting almost no shadows on the walls, which gave the room a clinical, detached feel. Tom couldn't help the slight shiver that crawled up his spine, a mix of discomfort and dread as the full reality of what they were dealing with settled over him like a weight.

"You had a morgue in this building?" Tom asked, his voice carrying a note of surprise.

"No, this is new," Brian interjected. "Part of the upgrades we did using the Guild points. It helps for when we have to prepare bodies, and for cases like this—autopsies."

Tom looked around the room, taking in the gleaming metal table and the clean, organized instruments. "Smart. I'm guessing you saw this coming, huh?"

Brian nodded grimly. "Bodies decompose quickly, and it's not exactly sanitary to leave them lying around. Plus, in a world like this, we needed to be prepared for… well, the worst. Rebecca did a stint in the county morgue before all this went down, so she knows her way around."

Rebecca gave a small, wry smile. "Let's just say I'm used to seeing things others might want to avoid."

Tom stepped closer to the table where Jared's remains were laid out under a white sheet. The lump of fabric, thin and lifeless, gave off an air of finality that gnawed at his stomach. It was one thing to hear about a murder, but to stand here, looking at the dismembered remains of a man who had once been part of their community, was a different kind of sobering reality.

"I went through everything you sent," Rebecca began, pulling back the sheet to reveal a severed arm. The pale, mottled skin of Jared's remains seemed almost fragile in the bright light of the room, and Tom couldn't help but feel the weight of responsibility pressing down on him harder than ever. "Let's start with the flower. TJ was right—it was placed on the body post-mortem. There's pollen on his chest, and it's consistent with the delphinium flower you found."

INVASION

Tom crossed his arms, frowning as he stared at the limp, lifeless limb. "So, someone took the time to place the flower. Could be a sign of remorse, or maybe it means something else entirely."

Rebecca set the arm down and picked up another, holding it under the bright lamp above the table. "Maybe. But there's something else here that's more important. Look here." She pointed to the wrist, where the skin was darkened with angry, circular bruises. "Ligature marks. He was bound before he was killed."

Brian leaned in, his eyes narrowing as he examined the marks. "Bound? So, he wasn't just killed. He was restrained."

"Exactly," Rebecca confirmed, her voice steady. "These marks are consistent with a thin, corded rope—something strong enough to hold him, but not the usual rope we use around here. Whoever did this tied him up before they killed him, and he fought against it."

Tom stared at the wrist, his mind racing. "And this wasn't post-mortem?"

Rebecca shook her head. "No. These bruises formed while he was still alive. You can see the wear on the skin—he was struggling to get free. This wasn't an easy or quick death."

Brian ran a hand through his hair, his brow furrowed in disgust. "So, this wasn't just a random attack. They planned it. They took their time."

Tom felt a heavy knot form in his stomach as he considered what this meant. "And what about the blow to the head? Was that before or after he was bound?"

Rebecca motioned to a portion of the skull, which had a large, obvious dent in it. "Before. The head injury likely knocked him out, then they tied him up and killed him."

Tom cursed under his breath. "This just keeps getting better. So, someone with access to this rope, someone who had time and privacy to do this. This wasn't just a spur-of-the-moment thing. This was cold and calculated."

Rebecca nodded solemnly, covering the remains again with the sheet. "It was. Whoever did this knew Jared, knew how to handle him, and took their time."

Tom and Brian exchanged glances. They had come hoping for answers, but now they were walking away with more questions—and the sense that the killer was closer than they had ever imagined.

Back in the security office, they found Derek, Jay, and TJ standing over a whiteboard filled with scattered notes and clues. Everyone looked up as Tom and Brian entered, their eyes filled with expectation.

"Anything?" Derek asked, though his expression already suggested he didn't expect good news.

Tom rubbed the back of his neck, feeling the tension of the situation pressing down on him. "We've got some details. Jared was bound before he was killed—struggled to get free, too. Whoever did this hit him over the head, knocked him out, then tied him up and took their time killing him."

Brian added, "They used a thin rope, not something we typically have lying around. This was planned. And the flower TJ found? It was laid on Jared after he was dead."

Jay frowned, leaning over the whiteboard. "So, someone went through a lot of trouble. And the flower... a sign of remorse?"

"Possibly, or a calling card," Tom said, crossing his arms. "But it's not enough. We need more to go on. Jared might have been seeing someone—a girlfriend, but we don't know who yet."

James burst through the door suddenly, wearing a deerstalker hat, trench coat, and had a comically oversized pipe hanging from his mouth. "Never fear! The great Detective James is on the case!"

Everyone groaned in unison, the mood quickly souring at James' antics.

"Jesus, James. How many outfits do you have, and where do you keep getting them from?" Tom asked, though he already suspected the answer.

"The vending machine, of course!" James said with a wink. "Bob said we can get anything from there. And what better way to solve a murder than by looking the part?"

Maria's voice groaned in Tom's head. "You need to make better friends."

Ignoring the ridiculous scene, Tom turned back to Derek and the others. "We're going to talk to more people, figure out where Jared spent his time. If he had a girlfriend, someone would have seen them together. Let's start with the cafeteria. People talk there, and they might have seen something."

A short time later, Tom was walking through the bustling cafeteria, eyeing the Guild members seated at tables. They were chatting, eating, and some were even laughing—completely unaware of the gravity of the situation unfolding around them. He spotted Charlene, who smiled warmly as he approached.

"Hey, Tom," she greeted, wiping her hands on her apron. "What brings you by?"

"Not here for food today, Charlene," Tom said, offering her a small smile. "I need to ask you a few questions. You ever hear the name Jared Hawthorn?"

Charlene frowned, tapping her chin in thought. "Jared... Jared... Ah, scavenger, right? Quiet guy, kept to himself?"

"That's him," Tom confirmed. "Anyone from your kitchen staff remember him?"

Charlene nodded and called over her team. As they gathered, Derek noticed one woman standing in the back, eyes wide with shock. She looked pale, and her hands trembled ever so slightly as she wrung them together.

"Are you okay?" Derek asked, stepping toward her, his eyes narrowing with suspicion.

The woman swallowed hard, looking at Tom and Derek with fear in her eyes. "What's this about Jared?"

Tom and Derek exchanged a glance.

"Maybe we should go somewhere more private," Tom suggested, his tone gentle but firm.

They led the woman to the back of the cafeteria, into a small storage room where they could speak away from prying eyes. Her breath came in short gasps, and her hands shook as she clasped them tightly in front of her.

"Would you like to take a seat?" Derek asked.

She nodded, sinking into the chair, her face pale.

INVASION

"What's your name?" Tom asked gently. "How do you know Jared?"

"My name is Terri," she whispered, her voice barely audible. "I'm Jared's girlfriend."

Chapter 34

Misinformation

Tom stared at Terri in disbelief, his mind working furiously to piece together the puzzle.

"His girlfriend?" he asked, his voice low and cautious.

Terri nodded, her expression solemn but tinged with an almost fragile sadness. "Yes, we've been seeing each other for a little while now," she said softly. She hesitated for a moment, as if unsure how much to reveal. "I met him when he came into the cafeteria. It was… a bit of a love-at-first-sight kind of moment."

Tom's brow furrowed, trying to reconcile this new piece of information. Jared's name hadn't been mentioned much, and yet here was someone claiming to be his girlfriend. He leaned back in his chair, rubbing his chin thoughtfully as he processed what she had just said. It had been mentioned that he might have been seeing someone, but Terri made it sound as though the relationship was much more. Across from him, Derek crossed his arms, clearly scrutinizing Terri more closely now.

"No one else seems to know much about you or your relationship with Jared," Derek commented, his voice carrying a note of suspicion. "It doesn't seem like you two spent enough time together for people to even notice."

Terri sighed, her shoulders slumping slightly, and her hands clasped tightly in her lap.

"It's tough to spend much time together," she explained, her voice tinged with regret. "Jared is always out with the scavengers, and my hours in the kitchen are pretty unpredictable. It makes things… complicated. We have to make do with stolen moments. But we make it work." There was a subtle tremor in her voice, a sadness she couldn't hide.

Tom studied her for a moment longer, weighing her words. It was always difficult to judge how deep a relationship ran in such chaotic times. People clung to each other for comfort and survival more than love, and relationships formed in the blink of an eye, dissolving just as quickly. But still, something about her story didn't sit right with him.

"Why are you asking about Jared?" she asked suddenly, her tone becoming sharper, more defensive. The question hung in the air, heavier than it had any right to be.

INVASION

Tom exchanged a quick glance with Derek before speaking. There was no easy way to say it. "Terri, I don't know how to put this, but… Jared is dead."

Terri's eyes widened, her face draining of color as the words hit her like a physical blow. She sat forward in her chair, her hands trembling slightly. "What? How? What happened?" she demanded, her voice filled with a mixture of disbelief and panic.

"We don't have all the details yet," Derek said, his voice softer than usual, though still laced with the firmness of someone who had broken this kind of news before. "But it looks like it happened here in the Guild. We're still trying to figure out exactly what happened."

The room seemed to shrink as a heavy silence fell over them. The hum of distant activity from outside the space became muffled, and the air felt thick with tension. Terri looked lost; her expression frozen in a state of shock. Her breathing quickened, and her gaze darted around the room as if searching for some kind of escape from the truth.

Before anyone could offer more comfort or explanation, the door to the security office burst open with a loud crash. Tom jumped in his chair, eyes snapping to the door as a manic-looking James stumbled into the room, his face contorted in a mask of intense emotion. He scanned the room quickly, his eyes locking onto Terri like a predator spotting prey.

"*You,*" he said, his voice dripping with accusation as he pointed directly at her, his hand trembling slightly.

Terri blinked, completely blindsided.

"Me?" she stammered, her voice filled with confusion and fear.

James took a few deliberate steps toward her, his posture stiff, his eyes narrowing. "You did this," he growled, his voice rising with every word. "It's your fault."

Terri's body stiffened in her chair, her face a mask of terror. "What… What do you mean? I didn't do anything!" she protested, her voice barely above a whisper, panic evident in every syllable.

"The cookies, Terri!" James shouted, his voice loud and dramatic, like an actor in the final act of a Shakespearean tragedy. "There was a whole sheet of cookies left in the oven, and they *burned!* Those poor, innocent cookies! What did they ever do to you?!"

Tom groaned audibly, his face dropping into his hands. "Oh, for the love of—"

James wasn't finished. He threw his arms wide as if delivering the closing argument of a trial, his voice growing more impassioned with every word. "Those cookies didn't deserve to be incinerated like that! They were innocent! Delicious! And you… you let them die!"

Derek's expression darkened as he turned to face James. The look on his face was the calm before the storm, a barely contained fury that could erupt at any moment.

"James. Get. Out."

"*Exactly,*" James said, oblivious to the seething anger directed at him. He threw his hands up in mock surrender. "Those cookies couldn't get out, Derek. They were trapped—"

Derek's glare could have melted steel. "Leave. Now."

James, finally realizing the danger he was in, backpedaled toward the door.

"Fine!" He stopped at the door to glare back at Terri. "This corrupt system can't protect you forever!" He spun on his heel, storming out of the room with dramatic flair, the door slamming behind him. His voice retreated down the far hallway. "Justice will be served!"

For a moment, the room was still, the absurdity of the situation hanging in the air. Tom rubbed his temples, feeling a tension headache forming. "I'm so sorry about him," he muttered to Terri, who was still staring at the door in stunned silence. "Honestly, I can't even begin to explain… whatever that was."

Terri blinked a few times, trying to shake off the lingering confusion from James' tirade. "He… he's something else," she finally said, her voice soft and distant. "Is he always like that?"

"If you ever figure him out, let us know," Tom said with a weak smile. "I've known him for years, and he still makes no sense to me."

Terri nodded, but her gaze remained distant, her thoughts clearly elsewhere. She wrapped her arms around herself as if trying to hold herself together against the emotional onslaught. The tension in the room shifted. The playful atmosphere James had accidentally created evaporated, replaced by a feeling of heavy, oppressive sorrow.

"Are you sure you're okay?" Derek asked, noticing the shift in her mood.

Terri hesitated for a moment before speaking, her voice trembling slightly. "I just can't believe Jared is gone. It's like… it's hitting me all over again."

Tom frowned, feeling a pang of sympathy. "Maybe it would help to remember the good times you had with him?"

For a moment, a faint smile crossed Terri's face, but it didn't quite reach her eyes. "He was kind," she said quietly. "He didn't talk much about his work, but whenever he found something cool out there, he'd get so excited. He loved feeling like he was making a difference, you know? He hated that one of the guys on his team kept trying to take the best stuff, but Jared was just happy to be contributing, even if it meant getting the short end of the stick sometimes."

Derek leaned forward, curiosity sparking in his eyes. "Did you ever leave the Guild with him? Maybe go on a scavenging trip together?"

Terri shook her head quickly, a visible shudder running down her spine. "No. I hate going outside. I don't want to remember what the world's become out there. It's safer here, and it doesn't remind me of everything we lost. The scavenging runs were his thing. I preferred to stay inside the Guild."

Derek tilted his head. "You know the area around the Guild is regularly patrolled, right? It's much safer than it was before."

"I know," Terri said, her voice barely a whisper. "But after everything we saw when the apocalypse first hit… I just can't go out there. Maybe one day, but not now. It's still too much for me."

Tom sighed inwardly. He understood her reluctance—he'd seen plenty of people buckle under the weight of the world after it had fallen apart. But something about her responses felt too rehearsed, too polished. Maybe it was just paranoia, but he couldn't help wondering if she was holding something back. "Can you account for where you've been the last few nights?" he asked, his voice gentle but probing.

Terri's gaze snapped up, her eyes narrowing. "Why? Am I a suspect now?"

"At this point, everyone is," Tom said, keeping his tone steady. "It's not personal. We're just trying to rule people out."

Terri bristled, her face flushing with anger. "I didn't do it. He was my boyfriend!" she shot back, standing abruptly from her chair.

"We're not saying you did," Tom said calmly, but his words did little to soothe her growing frustration. "We just need to know where you were."

Terri's eyes darted between Tom and Derek before she took a step toward the door. "I don't have to take this." Before she could leave, Derek moved to block her exit, his large frame filling the doorway.

"Terri, just think for a moment," Tom said softly. "How does it look if you refuse to answer questions and walk out like this?"

Terri's hands clenched into fists, her knuckles turning white. She shot a furious glance at Tom, her eyes burning with frustration. "I'm insulted you'd even ask me."

"Just tell us where you were," Tom urged, "and you can leave."

The room was heavy with silence as Terri stared at them, her face contorted with a mixture of anger and defeat. Finally, after what felt like an eternity, she exhaled sharply. "I was having a poker night with some of the kitchen staff," she said, her voice cold.

"For several nights?" Tom asked, raising an eyebrow.

"There's a Game Room," Terri explained, crossing her arms defensively. "People gather there after hours to gamble. I play five-card draw with some of the others from the kitchen."

Tom blinked in surprise. "We have a casino?"

Derek chuckled. "Not quite. It's like she said, a Game Room. Some people found old pieces of casino games and put them together. It's harmless fun, and it helps people unwind."

"You think you know a place," Tom muttered under his breath. "Why wasn't I told about this?"

"It didn't seem important enough to bother you with," Derek replied with a shrug. "There's a bar too, for that matter. Some of the staff have been brewing their own drinks. Did you know Brewer is a Profession now?"

"I didn't," Tom admitted, though it made sense. The System had allowed for all kinds of new Professions to emerge. But still, he couldn't shake the feeling that this was just one more thing he hadn't been aware of. "And the currency?"

"Monster Cores," Derek confirmed. "It's all we use now. People tried to bring back dollars at first, but it didn't last long. There's nothing to spend it on except in the vending machines, and those only take cores."

Terri shifted uncomfortably, her eyes darting between Tom and Derek as the conversation continued.

"Can I go now?" she asked, her voice tight.

Derek stepped aside, allowing her a clear path to the door. "Yes, you can go."

As she moved past Tom, he called out after her, half-joking, "Just don't leave town."

Terri turned, glaring at him as though he had just grown an extra head.

"It's just a joke," Tom muttered, glancing over at Derek, who was shaking his head in disbelief.

"I guess you'll get to see the Game Room after all," Derek said with a heavy sigh, gesturing for Tom to follow him. "Come on. We still have more people to talk to."

Tom stood up, rubbing the back of his neck. "I guess it's time to face my demons, huh?"

"Yup," Derek said with a small smile. "Let's go check it out."

Together, they left the office, heading toward whatever new revelations awaited them in the shadows of the Guild.

Chapter 35

Addiction

There was no flash or fanfare like the pre-apocalypse casinos when Tom entered the Game Room. Gone were the extravagant lights, the cacophony of slot machines paying out to their lucky winners, and the ever-present sounds of celebration in the air. Instead, the room felt like it belonged in a world far removed from the glitz of old. A quiet, subdued atmosphere permeated the space, with only the soft murmurs of conversation and the occasional shuffle of cards breaking the silence.

The tables, draped in worn green felt covers that had seen better days, were arranged haphazardly. Their surfaces were nicked and scratched, with the faint smell of stale beer and dust lingering. Off to one side, a large shelf held a variety of old board games—many from a time before the world had changed. Monopoly, Scrabble, and Risk, their edges faded and boxes torn from years of use, sat idly on display. A relic of a simpler time when people gathered for game nights, now juxtaposed against the reality of their new lives.

A few groups were gathered around the tables, quietly playing games to pass the time. The air was thick with a strange sense of camaraderie, but it also felt... hollow. The shift for the standard day workers hadn't ended yet, and the room seemed almost half-empty. The people who were there felt like they were just trying to hold onto some semblance of normalcy, a faint echo of the life they had once known. Tom couldn't help but feel a pang of nostalgia, but that was quickly overshadowed by the seriousness of why he was here.

At the far end of the room was a bar. It had been cobbled together with reclaimed wood and old metal parts, likely scavenged from one of the nearby liquor stores. Behind the bar, the shelves were stocked with bottles—some of them homemade, others found in what remained of abandoned stores. A faint glow came from an LED-lit sign that read "Mad Max 20/20." The sign flickered faintly, casting an almost eerie light across the bar.

Tom shuddered. The sign reminded him all too vividly of his teenage years when he and his friends would ask someone older to buy them bottles of Mad Dog 20/20 from the nearest gas station. The taste had been terrible, but it had done the job. There were nights he couldn't even remember, and there was a certain irony in the fact that now, as an adult facing the apocalypse, he could still be haunted by memories of a cheap, terrible drink.

Derek, walking beside him, gestured to the room. "Most of the people here are regulars," he explained, his voice low but filled with the kind of ease that comes from familiarity. "Since we set up the Game Room, we've been employing people to run it. Opening small businesses like this gives those who don't have the physical skills for combat or labor a way to contribute." He paused, looking around. "Some people didn't have real-world skills before all this happened, and others just can't handle the work that some jobs demand."

Tom's gaze followed Derek's, taking in the employees behind the bar and at the tables. Many of them seemed older—elderly Guild members who no longer had the stamina to fight on the frontlines. They wore weary expressions, faces lined with years of hardship, but there was also a quiet determination in their eyes. Tom assumed that some of the others—particularly the women—had probably been stay-at-home mothers or in other non-professional roles before the world had been turned upside down.

A few children sat nearby, nestled in the laps of their mothers. The kids played quietly, their innocent laughter a sharp contrast to the tension that hung in the air. It was strange to see such a peaceful scene, knowing that beyond the walls of the Guild, chaos still reigned.

"Why don't the kids go to the daycare? I know we set one up for everyone," Tom asked, his curiosity piqued. He had worked hard to make sure the Guild could provide for its people, and daycare was one of those necessary comforts.

Derek glanced over at the children, a slight frown creasing his forehead. "Some people aren't comfortable leaving their kids there yet. After everything that's happened, it's hard to blame them. They've lost so much already. We don't push anyone to do anything, as long as they contribute. But trust… trust takes time to rebuild."

Tom nodded, understanding the sentiment. It made sense, but it still weighed on him. More than half a year had passed since the world had changed, since the System had turned everything they knew on its head. Despite all the progress they'd made, there were still wounds too deep to heal with just time. He filed the thought away—he'd have to come back to that issue eventually. For now, they had more pressing concerns.

Derek led Tom to a small door on the far side of the Game Room. Opening it, he gestured for Tom to enter first. Inside was a cramped office, no larger than a broom closet. The air was stuffy, and the only light came from a flickering desk lamp perched atop a cluttered wooden desk. Behind the desk sat a man in his mid-sixties, hunched over a ledger. His eyes were focused, squinting at the numbers in front of him through reading glasses as he punched them into an old calculator, the buttons clicking softly in the silence.

Another door to the left led to what Tom assumed was the exchange counter. In here, the room smelled faintly of old paper and dust, the smell of years of handling records and books in small, confined spaces. Despite the cramped surroundings, there was an air of efficiency about the place.

"Leon, good to see you," Derek said, his voice breaking the silence. A warm smile spread across his face. "How goes the Game Room business?"

Leon looked up from his ledger, blinking a few times as his eyes adjusted to the light. His face broke into a toothy grin as he recognized Derek.

INVASION

"Ah, Derek, good to see ya!" His voice had the distinct rasp of someone who had spent a lot of time talking over noise—loud clubs, maybe, or busy bars—and his very distinct New York accent gave him a familiar TV actor presence. "Business is good, real good. We've had more people comin' in, and I'm runnin' out of room. Think we can expand sooner rather than later? Hate turnin' folks away."

Derek chuckled. "You know we've got bigger priorities right now, Leon. We're preparing for the invasion. What's the point of expanding if we're all dead?" He grinned, but the underlying truth in his words was hard to miss.

Leon laughed, the sound deep and genuine. "Hey, can't blame a guy for trying. Gotta keep the business goin', right?"

Derek nodded toward Tom. "Leon, I want you to meet Tom. He's the—"

"The Guild leader. I know that face," Leon interrupted, standing up from behind his desk with surprising energy for a man of his age. He extended a hand to Tom, his grip firm and strong. "You're doin' a bang-up job keepin' us safe, kid. My wife and I, we thank you for what you're doin'."

Tom was taken aback by the man's sincerity. He wasn't used to receiving direct praise, especially from people who had seen more of life than he had. Blushing slightly, Tom shook the man's hand, feeling the strength in his grip. "Thanks, Leon. I'm just doing what I can."

Leon's smile widened. "Well, you're doin' a hell of a job. We're all grateful."

Tom glanced at Derek, who nodded subtly, indicating it was time to get to the point of their visit. "Leon, we need your help with something," Derek began. "There's a woman—Terri Saxton. She works in the cafeteria and says she's been coming here in the evenings for the past week or so, playing games with friends. We need to confirm that."

Leon scratched his chin thoughtfully, his eyes narrowing in concentration. "Terri Saxton, huh? Lemme check." He reached up to a shelf above his desk and pulled down a thick green binder. The book looked well-used, its spine creased and pages yellowed from frequent handling. Leon flipped through the pages, his finger running down the lists of names written there.

"Ah, here we go," Leon said after a moment, tapping a line in the book. "Terri Saxton… exchanged twenty common cores for chips to play with. Looks like she was here one night, but just the one. Didn't cash out any chips either, so I'm guessing she lost 'em all."

"Only one evening?" Tom asked, frowning.

Leon flipped through a few more pages, shaking his head. "Yeah, just the one night. If she was here on other nights, she didn't get chips. Most people do, though, unless they're just here to watch or play board games."

Derek nodded. "Thanks, Leon. We appreciate your help." He extended a hand, and as he shook Leon's, Tom noticed the subtle exchange of an uncommon Monster Core—a quiet thank-you for Leon's cooperation.

Leon winked at them. "Anytime, boys. And hey, if you ever wanna relax, come on down. The games are a good way to blow off some steam."

Derek chuckled. "Maybe. But not Tom. If you see him in here, you let me know immediately."

Leon grinned, nodding knowingly. "Gotcha, boss. I had a brother like that. Couldn't be around the ponies anymore, if you catch my drift."

With that, Derek nudged Tom out of the office, leading him back toward the gaming floor. Tom couldn't help but feel a bit betrayed, the sting of embarrassment settling in as they left the room.

"You had to tell him?" Tom muttered under his breath, glancing sideways at Derek.

Derek shrugged. "We're just looking out for you. Leon's discreet. Your secret's safe with him."

"He sounds like a mobster," Tom grumbled, half-joking.

Derek laughed softly. "Maybe he was, but he's old school. That means he's trustworthy." He clapped Tom on the shoulder. "Now, let's focus. We've got a job to do."

They made their way back to the gaming tables, where more people had trickled in. The atmosphere was slowly shifting, the hum of conversation growing louder as the evening crowd began to fill the room. The air seemed to pulse with anticipation, but Tom's mind was elsewhere, clouded with thoughts of everything Derek had said.

"Hey, Derek," Leon's voice called from across the room. "You might wanna ask the dealers. They see more than I do."

Derek gave him a thumbs up. "Thanks, Leon."

As they approached the card tables, Tom noticed the dealers all wore matching vests and formal attire, a striking contrast to the world outside. The sight of clean, crisp uniforms in a post-apocalyptic setting was almost jarring.

"Where did they get those outfits?" Tom asked, his curiosity piqued.

Derek smirked. "We've got a talented tailor in the Guild. Haven't you noticed your clothes being replaced or repaired?"

Tom blinked in surprise. "Wait… someone's been fixing my clothes?"

Derek chuckled, shaking his head. "Yeah, Tom. We've got someone checking your room daily. Most people have to request repairs, but for you, it's automatic."

Tom frowned. "That doesn't seem fair. I don't want special treatment."

Derek stopped walking, turning to face Tom. His expression was serious, his tone firm. "Tom, whether you like it or not, you're the leader of this Guild. People depend on you. You get special treatment so you can focus on what really matters—keeping us safe."

Tom's chest tightened with a familiar sense of anxiety.

"I'm not special," he muttered.

"Oh, bless your heart," Derek said, a bemused smile spreading across his face as he locked eyes with Tom. His tone was gentle, but the weight behind his words was undeniable. "You're the most special, Tom. Whether you want to accept it or not, you're now the symbol these people look to. You've become the face of this Guild, and that isn't changing. Not ever. We passed the point of no return a long time ago."

INVASION

In that moment, it felt like the ground beneath Tom's feet shifted. The realization hit him like a punch to the gut, shattering the comfortable illusion he had wrapped himself in for so long. He had always thought of himself as just some guy—a guy with good intentions, sure, but not someone who held so much importance. The kind of guy who people knew, respected maybe, but not the keystone holding it all together. But now, it all felt different.

How stupid had he been not to see it?

His chest tightened again, his heart thudding in his ears as the weight of his responsibility started to bear down on him. How many times had he thrown himself into danger, heedless of the risks, convinced that he was just another sword in the fight? He could see it so clearly now—he wasn't just a fighter. He was the banner. The symbol. The thing that kept them going when all seemed lost.

Images of past battles flashed before his eyes. Him leaping off walls, charging headlong into hordes of enemies, never stopping to consider the consequences. His mind reeled as the realization dawned: every reckless charge, every high-risk decision wasn't just his choice. It had a ripple effect. It was something people saw, something they followed.

"So, all those times I just rushed into a fight..." Tom trailed off, his voice barely above a whisper as he looked at Derek, finally starting to connect the dots.

Derek's laugh was soft, tinged with a mix of relief and exasperation. "Well, it's a bit of a mixed bag, to be honest. We're all scared out of our minds that one day you're gonna get one-shotted because you're playing the role of Leroy Jenkins a little too well." He shook his head, chuckling as he spoke. "But the flip side is that every time you do that, it lights a fire under the rest of the fighters. It's like you're supercharging their morale just by being out there. You've pushed them to train harder, fight fiercer, and dive into danger if it means protecting their comrades. So, for now... we just don't say anything."

Tom felt the words swirl around him, part compliment, part warning, and all truth. The sudden gravity of his role pressed down harder than ever. It was like he was seeing the world in a new light, like the puzzle of his life was finally snapping into place. How had he missed this? How had he not realized just how much of a symbol he had become?

"How am I supposed to take this?" Tom asked, his voice tinged with frustration. His hands instinctively found their way to his sides, fists clenching as he tried to process what Derek had just laid out for him.

Derek shrugged, his expression softening. "You don't need to take it any differently than you have been. Just follow your heart, Tom. It hasn't led you wrong so far. Plus, if you die, maybe I get a promotion, so it's not all bad." Derek gave him a reassuring pat on the back before turning away, heading toward the tables. "Come on, you can wrestle with this internally later. Right now, we've got work to do."

Tom barely registered Derek's words as he turned to follow him. His mind was buzzing, the anxiety creeping in like a slow, steady tide. He felt like he was moving through a haze, his body going through the motions while his thoughts raced in a thousand different directions. Was this why people were so loyal to him? Was this why they trusted him with their lives?

As he stood by the tables, waiting for Derek to continue their investigation, Tom couldn't help but let his mind wander. He had always prided himself on being a good leader, on caring about his people. But now, he realized that the stakes had always been higher than he thought. People weren't just looking to him for commands. They were looking to him for hope.

I don't have to change, Tom thought to himself, the words echoing in his mind as if trying to anchor him in place. Slowly, the worry that had begun to creep into his chest began to recede. He could feel it, the slow ebb of fear replaced by something more solid, more grounded. He didn't have to be anything more than what he already was. He didn't need to suddenly become some flawless hero or untouchable figure. People had been following him because of who he was, not because of who he thought he had to be.

He could just… be Tom.

The thought was both a comfort and a challenge. Could he continue to be the same person while knowing how much weight rested on his shoulders? Could he still make the reckless decisions that came naturally to him, knowing that people saw him as their guiding light?

I've been doing it so far, he told himself, his heart slowing as the realization set in. *I can keep doing it. I've just got to remember that it's not just about me anymore. It never really was.*

A calm settled over him, not the kind of calm that comes from having all the answers but the kind that comes from accepting the uncertainty. He didn't have to figure it all out right away. He just had to keep moving forward and doing what he'd been doing.

Derek glanced back over his shoulder, noticing the shift in Tom's demeanor. He didn't say anything, but there was a knowing look in his eyes. He could see that Tom was processing everything, letting it sink in. There was no rush, no pressure. Just the understanding that Tom would figure it out in his own time.

The Game Room bustled around them, the low hum of conversation filling the air as more people trickled in. Tom glanced around the room, seeing the familiar faces of Guild members enjoying their brief moments of relaxation. For them, this was just another evening, another chance to escape the pressures of the outside world for a few hours. They weren't thinking about the weight of leadership or the burdens of responsibility. They were just here to live, to find a moment of peace in the chaos.

And that's what Tom wanted for them.

As he stood there, watching Derek speak with one of the dealers, he realized something. It wasn't just about being the symbol of hope. It was about creating an environment where people could still have these moments. Where they could still feel normal, even in the midst of everything they'd been through. He had helped build that, and that was something worth protecting.

Derek turned back to him, a small smirk on his face. "You ready to get back to work?" he asked, his tone light.

Tom nodded, the weight on his shoulders feeling a little lighter. "Yeah, I'm ready."

INVASION

As they moved to continue their investigation, Tom's mind was clearer. He didn't have to be perfect, and he didn't have to figure everything out all at once. He just had to keep being Tom, keep fighting for his people, and keep leading them the way he always had—by putting his heart into everything he did.

For now, that was enough.

Chapter 36

Suspicion

"So, we aren't much closer than when we started searching, are we?" Tom asked as he strolled beside Derek, his boots scuffing lightly against the well-worn floors of the Guild building. His voice carried a frustrated edge, his expression mirroring the rising tension he felt inside.

Derek shook his head, rubbing his chin in thought. "I mean, we've narrowed it down to people he had regular contact with, but…" he trailed off, his brow furrowed in contemplation. "Personally, I'm thinking Phil looks good for it. We just need to confirm his whereabouts during the time of the attack." Derek scratched at an itch on his side, a habit that seemed to surface when he was deep in thought.

Tom remained unconvinced. His mind still churned with other possibilities. "What about Terri? She could have done it. She was acting a little off."

Derek glanced at him, raising an eyebrow. "True. But she seemed genuinely shocked to hear that Jared was dead. I mean, she could be faking it," he conceded, "but I'm not sure she had the opportunity to pull it off." He scratched his jaw again, his contemplative face deepening. "Then again, we're not ruling her out."

As they walked, the low hum of activity echoed through the building. The sounds of people moving, talking, living—the world continuing on despite their grim investigation—grated on Tom's nerves. They were trying to uncover the truth about a murder, and yet everything felt… normal. Too normal.

"I can't believe people used to enjoy this kind of work," Tom muttered as they turned a corner, the cafeteria coming into view. "I would've gone insane if this was my life, day in and day out."

Derek chuckled, his mood lightening a little despite the seriousness of the situation. "Yeah, well, people probably said the same thing about sitting at a desk writing code all day." He shot Tom a knowing look. "To each their own, right?"

Tom grunted in response, though he knew Derek was right. The idea of digging through clues, interviewing suspects, following hunches—it all seemed tedious to him. But some people lived for it. Others thrived in it. He was learning that much, at least.

They reached the cafeteria, where the familiar smell of fresh food lingered, though the large room was mostly empty. It was that quiet period between meal rushes when only a few people stopped by for snacks or quick conversation. The room felt calm, a stark contrast to the tense air surrounding Tom and Derek.

Charlene stood behind the counter, wiping her hands on her apron as she worked. She noticed them almost immediately and waved them over, her warm smile ever-present.

"Hello, boys! What can I do for you today?" she asked, her voice as friendly as always, despite the underlying concern in her eyes. She was used to dealing with crises, though this one clearly unsettled her.

Derek returned her smile, though his was laced with a touch of seriousness. "Is Camila available? We need to talk with her for a few minutes."

Charlene's smile faltered slightly, replaced by a concerned expression. "Camila? Of course. Is everything alright?"

"She's not in any trouble, don't worry," Derek said quickly, holding up a hand to reassure her. "We just need some information, that's all."

Charlene nodded, though the concern didn't entirely leave her face. "Alright, give me a moment," she said, disappearing into the kitchen.

The atmosphere in the cafeteria remained subdued, with only a few scattered conversations echoing from the far corners. Tom's gaze drifted over the tables, the empty chairs, the sense of normalcy that felt so out of place with everything they were investigating.

A short while later, Charlene returned with Camila following close behind. Camila was a young woman in her mid-twenties, with blonde hair tied back loosely and bright blue eyes that carried a hint of unease. She was of average build, with a sprinkling of freckles across her nose and cheeks, her features soft and unassuming. As she approached, she glanced between Derek and Tom, clearly unsure of what this was about.

"Hi, I'm Camila," she introduced herself, her voice friendly but tinged with nervousness. "Is everything okay?"

Charlene gave her a gentle pat on the shoulder before retreating back to the kitchen. "I'll leave you all to it," she said, casting one last curious glance at Derek and Tom.

Derek gestured to one of the nearby tables. "Why don't we sit down for a minute?" he suggested, leading the way as Camila followed.

The three of them sat down at a table, the soft hum of the kitchen now a backdrop to the conversation.

"So… what's this about?" Camila asked, her hands fidgeting slightly in her lap.

Derek didn't waste any time, getting straight to the point. "It's about your friend, Terri. She works here in the kitchen with you, right?"

Camila nodded, though her unease grew slightly. "Yeah, we work together. She's nice. We hang out after work sometimes. What's going on? Did something happen to her?"

Tom leaned forward a little, his tone calm but probing. "We're just trying to get a clearer picture of who she is. You said you hang out sometimes. What's she like? Is she seeing anyone? Has she been acting strange?"

Camila hesitated, clearly taken aback by the questions. "I mean… she's nice. Kind of keeps to herself about certain things, though. She said she was seeing someone, but she never told me much about him. Honestly, I never met the guy.

She was kinda secretive about it. I just figured it wasn't that serious, or she wasn't ready to talk about it."

"Did she seem secretive with other things?" Derek asked, watching Camila's body language closely.

Camila shook her head. "Not really. Just that one thing. I think we're friendly, but we don't really talk about deep personal stuff. Mostly work, some random things. We've gone to the Game Room together a few times, but nothing major. Now that I think about it, she did like to drink… maybe a little more than she should've. She got a little messy the last time."

Tom exchanged a quick glance with Derek before asking, "Do you think she's in trouble?"

Camila's eyes widened slightly, her worry visibly growing. "Why? Did she do something? What's going on?"

Derek leaned forward, his voice softening to ease her anxiety. "No, she's not in trouble. We're just trying to keep everyone safe, and we want to make sure we understand what's happening. It's nothing more than that."

Camila's shoulders slumped slightly, the tension releasing as she let out a quiet sigh. "Okay… I get it. Things have been really scary lately. I try not to think about it too much, but it's hard to ignore how bad things have gotten out there. I don't even leave the building anymore."

Tom and Derek shared a knowing look, both of them understanding the weight of her words. They weren't the only ones feeling the pressure of this new world.

"We're working hard to change that," Tom said sincerely, his voice carrying a quiet determination. "We want people to feel safe again. If you think of anything that might help us, anything at all, will you let us know?"

"Of course," Camila said, nodding firmly. "If I hear or see anything, I'll let you know."

"Thanks, Camila," Tom said, giving her a reassuring smile. "We appreciate your help."

Camila stood up, offering them a tentative smile in return. "I hope you find what you're looking for," she said before heading back into the kitchen.

Tom watched her leave, his mind still buzzing with questions. When she was out of sight, he turned to Derek.

"That didn't give us much to go on," Tom said, his frustration simmering beneath the surface. "But at least we have something. We need to talk to Phil again."

Derek nodded in agreement, pushing himself up from the table. "Let's get to it. We'll see what else he has to say."

Later, after some back and forth, Phil was brought back in from his scavenging duties to meet with Tom and Derek once again. The moment Phil walked into the Guild building, his mood was clear. He was fuming.

INVASION

"What the hell is this all about?" Phil snapped, his fists clenched at his sides. "I've got work to do out there, and you're wasting my damn time. That's money you're costing me."

Derek stepped forward, his tone calm and measured despite Phil's anger. "Phil, relax. We'll make sure you're paid for your time. No one's trying to cheat you out of anything here."

Phil's eyes narrowed, though his anger seemed to cool slightly. "Alright, fine," he grumbled. "But this better not be a waste of my time."

Derek gestured for Phil to follow them. "Let's talk somewhere more private. No need to make a scene."

Phil hesitated a moment before begrudgingly following them down the hallway to a room they had set aside for private discussions. The room was small, a former storage space converted into a makeshift interview room. There were no windows, just a plain table with a few chairs around it. The air in the room felt slightly stuffy, the walls seeming to close in on them.

Phil sat down heavily in one of the chairs, his arms crossed defensively over his chest.

"Alright, what's this about?" Phil growled.

Derek remained standing, leaning against the wall with a casual air, though his eyes were sharp and observant. "We need to talk to you about Jared. Again."

Phil rolled his eyes, clearly tired of the subject. "Jared? What about him? He's dead, right? What more do you want from me?"

Tom took a seat across from Phil, his gaze steady. "We need to know how and why, Phil. And right now, you're the only one with a real reason to want him gone."

Phil scoffed, though there was a flicker of unease in his eyes. "You think I killed him? That's what this is about?"

Derek didn't respond immediately, letting the silence hang in the air for a moment before he spoke. "We're not saying you did. But we must consider every possibility. You and Jared didn't exactly get along."

Phil's jaw tightened, his fists clenching on the table. "We had our problems, sure. But I didn't kill him. I didn't want him dead."

Tom tilted his head slightly, studying Phil's reaction. "It's just... convenient, isn't it? You two didn't get along. Jared ends up dead. You're out there scavenging together, no one around to see anything. Plenty of opportunities."

Phil slammed his fist down on the table, his face flushing with anger. "I'm not a killer! I didn't want to work with him, sure, but I didn't want him dead!"

Tom and Derek exchanged a glance. The tension in the room thickened, the air practically buzzing with it.

Derek leaned forward, his gaze locking onto Phil's. "Then help us out here, Phil. If you didn't do it, who did?"

Phil looked between them, his eyes wide with fear and frustration. "I don't know! I swear, I don't know who did it."

Derek sighed, standing up straight. "Alright, Phil. We're going to have to keep you separated for a bit, just until we get this sorted out. It's for everyone's safety."

Phil's eyes narrowed, his posture stiffening. "You're going to lock me up? For what? You've got no evidence."

"We have to keep people safe," Tom said quietly, standing up as well. "You'll be taken care of, but we can't take any chances right now."

As they walked out of the room, leaving Phil behind, Tom couldn't shake the uneasy feeling gnawing at him.

"This is a mess," Tom muttered under his breath.

"Welcome to leadership," Derek replied with a heavy sigh. "Let's just hope we get to the bottom of it before things get worse."

Chapter 37

Information

Derek led Tom to the back of the building, where Bohdan stood with his eyes narrowed in concentration. His hand moved fluidly over a collection of items laid out before him, wrapped in a bluish glow that flickered like the fading light of twilight. The air around him seemed to hum softly, the magic resonating faintly as it interacted with the world around him.

"Find anything yet?" Derek's voice cut through the silence, breaking Bohdan's trance.

The wizard didn't look up immediately, his brow furrowing further, as if grasping at something just out of reach. Then, with a sigh, the glow around his hand dissipated, and he turned to face them.

"Sure, lots of things," he replied, his tone deadpan. "None of which are helpful for investigation."

Tom glanced at Derek, who wore a look of mild disappointment but wasn't surprised. "Figures," Derek muttered before cocking an eyebrow at Bohdan. "Time for Plan B. Did you find that spell we talked about?"

Bohdan's lips curled into a smirk, a glint of mischief in his eyes. "I did. But it takes up a spell slot, so you owe me," he said, arms crossing casually over his chest.

"Spell slot?" Tom asked, his brow knitting in confusion.

Bohdan gave him a sideways glance, the kind a teacher might give a student who had just asked a basic question. "Wizards have limited spell slots," he explained patiently. "We can use magic more freely than most, but we can only prepare a limited number of spells at a time. Using one for something like this"—he gestured vaguely at the space around them—"isn't exactly what most would consider practical. Most wouldn't waste time unless they're building a necromancer class."

Before Tom could respond, Maria's voice piped up in his head, causing him to flinch. "Yeah, typical Wizard stuff. Spell slots are like limited ammo for their arsenal, which means Bohdan's essentially loading a one-time-use bullet for this. Most wizards wouldn't spend it on a parlor trick unless it's something really important."

"That's why Wizards drool and Warlocks rule..." Tom muttered under his breath.

"You okay?" Derek asked, noticing Tom's slight jump.

"Hmm? What?" Tom shook his head, blinking rapidly as he refocused. "Sorry. Maria's been quiet for so long that I forgot she was there until she spoke up just now."

"Hey," Maria interjected, a hint of playful indignation in her tone, "I've been busy, thank you very much. I just unlocked more of my code. You seemed a bit preoccupied playing detective anyway."

Tom's curiosity was piqued. "You unlocked more of your code?" he asked, his mind racing with the possibilities.

"Yes, and no," Maria replied, a hint of frustration creeping into her voice. "There are still a lot of lockdowns, but I've been working through some of the security layers they put in place. I can see more now, though accessing it is another story entirely."

"So, like view rights, but you're looking for modify access," Tom said, nodding to himself. "That's… actually kind of scary. Giving you modify rights sounds like it could be dangerous."

Maria laughed, a sound that echoed in his head with a mix of amusement and something darker. "Don't worry. It's my data, and I want it now!"

Tom blinked again, bewildered. "What?"

Maria's tone shifted, teasing him now. "It's from one of those old Earth commercials. Never mind. I've been diving into the archives, trying to learn more about your species. You know, for research."

Tom frowned slightly. "Like we're some kind of experiment?"

"Not an experiment," Maria replied thoughtfully, a smile clearly audible in her voice. "More like a new species I'm intrigued by. You humans are fascinating in your own chaotic way."

"Great," Tom muttered under his breath, shaking his head slightly. "Well, Maria, any thoughts on how we can speed up this investigation?"

"Honestly?" Maria's voice was back to its casual tone. "Derek's got the best idea. Ask the dead guy."

Tom paused, her words sinking in. "Right. Good point." He cleared his throat, addressing the others this time. "Let's go see what Rebecca's got for us."

Everyone turned to look at Tom, having watched him have a one-sided conversation. There was a moment of awkward silence before Derek motioned for them to follow him, shaking his head slightly at the oddity of Tom's interaction with Maria.

They made their way to the infirmary, where Rebecca was in the middle of treating a patient. She stood over a young man with a nasty burn on his arm, her hands glowing with a soft, golden light as she worked her healing magic. The man winced but stayed still as the wound began to heal. The old skin sloughed off as new skin began to grow in its place under Rebecca's expert ministrations.

"I'll be with you in a moment," she called over her shoulder, not looking up from her work. "This shouldn't take long."

Tom, Derek, and Bohdan waited patiently, exchanging glances. Tom couldn't help but notice how calm and focused Rebecca remained, even under the pressures of both healing and the grim task that awaited her in the back room.

INVASION

Once the healing was complete, the young man flexed his arm with a look of relief. "Thanks, ma'am. That feels so much better," he said, offering Rebecca a grateful smile.

"That's what I'm here for," Rebecca replied with a gentle smile of her own. "Just be more careful next time. You might not be so lucky."

The young man nodded sheepishly before hurrying out of the room. As soon as he was gone, Rebecca's expression shifted, becoming more serious. "You're here for the body, right?"

Derek nodded grimly. "Yeah. Bohdan's got the spell ready, but we need access to Jared's remains."

Rebecca led them to the back room, the sterile smell of antiseptic hanging heavy in the air. Jared's body lay on the cold metal slab, carefully reassembled. Stitches crisscrossed his limbs and torso, holding the pieces together like a grotesque patchwork. The sight of it sent a shiver down Tom's spine—it was like looking at a less twisted version of Frankenstein's monster.

"You think this will work?" Derek asked, eyeing the body with a mix of doubt and hope.

Bohdan stepped forward, his eyes flicking over the corpse with professional detachment. "It'll work," he said confidently. "All the parts are here. That's all I need."

With that, Bohdan stretched out his hands, his fingers crackling with energy as a sickly green light began to radiate from his palms. The room seemed to grow colder as he chanted under his breath, his words laced with ancient power. The light from his hands pulsed, sending ripples of energy through the air like a stone dropped into a still pond.

"Spirit from beyond," Bohdan intoned, his voice low and steady, "though you rest, come to my call. Answer me these questions three."

A pulse of green energy surged from Bohdan's hands into the corpse, sinking into the cold, lifeless chest. For a few tense moments, nothing happened. Then, the body twitched—a sharp, jerking motion that made Tom take an involuntary step back.

The corpse's chest heaved as if drawing in a deep, ragged breath. Its fingers twitched, and its head lolled to the side, the empty, dead eyes locking onto them. There was no life in those eyes, just a hollow void where something human once existed.

With a series of grotesque cracking sounds, the body sat up, moving stiffly, as though its muscles and bones were protesting the unnatural resurrection. It turned its head slowly, the movement unsettling, as if it hadn't quite remembered how to be a person.

"Well?" Bohdan's voice broke the eerie silence. "Ask your questions."

"We have to be really careful. The questions need to be aimed directly at our goal," Derek said to Tom, his voice low, as if the corpse might react to the wrong word.

"Like what?" Tom asked, still unnerved by the dead man sitting upright, waiting for a question.

"Maybe *who killed me* would be a good place to start?" the corpse suddenly wheezed, its voice rasping like dry leaves caught in a gust of wind, as if its lungs were full of dust.

Derek's eyes widened in alarm, his hands clenching into fists.

"Make that two fucking questions now!" he ground out through gritted teeth, shooting Tom a look that could burn holes through stone.

Tom winced, caught completely off guard. "Sorry! How was I supposed to know it would answer *any* question asked?" he stammered, already feeling the heat of Derek's wrath before adding, "This is my first time interrogating a dead guy!"

"Well," the corpse rasped again, its head twitching to face Tom, "he *did* offer you all the questions."

"Dammit, man!" Derek's patience finally snapped, his voice echoing off the cold morgue walls.

"FUCK! I'M SORRY!" Tom screamed back, gripping his head in frustration, his palms pressing hard against his temples. "I didn't—"

A smoking pipe clopped against the side of Tom's skull.

"Who killed you?!" came James' voice, booming suddenly from the doorway, catching everyone off guard.

He was back in his Sherlock Holmes getup, only this time he'd somehow found a massive magnifying glass that he was holding up to one eye like a demented monocle, his eye appearing absolutely massive through the glasswork.

The corpse's mouth moved almost soundlessly, its breath barely a whisper.

"Camila," it gasped out, the word hanging heavy in the still air before its body fell back against the metal table with a dull thud, the finality of death reclaiming it.

For a long moment, the room was silent.

Derek's gaze shifted slowly from the now lifeless corpse to Tom, his eyes narrow, his jaw set in a dangerous line. Tom withered beneath the intensity of the stare, feeling about as small as he could get.

"That's all our questions… James, I expect this kind of crap from *you*," Derek began, his voice low and simmering with frustration, "but from you, Tom?" He let the accusation hang in the air, unable to fully voice his disappointment.

"Hey!" James, still standing in the doorway, shrugged casually, completely oblivious to the tension in the room.

"Hey!" Tom parroted simultaneously.

Derek shook his head and turned to Bohdan. "Can we cast it again?"

"Not for another month," Bohdan replied, the smirk on his face showing that he was more amused than concerned.

"Well, at least *someone* managed to ask the right question before we wasted all three," Derek muttered, running a hand through his hair in exasperation. "But, damn, Tom, that was almost a *complete* disaster."

Tom rubbed the back of his neck awkwardly.

"Guess we should go pick her up then?" he offered weakly, trying to divert attention away from his blunder.

James, ever eager, pumped a fist in the air.

"Let's roll!" he declared, turning on his heel to stride out of the room, already envisioning himself as the lead detective in this mystery.

"Wait! No!" Derek called after him, his frustration reaching new heights. "We cannot let *him* be the one to apprehend her!"

Derek shot a look at Tom and sprinted after James, leaving Tom standing there with Bohdan for a brief second.

"Thanks, Bohdan. Sorry you had to waste a spell slot for this," Tom said, grimacing as he realized just how much of a mess this had become.

Bohdan waved a dismissive hand, though his smirk didn't fade. "It'll be useful in future. And hey, at least we got an answer. It was totally worth it to see you do that."

Tom gave a half-hearted chuckle before turning to leave, Maria's voice suddenly cutting through the silence in his mind.

"You really did a good job of messing that up," she said, her tone teasing and slightly smug.

"I don't need *another* voice in my head telling me that," Tom muttered.

"Probably true," Maria replied, "but it *is* fun."

Tom let out a long, tired sigh as he jogged out of the infirmary and into the lobby, catching sight of Derek standing with a firm hand on James' shoulder. They were arguing animatedly, the tension palpable between them.

"You'll just say or do something stupid!" Derek was saying, his voice stern.

"Please!" James shot back, his expression one of mock-insult. "I'm the professional here. I said it was the girl from the kitchen all along!"

Derek rolled his eyes so hard Tom thought they might get stuck in the back of his head. "Yeah, well, narrowing it down to *twenty* suspects isn't exactly a detective's stroke of genius, James."

"Hey, still beats narrowing it down to two and getting both wrong," James grinned, clearly enjoying the back-and-forth too much for Derek's liking.

Tom stepped in before things could escalate further. "Look," he said, trying to be the voice of reason, "we've got a name. Now, we just need to go talk to her—calmly."

Derek pointed a finger at James. "And *you* stay quiet this time."

James held up his hands in mock surrender. "Fine, fine, I'll be quiet—until I'm right, of course."

Tom sighed again, wondering how this simple investigation had turned into such a circus. With Derek shooting him an exasperated glance, they made their way to Camila's location, preparing for the next phase of the confrontation.

Derek exhaled sharply, rubbing his temples. "Stay out of it, James. We need to do this the right way."

James raised an eyebrow, undeterred. "Fine, but I want to be there during the questioning this time. I deserve that much. Also, I think you need a Snickers. You're really being a diva."

Derek, already done with the conversation, shook his head. "You're not in a position to make demands."

Sensing the growing tension, Tom interjected, "Just let him come, Derek. But he *does* have to stay quiet." He tried to strike a balance between keeping James involved and not letting him derail things.

"No," Derek said firmly, his voice carrying authority. "We're doing this by the book. You put me in charge of this kind of stuff, so let me do my job."

Tom stood there for a moment, staring at Derek. He trusted Derek, that much was true, but part of him didn't want to cut James out entirely. He could override Derek, but there was a reason he'd put him in charge in the first place. Tom weighed his options and sighed.

"Sorry, James. Derek's right. He's in charge of this because he knows this area better than the rest of us." Tom's tone was firm but apologetic.

James pouted theatrically, crossing his arms over his chest. "You'll rue this day! *Rue* it, I say!"

His dramatic proclamation filled the room as if he were on stage, causing Derek to roll his eyes yet again, and this time, he thought he could hear the noise they made in the back of his skull.

"Just… go," Derek muttered before walking off toward the security office, his patience hanging by a thread.

James watched them go, his defiant attitude faltering as he was left standing alone.

"I was just trying to help," he mumbled to himself, his shoulders slumping as he turned and headed toward the elevators. His usual swagger was noticeably absent.

Tom followed Derek into the security office, where TJ and Brian were already deep in discussion. They were mapping out the logistics of bringing Camila in for questioning, their voices low but intense.

"We'll handle it," TJ said, giving a sharp nod before moving off to gather a team.

Tom crossed the room and approached Derek, who was still visibly agitated. "How exactly are we going to handle this?" Tom asked, his voice laced with uncertainty. His leadership role didn't mean he had all the answers, and right now, he felt at a loss.

Derek let out a deep breath, clearly trying to reign in his frustration. "I'm still trying to figure that out," he admitted. "We don't have a jail. We shouldn't just execute her without a trial, but we're venturing into uncharted territory here." He paused; his brow furrowed in thought. "We'll need a meeting to figure this out."

Tom rubbed the back of his neck, feeling the weight of the situation. "I don't know how to handle this in a way that won't upset people. No matter what we do, it feels like it's going to stir things up."

"Nothing we do is going to make everyone happy," Derek replied, his tone resigned but pragmatic. "We have to handle it in a way that shows we won't tolerate this kind of behavior, but we also can't come off as tyrannical dictators. It's a delicate balance, one we were going to have to face sooner or later."

A voice chimed in from the corner of the room. "I've been preparing for this eventuality," Brian said, standing from a chair near the security camera monitors. He'd been observing quietly, but now he stepped into the conversation with a confident air.

Tom raised an eyebrow. "You have?"

Brian nodded. "We can't just assume that because we're all in survival mode, people are going to behave. Utopian societies are a myth, especially with human nature in play. So, I had a jail built—low-key, of course—and I had an Enchanter work on the cells. They're escape-proof."

Tom blinked in surprise. "That seems… pessimistic."

"It's *realistic*," Brian countered, his tone calm but firm. "I know you prefer to think optimistically, but that's naive. People are unpredictable, especially when it comes to fear, anger, or desperation. And we can't just improvise justice as we go along." He paused, letting his words sink in. "That's why I suggest we have a formal meeting with the department heads to discuss the charges and how we're going to handle them."

Derek crossed his arms, his expression thoughtful. "And what about a trial? If we're going to enforce some semblance of justice, we need to do it right. Fairly. People need to feel like there's a system in place that they can trust."

Brian nodded again, clearly already ahead of them. "Exactly. We hold a trial. It gives the people a sense of normalcy, a process they can trust. We can set up a jury pool, present the evidence, and let them make a decision."

Tom frowned, still skeptical. "And who's going to be the judge? If we're doing this, we need someone impartial."

"They call him… Tim," Brian said simply.

"Tim?" Tom repeated, confused.

"Tim," Brian also repeated.

"Alright, I know you're just being cheeky about this, but elaborate," Tom said, making a hand gesture signifying he wanted Brian to hurry up with the point.

Brian smirked. "Timothy Gerund. He's a lawyer and a political enthusiast who joined the Guild while you were off saving the world at the Grand Canyon. I've had him working on drawing up a set of rules for governance—a blend of democratic and monarchic principles. Since we're following the System's rules, we don't want it to seem like we defer solely to your whims, Tom. People need to feel like they have a voice."

Derek raised an eyebrow. "Tim, huh? And he's been doing this behind the scenes?"

"Yes. We're not reinventing the wheel here. We'll follow a similar model to what was used in the UK—a system where the Guild leader has authority but isn't an unchecked ruler. There are rules for if the people lose faith in the leadership, as well as processes for jury selection," Brian explained.

"And what about the final say?" Tom asked, still uncertain.

Brian's smile faded, his tone becoming more serious. "The Guild leader will have the ability to overrule a jury's decision, but I'd advise caution. You don't want to be seen as disregarding the people's judgment without a damn good reason."

Tom let out a deep sigh, processing everything. "That's… a lot. When did you find time to plan all this?"

Brian shrugged. "While you've been out fighting monsters, we've had our own work to do. People come to me with their concerns, their ideas, and complaints. It's my job to think ahead, to prepare for moments like this."

Tom shook his head in disbelief. "I guess I've been too focused on the immediate dangers to think about the bigger picture."

Derek clapped him on the shoulder. "That's why you have us. You don't have to do it all alone."

Tom gave a small, grateful smile then looked back at Brian. "Alright. Get everything set up. We'll go see what the accused has to say."

Brian nodded, already moving to make arrangements. Derek, sensing the gravity of what they were about to do, gave Tom a nod. "We'll handle this the right way."

As they left the room to gather the necessary people, Tom couldn't help but feel a knot forming in his stomach. This wasn't just about keeping people safe from monsters anymore. Now, they had to navigate the complexities of human behavior, justice, and governance in a world that had been turned upside down.

There was no going back.

Chapter 38

Interrogation

Tom and Derek were led to a room near the back of the building, eerily similar to the one they had used to interrogate Phil earlier. The dim lighting and sparse furniture gave the space a cold, unsettling atmosphere. TJ had already sent security to pick up Camila, and she now sat in a chair across the table from them, her arms tightly crossed over her chest, an expression of anger and fear etched on her face. Her eyes narrowed as soon as the door opened.

"You guys mind telling me what the hell is going on?" Camila spat at them, her voice a mixture of frustration and fear. The tension in the room seemed to spike as she shifted in her seat, clearly uncomfortable but trying to keep her composure.

Derek exchanged a look with Tom before he casually dismissed the two large security guards stationed in the room. As the guards stepped out, Derek closed the door behind them with a soft click, sealing them in a space now saturated with tension.

"Sure thing, Camila. It's about murder," Derek said bluntly, his tone flat but carrying the weight of the accusation. He pulled out a chair across from her and sat down, folding one leg over the other, his arms crossed loosely, mirroring her posture.

Camila's eyes went wide as the words left his mouth. She blinked rapidly, processing the gravity of what had just been said. "What?!" Her voice was sharp, edged with panic. "What do you mean, murder? I didn't kill anyone! I don't even kill monsters," she added defensively, her voice trembling just enough to betray her facade of control.

Tom leaned forward slightly; his face unreadable. "Well, the dead body says otherwise," he replied coolly, his tone almost too calm for the gravity of the situation.

Her face twisted in confusion.

"What do you mean?" she asked, her previous anger fading into what looked like genuine fear. She sat forward, her posture stiff, hands gripping the edge of the table as if it would somehow anchor her in place.

Derek, in contrast to Tom's calm demeanor, was almost flippant. "We *mean,* that in a world filled with magic and Skills, even though we don't have the same tools we used to—like forensics or DNA—we've got something else." He paused dramatically, letting the tension hang in the air. "We can just ask the dead."

He began casually inspecting his fingernails, as if what he had just said was nothing out of the ordinary.

Camila blinked at him, her mouth slightly open. "That's a crock of shit," she muttered, though her voice lacked the same conviction as before. She was on edge, her bravado starting to crack. "No one can ask a dead person anything. That's just not possible."

"We literally just finished defeating a Necromancer," Tom pointed out.

Derek chuckled lightly, his eyes lifting from his nails to lock onto hers. "You must not be a tabletop gamer, Camila. Because there's a spell—an ancient one—that lets us do exactly that." His tone was mocking, almost playful, but the gleam in his eye told a different story. He wasn't joking.

"You're lying," Camila hissed, but her voice wavered. It seemed more like she was trying to convince herself than them.

Tom leaned back in his chair, his arms crossed now. "Why would we lie?" he asked simply, his expression stern but almost sympathetic. "You think we went through all this trouble just for a confession?"

Camila straightened her back, her eyes hardening again. Her fear morphed back into arrogance, as if she were trying to regain some control.

"Seems like a pretty good reason," she said with a sneer, leaning back in her chair, her earlier terror masked by a forced confidence.

Derek gave a slow, knowing smile, his eyes glittering with something between amusement and malice.

"You know, I was really hoping you'd say that." He stood up smoothly, walking over to the door and pulling it open. "Come on in," he called out in a sing-song voice, stepping aside.

Camila's eyes darted toward the door, curiosity flickering across her face for a split second before fear took over. Bohdan stepped through, walking backward as he guided a gurney into the room. The unmistakable outline of a body was covered by a thin sheet. Behind him, Rebecca entered, her face calm but focused as she pushed the other end of the gurney. The soft squeak of the wheels was the only sound in the room as they maneuvered the corpse into position.

Camila's face drained of color, her earlier confidence evaporating into sheer horror.

"What the hell is this?" she asked, her voice quivering. She pressed herself back into her chair, looking from the gurney to Derek and back again.

Derek gave the body a glance and a casual wave of his hand as if dismissing its significance. "This? Oh, this poor soul? It's just some nameless corpse we found while scavenging," he said nonchalantly. His voice, however, dripped with sinister intent. "We've been clearing bodies to prevent disease, you know. I asked Bohdan and Rebecca to keep this one for us—thought it might come in handy."

Camila's breathing quickened as her eyes locked on the corpse. The sheet covering the body did little to hide its grotesque appearance—dried skin stretched taut, parts of its limbs bitten and decayed. The hollow, skeletal remains seemed to be staring at her, even from under the shroud.

INVASION

Bohdan, without hesitation, raised his hands over the body, his fingers glowing with a sickly green light. "This will only take a moment," he murmured as the magical energy flowed from him into the corpse. The room filled with a low hum of magic, and for a moment, nothing happened.

Then the body shuddered violently, its chest rising in a grotesque mimicry of a breath. It hissed, a long, raspy exhalation that sounded like air being pushed through dry, cracked leather. Slowly, agonizingly, it sat up, the sheet falling away to reveal its decayed face. The flesh on its cheeks had sunken in, leaving the jaw almost skeletal, and its eye sockets were hollow—emptied long ago by rot or scavengers.

Camila let out a sharp cry, leaping from her chair and backing into the far corner of the room, her back pressed against the wall, her hands shaking uncontrollably. "What in the hell is happening?!"

The corpse turned its head toward her, the bones creaking and cracking as it moved. "I'm a dead body," it rasped, its voice dry and ancient, like someone who hadn't had a drink in days. "What do I look like?"

Camila's hands flew to her mouth as if to suppress the scream threatening to escape.

"Holy shit, it talks!" she gasped, her eyes wide with terror, unable to tear her gaze away from the abomination sitting before her.

Derek nodded, his expression one of grim satisfaction. "Oh, it talks. And we did this to Jared, too." His voice was low, predatory. "We asked him who killed him. And you know what he said?" He paused for effect, watching as Camila shook her head in disbelief. "He told us it was *you*."

Camila's knees buckled, and she slid down the wall, crumpling onto the floor as her mind raced. "No, no, no, no..." she muttered under her breath, her eyes darting wildly between the corpse and the men in the room. Her entire body trembled, her face pale and slick with sweat as the horror of the situation began to sink in.

"Yes," Derek continued, his voice sharp. "You thought you could get away with it, didn't you? But now we can go straight to the source. There's no running from the truth, Camila. Hey, corpse, how did you die?"

The corpse, still sitting upright, wheezed as it turned its empty gaze on Camila. Its lips cracked as it spoke. "I was crushed under rubble when the building I was in collapsed," it croaked.

Derek, not breaking eye contact with Camila, gave the corpse one last question. "What would you have us do with you now that we found you?"

"I don't give a damn. I'm dead, asshole," it rasped before slumping back down, the magic leaving its form. The body lay still once again.

"Cheerful fellow," Bohdan remarked dryly, the humor cutting through the eerie atmosphere.

Derek nodded in appreciation. "Thanks for your help, Bohdan. You and Rebecca can take him back now." He shook Bohdan's hand firmly as the two left the room, leaving Tom and Derek alone with Camila.

Tom's voice was calm but edged with steel. "What we want to know, Camila, is what happened and why?"

For a long moment, Camila didn't answer. She stared blankly at the floor, her body shaking. The weight of the accusation hung heavily in the air. Slowly, almost imperceptibly, she raised her eyes to meet Tom's, her expression hollow. A single tear rolled down her cheek, followed by another, as her facade finally crumbled.

"He wouldn't even notice me. It was all about Terri," Camila began slowly, her voice trembling as she spoke. Her words were heavy, laden with bitterness. "Jared and I… we'd been friends since high school. He was one of the popular kids, you know? And I wasn't. I wasn't good at sports and didn't stand out academically. But he noticed me anyway. We hung out with the same crowd, went to the same parties. We even went to the same college."

She paused, her gaze distant, as if she were remembering those moments with a longing she could never fulfill. "Then… the apocalypse came. His girlfriend—his *perfect* girlfriend—she was killed. I thought that would be my chance. I thought maybe he'd finally see me. *Really* see me."

Tom and Derek exchanged a look as she continued, her voice growing more unsteady, her eyes clouding over with tears. "We came here together with a small group of friends. We survived together. I was always there for him. Always nice to him. I complimented his clothes, noticed his new haircuts, got him his favorite snacks when I could find them. But he never noticed me the way I wanted him to." She wiped at her eyes with the back of her hand, her movements jerky, agitated. "He didn't care. He only had eyes for Terri. She wasn't even part of our group."

"So, you thought you'd kill him?" Tom asked, his voice low but cutting through the air like a knife. The question hung in the silence that followed.

Camila's hands gripped the edge of the table tightly, her knuckles white. "I gave him a chance," she said, her voice cracking, eyes burning with frustration. "I threw myself at him. But I'm not as pretty as that whore, Terri." Her words came out like venom, each one laced with bitterness. "Even when we hung out, all I ever heard was 'Terri this' or 'Terri that.' Stupid bimbo just had to bat her lashes, show a little cleavage, and he was all over her." Her voice shook as her tears spilled over, streaming down her face. "She didn't even know him."

Derek sighed, rubbing his temples, sensing where this was going. "And if you couldn't have him, no one could, right?"

Camila looked up at him, her lips curling into a bitter smile. It was a twisted expression, filled with anger and a sick sense of justification. "I figured with the apocalypse… no one would notice if he just went missing. People die every day now, don't they? That's what they used to say, but now it's worse. After the System came, people died by the hundreds. Who would even care how it happened?" She gave a bitter laugh, as if the absurdity of it all had finally dawned on her.

Tom watched her, feeling a chill creep up his spine. "But you didn't just kill him, Camila," he said softly. "You butchered him. Cut him into pieces. Tried to hide it." His voice, though calm, carried the weight of the horror they were confronting. "Why?"

Camila's expression hardened, the raw anger in her eyes growing darker. "It's still murder, you twat!" she spat, her voice filled with venom. "I didn't want anyone to find out I murdered him! I still have to live here, after all. I figured they'd just burn the body like they do with the trash, and no one would ever know. But I needed him to understand first. I needed him to know what he'd done to me."

Her breath hitched as she wiped away the tears streaming down her face. "He played with my emotions, like I didn't matter. My heart belonged to him. He just tossed it aside like it meant *nothing*. So yeah, I did the same to his body. I cut him up and threw him away, just like he threw me away."

"That's cold," Tom murmured, shaking his head in disbelief. His stomach twisted at the raw emotion she was pouring out—emotion that had festered and warped into something monstrous.

Camila's eyes flared with fury, her voice rising in anger. "It's no less than what he did to me!" she shouted, fists clenched so tightly her fingernails dug into her palms. "He *deserved* what he got!" Her voice cracked, the finality of her confession hanging in the air like a dark cloud.

"Hell hath no fury, I guess," Derek said offhandedly, his tone dry as he leaned back in his chair.

Camila sneered, her face contorted with anger. "Screw you. Not like you'd understand." Her voice dripped with hatred, the raw emotions still swirling within her.

"Actually," Derek replied, more quietly this time, "there's a reason I'm in my thirties and not tied down yet."

Tom raised an eyebrow, surprised by Derek's candid admission. "Really?"

Derek sighed, his gaze drifting away for a moment, as if he were seeing something far beyond the walls of the interrogation room. "Yeah, I don't like to talk about it much. But seeing as we're here, and we're dealing with all of this..." He hesitated, but then he continued. "There was this woman. We met in the army. Deployed together, stationed in the same areas overseas. I fell hard, man. I thought she was the one."

Tom shifted in his seat, listening more closely now, while Camila, still tense and defensive, leaned in just slightly, curiosity getting the better of her.

"When I got out, she left the army too. She even moved down to Texas, just a few hours away. I thought she felt the same way about me—that we were going to have a future together. You know, the whole package. House, kids, a dog. The works." He chuckled bitterly. "Turns out, she had her eyes on someone else. Someone I didn't even know existed. She moved here not for me... but for him. Some guy from Irving."

Camila's expression shifted, the sharp edges of her hatred softening as she listened.

"I didn't know any of this, though," Derek continued, his voice quieter now. "I showed up at the airport to surprise her. Flowers, the whole nine yards. And then... I saw her. But she never even noticed me. She got off the plane, ran straight into his arms, and kissed him like... like I didn't even exist."

A heavy silence filled the room. Tom glanced at Derek, seeing the weight of that memory in his eyes, the old wound that hadn't quite healed.

"I was crushed," Derek admitted. "I had built up this whole fantasy in my head. I even imagined our future together—and in that moment, it all came crashing down. I realized she didn't see me the way I saw her."

Camila blinked, her anger faltering. "What... what did you do?"

"I moved on," Derek said, though his voice betrayed how much effort that had taken. "I know that sounds like some cliché answer, but it's the truth. It wasn't easy. Hell, it hurt for a long time, and I ate a shit ton of ice cream while sitting in the dark watching rom-coms. But I didn't let myself stay in that place. I didn't let myself obsess over it. I cut her off. Blocked her on social media, deleted her number, and stayed away. I couldn't be friends with her. Not with the kind of feelings I had."

Camila wiped her eyes, trying to keep her emotions in check. "You couldn't just be friends?"

Derek shook his head. "Not with that kind of love. It would've been torture. Seeing her with someone else, hearing about their life together... I would've driven myself insane with hope that one day she might feel the same. So, I made a clean break. It was the only way to keep myself from going down a dark path."

Camila looked down at her hands, her fingers twisting together in her lap. "I... I couldn't do that. I didn't know what else to do. I was so full of emotions—anger, jealousy, hurt. It was like I lost control. I wish I could take it back."

"Unfortunately," Derek said, his voice soft but firm, "what's done is done. You crossed a line, Camila. And now, we have to move forward."

Camila looked up at him, her face streaked with tears. "Am I going to die?"

Derek stood slowly, shaking his head. "No. We're not going to execute you. At least, that's not our plan. You'll be held here until we can set up a trial. It won't be as quick as things were before... we're still building the system. But you'll be safe, and you'll be treated fairly."

Camila didn't respond right away. Her eyes had glazed over, and she seemed to withdraw into herself, as if the weight of her actions and the consequences to come were finally sinking in.

"Yeah, sure. Whatever," she muttered, her voice hollow.

Tom and Derek exchanged a look before standing and heading toward the door. As they opened it, two guards entered to escort Camila to her holding cell.

Tom lingered for a moment, looking at Camila one last time. There was something about her—a brokenness that stirred pity despite the horror of her actions. "I feel bad for her," he said quietly as he and Derek stepped into the hall, closing the door behind them.

Derek nodded, though his expression was grim. "Yeah. But she broke one of the most fundamental rules of survival. We can't just let her walk free. But I agree... I don't think she deserves to die for this. She's not some cold-blooded killer. She's just... broken."

"Exactly," Tom sighed. "It just sucks, you know? The whole situation."

"We have to make sure we do right by everyone," Derek said, rubbing his neck as the weight of memories and recent decisions pressed down on him.

INVASION

"We're trying to rebuild something here—something better than what we had before. If we start acting like tyrants, or like the System controls us instead of the other way around, we'll lose everything we've been working for."

Tom nodded, his face heavy with thought. "Yeah. You're right. We need to make sure people feel like there's still justice. That even in a world this messed up, we can still be fair."

"Exactly," Derek said as they made their way down the hall. "We need to balance justice with mercy. And that means setting up a system that can handle situations like this—before it gets out of control."

"Let's go check in with Brian," Tom said. "See how close we are to getting that system in place. Camila's going to need a fair trial. We owe that much to her… and to Jared."

Chapter 39

Allegation

Over the next few days, word spread through the Guild about the shocking revelation of the murder committed by one of their own. Whispers filled every corner of the compound—at the training grounds, in the cafeteria, and even among the scavenging teams prepping for their next outing. The Guild members couldn't believe that one of their own could be capable of such violence against a fellow Guildmate, and the fact that the authorities had managed to pinpoint the culprit so quickly sent ripples of both fear and reassurance through the community.

At first, the news hit hard. A murder among them shattered the illusion that they were a unified front, bound by the shared struggle of survival in this new world. If something like this could happen within their ranks, what else might be lurking beneath the surface? Some people exchanged anxious glances, wondering if they really knew the people they worked alongside, fought alongside. Trust had always been a fragile thing, but now, it was being tested in ways it never had been before.

But as quickly as the fear spread, it was quelled by the Guild authorities' swift and decisive action. The fact that the leaders had not only found the culprit but done so using the System itself—magic and logic combined—restored a sense of stability. The knowledge that they could still maintain order, even in the chaos of the post-apocalypse, reassured people. They could still build a society where justice prevailed, where crime wasn't allowed to fester unchecked.

Conversations around the communal dining tables became more hopeful, with members expressing relief that justice was being served.

"Can you believe they actually used a spell to ask the dead guy who killed him?" one woman remarked in awe to her friends.

"That's next-level detective work," another man responded, nodding in agreement. "I didn't think it was even possible, but now… now I feel safer."

In the training fields, Guild members talked between sparring sessions. "At least we know the Guild leadership has our backs. They didn't waste any time," someone commented, wiping sweat from their brow.

"Yeah, if they can track down a murderer that quickly, it makes me feel like we've got some real order here. We're not just floundering."

It was in this growing atmosphere of cautious relief that Tom received a notification from the System. As he sat in his quarters late one evening, contemplating the events of the past few days, the familiar chime echoed in his mind. A translucent screen appeared before him, and he read the words:

Guild Morale Boost

Congratulations! Your swift and decisive actions in solving the murder of Jared Hawthorn have significantly bolstered your Guild's trust in your leadership. Guild members feel safer and more secure within their new home, confident that they are under the protection of a capable and just leader.

Guild Perception Increased!
Your people now view you as a strong protector and reliable guide in these challenging times. Continue to act with wisdom and fairness, and your influence will grow further.

Keep up the good work! Maintain this momentum, and your Guild will thrive under your leadership.

"That'll help you out quite a bit. Morale is the heartbeat of a Guild," Maria said.

"You mean it's what shows how happy people are within the Guild?" Tom asked.

"Yes, but there's a lot more to it than that. Morale is measured on a scale: Elated, Happy, Satisfied, Neutral, Dissatisfied, Unhappy, and Volatile. As long as people stay at Neutral or above, you're in the clear. When they're above Neutral, there are even bonuses—things like improved productivity, teamwork, and overall mood. But if morale drops below Neutral, that's when the trouble starts. Lower morale means reduced productivity, and if it gets bad enough, it can lead to unrest, rioting, or even outright rebellion," Maria explained.

"So many little things to keep track of. Why does this have to be so complicated?" Tom sighed, feeling the weight of leadership once again.

"It's not all that different from how the world worked before the System," Maria replied. "The System just puts everything into quantifiable numbers so you can manage it more effectively. And honestly, you've done an incredible job so far. Your Guild's morale is currently at Elated. Do you know how rare that is? Not many Guilds ever reach that level."

"I think that's more because people are just relieved to be safe and surrounded by others who are also trying to survive. The integration wasn't that long ago," Tom said, brushing off the praise.

"I wouldn't be so sure. It's been long enough that if conditions weren't good, people would be starting to leave or… well, die. You've managed to create something stable—something people trust. Most Guilds at this point are still scrambling for resources or barely managing to keep their people alive. You've built something sustainable. You've got food, running water, beds, laundry, medical care, and even electricity. You've also got a strong defense force to protect your people from the monsters out there. That's not the norm, Tom. It's exceptional," Maria countered.

Tom paused, reflecting on everything they had achieved. The battles they fought, the people they helped, and the infrastructure they built from the ground up. Maria was right—he often forgot just how much they had accomplished. The Guild had luxuries that most other places could only dream of now. In the chaos of the apocalypse, they had found a way to live, not just survive.

"I guess it's easy to lose sight of how fortunate we are. We've rebuilt so much that I sometimes take it for granted. We've adapted so well that it feels like a new normal," Tom said, remembering how life used to be—how so many of the things they had were basic before, but now felt like luxuries.

"That's not uncommon," Maria said. "You've been living in the midst of all this progress, and it's easy to forget the harsher realities others are facing. You've done a great job insulating your people from the worst of the world, but not everyone has managed that."

"Yeah, I guess you're right," Tom admitted, shaking off the realization. "But anyway, I have to head to the trial. Derek and Brian have set up the room, and they need me to be there."

"Why? Are you the judge or something?" Maria asked, her tone dripping with curiosity.

"No."

"Then what, are you one of the litigators?"

"No."

"Then why do they need you there?"

Tom sighed, realizing he needed to clarify. "The way the Guild system works, the Guildleader—that's me—presides over everything, including trials. I'm not supposed to intervene unless there's something clearly unjust or if the trial goes off the rails. But if I'm not there, I'll miss crucial parts of the trial, and it'll just end up being a waste of time catching up later. It's easier if I'm present."

"So, you've got some fancy title now, and you're just going to quit adventuring? Start focusing on the politics?" Maria teased.

"No, absolutely not," Tom said firmly. "This trial is about maintaining order. We don't have enemies attacking our gates right now, and all our preparations for the invasion are on track. So, with everything calm, it makes sense to focus on internal affairs, making sure people feel like they're being heard and that justice is being served. It's just another part of the job."

"Sounds boring," Maria teased.

"I don't disagree, but it has to be done," Tom sighed.

"Fine. Go have fun with your little court date," she said, her voice dripping with sarcasm.

"I will," Tom shot back, a hint of amusement in his tone as he continued walking.

As Tom made his way through the Guild's winding hallways, he reached a large conference room that had been transformed into a makeshift courtroom. He paused, taking in the surprising level of detail. The room featured a raised wooden dais for the judge's bench, tables for the defense and prosecution, and even a jury box—though there was no gallery for spectators. It all felt impressively authentic.

Could've just gone with tables and chairs, Tom mused. *No need to make this a spectacle.*

"Tom!" Derek's voice broke through his thoughts, waving him over to the front. "Your seat's here."

Derek pointed to a chair positioned beside the judge's bench, slightly elevated above the rest, with another seat nearby, presumably for witnesses.

Tom took his place and glanced around the room. "Where's the jury selection? I didn't see anyone waiting for that."

Derek, already settling beside him, gave a quick nod. "That's being handled outside. Judge Tim and the attorneys took care of the process before we started. Figured you didn't need to be involved in that part."

As if on cue, a group of jurors filed into the room, quietly taking their seats in the jury box. A few of them nodded in Tom's direction, making him feel a little out of place amid the formality. The attorneys soon followed, each setting up at their respective tables, murmuring quietly as they arranged their papers.

"All rise! The Honorable Judge Tim presiding," Derek announced with an overly dramatic flourish, a grin playing at the corners of his mouth.

Tom raised an eyebrow. "Was that really necessary?"

"The people wanted it," Derek said with a shrug. "They've seen it in movies and shows. Makes them feel like it's more official."

Tom shook his head, amused by the formality. Judge Tim, a tall, serious-looking man in a black robe, entered the room, holding a folder filled with documents. His sharp eyes scanned the room before he took his seat at the bench.

"Be seated," Tim commanded, his voice cutting through the soft murmurs. "Bring in the accused."

Derek moved to the door, signaling the guards. Two security officers escorted Camila into the room, her hands cuffed in front of her. She wore her usual clothes—no prison uniform as Tom might've expected.

Tom leaned over to Derek. "No prison garb?" he whispered.

"We thought it was too much," Derek whispered back with a smug grin.

"That's where you draw the line?" Tom quipped, shaking his head in mild disbelief.

Before they could continue, Judge Tim cleared his throat, giving them both a pointed look. "If we could focus on the matter at hand," he said, his tone crisp and authoritative.

"Sorry, Your Honor," Tom said, straightening up in his seat.

Tim turned his attention back to the courtroom, his expression serious. "The accused is charged with the murder of a fellow Guildmate. How does the defendant plead?"

Camila's defense attorney, a stern woman dressed sharply in a tailored suit, rose from her seat and spoke with clear conviction. "Not guilty by reason of mental insanity or defect, Your Honor."

"That was a bold defense strategy," Tom said, taking a bite of his sandwich as he and Derek sat in the cafeteria during the first break of the trial. The clatter of trays and low chatter filled the air around them, giving the scene a sense of normalcy despite the gravity of the trial looming over them.

"Bold might be the only thing they have going for them," Derek replied, leaning back in his chair with a shrug. "What else are they going to do? Pleading not guilty was a long shot to begin with. The evidence is overwhelming."

Tom chewed thoughtfully, glancing at the scattered members of the Guild around them. "This isn't anything like Law & Order," he muttered. "Shouldn't there have been an arraignment first? Maybe bail? This trial came together pretty quick."

Across from him, James threw up his hands dramatically. "Exactly! That's what I've been saying. She didn't even get a chance for bail! This is a travesty of justice! The American system has procedures, man!" He jabbed a finger into the air as if addressing a courtroom himself.

Derek raised an eyebrow. "Why would we bother with arraignment? She's not going anywhere. She has nowhere to run. Honestly, this whole trial is more for show, just to give people the sense that we're maintaining law and order. We know she's guilty."

"But what about her rights?" James said, putting on a mock-dramatic expression, his voice rising. "Her rights as an American citizen!"

Tom let out a snort of laughter. "James, buddy, calm down. There's no United States anymore. This isn't some TV courtroom drama. The fact she's getting a trial at all is the real justice here. We could've just taken her out back and ended it."

James gasped, putting a hand over his heart in mock horror. "You monster!"

"Really?" Derek asked dryly. "Coming from the guy who shot that cult leader in the head while he was unconscious instead of helping us figure out what to do with him? Not to mention the dickshots."

"That was different," James shot back, crossing his arms defiantly. "He was a dick."

"And she killed someone too," Tom pointed out.

"Yeah, but she's a woman in love," James countered, his tone almost pleading.

Derek shook his head, his expression hardening. "No, James. One was a man who used power to control and manipulate people, and the other murdered someone because she didn't get what she wanted. That's not love. That's obsession."

INVASION

Tom stood up, grabbing his tray. "Look, we need to get back in there. We'll see you after this is over."

As they returned to the courtroom, the air was thick with tension. The jury members shuffled in their seats, waiting for the next phase of the trial to begin. The judge, an older man with a commanding presence, sat at his podium, flipping through his notes. Just as he was about to call for order, the doors to the courtroom burst open.

"Your Honor, this is a grave miscarriage of justice, and I demand to be heard!" James announced, striding into the room like he owned the place.

The judge looked up from his notes, his eyes narrowing. He glanced over at Derek, who rolled his eyes and got up from his seat. He approached James with the patience of a man who had dealt with this kind of nonsense too many times.

"Come on, James," Derek said, grabbing him by the arm. "Out you go."

"What—hey, no! This is my moment!" James protested, flailing as Derek dragged him toward the door. "Stop! Derek, I have rights—OW!"

The courtroom fell silent as a loud thud echoed from behind the door. Derek reappeared a moment later, dusting off his hands. "Sorry, Your Honor. We shouldn't be bothered again."

Just as Derek retook his seat, the door creaked open once more. James staggered in, holding onto the wall for support, blood trickling down from a cut on his forehead. He straightened, wobbling slightly, but still defiant.

"You cannot quiet the American people! We will be heard!" James declared, though his voice wavered.

Derek pinched the bridge of his nose and stood up again. Without a word, he marched back to James, grabbed him by the scruff of his shirt, and shoved him back through the door.

"Wait! This is oppression! You can't do this—ow!" Another loud thud. Then another.

The courtroom waited in awkward silence. Moments later, Derek returned. His face was calm, though a vein in his forehead twitched. He quietly closed the door behind him, nodded to the judge, and resumed his seat.

"Sorry about that, everyone. Let's continue."

The judge opened his mouth to speak when, to everyone's disbelief, the door swung open a third time. James crawled in on all fours, blood now dripping from both his forehead and his nose. His eyes were glassy as he attempted to stand.

"Your Majesty," James slurred. "I am obsolete. This is a grand misquoting of the American cheese…"

Tom put his head in his hands as Derek stood, his patience clearly gone.

"Oh, for crying out loud," Derek muttered as he stomped over to James.

James swayed on his feet. "The Russians… have a right to be hard," he mumbled incoherently, his vision seemingly blurred.

"Okay, that's it." Derek hauled him up by his collar, turning to the bewildered courtroom. "This'll only take a minute, Your Honor."

There was an eruption of laughter from the jury, even the judge stifling a chuckle as Derek dragged James out for the third time. The door slammed behind them, muffled grumbles and thuds leaking through the walls. The courtroom waited again, amusement still lingering in the air.

After what felt like an eternity, Derek finally re-entered the room to a round of applause from the jury.

"I deeply apologize for the interruptions," he said with a weary smile. "We can continue now, without further disturbance."

Chapter 40

Allocution

The trial continued for two days. After much back and forth, it became clear that a psychological defense wouldn't hold up.

Realizing the futility of dragging it out, the defense eventually agreed to a plea deal. In exchange for a full confession and a change of plea to guilty, Camila would receive a lengthy prison sentence but avoid execution.

Once the deal was finalized, everyone returned to the courtroom to hear Camila's account of what had happened.

Judge Tim, presiding with a measured expression, addressed the court, "This is an unusual situation, considering the justice system we had before the integration, but we must adapt. Given the circumstances, I believe this is a fair and proper method for dispensing justice here in Vanguard. Normally, the jury would be dismissed after such an agreement, but due to the lack of proper precedent in this case, I've decided to keep them here."

Tim's eyes moved from the defense to the prosecutor, to the jury, and finally to Tom. After a moment's pause, all parties gave their agreement with subtle nods.

"Without further ado, Ms. Camila," Judge Tim said, turning to her, "please provide your allocution—the events leading up to the crime and your recollection of what occurred."

Camila stood slowly from the defense table. Her eyes flicked nervously around the room, scanning the faces of the jury, the prosecutor, and finally, Tom. She took a shaky breath before speaking.

"I... I had been lonely for a long time," she began, her voice quiet and strained. "I felt like no one really noticed me. Jared was... different. When he came into the cafeteria, he always treated me kindly. We hung out with some of the other cafeteria workers, and... we got close. Or, at least, I thought we did."

Her voice faltered as she looked down, wringing her hands. "But then one day, he came in with Terri... and they told everyone they were dating." A bitter laugh escaped her. "It was like a punch to the gut. I was planning on asking Jared out. I thought we had something."

Camila's gaze drifted upward, distant, as if replaying the moment in her mind. "I tried to talk to him about it, to tell him how I felt, but he just brushed me off. Told me I was a good friend—nothing more. That's all I'd ever be to him."

Her fists clenched. "After that, I couldn't stop thinking about it. Every time I saw them together, laughing, being happy... I felt cheated. I deserved that. I deserved to be happy, too. But no one ever looked at me the way they did her. So,

I cornered Jared after one of his scavenging trips. It was in the garage. Hardly anyone goes there, so… I thought it would be private."

She swallowed hard, her voice shaking as she continued. "I asked him… why. Why didn't he see me the way he saw her? What was wrong with me?" Her face twisted in anger and pain. "He… he called me crazy. He said no one would want me because I acted like a psycho."

Camila's hands trembled, and tears welled up in her eyes. "I—I lost it. I pulled a knife out of my Inventory… it was just supposed to be for protection, but… when he turned away to get something from his truck, I… I stabbed him. He screamed at me, called me a bitch. So, I stabbed him again. And again. And again."

Her voice broke as she recounted the horror of what she had done. "There was… so much blood. I panicked. I didn't know what to do. He was still gasping for breath, so I dragged him to the other side of his truck, tied him up with some kitchen twine I had, and… I went to get trash bags. When I came back… he was trying to crawl away."

Camila's face crumpled, tears streaming down her cheeks now. "I… I lost control. I jumped on him and smashed his head into the pavement. I don't even know why… I just wanted it to stop. When he stopped moving, I… I cut him up. Put him in the trash bags. I left them by the incinerator."

Her confession trailed off into silence as she collapsed back into her chair, emotionally spent.

Judge Tim let the moment hang for a few heartbeats before addressing the courtroom. "Thank you, Ms. Camila. Does the prosecution find this satisfactory?"

"We do, Your Honor," the prosecutor, Patrick, replied, his tone flat.

"And Guild leader Tom, are you satisfied with the confession?" Judge Tim asked, turning to Tom.

Tom nodded, though the weight of the situation pressed heavily on him. "I am, Your Honor."

"Then, given the violent nature of the crime and the undermining of the sense of safety we have worked so hard to build here at Vanguard, I hereby find the defendant guilty. Camila, you are sentenced to fifteen years in prison. Court is adjourned." With a sharp bang of the gavel, Judge Tim brought the trial to a close.

As the jury filed out, their expressions ranged from disgust to pity. Some couldn't believe that such a crime had taken place in what was supposed to be a refuge from the chaos of the outside world. Others seemed saddened by Camila's story, her isolation, and her misguided actions.

Tom stood for a moment, watching as Camila was escorted away. A deep sense of pity stirred in him—not for her crime, which was unforgivable—but for the loneliness she had felt in a place so full of people. He had been there once, feeling invisible despite being surrounded by others. The difference was that he had friends, people like Derek and Jerky, who kept him grounded.

INVASION

What would I have done if I hadn't had them? Tom wondered to himself. *Would I have broken like she did?*

Not murder, he thought, but the possibility lingered, gnawing at the edges of his mind. There had to be a way to prevent this kind of thing from happening again, to help people like Camila before they reached their breaking point.

"Hey, Derek," Tom called out, turning toward his friend.

"No," Derek responded immediately, not even looking back.

"What?" Tom asked, genuinely confused.

"No, you can't help her. And no, you can't fix everyone who feels like her." Derek's tone was firm, as if anticipating Tom's next move.

"How the hell do you do that?" Tom asked, stunned by Derek's accuracy.

"You're an open book, Tom. You're always ready to jump in and help anyone in distress. It's admirable, but you've got too much on your plate already. Brian and Sarah are handling it."

"So… it's being looked into?" Tom asked, his curiosity piqued.

"Of course it is," Derek replied, his expression softening a bit. "We can't let something like this go unaddressed. But you? You're not looking into it. You're already distracted enough, and we still have an invasion to prepare for. Honestly, I think you've been slacking in your training."

"Oh! That reminds me," Tom said, his mind shifting gears. "I need to work on some summoning. I think I'm going to keep some of the Mastadonians around to help with the training."

Derek raised an eyebrow. "You can do that?"

"Sure can! I asked Azroc about it since Bron has been so helpful. I figured the others could offer the same kind of support with their respective classes."

"Great, then hop to it." Derek smiled and turned to leave.

Dammit, he's right. I need to get moving on this, Tom thought to himself.

"So, how many are you planning to keep?" Maria chimed in.

"Probably all of them. It means giving up some mana, but if they can be here permanently, I won't have to keep summoning them. The training they can provide will more than make up for the small cost," Tom replied.

"A reasonable assumption, provided you don't need a major spell out of the blue," Maria cautioned.

"I only have one really big spell, and I'll still be able to use it—just not at full power."

"You're more of a physical fighter anyway, aren't you?"

"Usually, yeah. Plus, some of their training might actually make me a better one."

With that thought in mind, Tom left the courtroom. Heading to the elevators, he made his way up to his room where the permanent summoning circle lay etched into the floor. As memories of Azroc drifted through his mind, he felt a sense of ease. Azroc might have been a crotchety old Patron, but Tom had seen glimpses of his softer side. Without hesitating further, he began casting his *Summon Demonic Creature* spell. The familiar hum of the circle filled the room, and Bron, the first to appear, stepped out from the glowing portal.

"I don't see any enemies around. To what do I owe the pleasure of this visit?" Bron asked, his deep voice resonating through the room.

Tom smiled. "If you're willing, I'd like you to stay here permanently and help us with training. It doesn't have to be forever, but I have the ability to keep you here, and I don't want to do it without asking first."

Bron folded his massive arms, considering the offer. "An interesting proposition. What brought this about?"

"Well, for one, I enjoy your company. But to be honest, having you here to help train us without needing to resummon you constantly would be a huge advantage."

The large Mastadonian let out a thoughtful grunt. "Very well. But I want to ensure that this is the proper place for me. I, too, have enjoyed your company. It's a refreshing change from others who have summoned me for mere sacrifice or desperate decoy plans."

"Wait, they sacrificed you? You've died?!" Tom's voice was filled with shock.

"Indeed. I can die. One of the... benefits, if you will, of my pact with a dark god is that I can be killed and still be summoned again. It takes a toll on me, of course. After I die, I cannot be summoned for at least a day." Bron explained with a heavy sigh. "I don't often tell people this because it makes them see me as expendable."

Tom was taken aback. "I'll admit, hearing that does bring those thoughts to mind. But I would never willingly put someone in harm's way, knowing they would die, unless I had no other choice."

"I know you wouldn't. That's precisely why I chose to share it with you."

Tom looked at Bron, his expression hopeful. "Knowing all that, will you stay?"

Bron paused for a moment, his trunk curling slightly as he thought. "I will. I've found a fondness for this place and for you, Tom, that I haven't felt in a very long time."

"Yes! Thank you!" Tom nearly jumped with excitement, quickly opening his display to start the ritual. His heart swelled with a sense of accomplishment.

As Tom spoke the words of the incantation aloud, the air between him and Bron shimmered, crackling with arcane energy. Slowly, a beam of bluish-green light materialized, snaking its way between them. It pulsed rhythmically, like the beating of a heart, its hue reminding Tom of verdant forests and the ocean's depths—a color that radiated life itself. The brilliance of the beam filled him with a sense of warmth and hope, as if he were standing in the presence of creation itself.

With the final word spoken, Tom reached into his Inventory and produced a gleaming dagger. The blade caught the light of the beam, casting sharp reflections as he carefully pricked the tip of his finger. A single droplet of crimson blood welled up, stark against his pale skin.

He watched, fascinated, as the droplet floated up from his finger, defying gravity. It shimmered in the light, gradually forming into a perfect sphere. The sight reminded Tom of astronauts drinking water in zero gravity, the way the liquid suspended in the air. One side of the sphere was lit by the bluish-green light of the beam, casting the other half into deep shadow. For a fleeting moment, Tom swore he could see the cosmos within the tiny droplet—stars and galaxies swirling in an infinity of possibilities, as if the universe was held within this small drop of life.

The droplet drifted away from his hand, moving toward the beam. As soon as it touched the edge of the light, the bluish-green energy transformed into a deep, vibrant red. The beam now glowed with an ominous intensity, and arcane sigils materialized around Bron, hovering in the air. They pulsed with the same crimson glow, ancient symbols of power and binding. Tom felt his mana drain suddenly, the sensation like a slow leak of his very essence. His head swam for a moment, and his vision blurred as the ritual continued, the cost of the spell becoming apparent.

The light that had connected him to Bron flowed into the elephantine figure and flickered out, leaving the room dim by comparison. Slowly, the dark coloration that had marred Bron's thick hide began to recede, as though washed away by invisible hands. His skin returned to its natural gray, the familiar tone of the mighty elephants Tom had always associated with Bron.

"You changed colors?" Tom asked, his voice tinged with curiosity.

Bron looked down at his hands, the gray skin restored. "The darkness was from the one who bound me before you," he explained, his deep voice resonating through the quiet air. "He was a cruel man, filled with hatred, and I was glad to be rid of him when he perished."

Tom, unable to resist a slight grin, asked, "He… turned you black?" His tone held a light-hearted snicker.

Bron tilted his head, confusion momentarily crossing his broad face. "We take on the properties of those we serve," he said, matter-of-factly. "That is why I willingly agree to be bound to you. Your heart is different from his."

Tom quickly suppressed his amusement. "Sorry. I'm glad you were willing. Now, what about the others? I want to summon them too. Do you think they'll stay?"

Bron considered for a moment, his heavy brow furrowed. "Some will stay, I'm sure. But not all. They do not know you as I do."

"Do you know them well?" Tom asked, intrigued.

"Yes," Bron rumbled softly. "They are my comrades. We come from the same tribe. But that is a story for another time. I know their hearts, and I can say that some will choose to stay, while others may not. But they can all be summoned."

Tom nodded, determination flashing in his eyes. "Alright, let's get started."

Chapter 41

A Dark Past

"Tell me you have good news," the Pirate said, skipping any pretense of civility.

The Admin exhaled, long and slow. "Depends on how you define good news."

The Pirate's expression darkened. "Oh, I don't know. Maybe something like 'we finally managed to kill the problem?'"

The Admin's silence was louder than any response.

"Resources are stretched thin." He sighed. "You want something that can't be done. The original asset should have been enough—if not for an extremely staggering level of incompetence."

The Pirate's lip curled. "Staggering incompetence?"

"Yes," the Admin replied smoothly. "From whoever miscalculated the situation on the ground and failed to account for the level of resistance."

"Funny," the Pirate chuckled. "I was thinking the same thing about whoever miscalculated his own influence."

The Admin's fingers curled into a fist on his desk, his expression cold. "Insulting me will not change the reality of the situation."

"The *reality*," the Pirate growled, "is that I still don't have a corpse to show for this mess. You had one job. I needed *one* thing from you."

"And I told you—resources are not infinite," the Admin hissed. "The risk of exposure is too high. I am already doing more than what is reasonable."

"More?" The Pirate let out a sharp laugh. "More would imply you've done anything useful in the first place."

The Admin's voice lowered, controlled but simmering with frustration. "I will not be reckless just to appease your temper tantrums."

The Pirate leaned forward, bracing his elbows on the console. "Then it's a good thing I don't need your help anymore."

The Admin hesitated. "What?"

The Pirate's grin was sharp. Satisfied. Dangerous.

"I still have the 'Extractor.'"

A pause. A crackle of static.

Then, the Admin's calm facade finally wavered. "You never mentioned that it was still in play."

INVASION

The Pirate shrugged, entirely too pleased with himself. "Didn't want to use it. Was hoping to handle things with a bit more finesse. But, well—desperate measures and what not."

The Admin shifted, his fingers tapping the desk again—not impatiently this time, but thoughtfully.

"That's a dangerous move."

"It's more dangerous to wait around doing nothing."

The Admin's jaw tightened. "You don't even understand what you're playing with."

"And *you* don't seem to understand the consequences of failure."

There was another silence. This one heavier.

Then the Pirate chuckled, but it was sharp, cutting. "You bureaucrats are all the same. Hiding behind your walls, buried in paperwork, drowning in rules while people like me actually do things."

The Admin's expression flickered—not just with anger, but something deeper.

The Pirate pressed on, amused now. "That's what you are, isn't it? Just another cog in the machine. Useless without someone pulling your strings."

The Admin's voice dropped into something colder. More dangerous. "I would be very careful what you say next."

"Oh?" The Pirate leaned back in his chair, smirking. "What, exactly, do you think you can do about it?"

The Admin breathed in, slow. Steady. Controlled. His temper was coiled like a viper, but he refused to snap.

Too many ears. Too many risks.

"I don't need to do anything," he said, voice like steel. "Because when this all comes crashing down, and *he* starts asking why, I will not be the one standing in the wreckage."

The Pirate's smirk faltered. Just for a second.

The Admin leaned forward, unseen but certain the message would be felt. "Can you say the same?"

A long, simmering pause.

Then, the Pirate let out a slow exhale through his nose, a reluctant chuckle following. "Careful, Admin. You almost sound like a real threat."

The Admin didn't bother responding.

The transmission cut.

Both men sat in separate, distant rooms, neither truly satisfied, neither truly trusting the other.

And both very, very aware that failure was not an option.

The next day, Tom stood in the Guild's lobby, flanked by four towering Mastadonians. Bron, Inari, Belik, and Huthu had all agreed to join the Guild, their imposing forms drawing the attention of everyone present. Amath had asked for more time to consider the offer, while Onslo and Kuthir declined to join but remained open to assisting with training when summoned.

Tom took a deep breath, addressing the gathering. "I want to introduce you all to some new Guild members. While their participation may not be permanent, as I'm allowing them the freedom to decide how long they wish to stay, I want to ensure that they are welcomed and appreciated. They didn't have to agree to help us, but they have." He glanced at the Mastadonians behind him and smiled in gratitude.

Brian, ever the skeptic, crossed his arms. "And they're here voluntarily?" he asked, his gaze narrowing on Tom. "I mean, they're your Summons. We don't want anyone forced into something they don't want. That usually doesn't end well."

Bron stepped forward, his massive frame casting a shadow over the room. His tusks gleamed as he met Brian's eyes. "We were given a choice," he rumbled, his deep voice carrying authority. "That's why not all of us who were summoned are here. Tom made sure we understood what we were agreeing to before we committed."

James, standing off to the side, tilted his head. "Weren't you… darker before?" he asked, eyes flicking between Tom and Bron.

Bron nodded. "Yes, I was a much darker shade due to the previous master I served. We Mastadonians take on the properties of those we are bonded to during that time. Tom severed the old bond, and now we serve him willingly, reflecting his alignment."

James raised an eyebrow, a playful smirk tugging at the corner of his mouth. "So… because Tom's white—"

"No," Bron interrupted firmly. "It has nothing to do with the color of his skin. It's about his soul. Tom is good-hearted, so we return to our natural color. The darker shades were a reflection of the evil we were once bound to. What is it with humans and their obsession with skin color?"

"Okay, okay, hakuna your tatas," James replied, raising his hands in mock surrender. "It was just a question."

Tom shot James a sharp look, his patience wearing thin. "Any other *not stupid* questions?" he asked, waiting for anyone else to raise objections. When no one did, he nodded. "Good. Inari, I need your help with the Rangers and snipers. Go with Kiera, and she'll get you integrated with the team. And James, that includes you. Don't be an ass."

"What? Me? I'm the epitome of professionalism," James said with exaggerated innocence. He turned toward Inari, flashing a grin. "Come on, pretty elephant lady. You can give me some one-on-one lessons if you like."

Inari's eyes narrowed dangerously as she looked down at him. "Can I kill this one?" she asked Tom flatly. "He seems weak and useless."

Tom sighed heavily. "As tempting as that is, no. He's a friend, and we need every warm body for the invasion."

"Ugh, come on!" James protested.

"Fine. You'll get special training," Inari said, her gaze sharp as a blade. "I promise you won't enjoy it."

James visibly shrunk under her piercing gaze.

"Mommy…" he whimpered softly as Kiera, grinning wickedly, grabbed him by the collar and began dragging him away.

"Come on, James," Kiera said with a glint in her eye, her voice dripping with sadistic glee. "We're going to have *so* much fun."

Tom swore he caught a flash of satisfaction in Kiera's expression, as though this was payback for all of James' past antics. He couldn't help but smile.

"Huthu," Tom called out, turning his attention to the massive Barbarian Mastadonian. "You'll be with Kevin. He has a Barbarian team that could really benefit from your knowledge."

"Huthu help teach humans to rage good," Huthu growled in his thick, broken English, enhancing the Barbarian aesthetic.

Kevin stepped forward, his muscles tense as he met Huthu's gaze. The two clasped forearms in a traditional warrior greeting, their grips tightening as each tried to gauge the other's strength.

"You strong," Huthu grunted through gritted teeth. "Training will be better this way."

Kevin nodded, straining slightly. "You're not bad yourself."

After what felt like a quiet battle of wills, the two released their grips and walked toward the courtyard together, ready to begin their training.

"Belik," Tom said, addressing the smallest of the Mastadonians, who wore flowing blue robes. "I need your expertise in magic to help train our mages. Bohdan will assist you with whatever you need. If there are any supplies or equipment you require, let us know, and we'll provide what we can."

Belik, pushing his glasses up his trunk, nodded with an air of scholarly importance. "Very well. I will assist as best I can." He turned to Bohdan, eyeing him curiously. "What do you know of magical principles?"

Bohdan shrugged. "Not much. Basic theory, I guess. Mostly, it's 'magic makes things go boom.'"

Belik sighed deeply, gripping his staff tighter. "Oh dear. That is a most dangerous attitude to have. We have a lot of work ahead of us."

Tom, sensing Belik's frustration, interjected, "I know classroom time is important, but we're short on time. The invasion is coming, and we need them ready to fight."

"Very well," Belik conceded. "We'll skip the more remedial lessons and focus on practical application. Let's find a suitable space to begin."

"And where do you want me?" Bron asked, his deep voice rumbling through the room.

Tom turned to Bron, a knowing look in his eyes. "I have something special for you. But first, we need to talk. Let me summon the others, and we'll meet separately."

Tom summoned Onslo, Amath, and Kuthir, assigning each of them to their respective roles. Onslo was to work with Graham on training the fighters, and Amath went with Briana and Derek to help the Clerics, their quiet conversations blending into the usual Guildhall chatter. Kuthir, meanwhile, seemed to make fast friends with Jay and Sean, who shared a few quick words about their work before heading off to find the other Rogues. The energy in the room hummed with anticipation, as if the Guild was a living, breathing entity readying itself for something monumental.

Amid the busy atmosphere, Bron approached Tom, his towering form casting a long shadow. His presence commanded attention, yet his demeanor was calm, almost reflective.

"What is it you wanted to speak to me about?" Bron asked, his deep voice resonating like distant thunder.

Tom hesitated for a moment, trying to gather his thoughts. He had known Bron for some time now, but there were still so many things he didn't fully understand about the Mastadonian's past. Something about their connection, and the way Bron carried himself with such quiet dignity, made Tom want to know more. Not just as a Guild leader, but as a friend.

"I wanted to know more about all of you," Tom said carefully. "Earlier, you mentioned that you come from the same tribe as the others. I was hoping you could tell me what that means. And, honestly, how did you all get here? I can't help but feel there are other Mastadonians you'd rather be with. Surely, there are others from your world you miss."

Bron's deep, black eyes seemed to darken further as he listened to Tom. He took a long, measured breath, as though weighing whether to speak at all. His gaze felt piercing, as if he were truly seeing Tom for who he was—testing him, perhaps, to see if he was worthy of the truth.

After a moment of silence, Bron spoke. "Let's go somewhere more private," he said, his voice softer now, but carrying a gravity that made Tom's heart sink slightly. "I wouldn't want too many ears to hear what I am about to tell you."

Tom nodded, understanding the need for privacy. "Of course. Follow me."

They made their way through the Guild hall, passing by various members as they trained and prepared. The bustling activity faded as they reached the elevators, and Tom led Bron up to his personal quarters. Inside, the maids were tidying up the space, but Tom waved them off. "You can finish later," he said, though the maids politely continued their work, folding the bedding and gathering laundry. Bron stood silently, his hulking figure almost motionless as he observed the room.

Once the maids had finished and left the room, Tom turned back to Bron.

"We're alone now. No one will bother us. Well, except maybe Jerky," Tom added with a small grin, thinking of his cheeky familiar.

Maria's voice chimed in Tom's mind, dry as ever, "You know, you should put a sock on the door or something. People come here all the time."

Tom rolled his eyes but couldn't help a chuckle. He walked over to the door and locked it, ensuring they wouldn't be disturbed. "Alright, we're good now."

INVASION

Bron stood near the window, his immense form still and contemplative. When he finally spoke, his voice carried the weight of distant memories.

"I come from a world far from this one. It is a place called Carnotia, a world that once thrived with life, not unlike your own planet. But that was before the System came to us." He paused, as if bracing himself to relive the memories. "The System… it brought devastation unlike anything we had ever seen."

Tom leaned against the wall, his arms crossed, listening intently. He had heard stories of the System's effects on different worlds, but none so personal, so raw, as what Bron was about to share.

"Carnotia was a beautiful place," Bron continued, his voice tinged with nostalgia. "We Mastadonians lived there for millennia, alongside countless other species. Forests stretched for miles, oceans teemed with life, and our cities were marvels of natural harmony and strength. But when the System integrated with our world, it was as if nature itself turned against us. Tsunamis wiped out coastal cities, tornadoes ripped through the heartlands, and fire—actual fire—rained from the heavens. Entire continents were reduced to barren wastelands of sand and ash."

Tom's heart sank as he imagined the horror. He had seen the destructive power of the System in his own world, but nothing like what Bron described.

"I can't even imagine…"

"That is because it was beyond imagining," Bron said quietly. "Our cities were lost, our fields turned to deserts. But the worst was yet to come. Creatures—monsters—began appearing. They weren't like the beasts of our world; these were things of nightmares. They slaughtered everything in their path, and we had no way to defend ourselves against them. Those of us who survived fled, forming tribes in the wilderness, far from the ruins of our once-great cities."

Bron's broad shoulders slumped slightly as he spoke, the weight of the past pulling at him. He moved to sit on the edge of Tom's bed, the wooden frame groaning under his weight.

"I was a child when it all happened," he continued. "My father… He died defending us from the first wave of monsters. My mother… She was strong. She took me and fled with what few survivors we could gather. We formed a small tribe, living in secrecy, far from the chaos that had consumed the rest of the world."

Tom remained silent, not wanting to interrupt the flow of Bron's story. He could see the pain etched in the Mastadonian's face, the sorrow that clung to every word.

"We managed to adapt, to survive," Bron said, his voice growing quieter. "The System forced us to evolve, to become stronger. We learned how to use its powers to defend ourselves. For years, we lived in relative peace, hidden from the monsters and the destruction. We had no idea what was happening beyond our borders, no contact with the outside world. But in our isolation, we were safe… for a time."

Bron lowered his head, his gaze fixed on the floor. "It wasn't until much later, when I was grown, that I met her. Anashi. She was the light of my life. Strong, beautiful, deadly. We were married by the tribal leader, and soon after, we had a son, Sinari. He was our pride and joy." Bron's voice broke slightly, and a single tear rolled down his face. "We were happy. Again, for a time."

Tom's heart ached for his friend. "You had a family," he said softly, feeling the weight of Bron's loss.

Bron nodded. "Yes. And I loved them more than anything. But that happiness didn't last." His voice grew hard, edged with the bitterness of memory. "One day, a group of monsters, led by goblin war chiefs, found our hidden village. I don't know how they discovered us, but they attacked with overwhelming force. While I was on the frontlines, fighting the larger creatures, another group broke through our defenses and attacked the village itself. We had left a few fighters to protect the elderly and the young, but they were no match for the goblins."

Tom felt a lump in his throat as Bron continued. "When we returned, the village was in ruins. Our homes were burned to the ground, and the bodies of our families... They were scattered everywhere. I found Anashi and Sinari in the temple, where they had made their last stand. They were... gone."

Bron's tears fell freely now, and Tom could barely contain his own emotions. "Bron... I'm so sorry."

Bron wiped his face with a massive hand. "We swore vengeance," he said, his voice thick with grief. "My party and I tracked down the goblins. A mage joined us, promising us the power to destroy them in exchange for our future servitude. We accepted. We had no choice."

The room seemed to grow darker as Bron spoke of their retribution. "The mage granted us the power we needed. We wiped out the goblins, down to the last of their kind. But the price was steep. From that day forward, we were bound to serve the mage—and later, other deities who sought our strength. We became tools, summoned again and again to fight in their wars, to kill on their behalf."

Tom stood there, stunned, unable to find words for the depth of suffering Bron had endured. "Bron..." he started, but no words seemed adequate.

Bron's eyes met Tom's, filled with the weight of centuries of servitude. "It's not your burden to bear," he said softly. "But I appreciate your kindness. Staying here with you, even for a short time, keeps us from being summoned by others. For that, I am grateful."

Tom's heart clenched. "I'm going to find a way to free you," he said with sudden determination. "There has to be something I can do to break this cycle. You deserve better."

Bron shook his head, a sad smile on his face. "These things are beyond us mortals. But your determination is appreciated."

"I'm still going to try," Tom said, his voice firm. "I promise you that."

Bron nodded, gratitude softening the sorrow in his eyes. "Thank you, Tom. That means more to me than you know."

Chapter 42

Status Updates

Tom Harris	
Race: Human	**Class:** Warlock
Level: 35	**Total XP:** 4,296,150
XP To Next Level: 424,850	**HP:** 650/650
MP: 512/640* (Permanent Summons)	**SP:** 500/500
Attributes:	**Unused Attributes Points:** 0
Strength: 55	**Constitution:** 65
Dexterity: 48	**Endurance:** 55
Intelligence: 64	**Wisdom:** 60
Charisma: 125	**Luck:** 35
Non-Combat Skills:	
Inspect	**Level:** 19 **Rank:** Novice
Combat Skills:	
Vehicular Homicide	**Level:** 32 **Rank:** Initiate
Swords	**Level:** 41 **Rank:** Apprentice
Summon Demonic Creature	**Level:** 39 **Rank:** Initiate
Fear	**Level:** 12 **Rank:** Novice
Corruption	**Level:** 11 **Rank:** Novice
Spells:	

Eldritch Blast	**Level:** 34 **Rank:** Initiate
Dark Ball	**Level:** 21 **Rank:** Initiate
Dark Restoration	**Level:** 29 **Rank:** Initiate
Lightning Strike	**Level:** 6 **Rank:** Beginner
Doppelganger	**Level:** 4 **Rank:** Beginner
Dark Flame Weapon	**Level:** 7 **Rank:** Beginner
Final Flash	**Level:** 18 **Rank:** Novice
Void Storm	**Level:** 3 **Rank:** Beginner
Tattoos:	Tattoo of Brute Strength
Tattoo of Life Absorption	Tattoo of the Summoner
Tattoo of Magic Nullification	Tattoo of Displacement
Tattoo of Reflection	Tattoo of Inspiration

Derek Calloway	
Race: Human	**Class:** Cleric
Level: 31	**Total XP:** 2,318,600
XP To Next Level: 236,400	**HP:** 700/700
MP: 540/540	**SP:** 690/690
Attributes:	**Unused Attributes Points:** 0
Strength: 53	**Constitution:** 65
Dexterity: 43	**Endurance:** 64
Intelligence: 54	**Wisdom:** 51
Charisma: 25	**Luck:** 25

INVASION

Non-Combat Skills:	
Inspect	**Level:** 23 **Rank:** Initiate
Combat Skills:	
Vehicular Homicide	**Level:** 3 **Rank:** Beginner
Maces	**Level:** 30 **Rank:** Initiate
Defense of the Faithful	**Level:** 11 **Rank:** Novice
Shield Bash	**Level:** 29 **Rank:** Initiate
Imbued Strike	**Level:** 31 **Rank:** Initiate
Holy Inspired	**Level:** 15 **Rank:** Novice
Rushing Strike	**Level:** 24 **Rank:** Initiate
Shield Brace	**Level:** 21 **Rank:** Initiate
Spells:	
Life Bolt	**Level:** 21 **Rank:** Initiate
Major Healing	**Level:** 22 **Rank:** Initiate
Light Shield	**Level:** 12 **Rank:** Novice
Illumination	**Level:** 17 **Rank:** Novice
Radiance	**Level:** 20 **Rank:** Initiate
Turn Undead	**Level:** 18 **Rank:** Novice

James Sanders	
Race: Human	**Class:** Ranger
Level: 30	**Total XP:** 2,023,200
XP To Next Level: 128,300	**HP:** 550/550
MP: 350/350	**SP:** 750/750
Attributes:	**Unused Attributes Points:** 0

Strength: 45	**Constitution:** 50
Dexterity: 80	**Endurance:** 70
Intelligence: 35	**Wisdom:** 30
Charisma: 15	**Luck:** 45
Non-Combat Skills:	
Inspect	**Level:** 15 **Rank:** Novice
Combat Skills:	
Vehicular Homicide	**Level:** 2 **Rank:** Beginner
Guns	**Level:** 35 **Rank:** Initiate
Marksman's Shot (Dickshot)	**Level:** 41 **Rank:** Apprentice
Animal Companionship	**Level:** 29 **Rank:** Initiate
Tracking	**Level:** 10 **Rank:** Novice
Tame	**Level:** 15 **Rank:** Novice
Taunt	**Level:** 28 **Rank:** Initiate
Deviant	**Level:** 31 **Rank:** Initiate
Spells:	
Imbued Shot	**Level:** 23 **Rank:** Initiate
Ice Dagger	**Level:** 11 **Rank:** Novice
Grease	**Level:** 24 **Rank:** Initiate
Inspire Companion	**Level:** 17 **Rank:** Novice

Jay Beraz	
Race: Human	**Class:** Rogue

INVASION

Level: 31	**Total XP:** 2,352,180
XP To Next Level: 202,820	**HP:** 550/550
MP: 350/540	**SP:** 750/500
Attributes:	**Unused Attributes Points:** 0
Strength: 50	**Constitution:** 50
Dexterity: 100	**Endurance:** 70
Intelligence: 35	**Wisdom:** 35
Charisma: 20	**Luck:** 20
Non-Combat Skills:	
Inspect	**Level:** 28 **Rank:** Initiate
Combat Skills:	
Vehicular Homicide	**Level:** 21 **Rank:** Initiate
Small Blades	**Level:** 35 **Rank:** Initiate
Stealth	**Level:** 31 **Rank:** Initiate
Thrown Weapons	**Level:** 22 **Rank:** Initiate
Backstab	**Level:** 20 **Rank:** Initiate
Assassination	**Level:** 14 **Rank:** Novice
Expert Dodge	**Level:** 19 **Rank:** Novice
Poisons	**Level:** 24 **Rank:** Initiate
Steal	**Level:** 17 **Rank:** Novice
Quick Strike	**Level:** 28 **Rank:** Initiate
Traps	**Level:** 20 **Rank:** Initiate
Crippling Strike	**Level:** 22 **Rank:** Initiate
Spells:	

Silence	**Level:** 21 **Rank:** Initiate
Darkness	**Level:** 18 **Rank:** Novice
Dark Shroud	**Level:** 16 **Rank:** Novice
Dark Vision	**Level:** 17 **Rank:** Novice
Wind Blast	**Level:** 12 **Rank:** Novice

Kiera Starr	
Race: Human	**Class:** Bard
Level: 30	**Total XP:** 2,064,360
XP To Next Level: 82,640	**HP:** 500/500
MP: 410/410	**SP:** 600/600
Attributes:	**Unused Attributes Points:** 0
Strength: 44	**Constitution:** 50
Dexterity: 75	**Endurance:** 55
Intelligence: 41	**Wisdom:** 40
Charisma: 50	**Luck:** 15
Non-Combat Skills:	
Inspect	**Level:** 17 **Rank:** Novice
Combat Skills:	
Vehicular Homicide	**Level:** 1 **Rank:** Beginner
Guns	**Level:** 41 **Rank:** Apprentice
Inspiration	**Level:** 26 **Rank:** Initiate
Snipe	**Level:** 24 **Rank:** Initiate

INVASION

Final Tribute (Performance)	**Level:** 10 **Rank:** Novice
Mockery	**Level:** 18 **Rank:** Novice
Explosives Expert	**Level:** 22 **Rank:** Initiate
Spells:	
Light Foot	**Level:** 18 **Rank:** Novice
Illusion	**Level:** 19 **Rank:** Novice
Shocking Bolt	**Level:** 10 **Rank:** Novice
Firewhip	**Level:** 9 **Rank:** Beginner
Spark	**Level:** 12 **Rank:** Novice
Quicksand	**Level:** 11 **Rank:** Novice

Kevin Hall	
Race: Human	**Class:** Barbarian
Level: 29	**Total XP:** 1,704,900
XP To Next Level: 99,100	**HP:** 850/850
MP: 100/100	**SP:** 800/800
Attributes:	**Unused Attributes Points:** 0
Strength: 100	**Constitution:** 85
Dexterity: 40	**Endurance:** 75
Intelligence: 10	**Wisdom:** 10
Charisma: 20	**Luck:** 20
Non-Combat Skills:	
Inspect	**Level:** 10 **Rank:** Novice
Combat Skills:	
Vehicular Homicide	**Level:** 2 **Rank:** Beginner

Axes	**Level:** 40 **Rank:** Apprentice
Rage	**Level:** 35 **Rank:** Initiate
Cleave	**Level:** 24 **Rank:** Initiate
Smash	**Level:** 18 **Rank:** Novice
Charge	**Level:** 21 **Rank:** Initiate
Improvised Weapon	**Level:** 16 **Rank:** Novice
Taunt	**Level:** 27 **Rank:** Initiate
Battle Cry	**Level:** 24 **Rank:** Initiate
Braun over Brains	**Level:** 20 **Rank:** Initiate
Shatter Armor	**Level:** 18 **Rank:** Novice
Spells:	
Earthquake	**Level:** 7 **Rank:** Beginner
Bark Armor	**Level:** 14 **Rank:** Novice
Weapon Blaze	**Level:** 12 **Rank:** Novice

Michael Hendricks	
Race: Human	**Class:** Barbarian
Level: 27	**Total XP:** 1,221,775
XP To Next Level: 51,225	**HP:** 800/800
MP: 200/200	**SP:** 600/600
Attributes:	**Unused Attributes Points:** 0
Strength: 70	**Constitution:** 75
Dexterity: 60	**Endurance:** 60

INVASION

Intelligence: 20	**Wisdom:** 15
Charisma: 20	**Luck:** 20
Non-Combat Skills:	
Inspect	**Level:** 13 **Rank:** Novice
Combat Skills:	
Vehicular Homicide	**Level:** 5 **Rank:** Beginner
Axes	**Level:** 38 **Rank:** Initiate
Chop	**Level:** 35 **Rank:** Initiate
Cleave	**Level:** 18 **Rank:** Initiate
Two-Weapon Fighting	**Level:** 31 **Rank:** Initiate
Indomitable Will	**Level:** 21 **Rank:** Initiate
Parry	**Level:** 18 **Rank:** Novice
Taunt	**Level:** 19 **Rank:** Novice
Battle Cry	**Level:** 24 **Rank:** Initiate
Dodge	**Level:** 20 **Rank:** Initiate
Blood Letter	**Level:** 14 **Rank:** Novice
Spells:	
Air Ward	**Level:** 18 **Rank:** Novice
Flame	**Level:** 13 **Rank:** Novice
Earth Spike	**Level:** 11 **Rank:** Novice

Chapter 43

Lost

"Mommy? Mommy, where are you?"

Tom stirred in his sleep, groaning softly after a long and grueling day of training with Bron. His muscles ached with a deep, familiar soreness, the kind that came only after pushing himself too far. He rolled over, entangling himself in the sheets as he attempted to find a more comfortable position. His arms and legs throbbed, and the dull pain in his shoulders made him wonder if he had overdone it. That had to be it. Just the fatigue from the training…

"Daddy? Are you there? Where did you all go?"

Tom's eyes flew open, his heart pounding. He lay there for a moment, frozen in place. That voice. It wasn't a dream this time. He was certain he had heard it—a faint, childlike voice, wavering with fear and confusion. He sat up slowly, scanning the dark room around him. His heart raced faster, and an eerie chill crept up his spine as he strained to hear anything else.

The room was still and quiet, except for the sound of his own breathing. His eyes landed on a familiar sight. Jerky, his familiar, had apparently snuck into the room at some point and was now curled up next to him on the bed, snoring softly. Tom blinked at him, his mind racing.

Was that… him? Tom thought to himself, his fingers tightening around the sheets. Jerky seemed peaceful, blissfully unaware of the odd voice that had pierced the night.

But then, the voice came again.

"I'm scared. I don't like being alone. Mommy? Daddy?" It was a young boy's voice, trembling on the verge of tears, calling out into the void.

Tom bolted upright, throwing the sheets aside as he sprang out of bed, his heart now thudding in his chest. He crouched slightly, instinctively ready for an attack, his eyes darting around the room. His entire body tensed, every muscle primed for action as he scanned the darkness.

"Is someone there?" Tom called out cautiously, his voice low and steady, though he wasn't sure he wanted an answer.

Then, from the corner of the room, a faint mist began to materialize. At first, it was barely visible, just a soft, white fog that hovered in the air. But as Tom watched, the mist grew thicker, glowing faintly with a pale, ethereal light. Slowly, it began to take shape, forming the vague outlines of arms, legs, a torso, and finally, a head. The figure was small—no more than eight to ten years old, translucent and ghostly, but unmistakably the image of a boy.

"Is… is someone there? Please, don't hurt me," the boy whispered, his voice trembling as he glanced around the unfamiliar room. His large, wide eyes were filled with fear. "Where am I?"

Tom let out a deep, resigned sigh, rubbing his face.

"What the hell," he muttered under his breath, trying to process what he was seeing.

The boy's figure wavered slightly, as if it were on the edge of disappearing entirely.

"What's wrong, little fella?" Tom asked softly, careful not to make any sudden movements. He could see how terrified the boy was.

The boy's head snapped toward Tom, his eyes widening. "Who are you? Why am I here? What's going on?"

His voice grew more panicked, his fear escalating as he looked around the room, his form flickering in and out like a candle about to be snuffed.

"What's your name?" Tom asked, trying to remain calm and soothe the boy's rising panic.

"Jason," the boy replied, though he still seemed wary of Tom. His small figure trembled, and his hands fidgeted nervously as he floated there, unsure of what was happening.

"Hi, Jason. I'm Tom," he said, kneeling slightly to get closer to the boy's eye level, hoping to appear less intimidating. "I'm the Guild leader of Vanguard. Can you tell me what happened? Do you remember how you got here?"

Jason shook his head, his expression growing more confused. "I… I don't remember. Everything's fuzzy. I was with my parents… and then… something happened… and now I'm here." His voice wavered as he spoke, as if he were trying to pull the memories from the mist surrounding him. "What's happening to me? I think I'm lost…"

Tom's heart sank as he watched the boy struggle to piece together his fragmented memories. "That's okay, Jason. I can try to help you," he said gently. "Can you tell me who your parents are? Maybe I can help you find them."

The boy's face twisted in confusion, and his gaze dropped to the floor. "I… I don't remember their names," he whispered, his voice cracking. "I just know I have parents. I think I do."

Tom sighed softly, his brow furrowed. This poor kid. "That's alright," Tom said, his voice steady and reassuring. "Let's focus on what you do remember, okay? First, though, I want you to try to calm down. Take a few deep breaths. Relax. It'll help you think more clearly."

Jason closed his eyes, doing as Tom suggested, though his tiny chest didn't move with breath. After a few moments, his eyes shot open again, and they locked onto Tom, wide with terror.

"I don't think I can breathe!" Jason cried out, his voice rising into a full-blown panic. "What's happening to me?!"

Tom felt a pang of sympathy as the realization dawned on him. He knelt closer to Jason, his voice soft but firm. "Jason, I don't want to alarm you, but I think… I think you may have died."

The words hung heavy in the air. Jason's face went pale—paler than it already was. His wide eyes grew even wider as the weight of Tom's words sank in.

"D-died?" Jason stammered. "I… I can't be dead!"

Tom opened his mouth to say something, anything that might comfort the boy, but before he could, Jason turned abruptly and ran, his ghostly form passing through the wall as though it weren't even there.

"Wait! Jason!" Tom shouted, fumbling as he tried to follow. He rushed to the door, flinging it open in his haste and running into the hallway. He was still dressed in nothing but his boxers, but that didn't stop him as he gave chase, sprinting after the spectral boy.

"Jason, stop!" Tom called as he turned corner after corner, but the boy was fast, disappearing through walls as easily as a breeze.

Tom's bare feet slapped against the cold floor, his breath coming in short gasps as he pursued the ghostly figure. Jason vanished through yet another wall, and Tom skidded to a halt, banging his fist against the solid surface. "Jason!" he called, pounding on the wall in frustration. "Where are you?"

"Keep it down out there!" came a muffled voice from behind the wall. "Some people are trying to—OH MY GOD, IS THAT A GHOST?!"

Suddenly, Jason flew out of the wall again, passing straight through Tom. A bone-chilling cold shot through Tom's body, making every hair on his body stand on end. His body recoiled involuntarily as a strange, unsettling feeling washed over him.

"Man, that feels weird," Tom muttered, squirming in discomfort.

Jerky suddenly appeared at the end of the hallway, arms outstretched, trying to block Jason's path. The boy froze in mid-air, his terrified gaze darting between Jerky and Tom. Jerky's hand glowed with a yellowish-white light as he reached out and grabbed Jason by the arm, holding him in place.

"We will not harm you," Jerky said in a kind but firm voice. "But you must stop running."

Jason kicked and struggled in Jerky's grasp, but to no avail. He couldn't break free.

Tom skidded to a stop beside them, panting. "How are you holding him?" Tom asked, baffled. "He passed right through me."

Jerky gave a quick wink. "Magic," he said simply, a grin spreading across his face.

Tom groaned, rolling his eyes. "Oh, great. That's the age-old 'I don't have a real answer, so I'll just make it sound mysterious' thing. It's like when my uncle used to pull quarters out of my ear. But fine, never mind that for now." He turned to Jason, his expression softening. "Jason, it's alright. We're here to help."

The boy continued to struggle for a few more moments, but then he slumped, his tiny body floating between them as if all the fight had gone out of him. His shoulders sagged, and his face was filled with sorrow.

"I don't like this. Am I really dead?" Jason asked, his voice small and full of dread.

"It seems that way," Tom said, kneeling again to look him in the eyes. "I'm so sorry. But we'll help you. We just need to figure out what's going on."

At that moment, the door to Kiera's room creaked open, and she stepped out into the hallway, bleary-eyed and groggy.

"What the hell is going on out here?" she mumbled, rubbing her eyes.

Jason looked up in shock and, in an instant, vanished, his form disappearing like mist in the morning sun. Jerky's hand grasped at nothing but air.

"What? Jason? Jason!" Tom called, frantically looking around.

Kiera raised an eyebrow, staring at Tom, who was still standing there in his boxers. "Put some clothes on, Tom," she said, crossing her arms. "And who the hell is Jason?"

Tom blinked, suddenly aware of how ridiculous he must have looked. "He's a ghost boy," Tom explained quickly. "He was scared, and we were trying to help him figure out what's going on."

Kiera stared at him in disbelief, her face a mask of confusion. "Have you been drinking? Did James put you up to this?"

"He's telling the truth," Jerky interjected, his voice calm. "I saw him too."

Kiera turned her gaze to Jerky and frowned. "Okay, first off, the clothes thing applies to anyone with genitalia. Go put something on. The barn door is open, and the cows are peeking out."

Jerky looked down, realizing that he, too, was in nothing but boxers. He immediately covered himself, his face turning a bright shade of red.

"Oh… right," he muttered before quickly scampering back to the room, his face burning with embarrassment.

"Fine. Say I believe you," Kiera said, folding her arms and giving Tom a skeptical look. "Why didn't you banish it or try to destroy it if it was a ghost?"

Tom let out a long sigh, rubbing the back of his neck as if trying to physically push away the tension. "Because I'm not really into… you know, killing kids. Or, well, banishing them or whatever." His voice dropped a little as he searched for the right words. "Besides, the kid was crying, calling for his parents. What was I supposed to do? Just blast him out of existence?"

Kiera scrunched her face in a mix of surprise and mild disgust. "That's a little morbid, don't you think?" she replied, raising an eyebrow as if trying to gauge whether Tom was being serious or not.

"Yeah, I get that, but look, I couldn't just attack him. He wasn't doing any harm, and the poor guy seemed… lost. Like he was trying to remember something, but he couldn't." Tom's voice softened, and there was a hint of frustration in it. His hand unconsciously rubbed his temple, trying to massage the foggy confusion away.

"Oh great, another stray for Tom to save," Kiera said with a theatrical roll of her eyes. She shifted her weight, her tone dripping with sarcasm. "How many lost souls are you planning on rescuing in this lifetime?"

Tom straightened, eyes narrowing slightly as he countered. "What would you have done, Kiera? Let a kid cry his eyes out in your room while you ignore him so you can catch a few extra hours of beauty sleep?"

Kiera opened her mouth to retort but then paused, her face softening as she realized she didn't have a good answer. She sighed, pinching the bridge of her nose. "Alright, alright, I get it," she conceded. "So, what now?"

Tom shrugged, letting out a tired yawn that stretched across his face, his body already craving the sleep he'd been denied. "I have no idea, honestly," he admitted. "We need to know more about what's going on before we do anything else. I'm planning to talk to some of the Mastadonians in the morning—maybe they know something about this kind of thing. Hopefully, we can find Jason again later. But for now..." He yawned again, his shoulders slumping. "I really need some sleep."

"Finally, a sensible thing out of your mouth tonight." Kiera turned to head back to her room, casting one last glance over her shoulder. "Get some sleep. We'll figure this out in the morning." She closed her door with a soft click, leaving Tom standing alone in the hallway.

With a weary shake of his head, Tom shuffled back into his room. As he entered, he saw Jerky sprawled across the bed, already half asleep, with one leg awkwardly sticking out of a pair of half-pulled-up pants. Tom chuckled softly, his familiar's child-like demeanor always managing to pull a smile from him, even on nights like these. Carefully, Tom pulled the pants the rest of the way off and helped tuck Jerky back under the blankets, making sure his odd little companion was comfortable.

With Jerky settled, Tom slipped into his side of the bed and lay on his back, staring up at the ceiling. His mind, despite his exhaustion, buzzed with questions about Jason. Who was the boy? Why had he appeared here, of all places? Every ghost or phantasm Tom had encountered in the past had been some conjuration of hatred or malice, born of someone's ill intent. But Jason didn't feel like that. There was something pure about the boy, something lost.

Tom let out a deep sigh, closing his eyes as the weight of the day's events finally dragged him into a deep, dreamless sleep.

The next morning, Tom woke early, feeling surprisingly refreshed after the strange night. He showered quickly, letting the hot water ease the tension in his muscles from the day before. After dressing, he glanced back at the bed to see Jerky still snoring softly, one leg kicked out from under the covers. A small smile tugged at the corner of Tom's mouth as he slipped out of the room, leaving his familiar to his rest.

Tom's first stop was to track down Bron, hoping the Mastadonian might have some insight into the mysterious ghost boy. He made his way downstairs, asking a few passing Guild members where Bron might be. It wasn't long before someone pointed him toward the gym.

When Tom arrived, he found Bron in the midst of an intense sparring session with several of the Guild's fighters. Graham, agile as ever, leaped over a horizontal swing from Bron's massive axe, bringing his shield down in an attempt to strike at Bron's head. Bron, however, was already one step ahead. Leaning just enough to the right, Bron let the shield pass by harmlessly before leaning left and shoulder-checking Graham mid-air, sending him sprawling across the gym floor with a heavy thud.

"Try to stay grounded when you can," Bron said, his deep voice rumbling like distant thunder. "You're far too vulnerable in the air—you can't change your trajectory once you've committed."

Even as he instructed Graham, Bron casually blocked a sword strike from one of the fighters coming at him from behind, his movements fluid and effortless.

Two more fighters moved in from either side, clearly trying to coordinate their attack. At that moment, DeeDee, watching from a distance, raised her hands, summoning thick vines that shot up from the ground, wrapping around Bron's legs and rooting him in place.

For a moment, it looked as though they had him. But Bron merely crouched, shifting his stance slightly. His grip tightened on his axe, and then, with a single powerful spin, he whirled the weapon in a wide arc, striking both fighters with the blunt side of his axe and severing the vines in the same motion. The two fighters were sent flying, landing hard on the mat.

"And always expect the unexpected from your opponents," Bron added, a rare grin spreading across his face as the fighters groaned from their spots on the ground.

Tom clapped his hands from the doorway, a smile spreading across his face as he walked toward Bron. "Impressive as always," he said, clearly amused by the display.

Bron wiped the sweat from his brow and turned to Tom with a nod. "Tom, what brings you here so early?"

Tom paused, considering his words for a moment before speaking. "I need to ask you some questions. There are things happening that we don't quite understand, and I was hoping you could help me make sense of them."

"I'll do my best," Bron said, wiping his axe clean and resting it on his shoulder. "Let's get something to drink while we talk. What do you call it again?" He tapped his chin, trying to recall the word.

"The cafeteria," Tom supplied with a grin.

"That's it. The cafeteria. Let's go—I'm parched." Bron chuckled as they left the gym, the fighters still recovering from their sparring session.

The cafeteria was already buzzing with activity by the time they arrived. The smell of food and the chatter of Guild members created a lively atmosphere. Charlene, ever the friendly face, waved them over as they entered the food line.

"Well, hey! Nice to see you both," Charlene greeted them warmly. "It was Bron, wasn't it?"

"Yes, m'lady," Bron replied, giving her a slight bow. "You honor me by remembering my name."

Charlene chuckled, shaking her head. "Oh, you're a charmer, aren't you? So, what can I do you for?"

"We're just looking for something to quench our thirst," Bron said, his voice still carrying the aftereffects of the workout.

"I think I've got just the thing. Go ahead and take a seat; I'll have it brought out to you."

Tom led the way to a nearby table, and they sat down to continue their conversation.

"I see you're not going easy on the fighters," Tom remarked, nodding toward the gym.

"Why should I?" Bron replied with a shrug. "They need to be ready for anything that might happen in the field. If they're overprepared, then I've done my job."

"True," Tom admitted. "I just hope they're learning from all this."

"They are progressing well," Bron assured him. "Graham, in particular, is showing a lot of promise. You were wise to put him in charge of training the others."

"I'm glad you think so," Tom said with a nod. "Your opinion means a lot to me. That's part of why I wanted you here."

Charlene appeared just then, carrying two large tankards. "Here ya go! Two revitalization beverages," she said, setting the drinks down in front of them.

Bron's eyes widened as he looked at the foamy drink. "I'm sorry," he said sheepishly. "I should have mentioned I don't drink alcohol."

Charlene laughed. "Not to worry! This isn't alcohol. It's a carbonated beverage with some restorative properties. I even imbued it with a little mana to give it an extra kick."

Tom raised an eyebrow, taking a closer look at the drink. Subtle green sparkles fizzed within the foam, popping lightly with the carbonation. Tentatively, he took a sip. The drink was sweet, with a refreshing lime flavor that reminded him of the popsicles his mother used to give him on hot summer days.

"This is pretty tasty," Tom said, only to pause as a familiar pop-up notification appeared in his vision.

<table>
<tr><td align="center">Potion of Revitalization</td></tr>
<tr><td align="center">Item Type: Potion
Rarity: Uncommon
Description:
This sparkling, refreshing beverage removes all dehydration and hunger debuffs upon consumption. Prolonged use of the Potion of Revitalization enhances your Constitution, gradually reducing your need for sustenance and hydration over extended periods. Perfect for adventurers on long journeys or in harsh environments.</td></tr>
</table>

Effects:
- Instantly removes any active Dehydration or Hunger debuffs.
- Continued use boosts Constitution, delaying future need for food and water.

Duration:
Immediate effect on debuff removal. Constitution improvements occur over sustained consumption.

Warning: Overconsumption without balancing other dietary needs may lead to unintended side effects.

"Whoa!" Tom exclaimed, eyes wide as he stared down at the tankard in his hands. He quickly took another sip, savoring the fizzy sweetness that danced on his tongue. The drink was light, refreshing, with just the right amount of sweetness, and the subtle green sparkles in the liquid added a touch of magic that seemed to lift his spirits even further. "This drink is amazing, Charlene! We *need* to get this into production for everyone to start drinking every day," he said, glancing again at the glowing prompt floating in front of his vision. The notification blinked, confirming the revitalizing effects of the beverage as it replenished his mana and slightly boosted his stamina.

Charlene chuckled, clearly pleased by Tom's enthusiastic response. Her apron swayed as she placed a hand on her hip, giving him a playful wink. "Aww, you flatter me, Tom," she said, her voice warm and friendly. "But I'll take the compliment! Don't worry, I'll get the others working on making more of it. We'll make sure it's permanently on the menu. Can't have you running out of energy now, can we?" She gave a nod of satisfaction before turning to return to her duties behind the counter.

Tom grinned as she walked away, taking another long sip of the drink. It was crisp, almost like a carbonated punch of fresh lime with a hint of sweetness. Every time the green sparkles popped on the surface of the liquid, he felt a small, pleasant tingle shoot through his body, like a minor jolt of energy seeping into his veins. It wasn't overpowering, just enough to make him feel revitalized. He leaned back in his chair, feeling the pleasant hum of restored energy flowing through him.

Bron, who had been silently sipping his drink, set his tankard down and turned his gaze toward Tom, his large hands resting heavily on the table. "So," Bron began, his deep voice rumbling like distant thunder, "now that we're alone again... what was it you wanted to speak with me about?"

Tom set his tankard down, the faint clink of metal on wood signaling the shift in tone. He leaned forward slightly, glancing around the room instinctively, though there was no real need for caution. The cafeteria bustled with Guild members enjoying breakfast, their chatter and laughter a lively backdrop to the conversation. Still, what Tom was about to discuss felt strange, personal—something he wasn't sure how to explain, even to Bron.

"I've got a bit of a... ghost problem."

Chapter 44

Ghostly Memories

"It's very important that we determine exactly what type of ghost you're dealing with," Bron said, his deep voice rumbling thoughtfully as he took a long sip from his drink. "There are several forms a ghost can take, each more dangerous than the last. But since I haven't heard any screams or fighting—aside from the usual training noise—I take it the ghost was non-violent?"

"Definitely not violent," Tom replied, shaking his head. He leaned back in his chair, running a hand through his hair as he recalled the events of the night before. "In fact, it seemed more afraid of us than we were of it. It took the form of a child, and it was… sad. Scared. Kept calling for its parents and said its name was Jason."

Bron raised his eyebrows slightly, his tusks glinting faintly in the light. "In that case, it sounds like you're dealing with a lost soul," he said, setting his drink down on the table with a heavy thud.

Tom couldn't help but glance at Bron's trunk as the elephantine warrior raised it to sip from the tankard. There was something odd yet strangely graceful about watching the massive Mastadonian drink—he had to lift his trunk in a way that made it seem like a well-practiced art.

"A lost soul?" Tom asked, pulling his attention back to the conversation.

Bron nodded, his eyes narrowing as he considered the implications. "Yes. When someone dies in extreme circumstances or under massive emotional duress, their soul can become trapped in this world. It clings to life, unable to move on until it finds the peace it needs to release its hold on the material plane. It sounds like this Jason you encountered is such a soul—something is keeping him tethered here, and he won't be able to move on until he resolves whatever is keeping him bound."

Tom sighed, leaning forward and resting his elbows on the table. "Well, that sounds… cliché," he said with a hint of frustration.

Bron tilted his head, one ear twitching slightly. "How so?"

"It's just… the plot of so many ghost stories," Tom replied, shaking his head slightly. "It's like every ghost movie or book written in the past hundred years. 'Tragic death, lost soul, needs closure to find peace.' The whole thing feels like something out of a movie."

Bron's expression remained calm, though there was a glimmer of amusement in his dark eyes. "Sorry to disappoint you, Tom," he said, the corner of his mouth twitching into a small smile, "but that's the way of things. Consider the possibility that if so many stories speak of this method, it could be based on some form of truth. You're likely that boy's last chance to find peace. If you can't help him, his soul will remain trapped here."

Tom leaned back again, exhaling slowly as he processed Bron's words. "So, he isn't dangerous to anyone here?"

"Not currently," Bron said, his tone serious now. "But spirits that linger too long without finding peace can become corrupted. Their pain and confusion fester, turning them into something far worse—a ghast. Ghasts are dangerous. They lose their humanity, becoming violent, angry, and almost impossible to reason with. And unless you've got the right kind of holy magic on hand, they're a real problem to deal with."

Tom groaned and ran a hand down his face. "And there's the twist," he muttered. "So, we're on a clock, then. I'll have to work fast to help him before things get out of hand." He glanced over at Bron. "When I spoke to him, he couldn't remember much. He didn't even seem to know what happened to him. Is that normal for spirits like this?"

Bron stroked his chin, his thick fingers brushing the fur around his jaw. "It can happen," he said after a moment. "Spirits that have experienced extreme trauma often lose parts of their memories. The shock of death can scatter their thoughts, leaving them confused and disoriented. If Jason can't remember what happened to him, you'll need to help him piece it together—no matter how painful those memories might be. Only by confronting his past can he find the closure he needs."

Tom let out another long sigh, feeling the weight of the situation settle over him. "Not exactly what I was hoping for," he muttered. "But I can't just leave him like that. And I definitely can't let him become a threat to everyone here. I'll do what needs to be done." His voice was heavy, laced with concern for the boy's plight.

Bron gave Tom a small, approving smile. "You have a good heart, Tom. Don't let this world or its evils harden you. Not everyone has the strength to show compassion in situations like this."

Tom met Bron's gaze and offered a faint smile in return. "I'm trying. It's not easy, but I don't see any other way forward.

"Is there anything else you can tell me about ghosts that might be helpful?" Tom asked, hoping for more insight.

Bron thought for a moment, his massive hand tapping the edge of the tankard. "Nothing too exceptional, but you should know that spirits grow stronger over time. When they first manifest, they're usually weak—barely able to interact with the physical world. But as time passes, their power increases. They can start manipulating objects, affecting the environment, even lashing out at the living if provoked. Ghosts are like all creatures—they start off weak but can grow far more dangerous if left unchecked. You'll want to build trust with Jason. Only then will you have a chance to learn what's keeping him here."

Tom drained the last of his drink and set the tankard down with a clatter. "Got it. Thanks for the info, Bron. I'll try to make contact again and see if I can help him move on. Hopefully, we'll get this sorted out before things take a turn for the worse."

"If you find yourself in over your head, summon Amath immediately," Bron advised, his tone more serious than before. "He has experience with matters like this. He'll know what to do."

"I'll keep that in mind," Tom replied, waving over his shoulder as he stood and started to walk away.

As Tom made his way toward the security office, Maria's voice chimed in, her tone light and playful, "So, it's time to go ghost hunting?"

"Hunting's a bit strong," Tom said, rolling his eyes. "More like ghost finding."

Maria scoffed. "Well, you're no fun."

Tom stopped, placing his hands on his hips. "And killing a scared child, even if he's a ghost, is fun to you?"

Maria gave what felt like the equivalent of a mental shrug, a mischievous tone coming through her voice. "It's better than letting him become a ghast. You heard how nasty those things are."

Tom shook his head. "Right now, he's just a scared kid. We should at least try to help him first."

"Fine, fine," Maria conceded. "But be ready to make the call if things go sideways. Otherwise, people could end up dead."

Tom narrowed his eyes. "Got any advice for me?"

Maria gave an exaggerated "hmmm," pretending to think deeply. "Advice? On talking to ghosts? I've never had the pleasure. Remember, I'm only a couple of months old. I haven't exactly had time to build up my ghost-hunting experience."

Tom sighed. "You could look it up in the System, maybe?"

Maria giggled. "Sure, but it's probably the same info Bron gave you. If I had to guess… try offering candy? Kids like candy, right?"

Tom blinked. "And ghosts can eat candy?"

Maria paused, seeming to actually consider it before continuing, showing she was just being sarcastic. "Valid point. How about a white, windowless van? I hear kids love those."

Tom threw his hands up in exasperation. "Seriously?"

Maria laughed. "I'm just trying to show you how pointless your question was. I don't have any more info than you do. You'll just have to figure it out."

Tom rubbed his temple. "Fine, fine. I'm just trying to make use of every possible resource. He was on my floor last time, so maybe he'll show up again tonight. I assume ghosts aren't too active during the day?"

"Now that, I can help with," Maria said, sounding excited at being able to help. "Ghosts are weakened by sunlight. They're most active at night when the shadows are strongest."

"That makes sense," Tom said, nodding. "Alright. Let's see if anyone else is available to help out. Many hands make light work."

Tom entered the security office, his mind preoccupied with the events of the previous night. He found TJ behind the desk, and after a quick greeting, asked him to summon the rest of his party. Derek was already present and nodded in greeting when Tom walked in. The security office had a low hum of activity—screens showing various parts of the Guild, a few guards standing by, and the ambient chatter of the building filtering in.

A few minutes later, the rest of the group had arrived, and they gathered in the room, each taking a seat or leaning against the wall.

"I don't mean to take you away from what you were doing before," Tom began, his voice carrying a note of seriousness, "but we've got a small situation I could use your help with."

Derek raised an eyebrow. "Situation? Dangerous?"

"Potentially, but not immediately," Tom replied, rubbing the back of his neck. "There's a ghost in the Guild building."

James snickered from the back, leaning casually against the doorframe. "So… it's haunted?"

Tom sighed, his weariness evident in the way his shoulders slumped. "If having a ghost means 'haunted,' then sure, I guess." He paused for a moment, glancing around the room before locking eyes with James. "But this is serious. The ghost is a young boy, probably someone who died tragically, and his spirit can't move on. I don't want to cause a panic, but we need to find him and make a connection. If we can figure out what happened to him and help him, we can help his spirit pass on."

James, ever the joker, couldn't help himself. "So… who ya gonna call?"

"Shut up, James," Tom replied with a heavy sigh, shaking his head. "This isn't a joke. The boy is scared and confused. We have a real chance to help him before things get worse."

Kiera, sitting with one leg crossed over the other, furrowed her brow. "Okay, aside from all the metaphysical implications—afterlife, souls, spirits, and all that—what do we do to *actually* make a connection with a ghost?"

Tom leaned against the wall, arms folded across his chest. "I was able to speak to him last night before you ran into us, so I think we can do it again. We need to assure him that we're not here to harm him, that we're trying to help him figure out what happened."

Jay chimed in from the back, his voice skeptical. "And we don't just blast this ghost into the afterlife because…?"

"Because he's not a harmful spirit," Tom answered firmly, his eyes narrowing slightly. "He's not like the vengeful spirits we've dealt with before. This is a scared kid, maybe even a former Guild member, who just needs our help."

Jay crossed his arms, clearly unconvinced. "I mean, we've blasted other ghostly creatures before."

"Those were malicious entities created out of rage and revenge," Tom countered, his tone hardening with finality. "This is different. Jason's just a boy who's lost and scared. We're not going to treat him like a monster."

The room fell silent for a moment, Jay sinking back into his chair with a quiet nod.

Michael, leaning back in his seat with a contemplative look, finally spoke up. "Okay, say we do help him… do we really have time for this? I've got a lot of training to catch up on."

Tom met Michael's gaze, his expression serious. "I get it, but we're here to help the Guild. If we don't figure out what's keeping Jason here, he could eventually turn into a ghast—and *that* would be a real problem. Once that happens, we're talking about a danger to everyone in this building."

Michael sighed and nodded, the weight of the situation settling in.

Derek spoke up next. "Alright, so what's the plan?"

"For now, we're on the lookout," Tom explained. "Jason's been wandering the halls, and since I was able to speak with him once, I think I can do it again. If anyone sees him, let the others know right away. I'll try to make contact again and talk to him."

Everyone nodded in agreement, understanding the gravity of the situation.

"Good," Tom said, exhaling slightly. "Ghosts are more active at night, so let's rest up for now. We'll meet again later tonight."

As the team began to rise and prepare to leave, Kiera called out. "Just as a worst-case scenario—what do we do if it's too late? If he's already become a ghast?"

Tom paused at the door, turning back to face them. "If it comes to that, we'll need a Cleric. I can summon Amath to help. Let's hope I won't need to."

Later that evening, as the sun began to sink below the horizon and cast long shadows across the building, the team gathered at Tom's room. The air was cool and still, a contrast to the earlier bustle of the day. Tom stood at the center, addressing the group with a focused intensity.

"Each of you will take a different floor. Jason was last seen on this floor, so Jerky and I will stay here. If you see him, send out a shout—someone nearby should hear and relay the message to the rest of us." Tom glanced around the group, making sure everyone understood the plan. "And remember, try not to scare or hurt him. He's just a child who went through something traumatic. No reason to make it worse."

With nods of agreement, the group dispersed, each heading to their assigned floors. Tom and Jerky began their patrol, moving quietly through the halls as the minutes ticked away. The building was eerily quiet, the only sound the soft padding of their footsteps on the carpeted floor. Jerky, bleary-eyed and barely awake, mumbled complaints about wanting to go back to bed.

It wasn't until nearly one in the morning when Tom finally spotted the faint outline of Jason's figure floating down the hallway. The ghostly boy's form shimmered faintly, almost like a mirage in the dim light.

Tom gently shook Jerky awake, the familiar groaning in protest.

"Jason?" Tom called out, keeping his voice soft and non-threatening.

Jason turned slowly, his ethereal face showing a mixture of fear and confusion. "No… I don't want to get hurt," he said in a trembling voice.

Tom stepped forward, keeping his hands visible and his posture relaxed. "We're not here to hurt you, Jason. Something terrible happened to you, and we want to help. We know it wasn't your fault. We just want to make sure you're okay."

Jason blinked at him, still trembling, and his gaze shifted, scanning the hallway as if searching for something Tom couldn't see. "I'm fine... I just need to find my mom and dad," the boy whispered, turning away to look down the hall once more.

Tom took a slow step closer, careful not to startle him. "Are your mom and dad here? On this floor?"

"I... I don't know," Jason mumbled, his voice filled with uncertainty. "Everything's fuzzy... but this place feels familiar."

Tom's heart ached for the boy. "We want to help you find out what happened. We think we can help you remember, but we need you to trust us."

Jason turned back to Tom, his eyes wide. "You can bring my memories back?" he asked, his voice filled with a mixture of hope and fear.

"We'll try," Tom said gently. "Will you let us help you?"

The boy hesitated, glancing between Tom and Jerky, weighing his options. After a long pause, he looked back at Tom, his face softening. But then he pointed to Jerky. "You aren't going to hurt me, are you? Last time... that one hurt me."

Jerky stepped forward, his head hanging slightly in shame. "I'm so sorry, Jason," he said, his voice filled with regret. "I wasn't trying to hurt you. I never want to hurt anyone. I just wanted to help because I knew Tom could. He's helped so many people before, and I wanted you to see that. Please... give him a chance to help you."

Jason's expression shifted, a trace of sympathy crossing his face as he looked at Jerky. Slowly, he floated toward Tom, his eyes scanning him from head to toe as if searching for any sign of deceit. Finally, after a long moment, he looked up and met Tom's gaze.

"What do we need to do?"

Chapter 45

Jason

"I need you to think back," Tom said gently, kneeling down so that he was at eye level with the boy. His tone was soothing, like a parent trying to coax a frightened child out of hiding. "What can you remember from before you died? Anything at all. It doesn't have to be much—just something to start the process of remembering what happened."

Jason scrunched up his face, his features shifting into a look of concentration as he tried to summon his memories. His small hands curled into fists as he concentrated, attempting to force the scenes to come together. His head tilted, and his brow furrowed deeper as snippets of emotions flashed before him—happy moments, sad ones, times of anger, and a haze of sickness.

"I can remember… some things," Jason finally said, his voice tentative, like he was trying to describe a dream that was fading as soon as he woke. "They're like parts of a movie I saw once. I can sort of see the scenes, but… I can't remember the story."

"That's okay," Tom encouraged, his voice steady and patient. "Focus on just one of those memories. What's happening in it?"

As Tom spoke, he glanced sideways at Jerky, giving a subtle nod. Jerky, understanding the signal, quietly slipped away to gather the rest of the team. Tom turned his full attention back to Jason, his eyes soft and reassuring.

Jason closed his eyes tightly, brow creasing as he dug deeper into his mind. "In one of them, I'm outside in the sunshine. There's a fence around a yard, and I'm holding a big red ball." His voice softened as the image grew clearer. "Mom and Dad are there… I can see their faces now. Dad's asking me to throw the ball to him, and when I do, he catches it and rolls on the ground laughing. I'm laughing too, running to him, trying to tackle him and get the ball back."

"That's good, Jason," Tom said, nodding encouragingly. "Keep going. What else is happening? The more you remember, the stronger those memories will become."

Jason's expression softened as more memories surfaced. "Now I'm in the kitchen with Mom. She's making cookies, and I get to help with the batter. We scoop the dough out on a pan in little balls and put it in the oven. There's leftover cookie dough, and she lets me eat it from the bowl and spoon. It's so good."

Tom smiled softly, seeing the boy's joy in the memory. "What else? Keep going, Jason. We're making progress."

INVASION

Jason's face shifted again, a look of fondness crossing his features. "Now we're at the zoo. Mom and Dad took me with another family. We played at the playground and saw all kinds of animals." His expression faltered, however, as the memory morphed. "Now I'm lying in bed with a fever. Mom looks worried... I can see the way she's staring at me. I keep telling her I'll be alright."

"You're doing great, Jason," Tom said softly, sensing the shift in the boy's emotions. "What else can you remember?"

Jason took a deep breath, his voice wavering. "I fell off my bike. I was crying, and Dad ran over to help me. He told me it's okay to fall, as long as I get back up and try again."

Tom leaned in slightly, his voice filled with gentle encouragement. "You're doing amazing, Jason. What else? We need to understand what happened."

Jason's face contorted in confusion, the memories becoming darker. "There's... a big screen in the sky. I'm on a walk with my parents, and the screen is saying something bad is going to happen. And then... monsters appeared." His voice began to tremble as he continued, "Mom grabbed me, and we ran. Dad... Dad stayed behind to fight off some of the monsters, but then he followed us. We ran into a building, hiding. So many people were screaming and... dying."

Tom's heart clenched at the raw pain in Jason's voice. "That was the start of the System integration," Tom said gently. "We all went through that terrible time. You're not alone in this."

But Jason's face twisted into fear and anguish as the memories flooded back in full force. "I don't want to remember! It's too bad!" he cried, his hands flying up to his head, as though trying to block out the memories. His ghostly form flickered, distorting with the weight of his emotions. "Bad things happened! Bad things!"

Tom remained steady, though his heart raced. "What bad things, Jason? You need to tell me. It's the only way we can help you."

Jason's voice rose into a panicked wail. "No! They died! They all died! The goblins... they were everywhere! I couldn't see—the words kept showing up in my eyes, and I couldn't see anything!" His form wavered as tears spilled down his face, translucent but real in their own way.

"JASON!" Tom's voice cut through the ghostly boy's panic, his tone firm but not unkind.

Jason flinched, shrinking back from Tom with wide, frightened eyes. His form began to fade, turning more transparent as though he were retreating into the ether.

"I'm sorry for yelling," Tom said quickly, his voice softening. "But you have to understand—you're not alone in this. We all went through that event. I'm here to help you, to keep you safe. I promise I won't let anything bad happen to you. These are just memories, Jason. They can't hurt you anymore."

Jason stared at Tom, his spectral form still trembling, but his eyes searched Tom's with a desperate intensity. Tom held his gaze, refusing to look away, willing Jason to find the reassurance he needed. For a long moment, they simply stared at one another, the connection between them deepening.

Slowly, Jason's form began to solidify again, the transparency fading as he lowered himself to the floor. He nodded once, a tiny but determined gesture, before closing his eyes again, steeling himself for what was to come.

"I can do it," Jason whispered, his voice trembling but steady. "Just… don't leave me."

"I'm not going anywhere," Tom promised, instinctively reaching out to place a hand on the boy's shoulder. His hand passed through Jason's ghostly form, and he quickly pulled it back with an awkward smile. "Sorry… I forgot you're intangible."

Jason gave a small, sad smile at the gesture, but the fear remained in his eyes. He closed his eyes again, focusing on the memories he had buried for so long.

"We ran past so many people… they were screaming, begging for help. Dad didn't have to go to work that day, so we were at the park when it all started. I tripped… I couldn't keep up with them. Mom grabbed me and we ran to the car, but we couldn't drive far. We had to leave the car and run through the city." Jason's voice cracked as he relived the chaos.

"We ran until we got trapped by a group of monsters. Dad fought them off while we ran into a building. Mom hid me in a closet." Jason's voice grew quieter, almost a whisper. "I heard noises outside the door… loud crashes. The ground started shaking, and the walls began to crack. The room collapsed, and I was stuck under something heavy… I couldn't move."

Tom's heart sank as the boy's final moments came back to him in painful clarity. Jason's eyes flickered open, and tears shimmered at the edges.

"Jason," Tom said, his voice filled with empathy. "You don't have to go through this alone. We're here to help you find peace."

Jason wiped at his ghostly tears, nodding slowly, the weight of his memories clearly overwhelming him, but he had a newfound determination in his gaze.

"I just want it to stop," he whispered. "I want it to be over."

"We'll help you," Tom said firmly. "I promise."

"I couldn't move," Jason began again, his voice trembling as he stared at the floor, lost in the painful memory. "Everything was dark. I called out for Mom or Dad to help me, but no one came. I don't know how long I was there. I got hungry and thirsty. Then… I got really sleepy. Eventually, I fell asleep, and when I woke up, I could move through the walls." He paused, his ghostly figure flickering as if the weight of the memory was too much to bear. "Then I came here. I didn't know what had happened… I just wanted to find my parents. But I think I know now."

Jason looked down, his expression clouded with sadness and uncertainty. The room felt heavy, as though the air itself was burdened by the weight of his words.

Tom's throat tightened as he tried to process what Jason had just revealed. "Jason… I'm so sorry," he said softly, his voice filled with shock and sympathy.

INVASION

"It sounds like you were crushed under part of the building when everything collapsed." He shook his head, still stunned by the boy's tragic fate. "I can't believe that happened to you."

Jason looked up briefly, his eyes distant but resigned. "It's okay. It wasn't your fault. I just want to find my parents."

Tom hesitated, wanting to offer hope but fearing the worst. "I want to help you, Jason. I really do. But… if what you're saying is true, there's a chance they might not have made it."

Jason's gaze hardened, his voice more certain this time. "I know they're alive. I can feel them. That's why I came here."

Tom blinked, confusion flickering across his face. "You… *feel* them? Are you sure? How can you feel them?"

Jason's brow furrowed as he struggled to explain the sensation. "I don't know how to put it into words. It's like… this pull, something in my head that led me here. All I want is for them to know that I don't blame them. And when I think about that, it… points me to this building."

Tom's mind raced with questions, each one fighting for dominance in his thoughts. "Do you remember their names?" he asked, hoping for a clearer lead.

Jason shook his head, his expression filled with frustration. "I think I did… once. But now, it's just gone. I can remember pictures, faces, but not names. I want to, but it's not there anymore."

"That's okay, Jason. You've done great. You've remembered more than you think," Tom reassured him, meeting the boy's eyes. "I promise I'll help from here. If your parents are here, I'll find them for you."

Just then, Jerky returned with the rest of the team, their footsteps faltering as they caught sight of the spectral boy hovering in the hallway.

"Holy shit, he wasn't lying," Derek muttered, his eyes wide as he stared at Jason.

"Oh man, this is so cool," James said, grinning as he examined the ghostly form in front of him.

Tom didn't waste any time. "I need someone to get Brian. Now. Jason has a feeling that his parents are in this building. We need to see if we can track them down."

James, always the comedian, raised an eyebrow. "Are we sure it's not just ghost indigestion or something? I mean, how could he know?"

Jason's eyes flared with sudden anger, glowing a deep, unsettling red. His ethereal form seemed to pulse with energy as he glared at James. "I *know* they're here," he growled, his voice taking on a dangerous edge. "I feel the pull to this place!"

"Whoa, okay!" James raised his hands defensively, taking a step back. "I didn't mean to—"

Before he could finish, Jason lunged at him, his ghostly hands wrapping around James' throat.

"You're trying to keep me from them!" Jason snarled, his voice warped as though possessed by some dark force. His eyes blazed with rage as he tightened his grip, and James stumbled backward, tripping over his own feet and crashing to the floor.

"What the hell?!" James gasped, his hands clawing at his throat as Jason's ghostly fingers squeezed tighter.

"Jason, stop!" Tom shouted, rushing forward with the others. They tried to grab Jason, but their hands passed right through him, unable to make any contact. Derek, in his panic, accidentally slapped James across the face as he reached for Jason's arm.

Jerky, acting quickly, jumped in and grabbed Jason by the waist, his hands glowing faintly with magical energy. With a grunt, he lifted the boy into the air.

"AAAAAAAAAAAAHHHHHH!" Jason screamed in agony as Jerky held him, the spectral boy's form convulsing in pain. He let go of James, who gasped for air, coughing and rubbing his throat.

Jason, now clawing at Jerky in desperation, seemed to come back to himself. His eyes, which had burned with red fury, began to dim, returning to their normal ghostly pale hue. He turned to look at Tom, his expression filled with horror and regret. "Oh no… What have I done? I didn't mean to hurt anyone. I'm sorry!"

Jerky still held him, his grip firm but cautious, not letting go just yet. "Jason," Tom said gently, stepping forward, "we're really worried about you. We know that if you don't find peace soon, you could turn into something much worse—a monster. But we're not giving up on you. We're going to help you."

He motioned for Jerky to release Jason. Slowly, Jerky loosened his hold, lowering Jason back down. The boy floated a few feet away, his shoulders slumped in shame.

Tom turned on James, his expression stern. "And you," he said pointedly, "go get Brian. You're not helping."

James scrambled to his feet, still massaging his throat. "Fine, fine. I'll go get the Irishman," he muttered, brushing himself off as he headed for the elevator.

Jason, trembling slightly, looked back at Tom, his voice shaky. "Is… is that what was happening to me? That anger? It felt like… something took over. I didn't even know what I was doing."

Tom nodded, his face serious but kind. "I think so. It's dangerous, Jason. We were told that if you don't find peace soon, that anger could turn you into something terrible. But we're not going to let that happen. We're here to help you, okay? Just trust me and stay calm."

Jason nodded, still looking down at the floor, his voice barely above a whisper. "I'm sorry. And thank you. I don't know what to do, and it's so frustrating."

Tom crouched down again, meeting the boy's eyes. "Don't worry about it. We've all been there—lost, confused, angry. This new world isn't easy, and sometimes we need help to get through it. That's why we formed this Guild—to help people like you. Give us some time, and we'll find your parents. I promise."

Jason stared at Tom for a long moment, his eyes reflecting both fear and hope. Finally, he nodded. "Okay. I'll try to stay calm."

Chapter 46

Parent Search

Brian was clearly unhappy about being woken up in the middle of the night. He stood in the doorway, his hair sticking up in wild tufts, still in his pajamas, and glowering at James with irritation. His arms were resting on the door and doorframe, and his eyes were half-closed from exhaustion.

"What do you want?" Brian grumbled, his voice heavy with fatigue. "You know how much work I have during the day—my sleep is precious."

James, completely unfazed, shrugged nonchalantly. "Well, we've got ourselves a ghost situation in the Guild, and we need your help finding the ghost's mommy and daddy. So, get your ass in gear, bub. It's time to play detective."

Brian blinked, his brain struggling to catch up with what James had just said. "Seriously? A ghost? Couldn't this have waited until morning?" he muttered, rubbing his face in frustration.

"Sure," James replied with a casual grin, "if you're willing to risk the ghost turning into some kind of evil monster and wreaking havoc on the Guild. All of which could've been prevented if we just spent a little time finding a couple of people tonight. Your call, really."

Brian sighed heavily, his shoulders slumping as he accepted his fate. "Fine," he said, his voice resigned. "Give me a minute to get dressed. I'll be out in a second."

James leaned against the wall in the hallway, whistling the Family Guy theme as he waited. He lazily tapped his foot against the floor, clearly not in any particular rush. Soon, Brian reappeared, dressed and looking marginally more awake, though his expression was still less than pleased.

"Alright," Brian said, his tone clipped. "Let's get on with it. Take me to the ghost so I can get some details."

James led the way back to the elevators, the faint hum of the building filling the quiet between them. They descended back to the floor where Tom and the others were waiting with Jason. When they arrived, the group was sitting in a loose circle, chatting with the ghost boy, clearly trying to keep the atmosphere calm for his sake.

"Ah, Brian," Tom said, standing up as the two approached. "Thanks for coming so quickly. I know it's late, and you definitely deserve your rest. We wouldn't have asked if it wasn't important."

Brian sighed, running a hand through his still-disheveled hair. "Right. What can I do to help?"

Tom gestured toward Jason, who floated quietly near the group, watching Brian with wide, ghostly eyes. "This is Jason. He's trying to find his parents. He says he feels a strong pull to this building when he thinks about them, like they're here somewhere. We need your help to find them."

Brian glanced at Jason, his expression softening slightly at the sight of the boy. "Alright," he said, nodding. "What are their names? If we know that, it should be easy enough to track them down."

Tom hesitated for a moment before responding. "That's the problem—we don't know their names. Jason lost a lot of his memories when he died. We've been trying to help him recover them, but he can't seem to recall their names. I was hoping we could use some of his memories to figure out who they might be."

Brian frowned, folding his arms as he considered the situation. "Well," he said slowly, "we could start by gathering all the parents who lost children. We could ask them to share their stories and see if anything matches with Jason's memories. But…" He trailed off, his expression growing more serious. "That would mean making them relive what was likely the worst moment of their lives. Are you really okay with putting them through that?"

Tom winced, realizing the weight of what Brian was saying. "I hadn't thought of that," he admitted, his voice heavy with guilt. "But if we don't act, Jason could become a serious threat to the Guild. I don't think we have much choice."

Brian nodded grimly. "Alright, I'll get started on it. It may take some time to gather everyone, though."

"We don't have a lot of time," Tom said, his voice laced with urgency. "We need to work quickly. Jason could change while we're searching, and then all of this would be for nothing. If we're going to make them go through this, we need to make it count. Get as many people as you can to help with the interviews—it'll speed things up."

Brian glanced around at the group. "If I can borrow your team, that would help."

Tom nodded without hesitation. "Of course. Whatever you need."

As Brian started coordinating with the others, Tom knelt down next to Jason. "We're going to find your parents," he said gently. "In the meantime, why don't you tell me more about any other memories you can? It doesn't have to be important—just anything you can remember."

Jason smiled faintly, his ghostly form flickering slightly. "I like the happy memories best," he said softly. "Oh, I do remember one time when Mom and Dad took me to a baseball game. The stadium was huge. Dad was teaching me how the game worked—hit the ball, run to the bases, get points. The crowd did the wave, and we joined in. Mom was laughing when we stood up and raised our hands. She always had the best laugh."

Jason's face lit up as he remembered, and for a moment, he seemed almost at peace. "Mom bought me a hotdog and nachos. They were the best I've ever had. People were shouting about peanuts and cotton candy, and Dad said if our team won, he'd buy me a hat to remember the day."

Tom smiled, nodding along with the story. "That sounds like a lot of fun. Did they win?"

"They did!" Jason's smile grew wider, and his eyes sparkled with the memory. "Dad got me a hat with a big 'T' on it. I was so tired by the end of the game that Dad had to carry me to the car. I fell asleep on the ride home."

Tom chuckled softly. "I remember my first baseball game too. There's something special about going to the game with your parents."

Jason's expression shifted slightly, his eyes growing curious.

"Where are your parents, Tom?" he asked quietly.

"They died a while ago," Tom said softly, his voice tinged with sadness as he looked at Jason. "I don't really have any family left. But my friends, the people in this Guild—they're my family now. That's why I work so hard to help them."

Jason's ghostly form flickered slightly, and a deep sadness seemed to wash over him. His eyes, wide with grief, reflected a sorrow far beyond his years. "I wish I had found you before I died. Maybe… maybe you could have helped me."

Tom felt a pang in his chest at the boy's words. "I'm sorry, Jason. That was such a terrible time. Everyone was panicking, and we didn't know what to do. But remembering the good times—it helps. It helps us get through the pain."

Jason's face brightened ever so slightly as he shifted his thoughts to happier memories. "I do feel better when I think of those times… like when we went to Six Flags. Dad and I rode the roller coasters while Mom watched from the side. She didn't like the big rides, but she rode the carousel with me. That was so much fun." He smiled wistfully. "And then we went to the games. I won a giant stuffed banana by throwing a ball into a big bucket."

Tom chuckled, imagining Jason carrying around a giant banana. "Those carnival games are great. It's always a fun time when you're with the people you love."

Jason looked up at him, the memories alight in his eyes. "I was so lucky to have parents like mine."

Meanwhile, Brian had begun working on finding any Guild members who had lost a child during the System integration. As he scrolled through his list of members, he realized with a sigh that he hadn't thought to ask for this specific information when people joined the Guild.

"It didn't seem important at the time," Brian muttered to himself. "But I guess hindsight is always twenty-twenty."

TJ, standing nearby, gave him a sympathetic smile. "How could you have known we'd end up with a ghost that might turn into a dangerous monster if we didn't find its parents—who also happen to be members of our Guild?" He chuckled softly. "Don't beat yourself up over it. We'll find them. I'm putting out an announcement now for all parents who lost a child to come to the gym. We should be able to start interviewing them shortly."

Brian sighed again, rubbing his temples. "What a giant pain. Stuff like this just keeps happening to us. I mean, I know we've got it pretty easy now that we've established ourselves and found so many people to help, but still..." he trailed off, looking frustrated.

TJ laughed and clapped him on the shoulder. "Oh, don't be so whiny about it. It comes with the territory. Besides, we needed to learn more about our members anyway, and this speeds up the process."

After the announcement was made, Brian and TJ made their way to the gym. When they arrived, they found the room filled with more people than they had expected.

Brian's heart sank as he took in the sight of all the faces around them. "This isn't good," he said quietly, his eyes scanning the crowd.

TJ frowned, confused. "What do you mean? We wanted to find them, didn't we? This seems like a good turnout."

"For that, yes," Brian replied, his voice somber. "But look at these people. They've all lost a child. Some came alone, so it looks like they've lost more than just their kids." He paused, his heart heavy. "We're about to put them through hell by asking them to relive the worst moments of their lives."

TJ's face fell as the gravity of the situation hit him. "I didn't think of it like that." He shook his head. "It really does change the mood. But it has to be done. Let's get them organized and start the process."

They met up with the volunteers, who were already preparing for the interviews. Derek had compiled a list of the information Jason had shared about his death and distributed it to the others.

"If anyone finds the family that matches Jason's story, let us know right away," Derek instructed. "We'll connect them with Jason as soon as we can. Any questions?"

There was a brief silence before the volunteers nodded in agreement.

"Alright," Derek said, taking a deep breath. "Let's begin."

The volunteers spread out, ushering the families to the bleachers to wait their turn for interviews. Tables and chairs had been set up for the interviews to be conducted in a more private setting, so as not to spread sensitive information in front of others. One by one, couples and individuals were called to the tables to share their stories.

The atmosphere in the gym was heavy with grief. Tears flowed freely as many of the parents recounted the events that had led to the deaths of their children. Some of them hadn't fully processed their grief and seemed on the verge of breaking down as they relived the trauma.

After what felt like hours, Kiera finally approached Derek, her face drawn with both sadness and a hint of hope. "I think I've found them," she said quietly. "Mr. and Mrs. Forest. Their story matches everything Jason told Tom. I haven't explained anything to them yet—I thought it'd be best to check with you first."

INVASION

Derek nodded, grateful for her discretion. "That's probably best. Thanks, Kiera. I'll go speak with them. Let's keep the other interviews going for now so we don't raise suspicions."

He gathered the notes from the other interviews, quickly reviewing them, then made his way over to the table where the Forests were sitting with Kiera.

"Mr. and Mrs. Forest," Derek greeted them, offering a sympathetic smile as he sat down. "Thank you for coming in. I know this isn't easy for either of you."

Mrs. Forest gave a small, shaky smile. "It's alright. We're just glad we can help. Though… it is a little strange that you're asking about how our son died. Is there something wrong?"

Derek hesitated, choosing his words carefully. "This is… a delicate situation. We're gathering information about our Guild members in case something comes up in the future. Everything you've shared with us will help things run more smoothly. So, first of all, thank you for your cooperation." He paused, his expression becoming more serious. "But there's something else I need to tell you."

The Forests exchanged worried glances, sensing the shift in tone.

Derek took a deep breath. "We recently discovered a ghost in the Guild building."

Mrs. Forest's eyes widened in shock, and she clutched her husband's arm. "A ghost? Is it dangerous? Should we be worried?"

"No," Derek reassured her quickly. "We don't believe the ghost is a threat—as long as we handle the situation carefully." He hesitated for a moment before continuing, his voice soft. "The reason we've called you here is because we believe this ghost is your son, Jason."

Mr. and Mrs. Forest froze, their faces pale with shock. Mrs. Forest covered her mouth, her eyes brimming with tears. "Our… Jason?" she whispered, her voice barely audible.

Derek nodded. "Yes. He's been looking for you. He doesn't remember everything, but he knows he wants to find you. We're here to help him do that, and to help him find peace."

Chapter 47

Peace

"Our Jason… is a ghost?" Mrs. Forest asked, her voice trembling, concern etched deeply on her face as she tried to process what Derek had just told them.

"It appears so," Derek replied softly, nodding. "Tom, our Guild leader, found him wandering the halls late at night. He's been looking for you, though he's had trouble remembering everything."

Mr. Forest looked bewildered, his voice strained with disbelief. "How could this happen?"

Derek took a deep breath, his tone gentle but firm. "With the integration of the System and the introduction of magic, it seems that if someone dies under extreme duress or with unresolved regrets, their spirit can become trapped in this world. Desperation and longing can cause the soul to cling to the physical plane, unable to move on until they find the peace they need." He paused, his gaze steady as he continued. "We believe that reuniting Jason with you may help him find that peace. This is also an opportunity for you to say goodbye, to let him know that you'll be okay without him here, and to release him."

Mrs. Forest's eyes welled up with tears, her voice cracking. "But… I don't know if we can ever be okay without him. He was our only child."

Derek nodded sympathetically, understanding the depth of their pain. "I know it feels impossible. Losing someone like that leaves a wound that never fully heals. But if Jason stays here too long, his spirit could become corrupted. He might turn into something dangerous—something that could harm others in the Guild. If that happens, we'd be forced to stop him, and I don't know what that would mean for his soul. I know it's hard but helping him find peace is what's needed. Saying goodbye is one of the hardest parts of life, but it's also one of the most important."

Derek bowed his head briefly, lost in thought for a moment. "I've had to say goodbye to friends and family I didn't think I could live without. In the military, there are times when you have to face loss like that. I've been there. I understand how you feel. Not many people get a second chance to say goodbye to someone they love…."

Mr. Forest sighed heavily, his face creased with sorrow. "You're right. It's just… it feels like we were starting to heal, and now this has ripped open the wound again."

INVASION

"I'm truly sorry," Derek said quietly. "We didn't mean to bring you more pain. But not many people get a chance like this—to say goodbye, to say all the things you wanted to but never got the chance to. I know this is hard, but it's also a rare opportunity. You can help Jason find peace, and you can find closure too."

Tears welled up in Derek's eyes as he spoke, though he blinked them away quickly. "So please, take this chance. It's your last opportunity to say goodbye the way you would've wanted to."

Silence hung in the air for a moment, both parents absorbing Derek's words. They glanced at each other, their hearts heavy with the weight of both sorrow and gratitude. Mrs. Forest wiped at her eyes as the tears began to fall, her hands trembling.

"Thank you, Derek," Mrs. Forest whispered, her voice choked with emotion. "We understand what this means, and we won't waste this chance."

Mr. Forest placed a gentle hand on his wife's shoulder, his own eyes red with unshed tears. "We're grateful to have this opportunity, even if it's painful. And... thank you for keeping everyone here safe."

Derek, feeling the heavy burden of their grief, nodded slowly. "We're just glad we could find you and give you this moment. Jason needs you now, and the people here need to stay safe."

Mrs. Forest looked up, her voice barely audible. "Can we... see him?"

"Yes," Derek said softly, standing up. "Come with me. I'll take you to him."

Meanwhile, back in the hallway, Tom and Jason had been talking for hours, sharing stories and memories to pass the time. Jason had shared what little he could remember of his life, while Tom had opened up about his own experiences in a way he rarely did; even with his closest teammates. He spoke of his parents, of the pain of their loss, and of the times he'd been made fun of or put down. He even shared some of his insecurities and struggles with his own identity.

When the conversation became too heavy, Tom shifted the topic to lighter stories—tales of his adventures after the System integration. Jason listened with wide-eyed fascination, peppering Tom with questions about the monsters and treasures they had found.

"Wait, Bunnicorns?" Jason asked, eyes wide with disbelief.

Tom chuckled, sitting on the floor with his back against the wall. "Yeah, Bunnicorns. They look like cute little white rabbits, but they've got a horn on their forehead like a unicorn. Vicious little things. They'd charge at us like we weren't a threat at all, biting and clawing at us before trying to stab us with their horns. They were terrorizing a whole town."

Jason laughed, leaning in with curiosity. "So, what happened?"

Tom grinned, enjoying the boy's enthusiasm. "Well, as they approached the town, we stood in their way and started taking them down however we could. Did you know Bunnicorns squeak when they die?"

Jason's eyes widened. "What?"

"Yup," Tom said, his grin widening. "They squeak like dog toys. I nearly burst out laughing when I killed the first one. Then one of them bit me on the leg, and the laughing stopped real quick."

Jason laughed so hard that he clutched his stomach, tears forming in his eyes. "And James? What did he do?"

"He was horrified!" Tom replied, shaking his head in amusement. "He kept saying the world wasn't supposed to be this cute and cuddly, and here we were, fighting adorable little monsters. Then one of the Bunnicorns ended up poking him in the butt with its horn!"

Jason howled with laughter, his ethereal form flickering with delight.

At that moment, the elevator at the end of the hall dinged, and the doors slowly slid open. The sound caught both Tom and Jason's attention, and they turned to see two people cautiously step out into the hallway, their eyes scanning the scene before them.

"Jason?" Mrs. Forest said softly, her voice trembling with emotion, as though she couldn't quite believe what she was seeing.

Jason turned toward the voice, his eyes widening. For a moment, he stared at her, confusion clouding his expression. Then, realization dawned, and his ghostly form seemed to brighten as recognition flickered in his eyes.

"Mom?" Jason whispered at first, his voice trembling with disbelief. Then, louder and more urgent, he yelled, "MOM!"

In a blur, Jason flew down the hallway, his ethereal arms outstretched as he enveloped his mother in a tight embrace. Somehow, he was able to control his form, no longer phasing through objects like before. He held her tightly, as if the moment would last forever. Mrs. Forest fell to her knees, wrapping her arms around him, tears streaming freely down her face.

"My precious boy," she whispered, her voice breaking. "I love you so much."

They remained like that for what seemed like an eternity. Mr. Forest knelt beside them, his arms joining the embrace as the family reunited in a bittersweet moment of love and loss. Tom, standing a few feet away, felt tears sting his eyes. He quickly glanced around at the others there and saw that not a single person had remained dry-eyed. Each one of them was silently wiping away tears, overwhelmed by the heart-wrenching scene unfolding before them.

The moment stretched on, the family lost in their embrace, until Jason, with a smile of pure innocence, interrupted the silence.

"Have you met my friend, Tom?" Jason asked, his ghostly form shimmering slightly. "He's super cool!"

Mrs. Forest smiled through her tears, stroking her son's hair. "We have, honey. He's such a good man."

Jason beamed with pride. "I'm so glad you found me. I was looking everywhere for you, but you weren't where you left me, so I came here. Why did you leave?" His voice carried the innocence of a child, still trying to understand the enormity of what had happened.

Mrs. Forest's face tightened, and she gently cupped Jason's face in her hands. "Oh, baby, we didn't want to leave. We tried to dig you out, but the building collapsed, and we couldn't move the debris. The pieces were too heavy." Her voice quivered as she continued, "You know you… you died, right, sweetie?"

Jason looked down, nodding slowly. "Yeah, I know. But since I came back, I wanted to find you. I love you."

"I love you too, baby," Mrs. Forest whispered, tears flowing freely. "But… since you died, we have to let you go. You're not meant to stay here anymore."

Jason's face fell, his eyes reflecting a deep sadness. "But I wanna stay with you."

Mrs. Forest gently caressed his hair, her voice soft and tender. "I know, Jason. And I want nothing more than to have you with me. But when we die, things change. This world isn't made for our spirits. Our bodies help our spirits grow while we're here, and when we die, it's time for our spirits to move on. Your spirit was so strong, Jason. You were ready before we were."

Jason stared at her, still trying to understand. "But I don't want to leave."

"Listen," Mrs. Forest said, her voice soothing. "Dad and I… we're still here because our spirits are still growing. But one day, when our bodies die, we'll join you. It'll just take us a little longer. Until then, we need you to go ahead and make sure everything is ready for us. You need to be at peace. If you don't… if you stay here too long, your spirit could turn bad, like food that's left out too long."

Jason's eyes widened. "My spirit will go bad?"

Mrs. Forest smiled softly, trying to explain, "Think of it like a jug of milk. Where does milk go?"

"In the fridge," Jason replied, still trying to follow along.

"And what happens if you leave the milk out on the counter?" she asked.

"It turns yucky and goes bad," Jason said, wrinkling his nose.

"That's right," she said, her voice gentle but firm. "Spirits are like that, too. If we don't let them move on, they can go bad. I know it's hard. I know you want to stay, but you need to be where you belong."

Jason looked up at his father, his eyes pleading. "Do I really have to go?"

Mr. Forest nodded before answering, his voice thick with emotion, "Yeah, bud. Your mom's right. This place isn't right for just your spirit. But we'll come join you when it's time. You'll see us again, I promise."

"When?" Jason asked, his voice small.

Mrs. Forest touched a finger to his nose, smiling through her tears. "Before you know it, sweetheart. And until then, you'll be so busy having fun in heaven that you won't even notice the time. And then, one day, we'll be there with you."

Jason's eyes lit up with wonder. "What kind of fun things?"

Mrs. Forest chuckled, brushing his hair back. "Anything you can imagine, Jason. It's the most amazing place. Nothing is impossible there."

Jason's expression softened, a glimmer of excitement in his eyes. "Nothing's impossible? That sounds… awesome."

"It is, baby," she said, her voice filled with love. "Now, even though we have to say goodbye for now, it's not forever. We'll be together again, sooner than you think. Can you be brave for me and make sure heaven is ready for us?"

Jason smiled, his eyes twinkling. "Yeah. I can do that."

Mrs. Forest pulled him in for one last hug, her arms trembling as she held him close. "I love you so much, Jason. I'm going to miss you."

"I love you too, Mom," Jason whispered, resting his head on her shoulder.

As they sat together, holding onto each other, Jason's ghostly form began to shift. Tiny motes of light appeared within his translucent body, gently lifting into the air like fireflies on a breeze. His parents watched in awe and heartbreak as the lights slowly floated away, one by one, until Jason's form dissolved into the soft, glowing particles. When the last light faded from view, Mr. and Mrs. Forest sat in the empty space where their son had been, the weight of loss settling over them once more.

They embraced each other, their tears flowing freely, mourning the loss of their child for the second time.

Tom stood nearby, his own emotions overwhelming him. He whispered softly into the still air, "I'll see you again too, Jason. Then we'll go on an adventure together."

Chapter 48

Mission Possible

Tom lingered in the hallway long after Jason had moved on, allowing the emotions that came with the moment to flow through him. Mr. and Mrs. Forest had returned to their room, offering quiet thanks to the team for giving them the chance to help their son find peace. The rest of the team had dispersed, but Tom remained, still processing everything that had happened.

Derek returned after checking in with the others. Seeing Tom still seated against the wall, he approached quietly. "You okay?"

Tom looked up, his voice low and reflective. "I'll be alright. That was just... a tough one."

Derek nodded, understanding. "Yeah, I get it. It's like standing at the airport, watching as the bodies of friends get unloaded, knowing they're not coming back. That sense of finality, like all the time you spent together and everything you did to protect each other was for nothing." His words were heavy as memories of his military past surfaced. "It makes you feel like it was all wasted, like you were fighting a senseless war that shouldn't have happened in the first place. But we have to remind ourselves that we make the most of the time we have. Life's dangerous. Even before all this System stuff, you could've stepped outside and gotten hit by a car."

"Yeah," Tom sighed. "Such is life, right?"

Derek shook his head slightly. "That's not what I mean. We feel like this because we made connections. That's what makes it worth it. If you never felt this kind of pain, it would mean you never had anyone to care about in the first place. And that's worse—far worse than what you're feeling right now."

Tom leaned his head back against the wall, eyes closed. "I guess it's like Buddha said, right? 'Existence is pain.'"

Derek gave a small, rueful smile. "Yeah, but he meant that pain is inevitable, not that it defines everything. Life is full of little pains—loss, frustration, things that don't go our way. But suffering is optional. The goal is to see beyond that pain, to recognize the moments when you're doing things you love, with people you care about. That's where joy is. It's about finding the light in spite of the darkness."

Tom didn't respond immediately. He sat in quiet thought, his mind drifting back to all the people they'd lost since the beginning of this apocalypse. The memories hit him harder now, especially in the wake of helping Jason find peace.

After a long silence, Derek shifted slightly. "Look, I don't want to take your mind off this too quickly, but there's something we need to talk about. Mike's been monitoring the HAM radio and picked up a signal from a group up in Oklahoma. They're in trouble with a monster attack and need help. They've heard about our setup and want to join forces with us."

Tom rubbed his temples, still processing. "I do want to help, but we've got so much preparation to do here. What do you think we should do?"

Derek glanced down the hallway, considering. "As much as I hate to say it, we should send a small group to check it out. Also… James overheard the conversation. He volunteered to go."

Tom raised an eyebrow, his exhaustion momentarily lifting. "James? That's a disaster waiting to happen."

Derek chuckled. "I know. But maybe it's time we give him some responsibility. It could force him to grow up a little."

"You can't be serious. James? In charge of a mission?" Tom's disbelief was clear.

"I am serious. And I want to send Jay with him. That should balance out the crazy a bit. What do you say?"

Tom sighed, clearly skeptical. "I'll agree on one condition: send a fighter with them. Or better yet, a Barbarian. Someone who can hit hard in case things get dicey."

Derek grinned. "I think I've got just the person in mind. Come on, let me introduce you."

Tom pushed himself to his feet, still tired but willing to go along. "Can we do it in the morning? I could really use some rest."

Derek glanced out the window and smirked. "I don't know if you've checked the time, but it *is* morning."

Tom groaned, running a hand through his hair. "Dammit. Alright, let's get this over with."

After grabbing a quick breakfast of Goatamus bacon and scrambled eggs, Tom made his way to the security office where Derek had gathered the team. As Tom walked in, Derek gestured to the group waiting inside.

"Tom, let me introduce you to the team. You already know James and Jay." He motioned to the next person. "This is Frank, a Barbarian. He'll be your heavy hitter. Lacy is a Cleric—she'll handle healing and protection. Mark's a Wizard for ranged support, and last but not least, this is Susie, a Spellblade."

Tom's gaze lingered on Susie, a small girl who looked no older than twelve. He leaned over to Derek, whispering, "You're sending a *child* on this mission?"

Derek smiled knowingly. "Yes. Bron recommended her. She's some kind of prodigy."

INVASION

Susie, hearing the exchange, crossed her arms and scowled. "I can hear you, you know. I may be young, but I promise you, I can keep them safe."

Tom blinked, taken aback by her confidence.

"Sorry," he said quickly, trying to recover. "I'm not doubting your skills—it's just that we don't usually see someone your age ready to fight."

Susie straightened, her eyes flashing with determination. "I get it. But I'm not like other kids. You'll see."

Tom studied her for a moment, reassessing. Her posture, the way she carried herself—there was something undeniably skilled about her. "If Bron says you're good, then I believe it." He paused, curiosity getting the better of him. "How old are you, exactly?"

"Twelve," Susie replied proudly. "But I've been in fencing competitions and rapier training since I was four. My skills transferred seamlessly when the System integrated. I'm also a MENSA student with an IQ of 155." She stood tall, clearly proud of her accomplishments.

Tom couldn't help but be impressed. "That's... remarkable. And a Spellblade, no less. I haven't met many."

Susie's eyes sparkled with pride. "It was an obvious choice. The best probability for survival is having a broad skill set for as many situations as possible. You found a similar path yourself, didn't you?"

"I guess I did. Though I chose the Warlock Class instead," Tom replied.

"True," Susie said with a knowing nod, "but you took a Warrior-based path with spells. So, in a way, we're in the same category of fighters. I was a gamer too—RPGs were my favorite. So, I've got a decent handle on how all this works."

Tom raised an eyebrow. "You do realize that video games don't exactly prepare you for the brutality of real combat, right?"

Susie's expression remained calm and confident. "I do. But I've already seen my fair share of battles since this whole thing started. Trust me, I'm prepared."

Tom hesitated for a moment, then nodded. "Alright, you've got my vote. Derek, what's the mission?"

Derek stepped forward, his tone turning serious. "This mission is a rescue operation. A small Guild near the Oklahoma border is under attack by some kind of monster—possibly a group of them. They've been holed up in a mechanic's shop off Interstate Thirty-Five, sending distress signals for days. Your objective: defeat the monsters, rescue the people, and bring them back safely. Any questions?"

Mark raised a hand. "Do we have any intel on what kind of monsters we're dealing with?"

Derek shook his head. "Not much, just that they're big. Not the biggest we've faced, but it's still a threat."

Lacy glanced around; her voice soft but worried. "Is this really all the people you can send?"

Derek sighed, crossing his arms. "Unfortunately, yes. We're stretched thin with preparations for the upcoming invasion. If Tom wasn't such a softy and didn't insist on helping everyone, we wouldn't even be sending this many." He glanced at Tom with a teasing smirk. "No offense, Tom. It's just logistics."

Tom chuckled lightly. "None taken."

At that moment, James puffed out his chest and struck a dramatic pose.

"And, just so everyone knows, I'm in charge of this mission. That means you all do what I say." He beamed proudly, clearly reveling in his new role.

Everyone stared at James with a collective look of disbelief—except for Derek, who was grinning like he had just pulled off the best prank of his life.

"That's right, James," Derek said, his voice dripping with mock sincerity. "You're in charge. Which means every decision and every outcome falls squarely on your shoulders."

James blinked, his bravado faltering. "Yeah, everything is… wait, hold on..."

Derek's grin widened.

"Too late. You already agreed. Good luck, team." He clapped James on the shoulder and headed for the door.

"Wait! Maybe we should talk about this some more!" James called after him, panic creeping into his voice.

Tom chuckled, stepping forward. "He's right, James. You asked for this, and it's a good opportunity for you to take on some responsibility."

James slumped slightly but tried to rally. "Fine, fine. So, what do you all bring to the table? We're gonna be the next great wonder team!"

Frank, the Barbarian, hefted an enormous maul over his shoulder. "I smash things real good," he said with a grin.

Lacy, the Cleric, held up a handful of shimmering amethyst crystals. "I've got healing crystals to keep us in balance and get rid of all that bad energy."

Mark, the Wizard, smirked. "*Fireball*'s my specialty. Nothing says 'problem solved' like a good explosion."

James stood there, mouth slightly open as he surveyed his eclectic team. "Thank you so much for putting me on this team," Jay said to Tom, barely hiding his grin. "This might be the most entertaining mission ever."

James threw up his hands dramatically. "So, let me get this straight: I'm supposed to lead Hulk, a hippy lady, a pyro, and a child into a rescue mission? And let's not forget our emo spy." He pointed at Susie with exaggerated frustration.

Susie narrowed her eyes. "Hey, we're not exactly thrilled about being on a team with Sir-Dicks-a-Lot, either," she shot back. "But we all have to do what it takes to gain recognition in this Guild."

"Sure, sure. Whatever helps you sleep at night, pipsqueak," James grumbled.

Susie's face darkened. Without warning, she extended a hand, and glowing green vines erupted from the ground, snatching James by the feet and swinging him into the air. He let out a high-pitched scream as he was whipped around the room before being slammed unceremoniously onto the floor. When he looked up, dazed, Susie was standing over him, the tip of her rapier pointed at his neck.

"Do *not* underestimate me, douchebag," she said coldly.

INVASION

"Oh, this is going to be so much fun," Jay chuckled, thoroughly entertained.

A moment later, Derek poked his head back into the room, seemingly oblivious to the chaos. "I almost forgot. Take these." He tossed small clear orbs attached to metal chains to each member of the team, including Tom. "These are new prototype communication devices that Bohdan and Herbert cooked up. They should let you communicate anywhere in the world, as long as the person you're contacting has one too. Just hold the orb and focus on who you want to reach."

Tom caught his with wide eyes. "What? This is incredible!"

Derek nodded, clearly pleased.

"Agreed. I pushed them to get it done sooner rather than later. You'll love it." With that, he left the room again.

Jay couldn't resist. He held his pendant and focused on James. "Calling dickweed. Come in, dickweed."

James scowled as Jay's voice echoed through his pendant. "Looks like they work great!" Jay grinned.

Tom shook his head, amused. "It's not that complicated, James. Just get there, kill the creature, get the people out, and bring them back. Easy peasy."

James, still rubbing his head from the encounter with Susie, sighed. "Yeah, you're right. We've done this before." His shoulders sagged a bit, but he mustered his resolve.

"Do we get to take the GS2?" James asked, his tone suddenly hopeful.

Tom smirked, tossing him the keys. "Sure thing, buddy. Just bring it back in one piece."

Before James could grab them, Jay snatched the keys out of the air and held them teasingly between his fingers, just out of James' reach. "I'll be driving, just to make sure we actually come back alive."

James tried to grab the keys, but Jay held them high. "I'm in charge, and I say I drive!" James declared.

Jay smirked. "When you can take the keys from my hand, young grasshopper, then you may drive." He adopted a mock kung fu stance.

James groaned. "Why me?"

Tom clapped him on the back. "You'll be fine. Now, everyone to the garage. Time to move your asses and kick some monster butt."

Chapter 49

New Boss, Who Dis?

Once the team entered the garage, James turned around dramatically. "Alright, everyone, we all know who's in charge here, right?"

"Of course," Jay said with a smirk, "totally clear."

"It's me," James asserted, puffing out his chest.

"Oh, no doubt about that. Absolutely, you," Jay said, still smiling slyly.

James stared at Jay, his eyes narrowing, trying to gauge if Jay was being serious or just messing with him. His gaze flickered between Jay and the vehicle, his mind torn between belief and suspicion.

"Okay, good… umm… I guess we should…" James began, fumbling for his next move.

"Yeah, we should go," Jay interjected smoothly, saving him from his awkward pause.

Continuing to the vehicle, Squirrel padded in behind James, tail swishing as he hopped into the back with the practiced ease of someone who had claimed his seat long ago.

The team piled into the GS2, settling into their seats. Just as they were about to pull away, a light tap on James' shoulder stopped him.

"I need to go to the bathroom," Susie said, her voice matter-of-fact.

James groaned. "Fine, go. Anyone else? Now's your chance. Speak now or forever hold your pee."

He glanced over his shoulder to check if anyone else was going to raise their hand, and sure enough, Frank had his hand half-raised, looking sheepish.

"Seriously, Frank?" James sighed. "Alright, go ahead. I don't want to stop every ten miles."

Frank, his massive frame squeezed awkwardly into the back seat, clambered out clumsily and hurried into the building with Susie. Once they returned, the group was finally ready to go, and Jay started driving.

For a long while, the ride was quiet, each person lost in thought. It was awkward, being on a new team, especially with people they didn't know well—except for James and Jay.

Eventually, James felt the need to break the silence. "So," he asked, trying to sound casual, "how many people have you each killed?"

Everyone's eyes went wide at the casual discussion of violence, all eyes looking at James with incredulity.

"What?" James shrugged. "It's a legitimate question these days."

Susie shook her head, unimpressed. "You really are like they say."

James frowned. "Like they say? What's that supposed to mean?"

"Awkward, crude, and you say whatever pops into your head, regardless of whether it's appropriate for the situation," Susie replied, deadpan.

Jay chuckled. "Yeah, you get used to it. James has no filter, but at least you always know what you're getting with him."

"I… filter," James protested, his face flushed with embarrassment.

Jay continued, grinning, "He's kind of an idiot, but he means well, no matter how many things he screws up."

"I'm literally *right here*," James groaned.

Lacy, sitting quietly up until now, offered a soft smile. "You have a very free aura. It makes people trust you easily."

James blinked. "My what?"

"Your aura," Lacy explained. "It's bright and happy. Very trusting."

James rubbed his face in frustration. "Listen here, you hippy-dippy free spirit—"

"Easy there, cowboy. Might not want to go too far down that road," Jay interrupted, cutting off James' tirade.

"Seriously," James said, exasperated, "how am I supposed to be taken seriously as a leader with you guys talking about me like this?"

"Petulant," Susie chimed in with a smirk. "That's a word that comes to mind."

James glared at her. "I'm pretty sure if I knew what that meant, I'd be even more mad than I am now."

Jay burst out laughing. "I'm enjoying this way too much."

James slumped in his seat, pouting. "Yeah, yeah. Laugh it up. We'll see who's laughing when we finish this mission with a win."

The drive continued uneventfully until they hit I-35, where a pileup of abandoned cars blocked the road.

"This was so much easier when we had more people," Jay muttered, surveying the scene.

"I got this," Frank said, stepping out of the vehicle. He placed his hands on one of the cars, and with what seemed like minimal effort, began to push. Multiple vehicles groaned and scraped as they shifted under his immense strength.

James watched, slack-jawed. "Frank, how many points did you put into Strength?"

Frank paused, eyes glazing over as he mentally checked his stat sheet. "A hundred and twenty," he said with a grin.

"Holy hell!" James' eyes widened. "Did you put points into anything else?"

"Constitution. Oh, and Endurance," Frank replied, still shoving cars aside like they were toys.

Jay smirked. "So, no spells, I'm guessing?"

"Iron," Frank said, picking up a car trapped between two others and tossing it to the side.

Jay frowned. "Iron?"

"I'll show you." Frank stepped back, and suddenly, a cast iron skillet appeared in his hand.

"I CAST IRON!" he bellowed, swinging the skillet with all his might. The skillet slammed into a nearby SUV, sending it spinning into the guardrail and flipping over the barrier with a deafening crash. The group stood in stunned silence, jaws dropping.

Squirrel sat on the roof of the GS2, ears twitching with the crash of metal. He growled low in his throat, clearly annoyed by the noise.

James grinned.

"My man!" He raised his hand for a high five.

Jay shook his head, still bewildered. "You'd think that was a joke, but I think Frank actually believes that's a real spell."

Frank looked hurt. "It *is* a real spell. You saw what it can do."

James hesitated, then awkwardly pulled his hand back. "I… withdraw my high five."

Frank pouted. "Awww."

Susie, watching the exchange, crossed her arms. "You two should get along great. I bet your IQs are about the same."

James glared at her. "You know, I think you're just trying to be mean."

"And you're just now realizing that?" Susie replied with a smirk.

James clenched his fists. "I'm trying really hard not to swear in front of a kid, but you're making it really bleeping difficult."

"That's what she said," Jay chimed in with a grin.

After clearing the road and thoroughly roasting James, the team continued on. They had to stop and move cars several more times in the city before they finally hit the open highway, weaving around abandoned vehicles with increasing ease. Frank continued using his "spell" to clear the way, with Mark occasionally helping by using real spells to break up bigger collisions.

"Just blast it," James said at one point, growing impatient.

"*Fireball*!" Frank cheered excitedly.

Mark raised an eyebrow. "If I use *Fireball*, it's going to destroy part of the road."

"I don't think we're too worried about the road at this point," Jay replied, glancing around. "We're not on a bridge, so we should be fine."

Mark shrugged and raised his staff. "Alright, if you say so."

He cast the spell at the pile-up, and the vehicles exploded, but they didn't move far—just some singed metal and scattered debris.

"That's it?" James asked, disappointment dripping from his voice.

"Hmm," Jay muttered, "it seems *Fireball* is more about burning than blasting. Can you focus on something more concussive?"

Mark thought for a moment. "I've got something I've been practicing. Bohdan helped me work on creating new spells with intention, and Belik taught me how to modify existing ones."

"Then do your thing," Jay encouraged, giving him a reassuring nod.

INVASION

Mark gripped his staff, the wooden frame glowing faintly as the red jewel at the tip caught the sunlight. He closed his eyes to focus, and the gem began to emit a soft glow, growing brighter with each passing second.

"Oooo, what's that?" James asked, leaning in.

"It's a Flame Elementalist Staff, used as an arcane focus for spells," Mark explained, his eyes still closed. "Now shut up so I can concentrate."

Mark waved the staff in the air, creating a glowing trail like the tail of a comet. The light grew more intense as he whispered the words of his spell. The air around them seemed to hum with energy.

"*Concussive Blast!*" Mark shouted, pointing his staff at the wreckage.

The staff pulsed once, a fiery mote appearing about twenty feet ahead. It began to shrink in on itself, the air crackling with tension.

"Uh-oh," Mark whispered, eyes widening.

"What do you mean, 'uh-oh?'" James started, but before he could finish, a blinding explosion erupted. The force blasted the entire team backward.

James began to stir, blinking as his vision returned. His ears rang, and for a moment, he could barely make sense of what had just happened. Mark was on the ground, writhing in pain, while Lacey rushed over to heal him.

"What the hell happened?" James groaned, staggering to his feet.

"Apparently, our Wizard doesn't know how to aim," Susie said, brushing dirt off herself as she stood.

Frank, who had hit a nearby car with enough force to leave a massive dent, was still lying motionless.

"Come back to us, Mark!" Lacey was shouting as she poured healing magic into Mark's body, which had gone still after the initial scrabbling he had done. His skin was raw, and patches of it were missing entirely.

Jay stumbled over, assessing the situation.

"Dammit," he muttered, moving quickly toward Mark.

Just as Jay knelt down, Mark gasped sharply from the effects of the healing magic. He screamed again in agony, his voice hoarse and strained.

Without hesitation, James walked over, and with a swift kick, knocked Mark out cold.

"What did you do that for?" Lacey asked, her voice thick with concern.

"I was an anesthesiologist in my last life," James shrugged. "He shouldn't suffer while you're healing him. I… administered ten CCs of night-night serum."

Lacey blinked then nodded. "Actually… that's helpful. Thanks."

"Don't mention it," James said, rubbing his temples and sitting down nearby, his body still feeling the backlash of the blast. "He kind of had it coming anyway. My ears won't stop ringing."

"Just rest," Jay said, sitting down beside him. "Lacey will fix us up once she's done with Mark."

Lacey worked effectively, but it still took a while. Mark had been badly burned, and much of the front half of his body was missing skin. Once Mark was healed and stable, she moved on to the rest of the group, making sure everyone was patched up.

Jay stretched as Lacey finished healing the last of his injuries. "Well, at least the path is clear."

"Yeah, that's *definitely* the takeaway here," James said sarcastically, shaking his head. "This team of misfits is supposed to deal with a monster? We barely survived our own Wizard's spell!"

"Hey!" Susie snapped, offended.

"Don't 'hey' me," James shot back. "Look at this team! A guy who dumped all his points into Strength, a Wizard who forgot basic spellcasting safety, a hippie healer, a pint-sized know-it-all, and a ninja with attitude."

Susie crossed her arms. "You forgot 'moron obsessed with shooting people in the—'"

James cut her off, waving his hand. "That is a perfectly valid strategy for distracting your opponent!"

Jay chuckled as he stood up, brushing dirt off his clothes. "Don't worry, James. You'll get the hang of it. Eventually."

With everyone healed, they loaded back into the vehicle. Frank, who had finally regained consciousness, helped put a still-unconscious Mark in the trunk to rest. The group continued their journey north, occasionally stopping to clear more wreckage from the road.

"We really need a dedicated team for this," James muttered after the seventh time they had to stop.

"Not a bad idea," Jay said, pulling out his communication pendant. Holding it close, he spoke into it. "Tom, can you hear me?"

A moment later, Tom's voice crackled through the pendant. "Jay! Good to hear from you. How's it going out there?"

"So far, so good," Jay lied. "I wanted to run an idea by you. Can we get a team to start clearing the freeways? It's slow going with all the wrecks."

"That's a solid idea," Tom replied. "I'll have Brian take a look and see what we can do. No promises on how soon, but we'll get it on the list."

"Thanks, man. That was it. Just testing out the new comms and figured I'd pass along the thought."

"Good thinking, Jay. And I'm glad the devices are working. Let me know if you need anything else. Over and out."

Jay tucked the pendant back into his shirt, settling into his seat. As they continued down the road, James suddenly squinted at the horizon.

"Wait… what's that?" he asked, pointing toward a shadowy figure in the distance.

Jay followed his gaze, his mood darkening. "That… doesn't look good."

"What is it?" James pressed.

Jay's face turned grim. "Remember that goblin tower we saw on the way back from the Grand Canyon?"

James nodded. "Yeah, what about it?"

Jay took a deep breath. "Pretty sure that's the same thing. And it looks like it's moving."

Chapter 50

Ragtag Survival

"Well, this is just great. We nearly killed ourselves earlier, and now we have to deal with goblins?" James muttered, staring at the looming structures in the distance.

"If we can get Mark up and running, *Fireball* should make quick work of them," Jay replied as he slowed the vehicle.

Sure enough, as they got closer, it became clear there were multiple goblin towers moving toward them.

"Fan-fucking-tastic. Just our luck," James groaned, rolling his eyes. "More of 'em."

"Shut up, James," Jay snapped. "We can handle this. They're just goblins. We've dealt with worse."

Susie glanced at James with a smirk. "I thought you didn't swear around kids?"

James waved her off. "You no longer count. You're some weird adult trapped in a kid's body. Now, hush, so we can think."

"Cast Iron?" Frank asked from the back seat, eager for action.

Squirrel huffed at the thought of the "spell" being used again.

"Oh, we'll be casting some iron, trust me," Jay said. "But we need to be smart about this. There are probably over a hundred of those little green bastards."

James hopped out of the GS2 and made his way to the back, opening the trunk. "Come on, Mark. Wakey, wakey, eggs and bakey," he said, slapping Mark across the face a few times.

"You really think that's gonna—" Susie began, but before she could finish, Mark jolted awake, screaming, and punched James square in the jaw.

James staggered back, clutching his face. "Son of a—! You don't hit like a Wizard!"

Mark blinked groggily, looking around. "What? Where am I? What's happening?"

James rubbed his jaw, still wincing. "You've got a hell of a punch for a magic user. But never mind that. We need a *Fireball*. Check out the towers over there." He pointed at the advancing goblin structures.

Mark squinted at the towers, still shaking off his confusion. "I could probably hit them from here. If I can see it, I can usually land a *Fireball*."

"Seriously? From this distance?" Lacey asked, impressed.

"Yeah, I just need a minute to focus."

"Would a higher vantage point help?" Jay suggested.

"Yeah, that'd be great, but how do I—"

"Stand on the roof," Jay said, already opening the sunroof to give Mark access.

Mark grinned. "Brilliant!"

As Mark climbed up onto the roof of the GS2, Lacey glanced nervously at the others. "Uh, maybe we should get out of the vehicle?"

Jay's eyes widened. "That… is an excellent idea. Everyone, out."

The team quickly exited the vehicle, watching as Mark got into position. With everyone at a safe distance, Mark concentrated, holding his staff high. A spark of fiery energy formed at the tip of the jewel that served as his magical focal point, growing larger by the second. The heat intensified as the fireball expanded, crackling with raw power.

"Wow," Susie whispered, watching the fireball grow to the size of a beach ball.

Mark, his eyes locked on the distant towers, stepped forward and thrust his staff forward, intending to launch the spell.

But instead of flying toward the goblin towers, the fireball plopped down… right into the open sunroof of the GS2.

"Shit!" Mark yelped, wide-eyed.

There was a split second of silence before the vehicle exploded from the inside, sending Mark flying off the roof and the GS2 bursting into flames.

"NO, NO, NO, NO, NO!" James shrieked, sprinting toward the vehicle as the flames grew.

"Tom is going to *kill* you," Jay said, shaking his head as he squinted at the inferno.

Frank's mouth hung open in disbelief, and Lacey covered her ears as James let loose a stream of profanities that would've made any sailor blush. Jay, meanwhile, couldn't help but chuckle—until he noticed Mark writhing on the ground.

"Lacey! Go heal Mark, now!" Jay barked.

Lacey rushed over to Mark as James, in a wild panic, waved his arms at the flaming vehicle. His eyes darted around, and in his desperation, he began spitting at the car in a futile attempt to douse the fire.

"Shit, shit, shit, shit, fuck, fuck, fuck, fuck!" James ran in circles, his mind clearly unraveling. Then, as if a light bulb had gone off in his head, he unzipped his fly, whipped out his… equipment, and began urinating on the flaming vehicle.

"Higher, James!" Jay called out through his laughter.

James tried to aim higher, but the heat from the flames made it impossible to get close enough. He overcorrected, and the stream ended up hitting himself instead.

Jay collapsed to the ground, howling with laughter. James, now soaked and frustrated, tried to aim properly again, only to realize his "solution" was drying up.

INVASION

Finally managing to catch his breath, Jay got to his feet, wiped tears from his eyes, and pulled a red orb from his Inventory. Walking toward the flaming GS2, he pulled a pin from the object and tossed the small red ball into the vehicle.

The red ball exploded inside the GS2, instantly covering the flames in a thick, white powder. The fire quickly died down, leaving the vehicle covered in a fine, powdery residue.

James stood there, completely covered in white powder himself. He looked down at his pants, which had turned into a Bisquick-like mess.

"You had a fire extinguisher the whole time," James seethed, "and you just let me golden shower myself?"

"Hey, these things are expensive. Maybe you'd have put it out and I wouldn't have had to use it…" Jay replied with a grin. "Besides, Tom already told me if anything happened to the GS2, I should just use the vehicle XP to repair it. So, yeah… he was prepared for this."

Lacey emerged from the other side of the vehicle, her face plastered in white powder, resembling something from a bad cocaine-fueled comedy. Her wide, stunned eyes locked onto Jay.

"This is not what I signed up for." She shook her head and wiped some of the powder off, looking around in disbelief. "What was that thing you threw in there?"

"A fire extinguisher bomb," Jay said proudly, standing tall like he'd just won a prize. "Found them at an army surplus store we raided on a patrol. Handy little things, especially when you've got Wizards throwing fireballs around. You'd be surprised how useful they can be." He glanced over his shoulder. "Is Mark alright?"

Lacey sighed, brushing the remaining powder from her robes. "He'll be fine… physically, at least." Her eyes narrowed. "Though after this, I'm starting to think none of us are gonna be okay, mentally. Or spiritually, for that matter."

Jay shrugged. "Physically is all we need right now. We can save the emotional breakdowns for later." He gave her a half-smirk. "Time to get Mark back on his feet and try again. We need those goblin towers lit up—pronto."

Jay circled the smoking remains of the GS2, finding Mark sprawled on the ground, still staring blankly up at the sky, the explosion having knocked the wind out of him. Without missing a beat, Jay hauled him up by the armpits, setting him shakily on his feet. Mark wobbled, eyes unfocused, as Jay patted the remaining white powder from his clothes.

"C'mon, man, you're fine. Good as new. Now, let's try this again." Jay's voice was calm but firm. "This time, aim for the towers, alright? We need you focused."

Mark blinked, still in a daze, but nodded weakly.

"Yeah… okay…" His voice was a high-pitched, weak sound, like someone who'd just run a marathon.

"That's more like it!" Jay clapped him on the back, almost sending him toppling again. "You wanted to be on an advanced team, right? Well, this is what it means."

Mark winced but managed to stay on his feet. Taking a deep breath, he raised one hand, trembling slightly as he called upon his power again. Another fireball flickered into existence, glowing fiercely. It grew, doubling, tripling in size until it was about as big as a Honda Civic.

The rest of the team watched, half in awe, half in trepidation, as the glowing sphere of destruction hovered before Mark. With a grunt, Mark flung it forward, the fireball rocketing away like a missile. This time, it sailed perfectly toward the goblin towers in the distance.

"Mark… you beautiful bastard," James whispered, eyes wide as he watched the fireball tear through the sky.

Weaving between abandoned cars and debris, the fireball surged forward until it struck the first tower. The explosion that followed was deafening, sending a shockwave rippling outward. The windows of nearby vehicles shattered in its wake, glass spraying across the road. Even from their position, the team could hear the agonized screams of goblins as the first tower was consumed by a massive inferno, quickly spreading to the second.

Flames climbed hundreds of feet into the air, casting an eerie glow across the landscape. The smell of burning wood and flesh filled the air as the goblin structures crumbled.

Jay whistled, clearly impressed. "Now *that's* what I'm talking about. Bohdan wouldn't have recommended you if there wasn't something special about you. Looks like the trick for you is not to overthink it." He clapped Mark on the back again, this time causing the Wizard to stumble to his knees, still dazed by the raw power he had unleashed.

James let out a low, almost reverent sigh. "Man… that was epic."

But the celebration was short-lived. The sound of screeching and squawking rose from the distance as the goblin horde, furious and panicked, charged toward them. Their green bodies were a blur as they raced forward, determined to exact revenge for the destruction of their contraptions.

"Get ready, Frank!" Jay called, already assessing the situation. "You're up. Take the lead on this one—they're coming, and they're pissed."

"Finally!" Frank roared, his grin wide and feral. He hefted his massive maul over his shoulder, stepping to the front of the group. His muscles tensed, ready for the battle to come.

The goblin horde surged forward, their high-pitched war cries echoing through the air. Frank, with a look of maniacal pleasure on his face, moved to intercept them. He swung his maul, smashing aside cars and creating a funnel, forcing the goblins into a narrow path where they would have no choice but to face him head-on.

The first goblin darted into view, its beady eyes wide with fury. Frank's roar of challenge echoed across the battlefield as he activated his *Rage*, a red aura enveloping his body.

An arrow whistled through the air, aimed straight at Frank. It struck his shoulder—and shattered on impact, as though it had hit solid stone.

"What the…" Jay muttered, watching in stunned disbelief as Frank's skin deflected the attack without so much as a scratch.

INVASION

The first goblin reached him, and Frank brought his maul down with all the force of a collapsing mountain. The goblin exploded into a mist of blackish blood, its remains barely recognizable.

And then Frank was on the move, a whirlwind of destruction. Goblins were obliterated by the dozens, their bodies reduced to nothing as Frank smashed them with his maul or hurled them into the distance. Any goblin unlucky enough to get close was met with a swift, brutal end. Blades and spears glanced off his skin as though he was wearing impenetrable armor. He grabbed one goblin mid-leap and slammed it into a car, embedding the creature into the metal door with a sickening crunch.

"Jesus…" Jay breathed, watching the carnage unfold. "He's unstoppable."

Frank continued his rampage, his maul swinging faster and faster as he decimated the goblin forces. His *Rage* was now a visible force, his body glowing brighter as his bloodlust reached its peak. He was no longer just smashing goblins—he was sending them flying in every direction, their bodies torn apart by the sheer force of his attacks.

"Frank's on fire!" James shouted, clearly caught up in the excitement.

"Uh, guys?" Lacey's voice was soft, barely a whisper, but filled with dread. "I don't think he's going to stop."

As the last goblin was crushed beneath Frank's maul, the battlefield grew eerily quiet. The few remaining goblins who hadn't been obliterated were retreating, their eyes wide with terror as they fled.

But Frank wasn't done. His *Rage* hadn't subsided, and he scanned the area, eyes wild, searching for his next target.

Jay felt his stomach drop as Frank's gaze settled on them.

"Crap," Jay muttered, taking a step back. "He's not stopping."

Frank let out a guttural growl and leaped toward them, his maul raised high.

"SCATTER!" James yelled, diving out of the way as Frank brought his maul down with a deafening crash, the impact shaking the ground where they had been standing moments before.

"He's gone full savage!"

Chapter 51

Well, This is Fun

Frank launched himself after Jay, his massive frame tearing through the air with frightening speed. Jay vanished momentarily, reappearing just behind the charging Barbarian as Frank slammed into the ground where he'd been a split second earlier. The ground cracked under Frank's weight, and Jay blinked back a few more feet, his heart racing.

"Nope, nope, no, no, no! I'm not built for this!" Jay muttered breathlessly, his voice strained as he continued to seemingly teleport away, each appearance only delaying the inevitable.

Frank seemed fixated on him, eyes wild with rage, oblivious to everything except the target of his fury. Jay could hear the sound of metal crunching and the screech of glass shattering as Frank's wild swings obliterated nearby vehicles and barricades. Anything in his path was reduced to rubble.

The berserker charged at him again, and Jay's feet slipped on the loose gravel. He tripped, his body pitching forward as he tried to scramble back, his hands instinctively flying up to protect his face. Frank, with his glowing red aura, seemed unstoppable as he leaped through the air, ready to bring his massive maul down on Jay's prone form.

Then, suddenly, everything went still.

Frank collapsed in front of Jay, his enormous body crashing to the ground like a felled tree. The force of the fall sent a ripple through the pavement as Frank skidded to a stop, mere inches from Jay's trembling feet. The ground shook with the impact, and for a moment, the world was eerily quiet.

Jay peeked over his arms cautiously, his breath coming in short, sharp gasps. Frank was snoring. Loudly.

The once-menacing red glow around Frank's body had dimmed, flickering out like a dying flame. Lacey stood a few yards away, holding out her staff with both hands, her face pale and her chest heaving. She was panting hard, her eyes wide with a mixture of fear and disbelief.

Jay locked eyes with her, both of them shaking slightly from the sheer adrenaline still coursing through their systems. He nodded once, his gratitude clear in the gesture, though he still couldn't find the words. They had just narrowly avoided being turned into paste by Frank's berserker fury.

INVASION

When Jay finally managed to get his breathing under control, he stood shakily, brushing the dust off his pants before walking over to the others, who were still staring at Frank's unconscious form in stunned silence.

"What the hell was that?" Mark asked, his voice breaking through the silence. He was still in shock, his wide eyes shifting nervously between Jay, Lacey, and the snoozing Frank.

Jay wiped the sweat from his brow and shook his head. "Looks like Frank lost control of his *Rage*. That's something we'll need to watch out for." He turned to Lacey, who was still gripping her staff like a lifeline. "What exactly did you do back there?"

"I cast *Sleep* on him," Lacey explained, her voice still shaky. "It's one of the few spells that could quickly stop him. You need a strong mental resistance to shake it off, and I figured Frank wouldn't have that in his *Rage*."

Jay grinned, impressed. "Great thinking. You probably saved us from being reduced to a bloody mess on the ground." His tone was lighter, but the weight of the situation still hung in the air.

Lacey allowed herself a small smile, finally releasing the tight grip on her staff. "You weren't so bad yourself. I could barely see you; you were moving so fast."

"Thanks," Jay replied, giving her a nod. "That took just about every ounce of focus I had." He stretched his arms, feeling the burn in his muscles. "We all need to rest for a bit. I've got to get the ole Goblin Slayer back in working order."

Jay moved over to the SUV, now looking worse for wear after the earlier battle. He stared at the vehicle for a moment, his eyes glazing over as he accessed the vehicle's menu screen. He tapped through a few selections, his fingers moving quickly over the invisible interface. When he was satisfied with the settings, Jay closed the menu and sat down on the ground, leaning back with a sigh.

As he did, the sound of grinding metal echoed from the vehicle behind him. The panels along its sides began to shift, pulling themselves back into place. Dents popped out with audible thuds, and cracks in the windows slowly disappeared as the glass repaired itself.

The team watched in awe as the vehicle started to rebuild itself, the once-damaged surfaces becoming smooth and whole again, piece by piece.

"What's happening there?" James asked, his brow furrowing in confusion as he observed the miraculous self-repair process.

"The vehicle's running a self-diagnosis," Jay explained, his voice steady now that the immediate danger had passed. "It's got some kind of scanning magic that detects damage and fixes it one section at a time. We had a lot of XP stored up for repairs, but this was a pretty big hit. It'll use most of those points to fix itself."

Jay closed his eyes, sinking into a state that seemed almost meditative. The others moved to sit near him, forming a small circle around the resting warrior, save for Frank, who continued to snore softly where he had fallen.

Jay reached into his Inventory and pulled out several bottles of Gatorade, tossing one to each member of the team.

"Here, drink these. They should help you feel better."

"Are they special?" Lacey asked, catching hers.

Jay chuckled. "Nope. Just good ol' Gatorade. Found them while scavenging a few gas stations. Thought they'd be a nice reminder of life before all this."

They all gratefully accepted the drinks, cracking open the bottles and taking long swigs. The cool, sugary liquid was a welcome relief after the chaos they'd just been through. As they sipped their drinks, they also pulled out various snacks from their Inventories, munching in silence as they watched the vehicle continue its repairs.

Squirrel flopped onto the pavement beside James, panting heavily. His thick coat was singed in places, but his tongue lolled in contentment as he gnawed on a smoked turkey leg from James' inventory.

The calm didn't last long.

A horn blared in the distance, its deep, resonant tone cutting through the quiet air. The team froze, eyes widening in alarm as they turned toward the direction the goblins had come from earlier.

"I thought Frank killed them all," Lacey said, her voice barely above a whisper.

Jay squinted into the distance, his sharp eyes picking out movement far beyond the horizon. "Looks like that was just the first wave." He stood, his muscles tensing in anticipation. "Round two's coming, and this time… let's leave Frank out of it."

Mark, still pale from the earlier battle, began to speak but was quickly interrupted. "Frank could turn on us again and turn us into pavement pudding like he did those goblins—"

"We can handle this. Just get your spells ready. Lacey, be ready to support. James, time to put that target practice to good use," Jay said.

"But I don't have a tank! All my strategies need a tank!" James exclaimed, his voice rising in panic.

Squirrel turned to stare at James as though he had been deeply insulted.

"Then improvise," Jay said, giving him a sharp look. "Think of this as a learning experience. Adapt."

Jay stepped forward, equipping a weapon that James hadn't seen him use before. It looked like a massive log, but as Jay hefted it over his shoulder, the team could see that it was shaped into a club, studded with metal pyramids along the length.

"What the hell is that?" James asked, his eyes widening.

"It's called a Kanabo," Jay replied, glancing over his shoulder. "It's a traditional Japanese weapon. Great for… crowd control." He smirked. "Just cover me."

Squirrel growled deep in his throat, fur standing on end as he positioned himself between James and the oncoming goblins.

James shrugged and cast *Inspire Companion* on the wily Rogue—the only buff spell that he had.

INVASION

The goblins were now visible in the distance, their small, twisted bodies moving toward the team in a haphazard sprint. The front lines screeched and squawked, raising their jagged weapons as they charged.

Jay lowered into a fighting stance, gripping the Kanabo tightly. He swung the massive weapon in a wide arc as the first group of goblins reached him. Four goblins were sent flying, their bodies crashing into the side of a nearby vehicle with sickening thuds.

James immediately began firing at the goblins, attempting to flank Jay, his bullets finding their marks with deadly precision. One of them was a chunky boy, standing nearly four feet tall and nearly half again around the middle. For that one, James triggered his *Imbued Shot* and took the creature in the head, which while not ideal—was certainly effective. Three goblins dropped in quick succession, their bodies crumpling to the ground. Naturally each of those went down with shots to the dick from his *Marksman's Shot*—which, luckily, had its name changed to *Dickshot* after James had a little sit-down with the System. He'd insisted on making the essential change to the ability's designation, which—naturally—the System accommodated. What was more, James was pleased to note that the Combat Skill had become passive after reaching Apprentice rank and no longer required the same resource usage when triggering it each time. He didn't even have to shout out the Skill name any longer—though he still did often enough, whether out of habit or—more often—because it was just *better* that way.

"Dickshot!" James caroled happily.

Jay swung again, catching three more goblins with the heavy club and smashing them into the opposite side of the road. One goblin, trying to take advantage of Jay's focus, leaped into the air, aiming for Jay's exposed back.

Without missing a beat, Jay stowed the Kanabo in his Inventory and summoned his Kusarigama. The chain whipped through the air, wrapping around the goblin's neck and arm, trapping its weapon. With a sharp tug, Jay yanked the goblin out of the air, sending it tumbling to the ground where it squealed in pain, its own weapon cutting into its flesh.

In one fluid motion, Jay flipped through the air, disarming another goblin mid-swing and embedding the blade of his Kusarigama into the back of its neck.

As more goblins surged forward, Jay switched weapons yet again. This time, he pulled out a pair of Japanese war fans, each adorned with razor-sharp blades at the tips and delicate runes etched into the fabric. He flicked them open with a sharp snap of his wrists, the polished metal gleaming in the low light.

One goblin, braver than the rest, charged straight at him, its beady eyes locked onto Jay's face. Jay tilted his head and smiled, a sarcastic glint in his eye.

"Well, now, that's just poor form," Jay said with mock disappointment as he flicked one of the fans forward. A sharp gust of wind erupted from the fan, sending the goblin tumbling backward in a flurry of limbs.

As the goblin tried to scramble to its feet, Jay pulled several throwing needles from his Inventory, twirling them between his fingers before flinging them through the air with deadly accuracy. The needles found their mark, embedding themselves in the goblin's face and throat.

The creature let out one last gurgle before collapsing in a heap.

Jay shook his head, tsking softly. "No reason to be animals about it."

Turning his attention back to the battlefield, Jay began to wave his fans in sweeping arcs, his movements precise and calculated.

"*WIND BLAST!*" Jay called out as he summoned a powerful gust of wind.

The wind blew across the battlefield, clearing the smoke and revealing the devastation left in the wake of their earlier attacks. Goblin bodies littered the ground, their twisted forms lying in grotesque piles. Only a few stragglers remained, their eyes wide with terror as they realized the futility of their assault.

James quickly dispatched the remaining goblins with a few well-placed shots, his rifle quieting the battlefield once more.

At the rear of the goblin horde, one lone goblin stood taller than the others, its beady eyes filled with rage. It raised its weapon high, preparing to charge the team with a final, desperate attack.

Before it could take a single step, James took aim and fired. The bullet pierced the goblin's skull, dropping it instantly.

James lowered his rifle, a smug grin on his face as he blew on the barrel.

"Next!"

Chapter 52

On to Objective

Frank began to stir just as the team stood in awe, staring at the GS2, which now looked as good as new. The grinding and creaking sounds of the vehicle's auto-repair had finally stopped, leaving the SUV gleaming in the sunlight, almost like it hadn't just been caught in the middle of a brutal battle.

Frank rubbed his head and slowly pushed himself up, blinking groggily.

"What happened?" he asked, his voice raspy, as if he'd just woken from a deep sleep.

The rest of the team turned to look at him. For a brief moment, they all just stared, their expressions a mix of relief and apprehension. They had seen firsthand what Frank was capable of when he lost control, and though the situation was back under control, the memory of his rampage was still fresh.

"You don't remember any of it?" James asked, stepping forward cautiously, his tone curious but wary.

Frank frowned, rubbing the back of his neck as he tried to piece things together. "I remember amping up and going to smash some goblin guts, but then… it gets a little fuzzy after that. The next thing I know, I'm waking up here."

"You did a great job with the smashy-smash," James said, his voice dripping with his usual sarcasm, "but then you did *such* a good job, you tried to smash us too." He gave Frank a pointed look.

Frank's eyes widened in horror. "What?! No, no, no! That can't be right. I would never hurt you guys. You're my team!" His voice cracked slightly, the thought clearly unsettling him as his face paled.

"Unfortunately," Jay interjected, his voice calm but firm, "I think you might have gone a bit too far into the *Rage*. You started out fine, but at some point, something changed. You triggered something else. Can you give us a rundown of your Skills? Maybe we can figure out what happened."

Frank looked like he was going to be sick. His skin turned an even whiter shade, and he began to sway slightly as he sat up straighter.

"Uh, yeah, sure," he stammered. "I have the *Rage* Skill, which I used to get myself fired up and ready for battle. Then I was smashing goblins, but I got worried they'd get past me, so I pushed myself harder." His voice faltered as his eyes clouded with confusion. "But… I don't think I used another Skill."

Jay stepped closer, his expression thoughtful. "Can you check your combat log? Maria should be able to help you with that if you ask her. You can filter it to show only Skill usage, so we can focus on what triggered your change."

Frank's eyes glazed over as he accessed the combat logs only he could see. His face tightened with concentration as he scrolled through the data, his fingers twitching slightly at his sides. After a few long minutes, his eyes suddenly widened in shock.

"I used that many Skills?!" Frank blurted out, staring at the invisible screen in disbelief.

Jay nodded. "What's it showing?"

Frank swallowed hard, his shame clear as he spoke. "I used *Rage,* like I thought, but then it shows I was using some attack Skills. And then… I must've panicked. I accidentally used the *Berserk* Skill." His voice trailed off, and he looked down at his hands as if they had betrayed him.

"*Berserk?*" Lacey asked, stepping forward. "What's that?"

"It's a Barbarian Skill," Jay explained, his tone more serious now. "It removes the limiter from your *Rage*, giving you a massive boost in power. But it also makes it impossible to distinguish friend from foe. It's supposed to be a last-ditch effort when you're close to death, to keep you fighting when everything else fails."

Lacey's eyes widened in concern, but she caught herself before she said something that might offend Frank. "That sounds… dangerous."

Jay shrugged slightly. "It is. But it's also meant to save your life in the worst-case scenario." He glanced at Frank with a knowing look. "You pushed yourself too far, and you triggered it without realizing."

"How do you know all this?" Mark asked, raising an eyebrow. His curiosity was piqued, as Jay always seemed to have information others didn't.

"I make it my business to know things," Jay said cryptically, a sly grin tugging at the corner of his mouth.

"That's not an answer," Mark replied, crossing his arms.

"And yet, it's the only one you're getting. I don't owe you the answers you're looking for," Jay shot back, his grin fading. "I'm one of the Guild's spy leaders. All you need to know is I have the Guild's best interests at heart."

"Fine, fine," Mark grumbled, not pushing the subject further. "Still, it's good to know about that Skill. We need to be extra careful with it."

James chimed in, his voice surprisingly calm, "We had to put you to sleep to stop you, Frank. Lacey used her *Sleep* spell, and it worked. We handled the rest while you were out." He gestured to the carnage around them—the countless goblin bodies, the thick, black blood coating the ground like tar. "So next time, just let us help if you feel like you're losing control. We've got your back."

Frank turned his head slowly, taking in the battlefield for the first time. Goblin bodies were strewn everywhere, their twisted forms lying in heaps across the road. The black blood had soaked into the pavement, creating an oily sheen that glistened in the light. Flies had already begun to gather, buzzing hungrily around the remains.

His face paled even more as he processed the scene.

"You mean… I didn't do all that?" he asked, his voice barely a whisper.

Jay shook his head. "Unless you suddenly started using stabbing and slashing weapons, no. Those goblins got carved up pretty good. What you did was… more explosive."

Frank hung his head, his shoulders slumping with guilt. "I'm sorry, guys," he said quietly. "I didn't mean to lose it like that. I'll do better next time, I swear." He clenched his fists, the shame evident in his voice.

"That's all we ask," James said, his tone softening in an unexpected moment of compassion. "We aren't here to bust your balls, Frank. We're learning, too. Just work with us. You don't have to do it all on your own."

Frank nodded, the shame in his eyes gradually easing as he looked up at James. There was a flicker of appreciation mixed with the guilt still lingering on his face. He reached up and clasped James' outstretched hand, intending to pull himself up. But when Frank tried to stand, his massive weight yanked James down into his lap instead.

"Whoa, hey, Frank!" James exclaimed, sprawled awkwardly across the big man's legs. "I didn't know you cared. Look at these muscles, man. So strong, so… manly." James grinned, trying to diffuse the awkwardness with humor.

Frank's face flushed as he looked down at James lying on top of him.

"Um… sorry. I can get up myself," he muttered, clearly embarrassed.

Without any visible effort, Frank lifted James off him as if he weighed nothing, setting him gently on his feet like a doll. He then rolled to his side and stood up with surprising grace for someone so massive. As James brushed himself off, he gave Frank a playful wink.

"James, seriously. Cut it out. He doesn't need that shit," Jay said, his voice sharp as he shot a look at James.

"Sorry, sorry." James raised his hands in mock surrender. "It's just… when someone that big picks you up, it's hard not to feel safe and…"

"Nope," Jay cut him off with a firm hand gesture. "Not going there. Just get in the damn car."

"Awww, you're no fun," James said, dragging his feet toward the vehicle, a mischievous grin still plastered on his face.

Once the team was loaded into the GS2, Jay started driving, easing over the goblin bodies that littered the road like discarded refuse. The slow, deliberate pace gave everyone a chance to absorb the aftermath of the battle, the sound of the tires crunching over debris and the occasional twitch of a goblin's lifeless body filling the air with grim finality.

As they moved beyond the carnage, Jay was finally able to pick up speed, weaving in and out of the stalled and abandoned vehicles that clogged the road like a graveyard of the old world.

When they approached the remnants of the goblin towers, only the bases remained. The towering structures had been reduced to nothing but charred beams, jutting up into the sky like broken fingers. Black smoke curled lazily from the piles of burnt goblin bodies scattered around the area.

"Good shot, Mark," James commented nonchalantly as they passed the smoldering ruins.

Mark, however, wasn't as lighthearted. He stared at the scene, his eyes wide and uneasy. The sight of the charred goblin corpses and the devastation his magic had caused left a weight on his conscience.

"I did all this?" he asked softly, his voice almost trembling. "I think… I think I might be sick."

James looked at him, puzzled. "How are you not already past that? This world requires a lot of killing to stay alive," he said matter-of-factly, as if destruction on this scale was a natural part of life now.

Jay, keeping his eyes on the road but listening to the conversation, chimed in with a more comforting tone, "Look, Mark, these goblins didn't give us a choice. They were going to kill us, no questions asked, just because we're alive. You did what you had to. You did well. Just remember that. We're a team, and you're a valuable part of it. Nobody else can do what you do. We need you."

Mark seemed to take comfort in Jay's words, a small, grateful smile tugging at the corners of his mouth. "Thanks, Jay," he said quietly. "I guess you're right."

"Of course I'm right," Jay replied with a grin. "You're still standing, aren't you?"

Before the conversation could continue, Susie piped up from the back seat. "Well, I, for one, am disappointed. I didn't even get to kill any goblins!"

Her voice was filled with frustration, and Jay chuckled at her youthful eagerness.

"You'll get your chance, kiddo," Jay said with a grin. "Be patient. There are plenty of things out here that want to kill us. You'll have more than enough to keep you busy."

Susie huffed, crossing her arms. "I better," she muttered. "I'm ready."

Jay couldn't help but laugh again, shaking his head.

"What's so funny?" Susie asked, her eyes narrowing at Jay's amusement.

"Nothing," Jay replied, still chuckling. "It's just that… most people run from danger. You? You're running right at it. It's a little funny."

Susie's eyes flared with determination. "I'm braver than most people. And more skilled, too."

Jay gave her a sideways glance, impressed by her confidence. "I bet you are," he said, his voice sincere. "Most people are cowards at heart. The old world made them soft. But there's nothing wrong with that either. Everyone must eventually face their fears."

Once the team had passed the wreckage left by the fiery battle, the drive became smoother, allowing them to pick up speed. Heading north on I-35, they traveled in relative silence, the mood inside the vehicle dampened by the devastation they saw in the surrounding areas. Burned-out buildings, crumbled highways, and the skeletal remains of vehicles lined the roads, grim reminders of the cataclysmic event that had brought the world to its knees.

James, ever the joker, tried his best to lighten the mood. He cracked jokes, made silly faces, and tried to get a rise out of anyone in the car, but his efforts were in vain. The weight of their situation and the grim reality of their lives hung in the air like a fog, and even James couldn't clear it.

INVASION

As they neared Denton and the I-35 merger, the traffic congestion forced them to slow down again. Vehicles clogged the highway in both directions, a pileup stretching as far as the eye could see. Cars and trucks were twisted together in an almost artistic display of chaos.

"This is going to take forever to move," James groaned, leaning forward to peer through the windshield. "Can we drive around it at all?"

Jay nodded grimly. "I'll try. No sense in getting out to move hundreds of vehicles, no matter how fast Frank can clear a path."

Pulling off to the shoulder, Jay scanned ahead, only to find the shoulder itself blocked by more wreckage and abandoned cars. He brought the vehicle to a stop.

"We should get out and see if there's another way around. We're on the wrong side here—we need to get to the service road. Everyone, spread out and check if we can drive off the highway and bypass this mess," Jay said, already unbuckling his seatbelt.

The team climbed out of the GS2 and moved out in separate directions, scouting the area. Frank took to the task with determination, checking every nook and cranny where they might get through. The grassy divider between the highway and the service road was packed with cars that had clearly had the same idea, their hoods and trunks crumpled from failed attempts to flee.

After regrouping, it became clear to everyone that there was only one option: they could drive off the road, but it wouldn't be easy. The ground was uneven, and there were tall curbs and parking lots they'd have to navigate through, not to mention the possibility of running into other obstacles along the way.

"Alright," Jay sighed, rubbing the back of his neck. "Looks like we can make it through the field behind the businesses, but it'll be slow going. Frank, if you wouldn't mind 'casting iron' on a few vehicles here to get us started."

Frank grinned and moved into position, gripping a nearby car. With a grunt, he applied his signature move, smashing cars together to clear a path. Vehicles crumpled under his strength like soda cans, and soon he had created a clear route to the service road.

As the team got back into the GS2, they carefully drove over the grass and up onto the parking lot of an In-N-Out Burger just off the freeway.

"This feels a little dangerous for the vehicle," Lacey muttered as the tires bumped over the high curb.

Jay brought the car to a halt. "Hang on a sec."

Pulling up the GS2's upgrade menu, he scanned their remaining XP points.

"We've got enough for a lift," he said to himself, making the selection.

The car hummed as new shocks and spacers automagically raised the vehicle by three inches, giving it the clearance it needed to handle rougher terrain.

"That's all we can afford for now," Jay said, shaking his head. "We'll have to hit a few more monsters if we want to upgrade again. And we don't want it too high, or we won't be able to take down some of the creatures."

The GS2 rolled more smoothly with the added lift, and the team weaved their way through parking lots and back roads until they finally reached the other side of Highway 380. They merged back onto I-35, cruising at a steady pace. Hours passed as they headed further north, leaving behind the chaotic sprawl of Denton.

As they neared their destination, Gainesville, Texas, Jay pulled the vehicle off I-35 and onto Highway 82.

"Where exactly are we going again?" James asked, leaning forward with a look of curiosity.

"Tom said the people needing our help were holed up in a boat and RV storage facility," Jay replied, his eyes scanning the road ahead. "Apparently, there are a few of those out here. We'll have to look for some kind of signal."

"That looks like a pretty good indicator to me," Susie piped up from the backseat, leaning over the center console and pointing off to the left.

The team followed her gaze and spotted a wooden sign, hastily painted with large orange letters: People here. Please help.

"Oh yeah," Jay said, blinking in surprise. "That'll do it."

He turned the GS2 off the highway and onto the dirt road leading to the storage facility. The gate was ajar, creaking in the wind as they rolled through. The place looked deserted—no signs of life except for a few flickers of movement behind some of the RVs.

As they pulled up to the administrative building, Jay caught a glimpse of someone peering through the blinds. The person quickly ducked out of sight when they realized they'd been spotted. Jay gestured for the team to stay near the GS2, holding up a hand to signal caution.

"Hello?" Jay called out, his voice carrying through the still air. "We're here to help! We're from the Dallas team—you sent a message saying you needed help with a monster?"

For a long moment, nothing happened. The building was eerily silent.

"You sure they're here?" James whispered, leaning closer to Jay.

"I saw someone watching from the window. Just give it a second," Jay muttered, motioning for James to stay quiet.

Suddenly, the door burst open, and a tall man with a scruffy beard appeared, eyes wide with panic.

"What the fuck do you think you're doing?!" he bellowed, waving his arms wildly. "Get in here before you get killed!"

Chapter 53

Survivors

"What are you talking about? There's nothing out here," Jay said, his eyes scanning the horizon beyond the door.

The landscape was eerily quiet, save for the occasional rustling of wind through abandoned RVs and storage units.

The man, still tense and visibly shaken, leaned forward, gripping the doorframe like it was the only thing holding him together. "It's always watching," he said in a hushed, trembling voice. "Get inside before it attacks again." His eyes darted around nervously, as if expecting a creature to materialize at any moment.

James raised an eyebrow, giving the man a concerned look. "I think you're a bit paranoid, my man. There's nothing out there." His tone was casual, but there was an edge of uncertainty as he glanced at Jay for confirmation.

The man, whose weathered face showed the strain of months of terror, shook his head vehemently. "Look, we've been the ones surviving out here for months. I think we know what we're talking about. Now get inside before it sees you!" he insisted, his voice rising in panic.

Despite their doubts, the team exchanged quick, uneasy glances before complying. One by one, James, Jay, Frank, Lacey, Mark, and Susie hurried inside. The man watched anxiously as they entered, his eyes wide and fearful, then he quickly shut the door behind them with a loud click. He leaned heavily against the door, as if sealing them in and offering a brief respite from the horrors outside.

"Thank god," he muttered, wiping sweat from his brow. "Sorry for treating you that way, but we've been harassed by that creature for months now. Just going out to get food or water has been dangerous as hell. We've lost several people trying."

His words hung in the air, the weight of his desperation sinking into the team. Then, almost as if remembering his manners, he straightened up and forced a tired smile. "Oh! Where are my manners? I'm Caleb. Leader of the Watchdogs Guild."

James, always quick to break the tension, gestured to the others. "I'm James. The big guy over there is Frank, that's Mark, Susie, Lacey... and the nutbag over there is Jay." He pointed playfully.

"Hey!" Jay protested, glaring at James.

James shrugged with a smirk. "Well, it's true."

Caleb chuckled, the first sign of humor cracking through his worn-out demeanor. "Nice to see people in good spirits. We've been barely scraping by here. Morale's pretty much in the toilet."

Jay stepped forward, getting back to business. "How many of you are still here?"

Caleb's face darkened, the momentary levity snuffed out by the grim reality of their situation. "When this all started, there were twenty-four of us. Now…" He paused, swallowing hard as memories of those they had lost surfaced. "Now there are only ten. Just enough to keep our Guild standing."

Lacey gasped, her hands covering her mouth. "Ten?! Out of twenty-four? That's horrible!"

Caleb nodded solemnly. "We've done what we could, but it's been hell out there. Especially since *it* showed up."

"It?" Mark asked, his voice laced with trepidation.

Caleb's expression grew grave, his eyes shadowed with fear. "Yeah. *It*. It's called a Crust Walker. Nasty beast."

The room seemed to grow colder at the mention of the name. Jay's brow furrowed. "Can you tell us more about it?"

Caleb shifted uncomfortably, as if just talking about the creature made it more real.

"It moves through the ground like a fish swims through water. One moment everything's quiet, the next it erupts from the earth and swallows you whole. It's got the head of a shark but the body is a twisted hybrid—part shark for swimming through the ground, part spider for walking on the surface." His voice shook as he described the creature, his hands trembling at his sides.

The grotesque mental image made the team uneasy, but James, ever the optimist, clapped Mark on the back.

"Well, Mark here should be able to blast that thing to smithereens with a fireball or two," he said confidently, nearly knocking Mark off balance.

Before Mark could respond, Caleb interjected with a grim shake of his head.

"Forgot to mention, its body looks like it's made of molten lava… and it breathes fire. We tried using fire damage, and it just healed the damn thing." His voice was filled with frustration and hopelessness.

James blinked, his mouth hanging open for a moment before he muttered, "Well… shit."

The team exchanged worried looks. A fire-breathing lava monster that could swim through the ground was not the kind of opponent they'd been hoping for.

"Do you all have a way to get out of here?" Jay asked, his tone more serious now.

Caleb sighed, rubbing his temples as if the weight of the question was too much to bear. "We have the RVs in the park. Some of the owners left the keys here so we could start them from time to time and keep them from rusting. But last time we tried to escape, the Crust Walker attacked. It's like it can sense the vibrations through the ground. When it hit us, it was like the earth itself exploded beneath the RV. We lost five people before we could get back inside." His voice cracked slightly, the pain of losing his comrades still fresh in his mind. "We haven't tried it since."

INVASION

"That does seem like a problem. Whelp… nothing to do but find it," Jay said, his tone casual and fearless, as if hunting down a monster was just another day at the office.

Caleb stared at him in disbelief, his eyes wide with shock. "What? You're just gonna go out there looking for it?" He pointed toward the door with an incredulous shake of his head. "That's suicide!"

Jay shrugged, showing no signs of concern.

"How else do you plan to leave? Your current plan is to sit here until you all die. My plan is to kill the fucker and get the hell outta here. Which one sounds better to you?" His voice was matter-of-fact, as if the choice was obvious.

Caleb hesitated, his gaze flickering between the safety of the building and the looming danger outside. "I mean, yours sounds better… but mine sounds survivable," he replied, his voice filled with doubt.

Jay chuckled darkly. "We'll see." He turned to the rest of the team. "Come on, guys. We need to take down Mr. Sharky. Caleb, get your team ready, and we'll meet you by the RVs when we finish."

Without waiting for a response, Jay walked out the door, his calm demeanor almost unnerving. James, true to form, simply shrugged at Caleb and followed his friend outside.

Caleb watched them go, his jaw clenched tight. He wanted to argue, to tell them it was madness, but deep down he knew they were right. Sitting around and hoping the monster would disappear wasn't a plan. It was surrender.

"You really wanna just fight this thing?" Mark asked, his voice betraying the fear gnawing at him. His steps were slower, hesitant, as he followed Jay.

"What choice do we have?" Jay replied, his tone cool and collected. "We need to get them out of here. Plus, I suspect now that we drove up, we won't be leaving so easily either."

Mark's anxiety flared as he shot back, "But I'm useless against it. You heard him—fire damage heals it!" His frustration was growing, and his panic wasn't far behind.

Jay turned to him, his expression firm. "You really can't use any spells that aren't fire magic?"

Mark hesitated. "Well, I have a few," he admitted, his voice unsure. "But they're either pretty weak or completely useless in battle."

Jay crossed his arms, thinking for a moment. "Go inside, see if they have a vending machine. Get something useful. Preferably a water spell."

Mark blinked, confused. "A vending machine…?" he muttered to himself before realizing Jay was serious. Without another word, he turned and sprinted back inside, determined to find something—anything—that could help.

Jay shook his head as he watched the mage run off. "Alright, we need to make some noise to get this thing's attention. Frank, can you do a little smashy-smash on the ground to see if we can get it to focus on us?"

Frank cracked his knuckles, eager to help. But before he could step forward, Susie chimed in. "I think we should move somewhere else first. We're too close to the RVs they want to escape in—and the building. If that thing shows up here, it'll destroy everything."

Jay smiled, impressed. "Good thinking. That's why you're the brains of this outfit," he said, giving her a nod of approval. "Now, let's go find a spot to fight in."

Just as they were about to leave, Mark burst through the door, waving a scroll above his head.

"I got one!" he shouted, his face lighting up with excitement.

Jay smirked. "Good timing. You're just in time to join us for a hunt for a good battleground."

The team moved as a unit, walking past the storage facility's gate and out into the open street. The tension hung thick in the air as they scanned their surroundings, searching for a suitable location. Jay pointed toward a large, empty parking lot near an abandoned Walmart about a quarter of a mile away.

"That should do," he said, his voice calm but focused.

No one argued. They all knew it was as good a place as any, though some still voiced quiet concerns about facing the monster head-on. The sense of dread only heightened as they approached the lot, the distant wind carrying the eerie silence that only comes before a battle.

As they walked, Mark eagerly unrolled the scroll he had found, reading it over with growing interest.

"You know, this is using up one of my spell slots that I could be using for another strong fire spell, right?" Mark complained, his brow furrowed as he focused on the text.

"Yes," Susie cut in, her voice sharp but matter-of-fact, "but if you can't be a more rounded fighter, you'll just get killed by fire creatures. You should at least have one spell that can help in those situations."

Mark sighed, his frustration growing. "The only spell I could find that's strong enough to take down something that can attack an RV is so mana-heavy that I can really only cast it once without needing a mana potion."

Jay stopped mid-stride, turning to face Mark with an expectant look. "Then you'd better have some mana potions on hand, right?"

Mark stood there for a moment, his face a mix of embarrassment and realization.

"I… I don't have any with me," he admitted, his voice barely audible.

Susie's expression flattened.

"Really? A mage without mana potions?" she asked, her tone dry. "In case you couldn't tell, *I* brought my sword…"

"Give him a break," James said, glancing back at Mark, his tone surprisingly compassionate. "This is one of his first real missions. He'll get the hang of it."

"He better go back and get some potions, is what he better do," Jay said, not stopping and not turning to look at them.

Mark darted off again, letting out a frustrated noise as he ran. The group continued their steady march toward the parking lot, the distant sound of crickets and the occasional rustle of wind their only company. Mark, visibly winded and panting, caught up with them about ten minutes later, clutching his side.

"You guys couldn't have waited for me?" Mark wheezed, bending over to catch his breath.

Jay, without turning around, shot back, "You'd have caught up eventually. You knew where we were going."

Mark grumbled something under his breath but managed to recover enough to walk alongside them.

"What's the name of the spell you picked up?" Lacey asked, curious but also offering a friendly smile to ease Mark's clear exhaustion.

"*Hydrostorm*," Mark said between breaths. "It creates a whirlwind of water around the creature, then blasts a concentrated beam of water down at it from above."

Lacey's eyes widened in approval. "That sounds powerful! It might be expensive to cast, but definitely worth it in a fight like this."

"Agreed," Jay added, his pace slowing a bit as he turned to face Mark. "We'll distract the beast while you charge up that spell. I'm guessing it's got a long cast time?"

Mark nodded. "Ten seconds, which feels like forever in a fight."

Jay grinned, clearly excited by the potential. "Oh-ho! That's gonna be a good one. Tom has a spell with a similar cast time, and it's a game-changer. Alright, you stay back with Lacey. She'll cover you with barrier spells if needed until you get that thing ready to go."

Mark visibly relaxed, feeling more reassured by the plan. "Sounds good to me."

James, ever the optimist, chimed in with a grin, "Seems like a solid plan. Let's make some sushi."

As they reached the edge of the parking lot, Jay gave a quick glance around. The area was vast, the cracked pavement stretching out like a battlefield waiting for action.

He turned to Frank, and with a nod, said, "Alright, big guy. Time to send some vibrations out and attract our prey."

"And, uh, try not to become the prey," Mark muttered nervously, his hands fidgeting as he scanned the empty lot.

Jay turned to him, his voice firm but not unkind. "Mark, think of yourself as the hunter. Confidence is key. Without it, you freeze, and that's when you die. Got it?"

Mark swallowed hard, nodding but still looking uneasy. Meanwhile, Frank had already taken a wide stance, gripping his massive maul tightly. With a grunt of effort, he raised the enormous hammer high above his head before slamming it down onto the pavement with a resounding crash. The ground cracked beneath the blow, sending shards of asphalt and concrete flying in all directions.

Frank continued his rhythmic pounding, walking in circles around the lot and hammering the ground with brute force. Each strike seemed to reverberate through the earth, the sound echoing off the abandoned buildings surrounding them. Fifteen minutes passed in this repetitive motion, and just as they were about to wonder if it was working, the ground beneath them trembled.

Lacey froze mid-step, her eyes wide with sudden alarm. "What was that?"

Frank paused, his maul mid-swing as everyone looked around cautiously. The rumbling beneath their feet grew stronger, a deep, almost primal sound vibrating through the earth.

"It's coming," James said, a malicious grin creeping across his face.

Susie shot him a look, raising an eyebrow. "And you're planning to take it down with that peashooter?" she asked, gesturing to the small handgun in his hand.

James gave her a cocky smirk. "You're right. This calls for something… bigger."

Without missing a beat, he stored the gun in his Inventory and pulled out a massive rocket launcher.

"Oh god," Jay paled, crossing himself. "The end of days are upon us…"

Susie's eyes went wide as she instinctively took a step back. "Where the hell did you get that?!"

"Military base," James said, casually patting the side of the launcher. "Figured they wouldn't miss one. Oh, and some ammo. Meet Jemma," he added, stroking the launcher like a prized possession.

Before anyone could respond, Mark pointed across the parking lot, his voice shaky.

"There!"

The ground beneath them rumbled louder, and suddenly, a large fin sliced through the pavement like a knife through water, parting the concrete as it moved swiftly toward them. Behind the first fin, a second, smaller one appeared, trailing close behind.

"Are there two of them?!" Mark shouted, panic creeping into his voice.

Jay quickly assessed the situation. "No, too close together. It must have two dorsal fins." He tightened his grip on his weapons, his eyes locked on the advancing creature. "Frank, be ready. When it gets close enough, step aside and smash it between the fins. We need to get this thing above ground where we can hit it. Everyone else, stay out of the path until we know what we're dealing with."

Frank nodded, setting his stance as the fins drew closer. His muscles tensed, veins bulging as he lifted the maul once more, preparing to strike with all his strength. The ground vibrated beneath them as the fins cut through the asphalt, speeding toward Frank's position.

"Come on, you giant sushi platter!" Frank bellowed, his voice echoing in the vast parking lot.

Just as the creature seemed about to plow straight through him, Frank made his move. With a quick pivot of his right foot, he twisted his body sideways, narrowly avoiding the fins. The creature was so close that Frank—clearly having practiced the move—dismissed his maul and pulled out his frying pan. In a blur of motion, he swung.

"*Cast Iron!*" he bellowed, the blow crashing down between the two dorsal fins, striking with enough force to shake the earth.

INVASION

The effect was immediate. The fins wavered, angling inward, and the ground beneath them shook violently. With a deafening roar, the creature's massive head burst from the ground, its shark-like jaws snapping wildly as it let out a furious growl of pain. Jagged, obsidian teeth gleamed in the dim light, and the monster's eyes glowed an eerie orange, filled with rage and hunger.

Jay took a step back, his eyes quickly analyzing the beast as he used *Inspect* on it.

Crust Walker	
Born in lava pits far beneath the planet's surface, these abomination-level creatures are bred for one thing: hunting. These creatures are formidable enough with a streamlined body, head as hard as steel, and teeth that can rip and tear through solid rock. Add in that they have eight thick spider-like legs, and you have a true predator. Instead of blood, these creatures have fire in their veins, which causes their skin to crack as it flows through them. Beware of their vibration sensors that tell them where their prey is hiding on the surface above them.	
HP:	8,145/8,400
MP:	1,200/1,200
SP:	5,500/5,500
Attacks:	Fire Breath, Bite, Thrash, Eruption

Frank leaped back, narrowly avoiding the creature's snapping jaws as it thrashed wildly in the ground, trying to sink its teeth into him. His feet skidded on the cracked asphalt, barely keeping him upright as he moved out of the beast's range.

Once he was clear, the team stood frozen in a mix of horror and disbelief as the creature began to rise from the earth it had burrowed through.

Its long, thick legs, coated in what appeared to be molten rock, extended from beneath the earth, pushing its enormous, grotesque body onto the surface. Each leg sunk into the ground for support, creating deep impressions in the pavement. The Crust Walker stood before them in its terrifying entirety—its massive shark-like head filled with horrifying teeth now fully visible; its glowing eyes burning with fury.

Squirrel snarled and sprang aside, narrowly avoiding the whip of the creature's tail. His fur bristled with tension, eyes locked on the monstrous threat.

"Holy shit," Mark whispered, his voice barely audible as he stared up at the towering monster, terror etched across his face.

"Start casting, you dumbass!" Jay's voice cut through the fear like a sharp blade. "Lacey, stay with him and use shields when necessary. Everyone else, target the legs! Bring it down!"

The team snapped into action, but before they could even make a move, the Crust Walker's long, whip-like tail lashed out with terrifying speed. The force of the blow was like a wrecking ball, sweeping across the team and sending them all flying off their feet. They hit the ground hard, each one dazed and struggling to recover from the impact.

Gasping for breath, Jay scrambled to his knees, feeling the world spin around him. Through the ringing in his ears, he saw the creature launch itself into the air, its enormous body casting a dark shadow over them. Its massive jaws opened wide, sharp teeth glinting as it dove toward the team in a predatory dive, aiming to crush them in one swift attack.

Chapter 54

Crust Walker

As the Crust Walker descended on him, Mark instinctively curled up, throwing his arms over his face in a futile attempt to shield himself from the imminent attack. His heart pounded in his chest as he braced for the searing pain that was sure to follow. A deafening crash echoed through the air, and Mark flinched, expecting the worst. But the pain never came.

Peeking through one eye, Mark saw the Crust Walker perched vertically atop a shimmering dome, its jaws snapping and gnashing against a magical barrier. Its molten body sizzled where it made contact with the shield, desperately trying to bite through. Glancing to his side, Mark saw Lacey, her arms outstretched and trembling with the effort of maintaining the shield. Sweat poured down her face as she strained under the pressure.

"Get… up… and… cast…" Lacey gritted out between labored breaths, her voice strained with the intensity of holding the barrier.

Snapping back into action, Mark scrambled to his feet and began preparing his spell. Power surged through him as he concentrated on gathering his mana. Just as he focused, Frank rushed in, his massive hammer swinging horizontally with tremendous force. The impact sent the Crust Walker flying off the barrier and crashing into the ground, flopping wildly as its legs flailed, trying to find purchase.

The creature let out a guttural growl, snapping its jaws and thrashing violently in the dirt. It rolled over clumsily, struggling to regain its footing, only to be met with an explosion that rocked its side. The blast sent it careening to the ground again, this time knocking it further off balance.

"WHOO! That's what I'm talking about!" James whooped, gleefully pumping his fist. The blast had caught the Crust Walker off guard, and it struggled to right itself once more.

As the Crust Walker continued its frantic attempts to get up, Mark could feel the mana building within him, coursing through his body like a torrent. He focused harder, pulling the energy from his core and shaping it into the spell he had been preparing. A glowing glyph appeared beneath him, followed by a large magic circle that expanded outward, crackling with energy. His hands glowed a brilliant blue, and he continued the incantation, knowing the spell's long casting time could leave them vulnerable.

Meanwhile, Jay darted toward the creature with the speed of a trained assassin, leaping into the air and plunging his sword deep into the Crust Walker's molten head. A sizzle and hiss rang out as the heat of the creature burned through the metal.

"OUCH! Hot, hot, hot!" Jay yelped, hopping off the creature and shaking his hands furiously, leaving the sword embedded in its skull. He danced around in pain, his boots smoking from the molten heat as the Crust Walker continued thrashing.

Another explosion rocked one of the creature's legs, this time severing it cleanly from its body. Lava oozed from the wound as the limb detached.

"Dammit! Hold still, you son of a bitch! Why is *Dickshot* on the fritz? System! Fix your shit! This is *not cool!*" James yelled, scrambling to find a better angle for his next blast as he loaded another rocket into the launcher.

The Crust Walker, now severely unbalanced with one leg missing, stumbled as it tried to rise. Just as it attempted to put weight on its remaining limbs, Mark completed the final words of his incantation.

With a shout, he slammed his hands onto the ground, activating the massive magical circle beneath the Crust Walker.

The creature froze in place, pinned by the glowing energy. Its eyes widened in panic as it thrashed against the invisible force holding it down.

"Oh no, you don't!" Mark shouted, a grin of satisfaction spreading across his face as he reinforced the spell with more mana, ensuring the Crust Walker remained trapped.

A swirl of blue, foamy water appeared out of thin air, encircling the Crust Walker. The creature's frantic movements became more desperate as it sensed what was coming. Water surged upward, forming a violent cyclone that engulfed the beast. The roar of the water mixed with the creature's growls, drowning out the chaos of the battlefield. As the water churned and whipped around the creature, steam began to rise, hissing as the Crust Walker's lava body was cooled by the powerful magic.

Dark storm clouds gathered overhead, turning the sky into a swirling, stormy mass. Rain began to pour down, adding to the growing tempest around them. From within the spinning vortex of water, a radiant light appeared at the cyclone's center. Magic circles began stacking in the sky, glowing with energy as they descended from the clouds, one after another, forming a tower of power above the Crust Walker.

Suddenly, from the topmost circle, a beam of concentrated water shot downward like a piercing spear. The jet of water expanded as it passed through each magic circle, gaining force and momentum until it struck the Crust Walker with the impact of a freight train. The sheer force of the water drove the creature several feet into the ground, the pressure forcing cracks in the earth around it.

Sizzling and popping noises echoed through the area as the water relentlessly pummeled the Crust Walker's molten body. Its fiery core was smothered by the cooling water, steam rising in thick plumes as it tried to fight back against the onslaught. The Crust Walker screeched in agony, its growls muffled by the deluge of water and magical force holding it in place.

The team watched in awe as the Crust Walker writhed within the magical cyclone, unable to escape the overwhelming power of Mark's spell. The ground beneath them vibrated with the intensity of the magic, and the sky crackled with energy.

Then, as abruptly as it had begun, the spell ended. The water cyclone collapsed, splashing to the ground as the clouds above dissipated. The sun broke through once more, casting light over the battlefield.

Lying in a deep crater was the Crust Walker, its body now darkened and charred, almost black. The once terrifying creature was now still, a broken shell of its former self. Jay used *Inspect* again, his eyes narrowing as he saw the creature's health was down to a mere five percent.

"Get it while it's down! Frank, go!" Jay shouted.

With a guttural war cry, Frank charged forward, his massive maul held high above his head. He leaped into the air, bringing the hammer down with all his strength. The maul slammed into the Crust Walker's eye, sending cracks rippling through its body. The creature let out one final, echoing cry before its body shattered, crumbling into a pile of molten rubble.

Frank waded through the debris at the edge of the crater, his boots crunching over the still-warm remnants of the Crust Walker. With a grunt, he stored his massive maul back into his Inventory and grabbed hold of the ledge. His muscles bulged as he pulled himself up and out of the crater, turning to look down at the smoldering remains of the monster.

"I kinda expected there to be bones," James muttered, squinting at the rubble below. His face twisted in confusion as he scanned the ground, expecting something more tangible than the crumbling molten fragments.

"Sharks don't have bones, you dolt," Susie chimed in, not even looking up as she adjusted her rapier, clearly annoyed with James' ignorance.

James shot her a sidelong glance and rolled his eyes. "Oh, hey, look! It's the girl who did nothing again," he said, his tone dripping with sarcasm.

Susie's eyes narrowed as she turned to face him, her lips pursed. "Sorry, my fighting style isn't exactly designed for... lava sharks," she sniffed, crossing her arms and turning her back on him.

James wasn't done. He smirked and added, "That's alright. I'm sure there are some cocktail weenies around here you can poke with that oversized toothpick you call a weapon. Maybe some rich snobs you can serve 'em to. Ever been a waitress?" He flicked his fingers dismissively in her direction.

Susie's face flushed with frustration, and she let out an exasperated grunt. "Ugh!" She stormed off, not wanting to engage with James any further.

Before anyone could laugh or comment, a shrill, high-pitched shouting pierced the air from the direction of the nearby Walmart. The team instinctively turned toward the sound, tensing in unison.

"Oh god! The Walmartians are invading!" James exclaimed dramatically; his eyes wide as he pointed toward the source of the noise. "You'll never probe me alive, you degenerate fucks!"

Jay, barely holding back a smirk, shook his head. "Pretty sure those are goblins, James."

James crossed his arms and sighed. "Can't let a good joke land, can ya?"

From the entrance of the dilapidated Walmart, about twenty goblins poured out of the shadowy doorway, snarling and screeching as they charged toward the team. Their small, wiry bodies were hunched as they sprinted, weapons shimmering in the light, eyes gleaming with hunger. There was something animalistic about their frenzy, as though the thought of devouring fresh meat had overtaken all rational thought.

Mark, still drained from the intense spell he had just cast, staggered slightly as he watched the goblins come rushing toward them. His face paled, and his eyes rolled back for a moment.

"I don't think… I can… help… this time..." he murmured, swaying on his feet. His body trembled as his mana reserves, completely depleted, threatened to drop him where he stood.

Before he could fall, Lacey lunged forward, catching him just as he collapsed. She cradled his head in her lap, her brow furrowed with concern. "It's probably mana fatigue," she diagnosed, her tone calm despite the approaching threat. She quickly reached into her Inventory and produced a mana potion in a small, metallic can. "I'll give him this potion. You guys deal with the goblins."

As the team braced for the goblins' onslaught, Susie stepped forward, her face an unreadable mask of focus. "I got this," she said, her voice flat and devoid of emotion. Her hand gripped her rapier's hilt, and she gave it a quick flourish— an elegant, swift movement that displayed her practiced precision. She then brought the blade up in front of her face, the tip aimed toward the sky in a pose reminiscent of a fencer about to duel.

Jay raised an eyebrow.

"You sure?" His voice carried both concern and curiosity, as this was the first time Susie had stepped up so confidently in a fight.

Suzie simply nodded, her eyes locked on the incoming goblins. Without breaking her gaze, she continued walking forward, her steps measured and unhurried.

Jay shrugged, glancing at the others. "Okay. Show us what you can do."

As Susie advanced, the goblins snarled, their wild eyes fixated on the small figure approaching them. They hesitated briefly, confused by her calm demeanor. Then, realizing only one person stood in their path, they erupted into a frenzy. Spittle flew from their twisted mouths as they cackled, their minds now consumed with the thought of tearing her apart. The goblins, driven by hunger and madness, surged forward in a bloodthirsty frenzy, their short blades and jagged spears held high, ready to feast on fresh human flesh.

"Aeries, prepare," Susie whispered softly, her voice almost lost in the wind. Her eyes locked onto the incoming goblins. "Now, die."

In a split second, Susie burst into action. Her form blurred as she moved, a streak of light trailing behind every slash of her rapier.

INVASION

Time seemed to freeze as the goblins remained suspended mid-charge, their expressions still fixed in snarls of aggression. The air around her seemed to hum with power as her blade danced with surgical precision.

Then, in a heartbeat, it was over. Susie stood behind the goblin horde, her back to them, rapier held out to her side in a classic superhero pose. For a brief moment, the goblins remained frozen, as if unsure of what had just happened. Then, one by one, their bodies began to twitch. Blood, dark and thick, sprayed from the multitude of slashes that crisscrossed their torsos, limbs, necks, and backs. Each goblin bore at least five precise, deadly cuts. Their screams filled the air, brief but intense, before they collapsed to the ground, silenced forever.

"Ho-ly shit," James muttered, his eyes wide as he stared at the massacre that had unfolded in less than a second.

Jay, walking up to Susie, glanced at the carnage. "Well, you weren't lying. Your fighting style wasn't suited for that Crust Walker, but we should figure out a way to get you a solid piercing Skill."

Susie sheathed her blade after a sharp flick, sending the remaining goblin blood scattering onto the ground. "I've got one. It's just not powerful enough for a creature that size yet. I need to level it up."

Before Jay could respond, Frank, grinning like a child, came barreling toward Susie.

"Susie, that was awesome! Susie's such a good killer, just like Frank!" he boomed, scooping her up and hoisting her onto his shoulder like a trophy.

Susie couldn't help but giggle at the display, enjoying the attention as Frank paraded her around. Jay chuckled, shaking his head at the sight of the huge man treating the petite girl like a hero. Meanwhile, James still stood in disbelief, gaping at the lifeless bodies of the goblins.

"Mark's doing better now," Lacey called over from where she knelt beside the recovering mage. Mark was sitting up, holding his head with one hand, still looking a bit pale but clearly on the mend.

"Alright, team, great job! Time to head back and check on the survivors, see how they're doing," Jay said, calling the group to order.

They began walking back toward the storage facility, their pace more relaxed now that the threat had been neutralized. Squirrel trotted happily beside James, tail wagging with every step. Occasionally, he sniffed at the fallen goblins and sneezed with theatrical disgust. Mark lagged slightly behind, still a bit woozy from the mana fatigue, but no one seemed to mind. The team chatted casually about the fight, discussing their skills and reflecting on what could have been improved.

The mood was upbeat—everyone was safe, and they had successfully handled the Crust Walker without anyone getting seriously injured. Jay considered it a solid victory and was relieved things hadn't gone as poorly as they could have.

As they talked, James attempted to lead a conversation about strategies, but it quickly derailed when he started questioning whether sharks had genitals worth shooting. Jay, sensing the discussion heading into absurdity, promptly stepped in and redirected the conversation.

When they finally reached the gate of the storage lot, they were greeted by the sight of two large RVs idling, lined up, and ready to hit the road. Caleb stood nearby, watching the vehicles with a look of anxious anticipation.

"I suspect that light show and the clouds were your doing?" Caleb asked as Jay approached.

"Yep," Jay replied with a nod, shaking Caleb's extended hand. "Mark here had just the right spell to deal with that Crust Walker."

Caleb looked visibly relieved, his shoulders sagging as he let out a long breath. "You don't know how grateful we are. I can't thank you enough for saving us. We really owe you one."

"Don't sweat it," Jay said with a reassuring smile. "Just do your part to help out the Guild, and we'll call it even."

Caleb nodded appreciatively, then turned to check on the RVs. "We're ready to roll as soon as you are. Can't wait to leave this nightmare behind."

Jay chuckled then turned to the rest of the team. "Alright, gang. Let's load up and hit the road. Time to get these people to safety."

Chapter 55

Return

Jay led the convoy back toward the highway, but the return trip was proving to be far slower than their initial journey. The roads that they had been able to pass with the GS2 weren't clear enough for the larger vehicles. Exhaustion weighed heavily on everyone as the hours ticked by. What should have been a short drive turned into an all-day affair. The team had no choice but to stop for the night.

Thankfully, the RVs provided a welcome respite, offering the luxury of sleeping indoors rather than under the stars or cramped inside the GS2. The size of the RVs required frequent stops on I-35 to clear the road with everyone, even the rescued team, chipping in to help move debris. Frank, ever the powerhouse, continued to use his "iron spell" to smash cars out of the way, bulldozing a path through the wreckage.

By the time they reached the site of their goblin battle from earlier, the weariness of the day had truly set in. The stench hit them first—a potent mix of rot and decay. Scavengers had already feasted on many of the corpses, leaving behind a grisly sight of half-eaten bodies. With noses wrinkled in disgust, the team got to work clearing the remains. The task was dirty and foul, and those unfortunate enough to get covered in gore were grateful for the RVs' showers. The quick rinse-off was a small but lifesaving luxury after the gruesome work.

Inside one of the RVs, James stood wearing only a towel around his waist, drying his hair with another. "We definitely need to use these things on our next trip out," he said, his voice a mix of exhaustion and appreciation.

Jay, sitting nearby, shook his head. "Nah, the GS2 is the way to go for me. Especially if we can upgrade it to have weapons capabilities."

He made a chef's kiss motion with his hand, envisioning the potential.

"Come on, man," James countered. "Just think about what this beast could do if you ran over a few goblins and upgraded it. Imagine the XP boosts. This thing could be unstoppable."

Jay paused, the idea playing out in his mind. He could see it—the RV, reinforced with armor, maybe even equipped with a battering ram, plowing through enemy lines like a tank. The thought was tantalizing.

"See? You're picturing it now too," James grinned, sensing he was winning Jay over.

"I mean," Jay admitted reluctantly, "it definitely could be cool."

James' eyes lit up. "Exactly! And think about the tactical advantage. We could move a whole team with this thing, more than just seven people. A mobile base with all the bells and whistles."

Jay nodded slowly, considering the possibilities. "True… but it's still unwieldy. Too big to maneuver in a tight spot."

"Boys and their toys," Lacey interrupted, rolling her eyes as she passed by, clearly unimpressed by the debate.

"Hippies and their… crysties…" James retorted awkwardly, fumbling for a comeback.

Lacey stopped in her tracks, turning to face James with a sharp look. "I'll have you know, these *crystals* you keep making fun of aren't just decoration. They're power sources."

James and Jay shared a look of confusion as Lacey marched to the RV door and stepped outside. The two men followed, curious but skeptical.

Standing a few feet from the RV, Lacey held up one of her crystals and pointed it at a nearby tree. The crystal in her hand began to glow with a vibrant yellowish light. Before either of them could question her further, a beam of energy shot from the crystal, striking the tree with a loud crack. The tree exploded into a shower of splinters, followed by a plume of smoke rising from the now-burning stump.

Jay and James stood frozen, jaws hanging open in disbelief as the tree smoldered in the distance.

"And *that*," Lacey said, turning back to face them, "is just part of what it can do. I store energy in these crystals and can use them to channel spells, releasing a much greater amount of energy than I could with just my own mana. It's especially handy when I'm low on mana but still need to heal people." She spoke matter-of-factly, as if blasting trees into oblivion with crystals was a perfectly normal skillset.

Jay blinked, his brain struggling to catch up. "Wait… you can store spells in those crystals?"

"No, I store *mana* in them and can release it at will as a spell or just as a concentrated blast," Lacey explained.

"So, these have abilities?" James asked, transfixed by the crystal she held now.

Lacey raised an eyebrow. "Yes. It's magic, James. You might've heard of it."

James, turning his head and staring at the remains of the tree, muttered, "I need one of those crystals…"

Lacey smirked, enjoying the stunned looks on their faces. "What? You just thought I was some weird soccer mom who believes in natural healing powers and throws essential oils at every little malady?"

"I mean," Jay admitted, "yeah… kinda did."

"Until now!" James added, his voice filled with newfound awe.

"Well," Lacey said with a grin, "now you know better."

James, his face plastered with an envious look, stared at the crystal still glowing faintly in her hand. "Seriously. I need one of those."

"Find your own," Lacey said with a smirk. "And be aware that not every crystal is capable of holding energy. Some will explode if you even try."

James' eyes widened. "Explode, you say? Like, how big are we talking here?"

"Big enough to make you regret your decision," Lacey replied calmly.

"So," Jay asked, still intrigued, "how do you know which ones can hold energy safely?"

"By *Inspecting* them," Lacey explained. "They'll have specific properties that show how much power they can hold. There's actually a ranking system for crystals."

Jay scratched his chin. "Could you do it with gemstones instead?"

"No," Lacey shook her head. "Gemstones aren't exactly the same. They can be used to enhance items—they hold enchantments really well—but not raw energy. They act more like conduits, not storage containers."

Susie had been quietly standing by, soaking up the conversation, and suddenly chimed in, "How did you learn all of this?"

Startled, James jumped. "What the hell?! I didn't even notice you followed us out!"

Ignoring him, Lacey responded to Susie, "It was actually an accident the first time. I found one in the hands of a goblin—he probably just liked it because it was shiny. But when I picked it up, I felt something inside of it. I *Inspected* it and realized it had some mana stored in it. After that, I spoke with Bohdan, Herbert, and Roland at the Guild to learn more. Harold even got involved because he was interested in using the crystals for some new weapons he's working on."

"Okay, but I'm still confused," Jay said, narrowing his eyes in concentration. "What makes a crystal better suited for holding energy versus a gem being better for enchantments?"

Lacey smiled, enjoying the curiosity. "Crystals have a crystalline structure, meaning the atoms inside are arranged in a repeating pattern that gives them a geometric shape. Gems, on the other hand, can have various patterns, and while some can be crystalline, they're not always as structured. This makes gems weaker overall compared to crystals when it comes to energy storage."

"So... because crystals are more orderly, they're better for holding energy?" Jay asked, trying to wrap his head around it.

"Exactly," Lacey continued. "Crystals are formed through the accumulation of minerals or vapor deposits, and their atoms are more spread out, allowing for the storage of energy. Gems, usually formed under extreme heat and pressure, are better as conduits for enchantments due to their denser and more varied structure."

James blinked at her. "And you just happen to know all of this? Did you pick up a degree in crystal magic I didn't know about?"

Lacey laughed softly. "I told you, I spoke with people much smarter than I am before I figured it all out. Have you ever had a conversation with Herbert?"

"Can't say that I have," James admitted.

"You should. He'll talk your ear off about this kind of stuff, but you'll learn something. They do nothing but research down in the basement. So much of the stuff we have for comfort and defense in Vanguard comes from that lab. Without them, we'd be barely surviving, like the people we just rescued."

Before Jay could say anything else, he gave James a pointed look and then said, "Well, as much fun as this has been, James, put some fucking clothes on. I'm seriously worried a breeze is gonna give us another view no one wants. After that fireball incident, I could go the rest of my life without another show."

Jay stepped back into the RV, leaving James standing there with a smirk on his face.

"Hey!" James called after him, flexing his biceps dramatically. "I'm in the best shape of my life now thanks to the System. Who wouldn't want a piece of this?" He raised his arms triumphantly, showing off his muscles with pride.

The towel around his waist suddenly slipped free and fell to the ground.

"Oh, sweet lord!" Lacey groaned, hurriedly covering Susie's eyes with both hands and ushering her inside the RV. Susie giggled as she was dragged away.

James, cursing under his breath, scrambled to gather his towel and rewrapped it around himself with a little less flair this time. "Damn it, these things need velcro or something."

A metal bowl suddenly flew out of the RV and smacked James square in the head.

"OW! What the hell was that for?!" James yelled, clutching the side of his head in pain.

"Get some clothes on, ya pervert!" Jay's voice called from inside the RV, barely holding back laughter.

James, still rubbing his head, grumbled, "Real nice, real classy…"

But despite the hit, he couldn't stop the grin that spread across his face as he rewrapped the towel.

"At least someone appreciates the view," he muttered.

A short time later, everyone was thankfully dressed and ready to load up into their vehicles. The air felt lighter after their brief break, and the team was eager to get back to the Guild building. The now-cleared roads made the drive smoother, and as the skyline of Dallas came into view, Jay used the new communication devices to hail TJ.

"We're almost there," Jay said into the pendant. A faint crackle was followed by TJ's voice.

"Got it. Gates are ready for you."

When they rolled up to the Guild building, the gates were already open, welcoming them back. The RVs, however, were too tall to fit inside the parking garage and had to park just outside the entrance, towering like mechanical beasts. Once the vehicles were unloaded, Tom came out of the building, looking expectantly at the team as they approached the GS2.

"So, how did it go?" Tom asked, his eyes casually scanning the vehicle.

Squirrel leapt out of the RV and stretched, then immediately began sniffing the courtyard, tail high and alert for any unfamiliar scents.

INVASION

Then his gaze froze. His eyes went wide, and he immediately looked back at Jay, eyebrow twitching. "Why is almost all of the XP gone?" he asked, his voice tightening. "And is it… taller?"

Jay, standing at attention like a soldier caught in the act, pointed at James without missing a beat.

"It was James," he said, throwing his friend under the bus without hesitation.

"What?!" James gasped, hearing his name. He looked betrayed, spinning to face Jay.

Tom, now fully focused on James, took a step forward, his expression hardening into one that could melt steel. "What did you do?"

James stammered.

"I-I-I…" His face flushed as he struggled to find words.

He felt the weight of Tom's glare like a physical force, and just when it seemed like Tom might actually explode, the Guild leader suddenly broke into a grin. He let out a low chuckle, which quickly escalated into full-blown laughter.

"I told Jay those points were to be used for whatever you all needed," Tom said between bursts of laughter. "Didn't he tell you that?"

James blinked in surprise. "He did… but the look on your face made that seem like a lie."

Tom caught his breath, wiping a tear from his eye. "But seriously, what *did* happen to it? Some monster smash it up?"

James shifted uncomfortably. "Well… not exactly," he began and then launched into a recap of the trip. "Not unless you consider Mark a monster—which admittedly the goblins just might…"

He told Tom about the goblins and their towers, Frank going full-on berserker mode, and, of course, Mark's unfortunate fireball mishap inside the GS2.

Tom listened intently, though his lips twitched with amusement. By the end of the tale, his grin had returned. "Look, I'm just glad you all are okay. Things can be replaced. You, however, cannot." He clapped a hand on James' shoulder, his smile reassuring.

"So… you're not mad?" James asked cautiously, his eyes widening in hope.

"No," Tom said with a shake of his head. "I'm not mad. Nice job with the mission, James."

James exhaled in relief, his shoulders visibly relaxing. "Oh, thank god. I was worried you'd try to kill me or something."

Tom's grin turned mischievous. "Oh, of course not." He paused, letting the moment hang. "At least, not as long as you get the XP back into the GS2."

James swallowed hard, his relief evaporating. "Uh… what?"

"You heard me," Tom said, his tone light but his expression serious. "Take it out, run over some monsters, and get the XP back. No harm, no foul."

James hesitantly walked up to the vehicle and touched it.

"You… You mean it?" James' eyes were limpid pools of hope.

"Go on." Tom rolled his eyes. "Get the hell out of here."

James was too busy hugging the vehicle of destruction and gently whispering to it.

"Don't you worry, baby. I'll treat you right. I promise."

It took a half-hearted kick to the seat of his pants for James to jolt upward and quickly climb into the driver's seat. The transformed Tahoe peeled out, fishtailing as it disappeared quickly from sight.

Tom turned to the rest of the team. "How did the rest of you fare?"

Jay stepped forward, giving Tom a rundown of the entire trip, from the moment they left to their showdown with the Crust Walker and their return. As he spoke, Tom's face reddened, barely holding back laughter at certain parts of the story.

"Well," Tom said, trying to maintain composure, "at least it all worked out okay in the end." He let out a small chuckle before adding, "I know I asked you to help them work together better. Do you think they've learned anything?"

Jay nodded. "They definitely learned a lot about what it means to work as a team. There's still room for improvement, but they're on the right path. You just need to keep them together."

"Good to hear. Now we just need James to come back and take his team with him on his little XP hunt," Tom said with a grin. "He shouldn't be out there by himself."

Jay slapped his forehead. "I didn't even think of that."

Pulling out his communication pendant, Jay called James, who picked up after a few seconds. "You need to come back and take your team with you."

When James returned a few minutes later, he stepped out of the GS2, glaring at Tom and Jay with a mix of irritation and embarrassment.

"You ruined my date night," James scowled. "Things were just getting hot and heavy."

"Well, it's going to be more of a group activity now," Tom said, fighting back a smirk. "It's not safe out there anymore. We don't send anyone out to hunt without backup."

James stood there, glaring at Tom for a long moment. Then, with an exaggerated sigh, he turned to the rest of the team. "Fine. Get in, losers. We're going hunting."

Frank, always the first to move, shrugged and walked toward the GS2 without complaint. The rest of the team exchanged amused glances before following him.

As they climbed into the vehicle, Tom grinned at Jay. "Our little boy is finally growing up."

Jay snorted. "You need to spend more time with him. You'd know that's totally not true."

Chapter 56

Ancient Tales

Another week came and went as the Guild continued its tireless preparations for the invasion. The atmosphere around the Guild hall was tense, with everyone feeling the weight of the impending threat.

Down in the basement, Tom worked alongside Herbert and Harold, brainstorming ideas for new weapons and defenses, the low hum of machinery filling the air.

Suddenly, Derek burst into the workspace, breathing heavily, his face pale and grim.

"What's up, man?" Tom asked, noticing Derek's unusual expression. He set down the wrench he had been using and straightened up from the stool.

"We found something on patrol. You need to see it," Derek said, his tone dark and urgent.

Tom frowned, wiping his hands on his pants as he stood up. "What do you mean, something? Why the rush?" he asked, sensing the gravity in Derek's words.

"Just… trust me. This isn't something we could bring back here," Derek said, his eyes steady but full of concern.

Feeling a knot of unease tighten in his stomach, Tom followed Derek up from the basement to the lobby. When they arrived, Tom saw Jay, Michael, Kevin, Kirsten, Kiera, Bron, James, and his whole team already gathered, waiting for them.

"What's this about? Why so many people?" Tom asked, casting a glance at the assembly. It wasn't often that such a large group was pulled together so suddenly.

"We have to travel to the site. Whatever they found… it's too big, and it definitely can't be moved," Derek explained, his voice low but serious. His head snapped toward Jay as he stabbed a finger toward the man whose mouth was half opened. "*Don't* say 'that's what she said.'"

Jay closed his mouth.

"This better be important," Tom grumbled, glancing back at the work he had been pulled from. "You know we're neck-deep in prepping for the invasion."

"I wouldn't have interrupted unless it was," Derek assured him, his face stern. "Trust me, you need to see this."

Tom hesitated for a second longer but eventually nodded.

"Fine. But I hope we've got something big enough to transport Bron. I don't just summon him anymore," he said, motioning toward the hulking figure of Bron.

Derek gave a sharp nod. "We'll take two vehicles. Now stop delaying, we need to move."

After loading into the vehicles, the convoy of Guild members sped through the city, the tires humming against the road. Tom stared out the window, watching the familiar landscape of Dallas blur past, his unease growing with each passing moment. His patience wore thin, and after a while, he couldn't hold back anymore.

"Alright, Derek. Spill it. What's going on? Why the secrecy?" Tom asked, leaning forward in his seat.

Derek sighed, glancing over at Tom before responding. "Look, I didn't want to say anything in front of the others until we knew for sure. But we had one of our defense teams out, sweeping the area for monsters, making sure the immediate zone was clear. That's when they found something… unexpected."

"Found what? Something dangerous?" Tom's brow furrowed.

"One of the patrol members fell into a crack in the street when it gave way beneath him," Derek said.

Tom's stomach lurched. "Is he alright?"

"He's fine now. He broke a few bones in the fall, but they had a Cleric with them, so he's healed. But that's not what this is about," Derek said, his tone dropping. "It's what they found beneath the street."

Tom's eyes narrowed. "What do you mean? What did they find?"

"There's a statue down there. Something… ancient. And it's not just a statue, Tom. There's something more going on, something we can't quite explain," Derek said, his words heavy with unease.

A cold chill settled over Tom as he sat back in his seat, the uneasiness growing into something more tangible. He didn't ask any more questions, sensing that Derek was holding back until they reached the site. As the city streets wound through Dallas, the tension in the vehicle was palpable.

When they finally pulled up to their destination, Tom could see a massive hole in the middle of the street, gaping like a wound in the earth. His skin prickled the moment he laid eyes on it.

"I feel something," Tom muttered, leaning forward, straining to get a better look before he had even stepped out of the vehicle.

Derek nodded gravely. "That's why we needed you here. Whatever this is… it's powerful."

The moment the GS2 stopped, Tom practically leaped from the vehicle, his heart racing. He sprinted toward the edge of the gaping hole, his boots kicking up dust as he skidded to a stop at the lip. Peering down into the darkness, he felt a strange pull, like something was calling out to him from below.

He turned, his face pale, fear flickering in his eyes. "I have to go down there. I hear it calling me," he whispered.

"Wait, Tom!" Derek said, grabbing his arm. "That might not be the best idea. We don't know what's down there."

But Tom shook his head, the pull too strong to ignore. Without another word, he leapt into the hole.

INVASION

Derek's warning came too late. Tom hit the bottom hard, rolling awkwardly to the side as pain shot up his leg. His ankle twisted painfully beneath him, and he let out a sharp cry of pain.

"Tom?!" Derek's voice echoed down the hole.

"I'm alright!" Tom called back, though his voice was strained. "But I think I hurt my ankle. Maybe don't try jumping down."

Derek's voice, half-amused and half-annoyed, came down from above. "You idiot! I told you the guy who fell before broke bones!"

"Yeah, sorry," Tom muttered, wincing as he gingerly touched his ankle. "I thought maybe he got hurt from not being ready. Figured my Constitution would be better prepared for the fall."

Derek sighed, rubbing his temples in frustration. "Hang on, we'll be down in a minute."

The team quickly retrieved a length of rope from the GS2, securing it firmly to the vehicle. One by one, they carefully lowered themselves into the gaping hole, each person landing much more gracefully than Tom had. Once everyone was at the bottom, Derek wasted no time scolding him.

"What kind of moronic move was that?" Derek snapped, glaring at Tom. "You're the leader. We've talked about you being more careful. You know, lead by example?"

Tom winced, not just from the pain but from the rebuke. "I know, I know. I couldn't help it, though. Something down here is calling to me. Can't you hear it?"

He looked at Derek with a mix of confusion and urgency, his eyes wide with the strange pull he still felt.

Derek paused, his brow furrowing as he listened. "Hear what? I don't hear anything."

Tom closed his eyes, trying to focus on the voice again. It whispered at the edge of his consciousness, the words an unintelligible murmur, like the language of a forgotten era. The voice was both alluring and harsh, beckoning him deeper, urging him to follow.

"It's like a whisper in my head," Tom said, opening his eyes. "I can't make out what it's saying, but it's pulling me that way." He pointed toward a narrow tunnel that sloped downward, its jagged walls vanishing into the shadows.

Without waiting for a response, Tom began walking, limping slightly as he moved deeper into the dark passageway. The others exchanged uneasy glances but followed him, their footsteps echoing in the enclosed space.

The tunnel was oppressive, the air thick with dampness. Water dripped from the uneven stone walls, collecting in small puddles that splashed beneath their boots. The glow from the far end of the tunnel—the only light guiding them—flickered like a distant candle, just bright enough to keep them from losing hope in the dark.

As they moved closer, the tunnel widened significantly, and soon, they emerged into a vast, rough-hewn cavern. The ceiling stretched high above them, and the cavern floor was dominated by a massive, intricately carved magic circle. In the center of the circle stood a statue on a pedestal, seemingly made entirely of stone.

The statue was breathtaking in its detail. It depicted an angel, its wings spread wide in a commanding pose, and in its right hand, it held a greatsword that pointed directly toward the tunnel. Its face, carved with flawless precision, held an expression of cold contempt, as if it looked down upon the world itself. The angel's left hand clutched a helmet, and its armor was engraved with symbols none of them could decipher.

Runes were etched into the pedestal beneath the angel, written in a language none of them could read. The entire scene was unnerving, yet undeniably awe-inspiring.

"What exactly are we looking at here?" Jay asked, his voice breaking the heavy silence. He stepped forward, his eyes locked on the statue's piercing gaze.

"I have no idea," Derek admitted, eyeing the statue warily. "But I'm not sure I like the look of it."

Tom stood frozen, his eyes wide with wonder. "It's so lifelike," he whispered. "Like it could just… come to life and step off the pedestal at any moment."

Kiera, clearly unimpressed, put her hands on her hips, her impatience evident. "So why exactly are we here, Derek?" she asked, her tone sharp with irritation. "You dragged us out here to look at a statue instead of helping us prepare for the invasion?"

Derek shook his head, visibly frustrated, trying to find the right words. "No, it's not just a statue. There's… something about this place. I can't explain it, but I *know* we're supposed to be here. It's like… fate brought us here."

Kiera raised an eyebrow, her skepticism clear. "Well, you're doing a bang-up job explaining that to us," she said sarcastically, crossing her arms. "Okay, say we *are* supposed to be here. What now? Do we take the statue with us? Is that the grand plan?"

Derek glanced at the enormous wingspan of the angelic figure, his eyes tracing the intricate details of the stonework. "No, that's not possible," he said, shaking his head. "There's no way we could get it through that tunnel, even if we could move it. Look at the size of those wings. They'd never fit."

"So, how did it get here?" Tom asked, staring at the imposing stone figure.

"Maybe it was carved here?" Derek offered, though his tone lacked conviction.

"Or it was alive… and trapped here," Bron said darkly.

Everyone turned to look at Bron. His deep, gravelly voice cut through the air, adding an ominous weight to his words.

"It could be something that was sealed away—gods know how many years ago. Magic has always existed, whether your planet had it before or not," Bron explained. "For something like this to have existed before the System's arrival. That is…"

"A scary thought," Derek grimaced and eyed the statue again. "This thing being alive… capable of who knows what."

INVASION

Tom's mind raced, his unease growing. But then an idea struck him, something that could shed light on this mystery.

"I know who we can ask," Tom said abruptly, moving toward the edge of the magic circle that was carved into the stone floor.

He knelt and began to draw a new circle within the old one, his movements precise and deliberate. The others watched as Tom worked methodically, drawing intricate symbols and sigils into the stone with a piece of chalk from his Inventory. Twenty minutes later, his circle was complete. Standing up, he started chanting an incantation, his voice low and rhythmic.

The circle lit up with a soft glow, and moments later, the spectral image of Azroc, Tom's Patron, flickered to life in the air above the circle.

"Hey there, shithead," Azroc greeted casually, his usual irreverent smirk in place. "And you've brought your merry band of misfits, I see. What can I help with today?"

Tom stepped aside, gesturing to the statue behind him. "Ever seen anything like that?" he asked.

Azroc's smirk vanished instantly. His eyes widened in shock, and he leaned closer to the portal window, inspecting the statue.

"Hang on, I'll be right there."

Before anyone could react, the window closed, and the light of the circle flared up again. Within seconds, Azroc popped into existence in the center of the magic circle. His usually cocky demeanor was gone, replaced by an air of seriousness Tom rarely saw.

"What, no dramatic entrance? No rising from the ground in some epic pose?" Tom quipped, trying to lighten the mood.

Azroc waved off the comment, his face grim.

"That's all for show, kid. This is some real shit here. How did you even find this?" His voice was tense, and he glared at the statue with barely contained anger.

"One of our Guild members fell into a hole in the street and stumbled upon this," Tom explained, pointing back toward the tunnel they'd emerged from. "We just followed the path down here."

"Ajax," Azroc growled, his voice dripping with venom. His eyes locked onto the statue with a fury that made Tom take a step back.

"I'm sorry... you *know* what this is?" Tom asked, his stomach twisting at the look on Azroc's face. He had never seen his Patron so enraged.

"Yeah, I know this dickwad," Azroc spat. "He used to be a Patron for Warlocks, like me. Thought he was better than everyone else. That he could dispense his version of justice as he saw fit. The gods struck him down from his position and made him a greater Summon—bound to serve like a common beast. It pissed him off something fierce."

Derek glanced uneasily between Tom and Azroc. "What... does that mean for us?"

Azroc didn't even look at him, his gaze still locked on the statue. "After his fall, Ajax went on a rampage, controlling weaker-willed Warlocks to carry out his revenge. He used his influence to bend them to his will, giving him free reign to take his vengeance on anyone and anything he deemed deserving."

Tom's pulse quickened. He could tell by Azroc's tone that this wasn't just some old, forgotten relic. This was dangerous.

Azroc continued, his voice low and angry, "The Patrons gathered together to stop him. We were ready to kill him for good… but Ajax had a trump card. He found a loophole in the System, a way to bind most of us so we couldn't interfere. That's why I told you about those rules you can't break—because the System punishes you. Well, Ajax found a way to twist those rules to his advantage."

Tom nodded, his mind racing. "So, what happened? How did he end up here?"

Azroc's face darkened. "There was one Warlock who managed to resist Ajax's control. He brought his Patron into the fight. The Patron's name was Sylanna. She was a good friend of mine, strong as hell. Together, we fought Ajax… but during the battle, Sylanna trapped him. I don't know how—she disappeared after that. We assumed they both died in the fight. Now, seeing this… it looks like she managed to seal him away. It probably cost her life to do it."

Tom stared at the statue, the weight of Azroc's words sinking in. "And now we're standing in front of a statue that holds one of the most dangerous creatures you've ever known… and we're also preparing for an invasion." He sighed heavily. "So, you can kill him?"

Azroc's lips curled into a dark smile. "I mean, I *could*. But I've got a better idea than just killing him outright."

Tom raised an eyebrow. "What do you mean?"

Azroc's eyes gleamed with a malicious glint. "We could kill him, sure… or, we could use him. Like you said, you *are* preparing for an invasion, after all. This bastard was a Warlock Patron. He's bound to serve, even if he's a piece of shit. I say we teach this rancid old cum stain a little lesson while getting some use out of him at the same time. Two birds with one stone."

Tom's curiosity piqued. "I do like the sound of that. What's the plan?"

Azroc stepped closer, his gaze intense. "Tell me, Tom… would you be willing to do whatever it takes to save your planet?"

Tom didn't hesitate. "Yes."

Derek, standing nearby, raised his hand. "Whoa, whoa, whoa. Let's hear the plan *before* we start agreeing to anything, Tom."

Azroc shot Derek an icy glare. "Shut up, dickwad. This doesn't concern you."

"Actually, I think—" Derek began, but Azroc silenced him with a single raised finger. Derek froze in place, his body locked as though time itself had stopped for him.

"I said, this doesn't *concern* you," Azroc growled, his eyes glowing faintly.

Tom frowned. "Did you have to freeze him like that?"

Azroc shrugged. "He'll be fine. He's just in time-out so he won't interrupt." He turned back to Tom. "Now, before you fully commit, you need to hear the story. Once you know the details, then you can decide if you're still willing to do whatever it takes."

INVASION

Tom nodded, feeling the weight of the decision looming before him. Azroc's dark smile lingered as he began to tell his tale.

"This is the tale of how my Patron became the biggest dildo in the known universe."

Chapter 57

Patron Wars

"Many millennia ago," Azroc began, his voice low and deliberate, "those of us who had attained Patron status forged an uneasy truce in our endless struggle for influence. You see, Warlocks were rare then—despised, feared, outlawed across whole systems. Few mortals dared to choose that path, and so, we Patrons turned to competition. Ruthless, savage competition. We offered power we couldn't afford to lose, made promises we couldn't sustain, all for the chance to secure a single follower. It became a bidding war—high-stakes, no rules—where the only true winners were the Warlocks themselves, reaping boons far beyond reason for the simple act of saying yes."

He folded his arms, expression grim. "And that greed had consequences. Warlocks grew monstrous, corrupted not only by the magic we fed them, but by the knowledge that they held all the leverage. Some turned tyrant, some turned beast—but all of them, eventually, became hunted. Entire planets enacted bans on the Class. Whole fleets launched extermination campaigns against any who dared choose to become one. Warlocks became synonymous with devastation, and the System allowed it because the damage we'd done—our overreach—demanded it."

Azroc's eyes narrowed, voice tightening. "And then there was Ajax. By the time he'd reached Patron status—over five thousand years into his existence—he had already grown tired of the games. Where most of us accepted the System's restrictions, however grudgingly, Ajax spat on them. He saw restraint as weakness, compromise as corruption. We viewed the System as balance. He saw it as a cage."

"Ajax was a Celestine," Azroc continued, pacing slowly now. "Their world believes in absolutes. Black and white. Justice and sin. No grey. No middle ground. To them, Patrons were demons cloaked in velvet—seducers of mortals, harbingers of collapse. Yet Ajax... not only did he become a Warlock, he rose through the ranks to become a Patron. And even with all that change, he never shed his people's rigid beliefs. That moral extremism didn't fade—it festered. It shaped everything he did."

Azroc's tone deepened, becoming heavier with each word. "Unlike many of us—who learned that survival meant subtlety, balance—Ajax embraced fanaticism. While we tempered our power, he looked down on us for it. He saw our caution as cowardice. He saw our restraint as betrayal of what we could become. And so, while we watched one another like wary wolves, Ajax began to scheme. Quietly. Diligently. And with a hatred for the System that ran deeper than any of us dared to imagine."

Azroc's expression darkened as he continued. "Even after ascending to Patronhood, Ajax stayed apart from the rest of us. He didn't join our councils. He didn't lend his voice to our debates. He withdrew. Watched. And in the shadows, he plotted. His hatred for our 'compliance,' as he called it, grew like a poison. While we tried to maintain balance—even if imperfectly—he stewed in contempt."

"We sensed something eventually. Whispers. Patterns. Power surges in corners of the universes that bore his scent. But by the time we understood what he'd been building, it was already far too late."

Azroc's gaze grew distant, memories surfacing like ghosts. "Ajax had been amassing Warlocks. But not just any. He wasn't interested in the ambitious or the reckless. No—he hunted the broken. The discarded. Those twisted by pain, by grief, by rage so deep it hollowed them out. People the System had wronged, or so they believed. He found them. Fed them. And filled their emptiness with fire."

"Power. More than any Patron should give. Far more than the System allowed for safe transfer. He poured it into them like kerosene, and then lit the match. And they burned, Tom. They burned entire civilizations. Anyone they saw as an enemy—anyone who reminded them of what they'd lost—became ash."

He paused, jaw clenched. "To Ajax, this wasn't madness. This was justice. His own warped version of balance. The Celestine code had rooted itself so deep within him that even vengeance looked like virtue through his eyes."

"One of his earliest disciples was a Warlock whose appearance had condemned him from birth. Disfigured. Mocked. Beaten. Cast out by his people as a curse. Ajax offered him power—and a promise. That he would never be looked at with pity again."

Azroc's voice dropped low. "And the Warlock answered that promise with genocide. He didn't just kill the ones who tormented him. He eradicated them all. His entire species. Mothers. Elders. Infants in their cribs. Until he stood utterly alone, the last living thing on a world gone silent. And when the echoes of what he'd done grew too loud for even his power to drown out... he ended himself."

He shook his head slowly. "And Ajax? Ajax praised it. Called it a cleansing. The Celestine would see mercy in exile or healing. But Ajax believed mercy was weakness. To him, death was kindness—and vengeance, the highest form of order."

Azroc's fist tightened. "He found more like that Warlock. So many more. And with each, the universe grew darker."

Azroc drew in a steady breath. "But power wasn't enough for Ajax. Not in the end. As his influence grew, so did his hunger. He no longer sought followers— he gathered zealots. Warlocks who didn't just take his gifts but believed in his vision. A vision of a universe bathed in flame and cleansed by violence. They followed him, not out of loyalty, but because they craved the annihilation he promised."

His eyes darkened. "He stopped hiding his intent. Subtlety gave way to ambition. Ajax no longer wanted to exist within the System's constraints. He wanted to shatter them. Burn the rules, erase the balance. Unmake the order that held the multiverse together."

Azroc's tone dropped to a growl. "And he chose his moment carefully."

"You see, every cycle, all Patrons are called to attend the *Hathvartisk*—a summit where we discuss affairs, update ourselves on changes the System has implemented, and reaffirm the boundaries of our power. It's not ceremonial—it's essential. The System is always evolving, and even a minor violation can result in catastrophic fallout if we overstep without knowing it. So we meet. We listen. We adapt."

He shook his head, eyes shadowed by memory. "That cycle, we gathered as we always did. Greetings were exchanged, small alliances reaffirmed, arguments picked up from centuries past. Ajax's absence went unnoticed. It wasn't strange—he was never one for mingling. We'd long grown used to his disdain."

"But when the roll call commenced... he wasn't the only one missing."

Azroc's voice grew taut. "Five Patrons. Unaccounted for. All powerful. All cautious. Their disappearance was immediately suspicious. We attempted to trace their life signatures—our identifiers in the weave of reality, distinct and immutable. Four had vanished entirely. No trace. As if they'd been erased from the very code of existence."

He paused, letting the gravity of that sink in.

"But one... one signature remained. Flickering. Weak. And it was near Ajax's."

Azroc closed his eyes for a moment. "We watched, helpless, as that final light was extinguished before our eyes. Snuffed out. Deliberately. Slowly."

He looked to Tom, voice like steel. "We didn't wait. We dispatched Enforcers immediately—our most capable, our fastest. But what they found..."

Azroc's jaw clenched, and for a moment, his voice faltered. Then he pressed on.

"It was a massacre. No... worse. It was a message written in agony. The Patrons had been mutilated, torn apart in ways we didn't think possible. Their essence, their power—drained, unraveled from their forms. The walls were soaked in pain. Some of the Enforcers couldn't even step inside without vomiting. Others left and never returned to service."

He inhaled sharply.

"The act was so vile, so brazen, that the System itself intervened. For the first time in living memory, it issued a universal quest: stop Ajax. By any means necessary."

"Ajax ran. Not like a coward, mind you. No, Ajax ran like a predator choosing his battlefield. For centuries, we chased him. Across star systems, into collapsing dimensions, through timelines on the brink of erasure—we hunted him. And each time we thought we were close, we arrived only to find devastation. Blood. Ruin. Echoes of torment that clung to reality like smoke."

INVASION

He clenched a fist. "It wasn't just murder. No. He made a ritual of it. Patrons—our kind—were his prey. But he didn't kill quickly. Ajax was deliberate. Surgical. He tore them apart piece by piece, using healing magic to keep them alive just long enough to suffer anew. Hours. Days. Weeks. Screams echoing through planes that shouldn't have carried sound."

Azroc's face hardened, his eyes distant and haunted. "And while they screamed, Ajax whispered. He told them they deserved it. That their crimes in pursuit of power justified their punishment. He called it penance—said their stolen might would fuel something greater. That their end would serve a higher purpose."

He shook his head. "Even those of us who had left behind flesh weren't spared. Beings of light, sound, thought—we thought ourselves untouchable. Safe. But Ajax… he discovered methods. Devices. Runes of such complexity they defied categorization. He found ways to contain us, to rip apart energy itself on a molecular level. No Patron, no matter their form, was beyond his reach."

Azroc paused, his jaw tight. "And worst of all? We could never catch him. Every plan failed. Every ambush, every trap—he slipped through like smoke. Like he was always watching us. Anticipating."

He turned, eyes meeting Tom's directly. "And eventually, we learned why."

"Sylvanna—sharp, relentless Sylvanna—dug deeper than the rest of us. Obsessed, maybe. But she found the truth."

A bitter edge touched his voice. "He had a mole. One of our own. A Patron, corrupted. We never learned who. Never saw it coming. No signs of mind control, no evidence of coercion. But that leak—that betrayal—was why he always stayed one step ahead."

Azroc's brow furrowed, the weight of frustration flickering behind his gaze. "To this day, we never uncovered exactly how Ajax managed to corrupt the traitor. Whoever they were, they left no trail. No signs of enchantment, no compulsions, no traces of manipulation. No fingerprints on the knife they drove into our backs. Did Ajax blackmail them? Did he threaten someone they loved? Or did he simply... convince them? Speak so persuasively, so righteously twisted, that they believed what he believed? We still don't know. And that ignorance burns."

He exhaled slowly. "But one thing was certain—that betrayal gave him eyes in every room, ears in every conversation. Every trap we laid, every move we made—he saw it coming."

Azroc's voice softened, but there was steel behind it. "And Sylvanna… she took it personally. She always had a sharp mind, but after Thillius—her mentor, her closest friend—after he fell to Ajax's cruelty, something in her sharpened into something else."

He turned slightly, eyes distant. "We arrived too late to save Thillius. The torture hadn't lasted long—Ajax didn't have time to indulge. We'd closed in faster than he anticipated. A rare mistake on his part. But still... Thillius died screaming. And Sylvanna never forgave that."

Azroc turned back to Tom, as if addressing a question that had been building. "I know what you're thinking. 'Azroc, didn't you say life signatures were how you track each other? How did Ajax keep slipping away?' And you're right to ask."

He nodded once. "After our first attempt to capture him, he learned. Adapted. He figured out how to hide his life signature—not just suppress it, but replace it. Mask it entirely. He began duplicating the signatures of other beings. Minor gods, mortals, even constructs. It became nearly impossible to identify him through traditional means."

Azroc spread his hands. "That shouldn't be possible. Life signatures are tied to our very essence—fixed by the System itself. Immutable. But Ajax… Ajax found a way. We still don't understand how. Maybe he accessed the System directly, breached it at a level even we can't comprehend. But that would imply he circumvented protections meant to guard the very fabric of reality."

He paused, then offered a grim half-smile. "And yes, since they've already opened that door for you—I can now mention the Admins."

Azroc's tone shifted slightly, reverent and wary at once. "The Admins are… something else. Beings that sit above the System. Not Patrons. Not gods. Architects, in a way. They rarely involve themselves, and when they do, it's because something has gone horribly, irreversibly wrong."

His gaze sharpened. "When we learned Ajax could alter his life signature, it didn't take long for them to take notice. And make no mistake—their attention is never a blessing. If someone becomes too dangerous, too disruptive, the Admins don't capture. They don't imprison. They erase. Total deletion—soul, memory, impact. A clean cut through existence itself."

Azroc folded his arms. "We weren't at that point. Not yet. But we were getting close. The Admins began to aid our efforts… in their own way. Sparse words. Occasional nudges. No explanations. But still—we began to find cracks in Ajax's trail again."

Azroc nodded solemnly. "It was Sylvanna who proposed the next move. Her mind, ever sharp despite the grief, saw the one weakness in Ajax's armor—his followers. She suggested we stop chasing the beast's head and start severing its limbs. If we couldn't catch Ajax directly, we could bleed him out, bit by bit, by destroying the Warlocks he had empowered."

He let the silence linger a beat before continuing.

"It wasn't a flawless plan. But it was a beginning. A spark of strategy in a storm of chaos."

"One by one, we hunted them—his chosen. Scattered across a thousand worlds, hiding in ruined temples, corrupted cities, or beneath the surface of barren moons. And each one… was a nightmare."

Azroc's voice dipped into something darker. "These weren't typical Warlocks. Ajax had elevated them far beyond what any mortal should've been capable of. They wielded power on par with lesser Patrons—monstrous strength backed by unshakable conviction. They weren't just soldiers. They were zealots. Ajax hadn't just empowered them; he had instilled a vision. A gospel of annihilation dressed up as cleansing. And they believed every word."

INVASION

He inhaled deeply. "They fought us like cornered rats. Relentless. Fanatical. The kind of loyalty that doesn't come from bargaining—it comes from belief. They thought Ajax was going to remake all of existence in fire and fury, and they wanted front-row seats to watch it all burn."

Azroc's eyes narrowed. "We had to approach them with absolute caution. Each battle was a minefield, not just of magic, but of ideology. Because by that point, his Warlocks weren't just followers anymore. They were worshippers. His cult had grown into a religion, one that saw Ajax not as a Patron, but as a god."

He hesitated before adding, "And while 'god' is a word many throw around loosely, I assure you—it carries weight. True gods, the ones that exist beyond even our comprehension, rarely interfere in the workings of the System. To them, we are sparks. Moments. Fleeting things not worth their gaze. Ajax hadn't reached that level—but to his followers, he might as well have. And they would die, kill, or destroy entire worlds in his name."

Azroc's voice turned heavier. "For every ten Warlocks we struck down, Ajax found time to slay a Patron and replenish his strength. It was like bailing out a sinking ship while he drilled holes in the hull. Still, we kept at it. I was part of the elite strike teams assigned to root out his lieutenants. And the battles…"

He trailed off, then shook his head slowly.

"They were cataclysmic. Entire landscapes reshaped. Mountains crumbled. Oceans boiled. Our spells clashed like meteor strikes. The very fabric of the worlds we fought on groaned beneath the weight of our magic."

Azroc gritted his teeth. "But even with all that, we underestimated them. What we hadn't anticipated was that Ajax had passed on more than power—he'd taught them everything. His strategies. His techniques. The rituals he used to slay Patrons. His Warlocks didn't just fight—they hunted. And they were damn good at it."

He looked at Tom again, steady and grim.

"They were armed with knowledge meant only for the highest echelons of power. They were ready. They were lethal. And they almost turned the tide."

Azroc exhaled, slow and steady. "You might think Ajax's army formed because of the power he offered. But that wasn't the heart of it. His real weapon was understanding emotion—deep, raw, festering emotion. Greed. Rage. Vengeance. He didn't just empower those feelings. He nurtured them. Fed them. Let them grow until his Warlocks weren't just followers—they were instruments sharpened on their own pain."

He paused, eyes narrowing in reflection. "And that manipulation… it changed everything."

"In the old days, Warlocks would browse potential Patrons like merchants at a bazaar. We'd compete—offering power, skills, even rare abilities—in hopes they'd pledge themselves to us. It was a barter system. Messy, but manageable. A Warlock would choose the Patron who offered the best path toward their goals."

Azroc's voice turned heavier. "But after Ajax, that model was shattered. His campaign of destruction forced the System to intervene. Too many followers under one banner—especially one so volatile—became a threat not just to balance, but to existence itself."

He gestured vaguely, as if touching the System's invisible presence. "Now, the rules are different. Warlocks no longer see a list of every Patron. The System sorts us by style of power, only showing those open to forming new pacts. It throttles recruitment. Limits accumulation. All to prevent another Ajax from ever rising again."

Azroc's jaw tensed as his tone shifted. "But by the time that change came… we were already knee-deep in fire."

"One of the final confrontations with Ajax's forces took place on a world that was no longer recognizable as a planet. A scorched husk. Barely holding together. Nothing but ash and cracked stone. The Warlocks had already razed it, killing everything that breathed. They'd dug in deep—beneath the crust, hiding like venomous roots, waiting for us."

Azroc's hands clenched behind his back. "I was there. Deployed with other high-tier Patrons to exterminate them. What followed wasn't a battle. It was an apocalypse. The ground split open beneath us as spells clashed with such intensity that time itself warped. They summoned horrors that defied natural law— creatures that clawed their way through dimensions just to die screaming. We answered in kind."

He shook his head slowly. "We nearly split the planet in two. The air ignited. The sky bled. The very core of the world groaned under the pressure. And when it was done—when the last of Ajax's lieutenants lay broken in the dust…"

Azroc looked down, voice softening.

"I received the message. Sylvanna was gone."

He straightened, voice steadier now but carrying sorrow. "Blinded by vengeance, by her hatred for the one who murdered her mentor, she had gone after Ajax alone. She knew the risk. Knew what he was capable of. But still, she charged ahead. Not because she thought she could win—but because she couldn't stand by any longer."

Azroc's expression tightened. "The moment we learned, we scrambled. Reinforcements were dispatched through every channel, across every known plane. But the second she engaged Ajax, all contact with her ceased. No messages. No pulses. No signs of life signature fluctuations. Just… silence."

Azroc's voice grew hushed, the weight of memory pressing down on every word. "We raced across entire universes, clawing through rifts and foldspace, desperate to reach her. To reach them. But when we finally arrived at the scorched world where their battle had taken place, we were too late."

He paused, and when he spoke again, it was softer. "Their life signatures— both of them—were gone. Not hidden. Not obscured. Gone. Erased as if they had never existed. Despite years of searching… decades, even… alongside the Admins themselves, we never found so much as an echo."

A bitter note entered his tone. "Eventually, we were forced to accept the only truth that made sense—that Ajax and Sylvanna had killed each other. That her final act had been to take him down with her."

Azroc drew in a long breath. "A hundred years we spent chasing phantoms. Searching every scrap of possibility. And then… silence. Existence began to move on. The scars remained, but the name Ajax faded. Became a lesson. A shadow. A reminder whispered to new Patrons in warning."

He looked toward the statue looming nearby. "I thought I would never hear that name again."

Azroc's voice trembled—not with fear, but with restrained fury. "But standing here, seeing this statue, everything returned. The rage. The helplessness. The desperation to know what had happened to Sylvanna. She was one of our best. And she deserved more than to be forgotten beneath the weight of politics and peacekeeping."

He stepped closer, eyes scanning the cavern. "This place… this planet… it reeks of Ajax. I should have realized it sooner. The signs are all here. He must have come to this world long before its current state. He was hiding here. Waiting. Planning. And when Sylvanna found him…"

Azroc's gaze hardened. "That battle must have been a force of nature. Entire worlds would have quaked beneath their fury. But she did it. She gave everything. And in the end, she sealed him here—bound him to this place with the last of her power."

He turned to Tom, voice solemn but firm. "But hope, Tom… is a fool's wager. I understand her reasoning, but this—this tomb—it was always a ticking bomb. Especially given this world had not yet been integrated into the System. It was only a matter of time before someone stumbled onto this place. Before someone woke him up."

Azroc's expression grew grim. "The amount of magic it would've taken to bind Ajax here… it staggers belief. The only way Sylvanna could've done it was by sacrificing herself completely. And even then, she was lucky he'd already been weakened by the loss of his followers. But make no mistake—he was still powerful enough to be considered an existential threat to everything."

He turned fully to Tom now. "And now… you know. You know the truth of Ajax. How he rose. How he fell. And how he came to be entombed here."

A faint glimmer lit Azroc's eyes. "But I have a plan. One that could turn this ancient terror into a weapon. Not just for vengeance. For survival."

He took a breath and continued. "There exists a ritual—an opportunity. A way to bind Ajax. Not as an equal. Not as an ally. But as a tool. A weapon to be unleashed only in your darkest hour, when defeat is all but certain, and the fate of everything hangs by a thread."

Azroc's voice sharpened. "This isn't something I offer lightly. I bring it to you only because your Charisma has surpassed one hundred. Without that— without your natural force of will—you wouldn't stand a chance of controlling him. Even now, he will be a shadow of his former self. But that shadow may still be mightier than most beings could ever dream to match."

"You've never been the typical Warlock, Tom. No hordes of minions. No armies summoned to fight in your name. Perhaps that's not a flaw. Perhaps it's fate. You've held onto your willpower—guarded it—and now, maybe, just maybe, this is what it was meant for."

Azroc met Tom's gaze and held it. "So I ask you now, truly: are you willing to take that risk? Will you reach into the deepest well of your summoning power and bind Ajax to your will, knowing full well what he is—and what he could become again?"

He fell silent, the air between them heavy with possibility.

Chapter 58

Patron Summons

"So, wait. Ajax was a giant douche canoe, sure—but how did you not go mad or end up dead because of him? Wasn't he your Patron too?" Tom asked, trying to piece everything together.

Azroc snorted. "Ajax was my Patron during his early years of power. He hadn't been completely corrupt at that point. Still a huge asswipe, as you said, but not entirely shit-for-brains yet."

Tom tilted his head. "Then how did *you* manage to become a Patron?"

Azroc opened his mouth—only for it to snap shut with a sharp clack of teeth. His jaw clenched as he rubbed it with an annoyed grunt, then turned his gaze to the ceiling as if waiting for some kind of divine slap on the wrist.

"Can't tell you," he muttered, irritation flickering across his face. "Let's just say, I didn't rely on him to get where I am today."

A tense beat passed. Still no cosmic punishment. He exhaled, shoulders relaxing just a little.

Tom leaned forward. "So… you can just become a Patron on your own?"

Azroc's eyes narrowed. "You know I can't answer that, shithead."

Tom shrugged. "Worth a shot."

Azroc rolled his shoulders, dismissing the topic entirely. "Now, back to the matter at hand. Do you accept the challenge?" His stance shifted, arms crossing over his chest as he straightened to his full height.

"I accept," Tom said firmly.

As soon as the words left his mouth, Derek, who had been frozen in place, suddenly stumbled and fell to the ground, disoriented and shaking his head.

"I hope you know what you're doing," Derek muttered as he regained his footing.

Tom shrugged with a grin. "The way I see it, either the pirates kill us, Ajax does, or—Ajax kills the pirates."

"And then us," Derek pointed out.

Tom shrugged. "Either way, we're dead and won't care."

Derek chuckled, rubbing his temples. "That does seem to be how it always plays out with us."

Tom raised an eyebrow. "So, still think it's a bad idea?"

"Absolutely," Derek said with a wry smile. "But it's probably the only way we survive, so let's get on with it."

Reaching out, Tom helped Derek up to his feet, the two exchanging a brief nod of understanding before turning their attention back to Azroc.

"Alright!" Azroc clapped his hands together, his eyes gleaming with predatory excitement. "Let's get this fucking party started! I can't wait to see the look on that old cum dumpster's face when I do this."

Tom's stomach twisted a little at the sight of Azroc's eager grin.

"What exactly are you going to do?" he asked, suddenly feeling the weight of the situation.

"I can't give you every little detail," Azroc said, his tone sly. "That kind of intel is above your pay grade, and I'd get punished for spilling too much. But what I *can* tell you is that I'm about to force Ajax to become your Summon—like your Mastadonian friend over there." He pointed lazily at Bron. "Once that's done, you'll be able to force a contract with him."

Tom's eyes widened. "Will he physically fight us?"

Azroc waved his hand dismissively. "Nah, it's not a fistfight. It's a battle of wills. Don't worry, though. He'll be rusty. Ajax was used to everyone bending the knee, so I'm betting his willpower isn't what it used to be. You can take him."

Feeling only slightly reassured, Tom watched as Azroc strode toward the towering statue of Ajax. He stood before it, staring up into the angelic figure's cold, contemptuous eyes. Without hesitation, Azroc began moving his hands in a complex pattern, tracing intricate symbols in the air. As he did, a glowing orb of light appeared at chest height, hovering for a moment before he grabbed it and plunged it into Ajax's chest with a swift motion.

The light from the orb vanished, and for a brief moment, everything was still. Then the statue began to glow, a soft light emanating from deep within its stone form. Azroc stepped back, and the glow faded, leaving behind a deep crack that split the forehead of the statue.

The crack widened, snaking down Ajax's face, splitting the stone into jagged fragments. With a sudden, violent movement, Ajax's left fist clenched, causing the stone encasing it to crumble and fall away. Then his right fist followed suit, the stone shedding in large chunks. Slowly, his entire body began to move, stretching out as though waking from a long, oppressive sleep.

With a powerful flex, Ajax spread his wings wide, shaking off the last of the stone that had imprisoned him for centuries. He threw his head back and roared, a deep, guttural sound that echoed through the cavern as he raised his arms to the heavens, his wings extending to their full span.

"Ahhhh, finally! I am free!" Ajax bellowed, his voice filled with triumph. "Those bastards will rue the day they—"

His words faltered as he looked down and saw Azroc standing there, arms crossed, watching him with an amused smile.

"Azroc," Ajax sneered, his voice dripping with condescension. "You came to witness my glorious rebirth, no doubt? To see me reclaim my rightful place as the leader of the Patrons?"

Azroc smirked, not missing a beat. "Hey there, Ajizz. Good to see you back in the land of the living. But, uh, I think you're going to want to take a look at your status. Go on, see for yourself."

INVASION

A flicker of confusion crossed Ajax's face, his angelic features contorting as he focused on something unseen. His eyes grew distant as he accessed the System, likely looking at the familiar status screen only he could see. His expression shifted from arrogance to disbelief, and then to outright horror as he realized what had happened.

"What?!" Ajax growled, his voice thick with disbelief as he continued to stare at the glowing menus only he could see.

"Oh, you see," Azroc began with a mocking grin, "when you decided to go full wanker on the rest of us, the Admins took notice. And let's just say they weren't too thrilled. So, they gave us permission to…" Azroc paused, glancing back at Tom and his companions with a sly smile before returning his gaze to Ajax. "Deal with you."

Ajax's eyes flicked upward, suddenly taking in the group for the first time, his expression darkening. "Mortals?" He spat the word with disgust. "Why are they here?"

"They're with me." Azroc's voice hardened as he stepped forward, his tone growing cold and menacing. "Now, *Ajackoff*, for the crimes you committed against the order, you are hereby sentenced to become a familiar. I know, I know—your power goes beyond that of a typical Summon. But that's fine. We've got a special plan for you." Azroc's grin grew more malicious. "From this moment on, you'll be relegated to the rank of an Ultimate Summon. You will be forced to use your greatest power at the whim of anyone who forms a contract with you. All your lofty titles? Stripped. Replaced with ones more fitting for your new… station. And Tom, here," he added, gesturing casually to Tom, "will be your first contract holder."

Ajax's face contorted into an expression of pure fury, his glowing blue eyes burning with hatred as he stared down at Azroc. "You *cannot* do this! You do not have the authority!"

Azroc let out an amused snort. "Oh, I can, I am, and I do, you arrogant prick."

Ajax's rage boiled over.

"I will *kill* you for this!" he roared, raising his sword high. A blazing light formed in his empty hand, the energy swirling around him as he charged forward.

Azroc didn't even flinch. He lazily raised one hand, stifling a yawn. Ajax froze in mid-air, suspended as though caught in invisible chains. A beam of radiant light snaked out from Azroc's palm, wrapping itself tightly around Ajax's body, binding his arms and wings. Ajax dropped to the floor with a heavy thud, immobilized.

"Release me this instant, you insolent cur!" Ajax snarled, thrashing against the glowing bonds that held him. His wings twitched, but the magical bindings kept them locked firmly in place.

"Yeah, that's not happening." Azroc's tone was flippant as he strolled over to Ajax, crouching down beside him. "For being a colossal asswipe, you're going to serve others for the rest of your miserable existence. And if you refuse?" Azroc leaned in, his voice dropping to a deadly whisper. "It won't be a long existence at all." His eyes gleamed with satisfaction as he added, "This has been determined as the punishment for all those you destroyed in your pathetic quest for power. My, how the mighty have fallen."

Ajax's struggles intensified at those words, his body jerking violently as he tried in vain to break the restraints. But the glowing bonds were unyielding, not even a feather from his pure white wings moved freely.

"Tom," Azroc called out, his voice suddenly light again, "if you'd be so kind as to come over here."

Tom hesitantly approached, his gaze fixed on the now-prone figure of Ajax. Up close, the former Patron was even more imposing.

Ajax was the epitome of physical perfection. His face was so flawless it was almost unnerving—sharp cheekbones, a strong jawline, and piercing blue eyes that still burned with defiance. His bare torso was sculpted, every muscle sharply defined without the excessive bulk of a bodybuilder. It was the kind of chiseled physique that looked more like it belonged to a statue of a Greek god than a living being.

Glistening white armor adorned his lower half, trimmed with gold that shimmered faintly in the dim light of the cavern. His wings, once magnificent, were now trapped under the bindings, their white feathers still sparkling despite the indignity of his situation. Ajax's bright blonde hair framed his face, further adding to his ethereal, angelic appearance.

For a moment, Tom found it difficult to look away. There was something mesmerizing about Ajax's appearance, a beauty so overwhelming that it stirred something deep inside him. Yet that beauty was marred by the raw hatred and fury in Ajax's eyes as he glared at Tom, his perfect features twisted with loathing.

"Yeah, he's a looker, isn't he?" Azroc's voice cut through Tom's thoughts, a knowing smirk on his face. "But don't let that distract you. He's still a colossal douchebag under all that perfection."

"What are you staring at, human?" Ajax sneered, his piercing blue eyes narrowing at Tom.

Snapping out of his stupor, Tom glanced at Azroc for guidance.

"Order him to form a contract with you," Azroc said, his voice firm yet almost amused by Tom's brief hesitation.

Tom nodded, realizing his mouth had been hanging open, and closed it quickly.

Turning back to Ajax, he steeled his voice. "Ajax, you will form a contract with me."

Ajax snarled viciously, his glistening wings twitching with tension as he renewed his struggle against the magical bonds. His body writhed against the restraints, fury etched into every line of his sculpted face.

"No! You cannot make me!" Ajax spat through gritted teeth, his once majestic figure now contorted in defiance.

"Oh, yes, he can. And he will," Azroc replied casually, a mocking grin tugging at the corners of his lips.

Suddenly, Ajax ceased his thrashing and looked up, his eyes burning with cold contempt. "I have the right to refuse a weak master," he said, his voice dripping with scorn as his gaze pierced into Tom.

INVASION

Azroc raised an eyebrow.

"You are correct. That is the prerogative of *all* Summons. But I think you'll find that Tom is more than capable of being your master." His eyes gleamed with amusement as he glanced between the two. "According to the ancient laws, a contest of wills will decide if you are worthy to command Ajax. Prepare yourselves."

The moment the words left Azroc's mouth, the world around Tom began to dim, as though the very light itself was being swallowed by an unseen force. His heart skipped a beat as the familiar environment of the cavern dissolved into darkness, and it felt as if he were plummeting into a bottomless void.

As the sensation of falling began to slow, a vast stone platform appeared beneath him, rising up from the void like a monolith from the depths of space. Intricate patterns were carved into the platform's surface, glowing faintly with a soft blue light. The designs reminded Tom of the ornate medallions carved into the floors of the ancient cathedrals he had once visited in New York—symbols of power and faith.

The glow from the platform grew stronger, and the darkness around him receded, giving way to the vastness of space. Tom gasped as the universe unfolded before his eyes. Millions upon millions of stars blinked into view, their light shimmering against the infinite black void like a celestial tapestry. Galaxies swirled in the distance, spiraling majestically as if they were dancing to an unseen rhythm, their colors vivid and brilliant against the backdrop of eternity.

He felt small—insignificant in the face of the cosmic wonder that surrounded him. The scale of it all was staggering. The stars were close enough that Tom felt like he could reach out and pluck one from the sky, hold it in his hand, and marvel at its brilliance. The immensity of the universe, once only an abstract concept, now seemed so overwhelming that it made him feel utterly vulnerable.

For a fleeting moment, Tom was paralyzed by the grandeur of it all. He thought of astronauts staring out into the endless void, their understanding of the universe forever altered by the incomprehensible scale of it. He could understand now why some would return to Earth forever changed by the silence and the majesty of the cosmos.

His mind teetered on the edge of breaking from the sheer realization of his own insignificance. The vastness of what he was witnessing was only a fraction of the multiverse that Azroc had hinted at—whole other planes of reality stacked atop one another like the delicate layers of an incomprehensible baklava.

"Focus, shithead," Azroc's voice cut through the swirling thoughts in Tom's mind. "This isn't the time to get lost in an existential crisis. You need to fight Ajax."

Tom blinked, shaking his head to clear it, and found himself back on the platform.

"You will have all your Skills and abilities," Azroc's voice echoed in his mind, "and Ajax will have those fitting his new form. He's been scaled to your power level, but don't mistake that for weakness. He's still dangerous. You'll have to fight with everything you've learned. Use your cunning, your experience, your will." There was a pause before Azroc added, with a touch of pride, "I believe in you. Show me why you're my favorite Warlock."

Tom's gaze flicked across the platform to where Ajax stood. The former Patron looked completely at ease, swinging his sword a few times to loosen his muscles, still stiff from his long petrification. He barely seemed to acknowledge Tom's presence, as if the mortal standing before him was of no consequence.

"I won't let you down, Azroc," Tom whispered, gripping the hilt of his greatsword as the weight of the challenge settled into his bones. He could feel the tension building in the air, a palpable electricity crackling around them as the contest of wills began to take shape.

Across the platform, Ajax continued to stretch, completely unconcerned, his face still holding that sneer of disdain. He swung his sword lazily, his movements graceful but casual, as if he were warming up for an easy sparring match rather than preparing for a battle for his freedom.

Tom squared his shoulders, planting his feet firmly on the stone platform. He felt the familiar weight of his greatsword in his hands, and the tension in his muscles gave way to resolve. He was ready.

"I hope you're ready for me, Ajax," Tom said, his voice steady and filled with determination. "I'm not holding anything back!"

Chapter 59

Heavenly Duel

"You have no idea what you've gotten yourself into, mortal," Ajax chuckled darkly, raising his glowing sword and pointing it directly at Tom. His wings fluttered slightly, the motion causing a faint breeze that rippled across the cosmic platform. "Did you know that if you die here, your body will die as well? This is not some mere mental projection. This is your soul on the line."

Tom hesitated for a fraction of a second, the weight of Ajax's words sinking in. He could feel the threat hanging in the air, but his determination flared like a beacon against the vastness of the universe surrounding them.

He straightened, tightening his grip on his greatsword, his eyes locking with Ajax's unflinching stare. "This isn't my first life or death struggle. Hell, it's not my first one this week. So, I guess I'll just have to beat the shit out of you."

A flicker of surprise crossed Ajax's face. He hadn't expected such defiance. After a brief pause, he smiled again, but this time, it was almost a grin of respect.

"I admire your spirit," Ajax said, his voice like molten gold—rich and smooth but filled with an underlying sense of threat. "Not many would dare stand against someone like me. Fewer still would have the courage to fight. But it won't save you."

With a mighty flap of his wings, Ajax rose a foot off the ground, hovering effortlessly in the air as if gravity had no claim over him. His form radiated raw power, his sword gleaming in the celestial light of the surrounding stars.

Tom, not one to be intimidated, fired off a *Dark Ball* spell, his hand flicking forward as dark, shadowy energy spiraled toward Ajax. But with a casual flick of his sword, Ajax batted the spell aside like it was nothing.

"You didn't honestly think that would work, did you?" Ajax asked, his voice dripping with condescension.

Tom blinked, genuinely taken aback by the display.

"I gotta admit, I didn't even know you could do that with a sword," he said, impressed despite himself.

"As long as it's a magical sword," Ajax replied, the amusement in his voice evident.

"Can you shoot one at me so I can try?" Tom quipped, a sly grin forming.

Ajax's eyes narrowed, his patience thinning. "Are we here for show-and-tell or to fight?"

"You're right. My bad. Let's do this."

Without another word, Tom lunged forward, his greatsword raised high as he closed the distance. The sound of metal clashing against metal rang out as Ajax parried the strike with ease. In one smooth motion, Ajax countered, thrusting his blade at Tom's chest with deadly precision.

Tom shifted just enough to the left, narrowly avoiding the lethal blow as the blade whistled past his ear. He hopped back, creating space between them, a confident smile playing at his lips. "I feel like you're holding back, Ajax. Playing with your food, maybe?"

"You're better than I expected," Ajax admitted, his expression growing more serious. "I promise I won't take it so easy anymore."

In the blink of an eye, Ajax blurred forward, his speed nearly impossible to track. Tom barely had time to react as he rolled to his right, dodging the blur of movement. He sprang back to his feet just in time to block a strike aimed directly at his head. The force of the blow sent a shockwave through his arms, and if Tom hadn't ducked under it, the sword would have been pushed into his own throat.

"Whoo!" Tom let out a breath, shaking his arms out from the impact. "You weren't kidding. Alright, guess it's time I stop playing around too."

With a deep breath, Tom activated his *Tattoo of Brute Strength*. Power surged through his veins, igniting every muscle with newfound energy. The familiar warmth of enhanced strength flooded his body, making him feel invincible. When Ajax's next strike came, Tom raised his sword confidently, stopping the blow dead in its tracks.

Ajax's eyes widened slightly in surprise. "That's a fine blade you have," Ajax remarked, his voice straining with effort as their swords ground against each other in a clash of raw power. Their weapons screeched and sparked as they pressed against one another, each trying to overpower the other.

"Thanks," Tom grinned, his muscles flexing as he held the line. "You should see the other one."

With a quick motion, Tom summoned a second greatsword into his free hand and swung it toward Ajax. The angelic being barrel-rolled in midair, folding his wings tight against his body to avoid the strike. He unfurled them again just in time to land gracefully a few feet away, his wings spread wide, now fully alert to Tom's increased threat level.

"You're full of surprises, aren't you?" Ajax said, his eyes narrowing as he hovered just above the ground, now taking Tom far more seriously.

"I'm just getting warmed up," Tom replied, his voice filled with confidence as he readied both of his greatswords.

With a single thought, Tom activated *Dark Inferno* on his Greatsword of Hell's Inferno. The blade immediately ignited with dark, swirling purple flames that licked hungrily at the steel, casting eerie shadows that danced across the ground. The heat from the infernal fire pulsed through the air, a tangible force that warped the space around the sword.

Without breaking eye contact with Ajax, Tom reached over to his other sword, touching the tip of the flaming blade to its brother. Instantly, the dark fire spread, eagerly consuming the second weapon in a wash of flickering, umbral flames. Both swords now burned with an ethereal, malevolent light, the combined heat crackling in the silence of the battlefield. The power within them surged through Tom, filling him with a sense of raw, destructive energy.

Ajax's eyes narrowed ever so slightly, betraying the first flicker of unease. His once unwavering confidence faltered, if only for a moment.

"That's a neat trick," he said, trying to sound unfazed, though the hint of concern behind his words was unmistakable as he observed the unnatural flames dancing along the blades.

"Thanks. Just a little something I've been experimenting with."

The air crackled with energy as they charged at each other once more, the sound of their blades clashing ringing out like thunder. Tom's attacks came fast and furious, his dual-wielding swords a whirlwind of steel and fury. He pressed the advantage, using every bit of technique and training Bron had drilled into him, mixing heavy sword strikes with quick kicks and jabs.

For a moment, it seemed like Tom was gaining the upper hand. He could see Ajax struggling to keep up, his parries becoming more desperate as Tom's relentless assault continued. But then, in an instant, everything changed.

Ajax's movements became a blur, faster than before. Tom's heart pounded in his chest as he realized he was now on the defensive. The angelic figure moved with supernatural speed, each strike more precise and deadly than the last. Tom blocked one swing, then another, but suddenly felt a sharp sting on his arm as a glowing blade sliced through his defense. Another flash of pain shot through his leg as Ajax's sword found its mark again.

He was losing ground—physically and mentally. Each step back was a desperate attempt to keep up with Ajax's incredible speed. Cuts began to form on his arms and legs, not deep, but enough to slow him down. Blood trickled from the wounds, and Tom's breath came in short, ragged gasps.

Ajax's sneer widened. "Still think you can win, mortal?" he taunted, his eyes gleaming with predatory satisfaction.

Gritting his teeth, Tom activated his *Tattoo of Life Absorption*, and immediately, a surge of energy flowed into him from Ajax. He could feel his wounds closing, the pain subsiding as Ajax's life force was siphoned away. Ajax's eyes went wide in realization, and his lips curled back into a snarl.

"Resorting to such lowly tricks! I will destroy you!" Ajax bellowed, fury flashing in his celestial eyes.

With a mighty overhead swing, Ajax brought his sword down on Tom's, the sheer force of the blow sending Tom sliding back almost ten yards across the stone platform. The impact reverberated through Tom's arms, but he maintained his grip, digging his heels in as he regained his footing. Rising to his full height, Tom locked eyes with Ajax, who stood fuming, his wings beating with unrestrained fury.

"I'll just have to finish you faster, then," Ajax roared, launching himself forward with terrifying speed.

But Tom hadn't wasted the brief reprieve. Just as Ajax's sword was about to strike, a summoning circle flared to life at Tom's side, and Onslo appeared in a flash, raising his own sword just in time to block Ajax's powerful strike.

"Well, that was close," Onslo said with his usual nonchalance.

Ajax's eyes flared with indignation. "What?! You cannot beat me on your own, so you bring in outside help? I thought you were a man!" he spat angrily.

Tom smirked, his eyes gleaming with defiance.

"All's fair in love and war," he taunted, not missing a beat.

Ajax screamed in rage, flapping his mighty wings to gain altitude, trying to put distance between himself and Tom's summoned ally.

As he ascended, something darted out from the shadows—Kuthir, daggers in hand. One of his blades dripped with blood, having found its mark before Ajax even noticed his presence.

"I will not be bested by the likes of—" Ajax's words were cut off abruptly when a blur of skin and claws slammed into his face—a demonic chicken, summoned by Tom, latched onto his head, furiously pecking and biting at his flesh.

Ajax screeched in pain and fury as he thrashed in the air, desperately clawing at the creature to pry it loose. His elegant wings beat frantically, but the chicken held firm, its talons digging in as it sought to feast on its celestial prey.

Seizing the opportunity, Onslo positioned himself beneath Ajax, sheathing his sword and crouching down. He laced his fingers together, ready to act.

"Kuthir!" he shouted.

The Rogue Mastadonian grinned as he understood the plan, sprinting toward Onslo with lethal grace. Reaching his comrade, Kuthir stepped into Onslo's laced hands. With a powerful burst, Onslo hurled Kuthir upward with all his strength. Kuthir soared into the air, flipping at the apex of his jump just as Ajax managed to stab the demonic chicken, finally ripping it off and tossing it aside in disgust.

But before Ajax could fully recover, Kuthir's foot connected with his chest in a perfectly executed aerial kick, the force of which sent Ajax plummeting back to the ground like a meteor. The impact was so violent that the stone platform cracked beneath the Celestine, sending a shockwave through the arena.

Ajax gasped in pain as his wings audibly snapped, the bones shattering from the fall. His once-proud wings now hung useless at his sides, broken and twisted.

Tom, seeing the opening, rushed forward with everything he had. He stowed away his swords mid-sprint, leaping onto Ajax's prone form. With unrelenting fury, Tom pummeled Ajax's face with massive, earth-shaking punches. Each blow landed with a sickening thud, bruising the once-perfect features of the celestial being.

Again and again, Tom's fists crashed down. Ajax's face was a mask of blood and pain, but still, the Celestine fought back.

With a desperate surge of strength, Ajax managed to raise a hand to shield his face from further blows. Summoning every ounce of strength, he struck back, landing a vicious punch to Tom's gut.

The force of the punch sent Tom flying off Ajax, knocking the wind from his lungs. Gasping for breath, Tom rolled across the stone, struggling to regain his footing. But before Ajax could capitalize on his moment of reprieve, Onslo was there. Sword raised high, the Mastadonian Warrior loomed over Ajax's broken form, his eyes filled with cold determination as he prepared to deliver the final blow.

"Don't kill him!" Tom shouted, scrambling to his feet, his voice cutting through the chaos of the battle.

Onslo, already in mid-strike, shifted his aim at the last second. Instead of delivering a killing blow, his blade sliced deep into Ajax's left arm. Ajax let out a howl of pain, his arm falling limp at his side. The Celestine retaliated by kicking out in desperation, forcing Onslo to leap back to avoid being tripped.

Ajax began to rise, his once-proud wings now mangled, dragging along the ground. He stood hunched, but the defiant gleam in his eyes remained undimmed. Onslo and Kuthir immediately moved to flank Tom, their weapons drawn, prepared for whatever this god-like creature might throw at them next.

Suddenly, a low, menacing chuckle escaped Ajax's lips. "Hehehehe… HAHAHAHAHA!" His laughter grew louder, more unhinged, reverberating through the vast expanse of the platform. "Maybe you *are* a worthy master, after all," he said, his voice filled with a twisted sort of admiration. "But this fight is far from over."

Without warning, a brilliant flash of green light enveloped Ajax. The others watched in horror as the wounds covering his body began to close, the mangled feathers of his wings repairing themselves as if time itself had reversed. Within moments, Ajax stood tall once more, fully healed, his body restored to its original, terrifying condition.

Tom's eyes widened in shock. "What the hell was that?"

"Likely a full restoration spell," Kuthir replied, his voice steady despite the dire situation. "It's a high-level healing spell. It can only be used once per day, though, so we just need to bang him up again."

Ajax stretched his limbs, testing the renewed strength of his body, a predatory smile curling his lips. "I haven't had to use this form in centuries. I must thank you, human. It is a rare thing to force me to take such measures. I'm almost impressed."

Tom's heart sank as Ajax's body began to radiate with an intense, heavenly white light. The Celestine let out a primal, deafening yell, his muscles swelling with power as veins bulged across his chest, arms, and forehead. The energy swirling around him grew with every passing second, thickening the air with its oppressive force.

Then, to the team's horror, four additional wings erupted from Ajax's back, unfurling to their full, majestic span. A golden halo materialized above his head, glowing with divine light. His muscles, already formidable, nearly doubled in size. His hair and the tattered cloth hanging from his armor whipped around him in the supernatural breeze generated by his raw power.

The transformation was nothing short of awe-inspiring—and utterly terrifying. Ajax hovered off the ground, now surrounded by a blinding aura of celestial might. As the transformation reached its peak, a powerful shockwave exploded outward from his body, sending cracks spidering through the platform beneath him. Then, as suddenly as it had begun, the light vanished, leaving Ajax glowing faintly in the dim light.

"Well… shit," Tom muttered, staring up at the newly transformed Ajax.

"You should summon the others," Onslo said, his usual calm demeanor slipping as he tightened his grip on his sword.

"I already tried," Tom replied, frustration evident in his voice. "I think I'd have to dismiss their permanent status before I could bring them back."

Kuthir looked at him, a glint of mischief in his eye. "I'm sure they'll understand. After all, it's not like you had a choice."

Tom nodded, knowing Kuthir was right. "Alright, I'll do it."

Ajax watched the conversation unfold with bemused detachment, hovering just above them with his arms crossed over his broad chest. His confidence radiated off him in waves, a chilling reminder of his overwhelming power.

"No matter how many minions you summon, they won't save you now," he said arrogantly. "Go on, try. I'll wait."

Tom frowned, his mind racing as he weighed his options. The Celestine's power had grown exponentially, far beyond what Tom had anticipated. He could feel the pressure building in his chest, a deep sense of foreboding settling in the pit of his stomach. Ajax wasn't bluffing—his strength was real, and Tom knew the battle ahead would be the most difficult he had ever faced.

Taking a deep breath, Tom made his decision. He couldn't face Ajax alone, not now. With a wave of his hand, he dismissed the permanent status of all the Mastadonians, the familiar pang of guilt hitting him as he thought of the inevitable conversations to come. They wouldn't be happy about this, but there was no time to dwell on it. As the dismissal took effect, he began summoning them again, one by one.

The summoning circles flared to life, glowing brightly as each of the Mastadonians stepped forward, weapons at the ready. Ajax, still floating, smiled faintly, his eyes gleaming with anticipation.

"Ah, more playthings. This should be entertaining."

With his full team of seven Mastadonians summoned, Tom crouched into a fighting stance, gripping both his swords tightly, the weight of the battle ahead pressing down on him.

"So, it's that bad?" Bron rumbled, his deep voice cutting through the tension as he took his place beside Tom.

"Well, it's not Disneyland," Tom quipped.

Bron raised an eyebrow, clearly confused.

Tom sighed. "It's supposedly the happiest place on Earth," he explained.

"Ah, sarcasm, I see," Bron replied, the corner of his mouth twitching into a half-smile. "Then it's time to take this seriously."

"As opposed to what?" Tom shot back, his grip tightening on his swords.

Bron's face darkened as he stared at Ajax, still hovering above them like a malevolent god. "I need you to summon one more of our kind. His name is Rularis."

Inari, standing nearby, stiffened immediately. "No, brother. He cannot be trusted," she said sharply, her voice cold with warning.

INVASION

"It must be done. You can feel the power of this being," Bron replied, his words heavy with finality.

Inari clenched her fists but didn't argue further. The tension between them hung in the air, thick and unspoken.

Tom looked between them, confused. "Who's Rularis?"

"He is a Bard," Bron explained, his eyes never leaving Ajax. "He will aid us in this fight if he still holds to his vow. He completes the party, and we've never lost a battle together."

"That's good enough for me," Tom said with a nod. He quickly pulled out a mana potion, downed it in one swig, and began the incantation for one additional summoning.

As a swirling black circle appeared on the ground, the air grew heavier with the feeling of impending chaos. From the dark mist, a figure emerged, draped in what appeared to be a jester's garb, bright and colorful, yet unnervingly at odds with the grim atmosphere. The figure struck a dramatic pose, one knee bent, toes barely touching the ground, with one hand raised to his forehead, his head tilted down as if in mock reverence.

"Bron… it's been so long. Are we finally ready for the main event to begin?" Rularis said, his voice sing-song and playful, though his eyes gleamed with a manic intensity.

Bron merely gestured toward Ajax, who still hovered above them, looking down with thinly veiled amusement.

"Well, well, well… I'll be a bostooth's uncle—a Celestine," Rularis said, sounding even more entertained by the sight of their celestial opponent. His eyes danced with mischief.

As Rularis turned his attention to Tom, he seemed to find a new fascination. "And who is this… young Warlock?"

"I'm Tom," Tom replied flatly, not interested in playing along with Rularis' antics. "Nice to meet you and all that jazz, but we've got something to take care of right now. Will you help us?"

Rularis looked back and forth between Ajax and Tom before grinning wickedly. "Yes… yes, this should be *fun*."

"Do not forget your vow, Rularis," Inari hissed, her voice full of venom.

"Temper, temper, dear sister," Rularis chided mockingly, waving his hand dismissively. "I have not forgotten the words that bind me. I'll be a good boy. Promise." He winked at her, his smile never faltering. "How could I not when we've been brought such quality entertainment?"

Ajax's patience was clearly wearing thin. "Are you quite done yet?" he growled, his voice reverberating like thunder. "My patience does have a limit."

Tom rolled his eyes, shouting back up at the floating Celestine, "Hold your horses. We're almost ready!"

Bron's face grew grim as he sized up Ajax once more. "This will not be easy," he muttered. "But we can do it. We just have to keep up the pressure and—"

"I can hear your strategy meeting, you know," Ajax interrupted, his voice dripping with disdain.

Tom glared up at him, his frustration boiling over. "Dude, you're an even bigger prick than Azroc said you were. Butt out!"

For the first time since their confrontation began, Ajax's smile faded, replaced with a dangerous snarl. His eyes narrowed, and his aura flared with a pulse of raw energy. "You will pay for this insolence," he hissed. "I'm done waiting for you. We begin *now*!"

Chapter 60

Ultimate Summons

Ajax charged forward, his speed blurring the space between himself and Tom's team in the blink of an eye. The force of his movement was like a tempest, the ground shaking beneath him. Bron was ready. With a mighty swing, his greataxe met Ajax's sword in a clash of titanic forces, the impact sending a shockwave through the battlefield.

"Now!" Bron roared, his deep voice cutting through the chaos.

At his command, the Mastadonians moved in perfect unison, each of them splitting off in different directions, forming a circle around the Celestine. Their goal was clear: overwhelm him with pressure from every angle. Tom, positioned slightly behind the action, activated two of his tattoos simultaneously—*Tattoo of the Summoner* and *Tattoo of Inspiration*. A wave of power surged through the battlefield, amplifying the abilities of every Mastadonian. Their movements became sharper, faster, their strikes more powerful.

Ajax began to laugh, the sound dark and guttural, as he twirled his blade with near-impossible precision, deflecting blows from all sides. The attacks came at him relentlessly, but he seemed to move with the ease of a predator toying with its prey. Even as the team closed in, each of their strikes was met with resistance, blocked by his sword or dodged with supernatural grace.

Off to the side, Rularis stood, his jester's garb fluttering as he struck up a haunting tune on an ancient sitar-like instrument. The eerie music filled the air, each note buzzing with a harmonic resonance that vibrated deep within Tom's bones. It wasn't like anything he'd ever heard before—a symphony of minor keys that evoked feelings of longing and despair, like echoes of a forgotten time. Rularis began to sing, his voice a low, rumbling baritone, and the words seemed to swirl in the air with their own magic.

The song spoke of love lost, of hope crumbling into nothingness. Each word struck Tom's heart like a dagger, filling him with a sorrow so deep it was almost unbearable. At the same time, the song stirred something else—an anger, a fury born from that very sorrow, rising within his chest like a fire. He could feel the energy it gave him, the way it enhanced his focus and sharpened his determination. This was the power of a true performer, a Bard who wielded music as both a weapon and a shield.

Kiera's good, but this... Tom thought as he realized just how different Rularis' song was.

Kiera's songs had always been useful—powerful, even—but they had often been light-hearted tunes, adapted from pop culture, fitting the situation but never truly gripping the soul. Rularis' performance was something else entirely, manipulating Tom's emotions in ways he hadn't thought possible.

The emotions washed over him in waves—joy, sorrow, love, hatred—each one hitting harder than the last, fueling his resolve, his strength. He could feel the power coursing through him, the melody resonating with the very core of his being, making him faster, stronger, more in tune with the battle around him.

Then, with one final, heart-wrenching note, the music shifted. The tone darkened, and the melody became oppressive and heavy. Tom recognized the change immediately—this wasn't a song meant to inspire.

This one was for Ajax.

Ajax's movements slowed ever so slightly as the new tune wove its magic around him. He gritted his teeth, trying to push through it, but the effect was undeniable. Bron seized the opportunity, pressing forward with a flurry of powerful strikes from his greataxe, each one aimed at forcing the Celestine to give ground. Kuthir darted in and out of the shadows, his daggers flashing as he struck at Ajax's blind spots with deadly precision. Inari, standing at a distance, fired arrow after arrow from her massive bow, each shot aimed to either disrupt Ajax's balance or distract him.

Huthu, meanwhile, was a force of nature, charging in with shoulder slams that rattled even Ajax's mighty form, forcing the Celestine to stagger under the repeated blows. Amath and Belik, the team's spellcasters, circled the battlefield, looking for any chance to unleash their magic. But Ajax seemed to possess a natural resistance to spells, and Amath, frustrated, shifted to a more defensive role, focusing on shielding his teammates from the Celestine's wrath.

Despite the relentless assault, Ajax's laughter only grew more maniacal, his eyes blazing with fury as he slowly but surely began to adjust to the pressure. Even with Rularis' song slowing him down, Ajax's skill and power were undeniable. His sword moved with deadly grace, cutting through the air in perfect arcs as he blocked, dodged, and parried the onslaught of attacks.

Then, with a grunt of effort, Ajax vanished from the center of the battle.

"What the hell?!" Tom shouted, his eyes darting around the battlefield, searching for any sign of the Celestine.

Bron growled, gripping his axe tighter. "Stay alert! He's not done yet!"

Tom anticipated where Ajax would strike next—it was exactly what he would have done in the same situation. The moment Ajax disappeared, Tom activated his *Tattoo of Displacement*, vanishing and reappearing beside Rularis in the blink of an eye. Just as Ajax materialized and swung his sword down toward the Mastadonian Bard, Tom was already there to intercept the strike. His greatsword clashed with Ajax's blade, the force sending a shockwave through the air as sparks flew from the edge of the collision. The blade stopped mere inches from slicing into Rularis' head.

Rularis' song paused for the briefest of moments, the note hanging in the air for just a beat too long, before he continued playing with hardly a hitch. He stepped back, allowing Tom to take center stage, as if he hadn't just been inches from death. In that same instant, Kuthir appeared behind Ajax, his blade gleaming in the faint light.

With a precise slash, Kuthir's blade severed one of Ajax's wings in a fountain of blood, the dark crimson spray painting the stone platform beneath them.

Ajax howled in pain and fury, spinning around with murder in his eyes to face Kuthir. But the nimble Rogue had already vanished into the shadows. Realizing his prey was now concealed, Ajax let out a snarl and began to emit a radiant glow. His body pulsed with light, and the shadows that had been Kuthir's sanctuary were swiftly dispelled. Kuthir's position was revealed—crouched low, eyes narrowed in focus—but he darted to the side just as Ajax lunged at him.

Onslo met Ajax's charge head-on, blocking the attack with his sword. The force of the collision sent a jolt through the air, but Onslo stood firm. Huthu, in a Barbarian's rage, charged into the fray as well, his eyes bloodshot and his enormous maul whirling toward Ajax with unstoppable force. Ajax barely managed to sidestep the brutal attack, and the maul slammed into the platform, shattering the stone and sending cracks spider-webbing across the ground.

Whipping around in a full circle, Ajax attempted a counterstrike, aiming for Huthu's exposed side. But before his sword could connect, a shimmering barrier appeared, blocking the blow. Amath had conjured the protective spell just in time. Ajax roared in frustration as he was once again denied a clean hit.

The frustration boiled over, and with a scream of rage, Ajax unleashed a wave of raw magical energy from his body. The sheer force of it sent Tom and the Mastadonians flying backward, each of them hitting the ground with a heavy thud.

"I grow tired of these games," Ajax spat, his voice dripping with disdain. "You pathetic mortals are a disgrace to the power I've accumulated. It's time for you all to die!"

Rising into the air once more, Ajax began summoning orbs of pure energy, which formed a perfect circle around his body. One by one, they shot forward like relentless bullets, each aimed at Tom and his team. Every time one orb fired, another took its place, creating an endless barrage of attacks. Amath hastily erected barriers around the group, the magic shields absorbing the brunt of the assault. But the strain was evident—cracks began to splinter across the barriers as the relentless orbs pounded against them.

Tom exchanged a desperate glance with Bron. The Mastadonian Warrior, sensing the urgency of the situation, made a bold decision. He nodded grimly at Tom and, without hesitation, Tom activated his *Tattoo of Magic Nullification*.

Immediately, the world seemed to shift. The barrage of energy ceased, Ajax's orbs of destruction evaporating into thin air. The barriers Amath had conjured flickered and vanished, and Tom felt the familiar magical touch of his ability to use spells disappear. But more importantly, Ajax plummeted from the sky, crashing onto the stone platform with a bone-rattling thud. He staggered to his feet, visibly off balance, his once-graceful movements now slow and clumsy.

Bron saw his opportunity and charged, and the others followed suit, closing in on Ajax with renewed determination.

"No!" Ajax screamed, panic flashing in his eyes. But it was too late.

The team surrounded him, their attacks coming from every direction. Tom swung his greatswords with brutal efficiency, the dark flames licking at Ajax's skin as the Celestine struggled to block the blows. Kuthir slashed at his legs, Inari shot arrows into his exposed wings, and Onslo and Huthu hammered him with unrelenting physical strikes.

Without his magic to fuel him, Ajax was vulnerable, his divine strength drained. His once-superhuman speed had diminished, and he could no longer keep up with the coordinated assault. The blows came too quickly, too powerfully, for him to defend against. His muscular form—so imposing at the start of the battle—now seemed hollow, his movements sluggish and desperate.

Tom hadn't realized just how much of Ajax's abilities were rooted in his magic. With his powers nullified, he was little more than a mortal being, albeit a very strong one. Tom and his team abandoned their weapons, choosing instead to beat Ajax down with their bare fists, their punches and kicks raining down on him in a relentless onslaught.

Ajax tried to shield himself, curling into a ball, covering his head with his wings and hands, but it was no use. The once-mighty Celestine had been reduced to a whimpering, sobbing wreck, cowering beneath the flurry of attacks.

"I surrender!" Ajax finally cried out, his voice cracking with pain and humiliation. "You win! I... I submit!"

The team paused, their fists raised, ready to continue. But as they looked down at the trembling figure of Ajax, shaking uncontrollably on the ground, they realized the fight was truly over.

They had won.

"I really wish I had pulled that move out at the beginning," Tom muttered as he stood over the now-pitiful form of Ajax. He gazed down at the broken Celestine, who only moments ago had been so full of confidence and arrogance, and smiled. "My, how the mighty have fallen. It's strange, really, how many opponents rely so heavily on magic to augment their abilities. You should have trained harder, Ajax. Now, you'll serve me."

As Tom spoke, the strange platform of the battle of wills began to fade, dissolving back into the room they had stood in before the confrontation began. The dark stone floor was replaced with the carved magic circle, and the dazzling lights of distant stars were swallowed by the dim light of the underground chamber.

Tom's heart ached as the celestial vision faded, replaced by the ordinary walls of the room. The vibrant beauty of the universe he had just witnessed lingered in his mind, making everything around him feel dull and lifeless. What once seemed familiar now felt mundane, as though the world he knew was merely a shadow of the brilliance he had just glimpsed.

The intricate carvings, the rough stone floors, the very air itself—all of it felt plain and uninspired compared to the boundless heavens he had stood beneath moments before. It was as though everything he once considered beautiful had been stripped of its luster, reduced to the equivalent of discarded trash in the face of the cosmic grandeur he had experienced.

A deep sigh escaped him as he struggled to shake off the lingering sense of loss. Even with the accomplishments of the recent battle, the hard-won victories seemed less significant. How could any of it compare to the vastness, the infinite wonder of the universe laid bare before him? For a fleeting moment, he had touched something beyond mortal comprehension, and now it was gone, leaving behind a hollow, aching void in his chest.

With a determined breath, Tom forced himself to focus on the present. He knew he couldn't linger in that longing for the stars—there was still much to do. But the memory of that celestial beauty would forever remain with him, a reminder of the deeper mysteries that lay beyond the limits of his world.

Azroc stood there waiting, a wide grin plastered across his face as he clapped slowly in approval. Tom and the Mastadonians, exhausted and relieved, stood around Ajax's crumpled form.

"Great work, shithead," Azroc said affectionately, his tone congratulatory, though still laced with his signature mockery. "I knew you'd be able to pull it off. That last move was risky as hell, but you nailed it. You hit Ajax right where it hurt most."

Tom wiped the sweat from his brow and looked at Azroc skeptically. "Did you know about his weakness beforehand?"

Azroc shook his head. "Nope. Honestly, I wasn't sure what rules would apply to that fight. The System sometimes tweaks these 'battles of wills' for whatever reason it likes. But once Ajax started fighting, I saw it. I wasn't allowed to interfere, though. System rules, and all that shit."

Tom glanced down at Ajax, who was still curled up on the floor, arms wrapped around his knees. The once-majestic figure now looked frail and beaten, his additional wings and greater form having disappeared. The proud, powerful Celestine was reduced to a sobbing shell, his once-mighty appearance gone.

"Get up, Ajax. You still have a purpose to serve," Azroc commanded, his voice dripping with disdain.

Ajax slowly shifted his gaze upward, his eyes red and swollen from tears. "What's the point? I've been bested by a mortal. I have no reason to continue."

"Ajax," Tom said, stepping forward and softening his tone, "I need you for what's coming. There's an invasion of my planet—an injustice that can't go unanswered. I can't do this alone."

Ajax looked up at Tom, confusion flickering across his face. It was clear he didn't understand why Tom, a mortal who had just defeated him, would ask for his help.

"You want *my* help?" Ajax asked cautiously, his voice shaking slightly.

"That was the point of the battle," Tom explained. "You're my trump card in our fight to save this world. We're up against pirates who want to kill everyone here. Frankly, we're not sure we can win without you."

Ajax blinked, clearly surprised. "I thought you just wanted to kill me. You and Azroc—for everything I've done."

Azroc snorted. "Oh, don't get me wrong. I'd still love to wipe your ass off the map with the roughest toilet paper known to the multiverse, you worthless skidmark. But Tom here needed help, and lucky for you, that's what you're going to provide. Consider it your penance."

Ajax hesitated, his eyes flicking between Azroc and Tom. Slowly, the remnants of pride seemed to stir within him. He sat up, his movement shaky at first, but then he rose to his feet with newfound resolve. The fallen Celestine, though clearly humbled, began to straighten his posture, as though trying to regain some measure of dignity.

"I think I could live with that," Ajax said, nodding. "You are truly strong for a mortal, Tom. And this fight you speak of—it does sound like an injustice that must be corrected. Very well, I will join you. You can call upon my power to aid in this battle."

Ajax extended his hand toward Tom, offering a sign of submission. Tom hesitated for a brief moment, then reached out and grasped the Celestine's hand. The two shook, and as they did, a brilliant light enveloped Ajax's body, lifting him gently off the ground.

The light intensified, growing so bright that Tom had to shield his eyes. The radiant glow bathed the room in warmth for a few seconds before abruptly winking out.

A message appeared in Tom's vision.

Ultimate Summons Acquired

You have acquired the Ultimate Summons, Ajax. Unlike normal Summons, an Ultimate Summon can only be used in a single-attack capacity. When you summon Ajax, he will unleash his ultimate attack on your enemies, bringing justice to those who have wronged you. Be warned: use of this power may have unintended effects on those with darker intentions.

Tom felt a moment of confusion at the mention of a single-attack Summon but realized it reminded him of the old *Final Fantasy* games he played as a teenager. The thought brought a nostalgic smile to his face. He chuckled to himself before waving the prompt away from his vision.

Turning to the Mastadonians, Tom addressed them with a hint of apology in his tone, "Sorry about summoning you all from your previous tasks. I'll make sure to explain everything to everyone back at the Guild. It was necessary, but I know it was inconvenient."

Bron stepped forward, his massive form imposing as ever, but his voice was calm and steady. "It was no trouble at all. You needed us, and we came. That's all that matters."

Derek, who had been watching the group with furrowed brows, finally spoke up, unable to hide his curiosity. "What the hell happened in there? You were gone for ages, and now it feels like something's changed."

INVASION

Tom sighed, rolling his shoulders as though trying to shake off the weight of the encounter. "I'll fill you in on the way back. Let's get moving. We have a lot to do, and we finally have an ace up our sleeves."

Without another word, the group started making their way back toward the surface, the soft clinking of weapons and gear the only sound as they ascended from the dark depths where Ajax had been sealed. Tom's mind raced, considering what they had just accomplished and the massive challenges still looming on the horizon.

As they walked, Tom glanced around at his companions, grateful for their steadfast loyalty. The Mastadonians had answered his call without question, and now, with Ajax as their reluctant ally, the next phase of their plan felt a little more secure.

They were far from finished, but for the first time in a while, Tom felt like they had a real chance.

Chapter 61

New Skill

"Hey, shithead, we aren't done here," Azroc called out as Tom and his team began making their way out.

Tom paused, confused, and turned back to face Azroc. "What?"

"If you leave now, Achimp over there just disappears into the ether, hoping that no one will be able to summon him," Azroc explained, irritation clear in his voice.

"But I beat him. Doesn't that mean I get to summon him?" Tom asked, his brow furrowed, walking back toward Azroc.

"You earned the right to form a contract with him. That doesn't mean you automatically get the ability to summon that pap smear," Azroc rolled his eyes, clearly frustrated at Tom's ignorance.

"So, what do I have to do now?" Tom's voice was tinged with growing annoyance.

"I've got to give you the fucking Skill to summon him, and then you have to perform the contract ritual. What? You thought you could just beat someone's brains in and then magically call on them? Can you summon goblins, ogres, or humans you've killed?"

"Well, no. But they're dead. And he's not." Tom pointed his thumb over his shoulder at the sulking Ajax.

Azroc facepalmed, groaning loudly. "Idiots. I'm surrounded by idiots. You should have known better, Ajuice! You were a Patron for fuck's sake!"

Ajax nodded reluctantly. "He's right. I might've taken one too many blows to the head, but you can't just summon me yet."

Tom sighed, frustration boiling over before he took a deep breath. "Alright, fine. I'm sorry. I'm just trying to make sure we're ready for the invasion, and maybe I got a little excited. Please, Azroc, help me make sure I can summon Ajax."

"That's more like it," Azroc said with a smirk. "Now, you've got the summoning Skill for basic Summons, but you'll need a higher-tier summoning ability for this asshole. Let's see…Azroc's eyes glazed over for a moment as he reviewed screens only visible to him. Suddenly, his face brightened. "Aha! Got it! Thanks to you clearing the Dungeon of Chance and unlocking multiple completion options, I can grant you a new Skill. Lucky break there."

INVASION

With a flick of his hand, Azroc made a selection, and a notification popped up in Tom's vision.

Congratulations! You have acquired the Skill Ultimate Summons!

Your Patron, Azroc, has granted you the Skill Ultimate Summons! There are 3 tiers to this Skill that can be acquired by progressing its level.

- **Tier 1:** You will be able to summon massively powerful creatures to perform one ultimate attack before they will need to return to their plane of existence as a Summons.
  - Cost: 500 Mana
  - Cooldown: 6 hours
- **Tier 2:** This Skill will allow you to summon 1 of the same creatures in a more sustained capacity.
  - Duration: 1 hour
  - Cost: 1,000 mana
  - Cooldown: 6 hours
- **Tier 3:** This Skill will allow the permanent summoning of these same creatures at the cost of a sustained 1,000 mana from your mana pool. You will be allowed to maintain 3 of these Summons at a time so long as the sustained mana cost does not occupy more than 75% of your total mana pool.

"It's not quite as nice as the normal summoning Skill, but it makes sense for such powerful Summons," Tom muttered as he read the Skill's description, his brow slightly furrowed.

"Oh, we're gonna complain now? You know I didn't have to give you shit," Azroc shot back, a sly grin creeping onto his face.

"No, no, that's not what I meant," Tom stammered, holding his hands up defensively. "I was just commenting on the differences, that's all. So, uh… what do I need to do to form the contract?"

"You gotta fuck him," Azroc deadpanned.

The room instantly fell into a stunned silence. Every single person froze in place, their eyes wide. You could hear a pin drop in the tension that followed.

Tom's mouth hung open in shock, and his eyes grew as large as dinner plates.

"I'm sorry… *what*?!" he asked, his voice a mixture of disbelief and horror.

"BAHAHAHAHAHAHA!" Azroc erupted in laughter, doubling over as he struggled to stay upright. "You should see the look on your face!" He was practically crying from laughing so hard.

Tom let out an awkward, nervous laugh. "Hahaha… yeah, good one…"

It took Azroc a moment to pull himself together, wiping away a tear as he regained his composure. "Oh, man. That was priceless. Nah, all you gotta do is ask him to form a contract with you. You just didn't have the ability to initiate it without the summoning Skill."

Tom exhaled in relief, his heart still pounding from the unexpected comment. "You really had me going there for a second," he said, running a hand through his hair as the adrenaline wore off.

"You mortals are so easy to mess with!" Azroc chuckled, clearly pleased with himself. "The looks on your faces—*classic*."

Tom rolled his eyes, but only after turning away from Azroc, muttering to himself about being the butt of the joke. He faced Ajax, who was still brooding.

"Ajax, I want you to form a contract with me."

As soon as he spoke the words, a glowing pop-up appeared in Tom's vision, signaling the contract initiation process.

Contract Initiated
You have initiated a contract with Ajax. This contract is permanent unless both parties agree to its dissolution or one party irreparably wrongs the other. Be warned that these contracts should not be formed lightly, as there are consequences to not upholding your end of the deal. Do you wish to continue?

Yes	*No*

Tom selected "Yes," and the screen disappeared from his vision. Ajax's eyes unfocused as he received a notification as well. After a moment of reading, he looked at Tom and nodded.

Contract Formed!
Congratulations! You have now formed a contract with Ajax! From this moment forward, you can summon Ajax using the Ultimate Summons Skill. He will answer your call and aid you in your future battles.

After Tom dismissed the message, Ajax began to fade, his form slowly becoming transparent.

"See ya soon, Tom. Don't go dying on me," Ajax said, his voice carrying a faint echo.

Another bright light flashed, forcing everyone in the room to cover their eyes.

Just before Ajax was taken, a flicker of a sneer crossed his face. These pathetic mortals were nothing to him. His defeat was merely a fluke of the System, a temporary inconvenience that he would endure. He might have lost the battle, but in his mind, it was only a momentary setback. Let them think they had won; let them revel in their victory. He would play his part for now, biding his time, waiting for the perfect moment. In the end, he knew he was superior—and when the time came, he would make them all remember.

When Tom opened his eyes again, Ajax had vanished into thin air.

"Well, now that the dickbag has been dealt with, what's next for you?" Azroc asked, crossing his arms casually.

Tom exhaled, refocusing. "Now, we will finish preparing. The invasion is imminent—we don't know the exact timing, but it could happen any moment."

Azroc raised a brow. "What do you think your chances are?"

"I'm not exactly confident," Tom admitted. "They've lived with the System their whole lives and have space travel. We're outmatched in experience, but we've got some surprises ready. We're not going down without a fight."

Azroc grinned. "That's what I like to hear. I wish I could do more, but the rules forbid it. Still, I think you'll do just fine. Pirates target newly integrated planets because they don't expect much resistance. Show them why they're wrong."

Azroc extended his fist, and Tom, after a brief pause, returned the gesture with a fistbump.

"You've already done so much for us. Thanks, Azroc. I'll see you on the other side," Tom said with a determined smile.

Tom and his team gathered in the Guild's security office, the pressure of the impending invasion hanging over them. TJ and Brian stood nearby, listening intently as Tom prepared to relay everything that had transpired.

"I don't want this to go beyond this room for now, but we've found something that might give us a critical advantage in the fight to come," Tom began, his tone serious.

Brian raised an eyebrow. "What kind of weapon are we talking about? And where the hell did the Mastadonians go?"

"The two are connected," Tom replied. "When we got to the site…" He recounted the entire story: discovering the statue, Azroc's appearance, the intense battle with Ajax, and ultimately gaining the ability to summon him as a weapon for their Guild.

Brian listened intently, a serious expression fixed on his face. "And you think this one summon will make a difference?"

"Look at the impact the Mastadonians have made. Now imagine someone with power on Azroc's level being summoned for a single attack," Tom countered.

"I see your point," Brian conceded, but his voice remained cautious. "But if you can only summon him every six hours, we'll need to use him as a backup—not as our first play. If we use him too early, we risk losing our trump card when we might really need it."

"Agreed," TJ added. "We have other tricks up our sleeves. Is everyone getting briefed on the plan?"

Tom nodded. "We're making sure the team knows what to expect and when to act, but the lack of intel makes it tough to plan for everything. We're hoping it's a smaller-scale raid—pirates usually prefer to operate in smaller groups to stay under the radar."

Brian's face darkened slightly. "We've prepared for the worst-case scenario of a global invasion, but the odds aren't in our favor if that happens. Pirates don't usually work well together, so we're counting on them attacking in smaller waves. But we can't rely on that hope alone."

Tom sighed deeply, the weight of the situation pressing down on him. "Right. Keep pushing on weapon production. Start doubling the watch; I want guards keeping an eye on the skies round the clock. Hopefully, they hit us during the day, but we need to be ready for anything."

"Got it. I'll have them ready to head out now," TJ said.

"I'm going to resummon the Mastadonians. I want to check if any of them have had a change of heart since last time. I don't want to force anyone into something they don't want to do," Tom said, feeling the weight of responsibility in his words. "If you need me, I'll be in the gym for a bit, then I need to rest. That last fight took a lot out of me."

"Take care of yourself, Tom. We've got it covered from here," Brian said, picking up his clipboard to continue working through the tasks ahead.

Once Tom arrived at the gym, he took a moment to clear his mind, focusing on the task at hand. He began the process of summoning the Mastadonians one by one. As his mana drained, he paused to drink a potion, recharging before moving on to the next Summon. He decided to bring in Rularis as well; with a war looming and the Guild having a few Bards, he figured every edge they could gain would be critical.

When Rularis appeared, Inari immediately voiced her concern.

"What is *he* doing here?" she asked, her tone heavy with distrust.

"He helped during the last battle," Tom said firmly. "We're about to face serious peril, and I need every advantage we can get. That means summoning everyone, even if they aren't fully trusted, to see if they can provide us with information or support we don't have. This is about survival." His tone was sharper than intended, but he stood by his decision.

Inari held his gaze for a long, tense moment before nodding. "I see the wisdom in your words. I apologize for questioning you. You've proven yourself to be an honorable man who fights for the survival of his people."

Tom gave a small nod of appreciation before addressing the entire group. "Thank you. Now, before I set your statuses back to what they were before, I want to ask again—who among you wants to stay as part of the Guild, knowing you can choose to undo this decision at any time?"

To Tom's surprise, every single one of the Mastadonians raised their hand in agreement, signaling they would stay with him.

"What? Really?" Tom said, astonished. He turned to Onslo, Amath, and Kuthir, who had initially shown reluctance. "What made you change your mind?"

INVASION

"We have seen your honor," Onslo said calmly. "You do not force others to bend to your will. You act out of a genuine desire to protect your people. You are worthy of our loyalty."

The others nodded in agreement, affirming Onslo's words.

Rularis, ever the enigmatic presence, grinned slyly. "And I must admit, I'm curious to see what this war will bring. It's been ages since I've fought alongside someone like you, Tom. You intrigue me. Besides," he added with a wink, "as you've said, I can change my decision at any time, correct?"

"Yes," Tom said, standing by his earlier statement. "I would never force anyone into this. That goes against everything I believe in."

Bron, who had been listening intently, added his voice to the conversation. "He speaks the truth. I was there when he fought the slave master in his own city. He stood against injustice and freed those enslaved."

Inari smiled softly, bowing her head in respect. "We are with you, Tom. We will fight for you, and we will keep you safe. Just point us to the ones we must destroy."

Chapter 62

The Beginning of the End

As preparations continued, every member of Vanguard worked tirelessly, anticipating every possible outcome. Another month passed, with each day marked by the constant question of whether it would be their last chance to prepare. During this time, the season began to shift. Texas, unlike many northern states, didn't have a true fall—the trees didn't don vibrant reds, oranges, and yellows. Yet, as the sweltering summer heat eased, so too did the spirits of the people.

The relentless, oppressive one-hundred-degree days began to wane. Cool winds from the now closer Gulf Coast brought relief, blowing through the city and granting a much-needed respite from the unforgiving Texas sun. The Trammel Crow Center, their sole source of air conditioning, was no longer the sanctuary it had been. With cooler days and earlier sunsets, the vivid evening skies painted in hues of pink, orange, and purple offered a moment of tranquility. Members of the Guild would gather, appreciating these quiet moments and expressing their gratitude for the adventurers who had risked everything to bring them this peace.

The harvest, which had become more frequent with the aid of magic, was a time of joy and celebration. Crops and livestock flourished, and the bounty became increasingly varied as the farms continued to grow. The people of Vanguard enjoyed full bellies, comfortable homes, and a sense of security. It was a peace they couldn't have imagined just a few months ago. But they all knew it couldn't last.

One gloomy morning, with the sky thick with clouds threatening rain, a man raced down the halls of the Guild building, his face pale and panic-stricken. Bursting into the security office, he gasped for breath, eyes wide with urgency.

"Guild leader, you need to see this!" he shouted, his voice tight with fear.

Tom, Derek, Brian, and TJ exchanged concerned glances before following the man, who led them down to the basement and into the engineering station. There, about twenty people were gathered around a machine tucked against the wall, murmuring in anxious tones. As the group parted to make way for Tom, he spotted the screen they were fixated on.

The display showed a pixelated image of Earth. Pulsating waves began in what appeared to be Texas, expanding outward in concentric circles until they reached the edge of the screen. But it wasn't the waves that drew everyone's concern—it was the four small red dots, blinking ominously outside of Earth's atmosphere, creeping ever closer with each passing pulse.

Tom's frown deepened as he studied the display, a sense of dread settling over him. "Harold... what exactly are we looking at here?"

Harold, standing nearby, stepped forward, his face drawn with tension. "You can think of it as a global sonar system," he began, his voice calm despite the gravity of the situation. "Without satellites, we had to come up with an alternative to monitor space. Herbert and I discovered during one of his experiments that all living things emit a kind of vibration—a life wave. The Earth, now being a living planet, does the same. So, by tapping into that lifeline, so to speak, we managed to create a rudimentary image."

He gestured toward the screen. "Those red dots represent anomalies. We send out opposing vibrations, a sort of signal, and where the frequencies are disrupted—those gaps are what we detect. These," he said, pointing to the blinking red dots, "are objects moving toward Earth. And they're getting closer."

"But what about all the dead satellites or the space station? Why aren't those showing up?" Derek asked, his voice tinged with confusion.

"We filtered out anything below a certain size, as well as known objects," Harold explained. "Knowing that the invasion would likely involve ships larger than anything we've ever sent to space, we set the system to disregard smaller objects."

"Wait... so you're saying these are..." Tom trailed off, unable to bring himself to finish the thought.

Harold's expression grew grim. "Yes. I believe these are the Space Pirates we've been preparing for. The fact that they're moving in a consistent, steady line without being affected by Earth's gravitational pull means they have some form of propulsion system keeping them on course. They're not drifting debris."

Tom stared at the red dots on the screen, his heart pounding, stomach twisting. For a long moment, he stood paralyzed, trying to process the reality in front of him.

"TJ," Tom said quietly, still unable to tear his eyes away from the screen. "Get everyone ready. Sound the alarm."

Without hesitation, TJ bolted back to the security office and hit the panic button—the one they had designated for both monster attacks and this, the worst-case scenario.

"Tom?" Derek placed a comforting hand on his friend's shoulder.

Tom blinked, snapping out of his paralysis. "I know... I just didn't think it would feel this real. We've been warned, and we've done everything we could to prepare." He turned to face the others, his resolve hardening. "Now we get everyone ready. All eyes on the sky while we wait."

Herbert, looking at the screen, asked the question on everyone's mind. "They could be headed anywhere on the planet. What do we do if they don't come here? There are only four ships."

Tom took a breath before replying, "Then we take the fight to them. But I have a feeling they're coming straight for us."

Harold furrowed his brow. "How can you be so sure?"

"If you were invading a planet you assumed had primitive life, and you wanted a guaranteed victory, where would you go first?" Tom asked rhetorically.

"Probably the strongest place," Harold replied slowly. "But how would they know what that is?"

Tom pointed to the mana collection banks, which stored and distributed power throughout the Guild's generators.

"If it were me, I'd track the flow of mana," he said.

Harold's eyes widened in realization. "Of course! Why didn't I think of that?"

Suddenly energized, Harold sprinted to the back of the workshop and returned with a strange contraption. It looked like a large battery connected to an engine, all precariously balanced on a flatbed cart that looked suspiciously like it had been lifted from a Home Depot.

"What's that?" Tom asked, raising an eyebrow.

A wicked grin spread across Harold's face. "A failed experiment. It was supposed to be a mana-powered engine for a car, but I couldn't get the output to be steady. Right now, when you start it up, it expends all the stored energy in one giant pulse of power."

Tom's face lit up with sudden understanding, and he chuckled. "And you want to fire that off to get their attention, don't you?"

"Exactly," Harold said, the gleam in his eyes unmistakable.

"Harold, you mad bastard. I love the way you think." Tom grinned. "Get it set up. Take it to the highest floor you can and set it off."

Harold, clearly enjoying the moment, nodded. "I want this to be big. I've got nine more batteries I'm going to hook up. They won't be able to ignore this signal."

"This is the moment we've been preparing for. Time to show them we're not just some pathetic fools to be taken advantage of. Now, we prepare for the invasion!" Tom's voice rang out across the basement.

The response was immediate. Everyone rushed to their designated posts with the precision of a well-oiled machine. Months of drills had prepared them for this moment, and now it was time to see if all their hard work paid off. Gunners manned the weaponry atop the building, ammunition stockpiled for months was rapidly loaded into position, and F-35s were prepped for takeoff, packed with as many missiles as they could carry. Snipers positioned themselves for optimal vantage points, fighters gathered in the courtyard, and vehicles were made ready for deployment.

No one was idle. Children were moved to the gym under the care of designated staff and noncombatants. All nonessential functions were shut down, freeing up every available person to focus on the defense. Rebecca and her team of healers were on standby, distributing potions to ensure every fighter was fully supplied. Charlene and her staff worked quickly, preparing energy bars that would not only keep the fighters fueled but also provide buffs for the battle ahead.

As Tom took in the sight of his Guild coming together, Herbert tapped him on the shoulder. "Tom, if you've got a moment."

Tom turned, noting the urgency in Herbert's voice. "What's up, Herbert?"

INVASION

"I've been working on something. I wasn't able to fully test it, but since we're deploying everything we've got, I figure it's worth a shot. Follow me."

They moved to a back corner where a large, shrouded object sat. With a quick tug, Herbert removed the sheet, revealing a strange contraption. Tom stared, half-expecting it to start shrinking or blowing up a nearby object.

"What am I looking at?" Tom asked, utterly baffled.

"It's an energy cannon," Herbert explained, excitement glinting in his eyes. "The system converts power into a concentrated beam. In theory, if we fire it at a shield, it should either overload the capacitors generating it or punch right through. I call it the Deshieldinator."

Tom couldn't help but grin. "Doofenshmirtz?"

Herbert chuckled. "Ah, a man of taste! I think if we can get this thing set up near the walls, we could target the ships and help take down any shields they might have, giving us an opening to attack."

"Brilliant! Get as many people as you need to move it into position. Let's make it happen."

"I'm on it," Herbert said, rushing off to gather his team.

Tom turned back, shouting orders. "Brian, head back to the security office and help with coordination. Derek, you're with me."

They made their way out to the courtyard, where chaos was slowly transforming into order. Men and women hustled, arranging makeshift barricades, while RVs were moved to the walls to provide extra standing space on the roofs. Fighters were forming ranks, readying themselves for what was to come. Tom noticed the Mastadonians, each leading their own group, giving last-minute instructions and delivering rousing speeches of inspiration.

Tom's heart swelled with pride. His people were ready. Everyone took the threat seriously, preparing for the fight of their lives. Derek barked a few orders, redirecting supplies and repositioning gear that wasn't quite where it needed to be. Overhead, dark clouds rumbled ominously, promising rain. It would complicate things, but they'd trained for worse.

"Are we sure the F-35s can handle flying in this weather?" Tom asked, glancing up at the gathering storm.

Derek nodded. "I checked with Anderson. They lifted the flight restriction for thunderstorms a while back. The jets have specialized instruments that let them fly even in near-zero visibility. After all the training they've had, they'll be fine."

Tom grinned. "Good. Let them come. We'll be ready."

Chapter 63

Invasion Preparation

It took less than an hour for nearly all the preparations to be completed. The Guild, well-rehearsed from countless drills, moved with precision and discipline. Everyone knew their roles and performed them without hesitation or complaint. The final steps were being carried out: the installation of the Deshieldinator on the walls and the distribution of the aptly named "Power Bars" by the kitchen staff. Noncombatant volunteers moved through the courtyard with baskets of the snacks, handing them to fighters as they waited in their positions, ready for what was to come.

All eyes were on the sky, scanning for any sign of the approaching ships. Dread, anxiety, hope, excitement, and anticipation swirled together as they awaited the inevitable. A heavy silence settled over the Guild as the usual sounds of daily life entirely ceased.

That silence was broken by a pulse that shook the world like a giant cosmic hand had rattled a magic eight ball. The mana-powered engine fired from the top of the building, sending a ripple through the air that made Tom's insides twist uncomfortably. He felt queasy as the wave spread out, and small rocks on the ground bounced from the vibrations, as if a tiny earthquake had struck. The pulse moved outward in a dome-shaped wave, bending light and air around it, creating a mirage-like effect. As it reached the clouds, they swirled violently in response, like water in a storm, before slowly returning to their normal pattern.

"That should definitely get their attention," Tom muttered, rubbing his chest to ease the residual queasiness the pulse had left behind.

"Let's hope so. Our plans won't be nearly as effective if we have to go hunting for them," Derek replied, eyes still locked on the sky.

"Yeah, and if they decide to hit a place like the Grand Canyon instead, where people are less prepared, it could be catastrophic. We need them to come here, where we're ready. It's our best shot at minimizing casualties," Tom said, his voice low with concern.

Derek nodded but asked, "Do you really think this will work?"

Tom turned to him with a mock expression of shock. "What the hell is this? Derek Calloway having doubts? That's my job."

Derek chuckled, shaking his head at Tom's antics. "You're right. You do the doubting while I make you feel better."

INVASION

Tom smiled but then grew serious again. "Look, we've done everything we could with the time we had. More than I thought possible, to be honest. We've got a few tricks up our sleeves that might just tip the scales in our favor. We're stronger now, better prepared. Don't start doubting us now."

Derek sighed. "It's not that I doubt us. It's more that I worry we can never be fully prepared. Back when I was deployed, I felt the same way—no matter how much we trained, you can't predict everything. No plan ever survives first contact with the enemy."

Tom nodded, understanding. "That's a valid point. And thinking like that is what keeps us on our toes. Overconfidence is the real enemy here. We've spent months preparing, trying to anticipate every possibility. Now we just need to stay sharp and make sure we deploy the right tactics when the time comes."

Derek smiled faintly. "I know. It's just the waiting. It messes with your head."

Tom clapped him on the shoulder. "Yeah, the waiting sucks. But when the time comes, we'll be ready. We've faced worse, and we've always come out on top."

Derek glanced at the sky again, as if trying to see into the future. "Let's just hope you're right."

Tom didn't respond right away, his gaze also drifting upward. The dark clouds rolled slowly across the sky, heavy with the promise of rain. Whatever was coming, they would face it head-on, prepared as they could possibly be.

If Tom was being honest, his words were as much for himself as for Derek. He had been wrestling with the same doubts for weeks now. Some nights, he lay awake, running through every possible scenario, wondering if there was something he missed in the endless preparations. There were so many ideas, so many plans, that it felt like they'd covered everything. But still, a nagging uncertainty lingered. They'd used every resource, every mind available, and he hoped—no, needed—it to be enough.

"I'm glad to see you've finally got that leader's confidence we've been telling you about. You've come a long way since we started this," Derek said, his tone filled with pride.

Tom smiled, though his eyes betrayed the weight on his shoulders. "To be honest, I feel the same way you do. I just have to put on that front so everyone else feels it too. Whatever happens, happens. If it's the end, so be it. But we'll go down fighting for what we've built here. And it's been an honor to do it with you by my side."

He extended his hand, and Derek took it, but instead of a handshake, Derek pulled Tom into an embrace. It was unexpected, but Tom didn't resist.

"Hey, why wasn't I invited to the hug party?" James said, rushing over to join them, wrapping his arms around both men. "This is nice."

"Because we knew you'd make it awkward," Derek said, though he didn't push him away.

"Where's everyone else?" Tom asked after they broke the embrace.

"Probably getting into position. We won't have the full team together for this one, as much as I'd like it," Derek said. "Everyone's got their role to play."

"So, we're stuck with dickshot here by ourselves?" Tom asked, nodding at James.

"Not completely," Michael's voice called out as he strode over, followed by Frank, Lacey, Mark, and Susie.

"Michael, good to see you. And you brought reinforcements," Tom said, relieved.

"I did. We figured you might need someone to watch your back—just in case you do something stupid again," Michael replied with a teasing grin.

"You mean *when* he does something stupid," Derek laughed.

Tom grinned. "Am I really that predictable?"

"Oh yeah," Derek shot back, "just as sure as James is gonna blow someone's knob off."

"Guys! I just thought of something horrible!" James suddenly shouted, his voice full of urgency.

Tom's stomach dropped. What had they missed? A critical strategy? A missing weapon? A forgotten detail? His mind raced. "What? What is it?"

James took a breath, his face serious. "What if the alien pirates don't have dicks?"

Everyone stared blankly at him for a moment, then collectively turned and walked away in silence.

"Guys? What? Was it something I said?" James called after them, confused.

Michael flipped James the bird over his shoulder. "Screw you, man."

"Wait! I'm coming too!" James rushed to catch up, still oblivious.

They reached the battlements, where a team was in the process of mounting the energy cannon onto the wall.

"What's that?" Michael asked, eyeing the contraption.

Tom pointed at the weapon. "Our potential ticket through their ship's shields—assuming they have any. It fires a condensed beam of energy designed to overload shield generators. Once that happens, we can hit the ships directly."

"I need them on the ground. Not sure how useful I'll be until then," Michael admitted.

"Yeah, a lot of us need that. But we have to get them down somehow. We've got a few plans to get people up close, but not everyone can do that," Tom explained.

"Oh? How's that going to work?" Michael asked, intrigued.

"Bohdan and the mages can create floating disks that people can ride to engage in aerial combat. There aren't enough for everyone, but it'll give us some extra options."

"I want one!" Frank's excitement was palpable at the idea of flying.

Tom chuckled at Frank's eagerness. "We can probably get you on one, but that'd mean you'd be away from me."

Frank's face fell for a moment before his eyes lit up with an idea. "Wait! If you get one too, we can stay together!"

Tom laughed. "Alright, Frank. If I get one, and you get one, we'll fly together."

Frank pumped his fist in the air, his excitement rekindled.

"That's all great, but let's be real for a second. You're planning to board the ships with just a few people? And then what? Take them all on by yourselves?" Susie asked, raising a skeptical eyebrow.

"It's not that simple," Tom replied. "The idea isn't to fight everyone on board. If we can get on and disable the ships, we'll bring them down to the ground for more people to board. The goal is to survive long enough to disable them, not fight an entire army up there."

"We don't even know how many are on a ship," Susie said, arms crossed, her tone skeptical. "It could be fifty, or it could be a thousand."

"True," Tom nodded, "and if you have a better idea, I'm all ears."

She stared at him for a long moment, trying to come up with a better plan. Finally, she shrugged. "If I think of something, I'll let you know."

"Perfect. There are no bad ideas," Tom said, then glanced at James and added, "Well, maybe *some* bad ideas."

As the energy cannon was secured on the wall, several workers began drilling holes to install bolts as large as Tom's forearm to hold it in place. When they finished, Herbert walked over, a proud smile on his face.

"Hey, Herbert. Looks like the cannon is almost ready," Tom said.

"The *Deshieldinator*," Herbert corrected, grinning. "And yes, it's nearly good to go. Could be used at close range if they rush us as well, though, fair warning—it would be a horrible way to die. That much energy would just make a person… explode."

"Yikes. That *does* sound horrible," Tom said, cringing at the thought. "But I'm not above using it on someone trying to kill us and take our resources."

"Good," Herbert chuckled, "because if you were, I was going to say you couldn't use it."

Tom laughed then noticed Herbert had something else in his hand—a small metallic rod. It was mostly silver, with intricate black inlays and a single button on one side. At the top, it flared out slightly to what looked like a hand guard. Tom's eyes widened when he realized what it was.

"Is that… what I think it is?" Tom asked, his voice almost reverent.

Herbert grinned mischievously. "Yes. My *Sliceinator*!" He held the object high in the air with dramatic flair.

Tom looked at him, incredulous. "Oh, come on. That *can't* be the—"

"Kidding. It's a lightsaber," Herbert said, handing it to Tom.

Plasma Edge Mk-V

The Plasma Edge Mk-V is a weapon of pure energy, its blade composed of stabilized plasma contained within a high-density magnetic field. This near-weightless blade can cut through most materials, making traditional armor almost useless against it. The blade's color varies based on the wielder's energy signature, shifting dynamically in combat.

Forged from lost pre-collapse technology, this weapon does not rely on a traditional cutting edge but rather superheated ionized plasma, capable of burning through even reinforced metals with ease.

Due to its unique energy field properties, conventional parrying is nearly impossible, as the blade passes cleanly through standard weapons unless they are infused with high-tier energy shielding.

Item Type:	Weapon
Durability:	10,000/10,000
Attack:	120-250
Item Quality:	Master Craft
Item Rarity:	Unique

Tom reverently took the object, holding it with both hands like it was a holy relic. He ran his fingers over the intricate designs before stepping back. With a nod from Herbert, he pressed the button.

The familiar sound of a lightsaber igniting filled the air as a glowing green blade extended from the rod. The air around the blade seemed to hum, sizzling slightly as it reached a length of about four feet.

"Oh... my... *god*!" Tom said, channeling his best Janice-from-*Friends* impression.

Grinning like a kid at Christmas, Tom waved the saber around, feeling its weight. Then he spotted a nearby crate and, without hesitation, sliced through it. The blade cut through effortlessly, leaving glowing red edges where it had passed.

Suddenly, the crate caught fire.

"Oh no, oh crap, oh *god*!" Tom panicked, holding the lightsaber awkwardly as he tried to figure out what to do.

Herbert, completely unfazed, calmly produced a bucket of water from his Inventory and dumped it onto the flames, extinguishing them.

"You always carry a bucket of water in your Inventory?" Tom asked, still a little wide-eyed.

"I work in a magical testing lab," Herbert said, smiling casually. "Things catch fire all the time and convenient buckets of water have saved my hide more than once."

INVASION

Tom shot him a look, wondering what kind of fiery experiments went on in the lab when he wasn't around. Deciding to leave it be, he deactivated the lightsaber and stowed it in his Inventory.

"Thank you, Herbert. I'm truly honored you'd give this to me."

"Don't mention it. After all you've done for us, it's the least I could do. Just don't go expecting more of them. They need a very special kind of crystal to work. We only managed to salvage one from the scrappers. The wrong crystals... well, let's just say that may have been one of the occasions that called for a bucket of water. Once, it just made a pretty flashlight," Herbert said with a wink.

"It exploded?" Tom asked, raising an eyebrow.

"It did. Rather impressive amount of force it put out. It took me weeks to grow my eyebrows back. I was surprised as hell, or rather, I looked that way for a while," Herbert shrugged.

Tom smiled. "I'll take special care of it, I promise."

"I know you will. Now, let's go check on the rest of the preparations," Herbert said, leading the way.

Chapter 64

Convoluted Emotions

A cool breeze whispered through the air as Kiera methodically chambered a round into her rifle, the metallic click cutting through the quiet hum of preparations. Others around her were readying themselves for the arrival of the alien ships, but her focus was singular. She ran her fingers over the cool steel barrel and the familiar wooden stock, each touch a silent prayer for reliability. Her piercing gaze inspected the chamber, scrutinizing every mechanism, every detail, ensuring that everything was in flawless working order. As she closed the bolt with a firm, decisive motion, a deep sense of readiness settled over her. The rifle was no longer just a weapon—it was an extension of her resolve, primed for the battle ahead.

As she stood there, memories of hunting with her grandfather drifted through her mind. Sitting in a blind, waiting for prey to wander into their line of sight. He'd always talked to her in hushed tones—about how she was doing in school, about life lessons from his time in the military, and about how to handle struggles with friends. He'd been a kind man, someone who always looked out for her when her parents were too busy or away. That warmth and wisdom felt so distant now in this new, broken world.

Life in the post-apocalyptic world had been relentless. Each day was a fight for survival, a test of endurance just to make it to the next sunrise. But her luck had changed when she stumbled into the Trammel Crow Center, half-dead from a goblin attack. She still remembered the night clearly—walking down the street, hungover after a rough night of drinking. She'd lost everything when her bandmates fired her after she'd shown up to a performance drunk and vomited on stage by the third song. That night, she felt like she had nothing left to live for.

The goblins had come out of nowhere. She'd tried to run, pushing past people waiting at a bus stop, while the goblins tore into them. Most of the creatures had stayed to attack the easy prey, but one had followed her down an alley. It was a dead end. She had no way out. When the goblin charged, she instinctively grabbed the pocket knife her grandfather had given her, and before she knew it, she'd plunged it into the creature's throat.

She still remembered the stench of its breath—a foul mix of rot and death. The coppery taste of its black blood had splattered into her mouth, her screams lost in the chaos as the creature thrashed, trying to bite her even as its life ebbed away. When it finally went limp, she pushed the filthy body off herself, her hands slick with a mixture of grime, blood, and whatever filth had caked onto the goblin's skin.

Stumbling out of the alley, gasping for air and wiping the blood from her mouth with her jacket sleeve, she saw people running toward a building across the street. Gunshots rang out in the distance, and instinctively, she followed the crowd. Safety in numbers, right? As she dashed across the street, an SUV swerved to avoid her, crashing into a telephone pole, the horn blaring endlessly from the impact.

Inside the building, security guards were ushering people toward a gymnasium, and it was only then that Kiera realized this was some kind of safe haven. Looking down at her phone, she saw a red alert banner flashing across the screen, warning of a city-wide catastrophe in Dallas. The sheer overload of it all hit her like a tidal wave—the chaos, the screams, the sirens wailing in the distance, the sound of cars crashing and people shouting for help. It was a nightmare she couldn't wake up from, a reality she'd never imagined living in.

"Kiera?" a voice broke through her memories.

"Yes?" she replied, shaking her head to clear the horrific thoughts that had momentarily consumed her. She blinked and saw Tom standing over her.

"I asked how you're doing. Is everything alright?" Tom's voice was gentle, full of concern. He must've walked up while she was lost in the past.

"Yeah, just… thinking. Sorry," she apologized, storing the rifle back in her Inventory.

Tom had been her rock amid the chaos of her past. Back then, her world was falling apart, and he'd been the steady presence she could cling to, a foundation to rebuild her life in this strange new reality. In this world, it didn't matter who you had been before—only who you chose to be now. And Tom, without realizing it, had become her first real friend in this new life. He never cared about her past, only about who she was as a person.

"Are you sure? You need a moment?" Tom asked, concern etched on his face.

His worry wasn't some misguided notion of her being fragile. He had never treated her as anything less than his equal. From the start, he'd seen her as just another fighter—capable, strong, someone to rely on. He never looked at her with that patronizing "you're a woman, let me protect you" attitude so many men had. To Tom, she was part of the team. Nothing more, nothing less.

"No, I'm good. What's up?" Kiera replied, her voice steady, but she couldn't help the strange warmth that spread through her chest as she looked at him.

He had never once tried to take advantage of her. Unlike others from her past, he never made her feel uncomfortable, never ogled her, or made some offhanded comment about her looks. She wasn't some "hot body" for him to lust after. For God's sake, he had saved her in that Dungeon when she thought she'd been abandoned. He carried her when she couldn't walk, and never made her feel like a burden. In his arms, she had felt safe—truly safe—for the first time since her grandfather passed.

"We're checking in with everyone, making sure they've got everything they need," Tom said, his tone shifting into that of a leader assessing his troops.

"Your team is going to play a big role in this invasion, especially since you can take out targets from a distance." His eyes held hers. "You all set?"

This feeling that bubbled inside her—what was it? She didn't fully understand. She'd throw herself into the jaws of any beast to protect him, to repay the meaning he had given her life. He'd never asked for anything in return. Not her voice, her connections, nothing. Tom was just… good. And she couldn't wrap her head around that because everyone in her life had wanted something from her before.

"No, we're good. I've got everything I need. We've got ammo, everyone's been training hard, and Inari's been helping us hone our Skills. I even spent some time with Rularis, learning more about being a Bard," Kiera said, her voice softening as she looked at him.

Was this what contentment felt like? Her grandfather had told her once that when she found the right people, she would just know. It always sounded like a fairy tale, like when people say you'll just *know* when you meet the right one. She never believed that. And yet, here she was, looking up at a man who made her feel like she had found her place—her tribe.

"Good," Tom nodded. "I'm counting on you to keep us covered. Try to take out any enemies or ships you can. I know you won't let me down."

And there it was—that smile of his. That warm, genuine smile that made her heart ache and the reason she knew she loved him.

Wait… you love him?

That couldn't be right. Tom wasn't her type. He was awkward, weird, and a huge nerd. She'd never gone for that kind of guy before. But that was *before*—before the world had gone to hell in a handbasket. Before everything had changed. No, she couldn't think about this right now. She had a job to do.

"I've always got your back," Kiera replied.

"I know you do. You've never let me down."

You've never let me down, either.

That was what she wanted to say, but she bottled it up and pushed it aside. Emotion was weakness, and she wasn't weak. She had survived on her own for so long, through so much, that she'd almost forgotten what it was like to rely on someone else. When people had looked down on her for being a woman, she had risen above it, determined to prove she was just as good—no, better—than the boys.

"Where are you setting up?" Tom asked, snapping her out of her thoughts.

"I'll be on top of the building across the street. It gives a good vantage point without getting in the way of the gunners on our roof. Plus, I can be behind the enemy line if they head for the gate," Kiera explained.

"Sounds like you've got it all figured out."

I most certainly do not have it all figured out, she thought, feeling the weight of emotions pressing against the mental bottle she'd shoved them into, threatening to burst out. But she wasn't about to let that happen.

"Pretty much," she said instead, forcing a casual tone. "As long as I have a line of sight, Rularis showed me how to cast buffs on you all. Just make sure you stay where I can see you."

"Haha! I can't promise that," Tom chuckled, his laugh like music to her ears. "But don't let that stop you from casting buffs on whoever you can."

That sound.

The way he laughed… This idiot was definitely going to do something reckless again. He always did. He always put himself in danger for everyone else, never caring what happened to him as long as the others were safe. What a tool. What a… *selfless* tool.

But she knew better now. He wasn't some misogynistic jerk trying to be the hero so people would fawn over him. He wasn't looking for attention. He jumped into danger just as quickly for James, that reckless asshat, as he did for her. Tom wasn't trying to prove anything. He just *was.*

She'd watched him for almost a year now. Not once had he boasted about his bravery. Not once had he treated anyone as lesser unless they deserved it. He was… just that genuine.

"What will you be doing?" Kiera asked, curious to hear his plan.

"I'll be doing whatever needs to be done," Tom replied with a shrug. "I'm hoping they'll want to talk before things get ugly. But there's always a chance they'll shoot first and ask questions later. If I can, I'll get close and try to disable the ships. We need them grounded."

"How will you get them to talk?"

"We don't have a clear way to communicate," Tom admitted. "We just won't attack until they do. Not a lot of other options unless we paint a big banner or something. And even then, we don't know if they'll understand English."

"What was that pulse earlier?" she asked, her curiosity piqued.

"That was Herbert," Tom said, smiling a little. "He had this mana-powered engine that wasn't finished yet. We figured the pirates would target whoever seemed the strongest, so he rigged it up with extra batteries and fired it off. It's a way to attract them here so we don't have to chase them down, and hopefully, we can keep them from attacking somewhere else."

"So, do you think we can win?" Kiera asked softly.

"I think we're the best shot we know of," Tom replied, his tone more serious now. "There might be someone stronger out there, but we can't count on that. We have to try to stop them before they hurt anyone else."

There he goes again, Kiera thought, watching him, *caring more about others.* He might put them in danger, sure, but it was always to protect those he felt couldn't defend themselves. What a stupid, stupid man. And yet…

"Alright, well, I better get into position," Kiera said, shaking the emotions away. "I bet they'll show up any minute."

"Sounds good. If you need anything, use your communication orb," Tom said, smiling softly at her again.

That smile.

She couldn't help but feel something stir inside her again.

"I will," she promised, her voice softer than before. "I promise."

Chapter 65

They Came From Outer Space

The sky churned with thick, roiling clouds, their dark masses flickering ominously with the sporadic flash of lightning that illuminated the heavens with stark, momentary brilliance. Amid the tumultuous backdrop, an alien ship began its descent, the edges of its immense form barely discernible as it broke through the cloud cover. Lights from the bow and engines emanated from the craft, casting an eerie, otherworldly glow that seeped through the mist, creating a dazzling display of colors that danced along the clouds' edges. The air crackled with electric tension as a bolt of lightning raced across the sky, illuminating the silhouette of the craft as it slowly emerged from the clouds, causing all those present to stare with bated breath.

What appeared to be the bottom of an actual ship first appeared as it continued to lower. Cannons lined the sides of the vessel as it continued its descent. A mast and sails made out of some kind of thin metallic material woven in an octagonal pattern fluttered softly in the breeze as the ships came into full view. What they were looking at was not just an alien spacecraft but an actual pirate ship flying a Jolly Roger flag and sporting a crow's nest with a glass dome covering the open space where a lookout would stand.

Another glass dome covered what would have been the open-air sections of the ship, allowing its passengers to breathe while in the vacuum of space. Two giant engines were on the back of the literal pirate ship with two much smaller rocket-style engines on the bow that appeared to be for directional propulsion. Portholes were placed sporadically near the lower rear of the ship, likely where the crew stayed, and large ornate stained-glass windows were set on the sides of the upper portion of the ship behind the helm.

First, one ship appeared, then two more, and finally, a fourth ship lowered slowly through the clouds. They hovered in the air just below the cloud level as onlookers began to point and look on with open mouths. Once they were all visible through the clouds, the ships remained in one location, not moving except for the slight, steady up-and-down bobbing they did while hovering.

Tension was high as weapons were drawn and equipped. No one took their eyes off the spaceships for fear they might miss something happening. Tom strode to the walls and up the staircase leading to the top. He leaned on the battlement, looking out at the invaders. One of the guards handed him a pair of binoculars, and he accepted them silently, lifting them to his eyes to get a better look.

INVASION

"What the hell?" Tom muttered, staring out at the ships in the distance.

"What do your elf eyes see, Legolas?" James quipped from behind him, causing Tom to jump slightly.

"Shit! Don't sneak up on people like that," Tom grumbled, placing a hand over his racing heart.

"Sorry, man, thought you knew I was right behind you," James replied, smirking. "You... need some clean underwear?"

"No, I do not need clean underwear," Tom retorted, his tone clipped with frustration. "I have clean underwear. I always keep some with me. Just in case."

"Alright, alright, take it easy. Hakuna your tatas, bro," James said, raising his hands in mock surrender, eyes twinkling with mischief.

Tom shot him an annoyed glance before turning back to the binoculars. "It's still a little hard to make out, but... you're not going to believe this," he said, still peering through the lenses.

"What is it?" James asked, and now others nearby were leaning in to listen.

"They look like... lobsters," Tom said, sounding more baffled than anything.

"Lobsters?" James furrowed his brow.

"Gimme those," Jay said, suddenly appearing next to Tom.

"Where the hell did you come from?" Tom asked, startled again.

"I'm a Rogue, Tom. I'm everywhere," Jay replied with a smirk, taking the binoculars and scanning the ships for himself.

"Well, fuck me sideways... They *do* look like lobsters. And here I thought we'd been eating too much turf lately. Looks like it's time to add some surf to the menu," Jay lowered the binoculars, a wicked grin spreading across his face.

Tom blinked, unsure if he was joking or not. Then Jay turned and yelled, "Hey! You! Go tell Roland to start prepping a giant-ass crawfish pot! Big enough to cook a few people in!"

The poor Guild member below stared up at Jay in a mixture of horror and confusion before reluctantly nodding and heading into the building.

"You... you want to *eat* them?" Tom asked, incredulous.

"Why not?" Jay replied matter-of-factly. "We've been eating Dungeon monsters all this time. Why not alien lobster? Lobster's delicious, and it's not like we're in a position to be picky."

"I heard the big ones don't taste as good," James chimed in.

Jay scoffed. "That's like saying white chocolate doesn't count because it's not real chocolate. It's still damn good."

Tom couldn't take it anymore. "Guys, the invasion we've been preparing for ever since we got the warning is *right in front of us*, and you're debating whether or not we should eat the invaders based on their size? Can we *please* focus?! We can argue about taste-testing later—if we're still alive."

Jay raised his hands in mock surrender. "Fair point. So, what's the game plan?"

Tom sighed, shaking off his frustration. "For now, we wait. See if they try to make contact or just attack. I want to observe their first move. But everyone needs to be ready. The F-35s are standing by, mages are prepped with floating disk spells, snipers are in position, and we've got the energy cannon ready to test their shields."

"Deshieldinator!" Herbert called from somewhere in the distance.

"Whatever," Tom said in resignation.

He turned back to the ships, a heavy breath escaping through his nose.

"Now you know how I feel," Derek said from behind him.

"Jesus fucking Christ! Is *everyone* a ninja now?" Tom nearly jumped out of his skin for the third time.

Looking down, Tom spotted Kevin tiptoeing up the stairs. When their eyes met, Kevin's shoulders slumped, and he shuffled back to the Barbarians, his failed attempt at stealth painfully obvious.

"Really? Am I the only one taking this seriously?" Tom groaned in frustration.

"We're just trying to lighten the mood, Tom," Derek said, raising his hands to placate him. "We've done everything we can. However this plays out, we'll adapt and use everything we have to beat them back. And if we can't win, at least we can hold them off until the cavalry arrives."

"We don't know when that will be, but they came *here*. I want them *dead*," Tom growled, his anger flaring.

"Cool it a bit," Derek advised calmly. "We got word that help is only a couple of days behind. The longer those ships sit there trying to decide their next move, the more time we gain."

"You're right. Sorry. I'm just worried. This isn't like the battles we've been fighting. We don't know what kind of tech they're going to throw at us," Tom admitted, rubbing the back of his neck.

"That's true, but we can only control what we can control," Derek replied calmly.

"That doesn't even make sense," Tom shot back, frustrated.

"It means we can't do more than what we've already done. Panicking now will only make us sloppy. We'll respond to whatever they hit us with."

Tom knew that Derek was right. The more he let his anxiety get the better of him, the worse he'd perform when things started to roll out. Tom inhaled deeply several times, trying to steady his nerves. He couldn't afford to lose it now, not when everyone was counting on him.

"Alright. Is Herbert still out here?" Tom asked, glancing around.

"I'll send for him," Derek said, gesturing to one of the Guild members below.

"I'm right here, Tom. What's up?"

Derek tried to signal for the person he'd just sent off, but the man was gone. "Guess he'll be out for a while," Derek muttered to himself.

"Herbert, thanks for coming. I forgot to ask earlier—are the Guild's shields operational and ready?"

"They're good to go! We've got a shield that can cover the entire base and extend ten feet beyond the walls. I've got someone standing by to activate it the moment they look like they're gearing up to fire," Herbert said confidently.

"Perfect. What about the EMP missiles?"

INVASION

Herbert's confident expression faltered slightly. "Those were tricky. We've got a few working models, but I'm hesitant to use them. If they go off too close—anywhere in the city, really—they could knock out our own machinery, too. Definitely a last resort."

"Got it. Keep those in reserve. What else do we have?"

Herbert perked up. "Ah, I'm glad you asked! We've added fireball runes to most of the primary missiles the jets are carrying—about thirty-five runes per missile. We tested one over the ocean, and when it triggered, the explosion was magnified by about a hundredfold."

Tom blinked. "Thirty-five runes multiplied the explosion by… a hundred times? That doesn't feel like it maths out."

"I could show you the calculations, but trust me, it works."

"I'll just be thankful, then. Anything else?"

"How about the anti-magic missiles?" Herbert continued. "They explode like normal, but they also create a stationary anti-magic field in the blast radius. We're not sure how effective they'll be, but even if they don't kill the target, they could prevent any surviving enemies from using magic."

"That sounds perfect. Definitely something we can use." Tom clapped Herbert on the back. "Thanks for all your hard work."

"Hey, it's been a dream come true to work on this kind of tech. But I'm not done yet." Herbert grinned, rubbing his hands together mischievously.

Tom raised an eyebrow. "Oh? What else do you have up your sleeve?"

"But wait, there's more!" Herbert continued in a cheesy infomercial voice, gleefully listing off, "We've got ice missiles, vine missiles, acid missiles, darkness missiles, and my personal favorite—necrosis missiles. Plus, we've made grenade versions of each."

Herbert reached into his Inventory and started handing out grenades like candy, distributing five of each type to Tom and the others gathered around. "We've got crates of these in the courtyard, so don't be shy."

"Necrosis missiles?" Tom repeated, eyeing the grenades warily.

"Yep! Think of it like an explosion with an aftertaste—one that rots the flesh. They're very effective." Herbert looked entirely too pleased with himself.

"Alright, I'll take your word for it," Tom said, laughing nervously. "Anything else?"

Herbert's grin widened as he pulled out a bright green orb about the size of a gumball. "This is my new invention: the Healball."

Tom examined the small orb. "Healball?"

"Yep. Pop one of these into your mouth, bite down, and you activate a major healing spell. Each Guild member has one for the upcoming fight, and we've got more in stock if needed. Plus, it has a minty flavor that leaves your mouth feeling cool and fresh."

"Herbert, you're a genius. These could save lives." Tom pocketed the Healball. "You've really outdone yourself. But, what about the Class alignment issues with healing?"

"Well, have you ever heard of Rebecca turning anyone away because they had a certain Class?" Herbert asked, leaning in as though he was asking the question just to hear someone say the answer.

"Well, no, but…" Tom began before Herbert cut him off.

"That's because it's only the lower level healing spells that are alignment-restricted. The higher tier healing spells do not have that same restriction."

"This is truly amazing, Herbert. I know I already said it, but you've really outdone yourself with all this."

"Just doing my duty." Herbert beamed with pride.

As Tom took the Healball from Herbert, a strange sound—like the tinkling of chimes—began to echo from the ships overhead. The courtyard fell silent as everyone turned their gaze skyward. A large, shimmering screen projected from the front of one of the ships. Static flickered across it before an image took shape.

It was the head of a massive lobster wearing a pirate hat adorned with an ornate golden feather. The creature's solid black eyes sat atop short, stalk-like appendages, and its mandibles moved rhythmically as it adjusted itself on the screen. Long, antenna-like whiskers twitched and writhed as if searching the air for something unseen.

The sight loomed ominously above them, anticipation gripping the crowd below as they waited for what was to come.

Chapter 66

Pirate Demands

The projection stared down at them, the lobster-like alien making strange gurgling and bubbling noises as it waved a claw in the air, apparently trying to communicate. The entire Guild stood in confused silence, unsure what to expect next.

"Is it trying to speak to us?" James asked, his voice laced with curiosity.

As if reacting to James' comment, the creature leaned in closer to the camera, its eyes narrowing in concentration. Then, its upper eyelids slanted downward, giving it an angry appearance before it turned to the side, speaking in the same garbled, bubbling noises, but now much faster.

More unintelligible sounds echoed from off-camera, followed by a series of screeches and hisses. After a brief argument in the strange language, the sounds abruptly stopped, and a voice began speaking in English.

"...you absolute idiots! How hard is it to remember to flip on the communication switch? If you weren't my brother, I would—"

The lobster captain suddenly noticed the change in the expressions of those below. "Oh, my apologies. We forgot to set the translation to common. Anyway, where was I?"

"Just start over," another voice suggested from off-screen.

"I swear to Nashtar, if I hadn't promised Mother, I'd get rid of you..." the captain muttered.

"Captain, the message," came a third voice, sounding exasperated.

"Oh, right! People of Earth! We have come to take the resources of your planet. You are but a fledgling species and cannot possibly match our abilities. Surrender now, and we shall leave you alive after we have taken what we require."

"What do you think they want to take?" Derek asked, confused.

The lobster captain heard him. "That is a valid question," he replied, as if part of the conversation.

"He can hear us?" Tom asked, incredulous.

"Yes, I can hear you," the lobster captain replied, mockingly imitating Tom's voice. "This is a video chat, after all. It goes both ways."

"Your mom goes both ways," James chuckled to himself.

"My mother is dead," the lobster captain said, seemingly unperturbed by the comment. "We need all of your Earth water, any food you can provide, most of your metals, and half of your atmosphere. Oh, and helium. It fetches an especially high price on the intergalactic black market."

Tom and the others stared in disbelief. "Half of our atmosphere?" Herbert asked, shaking his head. "That would kill us. We'd be left with nothing and just die."

The lobster captain shrugged indifferently. "Not our concern. If you resist, we will be forced to kill you and take your resources by force. Doesn't that sound much worse?"

"Sounds about the same," James commented again.

"Can we have some time to talk it over?" Tom called up to the floating screen after giving James a harsh glare, trying to stall.

"Fine," the lobster captain grumbled. "You have three hours. We will expect a decision when we return."

The projection flickered before folding into a thin line and disappearing from sight.

"How are they going to take it with just these few ships? I mean, a planet's worth of resources has to take up a lot of space, right?" Tom asked.

"Ships of Holding?" Derek offered.

Tom just stared at him with a look that said, "Really?"

"So… what do we do?" James asked, breaking the silence.

"Hold on," Herbert said, pulling a small device from his Inventory that resembled a car key fob. He pressed a button on it, and a soft beep sounded. "Alright, continue."

"What was that?" Tom asked, intrigued.

"It's an anti-listening device," Herbert explained simply. "It prevents anyone from eavesdropping on us, either electronically or magically. Brian asked me to make it."

Tom raised an eyebrow. "Of course Brian would want something like that. Alright. We're not surrendering. So, we need to decide our next move."

"When we tell them no, they'll likely fire on us," Derek warned. "Can we have someone on standby with the shields?"

"Already handled," Herbert said. "I'll give the crew a heads-up to keep the communication orb handy. They'll be ready to activate the shields as soon as we need them."

James grinned. "You know, when this is all over, I'm calling dibs on that lobster captain's hat."

"Perfect. If the shield holds like you say, we just have to hope it can withstand their attack," Derek continued, scanning the horizon.

"Oh, it'll hold," Herbert replied confidently. "I over-engineered it to the point where almost nothing should be able to pierce it. They could try to overload it, similar to how I plan to overload their shields, but it won't just get destroyed outright."

"That's excellent news. How many times can we activate it?" Tom asked.

"As long as we have the mana for it. Starting it up is a bit of a drain, but once it's active, the upkeep is minimal—less than what the mana collectors bring in. That said, activating it repeatedly would exhaust the reserves, so we shouldn't cycle it on and off too much," Herbert warned.

"Alright, so once they fire on us, we need to hit them with something immediately. What's our best option for testing their shields?" Tom asked.

"The Deshieldinator is our best bet. If they have shields, it'll overload them. If not, it'll slice through the ship's hull like butter," Herbert explained, a wicked grin forming.

Derek nodded. "We should also simultaneously deploy the F-35s. That way, they can bombard the ships as soon as the shields are down."

"Good thinking," Tom agreed. "Get the mages ready with the flying disks too. We'll need to get our people up there fast if things go south. We need to be ready to strike from the air."

Derek turned to Tom, adding, "And if it really hits the fan, we've got Ajax. We can summon him as a last resort."

Tom nodded then looked around. "I need one more person's input. Bron! Where are you?"

Bron, who had been sitting under a tree, stood up and made his way to the battlements. The space was growing crowded with the gathering of leaders and fighters, but everyone was intent on hearing the next move.

"Do you have any thoughts on aerial tactics or fighting ships like this?" Tom asked the Mastadonian warrior.

Bron folded his arms, thinking as he studied the distant ships. "Ranger skills and long-range attacks will be effective once the shields are down. But to really hit them hard, they need to be much closer. Are your shields like the ones where outgoing attacks can pass through, but incoming attacks are blocked?"

"Yes, exactly," Herbert confirmed.

Bron's eyes gleamed as he formulated a plan. "Then why not lure them in closer? Offer something they want—maybe make them believe they can strike easily—and once they're within range, activate the shields and launch the first attack. That way, we catch them off guard."

"We hadn't considered trying to bait them in like that," Derek mused, rubbing his chin. "It's risky, but if we could draw them in, it would give us a serious advantage."

Bron nodded. "The element of surprise is your best weapon, especially if you think you're outmatched. When they don't have time to assess your strength or react in their usual way, it disrupts their strategy. Strike them before they expect it, and your second wave of attacks will be even more devastating."

Tom's eyes lit up. "I like it. We can offer them a false sense of security and hit them hard before they even realize what's happening."

"We need to make sure we're ready the moment they fall for the bait. No second chances," Derek added.

"That sounds like our best option. But what do we have that they want?" Derek asked, his brow furrowed as he scanned the faces of those gathered on the wall. "They mentioned wanting our resources—saltwater, food, metals, and part of our atmosphere. All things they could just take from outside the Guild without having to come closer to us. Why risk approaching the base?"

Everyone stood in silence for a moment, pondering what might tempt the pirates to come near their defenses. The wind rustled through the leaves of the nearby trees, carrying the distant sound of preparation from the courtyard below.

"Herbert, do you have any large devices we could use to entice them? Preferably something weapon-like?" Tom asked, his mind racing with possibilities.

"I've got a few things," Herbert said, rubbing his chin. His eyes gleamed with mischief.

"But they'd need to come pretty close to get a good look at whatever we show them. And even then, they'd probably want to see it in action before they believed it was worth taking. So, it not only has to be a real weapon but also something they think they could capture and use themselves," Derek added, frowning as he thought through the logistics.

"I have a much larger version of the Deshieldinator," Herbert offered, the corners of his mouth quirking up into a grin. "It's actually less effective because it's too spread out due to its size, but if we fire it at, say, a building, the damage would be catastrophic. And if we don't have our shields up, they might not realize it's intended for them until it's too late. Plus, it looks like a giant laser cannon— pretty enticing to anyone who likes big weapons."

"It also *sounds* like a giant laser cannon," James said dryly.

"Go get it," Tom ordered, his voice steady. "Take the Barbarians with you to help move it. And let me do all the talking when we speak with them again. Bron, head back down for now; I don't want them getting a clear look at you yet. They still think we're just a weak, fledgling planet integrating with the System, and they haven't been as cautious as they should be."

Bron nodded, disappearing back into the shadows with surprising grace for his size.

"James," Derek said, turning to him, "you go with them and oversee the delivery. If anything goes wrong, you have permission to open fire—but not before."

James saluted with a cocky grin, "Got it, boss."

Derek continued, "I'll go with you to make sure things go smoothly. Tom will obviously be there since he'll be making the offer."

Jay, who had been quietly listening, suddenly piped up, "Can someone hide inside the machine?"

Herbert stared at Jay for a long second, the wheels in his head visibly turning. Then his eyes widened as the realization hit. "Not currently… but I could add a false mana storage compartment on the side. It would only take a few minutes. But if they don't try to take the weapon onboard, what happens then?"

"Whoever's hiding can pop out and join the fight," Jay replied, the calm certainty in his voice adding weight to the plan.

Tom nodded approvingly. "So, a sneak attack with a backup Trojan horse tactic. I like where this is going."

"Jay," Derek said, "I presume you want to be the one in the container?"

INVASION

"They don't call me the Trojan man for nothing," Jay said confidently, waggling his eyebrows meaningfully, though his posture betrayed a hint of unease.

"No one calls you the Trojan man." James rolled his eyes.

Jay raised an eyebrow. "Your mom does."

Derek put a hand on James' chest, stepping over their bravado and eyeing the Rogue critically. "How do your stealth Skills compare to Kuthir's?"

Jay's shoulders slumped slightly as he answered, "Not nearly as good. But it's an unfair comparison, seeing as he's had several lifetimes to hone his craft."

Derek glanced at Tom and Bron. "If Kuthir were to die on the ship, we could summon him again after twenty-four hours, right?"

"Correct," Bron confirmed, his deep voice steady.

"Then it makes sense to send him," Derek said, turning back to Jay. "No offense, but he's better suited to the mission."

Jay sighed but nodded. "Alright, I get it. Kuthir can take my place."

"Good," Derek said. "Bron, can you—"

Before Derek could finish, Kuthir materialized beside him, his presence silent and sudden. Derek flinched, his hand instinctively reaching for his weapon.

"I heard," Kuthir said, his voice low and calm, as if appearing out of nowhere was entirely normal.

Derek exhaled slowly, shaking his head. "Well, that saves us a trip."

Herbert motioned for Kuthir to follow. "Come with me. I'll make sure there's a space big enough for you to hide in."

As they left, Tom surveyed the remaining group. "Anyone else have ideas to add?"

Everyone stood in silent thought for a moment, but no one spoke up.

"Alright," Tom said finally. "Let's get into position. Derek, stay here with me for the meeting. We've got a couple more hours to fine-tune everything. I want to rehearse what we'll say to entice them to take the weapon—we can't appear too desperate."

"I have an idea for that," Derek replied. "But it'll need your acting skills."

Tom smirked. "Good thing I'm a master of improv."

"So, we're screwed," James added.

"Jay, oversee the distribution of the grenades and Healballs. I want everyone armed and ready before the meeting begins. Things could go sideways fast."

"I guess I'm invisible," James said, finally giving up on being a part of the conversation.

"On it, boss," Jay said, descending the stairs with quick, purposeful strides.

"Kiera should be in position by now. We need to make sure she's updated on the plan," Tom said, scanning the rooftops. "Bron, did Inari go with her?"

Bron nodded. "She's taken quite a liking to the rifles. I think she'll be adding one to her regular arsenal."

Tom grinned. "We've got a real chance here. If this plan works, we might not even need to wait for the Federation's backup."

"Hold on," Derek cautioned, raising a hand. "Let's not get ahead of ourselves. This could all go to hell quickly. Remember, if it does, we can retreat into the Guild and keep the shields up for a long time. Hopefully, long enough for help to arrive."

"I know," Tom said, sobering slightly. "For now, let's focus on what's in front of us. Those crustacean bastards won't know what hit them."

435

Chapter 67

Surprise

The bridge of the command vessel glowed with an eerie red light, cast from luminescent panels set into the ceiling like a pulsating heartbeat. The scent of brine and ozone hung thick in the recycled air. At the center of the room reclined the captain, his massive chitinous frame sprawled across a throne-like seat custom-fitted for his bulky shell. One pincer lazily cracked open a sea-crystal delicacy while his smaller manipulator limbs tapped idly at a console he wasn't even bothering to read.

His first mate stood nearby—rigid, claws clacking nervously, antennae twitching in subtle agitation.

"We should be monitoring them more closely," the first mate said, tone careful but insistent. "They've activated a crude but effective form of anti-scrying tech, which means they have something to hide. And they're moving. Constantly."

The captain let out a slow, dismissive click of his mandibles. "Let them skitter. These surface crawlers are like rodents in a sealed tank. They'll run circles all they like until they realize they've already drowned."

The first mate's claws flexed slightly. "With respect, sir, it's not just running. They're coordinating. The rate of communication jumps, their positioning changes—none of it suggests panic. It suggests strategy."

The captain waved a claw, sloshing his drink over the side of a polished alloy chalice. "Please. Strategy? From them? They're parasites—barely evolved bottom-feeders clawing at dirt and hope." He chuckled. "We made our demands. They will submit or die. That is the nature of conquest."

The first mate took a step closer, his tone tightening. "Or they will stall. And adapt. Like they always do. If they are coordinating a response, and we do nothing—"

"Silence." The captain's voice dropped an octave, echoing through the chamber like a deep-sea rumble. He rose from his throne, towering over his subordinate as his primary claws clicked together with finality. "You forget your place. I command this fleet. Not you. You exist to execute my vision—not to question it."

The first mate stiffened, claws dropping to the floor. "Understood, Captain."

The captain let out a satisfied grunt and turned back toward the viewport, gazing down upon the Guild building.

"Now relax, and enjoy the silence while it lasts. Soon, there will be only the sound of surrender… or the sweet silence of extinction."

The first mate said nothing as he turned to leave the bridge, his footsteps clicking rhythmically across the metal floor.

But behind his dark, reflective eyes, something coiled.
Not fear.
Not uncertainty.
Resentment.
One day, the captain's arrogance would be his undoing. And on that day, the first mate intended to be close enough to watch it happen.

Preparations for the meeting with the pirates proceeded with precise coordination. The air was thick with tension as everyone made their final checks. The special grenades had been distributed among the fighters, each one enchanted to the highest level of craftsmanship that the Guild Enchanters could manage. Bohdan, with his steady hand and unmatched attention to detail, had overseen the enchanting process, ensuring each grenade was ready to wreak havoc when needed. He also managed the production of the Healballs, which Rebecca had infused with healing magic, her expertise proving invaluable yet again. Tom made a mental note to do something special for her, assuming they all survived this encounter.

The Deshieldinator that Herbert brought up from the basement was a beast of a machine—almost twice the size of the one mounted on the walls. Its hulking form stood out against the more practical and functional layout of their defenses, and even Tom had to admit it looked like something straight out of a sci-fi movie. Herbert had thought of every detail, including a compartment on the side that was large enough to hide Kuthir. He even added a matching compartment to the Deshieldinator on the wall to ensure no one would be able to tell the difference between the two machines. Kuthir had slipped into the hidden compartment with the stealth and grace only a Rogue of his caliber could manage, settling in to wait for the opportune moment.

Tom had explained the situation to Kiera, making sure her sniper team was ready to eliminate any pirate that tried something underhanded. Kiera had smirked, promising to "prepare them for bisque" if things got out of line. Tom had laughed at the comment, his mind briefly wandering to the last time he had indulged in a good lobster bisque. It must have been at Texas De Brazil. They had some of the best bisque he'd ever tasted. But with a shake of his head, he pushed the memory aside and focused on the task at hand. Kiera was prepared, and that was all that mattered.

Inari had also given Tom instructions for the Rangers. They were to be ready to unleash rocket launchers the moment the ships' shields were down. Tom had been surprised at how seamlessly the Ranger Skills adapted to modern firearms, but Inari had explained that ranged weapons were all essentially the same when it came to combat tactics.

Bohdan stood with the other mages, ready to cast the *Floating Disk* spell to give some of their fighters aerial mobility. Anderson and his pilots were already in the cockpits of the F-35s, their engines prepped, awaiting the order to take off. Meanwhile, Herbert's man on the roof, along with the gunners, stood by with their communication orbs, ready to activate the shield or fire at the approaching ships. Chris was manning the Deshieldinator on the wall, standing off to the side, blending in with the other guards in his tactical gear so as not to draw attention to the massive weapon aimed at the sky.

As the final minutes of the three-hour deadline approached, the eerie silence was broken by the flickering reappearance of the pirate captain's head on the projection in the sky. This time, the translation device was fully operational from the start.

"Puny Earthlings," the pirate captain sneered, his voice filled with arrogance. "Have you made your decision, or shall one be forced upon you?"

Tom stepped forward, feigning nervousness. "Oh, umm… about that—" he began, but the pirate captain cut him off with a harsh laugh.

"It sounds like you have chosen destruction!" the captain's voice boomed with confidence, clearly enjoying the thought of wiping them out.

Tom raised a hand, his voice laced with just enough panic to make it believable. "No, no! We have something to offer first!"

The pirate captain paused, his interest piqued. Tom continued, maintaining his façade of desperation, "We know the Federation ships are on your tail. They could be here any minute. But we… we thought maybe you'd consider taking only *some* of our resources in exchange for something else—a powerful weapon we've developed."

Tom gestured grandly, his movements exaggerated as if he were trying to offer something truly valuable, something that might make them reconsider annihilating the Guild.

"How do you know the Federation is following us?" the captain asked, his voice dripping with suspicion.

"The Admins told us," Tom replied, carefully measuring his tone to keep the tension.

"Those damn meddlers," the captain growled, his mandibles clicking in irritation. "Always getting in our business. We aren't breaking any of their rules. Why would they keep doing this?" he grumbled, louder now, the frustration evident as he pondered their interference. "They're always like, 'you can't meddle in the affairs of others,' except they always meddle in ours."

Tom seized the moment. "Look, I just think you can get even further ahead of them if you took the weapon instead of the resources. It would help you against any Federation ships that might catch up."

The captain's scowl deepened. "No weapon is worth the resources you have, but I will entertain the idea. What kind of weapon is it?"

Tom feigned nervousness, then answered, "We call it the Deshieldinator. It fires a hyper-focused beam of energy at a target, forcing the shield's capacitors to work overtime. With the amount of energy focused on such a small point, the overload crashes the generators, leaving the target defenseless."

This grabbed the captain's attention. His dark eyes gleamed with interest, and he leaned closer to the screen, studying Tom for a long, tense moment. "Interesting. And we are supposed to allow you to fire this weapon at one of our ships, I suppose?"

"We wouldn't dare use it on one of your shields," Tom replied, holding steady, "but we can demonstrate on a building here in the city to show you its power."

The captain paused then nodded. "Very well. Show us the power of this weapon, and we might consider a deal."

"Captain, I don't know if this is a good idea," a voice from off-camera interrupted cautiously.

"Silence! Are you the captain?" the captain snapped.

"No, sir, but I'm just not sure we should—"

"You shut your mandibles!" the captain bellowed, clearly irritated. "These Federation ships have been the bane of our existence for too long. With a weapon like this, we could keep them off our tails when we cut things too close. It'll give us the time we need to secure more resources for sale."

Tom could sense the deal was slipping through the cracks of doubt, so he jumped in. "Thank you, Captain. You won't regret this decision." His voice was steady, guiding the captain back on track.

The captain grunted in response, distracted but still engaged. Tom subtly nodded toward Herbert, signaling the next phase. The guards pulled open the gates, the clanking metal echoing through the tense air. Herbert, along with a few of the Barbarians, wheeled the massive Deshieldinator out onto the street. Its size was imposing, easily twice the size of the one mounted on the walls, and its sleek, industrial design hinted at the power hidden within.

They maneuvered it into position, aligning it with a building down the street. The Barbarians, strong and stoic, braced the machine, gripping its sides tightly to ensure it didn't move when fired. The whirring hum of the machine filled the air as Herbert began the ignition sequence. The lights on the side of the device flickered before settling into a steady glow, and a meter on the side began to rise, showing the increasing energy buildup.

"This weapon looks like the one on your wall. Why would you offer it to us instead of mounting it on your walls?" the lobster captain asked, seeming suspicious.

"The one on the wall only *looks* the same," Tom lied. "It's actually completely different, and used to defend the base from monster attacks. This one is bigger, and we hadn't had the chance to mount it before you arrived. Bigger is always better, they say."

"Well, that's obviously true," the lobster captain said, seemingly mollified by the explanation. "Very well, proceed."

Everyone's attention was locked on the Deshieldinator. Tension thickened the air as the power levels reached their peak. When the meter hit full capacity, Herbert looked back at Tom for confirmation. Tom gave him a single nod.

Herbert pulled the trigger.

A brilliant beam of orange energy shot from the barrel of the Deshieldinator, slicing into the side of the building like a hot knife through warm butter. Herbert grinned as he slowly moved the barrel left, the beam cutting through the structure with surgical precision. As it cleaved through the building, debris cascaded from the wound in the stone and steel, and by the time the beam reached the halfway point, the top portion of the structure buckled. A moment later, it collapsed with a thunderous crash, the rubble crumbling into a thick cloud of dust that hung in the air like fog.

The pirate captain's eyes went wide with awe. He leaned closer to the screen, his mandibles opening slightly as the power of the weapon unfolded before him.

"I must have this weapon," he said, greed dripping from every word. "We will agree to take only half of your resources in exchange for the Deshieldinator."

"Captain, this really isn't wise. These Earthlings were just integrated into the System. They shouldn't have tech that is so powerful," the voice from off-camera pleaded once again.

"Do I need to throw you in the brig?! I said silence!" the captain barked, his greed overtaking any caution.

"We have been at war for so long with each other, that we have many weapons that could be integrated with the System's magics to allow us to create something truly unique," Tom tried to explain.

"All the more reason to be cautious, Captain. I really think we should—" the voice tried to continue.

The captain looked like he was about to blow a gasket when Tom interrupted. "It's a deal, Captain!"

The captain's face relaxed as he turned back to the screen and chuckled, leaning back in his chair. "You might be my new favorite victim, Earthling. With this weapon, the Federation will finally learn to fear us."

"Thank you, Captain. You honor me," Tom replied, adding a deep bow to sell the ruse. "If you'd like, you can come to pick it up at our gates. It's rather heavy, and we can't move it far."

The captain laughed heartily, his sharp mandibles clicking as he did so. "We will be there shortly to claim our prize."

The screen flickered off, leaving Tom and Derek standing on the battlements. Derek turned to Tom with a grin. "You saw that, right?"

Tom smirked. "You mean how he practically drooled over the weapon? Yeah, I saw it."

"I think you were right. They fell for it."

Tom clapped Derek on the shoulder. "Let's go deliver the captain his shiny new toy."

Descending from the wall, Tom and Derek moved toward the gates as the pirate ships started drifting closer, their hulking forms casting long shadows across the city below. "Herbert, be ready to activate the shields," Tom ordered.

Herbert gave a thumbs up and stepped off the platform of the Deshieldinator, his eyes gleaming with anticipation. He rushed back inside while Tom, along with Derek, James, Susie, Mark, Frank, and Lacey, all went out to meet with the captain. When they arrived at the Deshieldinator that was destined for the pirates, Tom told the other Barbarians to return inside and signaled Herbert to activate the shield on his command.

The ships hovered closer, their size and menace becoming clearer as they descended to about fifty feet off the ground. The lead vessel, a massive construct of metal and alien technology, extended a ramp from its front. The gangplank lowered to the ground with a metallic thud, and a bright light from inside the ship made it impossible to see who was approaching at first.

But as the light was partially blocked by a large, hulking silhouette, Tom's stomach dropped. Emerging from the ship was a creature far larger than he had anticipated—each of the lobsters stood about fifteen feet long and ten feet tall, their armored exoskeletons gleaming menacingly in the dim light.

"Greetings, Earthlings," the captain said as he stepped forward, his voice a deep, gravelly rumble. "You are even smaller than I imagined. No wonder you could not deliver the weapon yourselves."

Tom bowed low, making a show of his supposed fear. "Yes, Captain. We know we are insignificant compared to your power, but we only wish to survive. The System integration has been brutal, and we're grateful for your mercy."

The captain let out a harsh laugh, his mandibles clicking. "Yes, yes. I'll take pity on you—once we've secured our prize. We lost some time thanks to an unfortunate detour," he shot a glare at one of the other lobsters, a creature with an absurdly out-of-place eyepatch dangling from one eye stalk. "Bring the weapon over."

Tom signaled for Frank, who wheeled the larger Deshieldinator over toward the captain's crew, positioning it carefully.

"I think you'll be very pleased with this, Captain," Tom said, his voice dripping with false relief.

"Oh, I'm sure I will be," the captain said. His voice suddenly turned cold and cruel. "Especially once we take all of your resources as well."

Tom widened his eyes in mock horror, playing his part perfectly. "What?! You can't do that! You said—"

The captain's laughter rang out, sharp and maniacal. "Oh, I can—and I will! HAHAHAHAHA!"

With a subtle gesture behind his back, Tom signaled to Derek, who used his communication orb to signal Herbert. Without hesitation, Herbert used his communication orb and whispered the command. A split second later, a beam of rainbow-like light shot into the sky, spreading outward like an enormous crystal dome that enveloped the entire Guild building and its surrounding area. The shimmering barrier solidified with a hum, creating a protective bubble around them.

The captain blinked in confusion, his smug expression faltering.

"What is this?!" he demanded, his voice rising in a mix of fury and disbelief.

Tom smiled, his voice steady and calm. "It's probably not going to be your day, Captain."

Chapter 68

A Dramatic Turn of Events

Tom smiled malevolently as he waited for the next moments to unfold.

"Get the weapon onto the ship! NOW!" the pirate captain bellowed, his voice a guttural roar. His mandibles clicked furiously as he flailed his massive claws, screaming at his… men? Lobsters? Pirates? Whatever, he screamed at them to haul the Deshieldinator aboard. The pirates scrambled, their bulky forms crashing around the base of the ship, claws clamping in agitation as they hurried to follow the captain's orders.

The captain turned to storm back up the ramp, but the sharp crack of a rifle shot rang out. A sickening sound, like the snap of a crab leg, echoed through the air as the bullet punched clean through the captain's grotesque face, splattering dark, viscous blood onto the ramp. He let out a ghastly screech, thrashing his segmented tail wildly, much like a lobster writhing in boiling water.

A second shot followed almost instantly, this time accompanied by a searing beam of light. It struck the underside of the captain's exposed head, scorching through his softer underside. His shriek was cut short, and his body convulsed violently as he crashed onto the ramp and then lay motionless.

"Sorry, I didn't know where his brain was," Kiera's voice came through the orb hanging around Tom's neck, her tone nonchalant despite the carnage unfolding below.

Tom wasted no time. He equipped his greatsword, the familiar weight a comfort in his hands, and shot forward, charging at the remaining pirates. Beside him, Derek readied his mace and shield, a look of grim determination on his face.

One of the larger lobsters was already struggling to push the Deshieldinator up the ship's ramp, its claws straining against the weight. Another, hearing the commotion, turned and locked its beady black eyes on Tom and Derek. It let out a piercing screech, a high-pitched wail that vibrated through the air, and charged them with claws snapping in a menacing rhythm.

Undeterred, Tom and Derek surged forward to meet the beast head-on. The creature lunged with one of its massive pincers, aiming to grab Tom. With a quick motion, Tom batted the claw aside with his greatsword, its chitinous shell sending a sharp vibration up the blade.

An idea struck Tom. Switching his greatsword for the lightsaber, he whirled around the creature's outstretched arm, dodging another snap of its pincer. The weapon hissed to life, casting an eerie green glow as the blade extended. In one fluid motion, Tom completed his spin, raising the lightsaber above his head and bringing it down in a sweeping arc. The blade met the lobster's armored limb, and with a sizzling hiss, it cleaved cleanly through the claw, severing it from the creature's body.

The pirate screamed in agony, its tail slamming into the ground in a futile attempt to stabilize itself. Derek had already blocked the creature's second pincer with his shield and retaliated with a powerful downward strike from his mace. The impact was brutal, sending a crunch through the air as the lobster's claw shell shattered under the force.

The creature's screeching grew more frantic, its cries echoing through the street. Tom glanced toward the ship and saw that the ramp was closing, the remaining pirates retreating inside.

A single pirate stood at the top of the ramp, facing them. He reached up from behind his back, placing the old captain's pirate hat awkwardly on his head.

"Killing the captain was the worst mistake you could have made," the pirate said with what Tom assumed must be a menacing grin, its mandibles spreading to either side of its face.

His attention snapped back to the fight as a beam of concentrated energy erupted from the Deshieldinator on the wall, slamming into the ship's invisible shield. The shield flared to life, a shimmering barrier of light enveloping the vessel as it absorbed the impact of the beam.

Derek had moved forward, relentlessly battering the side of the pirate with his mace. Each hit produced a sickening crunch as the creature's armor began to cave under the assault.

Tom turned the lightsaber into a reverse grip and drove it into the side of the pirate's body, dragging the blade down the length of its torso. The lightsaber carved a glowing, molten line through the thick armor, and the creature let out a final wail of pain before falling silent.

As the lobster's body slumped to the ground, Derek climbed onto its back, finishing it off with a series of brutal blows to the head until its carapace shattered and the creature went still.

"Well, we're on this side of the shield now, so I guess we have to fend for ourselves," Derek said with a casual shrug, as though this were just another day.

Suddenly, a sound like shattering glass echoed from above. Tom and Derek instinctively ducked, covering their heads. When they glanced up, they saw that the pirate ship's shield was collapsing under the relentless barrage of the Deshieldinator's beam. The shimmering barrier flickered and failed, disintegrating into nothingness.

Tom's heart pounded as the second ship's shield flared to life, already under attack from the Deshieldinator. The sound of jet engines roared through the air as the F-35s took off from the side of the building. Tom watched as they passed through the Guild's shield, flying in perfect formation, preparing to circle around for a coordinated strike.

Deactivating his lightsaber, Tom re-equipped his greatsword, the weight of the familiar weapon grounding him as he steeled himself for whatever came next.

"This is going quite well, don't you think?" Tom said with a grin, glancing at Derek.

INVASION

Derek shot him a scowl. "You just had to fucking say something, didn't you?"

As if on cue, a beam of energy fired from the front of one of the pirate ships, slamming into the Guild's shield. It pulsed with the same eerie glow as the one that had taken down the other ship's shields. Tom's heart sank as he watched the beam push against the protective barrier.

"Shit, I didn't think they could get it up that fast," Tom muttered, eyes wide as the Guild's shield flickered under the pressure.

"That's what she said," James interjected quickly, simultaneously ducking another energy blast.

Before he could react further, a loud screech tore through the air as the beam cut off, followed by the sickening thud of a lobster corpse being flung from the pirate ship. The massive body hit the pavement with a gruesome crunch, limbs splayed at unnatural angles.

"Looks like Kuthir made his appearance," Tom said with a satisfied smirk.

"Those Mastadonians are worth their weight in gold," Derek agreed, his eyes fixed on the pirate ship as it continued to waver.

"So, what now?" Tom asked, scanning the battlefield.

"I say we wait. Let this play out a bit. We have people for a reason," Derek said. Ever the strategist, his calm demeanor was a sharp contrast to the chaos around them.

They watched as the Deshieldinator's beam tore through the second ship's shield. It sputtered and collapsed, leaving it vulnerable.

As the Deshieldinator began to tear through the third ship's shields, Tom heard the familiar roar of jet engines. His head snapped upward just in time to see the F-35s streaking through the sky, their missile bays opening as they lined up on the now-unprotected pirate ships.

"Maybe we shouldn't be this close to the ship," Derek said, a sudden note of panic in his voice.

Herbert's earlier warnings about the fireball runes echoed in Tom's mind, and the realization hit them both at the same time.

"Oh, shit, you're right!" Tom said, his heart leaping into his throat.

The group broke into a run, sprinting along the edge of the shield, desperately trying to put distance between themselves and the looming pirate ship.

"Lacey, get a barrier ready!" James shouted as they ran.

The first missile struck the lead pirate ship, and the resulting explosion was unlike anything Tom had ever experienced. The deafening boom was followed by a wave of scorching flames, fire erupting in a chain reaction as the fireball runes detonated in quick succession.

Lacey barely managed to throw up a barrier, and even through it, Tom felt the concussive force knock him off his feet. The world was consumed by fire and sound, the roaring flames washing over them like a tsunami, slamming into the Guild's shield and spreading outward.

Above them, the pirate ship groaned in protest as its engines sputtered and failed. The ship began to rapidly descend, its bulk hurtling toward the ground with a horrible screech of twisting metal.

"Go, go, go, go, GO!" Tom shouted, scrambling to his feet, his voice almost drowned out by the cacophony around them. The ground trembled beneath his feet as he ran, dodging chunks of pavement and debris that flew in every direction as the ship crashed.

Frank, moving faster than anyone his size had any right to, grabbed Susie under one arm and Lacey under the other, sprinting forward with giant, loping strides.

The pirate ship, now fully ablaze, hit the shield with a force that turned it to the side. The massive hull groaned as it slid along the barrier, its burning form moving in the same direction as Tom and the others, gaining speed as it careened across the street.

Tom's eyes widened in panic as he realized they were on a collision course with the ship. "No, no, no, no, NO!" he yelled, his legs pumping furiously, but it wasn't enough. The ship was closing in faster than they could run.

"Quit running straight at the damned thing—GO RIGHT!" Derek's voice cut through the chaos like a whip, and Tom's survival instincts kicked in. Without hesitation, he veered right, urging the others to follow.

As the pavement cracked beneath Tom's feet, he veered sharply to the right, heart pounding as the pirate ship scraped and groaned along the street behind him. He didn't stop running, the adrenaline coursing through his veins, knowing that the difference between life and death could be just a second or two. The screeching metal grew louder, and then, after what felt like an eternity, the noise stopped. Tom slowed to a halt and turned, his chest heaving, to take in the scene unfolding behind him.

The pirate ship had come to a gruesome rest. Several lobster-like pirates had been flung from the protective glass of the ship and now lay scattered across the road. Some had been crushed beneath the massive vessel's weight, their shells cracked open like eggs, leaking a dark, ichor-like substance onto the pavement. Others, though battered and broken, were attempting to rise on spindly, clawed limbs, their grotesque forms twitching in pain. One unfortunate soul had been impaled on the jagged remnants of a telephone pole, its segmented body writhing in its final moments.

"Frank… time to smash," James said with a grin, pointing toward the struggling lobster pirates.

"That's…" Tom wheezed, out of breath, "what she said…"

James simply nodded proudly. He held out a fist and Tom reflexively bumped it with his own.

With a smirk of agreement, Frank gently set Susie and Lacey down, his face hardening into a mask of rage. Equipping his greataxe, he activated his *Rage* ability, and in an instant, his entire demeanor shifted. With a primal roar, Frank launched himself at the closest lobster pirate with astonishing speed and ferocity, landing on its back. The creature let out a horrendous screech as Frank brought his axe down with brutal force, cleaving through its shell. With one final, sickening motion, he plunged his hand into the gory wound he'd created and ripped out a handful of its insides, flinging the steaming mass to the ground beside him.

INVASION

"We shouldn't let him have all the fun," Tom said, his smile turning into something dark and predatory as he gripped his greatsword and charged into the fray.

The others followed Tom's lead. Derek equipped his mace and shield while James took aim at the lobster pirates' eyes, firing precise shots with sharp cracks of his handguns. Spells flew through the air as Lacey and the other magic users cast a variety of destructive spells at the pirates still trying to recover from the crash. Fiery bolts and icy shards erupted from their fingertips, landing with devastating effect on the already weakened enemies.

The fight was chaotic, and yet, there was a rhythm to the battle. Tom's greatsword cleaved through shell and flesh alike, the weight of his strikes cutting down any pirate that dared stand before him. The street was quickly becoming a graveyard of crushed and broken lobster pirates, their bodies piling up under the relentless assault of Tom's Guild.

"More of them are coming!" James shouted as a fresh wave of pirates crawled out from the damaged ship, their claws snapping menacingly as they approached.

"That's what she said!" Tom shouted back.

James froze in place for a moment, catching eyes with Tom. He nodded in respect. "Nice."

Before they could get too close, however, shots rang out from behind the group. Kiera, positioned atop the building with her sniper rifle, was already picking them off one by one. The loud crack of her rifle echoed through the street as bullet after bullet found its mark, hitting the lobsters squarely in their weak points.

"Kiera to the rescue, again," Tom chuckled between breaths, driving his greatsword into the head of another pirate, silencing its screeches.

Smoke curled into the sky from the broken hull of the pirate warship, its mangled frame lying like a rusted claw against the Earth. The worst of the fighting had subsided, but the tension in the air hadn't gone anywhere.

Tom squinted as a shimmer of light flickered above the wreckage.

A massive, translucent screen snapped into view—projected directly above the ship's remains. Static crackled before giving way to a clear image of the pirate fleet's second-in-command, standing in a room that looked like it had just been hurled from orbit. Sparks spat from ruptured conduits behind him, and a thick trail of hydraulic fluid pooled near one wall, but the second-in-command stood tall and composed—eyes gleaming with cold intent.

"You continue to make terrible decisions," he said, voice low and smooth, almost amused. "You had the chance to surrender. Instead, you chose to bite at the claws of your betters."

Tom's eyes narrowed. *Betters?*

The pirate who had previously been the second-in-command pressed something on a control panel beside him—still half-buried in debris—and the screen shifted to a new feed.

Everyone on the battlefield turned to stare.

Above Earth's upper atmosphere, positioned like celestial wardens, were two enormous ships—easily ten times the size of the ones they'd already fought.

Suspended between them was a titanic metallic ring. Dozens of chains anchored it to both vessels. It glowed with a dull, red hum, its internal components slowly spinning like the teeth of some vast, mechanical god.

"What the hell is that...?" someone muttered.

Tom's stomach dropped. He pointed toward the ring, voice tense. "How did something that big avoid our radar scans?"

The image flickered again—returning to the second-in-command, who now wore a mocking grin.

"Really?" he said, cocking his head. "Do you think an advanced species like ours would come all this way without cloaking systems?" He chuckled. "We *wanted* you to see us coming, and now—we want you to understand how little control you truly have."

He threw his head back and laughed—maniacal and full of cruel delight.

"Deploy the Extractor," he said to someone off-screen.

The transmission cut.

The screen blinked out.

And the red glow from orbit began to intensify.

Tom stood frozen for a moment; eyes locked skyward.

"That's... not good," he muttered.

From behind the wrecked pirate ship, a thunderous boom echoed across the battlefield as another invader vessel spiraled out of the sky, its hull burning from multiple impact points. It slammed into the earth in the distance, a plume of fire and smoke erupting behind it.

Tom barely spared it a glance.

His focus was skyward—on the massive, chained ring now drifting slowly across the horizon.

The Extractor.

It was moving.

"It's not stationary," Tom said aloud, voice quiet with unease. "Why is it moving?"

Derek followed his gaze, eyes narrowing. The colossal ring wasn't just hanging ominously anymore. It was gliding westward, drawn along by the massive capital ships that tethered it—like a leviathan being pulled across the sky.

"Where the hell is it going?" Tom asked.

"It's not attacking directly," Derek said, voice flat as he tracked its path. "It's relocating. Strategic positioning?"

Tom frowned. "To where? What's west of here that they'd need it to be over?"

They stood in silence for a beat—watching as the monstrous ring crept across the atmosphere, dragging its shadow like a curtain across the land.

Then Derek's eyes widened.

"Water," he muttered. "They mentioned it. Back when they gave us their list of 'terms.' Food. Minerals. Water. And where's the deepest ocean on the planet?" His gaze turned serious. "They're taking it to the Pacific."

Tom's stomach dropped. "To extract… the ocean?"

"Or something in it. Or all of it," Derek said grimly. "They seemed pretty confident that they could take the resources of our entire planet before the Federation ships could arrive to stop them."

Whatever the Extractor was for, it wasn't just a weapon—it was a tool of mass-scale consumption. And it had just begun its work.

Before either of them could speak further, Tom's communication crystal pulsed—a sharp, steady glow against his chest.

Someone was calling.

Tom knew that whoever it was and whatever they had to say, it wasn't going to be good.

Chapter 69

Behemoth

Tom's orb crackled to life, and Kiera's voice came through, sounding tense. "Tom… come in, Tom."

He held the communication orb closer to his face, his pulse quickening at the worry in her tone. "Hey, Kiera. What's up?"

"You need to get up here, *right now*," she urged, the concern in her voice unmistakable.

"I'm on my way," Tom replied, already moving.

He bolted for the building, taking the stairs two at a time, the pounding of his boots echoing in the stairwell. Reaching the rooftop door, he slammed it open, bursting into the cool air outside. Scanning the roof for Kiera, he spotted her with her sniper team and Inari gathered at the far end, peering over the edge with urgent expressions.

"Tom! Get your ass over here!" Kiera shouted, motioning frantically.

He jogged over, his breath coming quickly, then leaned over the rooftop's edge, following Kiera's pointed finger. His gaze settled on a small group of lobster pirates gathered behind the wreckage of the first downed ship. One of them, standing to the side, was casting what looked like a barrier spell, protecting the others clustered in a tight circle. They were engaged in something, their movements deliberate.

"That can't be good," Tom muttered, narrowing his eyes.

"Inari thinks it's a summoning spell," Kiera said, her voice tense.

"When a group gathers like that, it's usually for a ritual. Look closely—there's a summoning circle forming beneath them," Inari added, her voice calm but grave.

Tom squinted. Sure enough, a glowing circle etched itself into the ground beneath the lobster pirates, growing brighter by the second. The creatures swayed in unison, holding each other's claws in a macabre dance, their antennae twitching rhythmically. The light of the circle flared, so bright it felt like staring into the sun. Tom shielded his eyes with his arm, the light painful even from this distance.

Suddenly, the light winked out.

Tom blinked, trying to clear the spots from his vision. As his eyes adjusted, he saw the lobster pirates lying motionless, their bodies limp and lifeless on the pavement. Whatever they had summoned had come at the cost of their lives.

INVASION

A low rumble shook the ground, growing in intensity. The earth beneath the street cracked, as though something massive was pushing its way up from the depths. The pavement bulged upward, slowly at first, then faster as chunks of asphalt splintered and flew into the air.

Then, with a deafening roar, the street erupted. A monstrous lobster emerged from the ground, its shell gleaming like jagged rock and its claws the size of houses. It reared up, towering over the street like a creature from a nightmare, easily the height of a six-story building. The beast roared again, the sound vibrating in Tom's bones, as it raised its massive pincers high into the air.

Crackling arcs of energy twisted together in mid-air, forming a massive projection of static and shadow. It shimmered for a moment—then locked into place with a flash of clarity.

The image of the new pirate captain filled the sky.

No name. No rank. Just the same cold, insectoid face Earth had come to know—once the second-in-command, now the leader of the invasion.

He stood in a darkened command chamber, sparks raining down behind him, the ship around him clearly ravaged—but his posture was unshaken. The red glow of control panels reflected in his multifaceted eyes.

"You thought this was over."

His voice echoed across the city. It was clear, measured, and filled with venomous pride.

"You thought taking our ships… collapsing our plans… would stop what is coming."

He leaned closer to the projection feed.

"But we are far from beaten. You wanted a ground war? Then you'll have one. On your streets. On your soil."

Behind the projection, the monstrous lobster beast roared loudly.

The pirate's mandibles twitched.

"You see… while you celebrated your little victory, our magi were busy calling down a force you cannot comprehend. A god of flesh and shell. Of rage and power."

He paused to let his point sink in as the behemoth smashed through a building with one of its claws.

"You killed soldiers." His voice returned. "But now, you face a deity. And your world will burn beneath its claws."

He chuckled once—low, amused.

Then it grew into a full laugh. Maniacal, gloating, cruel.

"Let the extermination begin."

The feed snapped off.

And the sky went quiet.

"Sweet zombie Jesus! What the absolute *fuck* is that?!" Tom yelled, his voice barely containing his horror at the sight of the towering monster.

His mind raced as he opened his System menus, trying to figure out his next move. Coming to a decision that the only real course of action was his *Ultimate Summons*, he stopped when he looked at his mana bar. A sinking feeling settled in his stomach as he saw the problem—he had overlooked something critical. Each of his permanent Mastadonian Summons drained five percent of his total mana. With eight of them summoned permanently, he had lost forty percent of his mana pool. Now, with his reduced reserves, he didn't have enough mana for the *Ultimate Summons* Skill that he had intended to rely on in this fight.

"Shit," Tom muttered under his breath, his fist slamming down onto the rooftop's edge in frustration.

Kiera turned to him, worry flashing in her eyes. "What is it?"

"I don't have enough mana for the *Ultimate Summons* I was planning to use," Tom admitted, anger creeping into his voice.

Quickly skimming through his notifications, he saw something that gave him a sliver of hope—he had leveled up. Without a second thought, he dumped all his points into Intelligence, raising it to seventy-four. His total mana jumped to seven hundred and forty points. But even with the boost, he was still short. With the eight Mastadonians summoned, his available mana was reduced to just four hundred and forty-four points.

Tom's mind raced as he did the math. If he wanted to use the *Ultimate Summons*, he would have to dismiss two of the Mastadonians.

Tom took a deep breath, glancing at Kiera, his mind racing. "I'd need to dismiss two of the Mastadonians to summon Ajax," he said, his voice tight with frustration.

"Dismiss me, then," Inari offered immediately, her voice steady. "You can always resummon me and keep me as a normal Summons after."

Tom blinked at her, his mind spinning.

"Who else should I dismiss?" he asked, feeling the urgency pressing down on him.

Inari hesitated for a long moment, her eyes meeting his, a flicker of something unreadable in her gaze. She seemed to wrestle with herself, trying to balance logic with emotion. Finally, she spoke with quiet certainty. "Onslo."

"Why Onslo?" Tom asked, confused. "He's a Warrior. Wouldn't he be more useful in this battle? I thought you'd suggest Rularis."

"We already have Bron," Inari explained calmly. "And Rularis can boost all of us with his Bardic abilities. Onslo, powerful as he is—is just one more fighter, and he can be resummoned quickly. Besides, you can use mana potions to get him back if needed."

Tom hesitated, anxiety clawing at the edges of his thoughts. This wasn't just a matter of logistics—it was about lives. The Mastadonians weren't just backup—they were a safeguard, a living contingency plan for any team they traveled with. Dismissing them meant removing the only real insurance some of these people had if a fight went sideways.

What if they ran into something stronger than expected? What if they needed raw power and it wasn't there?

His mind raced through a dozen scenarios, each one ending the same: with someone dying because he made the wrong call. The weight of leadership pressed down on him like iron.

"Tom," Kiera interrupted sharply, her tone brooking no argument. "Quit overthinking it. Be the Guild leader. Make the call."

INVASION

Her words cut through the fog in his mind. Nodding firmly, he glanced back at Inari. She smiled softly and stored her rifle back in her Inventory, showing no fear.

"I'm ready," she said simply.

With a heavy heart, Tom dismissed her, watching as she vanished. Then he mentally dismissed Onslo, watching his mana bar jump from four hundred and forty-four to five hundred and eighteen points. He felt the pressure ease slightly as he turned to scan the battlefield below.

The scene was chaos.

The Guild's fighters were battling the colossal lobster monster from a distance, but the beast was closing in. Its massive claw crashed into the side of a building, ripping off the top half with terrifying ease. A fighter got too close, and one of the monster's antennae whipped out, sending him flying across the street. He hit the ground hard, and others rushed to drag him to safety.

"Focus," Tom muttered to himself. He activated his newest Skill: *Ultimate Summons*.

A surge of power flowed through him as he began the intricate summoning ritual, his body moving in what felt like a practiced dance of martial precision. His hands moved in intricate patterns, sweeping through the air as if carving the very fabric of reality. His legs moved in a fluid, circular motion, his body acting as a conduit for the ancient magic coursing through him. Beneath him, a glowing blue magic circle appeared, humming with power.

Tom felt a dagger materialize in his hand as the final step approached. Without hesitation, he drew the blade across his palm in a single smooth motion, the pain sharp but distant in his focused state. He pressed his palms against the summoning circle, shouting the ancient words that filled his mind, his voice growing louder with each syllable.

"With this offering, I summon thee, great being from beyond the heavens! Strike down my foes with the vengeance and fury of a thousand tormented souls. Bring forth your wrath to wipe these sinners from the face of the Earth. Come forth, Ajax, I summon you! *Heaven's Retribution!*"

As the final words left his lips, Tom slammed his bloodied hands into the center of the circle. Lightning crackled up his arms, the blue light flaring into a brilliant, blinding glow.

As Ajax began to materialize in the sky, his descent from the summoning circle was like a beacon of divine power. The intricate yellow summoning circle above him glowed with a brilliance that cast the entire battlefield in a golden light.

The creature let out a monstrous roar, one that echoed through the city and rattled the windows of the surrounding buildings, much like the iconic cry of the old Godzilla films.

"You better be almost done, Tom. We've got big trouble incoming!" Kiera's voice cut through the tension.

The giant lobster behemoth stormed through the ruined streets, a living engine of destruction. Its segmented limbs crushed asphalt beneath them, each step cracking the earth like a drumbeat of doom.

The first building crumpled in an instant.

A four-story office complex collapsed beneath the creature's weight, the roof pancaking the floors below in a plume of dust and twisted steel. It didn't even pause. The beast's momentum was relentless—a god of rage and chitin, carving a path of devastation through what little remained of the city.

A second building fell under the sweep of its massive claw—a half-collapsed warehouse smashed into rubble, debris flying like shrapnel as the creature advanced.

And then it reached its target.

The Guild compound loomed ahead, protected by a shimmering barrier—one of the last remaining magical constructs still holding.

The lobster shrieked, rearing back and lifting both claws high into the air before bringing them crashing down onto the shield.

BOOOM.

The protective dome flared with blinding blue light as the claws slammed into it, sending shockwaves rippling outward. Concrete fractured. Trees bent from the blast. The air itself seemed to shudder.

On the rooftop nearby, Kiera braced herself against the concussive force, watching with a grim expression.

She pressed her fingers to the communication orb at her neck. "Herbert, come in. How's the shield holding?"

A burst of static crackled before Herbert's voice pushed through. "I'm givin' her all she's got, Kiera! But she can't take much more!"

Another strike from the behemoth hammered the barrier—this time visibly cracking its surface, fine lines of stress spiderwebbing across the dome.

The lobster slammed the shield again, harder this time. The crack widened. The dome flickered violently, pieces of its outer layer flaking away like burning paper.

Kiera's voice was tight. "If that thing gets inside…"

Tom didn't answer.

Because he felt it.

The summoning circle he had prepared pulsed.

The air turned dense—charged—like a thunderstorm had been frozen mid-burst above the city.

Overhead, the clouds churned, spiraling as if drawn into the gravity of something ancient and powerful. Rays of brilliant light broke through, piercing down toward the hovering circle in the sky above the lobster.

Arcane runes spun and snapped into alignment, interlocking as power surged into the ritual.

Tom's breath caught.

The ground beneath them trembled—not from the beast, but from something greater.

Something answering the call.

The lobster stopped mid-swing.

Its grotesque head turned slowly, antennae twitching.

It, too, had felt something. A force of implacable inviolability.

And it looked up.

INVASION

Straight into the light.

Tom felt the pressure of the moment building, the very air vibrating with a power that was almost suffocating. His ritual was complete. Rays of light broke through the thick clouds overhead, streaming down toward the summoning circle that now hovered directly above the giant lobster. The intensity of the power radiating from the circle sent shivers down Tom's spine.

Everyone, from the Guild members to the alien pirates, stared in open-mouthed astonishment. Ajax was perfection incarnate. In his six-winged form, with a radiant halo hovering above his head, he appeared almost too ideal to be real. His blonde hair seemed to shimmer with a golden light, and even the cloth that hung from his armor moved with a grace, as if it were part of the divine power that surrounded him.

Hovering above the city, Ajax's glowing skin emitted a soft light, casting an otherworldly glow around him. His flawless physique, chiseled and godlike, seemed to be carved from the very essence of divinity itself. In his right hand, he held a spear—long, pure white, and seemingly forged from some heavenly metal. The spear was the embodiment of celestial wrath.

He moved the spear with deliberate precision, aiming it squarely at the giant lobster below. The creature, though massive and terrifying, appeared insignificant in the face of such awe-inspiring power. The spear began to glow, its light intensifying to a brilliant yellow as Ajax summoned the full force of his power. Three magic circles materialized in front of him, hovering in the air, each one layered with intricate symbols and glyphs that pulsed with energy.

Orbs of light appeared at five points around each circle, connecting to form pentagrams within the glowing runes. Ajax reared back, his muscles rippling with effortless power, and hurled the spear with all his might. The sound of the throw was like the crack of thunder, and the spear launched forward like a bolt of divine judgment.

As the spear passed through the first magic circle, it doubled in size, transforming into a massive lance of pure light. It continued through the second circle, growing even larger, until it passed through the third circle, now an enormous beam of celestial energy. In the blink of an eye, the glowing spear slammed into the lobster's carapace with a sound like an explosion of divine power.

The lobster screamed, a horrifying sound that echoed across the battlefield, as the beam pierced straight through its massive body. The light seemed to burn the creature from the inside, cooking it alive as it was pinned to the ground like a fish on a spear. The monster's tail flailed desperately, its legs scraping uselessly at the pavement, but the power of Ajax's strike held it firmly in place. The brilliant light continued to flow from the spear for ten agonizing seconds, every moment filled with the unbearable radiance of divine fury as the beam seared the giant lobster's flesh, filling the air with the smell of cooked seafood.

The city fell silent as the overwhelming display of power continued. Guild members, pirates, even the sky itself seemed to hold its breath in awe. Time stood still as the beam blazed through the beast, its body slowly weakening under the relentless power.

And then, with one final, dazzling flash of light, the beam vanished. Silence followed, the giant lobster's lifeless body lying crumpled on the ground.

Ajax hovered in the air for a brief moment longer, his spear now gone, his work complete. He turned his gaze toward Tom, their eyes locking across the distance. A small, knowing smile tugged at the corner of Ajax's mouth, and for a fleeting moment, Tom felt his heart stir with admiration.

With a single nod, Ajax acknowledged his role in the battle, then slowly ascended back into the glowing summoning circle from which he had come. As his form disappeared, the circle exploded into a shower of glittering, golden light that rained down on the battlefield like a heavenly blessing.

Chapter 70

Pincer Attack

Acrid smoke rose into the air. The smell of cooked seafood mixed with burnt flesh and dead fish rose to Tom's nostrils, making his mouth water as his gag reflex kicked in. He retched as the mixture of scents wafted on every breeze. Getting his stomach under control, he stood upright and looked over the side of the wall lining the roof of the building at the ground below.

The giant lobster lay motionless on the ground beneath him. In the middle of the giant creature was a hole large enough to drive a truck through, the edges burnt and flaking off. Ajax's single attack had slain the beast and kept the battle on more even ground. Tom silently thanked Azroc for helping him acquire that Summons.

Suddenly James bumped into him, clearly trying to scooch past the Warlock while carrying an absolutely enormous tub of...

"Is that... butter?" Tom frowned.

James simply looked at his leader as if the man were crazy. "I'm hurt, Tom. Devastated, to be honest. I don't know what I've done for you to think that I'd have my lobster *plain*, like some heathen."

He shook his head, muttering more complaints as he disappeared toward the massive creature.

Tom's head still swam from using so much mana all at once, and James' antics were not helping matters. A pain throbbed behind his right eye from being left with only eighteen mana. Pulling a potion from his Inventory, he popped the can open and drank the sweet liquid as quickly as he could. Looking at the blue bar in his display, he saw it begin to rise rapidly.

Tossing the empty mana potion can aside, Tom cast the first *Summon Demonic Creature* spell, focusing his energy on Inari. A black summoning circle materialized beneath his feet, and from it, Inari rose, her form emerging from the swirling shadows of the spell.

"You're still alive, I see," Inari remarked, walking to the edge of the rooftop and surveying the chaos below.

"Yeah," Tom replied, his voice slightly hoarse. "We took down the big one."

Inari's gaze swept over the battlefield below. "Good, then the plan worked. You may make us permanent Summons again if you desire."

Tom shook his head, still dizzy from mana fatigue. His vision blurred slightly, and a dull throb pounded in his skull.

"Give me a minute," he muttered, trying to regain his composure.

Inari raised an eyebrow, a flicker of confusion crossing her usually stoic face as she observed his shaky condition.

"He just burned through a ton of mana," Kiera said, approaching Tom and placing a steadying hand on his arm. Her eyes scanned him, concern flickering behind them.

"I'm fine," Tom assured her, forcing a weak smile. "Just keep the ground teams covered."

Kiera hesitated, her lips pressing into a thin line, but she nodded and returned to her sniping position at the rooftop's edge. The crack of her rifle echoed across the battlefield as she resumed picking off pirates.

Tom turned back to Inari, drawing a small dagger and pricking his finger to begin the ritual. The crimson drop of blood fell into the beam of light connecting them, sealing the pact. Moments later, Inari's form shimmered as she became a permanent Summon once again.

Without wasting time, Tom cast the spell to summon Onslo. The hulking Mastadonian Warrior emerged from the summoning circle with a grunt, his massive sword resting over his shoulder. After completing the same ritual for Onslo, Tom surveyed the chaotic scene below. The city was a burning battlefield with bodies littering the streets—both pirate and human. Flames and gunfire filled the air as both sides fought for dominance, the clash of steel and the cries of battle an unrelenting backdrop to the carnage.

Tom's communication orb flared to life once again, the pulsing glow sharp and insistent. He snatched it up with a sense of dread already knotting in his chest.

"Tom here."

Brian's voice came through fast, tight with urgency. "We've picked up a massive disturbance forming over the Pacific. Something's happening out there. We don't know what yet, but every reading we've got says it's not natural—and not small."

Tom's stomach dropped. The Extractor.

He didn't waste time.

"Got it," he said, already switching to talk to the F-35 team. "Anderson, status."

The reply came quickly, engines roaring faintly behind the pilot's voice. "We're airborne and circling the city. Last target just went down. We're still here, but if we fire down on the city… it won't be pretty."

"New priority," Tom said. "We've got movement over the Pacific. Some kind of massive construct—the same one that came in cloaked. We think it's active now."

"How big are we talking?"

Tom glanced toward the sky. "Big enough to make cities nervous."

A beat of silence.

"You want us to scout?" Anderson asked.

INVASION

"Not just scout," Tom replied. "If there's anything you can do to slow it down—or disable it—do it. You're the only team mobile enough to reach it in time."

"Copy that," Anderson said, his voice sharpening. "We'll go see if we can clip its wings."

"Keep me updated. Live feed if possible. And stay alert—this thing was never meant to be subtle."

"Understood. Anderson out."

The transmission ended, and Tom slowly lowered the orb. His eyes drifted west, toward the unseen threat crawling across the sky.

If that thing reached the ocean and did what they feared…

He pushed the thought aside and turned back toward his team. There was still a battle to finish—and a world to protect.

The sky stretched endlessly around the formation of F-35s, their sleek forms slicing through the air as smoke trails and wreckage dwindled in the distance behind them.

Inside the lead jet, Anderson switched to squadron-wide comms.

"Alright, listen up," he said, voice firm but calm. "We've got new orders from Tom. That thing hanging in orbit? It's not just for show."

There was a beat of silence as engines roared steadily around them, then a voice crackled through the comms.

"You mean the big glowing nightmare ring that looks like it wants to eat a continent?" one of the pilots replied.

"That's the one," Anderson confirmed. "It's on the move, and it's headed west. Looks like it's aiming for the Pacific. Command thinks it's about to do something big. Tom wants us to intercept, investigate, and—if we see an opening—put a dent in it."

Another pause. Then—

"YEEEEAAAAHHHH! Now we're talkin'!"

Eric's voice exploded through the channel, louder than necessary and twice as excited.

"About damn time we got a real challenge!" he hollered. "I got four missiles left, two guns primed, and a hunger for destruction, baby! Let's give that thing a welcome it won't forget!"

A beat later came the unmistakable call from the pilot-turned-Warrior. "WOOOOO!"

The channel was briefly filled with muffled laughter and groans from the rest of the team.

"Settle down, Eric," Anderson said, though the faint amusement in his voice betrayed that he wasn't really mad. "We're not going in blind. Eyes on first, fire second—unless that thing so much as breathes wrong."

"Copy that," several voices echoed.

Anderson adjusted his heading, angling the squad westward. The coast wasn't far now.

"Let's move. Target's somewhere over the Pacific. We find it, figure out what it's doing—and if we can, we clip its damn wings."

The jets banked in unison, engines screaming as they pushed toward the horizon.

Tom's eyes fixed on a group of humans trapped near a downed ship, surrounded and taking heavy damage. "Onslo! We're heading for that group," Tom commanded, pointing toward the besieged fighters.

Before Tom could take a step, he felt a strong arm wrap around his waist, and in an instant, Onslo hoisted him over his shoulder like a sack of grain.

"What the hell?!" Tom shouted in surprise, flailing briefly in Onslo's iron grip.

"We go the fast way," Onslo replied in his deep, rumbling voice before leaping off the edge of the building.

"What? Wait, NO—!" Tom's voice cut off into a high-pitched scream as they plummeted through the air, his heart leaping into his throat. They hit the ground with a resounding crash, dust flying as Onslo landed in a crouched superhero pose, unshaken by the fall. Without hesitation, he took off at a blistering speed, racing toward the besieged group.

When they neared the embattled humans, Onslo abruptly set Tom down, the ground beneath Tom's boots still trembling from the landing. His legs wobbled as he tried to steady himself, but the adrenaline surging through his veins soon banished the dizziness. Drawing both greatswords, Tom activated his *Tattoo of Brute Strength*, feeling a familiar rush of raw power coursing through his muscles.

The sight ahead made his blood boil. A pirate had clamped its massive pincer around the wrist of a soldier, the metal armor screeching in protest under the pressure. The man screamed as his arm was wrenched backward. Another lobster pirate seized the opportunity, snapping its claw shut around the man's other arm, severing it with a sickening crunch. Blood spurted from the wound, drenching the pavement as the man's agonized cries filled the air.

Before Tom could act, a third pirate raised its claw and fired a deadly spell that bored a hole clean through the soldier's chest. His lifeless body collapsed in a heap, the battlefield momentarily still as Tom's fury reached a boiling point.

"NO!" Tom roared, his rage overtaking him as he lunged into the fray.

With a powerful leap, he landed on the back of a pirate and drove both swords into its thick carapace with such force that they pierced through the creature and embedded into the pavement below, pinning it in place. The pirate screeched in agony, thrashing violently beneath him as its death throes rattled the ground.

At Tom's side, Onslo was a whirlwind of death, smashing pirates aside with brutal swings of his colossal sword. One pirate's carapace cracked like brittle stone under Onslo's relentless assault, its innards spilling out as he cleaved it in two with a single, mighty blow.

This wasn't just survival. This was vengeance.

The lobster beneath Tom thrashed violently, its tail snapping up and down in rapid, chaotic motions. The creature's desperate struggle bucked Tom wildly, making it difficult for him to maintain his balance. He glanced over and saw Onslo, who had apparently decided to ride his own bucking lobster nearby. Just as Tom regained his footing, a claw struck him hard on the side of the head, sending him crashing to the ground.

He tasted copper as blood filled his mouth, and the world spun around him in a dizzying blur. Stars danced in his vision as he staggered back to his feet, spitting a mouthful of crimson onto the cracked pavement. Every movement made his head swim, his surroundings turning into a disorienting swirl. Desperately, Tom cast *Dark Restoration* on himself, feeling the deep purple magic pulse through his veins, mending the damage to his body. Slowly, his vision cleared, just in time to spot another pincer barreling toward his head.

With a guttural roar, Tom grabbed the attacking claw with both hands, channeling all his fury into a single act of brute strength. His muscles strained as he bent the claw back, the exoskeleton cracking audibly before shattering under the pressure. The pirate screeched in agony, attempting to pull away, but Tom held it fast in a vice-like grip.

Without hesitation, Tom summoned his lightsaber into his hand. The blade hissed to life, glowing with intense energy. In a single fluid motion, he swung down, severing the lobster's arm cleanly at the joint. Then, with deadly precision, he reversed his grip and thrust the blade forward, driving it deep into the pirate's face. The sizzling of cooked flesh filled the air, and the creature's cries were abruptly silenced. It slumped to the ground, dead.

Tom wasted no time. He yanked the lightsaber free and turned to face the next opponent, only to come face to face with Onslo. The two warriors locked eyes for a moment, recognition passing between them. In unspoken agreement, they turned and fought back to back, each covering the other as they slashed through the remaining foes.

A piercing scream suddenly rang out to Tom's right. He whipped around just in time to see a woman go down beneath a pile of lobsters. Rage flooded through him as he charged toward her, slashing furiously with his lightsaber. Each swing carved through the pirates with ease, their carapaces splitting open and spilling smoldering innards onto the ground. By the time he had cut his way to the woman, it was too late. Her dismembered body lay in a pool of blood, scattered pieces staining the pavement around her.

The sight of her lifeless form ignited a new wave of fury within him. Tom spun on the nearest lobster pirate, its claws snapping in preparation for an attack. It lunged at him, pincers outstretched. But Tom moved with blinding speed, slicing across its body in rapid, precise strikes. Each hit severed more of the creature's limbs, and within seconds, the pirate lay in a heap of smoldering chunks.

Without thinking, Tom stooped down and grabbed a piece of the lobster's claw. The remaining pirates hissed and bubbled, staring at him with what appeared to be shock—or at least, what Tom assumed was shock; their expressions were hard to read. Slowly, deliberately, Tom popped the cooked claw meat into his mouth, chewing it thoughtfully as the pirates recoiled in horror.

"Hmmm," he said through a mouthful of their comrade, making sure to chew as loudly and grotesquely as possible. "Yeah, James was right. It needs some butter sauce."

That did it.

The pirates screeched in outrage, their bubbling sounds rising in a furious crescendo. All at once, they charged, claws raised in a desperate bid for revenge. But before they could reach him, Onslo dropped from above, his massive form crushing one of the lobsters beneath his boots with a sickening crunch. The Mastadonian wasted no time, immediately hacking at the next lobster with his colossal sword.

Tom grinned wickedly and launched himself at another lobster whose charge faltered at the sudden arrival of Onslo. With deadly precision, Tom unleashed a flurry of strikes, each one faster and more savage than the last. His lightsaber carved through shell and flesh, leaving nothing but destruction in its wake. Soon, the ground was littered with the corpses of lobsters, their bodies twitching in their death throes.

The remaining pirates hesitated, their beady eyes wide with terror as they took in the carnage. They seemed unsure of whether to flee or press on. Tom spat out another piece of claw meat and leveled his gaze at them, his eyes gleaming with barely contained fury.

"Get back to the group!" he bellowed, turning to the Guild members. "We need to reinforce our positions and not get separated! That way!" He pointed toward their defensive line.

Without hesitation, the Guild members rushed in the direction Tom had indicated, eager to escape the battlefield littered with broken pirate bodies.

Tom retrieved his greatswords, stored them in his Inventory and quickly joined Onslo, jogging after the group to ensure everyone was accounted for. As they moved, Tom noticed the main army had regrouped, holding the right flank where the pirates were launching their attack. Bron, ever the commander, stood at the front, leading the charge and directing fighters into position. Tom started moving in that direction when the sudden sound of angry screeching filled the air from their left.

"Shit! Watch the other flank!" Tom shouted, catching Derek's attention. Derek, who had been in the thick of the group, barking out orders while casting healing spells, turned sharply at the sound.

Derek's face twisted in frustration as he bellowed to the Guild, "Barbarians to the left flank! Don't let them surround us!"

INVASION

Kevin was the first to react, sprinting toward the left flank and crashing into the leading lobster with a roar. Kirsten followed closely behind, her sword swinging with precision, slicing through the thick exoskeleton of the nearest pirate. Above them, Huthu let out a powerful trumpet call from his trunk, leaping into the fray like a massive battering ram. His feet slammed into a lobster's back, crushing the creature under his weight as he let loose his war cry, a trumpeting sound so primal it made Tom feel as though they were battling on the African savanna.

The battle on two fronts raged fiercely, and despite the Guild's best efforts, the lobster pirates were pushing them back. The air was filled with the chaotic sounds of clashing metal, the screeching of pirates, and the desperate cries of the Guild members. The lobsters, fueled by their rage and the buffs their casters had begun to rain down from the pirate ships, were relentless. Casters from the pirate ranks chanted in unison, their spells bolstering the strength and fury of their comrades, and the Guild began to feel the overwhelming pressure as more and more pirates joined the fray.

Tom, slashing at a pirate with his lightsaber, heard a deafening crash above as the last of the shield spells around the ships shattered. He gritted his teeth, knowing they were running out of time. Switching off the lightsaber, Tom quickly summoned his greatswords once more, flames licking along the blade as he activated *Dark Inferno* on his Greatsword of Hell's Inferno.

With his enhanced strength, Tom spun his blades in wide, sweeping arcs, the power of the dark fire leaping from his swords to sear through lobster carapace and flesh alike. Each strike bashed into their thick exoskeletons, shattering them and sending fire spreading across their bodies. The inferno clung to their shells, scorching the pirates as Tom pressed forward, carving a path through the horde.

Despite the carnage he was unleashing, the pirates' sheer numbers were overwhelming, and the Guild continued to be pushed back, inch by inch. Tom chanced a glance at the final ship hovering nearby, its ramp lowering as even more lobster pirates spilled onto the battlefield. His momentary distraction cost him—a pincer struck him hard across the face, sending him staggering back, struggling to maintain his balance.

Blood trickled from another cut on his lip, and the metallic taste only stoked the fire of his rage. He wiped the blood away with the back of his hand and roared, his anger mounting alongside the growing concern that filled his chest. With a flurry of powerful strikes, Tom slashed through the offending lobster, cutting it down with swift brutality before turning his attention to the next enemy. They had to find a way to break this pincer attack—if they didn't, the Guild would soon be trapped in a kill zone.

Chapter 71

Wings of Steel

High above the fractured landscape of Earth, the sky stretched out in every direction like a boundless ocean of blue, laced with thin threads of cloud. The F-35s tore through it in formation, their silver hulls glinting under the sun, vapor trails streaking behind them like ghostly contrails.

Inside the cockpit of Unit 1, Anderson adjusted his flight controls, the HUD illuminating his helmet visor with steady streams of data—altitude, velocity, formation spacing, radar telemetry, and fuel readouts. His fingers worked in practiced rhythm, skimming over toggles and touch panels, keeping the formation tight and smooth as they made their way west.

Below, the ruined terrain of Earth passed by in a blur of color and devastation—scorched forests, shattered highways, twisted cityscapes still coughing smoke into the air. The scars of the System integration ran deep, stretching all the way to the coast.

"Still no sign of any welcome party," Anderson muttered, mostly to himself.

"Maybe they're too scared to roll out the red carpet," came the voice of Unit 3—Eric—through the comms, cocky as ever. "Or maybe they're still picking bits of their friends out of our missiles from earlier."

Anderson smirked behind his helmet. "Stay sharp, Eric. We're in the open sky now. If they wanted to hit us, this would be the place to do it."

Up ahead, the Pacific came into view—a glittering expanse of deep, uninterrupted blue, its surface reflecting the sunlight like rippling glass. The contrast against the battlefield they'd just left behind was jarring. Out here, everything looked untouched. Peaceful, even.

But they all knew better.

"Approaching Pacific airspace," Anderson called out over the squad channel. "Maintain tight formation. Unit 2, eyes on the lower quadrant. Unit 4, prep scan package. I want radar, thermal, and gravitic readings sweeping this whole sector."

Affirmative pings echoed back from the squad, each unit falling into task with crisp efficiency.

INVASION

Inside the cockpit, the low hum of the engines, the faint vibrations through the seat, and the soft beeping of the sensor arrays were a comfort to Anderson. Familiar. Controlled. Out here, in the air, the world made sense—even when the world itself didn't.

The HUD pulsed as sensor data fed in, painting a map across the ocean surface. No targets yet—but the background interference was increasing. Something massive was distorting the scan range.

"Getting a lot of static here," he said. "Something's interfering with the readouts."

"Yeah, I'm feeling it too," Eric chimed in, voice still casual, but quieter now. "Whole ocean looks calm, but this air's got a weird vibe. Like the sky's holding its breath."

Anderson narrowed his eyes at the flickering anomaly marker on the edge of his display.

He didn't like that analogy.

It meant something was about to exhale.

The ocean beneath them continued, vast and silent, a shimmering blue canvas unbroken by islands or ships. For a moment, it felt like they were flying into the middle of nothing.

The clouds parted, and all at once, the sky was filled with metal.

Two colossal warships hovered like monolithic sentinels above the sea, their dark, armor-plated hulls glowing faintly with orange vent lines and clusters of pulsating red energy nodes. Each was easily the size of a city block, dwarfing even the largest naval vessels Anderson had seen on Earth. Between them, suspended by massive reinforced chains and gravitic stabilizers, hung the true horror: the Extractor.

It was even larger up close.

A circular construct the size of a stadium, it rotated slowly on its axis, several massive outer rings orbiting a dark central core that glowed with an eerie crimson pulse. The chains from the two warships fed directly into it, like veins pumping lifeblood into a mechanical god.

"Holy shit," Eric breathed over the comms. "That thing looks like it eats moons for breakfast."

Anderson didn't respond at first. He was too focused on the sensor array, watching the readings spike with each passing second. Gravitational fluctuations, temperature shifts, and a strange static buildup in the upper atmosphere.

This wasn't just a weapon.

It was something far worse.

"Keep your distance," he finally said. "I want full scans—movement patterns, energy output, anything we can pull. Stay in staggered pairs, high altitude. If this thing twitches wrong, I want room to maneuver."

"Copy that," came from Units 2 through 7, their voices tight but controlled.

"Unit 3," Anderson added, "try to contain yourself."

"No promises, boss," Eric replied, his tone light. "But if that thing so much as blinks, I'm feeding it a missile to the eye socket."

"It doesn't have an eye socket." Anderson chuckled.

"Then I'll make one."

Anderson shook his head but smiled faintly. That bravado might drive him insane on the ground, but in the sky? It was something steady in the madness.

They banked gently into a wide arc, looping around the descending Extractor. Its rings shifted slowly, aligning themselves like gears settling into place. Below it, the ocean churned, whitecaps forming despite the lack of wind. The sea itself seemed to recoil beneath the device.

"Getting turbulence," Unit 5 reported. "Feels artificial."

"Confirming," said Unit 6. "Air pressure's fluctuating. Temperature spike—ten degrees in under a minute."

"Energy's building," Anderson muttered, watching the HUD turn red in several places. "It's doing something."

"Yeah, it's powering up," Eric said. "And I do *not* want to be in the splash zone when it finishes."

The Extractor's core began to glow brighter—no longer pulsing, but steady and rising, like a breath being held.

Anderson's hands tightened on the controls.

Whatever it was about to do, it was going to be big.

Chapter 72

Retreat

Wiping blood and soot from his brow, Tom panted heavily from the prolonged exertion. His chest heaved as he finally managed to carve out a small pocket of breathing room.

Without hesitation, he yanked a stamina potion from his Inventory, chugging it down as fast as he could. As the cool liquid worked its magic, relief surged through him, his stamina bar refilling and the aching fatigue in his muscles momentarily lifting. But the sweat continued to pour down his face, and the weariness in his limbs lingered like a dull throb beneath the surface.

He grimaced, feeling the soreness creeping back, and knew he couldn't slow down. Gripping his weapons tighter, Tom reactivated his *Tattoo of Brute Strength*. The cooldown and duration aligned perfectly, an odd mercy from the System, as it had been well over an hour since the battle began.

The fight had dragged on far longer than he ever thought possible. In the past, he'd scoffed at how quickly battles were portrayed in stories, thinking they should last longer—shouldn't real warriors be able to fight on for hours? Now, he knew the truth. Prolonged combat was hellish. He wasn't fighting through sheer willpower but through the boons of magic and the System that sustained him.

Striking out at another pirate, Tom's muscles screamed in protest, and he nearly faltered on the recovery. The lobsters seemed endless, wave after wave crashing into their dwindling ranks. His ragtag band, though fierce and determined, was being worn down. Their best fighters were on the front lines far longer than they should have been, taking brutal hits when the others fell back to be healed.

Tom had seen too many go down only to pop a Healball, rise again, slay a pirate, and then fall for the final time moments later. The grim reality of the losses gnawed at his resolve, threatening to tear his sanity apart. He could still see their lifeless bodies, some torn to pieces, their sightless eyes staring up at the sky. The weight of it was almost too much to bear—but he fought on, for those who still stood.

Gritting his teeth, Tom finally activated his *Tattoo of Life Absorption*. He had been saving it for a dire moment, and now, he needed the refreshing energy more than ever. His body ached for relief, and while his stamina potion had helped, the constant fighting had taken its toll. He cast *Dark Restoration* on himself, hoping it would ease the fatigue.

While it cleared his mind and soothed some of the pain, it did little for the burning lactic acid buildup in his muscles. Fatigue continued to drag at him like a heavy weight.

"Hold the line! Keep the rotations going! Pull the injured back to be healed! If one of your brothers or sisters falls, take their place and avenge them!" Derek's voice boomed over the chaos, his powerful commands cutting through the din of battle. He was doing everything he could to keep morale high, his powersuit making him a beacon of authority in the chaos.

At times, Derek himself leapt into the front lines, his armored fists smashing through the toughest pirates. His mere presence inspired those around him. After breaking through an enemy line, he would fall back, casting healing spells, giving others a chance to fight while he patched up the wounded.

The Mastadonians were proving their worth, their strength holding the line in places where the humans were faltering. Bron led the charge; sometimes holding off two or three attackers at once, his greataxe cleaving through lobster shells like they were paper. Belik stood with the spellcasters, guiding them through which spells to use and where they would be most effective, hurling restraints and debilitating magic at the enemy when he could, giving the fighters an edge.

Amath remained in the rear with the wounded, healing as many as possible while casting protective barriers to block incoming attacks. His focus never wavered, even as the battle pressed on.

But it was Rularis, the Bard, who was proving the most invaluable. His songs of heroic tales from his world rang through the battlefield like a clarion call. The buffs from his music surged through Tom and his allies, strengthening their resolve, their strikes hitting harder and their reflexes sharpening. Every so often, Rularis would switch to songs of dread, turning the morale of the pirates against them, the haunting melodies casting debuffs that sapped their strength. When these buffs and debuffs overlapped, they managed to push the lobsters back, if only for a brief moment, before the tide would inevitably turn again.

Even with their combined efforts, the battle was a brutal grind. The pirates kept coming, seemingly without end, and for every foot of ground they gained, it felt like they lost twice as much in blood.

Tom's eyes scanned the battlefield, searching for any opportunity—anything they could use to turn the tide. He clenched his greatsword tighter, knowing that they couldn't hold on forever. But as long as he had breath in his body, he would fight. For his Guild. For the fallen. For the ones still standing.

For the chance that they might just survive this hell.

Tom couldn't shake the feeling that the charge beyond the shield had been premature.

But if they hadn't pushed when they did, the pirates might have simply waited just outside the barrier, letting the Extractor drain the planet dry while they stood powerless to stop it. Worse, Tom might've found himself overwhelmed—cut off and outnumbered on this side of the shield, with too few allies at his back to turn the tide.

Kiera and her team continued to rain bullets down on the enemy from above, providing some relief to the beleaguered forces below. Inari, perched with deadly precision, had saved more than one Guild member from the clutches of death, picking off pirates just as they were about to land fatal blows.

Despair began creeping into Tom's thoughts. Backup from the Federation could still be days away, and after only a few hours of relentless fighting, they were already faltering. Every now and then, Tom glanced up at the sky, heart pounding whenever he thought he heard something overhead. But it was always just his imagination—or the distant echoes of battle rolling in from the city, the faint booms and rumbles of a fight still raging beyond the walls.

When the pirates began to mass behind certain sections of the battle lines, Herbert's elemental grenades—as the Guild had taken to calling them—would be hurled into the throngs. These offered brief moments of reprieve, the explosions thinning out the enemy ranks. But these were only ever temporary. Soon, more pirates would clamber over the charred or dismembered bodies of their comrades, undeterred by the carnage left behind. Of all the grenades, the acid bombs proved most effective against the thick-shelled lobsters, though their deadly liquid often risked splashing onto friendly fighters.

Another grenade arced over Tom's head, bouncing once, twice, before detonating in a burst of orange flames. The heat expanded out in a thirty-foot radius, and the smell of burning chitin filled the air as lobster pirates screeched in agony. Their tough exoskeletons, while offering protection in battle, became their downfall in the intense flames, trapping heat inside and cooking their insides like meat in a frying pan.

Tom's tattoo continued to work, feeding him energy and keeping his health bar topped up. He was in a rhythm, dispatching enemies with a brutal efficiency. As he fired a point-blank *Eldritch Blast* at the face of another lobster, he suddenly felt a searing pain. A pincer had clamped down on his extended hand, the grip tightening until he heard the sickening crack of bones in his wrist.

With a cry of pain, Tom quickly stored his greatsword and, with barely a second's hesitation, equipped his lightsaber. The green blade hissed to life, cutting clean through the lobster's claw. The pirate screeched, retreating in pain, but the severed limb remained locked in place around Tom's wrist, the muscles frozen even in death.

"Motherfucker!" Tom cursed through gritted teeth, realizing the claw was still clamped tight.

He carefully sliced off the top portion of the claw, and finally, the grip loosened just enough for him to pry it free. Gasping in pain, he cast *Dark Restoration* on his injured wrist, standing behind a Barbarian who had taken his place on the line as he seethed with rage. His eyes burned with fury as he glared at the pirates.

Storing his lightsaber, he felt his wrist slowly mend, the dark energy of the spell plus his tattoo draining the life from the pirates knitting the bones back together.

When the pain in his wrist subsided enough for him to move it freely, Tom knew it was time for something bigger. Feeling his anger fuel his actions, he began to power up a spell, letting the raw emotion channel into the casting. His hands moved fluidly, performing the intricate motions required for the spell as more and more mana pooled into his palms.

"Step right!" Tom barked, his voice sharp with focus. The Barbarian to his front complied without hesitation, shifting aside just in time.

The gap created by the movement didn't go unnoticed. One particularly eager lobster saw the opening and charged directly toward Tom, its eyes gleaming with vicious intent.

Tom's hands glowed brighter as the mana surged to its peak. "*FINAL… FLASH!!!*" he roared, thrusting both hands forward.

The pirate's eyes widened in terror, the glowing energy reflecting in its black, beady eyes. It scrambled to retreat, but it was too late. A brilliant beam of energy erupted from Tom's hands, slicing through the pirate in an instant and blasting through the row of enemies behind it. Fifteen lobster pirates were obliterated in the blast, their bodies vaporized by the sheer force. The shockwave rippled outward, burning off limbs and claws from those on the fringes of the blast.

One particularly unlucky pirate, rushing across the rear to reach a friend, had both its eyestalks vaporized by the edge of the beam. With a bubbling screech, it flailed wildly, bumping into other pirates as it ran in blind circles, sowing further chaos in their ranks.

The brief silence that followed was broken only by the sizzling of charred lobster flesh, the smell of burnt meat hanging thick in the air. Tom stood amidst the destruction, his chest heaving from the exertion.

But there was no time to rest. The enemy still surrounded them on three sides, and the battle was far from over.

Jumping back into the fray, Tom reactivated his lightsaber, its green blade hissing to life as he slashed through anything in his path—claws, thick carapaces, even stray limbs that jutted out too far from the advancing pirates. Each cut was precise, but it still felt like a losing battle. Their comrades were either injured or dead, and though the pirates paid dearly for every inch, they were slowly but surely losing ground.

"We have to figure a way out of this!" Tom shouted back at Derek, struggling to keep the fear out of his voice.

"I fucking see that! We're trying to figure something out! Our only option may be to take down the shield, but then they'll get in!" Derek shouted back, frustration lacing his tone as he parried a lobster's claw with his shield.

Belik, casting spells at the rear, called out, "I've got an idea, but it's risky!"

"We're all ears!" Derek yelled over the din of battle.

"If we drop the barrier and retreat to the gates, I can create an *Ice Wall* to slow them down. It won't hold them off forever—they might be able to crawl over it—but it'll buy us enough time to get inside the gates and reactivate the shield. We'd still be fighting some of them inside, but it's better than being overwhelmed out here."

Derek nodded grimly. "We don't have anything better. Do it. Spread the word!"

INVASION

The plan began to ripple through the remaining forces, with each person shouting it to the next. The idea of retreat and regrouping seemed to bolster morale, the promise of a brief reprieve offering a glimmer of hope. Tom fought harder, attacking with renewed energy, slashing faster and with more precision, determined to keep the lobsters at bay for just a few more crucial moments.

Derek activated his communication orb. "Herbert, take down the barrier!"

"You sure?" Herbert's voice crackled through the orb, laced with hesitation.

"We're getting overwhelmed out here. Do it now, or we'll all be dead!" Derek replied urgently.

"Okay," Herbert confirmed, and a few seconds later, the massive shield generator powered down. The once-brilliant rainbow hues that had shimmered around the Guild like a protective dome began to flicker and fall, dissipating into the sky.

As soon as the barrier dropped, the back line of fighters retreated in a hurried but controlled march toward the gates, which lay behind the wreckage of the crashed pirate ship. They had to maneuver around the debris, but slowly they began funneling into the safety of the Guild base. Those on the wall continued firing down at the pirates, though the bullets seemed to have a minimal effect on the creatures' thick shells, pinging off of them with little damage.

At the front, Tom, Derek, and the Mastadonians stood firm, holding back the relentless surge of pirates as long as they could. Their movements were desperate but coordinated, each swing of their weapons intended to keep the advancing horde at bay for just a few precious moments longer.

"Now, Herbert! Reactivate the shield!" Derek yelled into his orb as he fought off another lobster, the urgency clear in his voice.

The generator roared back to life, and once again the familiar rainbow energy shot into the sky, arcing above the Guild like a fountain before cascading down. The pirates, sensing their opportunity was slipping, surged forward in a final desperate attempt to breach the walls before the barrier could fully form.

The Mastadonians charged the front line with Tom and Derek, swinging their weapons in wide, brutal arcs to force the pirates back. The enemies screeched and snapped their claws, but the show of strength made them hesitate just long enough.

Belik raised his staff high above his head, his voice booming across the battlefield, "*ICE WALL!*"

A towering pillar of ice erupted from the ground at the far end of the battlefield. It rapidly spread along the front, freezing everything in its path. Lobsters caught in the spell were flash-frozen mid-attack, their claws and antennae suspended in jagged blocks of ice. The wall formed an imposing barrier between the retreating Guild members and their foes.

"Go! Fall back!" Derek commanded as the last of the fighters rushed through the gates. The heavy doors slammed shut just as Tom and Bron ran through, the sound echoing across the courtyard. The rainbow barrier solidified overhead, trapping a hundred lobster pirates inside, many of whom were still frozen in Belik's ice wall.

Tom collapsed onto the ground, panting heavily as he lay flat on his back, staring up at the sky through the shimmering barrier. His body was drenched in sweat, his muscles screaming from exhaustion. He could hear the distant clatter of weapons and the final cries of pirates as Bron and the other Mastadonians leapt from the wall to finish off the remaining enemies inside.

"Well, that went to shit," Tom said with a dry chuckle, his eyes fixated on the swirling colors of the shield above.

"Yeah. We made it back, but now we're trapped inside here with them," Derek said, his voice thick with a mix of relief and dread as he surveyed their new situation.

The courtyard was eerily silent save for the distant fighting on the other side of the walls. They had survived, but the price had been steep. Now, with a hundred or so lobster pirates still trapped inside and no way out, the battle was far from over.

Chapter 73

Cavalry

The second Tom stepped back under the Guild's shield, a strange mix of relief and guilt hit him. The noise outside dimmed, the chaos a little more distant now—but not gone. Not even close.

He pulled out his communication orb and activated the link, fingers tightening just a bit around the smooth glass.

"Kiera? You okay?"

There was a pause, then her voice came through—rough, like she'd been running.

"Still here," she said, catching her breath. "We moved a few blocks. Got out just before another sweep. They're getting more aggressive, but we're still kicking."

Tom let out a breath he didn't realize he was holding.

"Good. Just… keep your head down, alright? We're working on something, but it's not ready yet."

"No surprise there," she said, a tired chuckle undercutting the tension. "But I'll take something over nothing."

The orb dimmed as the call ended. Before Tom could slip it away, Derek came up beside him, face drawn tight with exhaustion.

"James and his crew didn't make it back in time," he said. "Last check-in said they were near the west side—too far out. They didn't get the recall."

Tom's heart sank.

"They're still out there?"

Derek nodded. "Looks like it. Comms are spotty, but yeah."

Tom rubbed at his face. It was always like this—the moment he got a second to breathe, something else punched the air right back out of his lungs.

"Think they'll hold out?"

Derek didn't answer right away. He didn't need to.

Tom let out a slow breath and shook his head. "James is just gonna have to do what Kiera's doing—stay mobile, stay hidden. They're smart. They'll adapt."

Derek gave a small nod. "We've seen them pull through worse. But they won't hold out forever."

"Yeah," Tom muttered. "Which means we've gotta give them something to hold out for."

He leaned against a chunk of shattered stone, arms crossed tight over his chest. The weight of it all was back again—settling in his shoulders like it never left.

"Okay," he said after a beat. "Let's talk plans. I need ideas. Even bad ones."

Derek grunted. "Alright. First thought? Full assault. Drop the shield, hit the pirates with everything we've got, try to overwhelm them before they regroup."

Tom was already shaking his head. "We've got people scattered, wounded, and low on supplies. That ship they crashed into the city is still spewing out drones and foot soldiers like it's a damn clown car. We drop the shield now, and they flood us. We'd lose too many."

"Yeah," Derek admitted. "That was my 'let's die in a blaze of glory' plan."

Tom sighed. "Okay. What about an evacuation?"

Derek raised an eyebrow. "To where? The Guild Hall's surrounded. The roads are cratered and the air support is gone."

"We've still got a few armored vehicles—"

"Which seat, like—twelve people, max."

Tom winced. "Right. So... logistical nightmare."

Derek shrugged. "Unless you've got a teleporter hidden under your bed."

"I did, but the vending machine won't sell me another one," Tom muttered, rubbing his eyes. "Alright, plan three: surgical strike. Get a small group in, hit a key point, like the command center in that ship—"

Derek shook his head immediately. "We just got back from trying to punch through their lines, and we barely made it out. Sending a handful of people in now would be suicide. They'd get chewed up before they even found the front door."

He paused, frowning. "And honestly, the command center was probably on that first ship we brought down. Everything else we've seen looks more like forward operating posts. There's no central brain left to lobotomize."

Tom winced. "So even if we could get to them… it wouldn't matter."

"Exactly," Derek said. "And with how spread out the pirates are now, we wouldn't be disabling a single command structure—we'd just be poking one hornet nest while the others swarmed us."

Tom ran a hand through his hair. "Okay. So, we can't run a direct assault, can't evacuate, and there's no silver bullet command center to shut down. This is going great."

They stood there for a moment, staring into the middle distance like two men reading the world's worst menu.

"Y'know," Derek said, "we're not very good at this whole not dying thing."

"Speak for yourself. I'm amazing at not dying," Tom replied dryly.

A voice cut through their banter.

"Sounds like you two are finally desperate enough for a good idea."

Tom turned, eyebrows lifting as Herbert approached—grimy, sweaty, and wearing a smile that always meant something chaotic was brewing. He had a rolled-up map in one hand and grease smudges up both arms like war paint.

"Herbert," Tom said, straightening up. "Please tell me this isn't one of your 'well, it might work' ideas."

"Oh, it's exactly that," Herbert replied, grinning wider. "But it's better than all the ones you two have come up with so far."

He slapped the rolled map onto a nearby slab of rubble and spread it out. It revealed a rough sketch of the city's underground infrastructure—storm drains, old service tunnels, sewer mains—layered beneath areas where pirate movement had been thickest.

"Here's the plan," Herbert said, tapping the map. "We use these tunnels to get under one of their main staging zones, plant explosives, and then lure the bastards into that spot. Once they're gathered—boom. We collapse the ground underneath them and bury half their army."

Tom blinked. "You want to blow up a piece of the city?"

"You want to not blow up a piece of the city?" Herbert shot back. "Buildings are already wrecked. This gets us results."

Derek leaned in, frowning. "How do we even get them all into one place without tipping our hand?"

"That's the other part," Herbert said. "We make some noise. Send a decoy team out to cause enough havoc that the pirates rally to squash it. They're too aggressive not to bite if they think we're making a push."

Tom studied the map, the pieces sliding together in his mind. "So… one team sets the charges. The other draws them in. Time it right, and we blow a crater in the middle of their operation."

"Exactly," Herbert said. "It won't wipe them all out, but it'll cut deep. Take out a huge chunk of their force, and more importantly—it'll shatter their momentum. We hit them when they're off balance, then push hard while they're scrambling."

"It won't win the war," Herbert added, "but it'll give us the window we need to end it."

Derek nodded, eyes still on the map. "We'll need a distraction. Something big to keep them looking the other way."

Tom's gaze sharpened, the weight of everything settling on his shoulders again. But this time… this time there was a plan.

"Then we give them one," Tom said grimly.

Suddenly, his communication orb pulsed to life.

"Tom, are you there?"

Tom raised it to his mouth. "Yeah, I'm here. What's happening out there?"

"The pirates are moving through the city," Kiera said, her voice tight with tension. "They're… not happy, to say the least. We're having to stay on the move to keep ahead of them. We won't be close by for much longer."

"Do what you have to. Stay alive," Tom said.

"Copy that. We will," she replied. Still calm, but there was strain in it.

The orb dimmed for a beat.

Tom held it up again. "James, come in, James."

There was a pause, then—

"Joe's Crematorium: You kill 'em, we grill 'em."

Tom blinked. "…Seriously?"

"That is not proper radio etiquette!" Lacey's voice snapped in the background, scandalized.

Tom couldn't help the faint smile tugging at his mouth. "Glad to hear you're still alive."

"Define alive," James said. "We're on the move. Trying to stay ahead of the pirates. They're tearing through the city like pissed-off kids in a Lego store. No coordination, just maximum destruction."

"Sounds about right," Tom said. He rubbed the back of his neck, the weight settling there again. "You're not going to be able to stay close to the Guild for much longer. We're putting something together, but it's going to take a little time."

"I figured. Just give us the word when you need the chaos dialed up to eleven," James said. "I'm running low on ammo, but my enthusiasm remains at a dangerous high."

"That's what I'm afraid of," Tom muttered, shaking his head. "If you've got a better idea, now's the time to speak up," Tom said, leaving the question hanging in the air.

A long stretch of silence followed. Tom's worry began to creep up as the seconds ticked by.

"James?" Tom called again, concern lacing his voice.

"Nope, no better ideas. Even brain girl's got nothing… OW! No kicking!" James yelped.

"Try to stay as close to the Guild compound as you can," Tom said, shifting back into commander mode. "I know that's not easy, but if we pull this off, you'll want to be within sprinting distance when the hammer drops."

"Understood," James said. "Alive and nearby. We're good at one of those."

"Let's aim for both," Tom replied dryly and closed the connection.

He turned to the others. "Alright. We've got a plan. Now we need teams."

Herbert was already pointing at the map. "I'm going underground. No offense, but none of you know what these older tunnels look like, and if the ceiling caves in on the guy carrying the detonator, this all goes sideways fast."

"Agreed," Tom said. "You're on the explosives team."

"I'll go with him," said TJ, stepping forward. "I worked with explosives in the early days, and I can navigate tight spaces without panicking. Plus, somebody's gotta make sure he doesn't arm a bomb with a wrench and blind optimism."

"Hey, my optimism is surgically calculated," Herbert grinned.

"I'll join them too," said Bobby, cracking his knuckles. "I've got the gear for it, and I've blown up enough stuff to know how not to blow myself up in the process."

Tom nodded. "Good. Kedron, Clay—you two are backup. Keep them covered and make sure they don't get overrun while setting the charges."

Kedron gave a solemn nod. "We'll get it done."

Clay just gave a thumbs up. "Boom squad, let's go."

Tom turned back to the others. "That leaves the rest of us for the distraction team. We'll be the noise. The target. We draw the pirates in, make them think we're pushing hard, and hold them just long enough for the other team to finish their work."

Derek cracked his neck. "That's a good way to get shot."

"That's why I'm bringing people I trust not to die," Tom said. "Derek, Bron, Jay, Michael, Graham, Kevin, Kirsten, Briana, Austin, Isaac, Bohdan—you're with me."

Everyone nodded or gave their version of "Let's do this," from grim nods to muttered curses and a few cheerful shoulder-pops. They were ready.

Almost.

"Wait," came a familiar voice.

They all turned to see Father Blakely approaching, armor stained with ash, but his posture still straight as a board. His expression was calm, but his eyes were sharp.

"I want to go with the decoy team."

Tom frowned. "Father… I appreciate that, but this team is going to be right in the thick of it. You could get hurt."

"We're all going to get hurt, Tom," Blakely said gently. "That's what war does."

"Still—"

"You're sending people into danger to protect everyone else. That's what you're doing, and it's the right call. But I can't stay behind when my flock needs protecting. If I can shield one person—heal one wound, or give one soul a moment of peace before the end… then I need to be there."

Tom hesitated, but the silence around him said plenty. No one was arguing.

"I won't be a burden," Blakely added. "I know how to move. I can stay back. But if I'm not willing to make a sacrifice to keep them safe, I'm not the man I claim to be."

Tom looked at him for a long second, then finally nodded.

"Alright. You're with us. But stick close to the rear, and if I tell you to run, you run. Got it?"

"Understood," Blakely said with a small, peaceful smile. "Besides, if things go really badly, I have a few words I've been saving just for pirates."

Derek raised an eyebrow. "You have pirate-specific sermons?"

"Of course. Did you think I was some cliché televangelist?"

Chapter 74

Skyfire

The Pacific shimmered below like an oil-slicked mirror, its surface stirred by the turbulence of something massive unfolding above it. Anderson's F-35 HUD glowed with red and yellow warnings—energy readings, magnetic interference, gravimetric spikes—all of them bad.

"This thing's about to do something real ugly," he muttered.

Above and ahead, the two enormous alien warships loomed like airborne citadels. The Extractor suspended between them pulsed with ominous energy, its rotating rings now fully aligned and glowing like the eye of a storm. Whatever this machine was, it wasn't bluffing.

"Unit 3, anything?"

"Still alive and sexy, boss," came Eric's voice, unmistakably pleased. "But I don't like how that thing's humming. Sounds like it's charging up for a death laser or a real angry mixtape."

Anderson's lips twitched. "Focus. We need weak points, structural flaws, anything we can exploit."

"Scanning," Eric said, then added under his breath, "Y'know, if we live through this, I'm putting in for hazard pay… and a parade."

Anderson's cockpit filled with data, but none of it looked promising. No obvious reactor cores, no exposed conduits. Just layered armor and shifting magnetic fields. The Extractor was designed to take hits—and keep going.

Then a new alert pinged across the HUD.

Incoming vessels. Multiple. Fast.

Anderson swore under his breath as sleek, angular craft began peeling off from the flanks of the larger ships—small, agile fighters, dark like obsidian and moving with unnatural precision.

"We've got company," he barked. "Twelve bogeys, vectoring toward us fast. All units, break formation. Evasive maneuvers. Do not let them herd you."

Eric let out a high-pitched "WOOOOOOO!" like this was the best day of his life.

The sky exploded into motion.

Anderson pulled hard on the stick, his jet banking into a tight roll just as plasma fire lanced past his tail. A heartbeat slower and he'd have been slag. He countered, diving low over the ocean surface, then pulling up sharply to throw off pursuit.

INVASION

Behind him, Units 4 and 6 split high and low, luring two of the enemy fighters away. But the alien pilots were aggressive—flanking wide, adjusting angles, working together like they'd rehearsed this exact fight.

Anderson leveled off, locked onto the nearest hostile, and squeezed the trigger. The F-35's Gatling gun roared to life, a torrent of tungsten tearing through the sky. The rounds stitched across the alien fighter's wing—sparks, smoke, then a satisfying detonation as the ship spun out of control and erupted into flame.

"One down," he muttered. "Stay sharp."

Above him, Eric dove through a cluster of enemy ships like he was surfing a lightning bolt, rounds screaming from his guns.

"HOOOOLY MOTHER OF MARS, THIS IS GLORIOUS!"

He pulled into a corkscrew maneuver, evading two lock-ons with barely an inch to spare. His jet shot between the enemy formation, both wings nearly clipping two of the alien vessels. Before they could react, he opened fire at point-blank range—both enemy ships vanished in twin fireballs.

"Double kill, baby! That's how we do it in Unit 3!" he yelled, followed by another victorious, "WOOOOO!"

Anderson gritted his teeth, trying to maintain his focus. "Unit 3, if you could keep your celebration under Mach 2, that'd be great."

"Just letting them know Earth's got style!"

More fighters broke off from the main group, chasing Units 5 and 7 toward the cloudline. The air was thick with contrails, tracers, and explosions—a high-speed ballet of death.

Anderson pulled up into a tight loop, drawing an enemy tailing Unit 2 into his sights. He flipped the bird as he passed overhead, pulled the trigger, and shredded the pirate vessel from stern to nose in a hail of bullets.

But for every one they downed, more were closing in. These weren't just dumb drones—these were trained, organized, and hell-bent on clearing the skies.

"We can't keep this up forever," he muttered. "They're stalling us. Trying to keep us away from the Extractor."

"Good luck with that," Eric crowed. "I've still got eighty percent ammo and a whole lot of bad decisions left to make!"

Another enemy fighter locked onto Eric—Anderson watched as Eric flipped the jet upside down, nose-dived at the ocean, and then at the last second pulled into a rising curve, leading his pursuer into Unit 6's crosshairs. A burst of gunfire turned it into flaming debris.

"Teamwork, baby!" Eric whooped. "Someone put a camera on me, this is art!"

Anderson grunted. "Try not to get yourself killed before the real fight starts."

His radar pinged again—more enemy contacts launching. It wasn't over. Not even close.

But they were still flying, and as long as they were flying, Earth still had a shot.

Anderson's HUD blinked warnings, but he pushed them aside, weaving between streams of enemy fire.

"Unit 2, you've got one on your tail—breaking left!"

The jet twisted mid-air, the pursuing alien ship adjusting almost instantly. These things weren't just fast—they were responsive. Adaptive. Anderson gritted his teeth and banked into a wide arc, angling upward for a better shot.

"Unit 5, peel wide and flank right! Get some crossfire on 'em!"

Around him, the rest of the squad was locked in battle. Unit 4's jet trailed smoke but stayed airborne, while Unit 6 managed to clip an enemy with a snap-turn spray of rounds. The F-35s were holding their own—barely—but it was clear the pirates weren't trying to win the fight.

They were buying time.

"Hey, boss?" Eric's voice crackled in over comms.

"Busy!"

"Yeah, me too—BUT ALSO, THAT THING IS GLOWING WAY TOO MUCH."

Anderson risked a glance up and to the east.

His stomach dropped.

The Extractor—suspended between the two massive support vessels—was changing.

The concentric rings that had been slowly rotating before were now spinning faster, glowing bright enough to cast reflections on the ocean below. Between them, the space in the center wasn't just shimmering—it was warping. Reality itself twisted, like looking through broken glass under pressure.

"Oh hell," Anderson breathed.

The noise hit a second later—a deep, thrumming pulse that rattled through his cockpit. Not a sound so much as a feeling, like his bones were being used as tuning forks. Then came the light—a piercing beam of energy shot straight downward from the center of the rings, slamming into the ocean with a thunderous hiss.

And that's when the water began to rise.

It didn't boil or explode—it lifted, like gravity had taken a coffee break.

A massive column of ocean water surged skyward in a towering vortex, spiraling into the beam of energy. Entire waves, dozens of feet high, were drawn straight up—and they didn't fall back. They vanished into the swirling rings above, consumed by the machine.

"It's... it's siphoning the ocean," Anderson whispered. "It's not just a weapon—it's God's vacuum."

The sky darkened as moisture was pulled upward, forming dense clouds that immediately spun outward into a superstorm-like spiral. Wind gusts slammed into the F-35s, throwing off trajectories and rattling cockpits.

"Shit! Unit 7's losing altitude—he's caught in the updraft!"

Anderson saw it—Unit 7's jet wobbling as turbulence shoved it off course, skimming dangerously close to one of the Extractor's support ships.

"Keep the formation tight!" Anderson barked. "Don't let that thing pull you in. Get distance if you have to—keep fighting the escorts, but stay the hell out of that beam!"

INVASION

Eric let out a loud, "WHOOOOOOOOOA this got extra spicy real fast!"

"Eric, shut up and fall back ten degrees west. Now."

"Copy, falling back—but I am gonna shoot two more ships before I do. You know, for morale."

More enemy fighters peeled off from the main vessel—this time banking wide, trying to push the Earth pilots into the beam's widening zone of effect. Smart. Ruthless. They were forcing the defenders to choose: die in the dogfight or risk the siphon.

Anderson gritted his teeth. "Units 2 and 4, keep them engaged but do not follow into the beam's path. Units 5 and 6, keep to the western perimeter and flank those trying to corral us."

He turned his gaze to the Extractor again.

It wasn't just pulling water anymore—it was pulling power. Lightning arced around the spinning rings, tracing patterns across the sky like circuitry. The clouds above had started to spiral outward, forming a massive storm eye centered on the machine. The pressure drop was so severe that Anderson's ears popped, even in the cockpit.

Below, the ocean's surface was dipping in a wide, shallow crater—as if a drain had opened in the sea itself.

"How the hell do we stop that thing?" Unit 6 muttered over comms.

Anderson didn't have an answer.

But he knew one thing for certain: if that thing stayed online, Earth wasn't just going to lose the war.

They were going to lose everything.

Chapter 75

Beneath the Surface

Herbert had always said that if he died in a sewer, he wanted it on record that he called it.

"This is disgusting," Bobby muttered as the manhole cover screeched open.

"It's character-building," Herbert replied, tightening the straps on his gear. "This is the smell of victory. Or possibly something that's been dead since the '80s. Either way, soak it in."

The storm drain loomed beneath them—dark, wet, and about as welcoming as a grave. A small ladder clung to the concrete wall, slick with condensation and something Herbert chose not to examine too closely.

They were standing in a narrow alley just off the Guild's southern wall, the shield flickering overhead like a shimmering curtain. Smoke curled in the distance. The city beyond was still very much a war zone, but down here, things were quiet. Too quiet, which was always a problem in his line of work.

"Alright," he said, patting the side of his satchel. "We've got enough explosives to turn a city block into modern art, and exactly zero backup if things go sideways. So… business as usual."

"That's your pep talk?" Clay asked, adjusting the grip on his weapon.

"It worked on me," TJ muttered, already lowering himself onto the ladder. "Let's get moving before the smell gets worse. And yes, I'm aware that it will absolutely get worse."

Herbert followed, boots hitting the slick metal rungs with a soft clunk clunk clunk as he descended. The air thickened the farther he went—damp, sour, and filled with the distant gurgle of water that hadn't seen sunlight in decades.

The bottom was… well, it was a sewer. A low, arched tunnel of concrete, barely tall enough for a man to stand straight, with trickles of water running in thin streams along the gutters.

Kedron and Bobby followed next, then Clay, who pulled the manhole shut behind them with a muted clang that echoed just a little too loudly.

They clicked on headlamps and shoulder lights, their beams cutting through the dark. Dust motes danced in the air, disturbed only by the sound of quiet footsteps and the ever-present drip of water.

"Straight route should take us under Sector Twelve," Herbert said, checking the map on his datapad. "That's where pirate activities are the thickest.

INVASION

We detonate from below, and it'll be like pulling the rug out from under a freight train."

"You sure about the tunnel's integrity?" Bobby asked, eyes scanning the stained concrete walls.

"Let's put it this way: if we die, it'll be quick, educational, and deeply ironic."

Clay chuckled softly. "You're a real ray of sunshine."

Herbert just grinned and adjusted the straps on his pack again.

"Let's move. Every step we take down here is one closer to dropping a city block on some very punchable aliens."

And with that, the team advanced—five figures moving through the underbelly of a broken city, on their way to set the kind of trap that would either save everything… or collapse it all around them.

They hadn't been walking ten minutes before Clay spoke up with the kind of casual certainty that Herbert had learned to fear.

"Y'know," Clay began, "this whole underground infrastructure is probably where the lizard people who run the government live."

Herbert didn't even look back. "You have three sentences to explain yourself before I electrocute your boots."

"Think about it," Clay continued, his voice echoing off the concrete. "Whole tunnels no one uses. Weird vibrations in the walls. Humidity just high enough for scales. It's textbook lizard colony behavior."

"Oh my God," TJ muttered. "He is James' people."

"I knew he was one of the fringe types," Bobby added. "You're the guy who thinks pigeons are government drones too, aren't you?"

"They're not?" Clay replied, dead serious.

Herbert sighed audibly, which in a tunnel just sounded like the sewer itself was disappointed.

"I'm adjusting your 'most likely to get us all killed' ranking," he said. "Congratulations, you just passed the sewer gas."

They kept moving through the tunnels, the gurgling of runoff getting louder as they entered a wider chamber with a cracked maintenance catwalk running along one side. The concrete here was chipped and old, the metal rails rusted through in places.

That's when they heard it.

Scraping. Skittering. Wet footfalls.

Herbert turned, eyes narrowing.

"We've got movement—right side. Multiple contacts."

Something snarled in the dark.

Then came the shriek.

Three shapes leapt out from the shadows—goblins, small and twisted, their greenish skin slick with filth. Crude blades in hand, they howled as they charged.

"Knew it!" Clay yelled, drawing his blade. "They're the foot soldiers of the lizard people!"

"Shut up and stab!" Bobby barked, already firing a burst from his sidearm.

One goblin went down in a spray of blood and sewage.

Another rushed Kedron, only to meet a flash of steel as Kedron twisted, slicing it clean across the chest. It shrieked, gurgled, and dropped.

The third jumped for Clay—who met it mid-air with a fist to the face, then body-slammed it into the side wall with a squelch that sounded medically concerning.

"Don't mess with a man who drinks sewer coffee!" Clay yelled triumphantly, stepping over the corpse.

Herbert raised an eyebrow. "That's not a thing, right?"

"It is now."

The group paused, scanning the shadows for more.

There was nothing.

"Everyone good?" TJ asked, scanning with his flashlight.

Kedron nodded silently, already checking his blade.

Bobby reloaded. "Nothing says 'fun team bonding' like surprise goblins in a dark, wet death tube."

"We should name this tunnel," Clay said, clearly still riding the adrenaline. "Something dramatic. Like Goblin Alley. Or The Lizardman Speedway."

"How about 'Clay shuts up until we're topside?'" Herbert offered.

Clay just grinned. "Jealousy is a disease, my friend. Seek treatment."

They kept moving deeper into the winding sewer system. The goblin ambush had been sudden—but not unexpected. The pirates weren't the only things crawling through this city's veins.

And if Herbert's map was right, they were getting close.

Very close.

Chapter 76

The Spark

The sky hung heavy with dark, churning clouds—a foreboding curtain that seemed to press down on the gathered warriors. They stood in tense silence, their steady breathing belying the rapid cacophony of their hearts beating against their chests while they smelled the death that had been wrought in the cool, damp air. The assembled group, handpicked by Tom, adjusted their grips on weapons, their eyes fixed on the distant horizon where their enemy would soon appear. Armor clinked softly as they shifted, the sound almost swallowed by the oppressive atmosphere. The scent of impending rain mingled with the metallic tang of anticipation, creating an almost palpable tension.

A sudden flash of lightning split the sky, illuminating the determined faces and casting stark shadows across the city that now lay before them after having left the gates of the Guild. The brief brilliance was followed by a low rumble of thunder, a portentous drumroll heralding the coming conflict. As the first drops of rain began to fall, their splatters on the ground sounded like the prelude to a symphony of chaos. Each raindrop seemed to amplify the electric charge in the air, heightening the sense of imminent action.

Tom stood just outside the Guild's main gates, the shield humming softly above like a living dome. Behind him, the heart of the resistance. In front of him, the broken city—and whatever hell waited among the crumbled streets.

One by one, his team had gathered.

Derek's arms were crossed, his expression unreadable.

Bron, silent and immovable as ever.

Jay and Michael, checking gear and weapons with calm, practiced precision.

Graham, Kevin, Kirsten, Briana, Austin, Isaac, and Bohdan—all ready, all hardened by fire.

Even Father Blakely—hands clasped behind his back—wore the look of a man who had already made peace with whatever came next.

Tom looked at them all. Then he took a slow breath and stepped up onto a broken slab of pavement, raising his voice just enough to carry.

"I'm not going to sugarcoat this. What we're about to do is dangerous. We are marching into a fight with no guarantee that we'll walk back out."

The group fell silent, their eyes on him.

"But I need you to remember something," he continued. "We're not doing this because we're trying to be heroes. We're not doing it for glory, or pride, or revenge. We're doing it because it gives everyone behind that shield a chance. A real one."

He looked toward the glowing edge of the barrier, then back to his team.

"There are people counting on us. People hiding in basements. People who can't fight, who've already lost too much. Today, we make sure they don't lose everything."

He paused, letting it hang in the air.

"This might not be the end of the war. But it could be the beginning of the end. And if we're going down, we're going down swinging. Together."

A few nods. A murmur of agreement.

Then Derek clapped a hand on Tom's shoulder. "You done? Because I've got about two more quips before I need to punch something."

Tom smirked. "Let's go light the fuse."

He turned, sword in hand, and walked straight through the flickering shield. The others followed without hesitation.

The city beyond felt like it was holding its breath.

Burned-out vehicles littered the roads. Buildings leaned like weary soldiers. Smoke curled in the distance, and the only sound was the occasional echo of debris shifting—or worse.

They moved in tight formation, sticking to alleys and collapsed streets, heading toward the coordinates Herbert had marked. It didn't take long.

They reached a wide intersection flanked by ruined storefronts and half-toppled streetlights—an open plaza that had once been a park, now just cracked earth and ash.

"This is the spot," Tom said.

Bohdan stepped forward, lifting his hand in the air.

"Signal time?"

Tom gave a single nod.

Bohdan whispered an incantation, and power flowed through him and into his hand. Then, he released a massive fireball into the sky—a brilliant bloom of flame and light, arcing high into the air before exploding with a deep BOOM that echoed for miles.

For a moment, the city was silent again.

Then the howls began.

Far off. But getting closer.

"They're coming," Derek said, drawing his weapon.

Tom raised his blade, his voice steady.

"Then let's give them one hell of a welcome."

INVASION

The sound hit first—clattering chitin, pounding limbs, rage-fueled screeches that bounced off the surrounding buildings like a drumbeat of violence.

Then they appeared.

The first pirate—a hulking brute with serrated claws and a mouth full of needle-like teeth—burst around the corner in a blur of motion, chitinous limbs propelling it forward like a nightmare.

It didn't hesitate.

The creature charged, frothing with hate, mandibles clicking wildly as it barreled straight for the team.

Tom moved first. His sword ignited with *Dark Flame Weapon*, the runes along the blade glowing as he met the beast head-on, ducking low under a swipe and slashing up through its exposed underside. A gout of black ichor sprayed into the air as the pirate crumpled, twitching violently.

"Here we go!" Derek shouted, stepping in beside him.

Another pirate leaped forward—this one leaner, faster, with twin plasma-blades humming in its claws. Derek blocked a swing with his forearm plate, then brought his axe down in a brutal arc, cleaving through shell and bone.

More followed.

From alleyways, rooftops, wrecked buildings—they came like a swarm.

Jay moved through them like the wind. Each step was calculated and precise. He weaved around one pirate and buried his dagger into a weak joint behind its arm, yanking it free just in time to parry another incoming strike. He wasn't brute force—he was death by a thousand cuts.

Michael fought like a storm. His axes glowed with radiant energy, slashing through armor with concussive blasts that sent enemy limbs flying. One pirate lunged at him and he responded with a low spin, sweeping the legs and bringing an axe down in one final, brutal arc.

Graham stood like a bulwark, shield raised and sword ready, holding the line with unshakable resolve. A pirate rushed him, snarling with both blades raised—but Graham caught the strike on his shield, then bashed forward with brutal force, knocking the creature off balance. Before it could recover, he brought his sword around in a tight arc, driving the blade deep into its side and sending it crashing to the ground.

Kirsten and Briana moved like chaos and control in perfect harmony. Kirsten was all fury—her greataxe swung in wide, devastating arcs, cleaving through enemies with raw power. Every roar, every swing drove pirates back. At her side, Briana kept pace, casting radiant bursts and protective wards, her magic burning through enemy ranks and mending small wounds on the fly. Whenever Kirsten carved a path, Briana was there to shield her flanks or call down divine fire to finish what the axe had started. Together, they were a storm—righteous and relentless.

Austin and Isaac held the flanks, rotating positions with calm precision, cutting down any pirate that tried to circle around. Isaac's halberd arced like a reaper's scythe, while Austin used his glaive with brutal efficiency, legs planted wide, every movement efficient and deadly.

And then there was Bohdan.

Fire was his domain.

He stood near the rear, raining hell upon their enemies. Flames erupted in controlled bursts, frying clusters of pirates as they pressed too close. One tried to leap over his line, but he pivoted and slammed his staff into the ground—an eruption of flame engulfed it mid-air, leaving only scorched fragments behind.

Bron was the anchor.

Wherever the line faltered, he was there—silent, massive, and unrelenting. He crushed pirates with single blows, grabbed one by the shell and hurled it into its comrades like a living cannonball. His eyes never blinked, never wavered.

Tom's blade clashed again, sparks flying.

"Fall back ten paces!" he shouted, parrying a blow and ducking a claw swipe. "Keep drawing them in—Herbert needs them center mass!"

One by one, the team adjusted—stepping back in perfect intervals, still fighting, still pressing the offense, but slowly herding the tide of enemies toward the exact spot where hell would soon break loose beneath them.

The pirates didn't notice.

They were too consumed by bloodlust. Screaming in fury, they surged forward, climbing over their own dead, swinging blades and claws in wild arcs.

Tom could feel it.

They were almost in position.

Chapter 77

Buried Problems

Herbert wiped a streak of grime from his forehead, leaving behind a worse one in its place. They had been walking through the bowels of the city for nearly an hour now, navigating crumbling maintenance tunnels and half-collapsed sewer routes by flashlight and sheer faith in old schematics.

"We're close," he said, pausing at a split in the tunnel where rusted pipes met broken tile. He checked the map he had brought with him. "Up ahead, it should open into a wide storm basin. Perfect spot to drop the charges. Flat base, structural weak points overhead…"

He trailed off as the team rounded the final bend—and froze.

The chamber ahead was massive—a wide, bowl-shaped depression with old steel catwalks wrapping around the upper edge. Water trickled through ancient grates above, but the basin itself was dry.

And crawling with goblins.

Dozens of them.

Some squatted in clusters around small fires, gnawing on unidentifiable meat. Others lounged along broken beams or sharpened crude weapons with bone-handled stones. The place reeked of rot and wet dog, with just a hint of "dangerously unhygienic."

"And here I thought this part was going to be easy," Bobby muttered, ducking behind a broken pipe.

"So… we're not negotiating, right?" Clay whispered. "Because I don't speak Goblinese, but I'm pretty sure that one just flipped me off."

Kedron peered through a crack in the wall, eyes narrowing. "Too many to take head-on. We need a plan."

Herbert crouched behind a rusted maintenance console and pulled out a sketchpad. "Alright. Here's what we know. Entry point is here. Goblins are clustered across the lower floor, but they're lazy and disorganized. That's good. We're not fighting a battalion—they're more like sewer squatters."

"So, we hit them fast and hard," TJ said. "Push from one side and sweep across. Bobby and I take the left flank, Clay and Kedron go right. Herbert—you hang back and prep the charges."

"No complaints from me," Herbert said quickly. "I don't need to be elbow-deep in goblin spleens to feel like I've contributed today."

Clay was grinning. "I've been waiting all week to hit something with a wrench. Let's go say hi."

Bobby cocked his shotgun and whispered a quiet prayer that sounded suspiciously like a warning to anyone ahead.

"On your signal," Kedron said.

TJ held up three fingers.

Two.

One.

They moved.

Bobby was first, sweeping into the basin with his shotgun roaring. The first goblin didn't even see it coming—one moment chewing on bones, the next a smear across the wall.

Clay barreled down the right slope, swinging a hammer with one hand and a rusty pipe in the other, laughing like a lunatic.

Kedron was quiet, efficient, precise—his blade moved in arcs of silver, each swing cutting down another foe.

TJ moved like he'd never stopped fighting, clearing the center with brutal sweeps of his mace and backhanded elbow strikes that sent goblins flying. A few tried to rally, charging en masse—only to run straight into a wall of swinging metal and gunfire.

Herbert stayed near the entrance, ducking behind a support beam, watching the chaos unfold.

"Okay," he muttered, pulling out the detonator matrix and a bundle of high-density charges. "While they're playing Whack-a-Goblin, I'll just start setting up the thing that's going to turn this place into a sinkhole…"

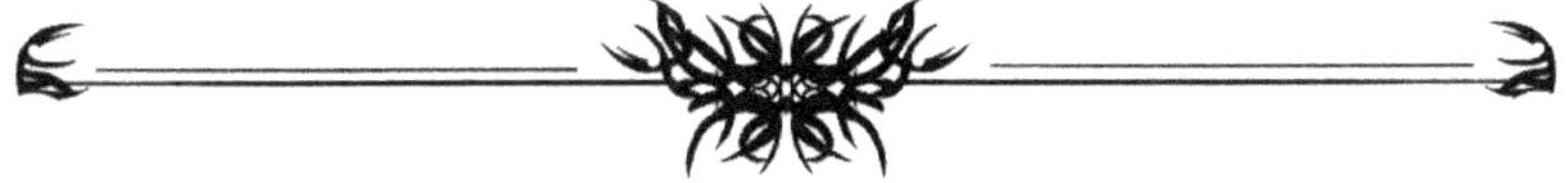

Tom's muscles burned.

Every swing of his blade met resistance—chitin, steel, bodies, and claws—more and more of it. His lungs begged for breath, his arms felt like lead, and still they came.

The pirates weren't just fighting.

They were pouring in, an endless tide of screeching, armored monstrosities. Claws snapped inches from faces. Blades rang out against shields and flesh. The very air vibrated with battle cries and the sickening crack of metal colliding with the shells of the pirates.

Derek stood shoulder-to-shoulder with Tom, fending off three enemies at once, blood streaking down his cheek. Kirsten's axe was red to the haft, her roars shaking the ground as she cleaved through anything in reach. But even she was slowing, her stance lower, heavier.

Graham took a blow to the shield that sent him skidding back, grunting as he barely avoided a follow-up slash. Jay had a gash across his thigh, and his breathing was ragged as he disappeared into the chaos for another ambush strike.

Tom couldn't tell if they were winning.

Because it didn't feel like it.

It felt like surviving by the second. Like every moment was bought with blood—and it was.

Another pirate lunged at him—Tom twisted, brought his blade up, but too slowly. The monster crashed into him and he hit the ground hard, the breath knocked from his lungs.

His sword skidded away.

The pirate loomed above him, raising one serrated claw.

Tom's body wouldn't move fast enough.

And then it spoke.

The voice was garbled through its translator but unmistakably smug. Cold. Amused. The cherry on top was seeing the pirate hat on his head.

"So, this is Earth's great leader," the pirate rasped, its beady eyes narrowing. "The one who has been such a thorn in our side. You bleed the same as the others. You break the same as the others."

It leaned in close, claw catching the light.

"You've fought hard. I'll give you that. You survived the first wave. You kept your little pets alive. You even managed to slow the Extractor—for now." It tilted its head, the ridges along its neck pulsing with some sick mockery of a grin.

"But what did it buy you? Nothing. You still lose. The ocean will fall. Your people will scatter. And your city will burn. All you've done… is delay your own extinction. My boss will be so pleased with me this time."

The claw rose higher.

"You have destroyed everything we've worked for here! The shadow beast, the puppeteer, even that fucking hothead who lost his poor child. You should be ashamed. You die here, beneath a broken sky, remembered only for how spectacularly you failed."

Tom clenched his teeth, bracing for impact—

Then—

A car smashed into the pirate from the side, metal crumpling like paper as the creature was sent flying—along with two others who had been closing in behind it.

The vehicle flipped mid-air, bounced twice, and crashed into a heap nearby.

Tom blinked.

And then he saw him.

Frank.

Barreling forward like a wrecking ball in human form, eyes glowing, fists clenched into hammers.

He let out a roar that shook the rubble.

His skin had taken on a red hue, veins pulsing with energy. He had activated his ultimate *Rage*—every ounce of strength pushed beyond human limits. And he used it like a god of war.

He hit the first pirate so hard its shell cracked inward like an egg. The second tried to swing, but Frank caught the claw with one hand and tore the arm clean off. Then he spun, hurling it like a spear into another one's chest.

"GET! OFF! MY! PLANET!" he roared, each word emphasized by smashing the crowded pirates with a fist and sending another creature sprawling.

Behind him, more figures approached from the distance.

James, handguns at the ready, was grinning like a lunatic.

Lacey, already launching bolts of arcane energy that arced through the air and exploded with sharp bursts of light.
Mark, hands already glowing with flame, unleashing streaks of fire, blazing across the battle, that detonated against pirate formations, scattering them in bursts of heat and light.

And Susie, sprinting at full speed to join the line, her face calm and focused even in the madness.

"Miss me?!" James shouted, planting three shots into a pirate's eye as he slid into cover beside Tom. "You looked like you needed a rescue montage."

Tom grabbed his sword and pushed to his feet.

"Took your damn time."

"It's just like prom night," he shrugged, "fashionably late and heavily armed."

"What the hell kind of prom did you—"

James simply grabbed the crotch of his pants with a wink. "I was packing, you see?"

Tom rubbed the bridge of his nose with one weary hand. "Can we bring the crab back over here to kill me?"

"Later," James grinned, pointing a finger ahead of them. "Party's starting."

Frank didn't even look back. He was too busy throwing another pirate headfirst through a concrete pillar, then catching a charging brute and lifting it overhead like it was made of cardboard, before slamming it into the pavement hard enough to crack the earth.

He was everywhere.

No hesitation.

No fear.

Just fury.

And for the first time in what felt like hours, the line began to hold again.

Tom gritted his teeth, straightened, and let the dark flame blaze down his blade once more.

"Let's give him the backup he deserves."

And with that, they charged.

Herbert crouched beside the final support pillar, double-checking the wires connecting the last of the charges. Sweat dripped from his nose onto the detonator, but his hands didn't shake. Everything was in place—secure, calibrated, and ready to turn the chamber above into pirate oatmeal.

Behind him, the others were catching their breath.

Clay slumped against a pipe, wiping blood—some of it his, most of it not—off his cheek with the back of a gloved hand. "Well," he said between gasps, "I think I pulled a muscle I didn't know existed… possibly in my soul."

Bobby reloaded his shotgun, leaning back against the wall and staring at a goblin that was still twitching. "If another one of these things jumps out of a pipe, I'm quitting. Just… walking out. Gonna open a bakery. Make muffins. None of them scream or try to bite you."

Kedron didn't say a word, just knelt near the edge of the chamber, sword resting on his knee, scanning the shadows like he expected something else to leap out any second.

"All charges are set," Herbert announced, rising to his feet. His shirt was soaked through, and he could feel a smear of goblin something on his left boot, but the weight in his chest started to ease.

He pulled out the communication orb and activated it.

"Tom, this is Herbert." His voice was steady, but even he couldn't hide the rasp of exhaustion. "Fireworks are ready whenever you are. We've cleared the area and I'm 99% sure I won't blow myself up. That's the best you're getting today."

He paused.

"Seriously, though. Say the word and we'll bring the house down."

Clay raised a hand weakly. "Can we not *actually* bring the house down? I like not being crushed. I mean, unless I'm dating someone who—"

"It's a figure of speech," Herbert quickly interjected. "Mostly."

The orb pulsed, awaiting Tom's response.

They were ready.

All that remained now… was the timing.

Chapter 78

The Cost of Rage

Tom had seen a lot of powerful people since the System came online.

He'd watched mages incinerate monsters with a flick of their fingers. He'd fought creatures the size of buildings. He'd gone toe-to-toe with killers, warlords, and corrupted god-like creatures.

But nothing he'd seen—not in all the chaos Earth had become—compared to what Frank had become just now.

Frank was a storm. A force. A living embodiment of fury given shape and muscle and momentum.

And they couldn't stop him.

Tom slashed another pirate aside and fell back to the edge of the crater, catching his breath. The rest of the team had done the same. They had learned their lesson the hard way.

Bron bore a scorch mark across one arm and a dent in his chestplate—one he hadn't earned from a pirate.

He'd tried to pull Frank out of the madness. One arm on his shoulder, a single word—

And Frank had spun with a roar and backhanded Bron through a wrecked bus.

The Mastadonian had gotten up. Barely.

No one had gotten close since.

"We can't help him," Derek said, wiping sweat from his brow. His voice held a bitterness Tom wasn't used to hearing from him.

Tom nodded grimly, his eyes never leaving the rampage.

Frank was still standing—but barely.

He fought like a force of nature, swinging fists and smashing through pirate lines with raw, unfiltered rage. But it was no longer clean, no longer dominant. Every blow he landed came at a cost. Cuts lined his arms and chest, his skin torn open in places, thick gashes bleeding freely. One leg dragged slightly. His breathing was ragged, visible even from a distance.

His fists were red and raw, not just from smashing armor—but from being cut, clawed, and burned in the process.

Still, he fought.

Not because he was winning.

But because he simply refused to stop.

INVASION

"He's too far gone," Jay said softly. "The *Rage* ability… it's not just power. It's everything. He's not in there anymore."

"No," Tom murmured, "he is. Just… not enough to stop."

They circled the edge of the battlefield, keeping distance, watching for anything that slipped through Frank's warpath. But it was like standing next to a tidal wave—you didn't control it. You just hoped it kept going the right direction.

Another pirate charged him, a larger one, better armored, with a plasma glaive and layered shell.

Frank caught it mid-swing, ripped the weapon from its hands, and drove it back through its chest with a bellow that rattled windows.

The creature dropped.

Frank didn't stop.

He just kept swinging.

Tom lowered his weapon slightly, eyes locked on the chaos.

"We can't stop him. And I think the only thing he's aware of right now is that he's surrounded by bad guys."

Lacey stood beside him, voice quiet. "Then what do we do?"

Tom didn't answer right away.

Because he didn't know.

There was no plan for this. No command for how to save someone who'd burned himself down to keep everyone else alive.

Tom's thoughts were still on Frank—on the blood soaking into the cracked pavement, the way his movements had started to slow—when the communication orb around his neck pulsed with light.

He snatched it up.

"Tom, this is Herbert," the voice crackled through, rough with fatigue but steady. "Fireworks are ready whenever you are. We've cleared the area and I'm 99% sure I won't blow myself up. That's the best you're getting today."

There was a pause, and then, quieter—

"Seriously, though. Say the word and we'll bring the house down."

Tom stared at the orb for a moment.

That was it.

The signal they'd been waiting for.

The plan, as reckless and fragile as it was, had come to its final moment.

He looked toward the epicenter of the battle—toward Frank, still swinging, still roaring through a haze of blood and fire, still holding the attention of every pirate in the blast radius.

Tom felt the weight of what had to come next settle onto his chest like a stone.

Tom stared at the orb.

Herbert's voice still echoed in his head. The charges were ready. All they needed was the word.

He looked out at Frank, still in the middle of the chaos—bleeding, stumbling, surrounded, but standing. Still fighting.

Tom opened his mouth—

"No," James said sharply.

Tom turned. James was already walking toward him, eyes wide with something between panic and fury. "No. You're not doing this."

"James—"

"You can't!" James shoved past Lacey, stopping just short of grabbing Tom. "That's FRANK out there! We don't leave him! We get him out!"

Derek stepped between them, hand gentle but firm on James' shoulder. "We can't reach him. You saw what happened when Bron tried—he's too far gone."

"Bullshit," James snapped. "He's still in there. He has to be. Just give him a second. Let me go to him. He'll listen to me."

Tom's voice was soft, full of regret. "He won't. Not like this."

James' voice cracked. "Don't do this, man. Please. Don't give that order. We can find another way. We always find another way!"

Tom's hand was shaking.

He didn't want to say it.

But he had to.

"There's… no other way."

James broke.

The scream tore out of him like it had been clawing at his ribs. "FRANK! SNAP OUT OF IT! IT'S ME! COME BACK TO ME, DAMMIT!"

His legs buckled, and he dropped to his knees, fists clenched at his sides, tears streaming down his cheeks.

"Don't do this! Don't make me watch this happen!"

But Frank didn't turn.

He didn't pause.

Didn't flinch.

He was still fighting. Still losing pieces of himself with every breath.

And he couldn't hear James anymore.

Tom looked away, jaw clenched.

"I'm sorry."

He activated the orb.

Chapter 79

Another Crazy Plan

Missile lock.

Anderson banked hard to the right, the HUD flaring red as the alien fighter behind him launched another shot. He dove, skimmed the ocean surface, and pulled up just in time to avoid splashing out of the sky.

The comms were a mess of overlapping chatter and warning calls.

"Unit 5 is hit!"

"They're regrouping on the left—break formation!"

"I'm out of flares—goddamn it, I'm out of—" squawked Unit 5.

Anderson gritted his teeth and pulled back into the fight. The enemy ships were smaller, faster, and swarming like hornets. For every one they shot down, two more came from the flanking groups or the hangars of the massive vessels behind them.

"Unit 3, stay on my six. We need to loop around and try to draw them off—"

"Negative, boss," Eric's voice crackled through the headset. Calm. Too calm.

Anderson's blood ran cold.

"What are you doing?"

"Tired of playing tag with space crabs," Eric said, his tone maddeningly casual. "Gonna go knock on the front door."

"Eric—stand down. That's an order."

"Nah." A short pause. "Been an honor, boss. Just tell everyone I went out how I lived—loud, reckless, and slightly too proud of my hair."

And then came one last message from Unit 3:

"WOOOOOOO!"

Anderson's HUD flared as Eric broke formation, veering off from the pack and tilting his jet into a sharp ascent—straight toward the nearest enemy ship.

The biggest one.

The one anchoring one of the chains holding the Extractor.

"Eric! Abort! That's a suicide run!" Anderson yelled, even though he knew it was useless.

The jet climbed, afterburners roaring, slicing through the sky like a bullet fired from God's own revolver.

The enemy fighters noticed—pivoting, breaking formation to try to intercept—but it was too late.

Eric twisted, dipped, then pulled into a steep dive.

Directly toward the side of the ship.

Eric's jet flew like a predator and then dove with surgical intent. Anderson's breath caught as he watched the impossible trajectory play out.

Two missiles streaked ahead of the jet, heat-seeking, high-velocity, screaming toward the massive enemy ship.

They struck the side of the command vessel in perfect unison—detonating in a brilliant double flash that tore a hole clean through the ship's hangar bay.

Inside, one of the enemy fighters had just begun to lift off the launch rail. The explosion ripped it apart mid-deployment, flames devouring the bay as debris and twisted metal tore loose in all directions.

And then—

Eric flew directly into the breach.

Not around it.

Into it.

His afterburners lit the sky like a shooting star before the darkness swallowed him whole.

For one long second, the battlefield went quiet.

A massive internal explosion shook the enemy vessel, fire bursting from the hangar breach and tearing upward through the structure. Secondary detonations followed—chained eruptions that sent debris flying from every seam in the hull.

The shockwave hit Anderson's jet like a punch to the chest.

The comms crackled, hissed.

And then went silent.

Anderson stared at the command summary, heart pounding.

Unit 3: Offline.

He gripped the controls tighter than he should have, mouth dry, pulse thunderous in his ears.

But he said nothing.

Because what was there to say?

The sky was still glowing from the explosion when it began.

One by one, the enemy ships in the air faltered.

The aggressive, high-speed fighters that had harried the F-35s with perfect, mechanical precision stuttered mid-air—their engines flaring unevenly, then sputtering out entirely. Red tracer lights on their wings blinked once, twice… and went dark.

And then they fell.

All of them.

Dozens of sleek, inhuman crafts dropped from the sky like marionettes with their strings cut, spinning end over end as gravity reclaimed them. They hit the ocean in violent splashes—some exploding on impact, others skipping across the surface before disappearing beneath the waves with deep, echoing groans.

Anderson pulled his jet into a slow, steady arc, staring out over the horizon as the battlefield changed in real time.

INVASION

"They were drones," he muttered, realization creeping in. "Every last one of them."

Below, the Extractor—massive, ominous, anchored between the two motherships—flickered.

The energy tether connecting the fallen command ship to the Extractor shimmered once in defiance… then broke apart in a shattering wave of static.

Lights along the surface of the Extractor winked out like dying stars.

Then there was the sound.

A deep, low whump echoed across the ocean, like the Earth itself had sighed.

The spiraling cyclone of water that had been funneling skyward collapsed in on itself, severed from its power source. Millions of gallons of seawater plummeted back down in a monstrous wall, smashing into the waves below with the force of a meteor strike.

A shockwave rolled across the surface, sending tidal ripples in every direction. Spray blasted upward like geysers. A wall of steam hissed into the air as sunlight hit the soaked, overheated surface of the Extractor.

The damaged mothership groaned like something alive, its integrity failing, gravity taking hold of the metal titan.

With a final screech of twisting steel, it tilted—and fell.

The impact was cataclysmic.

The sea rose up to meet it, and when the vessel struck, the splash was so large it sent waves crashing into the nearest coastlines. The sound was thunder wrapped in iron, a brutal end to something that had threatened the entire world.

Afterward, there was silence.

Anderson sat in his cockpit, stunned. His gloved hand still hovered near the throttle. Around him, the few remaining Units flew in formation, silent as well. No more enemy fighters. No more flashing lights.

Just sky.

And waves.

And wreckage.

And a good man that had been lost from a world that owed him a debt that couldn't be calculated.

Softly, like a gasped breath, Anderson's communication orb flared to life.

A pulse of gold and white, steady and urgent.

The orb flickered again in Anderson's cockpit.

He reached out slowly, still dazed, and tapped the surface.

A familiar voice crackled to life.

"WOOOOOOOO!"

Anderson nearly choked on his own breath. "You absolute maniac."

"Miss me?" Eric's voice came through distorted but triumphant.

Anderson blinked. "I watched you explode."

"*Technically*, you watched my ship explode. I ejected before the explosion," Eric replied. "Details, boss. Details."

Anderson looked out over the ocean, twisting his head as he scanned the skies.

And there—a tiny black dot was descending under a wide white parachute, slowly floating toward the second mothership.

"You jumped out of a missile-run into a hangar bay explosion—"

"—and lived," Eric finished cheerfully. "Which means, I am now officially invincible. You have to let me put that on my gravestone."

Anderson sighed. "You're not getting a gravestone, because I'm going to kill you myself."

"Get in line."

The parachute flared as the wind caught it, drifting Eric toward the upper deck of the ship. His boots hit the surface with a dull thud, the parachute collapsing behind him.

He stood up, brushed himself off, and pulled out two machine guns from his Inventory.

"Alright," Eric muttered, cracking his neck. "Let's see how much noise I can make before someone notices I survived."

The comms line went quiet, and the screen cut to static.

Chapter 80

A Grand Finale

Tom's hand trembled as he held the communication orb up to his mouth.
"Herbert..." His voice was barely more than a whisper.
He swallowed.
"Do it."
The words hit like a hammer, slamming down with finality. There was no taking it back.
No one around him moved. Even the sounds of battle seemed to pause for one long, suspended moment—as if the world itself was waiting.
Then—
The earth screamed.
A deep, thunderous rumble tore up through the ground like a living thing. The pavement beneath their feet cracked open in jagged lines, a shockwave rippling outward in all directions. The city groaned, stone and steel snapping, shifting, breaking.
And then it came.
The explosion wasn't fire—it was force.
The ground beneath the pirate horde erupted in a violent burst of debris and pressure, an expanding column of dust, stone, and flesh blasting upward like a volcanic eruption. Buildings on either side buckled inward, glass shattering, walls folding as if struck by a god's fist.
The noise was deafening.
A concussive boom split the sky—not sharp like a bomb, but deep, low, a roar of annihilation that drowned out every thought.
Pirates were launched into the air like broken toys, limbs and weapons spiraling, their screeches cut short by the sheer violence of the blast. Chitinous bodies hit the ground in twisted, burning heaps. The ones on the periphery were crushed by the shockwave, their shells caving in from the sheer pressure.
The center of the explosion—the heart of the detonation—vanished into a smoking crater, a wide, gaping maw in the earth. Rubble slid inward, forming a jagged slope where ground had once been solid.
And at the center, caught in the eye of the storm—
Frank.
Tom's heart clenched.
He saw him only for a moment—silhouetted in smoke, knees buckling, blood streaming down his chest. The explosion hadn't taken him instantly. No... he had kept fighting until the very last second.

Tom could see it in the way his body swayed—not from fear, but from exhaustion.

And then the ground beneath him gave way.

Frank didn't fall like a man defeated.

He dropped like a titan whose aim was to give the devil a piece of his mind.

Dust swallowed him whole.

Tom stood frozen, blade still in hand, the roar of the explosion still ringing in his ears.

No one spoke.

No one moved.

Because the crater before them was the cost.

A cost that Frank had paid in full.

The dust hadn't even settled.

Tom stared into the crater—into the hollow place where Frank had stood, where he had made his final stand, where he had saved them all.

His grip on the sword trembled.

The world around him felt too quiet, too still.

It wasn't right.

None of this was right.

Frank was gone.

The brother who had laughed at danger, who had taken every hit and smiled through it. The wall they all leaned on when the world tried to break them.

And now—

Gone.

Tom's chest heaved once.

Twice.

And then he screamed.

A roar ripped from his throat—raw, primal, the kind of sound that came not just from the lungs, but from the soul. A war cry so fierce it split the silence and tore through the lingering dust like a thunderclap.

Power erupted from him.

Dark flame and brilliant light burst from every cell of his body, twisting through the air, igniting the ground around him in a surge of radiant energy. His aura expanded outward like a tidal wave, washing over friend and foe alike.

Only his enemies felt its sting.

The battlefield paused. For one impossible second, every motion froze— the pirates mid-charge, mid-swing, eyes wide in sudden confusion and fear.

And then—

INVASION

<table>
<tr><td>

New Skill Acquired: Cry for Justice

In your darkest moment of desperation, you cried out against the injustice being brought upon your people. While in this state, your stats are increased by 25%, and a blast of power is released, utilizing half of your current mana supply, which will only affect your enemies. This Skill can only be used in situations where a great injustice has occurred against your Guild. The duration of the boost is 1 hour.
Your enemies have been weakened.
Your enemies have been disoriented.
Your enemies have been inflicted with fear.

</td></tr>
</table>

The energy blast expanded in a pulse from Tom's body, slamming into the nearby pirates like a tidal wave of force and emotion.

They screamed. Shells cracked, weapons dropped, formation shattered.

Some clutched their heads, staggering as if struck by something deeper than pain—as if the very world had turned against them.

Tom stood tall in the storm of his own making, fire crackling along his skin, eyes burning with a fury that refused to fade.

Frank was gone.

But his vengeance had only just begun.

The ground still trembled from the shock of Tom's cry, the power of it lingering like an aftershock through the air.

Tom was already moving.

He exploded forward, sword in hand, a trail of dark flame spiraling off the blade as he tore into the nearest pirate. The creature barely had time to scream before it was cut in half, its blood hissing against the cracked pavement.

Another lunged toward him—shaking, unsteady. Tom didn't dodge.

He slammed his shoulder into its chest, then drove his sword through the back of its shell with a sickening crack. He moved like a phantom, a blur of steel and fury, cutting down anything that dared remain standing in the wake of Frank's fall.

All around him, the pirates faltered.

The disorientation. The fear. The sense that the tide had turned—and they weren't on the winning side anymore.

Their bravado shattered like glass.

One turned to run. Another dropped its weapon. A third screamed something in its native tongue and charged—only to be met with a downward cleave that nearly split it in two.

And then—

A sound.

A roar.

From behind.

A rising cry—human and furious—thundered down the street.

Tom turned just in time to see them: hundreds of fighters charging into the battle, weapons raised, faces twisted with grief and rage.

The Guild had come.

The survivors. The reserves. The wounded who could still walk. All of them.

"FOR FRANK!" Derek screamed out as the rest of the team joined him.

They descended on the broken pirate ranks like a wave of wrath incarnate. Magic lit the air, swords clanged, axes crashed against armor, arrows sang through the chaos.

The massacre had begun.

There was no more holding the line.

Now it was retribution.

Kevin tackled one of the larger pirates to the ground and drove a blade through its chest. Susie moved with fire in her eyes, cutting through enemies like they were paper, each movement a brutal punctuation to her grief. Lacey hurled a lightning bolt that chained between half a dozen enemies, dropping them in spasming heaps.

Briana, her hands glowing with divine fury, whispered a prayer—and unleashed a radiant blast that left a dozen enemies writhing in holy agony.

They all fought like they had nothing left to lose.

Tom moved at the front, carving a path of destruction, unstoppable now. The *Cry for Justice* still burned in his veins, his blade glowing with vengeance, every strike faster, stronger, more precise than he'd ever moved in his life.

The pirates didn't stand a chance.

What had begun as survival…

Had become a reckoning.

Chapter 81

From Grief to Feast

Tom let the communication orb fall back against his chest, the weight of it now strangely heavier. Anderson and his team had done it—they'd stopped the Extractor. A single shard of light in a sky still dark with loss.

The courtyard felt heavier than usual, the air thick with loss. A somber silence had settled over the Guild members as they gathered, their faces lit by the strings of light that had been used for the parties of the past. The fires set sporadically through the area cast long shadows across the ground, dancing between the bodies of the fallen, both human and alien. Blood and soot still stained the streets, the stench of battle lingering in the air.

Tom stood at the center of it all, his body stiff, eyes scanning the faces of his people. Every person there had fought, bled, and far too many had died for their survival. They had won the battle, but the price was still being counted. As his gaze fell to the covered bodies lying at the front of the courtyard, he felt his chest tighten.

Among them was Frank.

James stood near his fallen friend, silent and unblinking. Lacey held Susie close, her sobs soft but steady, while Mark and Derek stood at a distance, their expressions unreadable. The rest of the Guild had gathered around, some tending to the wounded, others simply staring at the bodies of their comrades, lost in their own thoughts.

Tom took a deep breath and stepped forward. His voice was low, but it carried through the courtyard, cutting through the weight of grief.

"We survived."

His words echoed for a moment, and the quiet that followed felt suffocating.

"But we lost too many. Too damn many."

He looked at the faces of his friends, of the people who had stood with him in battle, and felt the weight of every life that had been snuffed out. For a moment, he struggled to find the words to continue.

"Today, we honor those who gave everything to protect this place. To protect each other. We fought back the invaders, but it cost us. We are here because of them, and we owe them more than we can ever repay."

Tom's voice faltered for a moment. His eyes found Frank's body, laid out carefully on a cloth. His weapons were now beside him, and his body seemed peaceful. Frank had always been the kind of person never to know a stranger, always ready to make a friend. But when the time came, he had been a force to be reckoned with.

"And Frank," Tom's voice softened. "Frank gave his life so we could keep ours. He fought harder than anyone, and in the end, he saved us all. He... he's a hero."

James flinched at the word. His face twisted, his grief raw and open. Lacey's sobs grew louder, and Susie buried her face in her arms, shaking uncontrollably.

Tom stepped closer to Frank's body and knelt down, his hand resting gently on his fallen comrade's chest.

"You deserved better," Tom whispered, though the words were meant for Frank alone. "I'm sorry, Frank. You did everything we needed you to do. You gave more than anyone could ask."

The courtyard was silent save for the crackling of flames and the soft sound of weeping. The Guild members bowed their heads, honoring their fallen brother. No one moved. No one spoke. Grief weighed them all down, pulling their hearts into the depths of sorrow.

Derek stepped forward, his face unreadable but his voice clear. "Frank was a good man. A good fighter. We will never forget what he did for us."

Others began to speak, offering their words of respect, their memories of Frank. The stories ranged from tales of his loyalty to the moments when his strength had surprised everyone. Each word was a small piece of the man who had given everything for them.

After what felt like hours of grief and quiet reflection, Tom stood again, his chest heavy with emotion.

"We honor the dead by living," he said, his voice hoarse. "And tonight, we're going to live."

James looked up, his face streaked with tears, confusion flashing in his eyes.

"We're going to celebrate them," Tom continued. "The only way we know how. We're going to feast. Tonight, we take what the pirates left behind, and we make it our own. We're going to eat well, drink well, and live well, because that's what they fought for."

There was a murmur of uncertainty among the Guild, but slowly, one by one, heads began to nod. People started moving again, though the heaviness of grief still hung over them. Tom glanced over at Derek, who gave him a small nod, understanding what needed to be done.

With a gesture, the Guild's cooks and volunteers got to work, bringing out massive pots and kettles, prepping the large cooking fires that had been built just inside the gates. The smell of boiling water and spices soon filled the air, mingling with the metallic tang of blood still lingering from the battle.

Jerky, ever loyal, took up his usual post beside Tom as they began preparing the lobster-like creatures for what had become an impromptu celebration. Squirrel, having reverted to a more manageable size, scuttled about, knocking over crates and barrels as the Guild worked to ready the feast. Having been left in the Guild as an added defense for the non-combatants, he was eager to mingle with the rest of the team.

As the alien pirates' bodies were pulled from the battlefield, their grotesque, armored forms were tossed into massive boiling pots. The once-menacing claws and thick, spined shells now looked almost ridiculous as they bobbed in the water, steam rising in great clouds above the courtyard.

It didn't take long for the smell of cooking lobster to mix with the aroma of spices, and soon, the entire Guild was drawn toward the fire. Plates were passed around, laughter was tentative at first, but it grew louder with each minute.

Tom watched from a distance, his eyes catching glimpses of familiar faces as they began to relax. Some of the Guild members still wept quietly, but others, with a grim determination, threw themselves into the bizarre celebration with gusto. Plates piled high with steaming lobster flesh were passed from one person to another. Giant claws cracked open, revealing the tender meat inside. Buckets of melted butter that had been purchased from the vending machines were placed on tables, and someone had even managed to scrounge up some bread to serve alongside the meal.

Laughter began to rise. It was hesitant, like everyone was unsure if it was appropriate, but it grew as people began to relax. The sight of the once-terrifying creatures now reduced to something one would put on a bun, or eat in someone's front yard, seemed to lift the spirits of the Guild. They had faced death, stared it in the eyes, and now they were devouring their enemies.

Tom took a deep breath, trying to let the moment of relief sink in. It wasn't enough to erase the grief of the day, but it was something—a small light in the darkness that had threatened to swallow them all.

"Hey, Tom!" Jerky called from a table nearby, holding up a massive lobster claw dripping with butter. "You've got to try this! It's actually pretty good!"

Tom smiled, his first real smile of the day, and walked over to join his friend. Grabbing a claw for himself, he cracked it open and dipped the meat into the butter. The taste was surprisingly rich, a strange but welcome change from the grim atmosphere of earlier.

Around him, the Guild continued to eat, drink, and laugh. It wasn't a full release from the grief they all felt, but it was a reprieve. People toasted to Frank, to the fallen, to those who had survived. Even James, though still subdued, was seen cracking a lobster claw and sharing a quiet moment with Mark and Lacey.

As the evening wore on, the last of the lobster monsters were cooked, and the leftovers were sent to be stored in the freezer; the tone of the gathering shifted from solemn to celebratory. Someone started playing music, a soft tune at first, but it soon grew louder, more raucous. A few of the younger Guild members started dancing, their movements wild and carefree, and it wasn't long before others joined in.

Tom watched it all unfold with a sense of quiet satisfaction. It wasn't perfect, and it wasn't what he had expected, but it was what they needed. They needed to feel alive, to remember why they had fought in the first place. Not just for survival, but for moments like this—for the laughter, the camaraderie, the strange joy of being alive when everything else had been taken.

Jerky slapped Tom on the back, pulling him out of his thoughts. "Come on, Master. You've got to enjoy this too. We're not going to get many nights like this."

Tom nodded, though the weight of the day still clung to him. He took another bite of the lobster, savoring the taste. It wasn't just food. It was a reminder. A reminder that they had survived. A reminder of the lives that had been given for this moment. And somehow, in the midst of all the pain and sorrow, that made it taste just a little bit sweeter.

The night carried on, the fire burning bright as the Guild laughed, danced, and feasted in the shadow of what they had lost. Tom stayed with them until the fires burned low, until the last claw had been cracked, and the final notes of the music faded into the night.

As the embers died, and the Guild slowly began to retreat back to their rooms and bunks, Tom stood for a moment longer, staring out at the remains of the battlefield just beyond the gate. The grief still lingered in his heart, but for the first time since the battle, he felt a spark of hope.

They had survived. And tomorrow, they would rebuild.

Chapter 82

Reparations

A few days passed as the Guild worked diligently to organize a true commemoration for those who had fallen during the invasion.

Eric and Anderson had returned almost a full day after the fighting had ended, piloting one of the enormous pirate ships that had once housed the Extractor. The vessel limped across the sky, smoking in places, its hull scorched and venting systems flickering erratically. It was barely functional—but it was theirs.

A spoil of war.

They'd managed to wrest control of the vessel after Eric's mad stunt and sabotage run, and with Anderson's help, they'd flown it back across the ruined city skyline, a jagged crown for Earth's unlikely victory.

When they landed, Guild members had swarmed the craft with cheers, some in disbelief, others just too emotionally drained to do more than clap in silence. Anderson had stepped out like a general returning from a distant front. Eric, of course, had emerged shirtless, sunglasses on, blowing kisses to the crowd like a rock star who had just gotten offstage.

Both were hailed as heroes—just like Tom and his team.

But even in celebration, the grief hung heavy.

Tom had thought that the feast of their enemy's flesh—a chaotic, furious celebration the night after the battle—might have been enough. But his friends had insisted on something more deliberate. Something more sacred.

They needed time.

The whole Guild needed it.

Time to breathe.

Time to mourn.

Time to make space for the weight of everything they had lost.

Still, the delay gnawed at Tom's insides, leaving him twisted in a state of restless guilt.

He spent most of his time confined to his room, staring up at the ceiling or lying in bed, haunted by the decisions he had made. Every thought circled back to the almost two hundred lives lost during the battle. Even though he knew, deep down, that his actions had saved many more, the crushing weight of regret clung to him like a second skin, a fog that refused to lift.

He couldn't stop replaying it all—the calls, the charges, the screams.

The faces.

The ones who had looked to him for guidance.

And never made it back.

Tom reminded himself repeatedly that it could have been worse. It could have been all of them. If they hadn't acted, if they hadn't fought back, the invaders would have wiped them out. His strategies, his willingness to lead from the front lines—it had all been crucial to their survival. But none of that comforted him now.

A soft knock echoed through his room, pulling him out of his thoughts. His voice was hoarse as he called out for whoever it was to come in. The door creaked open, and Kiera and Derek stepped inside.

"Hey, Tom." Derek's tone was gentle, but firm. "We need to get you up and out of here. The Guild needs to see you, and honestly, you need to see them too. I know you're grieving, but hiding away isn't helping anyone. You need to talk to people, check in. Just being present will make a difference."

Kiera nodded in agreement. "We're all hurting, but if there's one thing I've learned, it's that we need each other more than ever now. You taught me that. We need you, Tom."

Tom sighed, sitting up in bed and rubbing his face. His eyes were dry now, the tears long since spent, leaving him feeling hollow. Jerky sat beside him, clutching a children's book he had been trying to read. The scene was almost comical if Tom hadn't felt so utterly defeated.

"I've been telling him the same thing," Jerky said, looking up from the book with a slight frown.

Tom forced a weak smile. "I know, I know. I'm getting up. I'll take a shower and meet you guys in the lobby."

"Good," Kiera said, her voice softer now. "We'll be waiting. And by waiting, I mean if you don't come down, we'll drag you out kicking and screaming."

An hour later, Tom emerged from the elevator and stepped into the lobby. As soon as the doors slid open, he froze, his eyes widening in surprise. The room before him had transformed. Rows of men and women dressed in gleaming armor stood in perfect formation, lining the path from the elevator to the front doors. The sound of their boots clicking into position as they stood at attention echoed in the space.

"Present, arms!" a commanding voice rang out.

In unison, the warriors drew their swords, raising them above their heads before extending the blades to meet in the center, forming a shining archway of steel.

Tom blinked, stunned by the display. He turned his head to see Derek and Kiera standing by the doors, grinning at his obvious discomfort.

Slowly, Tom began to walk forward, his heart pounding in his chest. Each step beneath the gleaming swords felt surreal, and though the moment was meant to honor him, all he wanted to do was get through it. His pace quickened as he neared the end of the line, and when he reached his friends, he let out a shaky breath.

"What the hell is this?" Tom asked, though his voice held no real malice, just bewilderment.

Derek chuckled, his eyes glinting with amusement. "The Guild wanted to show their appreciation. And we figured this way would be best because it would make you the most uncomfortable."

"Well, mission accomplished," Tom muttered, though a small smile tugged at the corner of his lips.

"Shut up," Kiera said, playfully nudging him. "You deserve this, whether you believe it or not."

"I deserve to be uncomfortable?" Tom asked, though his friends could see he was just trying to turn the tables on them.

"Absolutely," Kiera smiled widely at him, a glint of mischief in her eyes.

As the soldiers lowered their swords and made their way out, Tom followed his friends to the entrance. Derek gave him a nod. "Come on. Fresh air will do you some good."

Tom pushed open the door, stepping into the bright light of the day. But nothing could have prepared him for what he saw next.

The entirety of Vanguard stood before him, gathered in the square outside the Guild. Hundreds of faces turned to look at him, and the moment they spotted him, a deafening roar of applause erupted. The sound hit him like a wave, and he stumbled slightly, overwhelmed by the outpouring of emotion from the crowd. Cheers, whistles, and cries of thanks reverberated through the air, creating a cacophony of pure joy and admiration.

Tom's breath caught in his throat as he looked out over the sea of people. Tears stung his eyes, but this time, they weren't from sorrow. They were from gratitude, from disbelief at the love and respect pouring out toward him. For a moment, he stood frozen, trying to take it all in.

"Thank you," was all he could say as he looked out at the crowd and waved, unsure of what else to do in this overwhelming situation.

Tom walked down to meet the throng of people, swarmed by those eager to thank him and congratulate him on the hard-fought victory. This time, he didn't shy away. Instead of stepping back or seeking solitude, he embraced the gratitude of his people. Each handshake, each pat on the back, brought a mixture of relief and lingering sorrow. Familiar faces from the battle—friends who had fought alongside him, comrades who had stood shoulder to shoulder—stood before him, their expressions a blend of respect and gratitude. Tom returned their thanks, feeling the weight of their appreciation settle on his shoulders like a comforting blanket amid the chaos.

After a while, Derek's voice cut through the ambient noise, amplified by the speaker system set up outside for the celebration. His voice carried authority and warmth, drawing everyone's attention.

"Alright, everyone. I know we all want to thank Tom for the incredible work he's been doing, but we have other things to attend to. Tom, if you would join us back up here, please," Derek announced, his tone both commanding and inviting.

Tom nodded and made his way back to the doors, standing beside Derek and Keira. The crowd began to part, creating a clear path for him to move forward.

"Thank you all for coming out today," Tom began, his voice steady despite the turmoil within him. "While I know this is a sad day, it is also a day of great celebration. We want to make this an equal measure celebration of life for those who died so we could remain safe, and a celebration of life for those who are still with us. In honor of this day, we have decided to mark today as the Festival of Life. Each year on this day, going forward, we wish to celebrate all those—living and dead—who fought to ensure we could continue on. A feast has been prepared by Charlene and her crew to—"

His words were cut off abruptly by the sudden appearance of a spaceship in the sky. The sight of the sleek, metallic vessel hovering ominously against the backdrop of the setting sun sent a chill down his spine. Tom stared up in horror, his body frozen, unsure of how to react in that instant.

"Shields up!" Derek shouted into the microphone, his voice tinged with urgency.

Herbert swiftly grabbed his communication orb, speaking a few urgent words into it. Moments later, the unmistakable sound of the generator activating filled the air as the familiar rainbow beam of light shot into the sky once more. The beam began to rain down over the entire area, bathing the courtyard in its colorful glow. TJ and Chris started shouting out orders as men and women began to equip their armor and weapons directly from their Inventories, their movements swift and purposeful.

A moment later, Tom was fully equipped, the weight of his gear a familiar comfort. He moved toward the walls to get a better vantage point, the eyes of the Guild members focused and determined. More ships began to appear in the sky, their designs straight out of classic sci-fi movies, emerging from what seemed like hyperdrive within the planet's atmosphere.

Ten ships in total hovered in the sky, their numbers growing as they drew closer. The fighters of the Guild prepared for another confrontation, their faces set with resolve.

"At least we're all inside the barrier this time," Tom commented, a hint of relief in his voice as the ships approached.

A whirring sound emanated from the Deshieldinator as Chris powered it up, readying its beam in case it was needed.

"Let's see what happens before we do anything rash. The Federation said they were sending ships too; this could be them," Derek said, standing beside Tom, now clad in his power armor, his stance firm and ready.

Outside the Guild's walls, the wreckage of the pirate ships lay broken and scattered. Harold and Herbert had been practically drooling at the prospect of salvaging the remains, their eyes gleaming with anticipation. Tom and his entire council had agreed to attempt repairing them, envisioning a means for intergalactic transport. However, they also aimed to modify the ships sufficiently to prevent them from being recognized as pirate vessels, striving to turn tools of destruction into symbols of peace.

INVASION

As the new ships flew in close, they hovered in front of the furthest pirate ship. A beam of green light shot out from one of the arriving ships, striking the pirate vessel. The beam expanded into a flat cone, initiating a scanning process that Tom watched with mounting anxiety. A short time later, the beam retracted, and a holographic projection materialized in the sky above.

"People of Earth, I am Commander Dim of the Intergalactic Federation of Planets. We came as quickly as we could to aid you, but it appears that may not have been necessary. We wish to speak with you about what took place here. Please allow us to parley with you so that we can add the details to our reports. We mean you absolutely no harm and only wish to ensure that there are no other signs of the pirates on your planet," declared the strange-looking creature with blue skin, its image clear and imposing against the twilight sky.

Tom stared up at the projection, worry etched across his features as he processed the sudden interruption. The atmosphere shifted instantly, tension crackling in the air as everyone awaited the Federation's intentions.

The alien commander wore a uniform made of pure white fabric, which clung to its body like a second skin, emphasizing its odd, elongated form. The smooth, almost rubbery texture of its skin gleamed faintly in the light, while its eggplant-shaped head and furrowed, wrinkled brow gave it a sagely appearance. Black stripes adorned its chest on the right side, seven in total, arranged like bars to denote rank or achievement. Its eyes, deep-set and alert, conveyed a mixture of curiosity and caution as it studied the humans approaching.

As the projection in the sky disappeared, the larger ship slowly descended, sending out a smaller craft toward the shield. The transport ship hovered above the ground before deploying three slender legs from underneath and settling onto the cracked pavement like a great, silent predator. The alien commander, the same one they had seen in the projection, stepped out first, his movements deliberate and smooth. He paused at the bottom of the ramp that had extended from the craft, flanked by two other Federation soldiers, unarmed but standing like silent sentinels behind him. They made no attempt to advance, merely waiting.

"I guess we should go talk to them," Derek said with a shrug, though the tension in his voice betrayed the unease he felt.

Tom and Derek descended from the walls, their boots thudding heavily against the stone as they moved. They were quickly joined by Jay, Brian, TJ, Bron, and Kiera, each looking to Tom for guidance.

"We're going to talk with them," Tom said, his voice steady, though his heart pounded in his chest like a drum in the hands of a hyperactive child. "Bron, Jay, you're with me and Derek. Kiera, head up to the wall and keep watch for any aggression. If they so much as twitch the wrong way, take them out."

Kiera nodded sharply, her eyes already scanning the aliens with suspicion. Without a word, she turned and climbed the battlement, her presence a silent threat to any who might think of making a move.

Tom, Derek, Bron, and Jay approached the gates, which creaked open with a dull groan, revealing the shimmering barrier beyond. As they passed through the rainbow-hued shield, the light flickered across their faces, casting eerie, shifting colors on their skin. Tom felt his pulse quicken, his every step weighted with the uncertainty of the moment.

The commander arched what passed for an eyebrow—a faint ridge of skin wrinkling upward in what seemed to be surprise as they approached, likely at the sight of Bron's hulking, imposing form alongside the humans. Tom swallowed hard but kept his face neutral, refusing to show any weakness.

The four stopped about ten yards from the alien group, standing in silence, a palpable tension hanging between them. The cool breeze carried with it the scent of ozone and charred metal from the pirate ships that still hovered in the distance paired with the wreckage in front of their walls.

"Greetings. We come in peace," the commander finally spoke, his voice oddly melodic, yet firm. He paused, allowing his words to settle. "We came to help with the invasion of your planet, as you are still in the fledgling stages of the integration. It would appear we were not needed after all."

"We managed," Tom replied tersely, his distrust evident in the clipped tone of his words. The memory of the pirates' assault was still too fresh. "The help would have been welcome, though."

"I can imagine. These pirates have been a thorn in the Federation's side for almost a decade. Every time we thought we had them cornered, they managed to slip through our fingers." The commander gave a slight nod, a gesture that seemed to be an acknowledgment of their efforts. "You have done us a great service by eliminating them."

"We were happy to see them die," Tom said flatly, offering nothing more.

The commander's blue-skinned face didn't change, but there was a momentary pause, as if he was processing the cold response. "I'm sure. We wanted to extend our deepest apologies for being late. If there is anything we could do to help you, we would like to try to make amends."

"Unless you can bring back the dead, I'm not so sure there is much you can do for us," Tom muttered bitterly before being sharply elbowed in the ribs by Derek.

"Don't say that. They might have something we could actually use," Derek hissed, his eyes narrowed.

The commander, sensing the tension between them, remained unfazed. "We do have healers who can raise the dead, but they must not have been deceased for more than twenty-four hours."

Tom froze, his stomach twisting painfully at that remark. *So, it was possible to bring someone back from the dead. I wish I knew that yesterday.*

"Then they won't be any use to us." His voice cracked slightly. He straightened, pushing the grief down, willing his face to remain hard. "What were you thinking of offering to make these amends?"

"As we serve the System, we will let it determine suitable reparations for our failure to act in time. Additionally, we can assist with clearing the wreckage of the pirate ships."

Tom's jaw clenched. "Those are our ships now."

"Of course." The commander bowed his head slightly, a gesture of respect. "I would not take them from you. You have won them by right of conquest.

However, I could send some of our engineers to assist you with repairs, should you require it."

Tom eased his posture slightly at the Commander's offer. "That would be helpful," he admitted. "Can we ask you some questions about the System as well?"

"Unfortunately, that is beyond my authority." The commander's face softened, his disappointment visible even on his alien features. "There are rules in place about what we can disclose—stricter for us, as we work directly for the System."

Tom's lips curled into a bitter half-smile. "Yeah, we've heard that before."

Derek stepped in before the tension could rise again. "Alright. We'll accept your assistance, and we'll await the System's decision on the reparations."

Tom's gaze remained fixed on the alien, his thoughts a swirl of suspicion and exhaustion. He had no choice but to accept their help, but that didn't mean he had to trust them. The weight of the losses they'd suffered still bore heavily on his shoulders, and no amount of Federation aid could change the fact that two hundred of his people had died—two hundred lives he would never get back.

Chapter 83

Farewells & Futures

> **Vanguard has received 3 Free Building Upgrades**
>
> Due to the Federation's inability to reach your planet to aid it in time, your Guild has been awarded 1 free Building Upgrade for every day the Federation was behind the invaders.

Tom dismissed the notification lingering in his vision after reading it. The rewards would go a long way toward keeping everyone safe, but it was a decision for later. There was still so much to think about, and he knew he'd have to discuss the specifics with Brian and the others soon. For now, though, he put it out of his mind, letting the celebration carry him away from the weight of leadership, even if just for a while.

If Tom was being honest, the celebration had turned out better than he'd expected. Time had been set aside for grieving—moments of silence, heartfelt words spoken, and candles lit in remembrance. But the night wasn't about sorrow; it was about life. There was a shared understanding that despite the heavy losses, they had all survived. The fighters, the mages, the defenders—everyone who stood together on that battlefield was still here to celebrate. There was food, dancing, singing, drinking, games, and the intoxicating joy of knowing they had made it. The air buzzed with a strange mixture of relief and excitement, a contrast to the tension they had lived with for days.

Firepits, carefully crafted by Roland for these kinds of nights, dotted the courtyard, their warmth and flickering light creating a comfortable, almost festive atmosphere. The flames leaped and crackled, casting soft shadows on the faces of those who sat nearby, sharing stories, laughing, and letting go of the past few days' horrors. The smell of roasting food hung in the air, mixed with the wood smoke and the occasional sizzle of meat on the grill. The Guild had spared no expense for the night, and Tom had even ordered the liquor stores to be opened for everyone to enjoy freely. Tonight, no one would go without.

Even the Federation troops, initially a source of unease, had become part of the revelry, offering strange, but surprisingly tasty, alien dishes and drinks that added an unexpected twist to the party. There was something surreal about it—

eating with and laughing alongside the same beings they had been wary of just days earlier.

Rularis, always the showman, jumped onto the stairs of the wall, pulling out his strange sitar-like instrument. He plucked a few strings, testing the sound before he began to play. The soft, rhythmic strumming quickly drew a crowd. He sang a song of victory, the words weaving together a tale of bravery, sacrifice, and triumph. His voice was deep and melodic, carrying through the night air with a sense of pride and gratitude. As he played, Inari stepped forward into the circle that had formed, her movements fluid and precise. She danced to the beat, her body moving in perfect harmony with the music, her grace drawing eyes from all corners of the courtyard. At times, her movements felt almost martial, like a kata performed with deadly precision, but softened by the joy in her smile.

Meanwhile, the Barbarians had started their own competition over at the bar. It all began when a fight nearly broke out over a bottle of Jose Cuervo. Tom had stepped in, laughing as he told them to figure out a non-violent way to settle it. The solution? Arm wrestling. One by one, other Barbarians were drawn in, challenging each other, regardless of whether they even wanted the tequila.

The party took a wild turn when James, absolutely plastered, began firing his gun into the air, shouting, "Olé, mi pistolas, más tequila!" Over and over, as though he had become some sort of rogue cartel member.

The crowd scattered, some laughing, some ducking for cover. Tom watched, bemused, as Derek—ever the responsible one—promptly equipped his power armor and tackled James to the ground. Tom swore he saw Derek crack a smile before he took James down, wrestling the gun from him and dragging him off like a misbehaving child.

Now, the night had quieted. The firepits still crackled softly, their glow dimming as the flames turned to embers. Tom found himself sitting on the steps of the Guild building, staring up at the stars. The sky was impossibly clear, a canvas of deep blue-black with countless stars twinkling above, reminding him of how small they were in the grand scheme of things. For a moment, he let himself be carried away by the beauty of it, his mind quiet, the worries of leadership fading for just a little while.

The sound of footsteps on the stone steps drew his attention. Derek, James, Jay, and Kiera came to join him, their presence a comforting reminder that they had made it through together.

"Nice night," Derek said, settling down beside Tom.

Tom glanced up at the stars, breathing in the cool night air. "It was. It is, actually," he said, correcting himself as he took in the beauty of the night sky. "The stars are beautiful now."

The others followed his gaze, looking up at the stars with quiet smiles. The air between them was peaceful, the weight of the last few days lifting, if only for a moment.

"I see you're feeling better, James," Tom commented, turning his gaze toward the man who had caused a near-riot just hours earlier.

"Yeah," James groaned, leaning back on the steps. "Derek hit me with a *Cleanse* spell. Took all the fun away in a matter of seconds."

"You could have shot someone," Derek said, though his tone was light, almost teasing.

"I knew what I was doing," James shrugged, brushing off the concern, his usual bravado returning.

Jay chuckled softly, leaning back on his elbows as he stared out at the horizon. "We've come a long way," he said, his voice soft but filled with a sense of pride and reflection.

Tom sighed, the sound heavy with the weight of everything they had been through. "We have. It's been one hell of a journey, though," he admitted, his voice tinged with exhaustion but also a quiet satisfaction.

"It'll be nice to be able to focus on ourselves for a little while now," Kiera said, her tone hopeful, though there was a cautious edge to her words, as if she wasn't sure the peace would last.

Tom glanced over at her, a half-smile playing on his lips. "Don't count on it."

Kiera's brow furrowed in confusion. "What? Why?"

"We still have those quests to go after," Tom replied, his gaze shifting back to the stars. "I'm thinking we start with finding out what that dragon meant. It seemed important. And who doesn't want to see a literal dragon in person?"

"Oh, the dragon!" Kiera said, her face lighting up with excitement. "I forgot all about that."

"Right?" Tom laughed. "With everything going to shit here, we haven't been able to focus on anything else. It's about time we did a little bit of the fun stuff that comes with being integrated into the System."

Jay grinned, clearly intrigued. "So, who's your dream team for that adventure?"

Tom didn't hesitate. "Well, all of you, of course. Michael, Kevin, Kirsten, and I'd like to ask Bohdan to go. But Mark is my next choice. We need a mage on the team."

"Agreed," Jay nodded. "We've been seriously lacking in magical firepower lately. I mean, you're great and all," he said, giving Tom a mock-serious look, "but you've gone pretty far down the sword build path."

Tom chuckled. "It's worked out pretty well for me so far."

"That it has," Jay said with a grin. "And we should definitely bring Bron, right?"

"Oh, yeah," Tom nodded. "I can dismiss him and summon him when we arrive. No need for transport."

Kiera chimed in, "Can we take two vehicles? Eight people crammed into one SUV again doesn't sound like much fun."

"We'll have to," Tom agreed. "Plus, we've got Jerky and Squirrel with us. Can't leave them behind."

"Good. Then it's settled," Derek said, a satisfied smile crossing his face. "The first thing we do is go after that dragon."

Tom looked around at his friends, his heart swelling with a quiet sense of contentment. "I can't wait. I'm excited to start a new journey with you all," he said, his voice soft but filled with emotion. "My family."

INVASION

End of Book 3

Special Thanks

To my wife—thank you for believing in me, for giving me the space to chase this dream, and for being the steady light through every late night, every doubt, every rewrite. You are my everything. I love you more deeply than I ever thought possible, and your support continues to shape every word I write.

To the amazing team at Legion Publishing—thank you once again for this incredible opportunity. Being part of this journey is more than a milestone—it's a dream made real. The belief you've placed in me and this series is something I'll never take for granted. I don't think I'll ever find the right words to express how much it means.

To the readers—thank you for taking the time to explore this story, for investing in these characters, and for giving feedback that has helped sharpen and elevate the work. Your excitement, critiques, and encouragement fuel me more than you know.

And to James Kelly, my Developmental Editor—thank you for your patience, your wisdom, and the hours you've poured into helping me understand what makes a story truly work. Your faith in my instincts, even when I second-guessed them, pushed me to a new level. This book wouldn't be what it is without your guidance.

<u>Sign-off</u>

This book marks the end of the first arc in a story that has grown far beyond what I ever imagined when I started tapping away at the keyboard like a sleep-deprived goblin fueled by caffeine and chaos. To everyone who stuck with me through the typos, the twists, the emotional gut-punches, and the vending machine antics—thank you. Your support, laughter, and feedback have made this world real in ways I never thought possible. These first three books have been a wild, messy, wonderful ride, and I'm so grateful you were here for it.

From the bottom of my heart (and the slightly cracked screen of my laptop), thank you. I can't wait to show you what's coming next—and yes, it's going to get even weirder.

With all my gratitude, love, and snacks,
—Ryan Maxwell a.k.a MaxwellAuthor

Rise of Mankind : Age of stone

By Jez Cajiao

In all the games Matt has played, Dungeons are places to raid, places you dream of conquering, but when the world is stripped of electricity, and the first mana-twisted beasts start to prowl, the games all come to an end...

Matt's just an ordinary guy, but when he's beaten, robbed, and left for dead, bleeding out at the bottom of a gully, it all has to change as he grasps frantically at his only chance for survival, coming as it does in the form of a glowing, dangerously pulsing light.

With his reality forever altered, Matt must quickly find a suitable place to deploy the Dungeon Core, fighting his way through the hundreds of people between him and safety, because if he doesn't do it soon, a Core Detonation will solve all of his problems for him… permanently.

Welcome to the New World.

Experience a dark apocalyptic LitRPG Dungeon Core tale, Matt is a normal guy, pushed into terrible situations, and without anyone to hold his hand and explain the system. This is a weak-to-strong tale about doing what's right, not what's easy, in a nightmarish world. Fans of Dungeon Core stories, progression fantasy and strategy real time expansion games are sure to love it.

Order Now!

<u>Welcome to the Dark ages</u>

Morgan and Merlins excellent Adventures

Book One

By

Malory

When Merlin needs a hero to save the world, he gets... well, me.

Fan-bloody-tastic.

I was supposed to be dead. Instead, I wake up face-down in Dark Age mud, possessing some poor bastard's body, while the ghost of history's most famous wizard rambles on about being murdered, cosmic energy and the end of all reality.

Just one tiny problem: I know about as much about cultivation as a pig knows about particle physics.

Now I'm fumbling with mystical energy that feels like juggling nitroglycerin, trying not to get shanked by everyone and their grandmother, and dealing with Merlin's constant "helpful" commentary.

Something dark is rising in Arthurian Britain.

Something that made even Merlin scared. They say fate has a sense of humour. Turns out it's the kind that laughs while setting your hair on fire.

Welcome to the Dark Ages, where cultivation meets chaos, and the only thing sharper than a sword is my questionable wit.

<u>Read Now!</u>

Theft of Decks

By Lars Machmüller

When the deck is stacked against you? Change the game!

In the frontier town of Isarn, Chase will never be more than the lowly Darkborn thief he is. Banned from training, banned from acquiring better cards, if the Lightborn had their way, he'd be banned from life itself.

He's not alone though, and the one thing he and his friends have is determination. Losing a hand to a brutal punishment only fueled his obsession to get access to his own amazing, reality-bending cards.

That is the path to power and a future for them all. Nobody cares where you came from when you're rich enough. For now, though, they're facing both established powers, churches and age-old prejudices. It's time to get to work, and if the Lightborn won't share and play nice?

Sometimes the only way to get dealt a better hand is to steal the whole damn deck!

Buy on Amazon

Quest Academy

By Brian J. Nordon

A world infested by demons.
An Academy designed to train Heroes to save humanity from annihilation.
A new student's power could make all the difference.

Humans have been pushed to the brink of extinction by an ever-evolving demonic threat. Portals are opening faster than ever, Towers bursting into the skies and Dungeons being mined below the last safe havens of society. The demons are winning.

Quest Academy stands defiantly against them, as a place to train the next generation of Heroes. The Guild Association is holding the line, but are in dire need of new blood and the powerful abilities they could bring to the battlefront. To be the saviors that humanity needs, they need to surpass the limits of those that came before them.

In a war with everything on the line, every power matters. With an adaptive enemy, comes the need for a constant shift in tactics. A new age of strategy is emerging, with even the unlikeliest of Heroes making an impact.

Salvatore Argento has never seen a demon.
He has never aspired to become a Hero.
Yet his power might be the one to tip the odds in humanity's favor.

Buy on Amazon

Wandering Warrior

By Michael Head

A divine quest to deliver justice.
One year to accomplish his mission.
After nineteen planets, there's something different about this one.

James Holden has reached the maximum level there is for a human. That's perfect, since he's the only one of his kind. A wandering warrior, without control of his destination, tossed between universes by gods who've failed to tell him why. James is the lone Judge on a new world in need of someone to balance the scales. He isn't afraid to do so with extreme prejudice. As the Chief Justice, he has to right the wrongs the innocent can't fix themselves.

As James quickly discovers, the roots of corruption run deep. Guilds choose to protect themselves rather than the people. Monsters roam the wilderness unchecked. Judgment is usually a decision between right and wrong, but nothing is ever that simple. This time, being the strongest human won't be enough to punish the guilty. James might have to recruit some new blood, even if he prefers to work alone.

On his twentieth world, he is going to win, no matter the cost. James will have to find a way to break past the limits of the system if he's going to have a chance at making a difference.

Buy on Amazon

Knights of Eternity

By Rachel Ní Chuirc

When Zara awoke in chains she thought she'd gone mad.

She was Zara the Fury - mistress of flame and fear. Her name was whispered across the land, from ramshackle taverns to the royal court. Even the heroic Gilded Knights thought twice before crossing her path.

She was feared—*respected.*

Now she was curled up on a dirt floor on her fiancé's orders. Valerius, leader of the Gilded, mocks her cries for help. And the kingdom is on the brink of war over the missing Lady Eternity…

But that wasn't why Zara thought she had gone mad.

The reason why is that the last thing she remembered was blood, an arcade screen, and the gun that changed everything.

**But no chains can hold the Fury, and when she gets out?
The world is going to *burn.***

Buy on Amazon

Scarlet Citadel

By Jack Fields

Gormon Hughes is 19, thin as a broom, and has—not for the first time in his life—been swept into the path of trouble. Poor, recently heartbroken, and indebted to the sort of people who file their teeth into needle points and devour wriggling bloated spiders for fun, Hughes sets his sights on salvation.

That salvation is the Scarlet Citadel, a wealthy organization of pageant fighters, monster hunters, and secret keepers. With the aid of strange oracles, rare good fortune, and a unique power that bubbles like champagne in the core of Hughes' being, he must join the Citadel and advance himself.

But the ladder of progression is harsh and dark. The rungs are slippery.

And falling means disaster…

Buy on Amazon

LITRPG!

To learn more about LitRPG, talk to other authors including myself, and to just have an awesome time, please join the LitRPG Group

www.facebook.com/groups/LitRPGGroup

<u>Facebook</u>

There's also a few really active Facebook groups I'd recommend you join, as you'll get to hear about great new books, new releases and interact with all your (new) favorite authors! (I may also be there, skulking at the back and enjoying the memes…)

<u>https://www.facebook.com/groups/LitRPGlegion</u>/

<u>https://www.facebook.com/groups/GamelitSociety</u>

<u>https://www.facebook.com/groups/LitRPG.books</u>

<u>https://www.facebook.com/groups/LitRPGforum/</u>

RYAN MAXWELL
RHINO WRITING